Truce
or
Consequences

Kelly Lopushansky

Cover Artwork By: SelfPubBookCovers.com/Insigna

ISBN: 978-0-692-09937-7

DEDICATION

To my dear friend and soul sister Richa Bhatnagar for all your support, enthusiasm, criticism, and encouragement. This book wouldn't exist without you.

ACKNOWLEDGEMENTS

No amount of thanks can properly acknowledge the assistance provided by my beta readers Richa Bhatnagar and Kiki Deans. Your thoughts and opinions shaped this book.

CHAPTER ONE

George Crewes stood next to his desk in his office at Gardiner D Associates, LLC flicking his favorite red yo-yo out and back a few times before beginning his looping tricks, having moved on from the traditional straight up and down so many years before that he hardly remembered the activity being new, when Taro Ng and Neal Ackerman entered quickly and nearly shut the door in Sergei Orlov's face as he trailed slightly behind. George stowed his yo-yo in his pocket and said, "Well?"

Neal nodded, "Lou's replacement is definitely starting today. Melissa confirmed it."

Taro took a seat at George's conference table. "That's good, right? We've needed to fill Lou's spot for months. Now we won't have to try to cover his team anymore."

George shrugged and sat on the edge of his desk. "Depends on who Gardiner hired." He crossed his arms and looked at Neal. "Did you get anything else?"

Taro shrugged too. "Just that this one has an M.B.A. or something."

"Naturally," Sergei said. "Couldn't possibly hire somebody with software programming experience."

George tried not to frown. "The only way that would happen would be to promote in-house. Gardiner made it clear he was going outside for this, so it really shouldn't come as a surprise. Maybe we'll get lucky and he'll have managed at another software firm."

George lost the struggle with the frown. The M.B.A. put a huge amount of pressure on him. George, just like his peers, was an in-house promotion from programmer to manager. He'd worked hard to make himself a good manager and had taken some classes, but he was far from earning an M.B.A. The division currently had two openings, one a manager peer, and the other, the Director. And he *wanted* that promotion. If this M.B.A. was worth anything, he'd have to convince Gardiner to promote him before the M.B.A. made too much of a showing, or he'd lose it.

Trying not to worry, he told himself that the fact that Gardiner hadn't hired the M.B.A. straight to the Director position gave him a solid chance. Maybe he still had a few months. Definitely two or three before the M.B.A. could show much of himself. Likely six before Gardiner would begin considering a newcomer for a promotion. *I still have time.*

The irritating part was that Gardiner had been sitting on both positions for so long already. It was confusing and he wouldn't talk about it. Lou had retired five months ago and the Director had left for another company just a week later. *Both positions should have been filled be now.* Well, George wasn't the boss and his name wasn't on the letterhead, so he couldn't do much but bide his time. At least it was clear that he was the in-house front runner for the Director Job. His team had the best productivity and even Sergei admitted that George had the promotion in hand.

He just wished that Gardiner had made the decision on the Director before replacing Lou with an unknown quantity. *Well, that's that.* He'd just have to make sure that he kept up the productivity and played a good game with Gardiner as a team player. *It isn't over until someone sits in the corner office.*

Taro crossed his arms too. "I don't like this. I would have thought he'd have had at least one of us sit in on the interviews."

"Never," said Sergei, the eternal pessimist. "Why bother if he wasn't going to listen to us anyway."

"Okay, okay," Neal said. "Let's not get worked up. Just because the new guy might take a little breaking in, doesn't mean we aren't up to it."

George had to force himself not to roll his eyes. Neal had only one goal in life, to keep everything around him peaceful. He had trouble with disciplining employees and he had trouble standing up to his peers much of the time, unless it made everyone relax. Here he was doing it again, trying to sooth some ruffled feathers that weren't meant to be soothed. Sergei was much the opposite; he liked things to be in turmoil. He didn't have trouble disciplining his employees, he had trouble keeping them. The ones he had now where the quiet kind who could keep their heads down and not get noticed.

George interrupted whatever Sergei was about to say with a simple question, "So when will we meet this M.B.A.?"

Taro frowned too. 'A bit out of character for him,' George thought. "With the way Gardiner's handling this, probably at the staff meeting in an hour."

Rachel, George's assistant, opened the office door squarely into Sergei. "Gardiner's on the floor," she said, in a loud whisper. Then she leaned around the door to see Sergei. "Sorry."

Sergei grunted something that could have been an acceptance of the apology or not. George had begun thinking of him as Eeyore from Winnie-the-Pooh recently; always expecting bad things, so not really surprised when they happened. But he definitely wasn't Eeyore in his temper. Eeyore kept his negativity depressing rather than volatile. Rachel didn't notice either way and closed the door as she headed to her desk.

"Well," George said, "we don't want to get caught in here planning a revolution." He looked at Sergei who barked a laugh and then turned to leave the office.

Sergei stopped with his hand on the door knob and looked back at his peers. "If we decide he has to go, we do it together, yes?"

"Go on, Sergei," George said, and he watched the three leaving and hoped Sergei wasn't starting to go off his rocker and actually meant something beyond getting the new guy fired. Every now and then Sergei was so far over the top that he worried George. Thank goodness Sergei liked him. He didn't feel he had to constantly watch his back.

But now, now he had a new threat. *Possibly a very significant threat.* He stood in his doorway a moment looking out across the cubicles. He had a good team. They had a good strategy and good production. M.B.A. couldn't affect that. M.B.A. was inheriting Lou's team who had been all but running amok since the announcement of Lou's retirement. M.B.A. was in for a big surprise.

He was about to return to his desk when he spied Gardiner out of the corner of his eye and paused to look closer. Gardiner was walking away from him, toward the break room, with Melissa from HR and another woman. The second woman he didn't recognize. She also carried a coat and had not just a purse, but another bag over her shoulder. *Oh, no.*

She wore black pumps and a fitted black skirt that went straight down to her knees from her hips, moving to nicely show off her curves when she walked as it moved with her. The blouse was a deep blue, kind of filmy in the arms, in the same shade, but in a different material. The group paused a moment as Gardiner caught Rachel carrying coffee. He apparently introduced Rachel and the new woman. Rachel smiled and shook hands, but didn't tarry long. As she moved to continue on her original course, the M.B.A. turned a bit further and George got a look at her face.

Holy. She was breathtaking. He couldn't make out her eye color from that distance, but he took in her face and thought that even if she had a terrible body, she might still have been one of the top ten most beautiful women he'd ever seen in person. And she didn't have a terrible body. The blouse wasn't as fitted as the skirt, but it still flattered her bust and showed off her waistline. He hadn't really paid any attention to her auburn hair from the back, but from the front he could see that even though she had it pulled back from her face, it was a loose style and she had those tendril thingies hanging down around her face, just wisps of hair that made her look soft and feminine and approachable, instead of cold and forbidding like a tight bun would have.

Gardiner turned back toward the break room and the beautiful face turned to follow and freed George from his staring. He turned and closed the door to his office and leaned against it. Only then did he realized that she was not just figuratively, but literally breathtaking. He wasn't actually breathing. He inhaled really deeply and tried to let it out slowly to still himself and instead muttered a curse. He walked to his desk and picked up his telephone and pushed the speed dial for Rachel.

"Yes?" Rachel answered.

"I don't suppose I just saw Gardiner introduce you to our new legal counsel that no one knew he was hiring. Perhaps a new accountant? Outside consultant?"

"Sorry."

"So you were just introduced to the new manager?"

"Yep."

"Thank you." He waited until he'd hung up the phone to curse again. Instead of sitting down at his desk, he took out his yo-yo and started sending it out in a forward throw and calling it back with a sharp tug so it slammed into his hand with a satisfying *smack*.

What to do? What to do? He stuffed Ringo back into his pocket and quickly headed out into the cube farm. He looked over the tops of the cubes as he walked, trying to catch a glimpse of Gardiner's head. He wanted a nice casual introduction.

"Good morning!"

George turned and realized he was blocking the way for Ishi to get to her desk. "Sorry," he said.

"What'cha doing?" She asked, as he took a side step and glanced over the tops of the cubes again.

"Nothing," George said, and glanced at her a moment. "Just thought I'd walk around before my morning meeting. Check in. How are things?"

Ishi tilted her head. "Things are fine. Who ya looking for?"

George shook his head. "Nobody." Then he peeked over the cube again.

"If you're looking for the boss, he's giving a tour to the new manager. I think they were headed toward her office next."

"Ah," George said. "Good to know." George tried to pretend he was still just walking around as he walked up the aisle by asking everyone how things were going. He didn't notice the looks behind his back as he went. At that point, he probably wouldn't have cared anyway.

Jillian Braden wondered why Rachel had seemed a little skittish when she was introduced. It wasn't until the tour reached the break room and Gardiner told her that Rachel wasn't her assistant alone, but her time was shared with another of the managers, that she realized that the introduction had meant more work was coming Rachel's way. *Great. I've already made one person's day.* Her internal sarcasm jumped into high gear with her nerves.

She'd been uncertain enough about taking this position. The company wasn't very big in comparison to where she'd come from, which was both appealing and unappealing. It would be easier to get noticed here, where the boss knew everyone. It would also be harder to hide, if things weren't going well. But it had been the step up she was looking for. Her previous job had moved her up to an acting-manager position, but after six months it had become clear she wasn't going to get the full-on promotion, so she'd started looking.

Gardiner D seemed like the perfect place to start as an actual manager when she'd interviewed. But as she'd drawn closer to the obtaining the position, she'd learned things she didn't expect. For one, she was the only female in management in the Software Division, the Hardware Division, or the Manufacturing Division. Gardiner had women in management positions in his HR and Accounting, but not in the design or production side of things.

Malvinia, Jillian's best friend, had been a bit discouraged at that. "You're trying to rise to the top. Perhaps it'd be wiser to start somewhere that the glass ceiling isn't quite so low."

Jillian had thought about that long and hard. In the end, it had been Gardiner himself who'd won her over. He really did know all his employees and it was obvious that he thought of them as family. She wanted to be part of a smaller, family type of business, rather than the colder corporate world. *At least for a while.*

So she'd accepted his offer and on her first day found herself getting the tour from Gardiner personally. That was a nice change too. How many people can say they've been introduced around by the owner of their company? *Not enough.*

After pouring a cup of coffee for both Jillian and himself, he led the way around the cubicles to Jillian's new office. They passed another manager's office and Gardiner made a weird sound, and then said, "I guess George isn't in his office. You'll have to meet him in the staff meeting at nine. He's the manager you'll be sharing Rachel's time and talent with."

Jillian nodded and glanced through the doorway and then the windows in George's office as they proceeded. George had a lot of sports memorabilia on his walls. A picture of a stadium, she wasn't even sure which one, graced the right, and he had a framed jersey on the wall behind his desk. His bookcase sported a glass encased baseball and two trophies. *Well, I guess that defines George.*

She liked basketball. But baseball wasn't her thing. She might have to bone up a little on the sport in order to have something to talk to him about. *Lovely. Homework.* Well, it wasn't like she wasn't up to it.

The door to her office was to the right of her two windows that looked out onto the floor. Her office was, of course, barren. The walls had clearly been repainted in the last two days; the paint scent was still lightly in the air when Gardiner opened the door. The bookcase was empty and the desk was nearly the same, holding only a phone and a docking station. The desk's right side when sitting at it, like George's, was pressed up against the wall, providing a little more walking space.

Melissa jumped in as they entered the office. She'd been carrying a few things since she'd signed Jillian in at the security and reception desk. She handed Jillian her copy of the employee manual and then a laptop and a paper with all her login information on it. "Be sure to shred it today, before you leave."

Right. Jillian pondered how many employees could memorize logins and passwords in just a day. Then Melissa handed her a cell phone. "And this is your company cell. I have a few of the more important numbers programmed in for you. Gardiner's of course, and mine, just in case. Rachel is in there, just like she's number one on your desk phone's speed dial. The other Software Managers are also in the contacts. And the desk numbers for your team."

"Oh, my," Jillian said, accepting phone after setting down the laptop. "Thank you, so much. That's so helpful."

Melissa smiled. "No problem. Rachel can help you stock your desk. Here are your keys." She showed her the office door and then the desk key.

Gardiner moved toward the door, after leaving Jillian's coffee on her table. "I'll let you get settled and come by to get you for the staff meeting. After the meeting, I'll take you around to your team."

"Okay," Jillian said. "Thank you both." Melissa left with a kind smile and a 'good luck.' Gardiner delayed a moment and when Melissa was out of ear shot, he moved a little closer to Jillian and lowered his voice.

"Don't forget what we talked about when I made you this offer. I'm looking for a fresh perspective and for leadership. When you see something that needs fixin', I need you to jump right in and say so. My management team here in Software is a good bunch, but they need someone to look at things with fresh eyes too. I can't guarantee that everything you suggest will go forward, but I do guarantee there'll be discussion."

"Of course," Jillian said. On that note, Gardiner exited and she moved the door partially shut behind him and looked at her office. It was a nice size, with a conference table that could seat four, in between her desk and her windows. She'd have to bring in some things to liven it up. *Definitely a plant or two.* She wasn't sure what she was going to hang on the walls yet. She wanted to show her personality a little, but not like the sports bar next door.

She picked up her desk phone and pressed the speed dial for Rachel. When Rachel answered Jillian reintroduced herself and asked Rachel where she sat.

"I can take you," a deep voice came from her doorway.

"Oh!" Jillian said, a little startled, as she looked up and her door swung open. A rather tall and fairly broad man leaned against her door frame. He was nice looking at a glance, clothed in a dress shirt, tie, and slacks, with just the thinnest shock of graying hair at his temples amidst his otherwise dark brown hair.

"Sorry if I scared you," He said, and then walked forward extending a hand. "Hi, I'm George Crewes. I'm just next door."

"Oh, yes, thank you," she lifted the receiver back to her ear. "Never mind, Rachel. I've just met someone who's offered to show me the way." Placing the receiver back in the cradle, Jillian extended her hand.

George closed the gap between them and took her hand in his. As she gripped George's hand firmly, she waited for him to show his colors. She'd had a wide range of handshakes from male colleagues. Some took the handshake as a way to assert dominance with a painful grip and some were too solicitous and were rather weak.

His handshake was nice, firm and warm, not moist, or limp, or anything else she could make a negative comment about. It was a manly handshake, solid and confident. As she looked into his eyes, he smiled and she felt a faint shiver run down her spine. His eyes were quite nice, a really surprising shade of blue, bright and inviting. Her breath caught. *Oh, my. I think I just met the office Casanova.*

"And your name is?" He prompted.

"Oh, right." Jillian laughed slightly and shook her head. "Um, Jillian Braden."

Continuing to shake her hand, George's smile widened. "It's nice to meet you Jillian. Do you prefer Jillian or a nickname?"

"Just Jillian, please."

"Ok," George said, as he let go of her hand. "Follow me, Just Jillian."

"What?" Jillian asked, before she could stop herself, remembering just after she'd said it that she was heading for Rachel's desk. "I mean, um, right. You're going to show me where Rachel sits." *Can I possibly make a bigger idiot of myself? For Heaven's sake! He's not that good-looking.*

George led the way, sadly it was only a short distance and all Jillian could manage to ask him was how long he'd worked at Gardiner's.

"Eight years," He said, as they turned a corner. "And here we are." He spread a hand out toward the desk.

Rachel rose from her chair and Jillian couldn't think of anything to say to George except, "Thank you. I appreciate the help."

George nodded. "Anytime, Jillian. Remember, I'm just next door."

"Right," she said to his back, and had a moment to glance at his backside. *Nice there, too. Oy. Maybe my mental lapse when we met was excusable after all.*

Turning back to Rachel, Jillian focused on more important things.

By the time Gardiner showed up at Jillian's office door, she'd managed to get a fully stocked desk and arrange herself a little. She was using the top corner of her bookcase as a coat rack *mental note: purchase a coat rack or a hook* and had figured out which drawer to lock her purse in. She also set out the two small framed pictures she'd brought in with her, so the desk looked a little less sterile.

She had decided that art work on the walls was her next priority. She'd worry about the empty book case some other time. *And the plants...don't forget the plants.*

Heading into the unknown of the staff meeting, she decided to take her bag with her, loading her laptop and company cell into it, along with a note pad and pen. If all of the other managers had their computers, she would too. If not, well, it wasn't that heavy.

When she and Gardiner entered the conference room, the talking inside stopped in its tracks. She felt the weight of the silence. The conversation hadn't petered off and died, it had just stopped. *Great!*

She looked around the table at the faces. Three men. Exactly as she expected. Apparently she wasn't what they'd expected. They were openly staring at her.

Gardiner didn't help to brush the whole *it's a girl* moment under the rug. He pulled out a chair for her. She managed to keep her face fairly neutral and murmured a thank you as she sat and he rolled it up to the table. *I wonder where George is.*

But Gardiner then proceeded with introductions, making for the awkwardness of her having to stand and lean over the table to shake Sergei's hand, Taro's hand, and then Neal's hand.

Sergei appeared to be about her height in her heels, had a medium build, and brown hair and dark eyes. His hand shake was a bit hesitant; as if he was afraid he'd break her. Taro, black hair and dark eyes, was tall and thin. Taro didn't seem hesitant in his hand shake, but his hand was sweaty and Jillian had to consciously stop herself from wiping her palm off afterward. Neal was also about her height, blond and blue-eyed, with a smile that didn't look phony. Neal was a little overzealous in his hand shake, pumping her arm a little too much. Jillian sat down and wondered about the backgrounds of her peers.

George appeared at the door right as the clock turned the hour. He hopped in a chair and lifted his feet so that the chair rolled with his momentum and he ended up next to Jillian. Then he turned the chair to properly sit at the table, dropped some papers he'd been carrying onto the table, and waved at Gardiner.

"You're-"

"On time," George said, with a grin. Jillian hid her grin behind her hand.

"Right," said Gardiner. "I was just introducing everyone."

"We already met," he said, motioning between Jillian and himself. "So, we're good." Then he turned to Jillian. "Right?"

Jillian smirked a little. "Well…"

"Oh, well, then," George said, and held out his right hand across his body. "I suppose it's been a little overwhelming meeting a lot of people this morning. Just to refresh your memory, I'm George."

Jillian took his a hand a moment and enjoyed the nice handshake a second time. "How nice of you, George."

"Well, terrific," said Gardiner with a tight smile, apparently oblivious to the by-play, as George and Jillian released each other, and launched into his agenda.

The meeting was scheduled for an hour and about halfway through George rolled his chair back a bit and dug in his pocket. Then the yo-yo started. In meetings, George kept it to a sedate and relaxed up and down. He didn't let it smack his hand noisily.

After the first few repetitions he realized that Jillian, he was still letting the name settle in a bit, was staring at him. He looked over at her and saw a look of irritation. *Uh, oh.* He stopped the yo-yo and focused back on Gardiner.

Several minutes later, George's hands were twitching. He couldn't help it. So he took out Ringo and did a couple of reps. There was something about the yo-yo that was soothing and helped him focus. When he saw Jillian glance over again, frowning, he stopped again. He didn't want it to become a big deal.

Gardiner was starting on the results for the last month. George knew this was where he needed to shine if he was going to get that promotion. He shuffled through his papers a moment to find his copy of the sheet he'd handed in to Gardiner.

The review was much the same as always. How many releases had each team completed? Had they met their time frames? Had they included everything they'd committed to for those releases? What had their client feedback been like? Was the documentation in order?

Gardiner slid a copy across the table to Jillian and George leaned over and whispered, "I was going to offer to share. Not fast enough, I guess."

She looked at him, smiled, and then whispered back, "Speed isn't everything. It's the thought-"

"Everything all right?" Gardiner asked.

George and Jillian both nodded and replied, "Sure." "Of course."

The review dragged on and on and as George kept glancing at Jillian's profile, he started thinking about asking Jillian to join him for lunch. It was risky to go for a whole meal. If they didn't have anything to talk about, he'd be stuck. But he considered that if that happened he could always let her drone on about whatever she wanted and he could just enjoy the view. Gardiner dimmed the lights and started on his slide deck.

George reached over to her notepad and slid it in front of him. He scribbled, "Got lunch plans next week?" He glanced at her and she mouthed, "Next week?"

He wrote, "We'll all need to eat when this meeting *finally* ends…"

When he slid the notepad back to Jillian her shoulders started bobbing up and down as she tried not to laugh.

He hadn't even realized he was playing with his yo-yo again until Gardiner asked him a question. Thank God he'd started half-listening again and was able to work out what the question likely was and provide an answer.

Jillian scribbled something on her notepad, but she wasn't able to slide it for George to see because the last item on the agenda finally came up and so did the lights. The rolling schedule for the next twelve months was always the end of the review meeting. Gardiner handed out hard copies, made a point to tell Jillian where she could find it in the company network share folders, and then ran through the schedule.

George saw Jillian frowning at the schedule and gave it another glance, it was a little ugly when it came right down to it. Everyone else was used to it and could make out what they needed. Maybe it wasn't so obvious to someone new. Or maybe she was worried about everything on her teams' plate. He would be worried, if he were her.

When Gardiner finished running through the highlights for the month, the meeting would normally have broken up, but Jillian cleared her throat. "Uh, Gardiner? I know I'm new, but when I look at this schedule I'm seeing the *traditional* way of handling software development. Have you all considered trying *Agile*?" All the other managers sat back in there chairs, away from the table as if to distance themselves from the comment. All, except George.

George shook his head, wearing what looked like an indulgent smile. "*Agile* is only really effective for larger groups than this. And besides the bug fixes and small requests that go into the new releases just don't lend themselves to the *Agile* method."

Jillian looked at George. "Actually, small requests and bug fixes are perfect for *Agile*."

Seeing Jillian shake her head in disbelief, George tried harder. "We've been doing it the way we do it for years. Before any of us became managers."

Jillian sat back and crossed her arms. "And that's a good enough reason to keep doing it? Have you tried *Agile*?"

It was George's turn to cross his arms. "No, not really. But the current system works. Everyone knows their part-"

"I understand that it's easier to continue with what you know. But if applied correctly, *Agile* can save time and speed up development."

"I-" George started.

"Interesting," Gardiner said. "I don't know much about this *Agile* thing either, other than it's been around for quite a while. Let's revisit this at the next meeting. In the meantime, Jillian, I'd like you to write up how this *Agile* would work. Put together a presentation on how you'd implement it. Thank you all-"

"Um, Gardiner?" Jillian said, a little tentatively.

"Something else?" Gardiner asked.

"Yes. I don't see anything on the schedule for the next year supporting Hardware."

George sighed and Sergei mumbled. Taro spoke for the group this time. "That's because Hardware refuses to give us any type of schedule."

"Excuse me? Don't we support pretty much everything they produce? At the minimum, we produce drivers, right?"

"Indeed we do," George said, and not only sat back in his chair but rolled it a little away from her. "But they won't give us timelines."

"So, how do we know when we need to put together something for them?" Jillian asked the table in general.

Sergei exhaled. "When the first one rolls off the production line, they give it to us."

"Are you kidding me?" Jillian asked.

Every one of the manager's shook their heads. Even Gardiner looked a little sheepish.

"Okay," Jillian said. "Can I safely say that we all agree that that is completely unacceptable? That it needs to be remedied? At the very least we should be represented at development meetings?"

"That's been tried. Our previous director tried for a year and a half. They won't keep us in the loop. They won't invite us to meetings." Taro said.

Jillian looked at Gardiner. "They haven't talked to *me* yet. I can get this straightened out."

"Okay. Run with it," said Gardiner.

"Really," said George to Jillian, his face a little red. "Just like that. Wow, good luck." He looked up at Gardiner. "We done?"

"Unless-"

"Good," he stood up, grabbed his papers, and left the room. Taro, Neal, and Sergei jumped up and followed him.

Jillian blinked and then looked at Gardiner. "Was it something I said?"

"Probably," Gardiner said. "Don't let it bother you. You're doing exactly what I asked you to do. Keep it up."

"I can understand that everyone might not like my suggestion to change how we handle our own workload."

Gardiner waited for her to pick up her things. "Don't worry about what these guys like. Worry about efficiency. And get Hardware to cooperate with Software."

Jillian slung her bag on her shoulder. "Why don't you do it?"

Gardiner looked into the hallway and then closed the door. "I want the problems in this company to be fixed organically, not dictatorial command. We need bridges, not walls. I don't know what you'll hear about this around here, but the truth is there is a real reason I didn't fill your position until now. And why I'm not even trying to fill the Director position."

"What reason is that?" Jillian asked.

"Something is broken. And it needs to be fixed from the inside out. I gave my guys five months after the previous director left to make progress, but I haven't seen anything. You are outside material because I need a new perspective. Everything we talked about and everything I heard from anyone I asked during the hiring process, gave me cause to believe that you believe in whole company teaming. Now, I'm hoping to see that proven true."

Jillian took a deep breath. "So, it's my job to build the bridges between Hardware and Software?"

"Yes. You did just volunteer, didn't you? And see what you can come up with to fix Software. My people are working too hard for too little results. I'd say you picked up some of the big stuff already. I don't know what the little stuff is. While buy in from your peers may be a challenge, I trust you can get it."

"What if I fail?"

Gardiner sighed. "Don't." Then he reminded Jillian that she had a one on one meeting with him that afternoon and he invited her out to meet her team.

Gardiner was still very serious as he opened the door for Jillian. He let her lead the way out of the room. "I'll let you drop that in your office and then we'll make the rounds. Be right there." He headed off in a different direction.

Jillian turned to head to her office and found George was standing just around the corner, leaning against the wall, yo-yo in hand, going not up and down, like in the meeting, but rather being thrown out ahead of him so that it flipped up more than horizontal with the ground and then returning to his hand with a very forceful smack. It reminded her just a little of something out a movie that had gangs in it. It wasn't the move he was making that was threatening; it was the tone of what he was doing, the fact that it felt hostile.

But, Jillian noted, it was also childish. "Nice yo-yo," she said, and veered to walk outside the radius of his throw, trying not to feel nervous and failing.

"What's your problem?" He asked, catching the yo-yo.

"I don't have a problem," Jillian said, over her shoulder. She felt defensive. It was obvious he was the one with the problem. But she didn't want to talk to someone bigger than her who seemed to be about to lose his temper.

George decided to follow her and kept up the yo-yoing while he walked. She'd talk to him eventually, if he didn't leave her alone. *I'm mad.* It was a bizarre thing to actually think about it, to notice that he was angry, but he was. He was actually skirting furious.

She could hear the loud smack of the yo-yo against his palm and knew he was following her. She chose to ignore it. Ignore him. His office was next to hers. He wasn't necessarily following her. He could just be walking behind her.

She went into her office and set down the bag and fished out her keys. She was going to have to get a key ring that would go over her wrist, or invest in adding pockets to her skirts. For now, she decided to just carry the keys.

As she turned back to the door she heard the *smack* of the yo-yo. There was George. Actually taking him in a little again, she realized he was even taller than she'd thought earlier. And he was blocking her entire doorway, while his red yo-yo was flying at her and then back. It was still very threatening. She wondered if she'd be able to convince anyone that it was a threat. The behavior was completely unacceptable for the workplace. She watched a few throws, trying to figure out what to do, and then looked him in the eye.

He wasn't even looking at the yo-yo. He was just staring, no *glaring*, down at her. She glared back for a few more throws and then she marched straight toward him grabbing hold of the yo-yo as it came at her. "Take this out of my office, please." She dropped the yo-yo so it fell and dangled on the string, spinning.

"Don't *ever* touch my yo-yo," George said, through his teeth, as he fought his inclination to actually grab her arm and squeeze, and instead wound his yo-yo while stepping back to let her out of her office.

She meant to simply let it go, at first. Then she thought to try to make a joke to lighten the mood. But she didn't have any inspiration for a joke. She decided the most winning move was to walk away. As she moved to lock her office door, George threw the yo-yo out at her again and she had to side step a little to keep it from hitting her. "Oh, honestly, how old are you? Twelve?"

"No," George said, finally putting Ringo in his pocket. "Yesterday was my birthday. I'm thirteen now."

"What's *your* problem?" Jillian asked.

George's eyes narrowed and he said, "Oh, nothing. Good luck with Hardware." Then he turned and walked the three paces to his own office door and went inside.

Jillian closed her eyes a moment as she locked her office door. *Well, Casanova and I aren't going to be getting along after all, are we?* It was not the kind of start she'd been hoping for.

By the end of the day, George was more grateful than he'd ever been that it was court day. He, Taro, Neal, and Sergei played basketball at the recreation center after work twice a week and he needed it today like he needed air. He'd been so angry he could hardly breathe when she'd grabbed his yo-yo. Of course, that hadn't stopped him from looking for her every time someone passed his office, or when he was out in the cubes, or the break room. He kept looking for her.

As soon as he'd had a chance to cool off, he'd felt like an idiot. *I was acting like a kid, a grade-A fool.* Not only had he overreacted to what was said in the meeting, he'd tried to smack her with his yo-yo. She was right; he was twelve, if that.

And she was still pretty. And she seemed smart. And gutsy. And he liked all of it, even the attitude that had grabbed his yo-yo. He just didn't like it when it was aimed at taking him down. But, unless she was prepped beforehand, she hadn't known his part in any of it. *So it wasn't personal. Probably.*

When he'd flirted, just a little, she'd responded. He'd actually thought he was getting somewhere. And then, she was brilliant and he was an idiot. Thank God for basketball.

George and Taro took an early lead, up ten points to two. George had the ball and was trying to decide which way to move around Sergei, checking to see if he could pass to Taro, when Sergei smirked at him. "What?" George demanded, trying to keep some focus on his dribble. Sergei shrugged a little and George charged, making the layup and another two points. "What?!" He said *at* Sergei, more than *to* him.

Sergei shook his head as if he had no idea what George was talking about.

Glancing at Taro and Neal, it was easy to guess and George cracked. "This about little Miss Bossy, Control Freak?"

This time Sergei laughed.

"What is so frigging funny, Orlov?"

"I wish you could have seen your face when she said that Hardware hadn't dealt with *her* yet. I thought you were going to explode."

"And here I thought I kept myself under excellent control," George said.

Sergei laughed again. "You didn't lose it in the meeting, but you turned red. I heard about you threatening her later."

"I didn't threaten anybody. Where'd ya hear that?" George looked at Taro who had the ball. "Let's go."

It was a fairly even match for the next few minutes, as they all blocked and the score remained the same. Sergei spoke again. "Hey, Neal! You think she can succeed where Georgie-boy failed for months and months?"

George knew Sergei was just doing it to screw with his head. So what if he'd been trying to get some cooperation from Hardware for a year? So what? If she succeeded, it would be because she wore a skirt which covered some well above average legs. George blocked Sergei again and Sergei grinned. "She's going to mess up your development system too."

"It's not *my* system," George replied. "I didn't think it up."

"But you defend it to the death!" Sergei pantomimed being stabbed in the heart.

Taro tossed the ball to Neal who took it back to the top of the key. George moved to guard Neal and tried to refocus on the game. He was holding his own until Sergei spoke behind him. "I think she's hot."

George turned to Sergei. "What?!" And Neal scored three points.

Sergei winked at George. "So do you."

George tried to make light. "Fuck off."

Sergei laughed harder. "Even better!"

"What's going on?" Neal asked, as Taro took the ball to the top of the key.

Sergei looked at Neal and pointed at George. "He's hot for the bossy, control freak."

"Are we playing ball or not?" George asked, and accepted a pass from Taro and made the layup. When he turned, ball in hand, none of the guys were moving. They were all just standing still and looking at him.

"This is going to be good," Sergei said.

"Twelve to five," George said, throwing the ball at Sergei.

"Uh, I believe it's fourteen after your score." Sergei said.

George winced, "You should have taken the twelve, Orlov. You're going to lose."

"I'm not so sure," Sergei said, as he dribbled to the top of the key.

"You're a bit distracted now, Crewes."

George moved up to guard Sergei. "Try me."

Sergei just kept on grinning while the score moved again. By the time it was eighteen to fourteen, George was able to ignore Sergei and get back in the game for real.

A three pointer would win the game for George and Taro, and Taro had passed to George to set him up. Sergei was guarding him and George kept moving for an opening. He was about to pass back to Taro and hope he went for the two points, when Sergei said, in a whisper, "I watched you both in the meeting. She likes you, too."

Before George knew what had happened, Sergei had the ball and dunked it.

"What the hell was that?" Taro shouted while George blinked and ran his hands through his hair.

Sergei was showing off, dribbling between his legs. "Psyche out!" Neal was right next to Sergei.

George didn't think, he just charged at Sergei, grabbing the ball, passing it back to Taro, who was able to take the three point shot from the top of the key. "Boom!" George shouted at Sergei and then high-fived Taro.

Taro said, in a low voice, "We still need two more to win."

"We'll get it," George said. "Sergei played his last card."

They played two more games, Taro and George also taking the third. George was happily exhausted. He made a point to keep his distance from Sergei in the locker room, though. He didn't want to hear any more about Little Miss Trouble, if he could avoid it. He was irritated enough without Sergei's help.

Sergei caught him on the way out the rec center, though. He hit George on the back a good deal harder than necessary. "You got your head back in the game better than I thought you could."

George sort of grunted. He knew anything he said would just make matters worse.

"You're going to have to deal with it, you know," Sergei said. "She's in the office next to you. You'll be hard-pressed to avoid her."

George swallowed. *It's true. I'll have to deal with her.* Even if Taro and Neal weren't as aware of it as Sergei, though maybe they were just less inclined to give him grief about it rather than being clueless, he already had a bit of a thing for Jillian.

Clearly, like Sergei had said, she was hot. And he'd liked how she'd been a little nervous talking to him when the first met. She hadn't been nervous around anybody else, as far as he could see.

His tell, however, was that she'd made him a lot madder than he should have been. Just thinking about the bit with the Hardware guys and then her grabbing his yo-yo made him hot under the collar again. It was stupid.

He had options. He could try to make peace. At least act a little like a grown-up. He could try to drive her out. Not grown-up but very appealing in its own right. And there was always option number three, don't do anything regarding her at all.

On his way home on the train, he decided to do nothing for the time being. If he let the animosity subside a little, the rest would fizzle out on its own. It wasn't as if they had even exchanged more than a few sentences. He'd take it as it came.

As he relaxed against the hard plastic seat, he thought of a fourth option. He could try to get in on her attempt to negotiate with Hardware. Maybe he could share in the success. And maybe he could make up for his early behavior by being helpful.

His mind wandered a bit. Maybe she'd be grateful if he helped. And eventually he could start over and ask her out. *Yeah. And maybe I'll win the lottery too.* He sagged a little in the seat. *That'll happen.*

Jillian met the rest of the Fab 5 for drinks, as planned. Malvinia wouldn't allow anyone to start a new job without a first day debriefing and then a first week debriefing. Kai was the last to arrive, while Christy kept looking at her watch. "I've got a date, you know."

Malvinia frowned. "You've had this on your calendar for two weeks."

Christy shrugged, "I only just met him last night."

Lacey sipped from her Martini and then asked, "Why'd you put him off to tonight?"

Christy crossed her arms. "I had a date last night too."

Kai joined the group and ordered a coke. "What'd I miss?"

Malvinia touched Christy's shoulder. "Christy has plans. Other than that, Jillian had a long day."

"Oh," Kai said.

Jillian provided her account of her day. She tried very hard to downplay the ridiculous scenes with George, the ones where she drooled on him and the one where they had a fight and she didn't even know why. She made a point not to mention anything about his looks. Apart from George, the day had gone fairly well. In her one-on-one with Gardiner, he'd told her about what he was expecting of her and that he was interested in seeing his Software Division work better as a whole, which she already knew. She was pleased to hear that he felt the teams were a little disconnected, because she thought so too, and that was at first glance. But mostly, he talked about wanting to see a productivity increase from her team. Her predecessor had sort of checked out before he'd left and the team had been floundering ever since, missing deadlines and not completing everything they agreed to have in a release. Not surprising, the team had been a little wary when they'd met her.

Malvinia was nodding, "Of course, they're wary. Someone is actually going to be watching what they do from now on. It'll be fine. Just step in and make your expectations clear and go for it."

Jillian leaned on her hand, so exhausted she only wanted to drop into her bed and wake up to another new job. "Since when did the doctor acquire management skills?"

Malvinia's eyebrows rose. "You know I want to go into administration at the hospital as soon as possible."

"Oh, right," Jillian said.

Kai, always the one to deal with the touchy feely subjects, asked, "How was it personally? Do you think you'll like it or not? How do you feel about fitting in?"

Jillian weighed the day in her mind. If she could have George banished to another dimension it would be perfect. "I think the job will be fine. I'm a little worried about my peers, though." She grimaced at Malvinia. "I should have listened to you, Mal. I'm not sure I fit in very well. Not that I had much chance to get to know anyone today. Maybe it'll be better tomorrow."

Lacey drained her Martini and asked, "What happened?"

Jillian shrugged. "Gardiner pulled out a chair for me at the manager's staff meeting."

"Ugh," Malvinia said. "Idiot."

"I think that's nice," Kai said.

"You're a lawyer, Kai," Christy pointed out. "Special treatment in the workplace due to gender is a no-no, isn't it?"

"Well…"

"That's not the point," Jillian said. "I just felt funny. That's on me. I have to try to fit in. I can't blame them for not knowing how to make that work. They haven't tried before either. I'm just wishing I wasn't the first."

"Did anything else weird happen in the meeting?" Malvinia asked.

Jillian debated and finally told them what had happened with her analysis and then George's reaction.

"Nice work," Malvinia said, toasting Jillian with her White Russian.

Kai didn't look very pleased, but she didn't say anything.

Christy grinned, "The only time men are worth anything is when they're pants are down. Catch 'em that way as often as you can. Go, girl."

Lacey was also quiet. Jillian knew that she'd flubbed it. Although Malvinia and Christy had both had plenty of success in the workplace, it was Kai and Lacey who had the stronger centers and were, quite frankly, happier in their jobs and their lives.

Maybe flubbed wasn't a strong enough word. She should have never jumped in quite so quickly, regardless of what Gardiner told her to do. She was too new to the culture. It was obvious to her now that George had taken some of her comments as a personal attack on him. He was probably responsible for something that she'd picked apart. He had defended the convoluted mess in the existing schedule and he'd been pretty adamant that Hardware was never going to cooperate. She had poked at something she shouldn't have there; she just wished she knew what. On the other hand, it didn't matter, because she wasn't about to apologize to him for it.

A second round of drinks came with a general loosening of the conversation and everyone had a chance to share their lives. Jillian listened as Kai talked about a case she'd just prosecuted with all the fervor of a television drama. Kai was so passionate about the law, it was almost intimidating.

"You need to start making more contacts to get you on the bench," Malvinia said, when Kai finished.

"Not right now," Kai said. "I'm doing really well where I am."

"Yes, right now," Malvinia said. "You need to look ahead every day, or you're looking back. When you're on top isn't the only time to make connections. If you wait until you're ready to make the leap, you'll have to do a lot of legwork and wait. Now is the time. And you can start racking up favors owed at this point too. Look for any and every opportunity to do someone a favor."

When everyone at the table just looked at Malvinia in silence, she frowned again. "What? I started racking up favors day one. I covered two extra shifts my first two weeks at the hospital. That put both administration and the two I covered for in my debt right off. I keep going like that until the weight on the scale is so heavy on my side that they can't say no, and then I make my move."

She looked at Jillian. "You should start it to, Jilly. Do what's-his-name a favor and you'll throw him off balance again *and* put in him in your pocket."

"Not George," Jillian said.

"George?" Christy said. "You didn't tell us he was that old."

"He's not," Jillian said. "He's close in age to us."

"Who named their kid 'George' when we were born?" Malvinia asked.

"Apparently, George's parents-"

Kai cut in. "You know 'George' is reviving yet again thanks to the English Prince. You know, I like the name. It's sort of... staid."

Jillian let the conversation go on its' sidetrack. She didn't want to dissect his name. She didn't want to talk about him anymore. She just wanted to go home and go to sleep. Hoping to encourage the rest of Fab 5 to quit for the night, she downed the rest of her wine and waited for someone to do the same.

It was Lacey who noticed Jillian first. She nodded at her and finished her drink. "Let's call it a night. Tomorrow is another work day."

"And I have a date," Christy chirped.

Malvinia crossed her arms. "I don't think this meeting has met any of its objectives. We can't go yet."

"Ma-a-a-l-l-l," Christy whined.

"Come on," Malvinia said. "We started the 'Fab 5' so that we'd help each other get ahead. Jillian has only gotten one suggestion tonight, mine. Everybody else needs to give her some advice and then we'll adjourn."

Christy leaned toward Jillian, "Unbutton one button on your blouse tomorrow. They won't be able to think."

"Christy!" Both Malvinia and Kai admonished.

Christy frowned and crossed her arms too.

Lacey tapped the table. "Okay. I've got useful advice." She turned to Jillian. "Focus on your team and not the other managers for this week. Your immediate success at Gardiner is dependent on shaping up your team."

Malvinia seemed to mull it over. "But keep your eyes open for opportunities to accumulate debt owed."

Kai spoke up. "It might be advisable to make a friend or two in the other departments that do have women managers. You might be able to get some insider advice and maybe even some background on your peers. Not gossip, though."

Christy sighed. "Since no one liked my button idea, I'll give you something else. Pay attention to the dynamics with your peers. See if you can figure out who are the leaders and the followers. You might be able to help a follower and bring him to your side."

"That's a little better," Malvinia said. "A riff on my advice, but all the same."

Christy's mouth curled into a near snarl. "Why do you invite me to these things if you're just going to dismiss everything I say?"

Malvinia rolled her eyes. "You just want to get to your *date*, you aren't even trying."

"Nice!" Christy said, and stood up. "Good luck, Jillian."

Kai put her hand on Christy's arm. "Christy, honey, sit down. Malvinia didn't mean anything by it."

"You know she did," Christy said, but sat down anyway.

"Please," Jillian said. "Please don't fight. I appreciate the advice from all of you. You know I'll consider *all* of it."

"I know you all think I'm a slut," Christy muttered.

"Oh, brother!" Malvinia said, and slammed the rest of drink.

"On *that* note," Lacey said, as she stood. "Come on Christy. Let's get a cab."

"Vi!" Kai said, watching Lacey and Christy head for the door. "Could you just lay off Christy?"

"Me?" Malvinia said. "She's the one who can't put two seconds of thought into helping a friend because she's got a man waiting for her. If she was genuinely in love, I'd cut her some slack, but she just keeps on with these one-nighters."

"That's her choice, Vi," Kai said. "Just like it's Jillian's choice to handle work the way she wants. And me. I have a choice-"

"You know one of these days she's going to pick up a monster and he's going to really hurt her," Malvinia said.

"Then say *that* to Christy. Tell her you're worried for her safety. Don't pass judgment on her."

"I'm not!" Malvinia said.

Jillian stood up. "Goodnight, ladies. It's been an eventful day. I'm going home."

Kai jumped up. "I'll walk with you."

Before they were out the door, Jillian was already looking back at Malvinia. "We probably shouldn't leave her alone, like that."

"She wants to be alone, or she'd be nicer."

Jillian stood straighter in her surprise. "I've never heard you say anything like that."

"Like what?"

"Calling someone 'not nice.'"

Kai snorted. "Malvinia is... starting to lose her perspective, I think."

"Kai," Jillian said, as they walked out onto the street, "You don't want to be a judge, do you?"

Kai sighed and stopped walking. "No. I want to be the D.A., maybe later a state attorney general. But I don't want to sit on the bench. Maybe I'll change my mind in a few years, but I don't think so."

"You need to tell Mal."

"I know. But she doesn't let me say it."

"If you don't tell her, she may start working on your judicial appointment without you."

Kai laughed with Jillian. "Yeah, that's Vi."

Jillian started walking again. "You know she's got her sights on the Supreme Court for you."

Kai caught up. "I know. I guess I'll tell her soon."

Jillian smiled and linked her arm through Kai's. "Even if she throws you out of the 'Fab 5,' I'll still be your friend. And I bet Christy will leave the group and join you."

"I don't want to break up the group, Jill," Kai said.

"No, I don't either."

"So... what weren't you saying in there?"

Jillian didn't respond for a minute. "Do you win your cases because you're psychic?"

"Not psychic. Just incredibly interested in others."

"Oh."

"Well," Kai said, and nudged Jillian in the ribs.

"Nothing important," Jillian said, as George's face flashed in her mind, red and fuming.

"Okay. If you change your mind and want to talk, give me a call."

"Thanks," Jillian said.

Later that night after she crawled into her bed with Charlie, Jillian scratched the black cat's ears and asked him, "Have I lost my mind? I jumped in the deep end without knowing how to swim. I got into an argument with a peer and I don't even know what it was about. I'm in way over my head."

Charlie purred.

"Thanks, Charlie. You're the best."

She tossed and turned a while, thinking through all the ways she could have handled George, some in the meeting, some after in the hall. Now that she had some distance, she could see the subtle and less subtle cues he'd given off that he didn't like what he was hearing. If only she'd taken a different tack and hadn't made him that mad.

I need a strategy if he shows up with that stupid yo-yo again. Something that'll get him to put it away. I can't believe he was that angry with me.

And then she thought about how nice he'd been briefly before that. How he'd smiled so warmly at her. And his entrance to the meeting. She rolled over again and adjusted her covers. *He was showing off.* She almost smiled at that, except that he wasn't going to show off for her again. It had even seemed like he was on the verge of asking her to lunch for real, not just a joke. That wasn't going to happen either. That was for the best. She wasn't going to date anybody at Gardiner D. *Too risky. Can mess up your reputation.*

As she was drifting off to sleep, she replayed grabbing his yo-yo and this time instead of him telling her not to touch it, she imagined him backing her against the wall and kissing her. A solid, knee-weakening kiss that made her sag into him and she couldn't help but kiss him back.

Jillian bolted upright in the bed. "Oh, no." She clutched arms around herself. "I can't have him in my head like that already. Not when we have to work together. Not when I have so much to do there." She rubbed her arms. "Not when he hates me." She sat there a few minutes trying to talk herself out of it, and then gave up and walked out to living room to turn on the television.

CHAPTER TWO

One year later…

George had taken to using the back stairs, so he wouldn't have to pass by Jillian's office and it wouldn't be obvious that he was avoiding it. He could, of course, simply have made a detour around the cubicles, but eventually someone was bound to notice, so he took the other option. It was early on a Wednesday morning and he didn't expect her to be in her office already, but he'd quit taking chances months before.

The tentative 'peace' they'd forged months ago rested squarely on dealing with each other as little as possible. He hadn't even set his bag down when Taro was knocking on his open door. "Morning," George said.

"Morning, got a minute?"

"Sure," George answered. Taro closed the door behind him. *That can't be good.* "What's up?"

Taro scratched his cheek just aside from his eye. "Gardiner's doing the next review tomorrow."

"I know," George said. He'd worked damn hard to make sure that all his team's releases had gone out on time and complete last week.

"The rumor in HR is that he's finalizing the short list. Or should I say, he's finalized it."

The Director Position. George had waited and waited. Gardiner had sat and sat. It'd been almost a year since Jillian had started and still nothing had happened. George had started to wonder if Gardiner had decided it was best to have his software folks report directly to him, rather than put back that layer of management. "I take it Melissa's seen the list."

Taro nodded. "I think you know what it says."

George took out his yo-yo. "At least tell me I'm on it too. Not just her."

"Got it in one." Taro sat on the edge of George's desk. "And it's just you and the Ice Queen."

"Does it bother you?"

"Nah. I've always known that I wasn't in the running. Sergei is taking it fairly well too. Although, he's definitely on your side. He figures if she's promoted, you'll be the first out the door and he'll be right behind."

"So positive, that Sergei."

"Mmm," Taro nodded. "Neal's a bit miffed."

"Should I talk to him?"

"Nah. Let him wind down. Deep down he knew he wouldn't make the short list either. He's good at keeping things calm, not at pushing ahead. Gardiner is looking for a leader, not a pacifist."

George stopped his yo-yo. "I never figured you for a philosopher, Taro."

"There's a lot you miss, these days," Taro replied.

"Like what?"

Taro scratched next to his eye again. "Little stuff and big stuff. Jillian's team upped their output again." He paused and George grunted. "Rachel got engaged."

"Engaged?"

"Two weeks ago. She told me you're the only one who hasn't said anything."

"Damn," George muttered under his breath. "I guess I've been a little focused lately. What else?"

"Well, Melissa and I got engaged too."

"Ha! That's fantastic, Taro. Congratulations man!" George dropped his yo-yo on his desk to give Taro a good manly hug with several claps on the back. "That is really terrific! Am I the last to know?"

Taro was sporting a grin a mile wide. "Actually, apart from our families, you're the first. I thought I might ask you to be my best man. That is, if you can get your head out of your ass long enough to do the job."

"Oh, yeah. I'm there. I'm honored, man. Sending Taro off into the afterlife."

"Don't give me that crap, George. I'm a lucky man and I'm damn happy."

"You are lucky. It's hard to believe you ever got Melissa to go out with you at all."

"No kidding," Taro said. "I was so nervous asking her I... well, that's not important. Anyway. We've um, ha, we've decided to do a planned elopement."

"What is that?"

"A month from now, City Hall. Small guest list. Say, I guess you're on the short list there too."

George laughed with Taro.

"The reception will be at Gino's, where I took her on our first date, with the same small crowd. We're trying to keep it simple and relatively inexpensive."

"All that was decided in one night?"

Taro, still grinning, cleared his throat. "Apparently, Melissa's been giving this some thought for a while now."

"All the nerves for nothing, then."

"Yeah."

George gave him another manly hug. "I'm so happy for you."

"Now, I'm going to go break the news to Sergei and Neal."

"Are they invited too?"

"Of course. I told Melissa that if I couldn't have you three there, I wouldn't do it. And she believed me."

"I'd call her a sucker, but I think she might have just wanted to make you happy. Don't worry; I'll keep Sergei from making a toast."

"For that, I owe you," Taro said.

George sat at his desk when Taro had gone. *Married.* Of all his buddies from work, Taro was the most likely, he supposed. He was the most together, in just about every respect. He didn't work anymore overtime than he had to. He had activities outside of work. And, of course, when he'd decided he wanted to date Melissa, he'd jumped on it and asked her out right away. None of the guys had known he was the least bit interested in her before. He'd decided and gone for it.

Knowing Taro on that account, he'd probably decided to propose to her yesterday, gone and purchased a ring, and asked her in the span of a few hours.

Well, good for him. He was getting everything he wanted. George hoped they'd be happy. He also hoped Taro would still play basketball with them some of the time. *Selfish, but true.*

Taro had started dating Melissa right about the time that George and Jillian had declared their armistice. That was a little over six months now. *Hard to believe it's been a year since she started.* No wonder Jillian had been able to get on Gardiner's short list.

He picked up his yo-yo again and tried to relax. *Her or me.* He'd been a good boy, he hoped. He hadn't tried to get her fired, despite the many times he'd thought about it. He'd even come up with a few really good plans to at least see her professionally embarrassed, if not forced out. But he'd never set any of them in motion. It wasn't so much the irrational fear of karma getting him right away, though he did consider that too. No, it was simply that he'd decided he needed to beat her the right way, sort of a man-to-man thing. It would have been cowardly to sabotage her.

Now he was facing a very hard truth, she might well be winning. Her

25

team's productivity kept going up and up. In the beginning, that made sense. Given that they'd had no leadership for so long, anyone could've gotten *some* results. But a year later they were still making strides. He almost didn't want to see the latest results, wishing she'd plateaued earlier.

It was going to make it easy on Gardiner to make a choice. Too easy. *Who would I pick?* And there it was. He was going to be working for her. He closed his eyes a moment. That was the nightmare.

He heard her unlocking her door and, for the first time in so long, he didn't just want to see her, he wanted to talk to her. It was only a few steps and he could see her in her office, putting her things away to start her day. She'd done a really nice job decorating. He'd expected to see her degree on the wall, but instead she'd put up some lovely prints. One was a waterfall with a pool below. She'd also put up a view of some mountains. Both were spectacular. When he wasn't thinking how much he hated her, he couldn't help but wonder about where she lived and what it was like. What *she* was like.

She'd brought in plants too. A cute little flowering something sat on her desk and a viney thing sat atop her bookcase. He liked her office.

That morning, as she hung up her coat, he realized she'd left her hair loose, for once. She usually tied it back or twisted it or piled it on her head. He watched the hair move with her, and then watched as she tucked one side behind her ear as she bent over her desk to deposit her things inside. *She's so beautiful.*

That was the other reason he avoided her, the one he tried to pretend wasn't there. He didn't want to think thoughts like that anymore. He kept hoping he'd work her out of his system. He didn't expect to quit thinking she was pretty. That was absurd because she *was* pretty. But he did hope that one day he'd quit wanting to touch her. Okay, that was absurd too. *Who wouldn't want to touch her?* But maybe he'd quit fantasizing about her… so often. There was some hope there. But after months and months of only seeing Jillian when he had to, he hadn't made much progress there either.

She looked up then and saw him. Somewhere, deep in a dark place in his mind, a place he hated for lurking there and would have destroyed could he have reached it, he wished she'd smile when she saw him. Smile with genuine pleasure at his presence. Smile because she was glad to see him. Smile because she thought of him constantly, like he thought of her.

No chance. The ice in her eyes never melted for him.

Jillian had a weird feeling, like she was being watched, and looked up. *Oh, great! Just what I need this morning.* She stood up and walked to her door. "Can I help you?" she asked, in a tone that clearly indicated she had neither the time nor the desire to help him at all.

"Not really," George said, and walked up to her. "I have news. You might like to hear it."

"Oh, right," Jillian said, her voice thick with sarcasm. "Then, by all means." She held up her arm in a gesture of welcome into her office. Assuming he was up to something, she crossed her arms and gave him space, making sure that his stupid yo-yo wouldn't hit her if he decided to fling it at her.

George closed the door behind him. "I'll be brief. I promise. The short list for the Director position is complete. It hasn't been announced, but it's done."

"And," Jillian prompted. *He's so exasperating.*

"As expected. You. And me."

Jillian inhaled deeply. "Mmm. Yes. I guess that's what everyone expected. So why tell me?"

"Just thought you'd want to know, since everyone else does or will very shortly."

"Oh," Jillian said, and nodded slightly. "Well, then, thanks."

George nodded back and then opened the door and left.

That was weird. She sat at her desk and tried to concentrate and it didn't happen. She got up and closed her blinds and her door, then returned to her desk chair to wheel it against a wall and lean her head back.

No matter how much she wished it, George wasn't going away. And no matter how much she tried, he kept popping up in her thoughts. She'd already lost one guy she'd been dating, thanks to George. At least, that's what he'd said when he ended it with her. 'Some other guy is always on your mind. It's obvious. And I don't even know who he is.'

"Well, neither do I," Jillian said to herself, in response to the memory. She didn't know anything about him beyond his yo-yo and his baseball memorabilia. She avoided him and yet she thought about him all the time. She'd hear something from his office and wonder what it was. Who he was talking to? Was he wearing the blue shirt she liked on him so much? What he was laughing about? Where did he go after work and who has was with? And that was where she tried to draw the line.

More than once, she'd thought of following him, just to know. But she'd controlled herself. And she hadn't shared her weird obsession with anyone. Not Mal. Not Kai. She had confessed to Charlie, but that was different. He could keep a secret and he never judged her.

Now she was faced with the prospect of working for him. Not good. Perhaps she should start looking for a new job now. She'd been with Gardiner a year. It wouldn't look too bad to leave now. And she had the clear and simple explanation that she wasn't going to get a promotion here. Who could fault her for moving around if she was looking to go up?

But should she? Would that be like giving up on the possible promotion here? She imagined herself in the corner office, so much larger than the one she had now, with windows to the outside world, as well as the inside. If George wasn't lying, and she was fairly certain he wasn't - *What could he have to gain by that?* - then she was on the short list. It could just as easily go her way as his. And she had the numbers on her side. Her team was outperforming the others. She had good development too. All but one of her team had taken classes to grow their skills. Several had even voluntarily taken some 'soft skills' classes.

She swallowed at the thought of being the boss. It sounded good on the outside, just what she wanted. But on the inside? She hated the idea of providing direction to either George or Sergei. Neither of them would want to listen to her. She might be okay with Neal and Taro. Neal was so interested in keeping everything around him calm that he'd probably take whatever she shoved at him. Taro was focused on having a life, so he'd just go with the flow. But Sergei and George. Ugh. They were not fun. She wasn't entirely sure how Sergei still had a job there since Gardiner had been dealing with him directly. *I would have let him go years before.*

Oh, well. What would come would come. If she was promoted over George, she'd just have to be gracious about it, but not solicitous. She'd treat him like everybody else. And if he didn't like it, he could leave. And that might be for the best, because then she'd get over him and quit thinking about him.

She got up from her chair and headed for the break room, careful to lock her office. She'd had enough of George's jokes and her fear of him taking something she needed or doing damage to something was as strong as her curiosity about him. The greased doorknob had been particularly gross. And finding some of her property scattered around the office one day had been annoying. Most of the time the *jokes* just hid her things, or made her life just a little inconvenient. The tape over the laser of her mouse had only taken a few moments to sort out. The small little explosive things that had been laid on her office floor that gave her a jump when she stepped on one had been a sign that things were escalating. Of course, the pièce de résistance had been the stopping up of the toilets in the ladies' room on their floor. That had inconvenienced a lot more people than her.

She poured her coffee as Taro and Neal walked in. They looked surprised to see her. *Probably talking about the list.*

"Good morning," she said, brightly, just to throw them off.

Taro and Neal nodded at her and chirped back with "Morning."

She poured in her creamer and then said, "Congratulations, Taro. I'm sure you'll be very happy," and headed back to her office. Behind her she heard, "How did she know?"

That was easy. She'd seen Melissa bouncing up and down on her way in this morning. Melissa was squealing and hugging everyone in sight. Jillian smiled. It wasn't exactly a secret.

She unlocked her office and glanced into George's office while she did. He wasn't there. That was for the best. She didn't want him to see her looking at him. She reached for the doorknob and gave it a turn, it slid through her hand. She closed her eyes a moment to take in the very slimy feeling her hand was now experiencing. *Again!*

Jillian turned around looking for something to wipe her hand on. She didn't want to stray far from her office with the door unlocked though, as this could be the prelude to something bigger. "Rachel?" She called. "Ishi? Anyone there?"

When she didn't get a response, she decided to lock her office door, wash her hands, and bring back some paper towels. It took a little finagling to get a hold of her keys with her 'wrong' hand and when she finally moved to lock it, she transferred her coffee cup to her 'slimed' hand. She hadn't even put the key in the lock when the coffee cup slid through her fingers and dumped on her blouse and skirt on its' way to the floor, where it managed to splash a little on her shoes and stockings.

The only thing that kept her from screaming was that she couldn't think of a word that was foul enough to cover how she felt at that moment. Not even touching the coffee cup, she headed straight for the ladies' room. After washing her hands, she discovered that the handle on the inside of the door had also been greased. She washed her hands again, cleaned off the door handle, and then took more paper towels to her office.

The office door was standing wide open and she tried not to think about what may have been done to it before she returned. She completely cleaned off the doorknob and wiped up the coffee, tossing the cup and the paper towels in her waste basket. She shut her door, but didn't bother to lock it as she stepped next door.

George's door was open, but he wasn't in. She quickly walked into his office and unplugged his laptop docking station from the wall. It was silly and not at all a good revenge for the coffee she was wearing, but she hoped he wouldn't realize that it was unplugged until his laptop died on him. And maybe that would happen in the middle of a meeting where he couldn't plug it in easily.

She quickly returned to her office and pursued the first order of business, to check her purse. Not a quick exercise, it took almost five minutes but she was then confident that nothing had been taken. She couldn't be sure no one had written down a credit card number, but she hoped it was unlikely that George would commit credit card fraud just to get under her skin.

The search of the rest of the office took another fifteen minutes. By then she was fairly sure that nothing had been taken. The one question that remained then was had anything been sabotaged or had the door been opened just to mess with her? *As likely as not.* She looked down at herself and tried to decide if she wanted to drive all the way home to change or not? *Correction.* Had *to drive home and change.*

She had yet another meeting with Hardware in an hour. This time she was supposed to take George with her. That had been Gardiner's idea. She'd made excellent progress in securing invites to the meetings, but the folks in the meetings were purposely talking over her head or using jargon that she couldn't follow. At least it *seemed* purposeful. When she gave a progress report at the most recent of Gardiner's staff meetings, he'd told her to take George with her.

If traffic isn't too bad... She mulled over going home to change. Just as she was picking up her purse, she heard George in the hallway, his voice getting louder. She stood up as he was just visible through her open door. She slammed her drawer and heard a loud bang and screamed. George, coffee in hand, and Ishi came running.

"You ok?" "What happened?"

Jillian opened her drawer and smelled the remnant of gun powder waft a little stronger. She pulled her drawer out of her desk and found three little popper things had been taped together to the back of her drawer.

She shook her head and then stood up and grabbed her purse. "Out," she said, in a firm voice.

Ishi and George stepped back into the hallway. "Are you all right?" George asked, and glanced at her clothes and the coffee stains. "What happened?"

It was the last straw. Jillian smacked his cup and spilled his coffee all over him. Ishi stifled a laugh and stepped further away.

"What the hell?!" George said. Jillian locked her office door in a quick movement and headed down the hall muttering under her breath about his pedigree while George shouted at her.

Unlike Jillian, George didn't go home to change his clothes. He liked the idea of having the Hardware people ask him what had happened to him while she was right next to him. He wanted to see her squirm.

Ishi had tried to help him clean up a little. She'd gotten the coffee off of his tie without it setting. His white shirt didn't fare so well, it had a nice big brown stain on his chest.

Well, it'll just have to be my badge of honor.

He waited until the last possible moment, for Jillian to return to her office, before he headed down stairs to the meeting without her. He was welcomed, though not warmly, and sat only to learn that Jillian had one upped him again. She'd called in to the meeting.

Jillian met Malvinia at a restaurant near the hospital for lunch; she called and told Malvinia it was an emergency. She spent the first ten minutes ranting about George and his childish pranks. Once she'd calmed down, she was able to take a bite of her salad.

"It's been a year," Malvinia started. "Are the other managers treating you any better?"

"Eh," Jillian replied, shrugging her shoulders. "I'd say that Taro and Neal are polite, but remote. Sergei, well, Sergei clearly doesn't like me. He keeps a bit of distance. Until today, I thought that George and I were doing something similar, keeping our distance. I can't believe he did the greased door handles again. That shows a real lack of imagination."

"Okay, then let's get to the nitty gritty. Promotion prospects?"

Setting her fork down to pick up her water glass, Jillian answered, "I made the short list. I just heard this morning. It's me and George."

Malvinia leaned forward and lowered her voice. "Then why are you surprised? Didn't you tell me months ago that you figured out he wants the Director position too? He's playing dirty. And you got him back. I say, it's time to look for a big play. Something to take him out of the running." She sat back. "Set him up, if you have to."

Jillian's eyes widened. "What do you mean?"

"I mean, take him out. Get him fired. Set up something that even Gardiner will have to fire him for. Who's pretty? Set him up for sexual harassment."

"I couldn't do that," Jillian said, aghast. "I mean, it's one thing to unplug someone's computer and spill coffee on them. It's entirely different to get him fired for something like that. If word gets out about it, he might have trouble getting another job! It's just… just…"

"Necessary." "Mean!"

Malvinia sipped her water for a moment and then sat up very straight. "Survival of the fittest, Jilly. In this case, the smartest and the fastest."

"No. I could never do that."

"Well, then you could start looking for a new job."

"Oh! Don't *say* that," Jillian said, and speared some lettuce. "I was thinking about that this morning. Don't you think it would make me a quitter?"

Exhaling loudly, Malvinia studied Jillian's face for a moment. "Let's think about this on the simplest of levels, ok? It's you or George. If it isn't you, you'll be working for him. Do you want to work for him?"

"No."

"Then it's quit or win." Malvinia said, very flatly and then returned to her soup.

Jillian sat back, not feeling hungry all the sudden. "I don't want to quit, but I don't want to cheat to win."

This time Malvinia full-on sighed. "You have got to be kidding me. Cheating? Do you think it was fair play when he started playing all his little pranks on you? Today it was a miserable mess that ended with small explosives. It could have gone much farther.

"You have got to take this seriously," Malvinia said. Then she considered. "Fine. I wasn't going to tell anyone about this, but I think I had better. You know that I recently made department head."

"Of course," Jillian nodded. That had been a fun night of celebrating.

"You know that I was far from the only candidate. I'd done my part, covering extra shifts, taking on extra paperwork, pushing through new protocols and procedures. I earned it."

"Right."

"Martin announces he's retiring and that he'll work with the Chief of Staff to name his replacement. I learn that Tedi is on the list, too. She's also worked hard, not as hard as me, but she's friends with some of the right people. I realized *my* position was in jeopardy. So, I took care of it." Malvinia looked straight at Jillian. "She left her birth control pills in her locker. I changed the active ones for inactive ones. Now, she's going to be a mom and I'm head of the department."

Stunned, Jillian sat back in chair. *How could you do something like that?* "Mal! That's... that's..."

"Business. If she had a brain she would've noticed the pill packages had been swapped. The colors aren't even the same for inactive pills. But she didn't pay any attention."

"Are you saying she asked for it?"

"No, I'm saying I wanted the job more than she did. You don't have to act so shocked."

"This isn't acting."

"When we formed the 'Fab 5,' we all agreed to do what was necessary to succeed." Malvinia took a quick drink. "And Tedi isn't unhappy. She's married now and she's going to work in a clinic where she'll have better hours. She's not complaining at all.'

Would you complain? It must be mortifying to be a doctor and have an unplanned pregnancy.

"Fine, if you're such a goodie-goodie. Look for another way. But mark my words, men play for keeps in the business world too. Take him out before he gets you. He may well have been improvising today, just some subtle things to make you want to go on your own. Tomorrow may be much worse." Malvinia punctuated her words with a wave of her fork.

Jillian quit talking. She let Malvinia change the subject to the hospital and go on and on. *Why say anything else?* Malvinia had clearly gone to the dark side and she was inviting Jillian to join her. She couldn't imagine wanting anything so much that she'd do something like Malvinia had done. As much as the idea of sinking George sounded appealing after the explosive thingies, she couldn't set him up for a fall. Not like that. It was... evil. She didn't want the job that much.

But if she didn't get it, she'd have to come up with a good next move, and it'd have to be a move out of the door. Feeling a little lump form in her throat, she started to wonder if she could do something small and get him out of the running. Not the size of Mal's suggestion. The lump got bigger as she thought about it. *Why did I take this job? I could have taken the job at Chase and been in the big bad corporate world and changed companies to get promoted. It'll be so much harder to move from this small company up to the big ones.*

I need that promotion.

George decided to wear Jillian's coffee all day, rather than leave to change. By the time lunch was over, the story had spread like wild fire and he was hoping that it would get back to Gardiner, but he never heard whether it did or not. And when the day was over he went down to the first floor bathroom and changed into his casual clothes and headed for Whistling Elms. The weather was decent, so he walked the nearly two miles.

Whistling Elms wasn't a particularly large retirement community and assisted living facility. They had a capacity of ninety-eight residents, which meant that everybody knew everybody. George walked up to front counter and handed Mariah his bag with a big smile and a 'thank you.' She stowed the bag for him and watched him sign in. "He's waiting for you in the community room."

"Thanks, Mariah. How're the kids? Did Junior have his dentist appointment?"

Mariah leaned over the counter a little. "No cavities. How do you remember?"

George stepped back to shrug out of his jacket. "It's easy. I don't clutter my mind with friends outside of here."

"Pssh," Mariah said, and took George's jacket to hang on coat rack. When she turned back, George was already heading down the hall. "I should probably tell you..."

Orville had the game console hooked into the smaller television already when George found him. "Are you playing without me?" He asked, and Orville looked up and grinned. "Planning on beating me today?"

Orville tossed him a controller. "I plan on it every day. Just don't often succeed."

"Ah," George said, and sat down. "Start 'er up."

Starting off with Need for Speed, Orville didn't talk much in the beginning. "How are you today, Orville? How's the sciatica?"

"It's the arthritis that's getting worse. My knees are shot."

"And how is Delaney?"

"Still an idiot. They caught him trying to sneak food. I don't blame him for hating his diet, but diabetes is serious."

"And Marcia?"

"Still the prettiest woman here."

"Are you still chasing her?"

"Not as fast with my knees going on me. So, how's work?"

"It's work." George said, automatically and then realized he was neglecting the big news. "I did make the short list for the Director position."

"Oh," Orville said, moving with his controller.

"Oh?" George said. "I thought I'd at least get congratulations."

A snort and a small cough. "Right. Congratulations."

"Well, that was flat," George said. "I've been working really hard for the job."

"Wrong job," Orville mumbled and ran George off the road and laughed. "No concentration. Are you letting me win today?"

"Never." George shifted in the seat. "Why do you keep going on about it being the wrong job?"

"'Cause it is," Orville said. "I remember when you first visited me. This nonsense isn't what you talked about, all this management crap. You wanted to create, design, and build. It's hard to see you killing yourself on something you don't even want."

"Things changed, Orville. I want it now."

"No, you don't. But don't pay me any mind. Nobody else does."

"Yeah, right. Let's race."

"What about the woman in your life? I haven't heard a word about, oh geez, what is her name? Kathy?"

George nudged Orville's car a little. "Yeah. That's over."

"Over? Why?"

"Good question. She didn't exactly give me a reason the last time we talked."

"Hmmph," Orville scoffed. "I suppose you didn't ask."

"Ack!" George plowed into a barrier. "I was a bit relieved, to tell you the truth."

Orville snorted again. "Why is that? What was wrong with her? I thought you liked her."

George glanced at Orville. "It fizzled out."

"Mmm," Orville nodded. "Anyone new on the horizon?"

"Leave it be, Orville."

"Can't. You're too young to be alone and too old to be goofing around."

"I'm not goofing around. She just wasn't the one and neither was I. In a way, it all worked out just fine."

"Idiot stick."

An hour later, when the nurse had actually walked up to them to announce 'third and final call for dinner,' George told Orville to go ahead and he'd put away the game system. Orville tried to argue. "Come on, Orville. You know you've got to go to dinner when they want you. I'll clean up and see you in a few days."

"Oh, fine," Orville grumbled. "I had fun." He patted George on the shoulder and headed off to the dining room. "Good to see you, Kid. Come at the usual time on Saturday."

George packed up the game system and returned it to the front desk as he signed out. "Working late?" He asked Mariah, who should have been gone by then.

"Margot's sick. I'm covering half her shift. Damon will be in early to cover the other half."

"Ah. Well, take care of yourself. Don't get sick too."

"I won't," Mariah said, handing him his coat and bag. "How was Orville?"

"The same as usual. Though he's getting better at the racing games."

Mariah tightened her lips. "His son cancelled his visit again."

"Oh," George said, feeling all the air go out of his lungs. "Not surprising, I guess," he said, after he took in air again. "Cancelled the last two, didn't he?"

"Three," Mariah said. "I was going to say something when you came in..."

"Better you didn't. You know Orville doesn't want anyone feeling sorry for him. It was probably better I didn't know." He shrugged into his jacket. "Do me a favor and let me know if he's particularly down tomorrow. I'll come by for a while and let him pick apart my life again. That'll cheer him up."

"You're a good man."

"Nah, but thanks for saying it."

Charlie meowed loudly when Jillian opened the door to her apartment. "Hi, baby." She brought in her bags of groceries, set them down, and gave Charlie a scratch before she took off her coat. "It was a long day for me. How was yours?"

He meowed again and then started to purr and rub against her legs. "Lots of napping? I bought you some tuna."

Unpacking her bags didn't take long and she started an omelet on the stove for dinner. Her company cell started chiming just as she plated the omelet. Taking care to turn off the stove first, Jillian answered her phone. "Hello. This is Jillian."

"Manager's meeting at 7 am tomorrow," Gardiner's voice came through clearly.

"Seven? All right, I'll be there."

"Good. This is important. Tardiness will not be permitted."

Click.

Ohhhkay. That was weird. "Early morning tomorrow, Charlie. A very odd omen for a Thursday. Looks like it's only one movie tonight. What do you think? Musical? Comedy? Drama?"

Charlie ran into the living room and jumped up on the coffee table looking at the television. Jillian brought in her dinner on a tray. She pulled a few DVDs off of the shelves and asked him if any were acceptable. Charlie sniffed each case in turn, but didn't react. She pulled off another four choices. This time he pawed one box. She turned it around. "It's a Wonderful Life. That's one of your favorites isn't it?"

She slid the disc into the player and let it start. "Tuna now or at intermission?"

"Meow!"

"Of course. Follow me while the disc plays to the menu." She served him his tuna and then returned to the sofa to start her dinner. She waited for Charlie to hop up next to her to start the movie, though. He didn't like to miss the beginning, even if the cards were boring. He loved the opening music of It's a Wonderful Life.

Jillian was early, and she arrived with some other female managers. But she didn't sit until the Hardware folks showed up and she made a point to sit next to one of them. The remainder of the software team arrived last, save the boss.

Jillian looked around the room and whispered to herself, "Managers, Directors, and a VP, oh my." Everyone at every level of management was present.

George picked a place to stand near the front. The personal phone call from Gardiner the previous evening had really thrown him. Gardiner was particularly cryptic, and as far as George could find out, he'd been that way with everyone. He looked around the room. "Managers, Directors, and a VP, oh my," he said to himself.

Right at the stroke of seven, Gardiner walked into the room and shut the door. "I apologize for all the late calls and the early meeting. I want to share this with you all before it comes out another way.

"I'll keep this brief. The important information to share downward is already in a memo that everyone is going to find on their desk this morning, so don't worry about having to communicate this word for word. But I want you prepared.

"As you all know, we've had a few product flops over the last two years. Thanks to that, we're not in the cash position we should be. I've spent a great deal of time with finance and with banks trying to secure a loan to keep us going while we bring out our next Server, the Mark VIII, and our next hard drive, the Infinity.

"Unfortunately, neither finance nor I have been able to find a traditional lender willing to give us a go."

At that, the room buzzed with whispers of worry and even panic.

"All right," Gardiner said, after a time. "Let's not go too far here. I'll give you the short-short right now.

"If we are unable to secure a loan, I'll be laying off about twenty percent of the staff in about a month and a half. We'll be able to bring out our new devices and hopefully make a big enough splash to bring everyone back in about six months. We also have a new software product that will be rolling out in about four months and depending on how it does, we may find ourselves in that position sooner.

"The big question, right now, is can we find a lender to give us enough to get us through? Having exhausted the banks, we've moved on to another traditional form of finance, the private investor.

"I can't make promises as yet, but we found a man who is looking to invest in Tech companies. I've been meeting with him personally and I can tell you that he has been interested enough that he's going to come check out the operation here.

"He is aware of the urgency. I won't say he's the last chance, but he may be. I'm still quite confident of our comeback later in the year, but for the now…"

Gardiner looked around the room, his face grim. "I know you're all here because you want to be. I'll do everything I can to keep you all on. I'm not looking around at who I'll let go, if it comes to that. I'm going forward with the expectation that Mr. Grec will decide to back this company.

"But it was only fair to tell you all what might be coming. I'm sure you have questions. I'll answer a couple right now. As I've said, there isn't a list of who stays or who goes. Six weeks is when I'll have to make those cuts. I don't want anyone to leave, but if you or your people feel they have to look for new jobs, I'm hoping I gave you adequate notice."

Gardiner paused again; Jillian thought that he looked as though he was tearing up. "I'm very sorry." He left the room quickly and the staff remained, staring after him for a moment and then all talking at once.

Melissa came into the room holding a stack of paper in her hand. "One for everybody," she said. When people started filing out, Jillian found herself holding back. The disappointment wasn't just real for her and the job that she wasn't likely to be getting now; it was very real for the boss. She'd never seen Gardiner like that before. It was unsettling. He didn't believe he was going to get the money. That much was clear.

Jillian noticed George as the staff slowly filed out. He too held back a few moments. When he finally wandered up to the door, Melissa handed him his copy of the letter and then said, very quietly, "Gardiner's office. One hour." George looked at her, surprised. "Okay."

He found Taro and Neal down the hallway. Taro shook his head. "I didn't know anything about it. I'm betting Melissa didn't know either until she came in this morning."

"You don't have to be defensive, Taro," George said. "Bad news travels fast. I'm thinking they've been keeping a pretty tight lid on this."

Neal cleared his throat. "Melissa told me to be in Gardiner's office in an hour."

Taro and George looked at each other and then at Neal. "Me too." "And me."

Neal exhaled in relief and sagged in the knees a little before bouncing back up. "Thank God. I thought maybe he'd decided to tell me I'm on the chopping block, as a courtesy."

"I bet it's all of Software," George said. "He's probably going to go over the schedule again and make sure all our ducks are in row for this investor."

"Right," Neal said. "Makes sense."

Sergei came out of the washroom a few feet away and walked over. "Bummer morning, eh?"

"Yeah," Taro said. "You get a personal invite to Gardiner's office too?"

"Not just me? Good. Yeah. In one hour."

"That's four out of five," George said, and glanced back toward the conference room. "I wonder if it's a clean sweep."

Jillian took her copy of the letter and also her whispered command to attend Gardiner. She'd delayed long enough that she felt comfortable asking Melissa, "Know what it's about?"

"No," Melissa shook her head and frowned. "I wish I did. It's you and the four musketeers, though."

"Mmm," Jillian said. "Thanks."

She walked out into the hall and saw her peers looking her direction. Gritting her teeth a little, she walked over to their group and joined them. "Sounds like a review in an hour."

"Yeah," said Neal. "We're guessing schedule review."

She nodded. "I guess, I'll see you all then," she said, and started up the hallway toward the stairs. George stayed with the others, all silent, for a few moments and then he mumbled a 'later' and he too walked up the hallway. He caught up to Jillian on the stairs.

"Looks like the promotion is on the back burner," he said.

Jillian paused and looked at him. "If it's as bad as what he said, I'd say the promotion is completely off the table for at least a year. Our cash position has to be very bad. He's downplaying it."

"Really? Laying off twenty percent of the staff is downplaying it?"

"Not that. I mean, we must be up to our eyeballs in debt. If he can't find any other lenders, then he's probably mortgaged everything here. All the equipment in the factory. All the lab equipment. Maybe even the furniture. Surely the building."

"Wow, aren't you Little Miss Sunshine?" He said, with a half-smile.

Jillian gave him a grim, tight smile back. "It's bad. I'd say he's being optimistic about bringing anyone back. Unless the new server and the new hard drive really take off in the market, I bet this place doesn't have two years." She started back up the stairs again.

Letting out his breath, George followed her up. "Yeah. I've never seen Gardiner like this. It's bad all right."

When they reached the top of the stairs, Jillian went left and George went right. George took a few steps, paused to glance back at Jillian, and then kept on. Jillian took a few more steps and glanced back at George for a moment. She didn't pause in her steps though.

"I know it's a little unorthodox," Gardiner said, as his Software leadership gaped at him. "But Mr. Grec seems to believe that our Software Division is more important for the long term sustainability of the company. And he does have a point. Software has all the recurring business, the base we can count on monthly. And it's where I started this company. Hardware tends to be a flash in the pan with each new product. Sometimes we make back our investment, sometimes we don't."

George was the one to work up the nerve to speak first. "I don't think I understand correctly what you want from us."

Gardiner sat on edge of his desk. "Look, I don't know why Cisco Grec is so set on this little challenge. But if it gets us the funds to keep moving forward, then I'm all for it."

Jillian had to keep from hiding her hands. "It'll set us back on our schedule. We can't drop everything just like that. If we're the money farm, shouldn't we keep farming?"

"Okay," Gardiner said. "You're absolutely right. But we need this money, Cisco's money."

Taro leaned forward in his chair. "How bad is it? Is it worse than you told us?"

Gardiner didn't say anything for at least a minute. "Okay. I'm going to do something I hate doing. Jillian and George can testify to it with regard to the communication problems between Software and Hardware. I'm playing the boss card.

"You and your teams will drop everything and work for the next four weeks on a brand new tool. At the end of the four weeks, each team will get a chance to demonstrate what it's capable of putting together in a month. If we impress him, we'll likely get the money. You'll save a lot of jobs, some your own. The few requirements for the tool are laid out in an email that'll be in your inboxes before lunch."

"You do realize that Thanksgiving falls in there, don't you? Sir?" Neal asked.

Gardiner absently tapped his desk with fingers. "Yes, I know that. You'll just have to figure it out."

Everyone sat back inhaling in an attempt to bite back what they all wanted to say.

Sergei changed the subject. "Is this a competition or-?"

"A competition. If we fail to impress him, it'll be easy to see which team is the bottom twenty percent."

Jillian gasped a little and then flushed in embarrassment at the uncontrolled sound. She'd never heard Gardiner talk like that either. She tried to get him to be strong like this with Hardware but never seen a tenth of the firmness.

Gardiner looked at her and swallowed. "I'm serious."

"I know," she said.

"Good luck," Gardiner said, as a dismissal.

CHAPTER THREE

An emergency meeting of the 'Fab 5' was more than a little unusual, and everyone but Kai, who was trying a case, made it. Jillian only waited for the waitress at the 'Leaping Lizard' to take their order before she launched into the story. Lacey didn't seem particularly interested until Jillian got to the competition part. "So each team is supposed to develop a whole new tool from scratch over the next month and then present it. If this Cisco Grec likes what he sees, he saves us. If he doesn't, the bottom team is the first out the door."

"You're kidding," Lacey said.

Jillian shook her head. "You can bet this is going to get ugly. And my team is really strong in database, not fancy GUIs or reports. I think I'm done before I start."

Christy tapped her fingers on the table in a little rhythm. "What rules were you given?"

"Not a lot of rules. Just a lot of requirements."

Malvinia signaled the waitress and ordered Jillian a glass of wine. "You need to relax. You're shoulders are almost covering your ears."

The four kicked around the problem for a while with little to no success and ate their chicken salads, or linguini alfredo, or hamburger. Jillian looked around the familiar restaurant and sighed. Many a problem had been talked over in that place. "Thanks for coming, anyway, guys. I appreciate your support."

Malvinia shook her head. "We're not done yet. We just need to warm up."

Jillian smiled and finished her wine. "I don't think there's much to do, except give my team the biggest pep talk ever and then pray a lot."

"Is there a rule about working with another team?" Lacey asked.

"I don't think there's a rule exactly," Jillian answered. "But Gardiner said it was a competition."

"Oo," Malvinia said. "I like where you're headed with this Lacey." She looked at Jillian. "Join forces with someone else. Guarantee the win. Get either the GUI team or the reports team."

"Wait. Wait. Wait. Gardiner was really clear about the competition thing. If my team partners with another, we may get the boot for it."

Christy shrugged. "This sounds like the kind of situation where you do what you have to and ask for forgiveness later. Just be sure that no one knows what's going on until you have to put your cards on the table."

Jillian looked at Lacey, Christy, and then Malvinia in turn. "Okay. How would I pull it off? I'd have to suggest it to someone, have them accept, and not have anyone else hear about it. If I ask one of them and they say 'no' you can bet Gardiner will hear about it."

"Well, yes, that is a tricky point," said Malvinia. "You could always go the other way too. Sabotage everyone else. Stay late and steal the notes people leave on their desks. Maybe do something to set them back with the servers. I don't really understand any of this tech stuff."

"I couldn't do that," Jillian said. "No, Mal. That's out of the question."

Malvinia shrugged. "Well, then I suggest you go with Lacey's idea."

Jillian handed her credit card to the waitress. "George's team is GUI. Taro's is reporting."

"So?" Lacey asked.

"So. I don't know that I can trust either of them to team up. If I start with the wrong one... I won't have a chance to try the other."

Malvinia leaned forward and rested her elbows on the table. "Jill, it's time to grow up. You don't win by playing nice. And you don't get ahead watching everyone else play the game. What happened to the girl who jumped in on her first day and said she'd take on the problem with that other division...?"

"Hardware," Jillian supplied.

"Exactly." Malvinia continued, "This is the moment to take chances and shine. If you don't, you may still have your job, but you won't be looking at the promotion."

Christy chimed in. "That's right. Play it safe and stay where you are. Or, take control and show them all who you are."

Lacey just nodded.

"Okay," Jillian said. "Okay. I'll go for it."

As they headed for the exit, the bartender called to Jillian. "Excuse me, Miss?"

She walked over to the bar. "Yes?" She asked the woman she didn't recognize.

"I'm sorry to bother you. Did your waitress get your wine added to your tab? I still show it open here."

Jillian took out her receipt. "Um. Let's see. No. Can I pay you here?"

"Sure," the woman took her credit card and swiped it.

Jillian tried to make conversation. "Are you new? I don't recognize you."

The woman smiled. "I'm very part-time and yes, I'm new. I'm Juliette. I take it you're a regular?"

"You could say that," Jillian said, and smiled. "My girlfriends and I come here almost once a week."

"Well, I'll see if I can remember your wine preference for next time." Juliette said, handing Jillian her credit card and a slip to sign. "You four looked pretty intense back there."

"Mmm, yes," Jillian said, and returned the slip and waited for her copy. "I needed their advice. Trouble at work."

"Oh, really?" Juliette asked. "Want an opinion from an impartial third party?"

"No, thank you. I've got a plan. Sort of. I just need to figure out who to try it with." She took her receipt and started to turn.

"Who are the choices?"

Jillian turned back. "One of any of four of my peers who pretty much hate me. Although, the better choice is between just two of them."

"Tell me about them."

"Well, I'm competing with one of them for a promotion and the other hasn't been as mean to me directly."

"And the plan is to…"

"Team up to win a completely separate competition."

Juliette tilted her head. "I'd team up with the competition for the promotion."

"Oh, why is that?"

"It's like that old game show. What was it called? 'The Weakest Link.' In the beginning everyone votes off the weak players so they can accumulate more money. Later on they vote off the better players so they have a shot at winning. In your case, better to team up with someone you're competing against, so you share the credit equally. That would also limit the risk of him doing better than you and showing you up."

Jillian thought about that a moment. "Share the success. Keeps the status quo doesn't it?" She tapped her hand on the bar. "That is excellent advice."

"Unless you think you have a better advantage with the other one."

"No. I don't think so. I think you're right on."

Suddenly, she had a much bigger problem. If she was really going to try this, she was going to have to think about how to approach George.

Sergei was in fine form. "We're doomed. Especially me and Neal. Testing and Documentation. We're screwed."

Taro shook his head. "Just relax, Sergei. Worrying will only give you an ulcer."

Neal made a face. "Easy to say when your people produce reports. At least you have a product to show off. I'm sure this investor guy will be ever so impressed with stacks of documentation on a tool we can't build. And then I'll be out."

George just slouched low in his chair and played with his yo-yo while the conversation went on and on. Finally, Sergei looked at him. "Why are you so quiet?"

He looked at all of them in turn. "I'm not as worried as all of you that we can't impress this Mr. Grec. I'm more concerned about losing to Jillian."

The group fell silent for a good minute after that. Neal broke the silence. "I guess it's better than losing our jobs."

George snorted. "And then she'll definitely get promoted over all of us."

Taro got up. "I'm so tired of this. All of this." He shoved his chair into the table. "I'm taking mine to go and going back to the office to figure out my game plan."

George and Neal looked at each other. "Well," George said. "That was surprising."

"He's getting married in a month," Sergei said. "I bet you ten dollars he starts working on his résumé before we get back."

Neal hmmphed. "Could be."

"Well, I'm not quitting just yet," George said, and pulled out his smart phone. He started looking for information on the investor Gardiner had found. "We'll impress Mr. Cisco Grec, so help me."

The walk back to work was a little quiet. Between the somber mood from the work situation and Taro having left early, it seemed even negative Sergei didn't have anything left to say. The breeze seemed to pick up a little and George turned his head and saw the carpet cleaning billboard out of the corner of his eye. For a moment, not even a second, he thought it said 'Trust Jillian' instead of 'Trust Sullivan.' But when he took a good look, it was as it had been for the month.

He blinked a few times and assumed that he'd made it up because his impending loss to her was heavy in his mind. *Not normal.* He almost said something to Neal and Sergei and then figured it must be the stress and kept it to himself. The last thing he needed was to have the guys start giving him crap about Jillian again.

He'd called a team meeting for 2 pm so he could layout his strategy with his people, hoping that they'd all remain fairly calm. It was a bit of a worry that some people might decide to jump ship and manage to do it inside the month they had to put together their new tool. If he lost the wrong people, or too many of the right ones, he and whomever remained would be sunk.

In his office, he couldn't sit at his desk. He stood, doing looping tricks with Ringo, while he talked to his dictation program, attempting to lay out a plan.

He heard the knock on his door and glanced at the window to see Jillian. *That's a surprise.* He paused the dictation and opened the door himself. Several greetings came to mind. 'What do you want?' 'Hello.' 'I'm busy.' But before he had a chance to settle on one, Jillian spoke first.

"Hi. May I come in? I come unarmed." She held out her hands from her sides.

"Sure," he said, putting the yo-yo in his pocket. "I guess."

George watched her with caution. She entered and then shut the door. "I'll try to be brief. I know you're busy."

"We're all busy." George walked back to his desk and then changed his mind and walked back to his table and said, "Please," and motioned her to take a chair.

"Thank you," she said, sitting. George sat after she did. *Just like him to behave all manners now.* "First, I want to apologize for the coffee yesterday." In truth, she wasn't sure that bringing it up was a good move, but she was fairly certain that an apology was in order, if this was going to work.

"Oh?" George said, and crossed his arms.

"Yes," she said. "It was a childish reaction. And I'm sorry."

"Okay," George said. "I accept." His curiosity was in overdrive. When they'd called the last truce, neither of them had apologized. They'd just agreed to let it go.

Jillian took a deep breath then. It was too much to hope he'd apologize, too. *Oh, well, just get on with it.* "Thank you. Okay. So, I wanted to see you about this new project nightmare."

"Yes?"

"Well, here's the thing. None of us is really equipped to produce anything alone."

"You're right," he said.

"I know," Jillian continued, "that our teams work differently. But our teams are each strong in particular areas. So, I'd like to propose something."

George's eyebrows rose. He was more than casually curious now.

"I think that your team and mine should take this challenge on jointly."

His right hand rubbed across his mouth. "Really?"

Jillian stood up. "Gardiner has to know that our groups independently aren't going to impress anybody in this short a time period. The requirements could keep my people busy for a nearly a year." She grabbed the back of the chair she'd been sitting in and leaned toward George just a little. "But together, we can do so much more. My people are good at the bones. Your people are good with the flesh. I don't know if we can create a soul in a month, but we'd have something much better than either can do individually." She stood up straight. "What do you think?"

Was it wrong to like the fact that when she asked what he thought, she bit her lip? She almost never showed her nervousness with a habit like that. It was a little distracting in other ways too, if he was honest.

"What do I think?" George said, and took out his yo-yo. He didn't think about it until he'd moved it up and down a few times, the fact that she hated his yo-yo. When he looked at her, she was looking at his face and not the yo-yo. *She wants this team up pretty bad.*

But do I? It would save me from losing to her, or her to me, if a miracle occurred. But how would it even work?

"You know our people can do more together," she said. "Do you need time to think about it?"

"Did you ask anybody else?" George asked, and tried to keep the surprised look off his face. The idea hadn't even occurred to him until it was out of his mouth.

"No," she said, and stood up from the lean against the chair. She lifted one hand up to her hair and patted it. "It's evident that Gardiner is expecting more than one tool to demonstrate for his investor. We can't all work together and undercut that. It may cost us the investment. But just two of us... We might be able to get away with it. Ask for forgiveness, rather than permission." She stole Christy's words without compunction.

"Why me?"

"Good question," she said, and then paced his office. "Okay. All our cards on the table? We need help with GUI. We can fake reports. We can provide some functionality. But we're just not good with the pretty."

"That's all your cards?"

"And then neither of us will get a leg up on the other for the promotion we both want."

George rocked back in his chair. "You're worried that I'll get the job because of this?"

"More like I'm worried there won't be a job to get. And then, if there is a job, yes."

George stood up and walked over to Jillian, crossing his arms and frowning. "How would it work?"

"Actually, I was thinking of letting our people figure that out. We could pair them up to get them started, but, in the end, let them figure out the how and what and when and who."

George blinked. "You want to let them plan it and build it."

"You know how my team had another increase in output this past month?"

"Yes," George said, and successfully fought the urge to grind his teeth.

"I've been letting them make suggestions and decisions on how to streamline our work load. Every month it gets better and better." Jillian lifted a hand to her neck and rubbed the back. "I facilitate discussions and brainstorming, but I let them make the decisions and the commitments. It can work with your people too."

"New Age Management..." He stopped himself from adding anything else. "I don't know that I can be comfortable with it. I don't know how my people will respond to it. Especially because there is a lot of resentment toward your team. You all have been making the rest of us look bad for a really long time."

"Here's a chance to join us," Jillian said.

"What about Taro, Neal, and Sergei? Their people?"

"Save ourselves, save us all." Jillian said. "Their product may not look as good, but we can save their jobs and 20% across the rest of the company. Perhaps one hundred percent, if Hardware's work flops on release. I don't like thinking that way, but it's possible that the whole company is going down if nothing is done to save it."

"And we're the ones to do it?"

"No. But our teams are, if we get them together and then get out of their way."

George rubbed his face and then walked the length of the room, throwing his yo-yo. "I can't decide whether to say 'Wow' or 'Yikes.'" He turned toward Jillian and she looked like she was stifling a laugh. "What?"

"'Yikes?' I didn't know anyone still used that word."

"Yeah, well, I guess I'm older than I look," George said.

Jillian smiled openly and George almost took a step toward her in reaction. "Are you?" She paused a moment and then said, "And here I thought you were thirteen."

Trying to keep the light, teasing feeling going, George threw his yo-yo out toward her and she didn't even flinch. "Nah. Twelve. I lied."

"Okay, twelve. You in or out?"

George pocketed his yo-yo again. Thinking about the absolute mess he'd been dictating and his presumed upcoming defeat at her hands if he said no. *I'm both cornered and tempted.* He didn't really have a choice, not if he wanted to stay at Gardiner, not if he wanted a shot at the Director position. But it meant... *I guess I'll trust you.* He held out his hand. "Okay. You got a deal."

Jillian pressed her hand into his and George's shoulders dropped. "Wonderful." Her heart started to beat a little faster and she thought she felt a flutter in her stomach. *Please don't let this be a mistake.*

George looked into her eyes and caught himself just before he sighed. "I'm going to need your help with this New Age stuff," he said, as he let go of her hand and quickly hid his own in his pocket.

"That's no problem," Jillian said. "We'll sit down and hash out the general plan, then we present it to our folks together, and *then* we see what happens next."

"That's a lotta faith."

"Mmm," Jillian shrugged. "Expect the moon, they'll try not to disappoint. Expect a pit; they'll drop you in one."

"Is that a New Age Management philosophy?"

"Actually, my mother, the teacher, told me that one. It was the same with students. The more you expect of them, the more you get. She was right, too."

A silence fell. "Okay," George said. "I called my team together at two. You think we can be ready by then and bring yours in too?"

"Follow me," Jillian said.

"Where?"

"My office," she said. He followed, not sure that he liked the fact that she was going to use her desk as a power play, but he followed anyway.

After putting out a message to her team to meet at two, she handed George a dry erase marker and took one for herself and stood at the board on her wall. "Let's iron out what we're going to tell them."

So much for my worry of a power play. Good sign. George walked over to her windows and looked out. "How are we going to keep this little team up from everyone else?"

Jillian followed him over and closed her blinds. "I don't know. But Taro, Neal, and Sergei don't talk to me." She picked up the requirements that Gardiner had given them for the new tool from her desk and walked up to the dry erase board. "Let's start with…"

Jillian was pretty good at teaming, George had to reluctantly admit. She made a point to ask him for his input and never shut him down when he said something. Everything went on the board and then they agreed together what stayed and what went. By the time they had all their employees meet them in big conference on the first floor, they had a plan. It was a loose plan, with plenty of room for maneuvering.

The meeting between Jillian's team and George's team had been what George generously called thought-provoking. She talked at the beginning, outlining what she and George were expecting by way of cooperation, communication, and, eventually, the presentation. George ran through the requirements for the new tool and Jillian handed out the documentation.

Then Jillian laid out the starting plan for who was to partner with whom, being certain to mention that this was just a suggestion and that it could be modified. Finally, much to George's consternation, she said that they'd meet again the following morning, before lunch, to hear what the group had planned amongst themselves. And then she left.

George had trouble convincing himself to head out the door and leave his team and Jillian's without any more direction. But when he finally convinced himself to go, he covered his reticence by saying, "Good luck," and then heading out.

He followed Jillian to her office two floors up. "Are we really sure about this?" He asked when she'd opened her office.

"Sure about what? Joining up?"

"Letting them work out the details. It's a lot of details."

Jillian leaned against her door. "They're the ones who'll be providing the results. I think they should decide how to get there. If the meeting tomorrow doesn't show significant progress, we can always decide to step back in." She let out a quick breath. "You'll be surprised. Give them a chance to impress you."

George leaned against her door frame and crossed his arms. "I don't know how you talked me into this."

Jillian smiled and stood up from the door. "It wasn't actually that hard." Then she walked over to her desk and sat down. He watched for a moment, through her doorway, while she opened up a folder on her desk and then started to type on her computer.

"What have I done?" He asked himself, and walked the few steps to his office. His stomach was beginning to knot up a little or something. He felt really tight and nervous, no not nervous, similar but different. He couldn't stay still. He had to move. His breathing was a little a fast too. "Oh, God. I can't believe... am I having a panic... attack?"

He wasn't sure what to do for something like that, so he decided to get out of the building to his quiet thinking spot. He took the stairs to the roof and tried to breathe deeply and slowly while walking quickly around and around. A few tries and he finally felt himself calming.

"Well, that was an overreaction, if ever there was one," he said to the air. He didn't stop the fast walking, but at least he was breathing again. He felt like he wanted to jump out of his skin.

"Distract yourself. Distract yourself." He took out his phone and called Whilstling Elms and asked for Orville.

"Hello?"

"Orville. It's George. How are you today?"

There were a few moments of silence and then Orville spoke. "They told you, didn't they?"

Still tearing around the roof, George answered. "Yes. But that's not why I'm calling. I'm trying to get a grip on myself. I think I had a panic attack."

"Oh," Orville said. "A panic attack? Why?"

"Everything went sideways today, that's why."

"Illuminate me."

George found once he started talking he couldn't stop. It felt great to get it out with someone who wasn't in the midst of it too, someone who only cared about what happened to him. While he dribbled out the story, he had a few 'uh-huhs' and some 'mm-hmms' but mostly Orville just listened.

"And now I feel like I'm coming apart, literally, like I don't fit in my skin. I can't stop moving. For a few minutes I had trouble breathing. This has never happened to me before."

Orville gave him time, making certain that he was finished, and then said, "Interesting."

"That's it?!" George asked.

"What do you want, George?"

George walked the perimeter of the roof. "I don't know. Sage wisdom? Something that makes me feel better."

"You know, as well as I do, that you don't like my wisdom. My advice to you right now is to quit. Quit and don't look back. Find a job that you actually love."

George walked faster. "I guess you're right, Orville."

"Oh, yeah?" Orville said, surprised.

"Yeah," George said. "I really don't like your wisdom."

"Smart ass," Orville said.

"Yeah, well, you know who my role models were growing up. And now I have you."

Orville snorted. "If you took me at all seriously, you'd listen to the amazing advice I give you. But, since that obviously isn't going to happen, tell me this, do you feel any better yet?"

"I don't know. I still feel like I'm coming out of my skin. It's unsettling. At least while I'm walking I'm less tense about it. Or something."

"You breathing all right?" Orville asked. "Quit breathing and you die."

"Yeah, that's back to normal." George paused. It was actually hard to tell, he was walking so fast he was breathing a little hard. "I think."

"Let me know if you think you're going to hyperventilate. I'll hang up and call 9-1-1."

"I don't think that'll be necessary."

"Where are you anyway? Taking a walk around the block?"

"Around the roof. It's perfect. Nobody comes up here, so it's private. And there's an amazing view of the river."

"If you don't feel better soon, you should go for a walk by the river. It'll still your soul."

George smiled a little. "Orville, your poet is showing again."

"Yeah, yeah, yeah. You just want to change the subject now. Though why is beyond me. I believe you called for advice."

"More like for sympathy," George said.

"Well, call somebody else. I'm not going to sympathize with you when I don't think you're doing the right thing."

"We agree on that, at least. I should never have let her talk me into giving up that input."

"Control, you mean," Orville said. "You're a control freak. And do you know why?"

George shook his head and realized he'd slowed his pace without noticing. *Well, that's good. I'm really calming down, anyway.* "No. Why am I a control freak?"

"Because you're unhappy. Your soul's unchallenged. Everything that makes life worth living is missing from your life, so you try to manage the daylights out of what's there. Shape it into the most convenient and comfortable form possible."

"That's an interesting idea. I don't think there's a whole lot of basis in psychology though."

Orville snorted. "I don't need any psychology to tell me that your problem is you aren't happy. Start working on that, will you?"

"I am, Orville. I'll be very happy when I get the Director position. I'll be able to say I really made something of myself."

He could hear the frown in Orville's voice. "Yeah. But *what* will you be?"

George gazed toward the river. "I'll be satisfied with myself, Orville. And while I appreciate you, probably a great deal more than you know, it's my opinion that counts."

"You're right, George. Your opinion counts much more than mine. Just think about what I said. Now," he paused, "when are you coming again to play. We got an old one I've never played before. Some kind of shoot 'em game."

George crossed his free arm. "You do know they don't like you playing violent games there."

"What am I going to do? Turn into a serial killer?" Orville laughed. "I'll terrorize everyone here, hobbling up and down the hall slower than a turtle. Watch out! It's the Octogenarian Off-er!"

George found himself smiling, finally. "That's it. And I'll be in trouble as some kind of accessory."

"My friend, you are no accessory. You're an enabler. Completely different. Anyway, when are you coming?"

"Well, that's a good question." George knew he had some late nights coming, and probably a great deal more weekend time. "I'll try for tomorrow, but after that, it may not be until the next Saturday. There's going to be some overtime coming."

Orville made some kind of sniffing sound. "You see. Just more proof. Your priorities are all out of whack. You should be having some fun. And whether you admit it or not, you like coming by to see me."

"I'd probably like it more if you didn't try to tell me how to run my life. I moved out here to get away from a family that did that, if you recall."

"Ha. You came out here to get away from the family business. And if you didn't need me to tell you what's wrong with your life, I wouldn't do it." Orville said. "Now, you sound better. Got yourself back together, hmm?"

George smiled again. "Yes. I guess so."

"Good," Orville said. "I'll see you on Saturday. Then get your priorities straight and be sure that you're here next Wednesday, as usual, if not sooner."

The line went dead and George lowered the phone. He chuckled and said, "Bye, Orville." He shook his head. "Gee, can't wait to see you."

He put the phone in his pocket and took out his yo-yo from the other. He proceeded to run through one of his old trick routines, enjoying the side mount and trapeze and a few inside and outside loops, before moving into an arm wrap, a stall, a leg wrap, a double stall, and the guillotine. He finished up with a picture trick of the Eiffel tower, to go with the guillotine, and then pocketed his yo-yo. He'd put together routines that lasted almost twenty minutes when he was serious and competing; not that a competition ever allowed much over three minutes. Now, it was just fun. The one thing he missed was the audience. It was a lot more fun to do the tricks with someone else appreciating it.

Mostly feeling back to his old self, George descended the stairs and returned to his office. He still had one other thing to worry about... how he was going to keep this all from Neal, Taro, and Sergei... and live with it.

Jillian spent most of the rest of the day trying not to think too much. There was too much to think about. *Far too much.* And how her employees and George's were getting along and planning was probably the smallest of them. Her stomach felt funny, almost like she was hungry, but not.

He'd been standing next to her at the dry erase board when she first noticed it. It came on when she'd detected the slight spice in the air, either cologne or aftershave. The scent was subtle and masculine and went straight through her. But after her head and knees had mostly recovered, she still felt almost queasy, probably because her heart started racing a bit and hadn't really slowed down until she was alone in her office.

But being alone with her thoughts was not a particularly good thing, as her thoughts kept turning back, far back, to when they'd first met and he'd been nice and she thought he was even flirting with her. She'd liked it. As bad an idea as it would have been then, if he'd asked her out, like he'd sort of maybe started to in that first meeting, she might well have said yes.

Now it would be an even bigger disaster, not that he'd ever ask her out after everything that had happened since that first day. It had become clear that he wasn't going to lose without a fight. Even a few weeks of cooperation hadn't a chance to change that.

"I've got to stop thinking about this," Jillian said to herself, and stood up. "Coffee would be good."

Walking briskly to the break room, she tried to still her thoughts enough to listen as she went along and detect if anyone from the other Software teams had noticed that both her team and George's had disappeared. About half of Sergei's team appeared to have taken the afternoon off, as the area they sat in was awfully sparse for that much before quitting time. Neal had his people in one of the conference rooms on that floor. As she walked by she could see a little through the blinds. They looked stressed and Neal looked stressed.

"Not good," she muttered.

As she rounded the corner into the break room she found George and Taro talking. "Hello," she said, like she usually did, attempting to keep up the appearance that absolutely nothing had changed.

Taro said hello back and George made a small waving sort of hand gesture. *Oh, George. If you don't at least act a little like yourself, someone will figure out something's up.* She considered spilling a little coffee on him again, just to keep up appearances, but thought better of it. After all, everyone had the excuse of some major stress.

Instead of coffee, Jillian filled a mug with water and ice. Turning to leave again, she tried to smile at Taro and George, and Taro held out a hand as a plea to stop. "Do you have a game plan, yet, Jillian?"

Watching George's face told Jillian all she needed to know about his acting abilities, he had none, so Jillian answered to keep Taro from looking at George. "Of a sort. I laid out a broad plan for my people and I'm letting them fill in the blanks. You?"

"Ha, um," Taro made an almost amused sound. "Let's say, not so much. I was trying to make a plan with everyone and there was so much negative energy in the room that I had to call for a break."

"That's tough," Jillian said.

"Meh," Taro said, and shrugged. "It could be worse."

George suddenly joined the conversation. "Yeah, you could be Sergei. Half of his team just up and left. I'm not even sure they're coming back."

"I wondered," Jillian said, her hand rising a little to motion toward the empty cubes. "Neal doesn't look to happy either. I just passed him and his team in the conference room."

Taro stuffed his hands in his pockets. "This is stupid. I don't know what Gardiner is thinking. We're better together."

"Except when we're not," George said. "It's a test from top to bottom, front to back."

"Yeah, well, I can think of better ways for him to decide between the two of you than this."

Jillian shook her head. "It's not about the Director position. But I don't get it either."

"If Gardiner's being straight with us," George said, "and I believe he is, and then it's about this investor guy. But what he thinks he's going to figure out from this is beyond me. If he thinks the programmers don't cut it, is he just not going to invest? Or will he invest on the condition that half are let go?"

Jillian shook her head again. "I don't have a feel for this, at all." *If we were talking about anything else, I'd stick around. Even baseball.* "But, I should get back. I need to find out what the masses have decided to do. I'd planned to give them until tomorrow to present their plan, but now I'm getting the feeling I should at least check in and make sure that there isn't much... disagreement."

"I'm going that way, too," George said. "I'll walk back with you." He looked at Taro. "Good luck."

"You, too," Taro said.

Jillian purposely didn't look back. She didn't want to see Taro's face as he tried to figure out when she and George had suddenly started walking places together. When they were out of earshot, Jillian lowered her voice, "What are you doing?"

"Walking," George said. "Is that a trick question?"

She just sighed. "Don't you think someone will notice if we're suddenly being somewhat friendly-ish toward each other?"

"Your point?" George asked, and when Jillian looked at him he had a very obstinate expression on his face. She'd seen it before when she'd tried to change things that 'had always been' a different way.

"Might be a giveaway," she answered. "Our joint venture."

They walked in silence halfway around the cubes. George grinned then. "I thought about it when you came into the break room while I was talking to Taro. We have nothing to worry about. No one would believe we'd team up on anything."

"What if you're wrong? What if they ask? Are we going to lie?"

"Didn't you already lie?" George asked, and looked away from her face.

"In the strictest sense... I suppose I implied..."

George snorted and shook his head. "Oh, Jillian. Either you lied or you didn't." He stopped at her office door.

"I," Jillian started and then stopped. *I don't like to think of myself like this.*

"Oh, now don't go getting all up about lying. Don't think of it like that."

Jillian unlocked her door and then, even knowing she'd regret it, she looked up at him and asked, "How am I supposed to think of it?"

"Just think of it as strategy." Then came the big reason she knew she'd regret it, he smiled at her. The full of himself, macho smile that she hated intellectually and loved in every other way. Her heart sped up again. "We're playing chess," he said, "and we're winning."

"It'll only count if we actually win the game," she said.

"We will," George said. "If anyone can, we will."

"Okay." She started to turn back to her office.

"Aren't we going downstairs for a progress check?"

"That was just an excuse to leave you and Taro." Jillian went into her office and returned to her desk. Now she was thinking about his self-satisfied smile. *That will never do.* She opened up Irene's file and started to work on Irene's end of year review, using her time as wisely as she could.

CHAPTER FOUR

George didn't know what he'd said wrong, but clearly he'd done something to piss off Jillian, yet again. They were talking and having a half-way real conversation, and then they weren't.

He took out his yo-yo and walked a lap of the floor. He knew it would look unusual, if anyone noticed, but he'd figured that, today at least, most everyone was pretty well focused on themselves. Between the worry of being laid off and the nutso challenge, it was certainly understandable. If anyone on the floor wasn't completely self-centered at the moment, it was Taro. And he probably still had plenty of other things on his mind.

That's when George remembered Rachel. He took a partial second lap and stopped at Rachel's desk. She was typing away, sitting up straight in perfect typist form, and only paused a moment when she saw him. "Just one minute, if it's alright."

"Sure," George said, and pocketed his yo-yo in an attempt to show that he was going to pay full attention to the conversation, once it started. It worked, he saw her eyes flicker from the screen to him and she stopped.

"I'm sorry. This is important, isn't it?"

Score. "Yes," George said, and grabbed Vidar's chair from across the aisle to sit down. Once he sat, he tried to smile, but he was sure he just looked sheepish which he felt anyway. "So, it looks like I missed some news." He gestured toward her hands. "I just wanted to take a moment and give you my very best wishes."

"Oh," Rachel said, sitting back a little. "Well, thank you. I started to think you didn't approve or something."

"What?" George asked. "Why wouldn't I approve? Do I even know him?"

Rachel made a strange sound, like a suppressed laugh. "No. I don't think so. I just thought... I don't know. I thought maybe you were worried I'd get married and quit. I know you don't like change."

"Well, I'd hate to see you go, that's true. But, I honestly just didn't notice the ring. If you'd announced it, I'd have been happy for you then." *I'm pretty damn self-centered too, aren't I?*

"Okay. Well, thank you, George."

He stood up and returned Vidar's chair.

"Oh, George?" Rachel said.

"Hmm?" He turned back to her.

"Thank you, really. I appreciate it. And, just for your peace of mind, I'm not quitting." Rachel said, with a smile.

"You know," George said. "If you were, I'd still be happy for you." *And what do you know? I think I really would be.*

Jillian held off checking on the new consolidated team as long as she could keep herself in check, but when the time came for some of the earlier birds to start heading home, she couldn't wait any longer. Her fake excuse to Taro and George had become a prophecy. *What if they're just arguing and not making any plans?* She knocked on George's door on her way, told him where she was going, and then headed for the stairs. He caught up to her by the time she was on the first floor and they walked together to the large conference room. She knocked once and went in first.

Before she or George said anything, the entire group stopped what they were doing and covered up everything. People jumped in front of the dry erase boards and flipped over papers on the table. "Hello," Jillian said, her voice rising in tone to convey her surprise. "And how are things going? We were just coming to check on your progress. It's nearly quitting time for a few of you."

George peeked in around Jillian who had stopped most of the way in, with her hand still on the doorknob. "Everything all right?"

There were a few moments of silence as the team shared looks at one another, finally Irene, one of Jillian's programmers, stood up. "Everything is coming along just fine. We'll be ready to talk to you about the plan tomorrow as scheduled."

Irene sat back down and the room stayed silent. Jillian moved out of the way and George followed her in and then shut the door.

"So… it's going well?" Jillian asked.

Another few moments of silence, then Irene spoke again. "Yes. Thank you."

George took a few steps toward the nearest dry erase board. "Mind showing us?"

"Actually, we do," Mahdi said, from across the room. "We'll tell you all about it, tomorrow."

George walked backwards to where Jillian was standing. "Do you get the feeling we're not wanted?"

Jillian nodded. "Mmm, yes. I'd say so." She cleared her throat. "If there's anything you need, you know how to reach us," she said, and gestured toward the phone on the conference table.

When she received no reply, save staring from nearly every direction, she looked at George. "We seem to be superfluous."

"Uh, yeah," George said, and opened the door. "After you."

"Thank you," Jillian said, and led the way out. As soon as George shut the door behind him, she said, "That was interesting."

"You can say that again," George said, "that is the least welcome I've felt since my last girlfriend and I broke up. She said, 'we're done,' and opened the door. This was almost as warm."

Jillian crossed her arms. "Do you think we should be worried?" *It's hard not to be. My team has never done anything like that to me before.* She ignored the information George had just shared about his break up, not wanting to delve into that particular area at the moment, if ever.

George started for the stairs and said, "You're the new age manager. You tell me."

"Oh, please," Jillian said. "You and your aversion to change. You just have to label everything in some derogatory way so that you don't have to consider it viable."

"'Scuse me?" George stopped and gave Jillian a frown.

"Forget it," Jillian said, and charged ahead of him. She didn't want to make him mad, but it was true. She might not know a whole lot about him personally, even after working so near each other for so long, but she'd picked up a few things. For example, he didn't react well to change. He fought it tooth and nail. He also liked to call her a 'new age manager' to belittle her style. It made it easy to dismiss her methods without even finding out what they were. She'd seen him do a similar thing with new processes.

"Hey!" He called out as she hit the third step going back up.

She froze before she transferred her weight to move up to the next stair. "What?" The door to the stairwell shut with a click.

"I was hoping you'd say something encouraging. Not get your back up."

She rolled her eyes. "Why? I asked you what you thought and you insulted me."

"Hey," he said, again, and she pivoted and put both feet on the same step. "Look, this whole 'let them figure it out' idea was yours. I'm following your lead. Do you think you could just go a little easier on me? I don't have any idea how to just throw my trust into a room that I'm not even welcome in.

"I thought we weren't going to check in until tomorrow. You came down. They seemed mad. I don't know what to think." George ran his hands through his hair and then shook his head. "How do you do it?" He looked up at her and held his hands out from his sides. "How do you just let them go without any... *should* we be worried?"

Feeling her stomach turn over, Jillian took a deep breath. He looked human when he did stuff like that, showing that he was genuinely feeling worried. He looked mad and tense some of the time, at least he looked that way when she was around. She always suspected that that was how he covered up the worries and the fears. *Come to think of it, I guess I do too.* She thought about how she'd just rolled her eyes. *And I guess I put him down too.*

She leaned over the railing and looked up the stairwell just to be certain no one was coming down then, having already considered that she was wearing a black skirt and it wouldn't show the dirt, she sat down on a stair. "Let's sit a moment."

George's eyebrows rose, but he took a stair and then sat down next to her.

She took a moment and then looked at him. "Do you think your people are good at what they do?"

"Yes," George said.

"Do you think mine are good at what they do?"

George paused a moment and if they'd been friends, Jillian would probably have given him a shove. "Yes," George said, reluctantly.

"Then tell me why they can't make the plan? They're going to do the work."

"It's not that they can't..."

Jillian put her elbow on her thigh and leaned her head on her hand and looked at him. "Do you think they work better when you tell them what to do?"

He shrugged and exhaled.

"You do, don't you? Why? Do they need you to motivate them? Is it because they don't really know what they're doing? Why?"

He looked away and shrugged again. "I don't know. It's just better."

Jillian patted his thigh once. "You've never let them try to be self-directed before, even a little, have you?" George looked down at his leg and then at her. She realized how she'd touched him and tried to casually drape her arm across her lap.

"Uh, no," George said.

"All right," Jillian said. "Well, there's a first time for everything." *Like inappropriately touching a colleague. Oh, my God.* At least it had been a very quick pat and she hadn't left her hand there. *I can't believe I did that. Is he going to report me? Would that be enough to get me thrown out of the running? Or worse, fired? Is this karma for something I've done? Just pretend it didn't happen. It didn't happen.* "I can't tell you how exactly to let go. I can tell you that the only way to do it is to do it." She swallowed. "And you can see for yourself that even with plenty of experience, I still botched it today by pushing back in when we'd agreed to meet in the morning. It was an amateur blunder, we didn't learn anything, and..." Jillian sat up straight.

"And?" George said.

Jillian smiled. "Actually, we did learn something. I can't believe I didn't see it immediately. Must be the stress."

"What?" George asked.

"Well, we might not be able to say how much progress they've made in planning, but they certainly made progress in one area." She paused. "They're acting like a cohesive team, aren't they?"

George took a moment and then nodded and started to smile a little too. "They are," he said, still nodding. "Yes, they definitely are on the same side."

"Then we need to hang our respective hats on that accomplishment and give them time to finish the plan."

"I suppose so," George said.

"They'll tell us the plan in the morning," Jillian said. "And it'll be good."

"Okay," George said.

"So," Jillian said, grabbing the railing and pulling herself up. "In order to keep up appearances that we aren't up to something, I'll say 'good evening' now, go back to my office and not speak to you again until tomorrow." She'd taken two steps when George cleared his throat.

"Unless..."

She stopped and turned. He was still sitting on the stair where she'd left him, but he'd swiveled to look at her. "Unless...?"

He grabbed the rail and stood up, looking into her eyes. "Unless you'd... You know what? Never mind. Have a good evening."

Jillian nodded. "Right," she said, and turned and took the stairs as quickly as she could. *What was that? Unless you'd...what? Oh, my. Oh, my. Oh, my. Did that sound like the beginning of an invitation to... what? Forget it. Just, forget it. It probably wasn't. He was probably going to ask to talk more. Either way, it doesn't matter.* She opened the door to the third floor and headed for her office.

She closed the blinds and then shut the door, sliding down it to the floor and covering her face with her hands. "I can't believe I touched him like that," she moaned to herself. "I am such an idiot."

She stayed on the floor for a time, before she convinced herself to get up and do some work. She made it as far as sitting at her desk and opening a file before she put her head down on the desk and moaned again. "I hate myself."

George stayed on the stairs after she'd gone, mentally kicking himself. That had been a close one. He almost asked her to dinner. She'd touched him and he'd lost his mind for a second thinking that he might be able to coax her into doing it again. *What a mess that would have made.* He wasn't even sure which would have been the worse answer, had he asked; her saying 'no' or 'yes.'

He let out his breath in a slow controlled exhale. He could come back from today. He'd floundered more than once, but he could get it together. *No problem. Just move forward. And breathe.*

He took the stairs two at a time to make it harder. Then he made a beeline to his office. He'd had enough. Every time he thought he had it together since the bad news had been sprung, he showed himself that he didn't. It was time to go and come back the next day with a fresh mind. He packed up as quickly as he could and shouldered his bag. As he shut of the lights in his office, he remembered to let Rachel know that he was leaving and would be available by his company cell.

The lock clicked and then he walked over to Rachel's desk only to find Jillian there. She, too, had her bag and coat. *Ah, hell.* "You bailing, too?" He asked when Rachel and Jillian looked up at him.

"I, er, yes," Jillian said.

"Well, then," he said. "Rachel, you should put a message on the phone and go home too."

Rachel looked at Jillian and then back at George and the back at Jillian.

"Good idea," Jillian said.

"Thank you!" Rachel said, before anyone could take it back. "Have a good night." She waved at them.

Jillian looked at George a moment and then headed toward the elevator. George followed. "I didn't realize you were leaving," he said.

"I'm having trouble focusing," Jillian admitted.

"Yeah," George said. "It's been a bad day."

"Not all bad," Jillian said, as the doors opened. She stepped in and turned to face the front. George hadn't moved, he was thinking about what hadn't been bad. "Are you coming?"

George stepped into the elevator and turned. "Yeah."

Jillian was looking at him, and he looked at the doors. "You look like you need a drink," she said, as the doors slid shut.

"I need something a lot stronger than a drink," George said, turning his eyes toward her.

"I guess my attempt to be encouraging didn't work," Jillian said, and she set down her bag to put on her coat.

George turned toward her. "I guess not. Let me help you with that."

He took the coat from her and held it up.

"Thank you," she said, and told herself to accept the gesture as nice and not demeaning. As she slid her arms into the coat sleeves and he lifted the coat up, she felt the backs of his fingers brush her neck before he let go. She immediately picked up her bag.

The elevator doors slid open and she headed away from the front doors. Curious and confused, George followed. She stopped in front of the big conference room. *Ah.*

She knocked and leaned her head in. "Go home, everybody. Pick it up in the morning. George is here with me and we promise not to bother you again until 10 am tomorrow. Good night."

She stepped back and motioned George to the door. He wasn't sure what she expected him to do or say, but he leaned in and came up with very little on the fly. "You've all earned an early night. Go home and rest."

When he leaned back and closed the door, he looked at Jillian and shrugged.

"What?" She asked, and started toward the front again

"I couldn't think of anything to say."

Jillian smiled. "You were fine. Let's go. We deserve it too."

"Where are you headed?" George asked.

"Oh, I'm heading home. Charlie will be glad I'm early tonight."

"Ah," George said, as they reached the lobby. "Have a good night." He headed out of the door and then held it for her.

"You too, George." She said, and then turned toward the parking lot.

George noticed the chill in the air and headed toward the mass transit station in the other direction. *Of course she lives with somebody. A woman like that wouldn't be single for long unless she wanted to be. She wouldn't have to wait twenty-four hours after a break up to find someone asking her out. Thank God I stopped myself from saying something about dinner. Not that I couldn't have played it more casual... No... I probably couldn't have played it more casual.*

He was on the train before it occurred to him that he hadn't said anything to Taro, Neal, or Sergei about leaving. Well, that was probably for the best too. *My poker face is probably in the wind right now. They'd see right through me. I've gotta get it together before tomorrow.*

It was a short three block walk from the station to his house. By the time winter was at its' peak it'd be a pretty miserable three blocks, but it was worth it. His house was a detached 2-story in a decent, but old, neighborhood. The house was also old, but decent. Actually, it was beautiful, made of stone and brick from the days when real masons did that kind of work. Apart from the roof replacement, the electrical replacement, and the insulation additions he'd had to do before moving in, it hadn't needed any substantial work. The plumbing was solid, as was the structure. And, most importantly, it had character.

The plumbing and electrical had been added after the house was built, so there were a few places, here and there, where the floors were raised. Each bathroom had a step up to enter. But he could live with that. He'd been lucky with the house. There weren't any problems with the foundation or water leakage. The heating system had been re-done by the previous owner and they'd put in both forced air and some heated flooring. The heated flooring had been confined to the upstairs. The downstairs still had beautiful hardwood floors.

The crown molding was all still original. He'd had the contractors save it and put it back up after the insulation was added. The windows, on the other hand, had also been replaced by the previous owner. George had had mixed feelings about that. The originals wouldn't have made for a very warm house in the winter, but in that neighborhood at that age, they would have been beautiful. Then he'd made the discovery in the basement. The desire to replace the windows hadn't overcome sentiment. Many of the original windows were in the back of the basement. They were beautiful with stained glass set-ins and beveled edges.

He'd taken a few panes and had them mounted in sturdy wooden frames and hung them just inside some of the windows on the main floor. He could just make out the reds in the living room window as he headed up the walk to the porch.

As his key clicked in the lock, he sighed and felt his shoulders drop a little. *It's good to be home.*

He flipped on the lights and locked the door and headed for the kitchen, shrugging off his coat along the way and tossing it on a hook. He opened the fridge, took out a Michelob, and sat down at the kitchen table.

When his phone rang, he looked at the clock and realized he'd been sitting at the table holding the cold unopened bottle and staring into space for nearly twenty minutes. He walked over to the wall phone and glanced at the caller-id. *Oh, goodie. Mother.* "Hello, Mom," he said.

"Well, George. I'm so glad you answered. You haven't called in ages and I started to worry something had happened to you." Her voice was sweet and light over the line.

Ah, concern and guilt. The Crewes family specialty. "I'm fine, Mom. How's everyone?"

"Well, your Uncle's back is bothering him again. The doctor says he shouldn't be in the field anymore, and you know how Uncle George took that."

Yeah. His Uncle George, 'officially' the origin of his name, was especially stubborn. *When someone in the Crewes family is labeled stubborn, it really means something, since we all have rocks in our heads.* "I'm sure that you're all trying to get him to listen to reason."

"Well, Sally is, dear girl, but she hasn't a prayer and we all know it.

63

You're the only one he ever listened to."

A lie. A big ol' lie. She must want something mighty bad. "What do you want, Mom?"

"Now, George, you know I don't want anything more than to have the whole family together for the holidays. I'm making a turkey for Thanksgiving-"

"I already told you that I won't be home for Thanksgiving. I'll be home for three days at Christmas. That's it."

The sweet voice turned sour. "Just you think about your family, young man! We fed you, clothed you, and raised you. We don't deserve to be treated like last week's trash. You get your priorities straight and come home for Thanksgiving!"

George heard dial tone in his ear. "Well, that was new," he said to himself. Usually he had to beg off the phone. He wasn't crazy about her being so upset that she hung up on him, but it was a nice change of pace. Sort of.

The moment he put the handset back in cradle, the phone rang again. He glanced at the number. *Oh, good. That'll be Dad call to chew my head off for upsetting Mom.* He let it ring twice before he answered. "Hello, Dad."

"Don't you 'Hello, Dad' me you selfish brat! Your mother is crying her eyes out because not only won't you come home for Thanksgiving, but you yelled at her. How could you treat your mother like that? If I was in the room with you, I'd teach you some manners, by God!"

George held the receiver away from his ear a moment and looked at it. His father had never laid a hand on him. He'd scolded him, sure, but he'd never threatened him like that. *What the Hell is going on at home?* "Dad, is Uncle George all right?"

"Don't you change the subject, young man. I'm going to put your mother on the phone and you're going to apologize and tell her you'll be here for Thanksgiving."

"I'll apologize, but I won't be home for Thanksgiving," he said, firmly.

He heard dial tone again.

This time he only put the phone on the hook for a moment before he picked it back up and dialed one of her older brothers.

"Hello?"

"J.P., it's George."

"Hey, G. How's things?"

"Well, I would tell you, but since I got home and answered the phone, I've apparently put our mother to tears and Pop's telling me he's going to teach me some manners. Is something up? I'm used to the guilt for moving away, but this is much bigger-"

"Uncle George has cancer," J.P. said, in a very matter-of-fact tone.

"Oh," George said, and sat down on the nearest chair, feeling like a rug had been pulled out from under him. "I asked Mom, but she just went on and on about Thanksgiving."

"He may not make it until Christmas," J.P. said.

George shook his head. "Why doesn't she say that, rather than some bull about his back and then try to guilt me into coming home?"

"Because that isn't how our mother operates, G. I would have told you, but I just heard the news an hour ago and I haven't had a chance to, well, process it myself."

George and J.P. held the line in silence for a while. "I don't know if I can get away for Thanksgiving, J.P.," George said, quietly. "We have some real trouble at work. A big project just started, and its chaos."

The reply took a moment. "Well, I guess that's up to you, G. Think about your priorities and do what you have to do. If you can't make it for the holiday, maybe you could just fly in for a weekend soon? Something like that?"

"Maybe, something like that," George said. "I gotta go, J.P."

"Yeah, me too."

"Well, uh, bye."

"Yeah, bye."

George hung up the phone and took his unopened beer with him to the window to look out at the leaves in his backyard. They were calling to him to come and rake. *An awful lot of people are telling me I have messed up priorities.* He set down the beer and went to the detached garage for supplies.

He raked in his work clothes, despite the cold, without a coat. He didn't even notice the cold and the wind. After filling two bags, he walked over to his favorite tree, the sycamore, and patted its' lowest branch. "How you doing today, old girl? You still got a lotta leaves up top. Are you hanging on late before you go dormant?"

Funny, how just being near the tree helped him feel a little better. She, he firmly believed all trees were girls, save the redwoods, something about them made them boys, had been around before he was born, and unless something catastrophic happened, she'd be around long after he'd gone. There was something about the continuity, and maybe the daunting stubbornness to have that continuity, that made his own small life feel like a part of something bigger. He couldn't climb up and sit in the branches then, at least not in his work clothes, so he patted her again.

"I wonder what you'd say if I told you my uncle's dying. He chopped down an awful lot of your distant relatives over the course of his short life. Would you be glad to see him gone?" He patted her again. "No, I suppose you wouldn't. You've been around long enough to appreciate what life is and what it isn't, haven't you? You'd no more wish him dead then one of your sisters."

He sighed and finally noticed he was cold. "Brr. I guess, I didn't think this through. A lot of that happening with me today, old girl. I've done tons of thinking and none of it has done me any good, I'm thinking about all the wrong stuff or something. Any suggestions?"

He smiled as he looked up through her branches into the leaves. "I'm getting the message," he said, and patted her branch again. "Live on."

"I guess I have to figure out how to go home over Thanksgiving. You'll be here when I get back, of course. Maybe you can remind me who I am. God only knows what mixed up mess my mind will be when I come back from a family holiday." He snorted then. "Come to think of it, I guess you'd already know that too, wouldn't you? Seen it a few times."

He walked back to the leaf filled bags and hefted them to his shoulders. As he headed for the garage, he stopped and turned, "Thanks, old girl. For being you." The bags would remain in the garage until collection day.

Jillian had tossed and turned most of the night. When she'd slept, she'd had frustrating dreams where she was trying to get somewhere or get something and she couldn't move fast enough. When the alarm had gone off, it was almost a relief. But the lack of REM had taken its toll and she was on her third cup of coffee, by the time she unlocked her office.

George's door was open and his light was on, so he must have beaten her in. Just a few days prior, that would have irritated her. She liked being settled before facing the possibility of running into him. But today she was too tired to care. And, if she was honest with herself, she was sort of looking forward to seeing him. Just a little.

When she'd been awake, she'd run through her day over and over in her mind. And she kept stumbling on little things, like when he'd said, 'Unless.' It could have been the start of a thousand different things. In fact, they'd ended up leaving together - *at the same time, not together* - and he could have meant something like that. But somewhere in the wee hours, when Charlie had gone on his early morning apartment prowl and she was alone in her bed, she finally accepted that she wanted him to mean something else, she wanted him to flirt with her again. Despite everything he'd done to torment her, she was still attracted to him and when he wasn't acting all superior, she found that she even liked him. His human side was very appealing. Not that she saw it very often.

The one thing she hadn't resolved was the inappropriate pat on the leg. When she'd done it, the actual act, it had seemed completely natural, somewhat consoling in nature. If he'd been sitting and she standing, she'd have patted him on the shoulder. Yet, that would have been inappropriate too. Of course, the leg was worse, and in the end, that's where she'd touched him. And it wasn't like he hadn't noticed it. His eyes had popped. She couldn't stop wondering if he was going to see her punished for it.

She had barely logged into her computer when she decided to resolve it. She couldn't have it hanging over her head. Even without any idea of what she would say, or how she might go about finding some kind of resolution, she jumped up and walked to George's office.

He wasn't in. *Naturally.* She held the door frame and leaned in a little, just to be sure. Silly, since unless he was under his desk or his table, she'd have seen him at a glance.

Jillian turned and found George was right behind her. "Ahh!" She gasped, startled. "Oh, you surprised me!"

George took a step back. "Sorry." Then he smirked and said, "Of course, that is my office you were leaning into. Afraid to go in?"

"Well, it would be rude to go in when you aren't there."

"Ah," George said, and winked at her. "Not what you were thinking when you were pranking me, though."

"Now, wait a minute," Jillian started and George stepped closer and motioned her into his office. She crossed her arms and walked in, trying to think and speak at the same time. The wink threw her a little. "I can't believe that you'd even bring that up. You put explosives in my desk-"

"Now, *you* wait!" George closed his door with loud thud. "*I* put an *explosive* in your desk?"

She scowled. "Don't pretend with me-"

"I didn't put an explosive anywhere! I would never put an explosive near people or-"

"Oh, right! I suppose you didn't put those things on my office floor so that when I stepped on them it scared me half to death."

"Absolutely not!" He crossed his arms. "That is absurd! I would never do something like that! Even little things can be dangerous..." He trailed off and his eyebrows raised and he put his hands on his hips. "Is that why you dumped the coffee on me after the bang and scream in your office? You thought I did something to you?!"

"I know you did," Jillian said. "And while personally I'd consider that the worst of it, the other women on the floor might just say that stopping up all the toilets in the ladies' room on this floor was worse. You know, I wasn't the only person who had to use the ladies' room on the next floor. There are a lot more women working on this floor than just me. That was a pretty major inconvenience."

George uncrossed his arms and rubbed his face. "I don't know what you're talking about. I *never* did anything like that. I admit to messing around with the connections to your computer. I admit to taking all the pens in your desk. I'll even cop to the time I picked up your keys and slipped them onto Rachel's desk."

"I thought-"

"But I *never, ever* did anything that would actually cause damage! I would never mess with anything explosive! And toilets? That's just ridiculous!" George leaned down toward Jillian and was pleased to see her duck a little. "For the record I quit messing with you when you quit messing with me. I sure as anything didn't start up again, because I don't want to have another prank war." He leaned further and Jillian took a step backwards and connected with the wall. "Did you unplug my docking station?"

Jillian swallowed. "Yes. After you greased my office doorknob and the bathroom door handle."

George took a step closer and Jillian glanced at the door. If he struck her, he could do some serious damage. She debated a quick lunge for the door, but as she looked back at George, he didn't look angry anymore and he took two steps back. "I didn't do any of that," he said, shaking his head and holding up his hands. "I swear I didn't. I'll swear on a Bible or whatever you want. But I didn't do it."

Still pressed against the office wall, Jillian tried to sort through his denial. He seemed sincere. Very sincere. But... "Then who did?"

"I don't know," George said. "If I knew..." He sat on the edge of his desk. "This is going to sound silly, but, would you mind making a list of all the pranks that have been pulled on you?"

"Whatever for?" Jillian asked, finally comfortable enough to stand straight.

"You just listed three things that you're blaming me for that I didn't do. I bet there are more. Maybe I can figure out who did it, if I see a list."

Jillian blinked. "What difference would that make?"

"One, I clear my name. Especially with the bathroom thing. I really don't like the idea that anyone blames me for something like that. Two, I'll stop him."

"You'll stop him," Jillian said, incredulously. "That's-"

"Wouldn't it be nice not to have to lock your office every time you step out?"

"Yes," Jillian conceded.

George turned and picked up a notepad and a pen and held them out to her. "Everything you remember and if you know approximately when, that might help."

Jillian shook her head and moved quickly for the door. It was all so far-fetched. Of course, he'd been responsible. But he just seemed so sincere. And so indignant when he'd been accused. She opened the door and then said, "I already have a list."

CHAPTER FIVE

George followed Jillian toward her office, but she stopped just outside his door and he bumped into her. "What?"

She whispered over her shoulder, "Who's that with Gardiner?"

George followed her gaze out over the cubes. Gardiner was walking with a gentleman who appeared to be just a little older than Gardiner, though it might have just been the very gray hair. "I think that's the investor, Cisco Grec."

Jillian shrugged and then turned back to him. "Just in case, let's discuss childish pranks later. I'd rather at least look busy."

George nodded and Jillian scurried the few steps to her office. He returned to his desk and brought up his team's schedule, prior to the insane reassignment, planning to look through it and see what kind of impact the reassignment was going to have. It had occurred to him that he might be able to pull a few people back to work on the real work. Even if Gardiner was certain about what he wanted, George couldn't help but think that angry customers, who'd been promised bug fixes and so on, weren't going to be to particularly sympathetic.

As he looked through the schedule, his mind wandered to the conference room downstairs where his team and Jillian's were working again that morning on a plan for the new tool. How were things going down there? If Gardiner was indeed touring Mr. Grec, would it be a big deal that half the floor wasn't at their desks? Maybe he and Jillian should 'disappear' too, so that it might be supposed that they were sequestered with their people.

He stood up and headed for his door, only to overhear Gardiner speaking. "Ah. Good. Jillian, I'd like you to meet Cisco Grec. He's considering an investment in our business. Cisco, Jillian Braden is a manager in Software."

He heard Jillian's 'nice to meet you' and then a deeper voice, with a faint accent he couldn't place, speaking. "The pleasure is definitely all mine." Then a pause. "Mr. Dabney, would you mind terribly if I speak to Ms. Braden alone for a few minutes."

"Uh, no, of course not. I'll just check my messages and be back in a few minutes."

"Very good." Then the door to Jillian's office closed. George couldn't help but disagree. *That doesn't sound good at all. That's strange behavior. Alone? With the door closed?* He was pretty certain her blinds were closed earlier too.

George popped quickly into the hallway and caught Gardiner. "Hey, Gardiner! Did I just overhear our investor is in Jillian's office?"

Gardiner turned to George with a strange look on his face, sort of the 'deer in the headlights' look, but slightly more comprehending. "Yes."

George didn't like the vibe he was getting from Gardiner. He almost asked Gardiner what was up, but instead he listened to his gut and walked straight to Jillian's office, knocked on the door, and opened it. "Hey, got a minute?" He asked, doing his best casual impression.

As he leaned into the office, he saw Jillian sitting in her desk chair and the gray haired man was sitting on the edge of Jillian's desk right next to her. Whether he was trying or not, and George definitely suspected he was trying, he had effectively penned her in. Gray hair turned to look at George with a frown, Jillian, on the other hand, looked like he'd just saved her from a fate worse than death.

"George!" She said, and stood up, pushed awkwardly passed gray hair, and then motioned him into to her office. "This is Cisco Grec. He's considering an investment here."

"Oh, sure!" George said, trying his casual bit again. He held out his hand to gray hair and received a decent enough handshake and a rather displeased look. "George Crewes. Pleased to meet you."

"George is a peer of mine, Mr. Grec," Jillian said. "His people are our GUI specialists. He's also the person with the most time in software management here at Gardiner D. I think he'd be a good addition to our dinner party. He can answer so many more questions than I can."

Uh-huh! Thought so.

"Oh," George said, playing as stupid as possible. "Dinner? That would great. I'm free tonight, if that's the plan."

"Uh, yes," Mr. Grec said, and stood up from the desk. "Perhaps, it would be best if we got together for dinner another evening. I just remembered another commitment for this evening."

"Oh," Jillian said. "Of course. Please let me know. We could invite all the managers. There are five of us in total."

"Yes, right," Mr. Grec mumbled. "A pleasure," he said, and held out his hand to Jillian.

She put her hand in his and smiled a bright, innocent smile. George nodded at Mr. Grec as he exited. Jillian and George peeked out the door to see Mr. Grec catch up to Gardiner. As soon as the pair had their backs turned, George saw Jillian cringe and shiver a little.

George lowered his voice. "I take it that was what I thought it was."

Jillian looked at him and then away and cringed again. "I have never been propositioned quite like that before. 'Let's have dinner on my yacht and talk about your work here. Then we can talk about my investment and the opportunities it could provide. Perhaps you can *convince* me it's a good investment.'"

"Unbelievable," George muttered. "And not very subtle." His stomach turned a little.

She wrapped her arms around herself. "I don't give off some kind of slut signal, do I?"

George blinked in surprise. "Uh, no."

She looked down at herself. "I don't dress provocatively, do I?"

Well, I certainly wouldn't say that. "No." *You're just beautiful without any assistance.* He looked down at her clothes and shoes. "No. You look professional."

"I can't believe…" She rubbed her upper arms and shook her head. "I just… I feel… ick." She looked back at George. "Thank you so much. Was that a happy coincidence?"

She looked so uncomfortable and so miserable. She lifted a hand to push her hair back and he could see it was shaking. She saw it too and immediately hid her hand. Something within George made him desperately want to fix it. "Actually, I overheard the conversation before the door closed. It seemed a little… shady."

She closed her eyes a moment. When she opened her eyes again, she looked at him gratefully again. "I don't know how to thank you. I didn't have a clue what to say. I was so floored. And he just kept moving closer. Thank you. I owe you. I owe you big."

"No," George said. "You don't owe me anything. It should have never happened in the first place."

"But it did, and you're my hero," Jillian said, in seriousness. "Gardiner…"

"Yeah," George said, unhappily. "I'm pretty sure he knew what was going to happen. I'm going to have a word with him about it later."

"Oh, no-"

"I don't care how desperate he is for money. He can't begin to turn out his employees." He saw Jillian cringe again. "I'm sorry." He reached out and put his hands on her upper arms. "I'm sorry." As her face fell, he was sure she was about to cry. *Oh, God. What do I do?* He let go of her and picked up her desk phone. "Rachel, can you please come to Jillian's office?"

He left Jillian in Rachel's care. It seemed the wisest course of action. If he'd stayed, he'd have had to try to comfort her and he couldn't think of a single thing that he could do to make her feel better. Now, he needed something to make him feel better. *My fist in Grec's face might do it.* But, that would probably land him in jail. He'd looked up Cisco Grec and knew enough about the man's money to know that if he ever did hit Grec, Grec would find a way to keep him in jail too. He had enough money to believe that no one could cross him, or they would pay if they did.

Well, George had pulled his cross in a decent enough disguise that he didn't think Grec would retaliate. But that was worth bringing up to Gardiner too. The idea that Gardiner would still want to have a business relationship with someone who'd do something like that was disgusting all on its own. But if Gardiner wouldn't give up, then George owed it to himself to tell Gardiner what exactly he'd done, in case Grec pulled out of the deal.

The more George thought about it, the more he moved from being concerned about Jillian to being mad at Grec and at Gardiner. He stood in the stairwell, breathing awfully fast again. He couldn't just let this kind of crap go. He didn't know how long he'd stood there, he didn't even remember going to the stairwell, but finally he'd thought about it enough.

When he made his decision, he was down the stairs without even noticing, and then he was outside Gardiner's office. Gardiner's assistant and Melissa walked up to him and grabbed his arms, dragging him to the HR cubes, before he could even knock. "What is this?"

"Shh," Melissa said. "Whatever it is you're about to do, don't do it."

George shook off their hands. "I need to see Gardiner. That's all." He glanced over his shoulder to look toward Gardiner's office and saw more women walking up, circling around him. "Uh," he started.

"We've heard what you did," Melissa said.

"How could you have heard already?"

Melissa shook her head. "Don't ruin it by doing something stupid now and getting fired. We need decent men, like you, here."

"Well, that's-"

"Please, just go back upstairs and leave it alone. You've done enough, more than enough. Okay?"

He turned a little again, looking at the faces surrounding him. They were looking at him with admiration, as though he'd just cured a disease or something. No, they were looking at him like he was a hero. Just like Jillian had said. He found himself blushing a little. "I really should say-"

"Please," Melissa said. "You may be needed again. Just let it be."

"All right," George said, and when he started to walk, the circle of women parted for him. He'd never experienced anything like it. He felt more self-conscious then when he was going through puberty. *This can't be how the Lone Ranger felt, or he'd never have helped anybody. Then again, he didn't stick around to be appreciated either, come to think of it.*

The rest of the early morning didn't get any less uncomfortable. Rachel kept offering to bring him coffee. One of the women on Sergei's team kept bringing him his papers from the printer. He started to wonder if he'd have to lift a finger ever again.

Just before 10 am Jillian appeared in his doorway and he stood up immediately. Her eyes were red. "Hi," he said.

"Hi," she answered, quietly. "It's, um, about that time, to, um, go hear…"

"Yes, I know," George said, and tried not to frown at her sudden timidity. He'd been annoyed by her more aggressive behavior, but this was just wrong. "Should we go together?"

"Yes," she said. "That would be good."

And she waited for him. And she walked beside him. *No, this is not good.* As soon as they were in the stairwell, George turned and asked her, "Are you still upset?"

"No," she said, unconvincingly.

"Jillian," he said. "It's going to be okay."

"Sure," she said, quietly and nodded, then gave him a tight smile.

He exhaled and frowned. "Jillian…" *I want to make this better for you, but I don't know how.*

"I hate this place," she said, suddenly and turned toward the stairs.

"Ji-" George had to follow now, as she moved quickly down the stairs. At least that was more toward normal. So he followed behind and was the last into the conference room. *This had better be good.*

Jillian knew that everyone in the conference room was looking at her, wondering about her. She'd tried to pull herself together, but she couldn't do anything about her eyes, and she noticed that her hands would shake when she reached for things, so she just kept her hands together, or in her pockets. *I can't believe I'm acting like such a child. Nothing happened.*

George took control when it seemed like no one was going to say anything and got the meeting on track. When Irene and Faisal had finished, Mahdi and Vidar chiming in here and there along the way, George was the one who thanked them all. He then looked at Jillian and waited for her to say something. "Excellent work," was all she could manage.

She sat quietly while George congratulated everyone and asked them about their timeline. Irene had obviously stepped up during the planning stages; she was the one who ran through the timeline and paused to look at several people as she shared that they'd all agreed to work weekends, starting the following day.

At that, Jillian finally found her voice. "That's going to be tough on everyone. Are you sure you want to do that?"

Irene nodded. "We discussed it. Majority vote decided to work the next four weekends, but take off Thanksgiving and the day after."

"I like how you've laid this out. You've got plenty of flexibility." Jillian looked at George. "Any concerns or objections?"

"No," George said, and then smiled at her.

What is that about? "Well, then I say, plan approved. I'll check budget and see what I can do about providing some meals on the weekends. I'll let you all know." She looked around the table again. "This is a very ambitious plan. For what it's worth, I'm impressed and I hope you're impressed with yourselves." She looked at George again. He was still smiling at her. "I think I speak for both of us, when I say that." She looked around the room. "Okay. So going forward, everyone needs to check-in daily. Just two minutes in the afternoon before you leave to give a quick status. Nothing too detailed. If anyone has a concern, please come to us at once. We'll do our best to help. But, apart from that, we'll do our best to stay out of your way." George was still smiling when she looked at him again. "Let's not keep them."

He nodded and they stood up and watched their people file passed them.

"Why are you grinning like that?" Jillian asked, in a hushed tone even though they were alone in the room.

"You seem more like yourself again. Taking charge."

"Oh," she said.

"I was concerned," George said.

Jillian felt herself flush a little. "Don't be. I just..."

George smiled again. "It's okay. I'm just really used to you like this. Not... timid."

He turned and motioned her to head through the door first. She nodded politely and instead of heading for the stairwell, she detoured toward Accounting and ensured that she wasn't going to have to talk to George for at least a few minutes. "Thank God tonight's yoga," she said to herself.

By midafternoon, George was certain that Jillian was avoiding him. It was obvious. And he was annoyed by it. And he was annoyed that he was annoyed. He could understand her wanting to avoid Gardiner, though, if it were him, he'd want to kill Gardiner. Come to think of it, he sort of wanted to kill Gardiner anyway. But why did she need to avoid *him*? Their teams had jumped into work right after the meeting broke up, and Jillian had disappeared.

He'd watched for her to return to her office, but he'd finally decided to join Taro, Neal, and Sergei for lunch in the cafeteria when she hadn't shown. Lunch conversation mostly consisted of Sergei detailing how he was going to look for another job because the company was going down.

When George came back, having escaped the miserable lunch conversation, the light in her office was still off, or off again, depending. So he'd taken a walk around the cubes and still hadn't found her. This time he asked Rachel if she knew where Jillian was. That had gotten him the worst evasive babble he'd heard in a long time. He took that to mean 'yes' and 'I'm not supposed to tell you.'

Still annoyed that she wasn't around, he spent the rest of the afternoon updating the schedule and writing up notifications to clients about the delays to their requests. He held off sending of the notices, figuring a fresh eye on them in the morning would be a good idea.

He took another walk around as the clock closed in on quitting time, and then wandered into Taro's office. "Hey, man. I don't suppose you're available for some b-ball tonight?"

Taro looked up from his computer. "I could use some stress-relief. One-on-one?"

"I was thinking the foursome. Although, if you'd rather not, one-on-one is good by me."

Snorting, Taro replied, "Well, if we could glue Sergei's mouth shut..."

"I'll see about getting a reservation. It's pretty last minute. We may have to go uptown a little."

"No problem," Taro said. "I suppose we can invite Neal and Sergei anyway."

"Yeah," George said. "Is Melissa going to mind?"

"Nah. She has Pilates tonight," Taro answered.

"Ah."

Four hours later, George was happily exhausted with his best friends and carrying a basketball as they walked off the court. "Good games tonight," he said.

"I needed it," Sergei said.

"Me too," Neal chirped. "It's been a long rough week."

Taro barked a laugh. "Understatement of the year!"

"Yeah, yeah, yeah," George said. "Let's not talk about it anymore tonight. We'll all just stress out again."

Sergei grunted and grabbed his bag from the court-side bench. "Good find here," he said, looking at George and motioning around him at the building. "I like the court."

"Agreed," said Neal. "Nice place. Quiet, but not too quiet."

George grabbed his bag from the court-side bench. "Yeah, not bad for last minute."

They were about to head toward the locker room as a class from one of the several smaller exercise rooms, just passed the court, let out and a gaggle of the predominately female participants crossed their path, taking up a great deal of space to carry their bags and rolled up mats. Not one for patience, Sergei stepped into the mess and tried to make his way forward. "Serge, hold up," George said, and took just one step forward to get him closer to catch Sergei's attention.

"Ah, just let him go," Taro said.

George turned back and shrugged with a hand out from his side and whacked someone with his bag, causing him to drop the ball as well. He turned back and apologized to the blonde, who smiled at him, taking his apology with good humor. George was glad that she'd been working out too, as he'd hate to have gotten sweat all over her.

"Christy, are you all right?" A familiar voice asked from behind the blonde, who turned for a moment and let George make eye contact with the auburn haired beauty who'd been avoiding him. He wondered if he looked as startled as she did. "George!"

"Well, if this isn't a surprise," George said, trying to sound casual. "Hello, Jillian."

"George?" Christy asked Jillian. "Not George-from-work?" Before Jillian even answered she turned back to George. "Hi, I'm Christy Joukers." She shuffled her mat from one arm to the other and extended her right hand and smiled really widely, looking him up and down.

George ignored the look. "Hi," he said, and shook her hand while he looked at Jillian.

"We're just coming from yoga," Jillian said.

Yeah. Okay. "Ah," George said, extricating his hand from Christy's just as Taro and Neal walked over.

Only a few people were left from the yoga class and Jillian stepped around Christy, giving George a good look at her in a stretchy bright blue top and black yoga pants. *Whoa.*

"Hey, Jillian," Neal said. "How are you?"

"Fine, Neal, thanks," Jillian said. "And you?"

"Fine too." Neal looked at Christy and then at Jillian and sort of shook his head toward Christy.

Jillian looked around and smiled tightly. "I guess I know everyone here. How about I make some introductions?"

George met three other women, and apart from the brunette who glared at him, Mal-something-or-other, he completely forgot their names before Sergei had even come jogging back to see what was holding up his friends.

George stepped aside to pick up the basketball.

"Oh," Sergei said, flatly when his spied Jillian. "Small world."

"Yes," Jillian said, in crisp tone. "Too small."

"We're going next door for smoothies," Christy said. "Would you all like to join us?"

George saw Jillian elbow Christy. "I don't th-" he started, trying to be sensitive to Jillian's obvious desire to have them disappear into thin air, but Neal cut him off.

"Sure," said Neal and George remembered that Neal was single and in the presence of five attractive and very fit women. Of course he wanted to go, even if one of them was a nightmare from work.

"Great," Christy said, and started toward the women's locker room. "Twenty minutes?"

Neal was nodding and following along. George hoped Neal would remember not to walk into the women's.

George looked at Jillian who had crossed her arms again and was shaking her head. He lowered his voice as the others started to move too. "Did we mess up something?"

"Nope," Jillian said, and looked at him, her eyes dropping to the basketball and then returning.

"We were just playing basketball," George heard himself say. *Well, that was obvious.*

"I see that," Jillian said, and took a step.

George saw her looking at the other guys and he suddenly felt overwhelmed by how separated she was from the rest of the Software Managers. He opened his mouth again. "We're in a rec league, so we practice as often as we can."

"Ah," Jillian said, and nodded and took another step.

"We've been playing for three years. We already have a team. That's why we didn't invite you," George said.

Jillian turned and looked him square in the eye. "So?"

"I don't want you to feel bad," George said. "I'm sorry if you do."

Jillian shook her head and then took a step toward him. "Are you kidding me?"

"N-"

"You're going to apologize now? After a year?"

"Well, I ju-"

"How magnanimous of you!"

"Hey! I just felt bad that we've never invited you to be a part of anything," George said. "It must be hard."

Jillian shook her head again. "You think?! You think it's hard to be an outsider?"

"You're no-"

"Oh, I know," she said, in a low voice. "It's just because I'm a girl. And after what happened earlier today with that pig, instead of feeling challenged or threatened by me, like you have been for so long, now you feel protective of me. That's it, isn't it?"

"Well," George started. "Actually-" He wanted to say that that really didn't have anything to do with it. After all, she hadn't exactly made friends by jumping all over everything her first day, making everyone else look bad. But, it was partly true too. "Look. I'm just sorry. Okay."

"Is this on behalf of all of you?" She motioned toward the other men waiting a little distance away.

"Well," George said, again and found himself uncertain of how to continue.

"Of course not," Jillian said. "It's just you. You put yourself in my shoes for a whole footstep and now you feel bad. Well, George, let me tell you this. It takes a lot more than being hit on to take me completely apart. Yes, I was upset. Yes, I was taken aback, but I'm fine now. You think you know something about me? Well, you don't. You had the tiniest glimpse at one miniscule aspect of my life.

"But if you think that apologizing will help, why don't you apologize for all the times I was told that girls aren't good at math? Or for the professor who told Malvinia that we women just weren't cut out for business or science and that we'd all be a lot happier if we studied philosophy or poetry and took some cooking courses so our husbands would be happy?

"Perhaps you'd like to apologize for all the wolf whistles I've heard over my life? Care to say anything about the guy who dumped me because, in his words, I made him feel stupid?

"At my last job, it became obvious I was never going to get promoted, so I left, because that's what smart people do. Take a guess what was said to me after I turned in my resignation. 'I knew a woman couldn't handle this job.' Do you think I said anything about it, though? Of course not. Because then I'd be black-balled everywhere.

"George, you choosing not to invite me to play with you and the boys is barely a blip on my radar." She dropped her mat and took the ball from him. She dribbled onto the court, and then shot from just outside the three point line, swishing the ball through the net without any backboard or rim. She turned and walked back to him, scooping up her mat. "Besides, I'm not really into basketball."

Fetching the basketball from the court floor, George watched her walk away. Sergei was staring open mouthed at her as she walked passed. Taro's eyes were a little wide, but nothing else gave away his surprise. "Dear, God," George mumbled to himself.

Jillian was muttering under her breath the entire time she cleaned up with a quick shower. *The very idea of him apologizing to me now! What a... a...* She stopped herself from concluding the thought since so many varied words were available and appropriate. She tried to hold on to the anger and the irritation; she needed that because it took all the anger she had not to wash her hair in anticipation of being seen by him. She hated herself for caring what he thought when he looked at her.

She'd seen the admiration in his eyes after her shot. She wasn't certain if it was her physical shape or her basketball skill, or perhaps her attack on him, that he'd admired, so she told herself she didn't care. It didn't matter at all what he thought of her beyond the office. And even there, so long as it didn't jeopardize their agreement and efforts, it still didn't matter.

And yet, she didn't want to look like a sweaty mop when she saw him again, should he end up next door for smoothies. It was obvious that Neal had already committed. Unless Taro had somewhere else he needed to be, he would be there to watch over Neal. If Taro went, the odds were that Sergei would also go for the entertainment of watching Neal. That was how the situation usually played when they were at lunch. She'd seen them once or twice, when they hadn't known she'd seen them. Normally, she'd have bet on George too, but she wasn't certain after her attempt to cow him a little. He might beg off.

Do I want him to beg off, though? Oh, God. What a nightmare! The anger had faded fast, she'd excised so much of it in her rant at George and then with the basketball shot, and before she could stop herself, she shampooed her hair.

A few minutes later, Jillian was hurrying to get herself together, feeling way behind her friends.

"You didn't tell us George was gorgeous," Christy said, with a tinge of accusation in her tone as she applied her lip gloss.

Jillian pulled her hastily dried thus still damp hair into a low, loose ponytail. "I didn't think his looks were important."

"Oh, really?" Malvinia asked, as she applied her blush. "Why don't I believe you?"

Jillian rolled her eyes and dug into her gym bag for her smaller makeup kit. "In what way does that play into anything?"

Christy put in an earring and then looked at Jillian. "Well, I for one, feel like you've been hiding him. Is there any reason I shouldn't go for him?"

Putting on a light layer of powder, Jillian took a moment to respond. "Christy, I haven't been hiding him. If you want him, go for it."

Malvinia stood behind Jillian and met her eyes in the mirror, then raised her eyebrows. "Really?"

"Sure," Jillian said. "Why not?"

"I'd have thought if his looks didn't matter, you'd have said something."

"I'm not interested in George, his looks, or anything else about him." When Jillian saw Malvinia frown and cross her arms, she said, "Except, or course, anyway I can use him to get ahead at Gardiner D."

Malvinia's frown lessened, but didn't fade entirely. As they exited the women's locker room, Malvinia leaned over and whispered a question to Jillian. "Then why did you wash your hair?"

Jillian exhaled and didn't bother to answer. It was pointless. She raised her voice. "You know, I'm not in the mood for a smoothie. I think I'll head home."

"What?" Christy turned and walked backwards. "You *have* to come. I need your help with George."

Malvinia looked at Jillian again and smirked.

Jillian ignored her. "You don't need any help from me, Christy. Really. Just be your usual bubbly self."

"Ugh! Useless! You're utterly useless." Christy turned and led the group out of the recreation center.

"Call me later," Malvinia said to Jillian. "And be in the mood to be truthful."

Jillian sighed. "If I come and help Christy, will that exempt me from the interrogation?"

"Mmm?" Malvinia tilted her head. "Oh, this will be interesting."

Rolling her eyes again, Jillian caught up to Christy. "Okay. I'll come."

Christy exhaled, "Thank you!"

Jillian smiled as best she could and made a point to keep ahead of Malvinia, completely counter to her desire to walk as slowly as possible. *I really don't want to be a part of this. I love Christy, but I really don't want to be a part of this.*

The chill in the air made Jillian regret washing her hair. The temperature was dipping really low at night and she wished she had brought a hat along. *Perfect.*

As the group entered the juice place, Jillian tried to put on a good smile, but could feel how fake it looked. She glanced around and spied Neal and Taro. "I'm skipping the smoothie," she said to Kai, and headed over to the table.

Plunking her bag on a chair at the next table, she looked at Neal and Taro. "Hey."

"Hey," Taro said. "No drink?"

Jillian sat, reached into her bag, and pulled out a water bottle. "I'm good." She looked at Neal and saw him looking at her friends in line. Glancing back at Taro, she asked, "Did we lose Sergei and George?"

"Yeah," Taro answered. "George bailed and then Sergei did too."

"Ah," Jillian said, nodding and finding a real smile cross her face.

Christy hid her disappointment that George hadn't joined them until the group broke up some fifteen minutes later. As Jillian held back to return a few chairs to where they belonged, Christy got her attention. "Would you give this to George the next time you see him?" She passed Jillian a piece of paper.

"Oh, Christy," Jillian said, and shook her head. "Really? You're not desperate. Why-"

"I like him," Christy said, emphatically. "A lot."

"After a minute? Wouldn't it be bet-"

"Please, Jillian."

Jillian held in a sigh. She folded the paper and placed it in her jacket pocket. "Of course. But that's it."

Christy hugged Jillian. *"Thank you!* You're the best!" She bounced out of the juice place and disappeared.

When Jillian shouldered her bag and turned, she discovered she wasn't the last of the group, as she'd thought. Malvinia had her hands in her coat pockets. "Calling it a night?"

"Oh, yeah. I need some sleep. I'll be working all weekend."

"Oh? That's unusual, isn't it?"

Jillian pushed open the door to the street. "A full weekend? Yes. But my team is putting in weekends on this new project. So, I am too."

"Oh," Malvinia said, and walked next to Jillian to the parking lot.

Unlocking her car, Malvinia let out her breath. "Jillian?"

Jillian was parked next to Malvinia. She turned around to see her. "Hmm?"

Malvinia paused before continuing. "Don't work too hard, okay?"

"Thanks. You too."

CHAPTER SIX

Saturday morning had come fast for Jillian. She'd been exhausted, so despite all the things that could have been on her mind, she'd fallen asleep quickly. Still tired, she drank her coffee and made her way to the office.

George was already in his office when she walked up to hers, but she put off handing him Christy's note. As she opened her door and flipped on her lights, she blinked at the strong flowery scent. On her table stood a large vase with, at a glance, perhaps three dozen red roses in it and a big white envelope protruding from the flowers. "What *is* this?"

She dropped her things on her desk and didn't bother to take off her coat. There was a yellow sticky note on the table in front of the vase. She picked up the note.

These arrived just after you left on Friday. —Rachel

The envelope was addressed in beautiful lettering to Miss Braden. *Well, that narrows it down.* She plucked out the envelope. It contained a thick white paper that was folded a single time. Half-curious, half-afraid, Jillian opened the folded paper.

I was an overzealous, forward fool. Please accept these blooms and my sincerest apology. If you can find it in your heart, please forgive my shameful behavior. - Cisco

Jillian pulled out a chair and sat down, uncertain of what to make of the whole thing. He hadn't asked for anything, except forgiveness. And he hadn't asked her to do anything if she did forgive him. There wasn't a 'please call me' or anything like that. Perhaps this was an apology and a good-bye all in one.

The roses were certainly lovely. The fact that they were red, however, she didn't miss. "I thought apologies were usually made with yellow or white or something other than red," she said to herself.

She stood back up and took the paper and envelope and stuffed them in her purse and locked her purse in her desk, then hung up her coat. Inside her computer bag was not just her computer, but Christy's note too. She set up her laptop in the docking station and while it was booting, she looked at the folded piece of paper. She didn't know what Christy had written. Probably her name and phone number.

Logging into the computer, Jillian tried to ignore Cisco's flowers and Christy's note. She checked her email and after responding to a few, decided to just get it over with.

George had hardly slept. His mind kept going over the week in detail, highlighting all the places where he'd made mistakes. He was hard pressed to decide which mistake was the worst. And he was still more than a little uncertain about this team up with Jillian. *Mistake or not?* He wasn't even sure why he'd said yes. She'd thrown a few perfectly good reasons his way. But he wasn't sure that he'd gone for it for any of those reasons. But all the same, he'd gone for it.

After that, nothing had made sense. Not really. He'd been outside of his element ever since he'd said yes.

The image he'd been fighting all night sprung back up in his mind, Jillian in a tight blue top telling him how he was barely a blip on her radar. *She's a wildcat with claws and fangs.* And he liked her that way even more.

He'd finally given up on getting any real sleep and come into the office early, uncertain of what he'd do once he got there.

Two cups of coffee and a few Advil later, he was editing his emails to whom he was sure would be angry customers about the delays in the schedule. As he re-saved the last one, Jillian entered his office with a light rap on the door.

"Morning, are you busy?"

"Morning. No," he said, surprised to see her voluntarily in his office. "Well, yes." He stood up. "But, I've got time."

She looked casual, much more so than he ever remembered. Well, except of course for the workout clothes the night before. Today, she was wearing slacks. Her hair was down again, completely loose. Instead of a blouse, she was wearing a sweater.

Or course, he'd gone casual too. Though he'd gone further. He'd put on jeans and a dress shirt without a tie.

She gave him a very fake smile and walked up to his desk and handed him a folded piece of paper across the desk. "Here," she said.

"What's this?" He asked.

She stuffed her hands in her pockets. "It's from my friend, Christy. I agreed to give it to you and now I have." She started to turn.

Oh? What is this? "Which one was Christy?" He asked.

Jillian turned back, her face wide with surprise. "The blonde."

"The one I hit with my bag?"

She looked away a moment and then looked at him. "Yes. That's Christy."

"Oh," George said. "Well, then, thank you." He waved the paper at her.

Jillian pulled her hands from her pockets, crossed her arms, and turned, saying, "Oh, absolutely. Anytime," as she exited his office.

George dropped the paper on his desk and sat back in his chair. *That was weird.* He ran his hands over his face. It was the first time since high school that someone had passed him a note. *Well, maybe college. That was really weird.*

After a few moments of thinking that same thought over and over again, he picked up the paper and opened it to see Christy's name and number and the words 'call me' with a smiley face. It was cute, in its own way. And forward. Which was an excellent sign. He folded the paper and stuffed it in his pocket. *Later.*

He debated for a moment what he should do with his time, and then wondered what Jillian intended to do with her day. He got up and walked to Jillian's office. He rapped on the open door, walked in, and found himself aromatically assaulted. "Gah," he mumbled and focused on the flowers.

Jillian was already back sitting at her desk, and she looked up as he entered. "Did you need something?"

He motioned to the flowers as he looked at her. "Wow! What did we do to merit this?"

Jillian crossed her arms. "*We* didn't do anything. And even if *we* did do something, it wouldn't be any of *your* business."

"You're right," George said. "Absolutely right." He pulled a chair away from her table and up to her desk and seated himself. "None of my business."

She was looking at him like he'd just flown in from Pluto. "Have a seat?" She asked, sarcastically.

"Thanks," he said, as if she'd meant it and crossed his left ankle onto his right knee. He smiled briefly and then glanced back at the flowers.

"Did you need something?" Jillian repeated.

"Well," George said, still looking at the flowers. *Sent to her workplace.* "I was wondering…"

"Yes?" Jillian prompted.

No way! George whipped back around. "Are those from Grec?!" When Jillian looked away and didn't answer, he knew. "Unbelievable." His foot dropped to the ground and he sat forward. "What are you going to do?"

"Nothing," Jillian said. "Now, if you don't want anything else, please be-"

"Oh, I do." George interrupted. "But, first," he motioned toward the flowers with his thumb, "may I do something about this?" *Like find him and shove them up his-*

"No, you may not. Now, what do you want?"

George frowned and then exhaled. "Fine." He sat back again and tried to relax. "I was just wondering what you plan to do with your time while we're here all weekend. For that matter, if you're not holding staff meetings and so on, what all do you plan to do all week? I've been working on email notices to our clients that they won't be seeing their requested updates this month. But, for the usual, there isn't a point in putting together status reports, since they'll all say nothing. What do new age managers do?"

Jillian tapped one finger against her opposite arm as her only response. George waited her out and she finally broke.

"Okay. Very well. Since you asked… I'm starting on the year end appraisals."

"Ah," George said, and nodded. "That's… that's very smart."

"I'll also be ordering lunch for everyone. Not exactly the most time consuming activity, but I didn't want to ask Rachel to come in on her weekend, so…"

"Why don't you let me handle it?" George asked. *Excellent idea, George. Very modern. The guy handles lunch.*

Jillian uncrossed her arms. "You want to order lunch?"

"Sure," he said.

"Well," Jillian looked a little hesitant for a moment. "Okay," she shrugged a little. "Thank you."

"Cool," George said, and stood up to go. As he turned, he paused and looked at the flowers. "Are you sure I can't do anything about this?"

Jillian rolled her eyes. "I have it all under control now. Go," she waved and made a shooing motion.

George hesitated. "What'd the card say?"

Shaking her head, Jillian crossed her arms again. "This is none of your business. Need I repeat myself?"

George walked back to her desk, placed his palms on the top, and leaned over toward her. "What'd the card say, Jillian? He was completely inappropriate yesterday and now he's sending you red roses."

"Actually they came yesterday, after I left," she said.

"You were visibly shaking when he left your office, Jillian. What'd the card say?"

She exhaled loudly. "If you really must know, it was an apology."

George stood up straight. "An apology?"

"Yes," she said. "A simple apology."

"Nothing more?" George asked.

"Nothing more."

Interesting. "Okay," George said. "But, you do know that apology flowers are supposed to be yellow. These are red. And there are - what? - three dozen of them."

Jillian slid one of her hands up to her neck. "I know." She stood up and walked around him to the flowers. "I was hoping that maybe he just made a mistake."

"A guy with money like Grec will have staffed it out. And if he told whoever handled it that this was an apology, they wouldn't have been red. They wouldn't make a mistake like that."

"So," Jillian said, "maybe it was a miscommunication with his staff."

George shook his head when she looked at him. "I don't buy that. But if it makes you feel better…"

"Oh, stop it," Jillian said. "I don't want to talk about Cisco Grec anymore. Please let it alone."

"I will. But-"

"No! No buts or maybes." She walked back to her desk, unlocked her drawer, and pulled out the note. "Read this, appease your curiosity, and then don't mention it again."

George glanced at the note, turning it over once. "Well, you're right it's a simple apology." He handed the note back to her. As she once again secured it in her desk, he pulled out his yo-yo. "I'd be prepared for something else, if I were you. Not sure what. But, I doubt that's the end of it." He started the yo-yo.

"Oh, you do, do you?" Jillian's tone dropped. "What do you know about this kind of thing?"

"Personally?" George asked, and caught Ringo, so he could bring his hands to his chest in a *'who me?'* gesture. "Nothing. But those aren't a mistake and they certainly say he isn't giving up."

Jillian's shoulders sagged. "That's the way it always is. Getting flowers from someone you wish would disappear and nothing from someone you wish would pay attention."

George lightly tossed Ringo toward Jillian with a grin; he didn't come anywhere near her. "Ah. So who isn't paying attention? Charlie?"

Jillian pushed back her hair as her brow furled. "Charlie?"

"The other night you said Charlie would be glad you were home early."

Then she laughed. "Charlie is my cat."

"I thought…" George stuffed Ringo in his pocket as he felt a slight heat in his face. "I assumed you were living with somebody."

"Well," Jillian said, "you know what they say about assumptions."

"Yes," George said, trying to cover his embarrassment by continuing the conversation. "Speaking of assumptions… you still haven't given me the list of pranks."

"Oh," Jillian said. "I guess not. Are you still denying-?"

"Yes," George said, emphatically. "Just how many, we'll see."

"All right," Jillian said, shaking her head. She sat down at her desk and put her hand on her mouse.

"You typed it up?"

Jillian didn't look at him. "I didn't put it on a shared drive or anything," she said, as if that was an answer. But he didn't ask any more questions, he just fetched the three pages from the printer and glanced at them as he returned to her office. She'd listed the prank and the date and time. He couldn't decide if she was thorough or pathological.

"May I borrow a pen?" George asked. Jillian handed him a red one. "Thank you."

He sat back down across from her and started at the top. "Nope." He put a big X next to the very first one. "Nope." Another big X. "Yep. But in retaliation." He placed a big R next to the third. He kept on down the list. By the time he was halfway through he was beginning to seethe. *Okay, I've been responsible for less than a quarter of these.*

Although the majority of the pranks were little, annoying, and stupid, there were some things that he couldn't call pranks. More than once someone had put the little popper things on her floor. As unlikely as they were to do any real damage, it was still a really mean thing to do. And the toilets pissed him off. He looked at the date and tried to remember what had been going on that week. He was going to have to look at his calendar.

But when he'd finished, what struck him most was that he hadn't been responsible for the very first and second pranks. "Looks like I wasn't the only one assuming."

"What's that supposed to mean?"

He turned the list toward her. "One and two. I'm innocent. You assumed it was me and started to get me back. That's why I did number three."

"Right," Jillian said, and crossed her arms, a pose George was becoming more and more familiar with. "I believe you." Then she leaned forward. "My first retaliation was after the sixth. I put up with it until then. Don't try and tell me the third was in retaliation to something *I* did."

George could feel the roil starting in his blood and took a deep breath. "If that's true then somebody else started it. They played both of us."

Jillian's face morphed from disbelief to surprise and back to disbelief. "Look, it's not important. We're passed it, right? I apologized for the coffee and it's over. We can shake on it, if you like. Let's not get bogged down in this."

George turned the list around and flipped through it. After a moment he sat back and looked at Jillian. "When I find who did this, and I will, then I'll put it behind me. But I can't let this," he lifted the papers up, "go."

Jillian rolled her eyes and George had to take another deep breath. But rather than argue anymore, or try to convince her of his innocence, he stood up and left. *It's my good name being besmirched. She hasn't the right to act like I'm making a fuss over nothing. I wonder how many of the things that I assumed she did were really somebody else. If I had a list like this, she'd feel the same if things she hadn't done were on it.* He laid the list out across his desk and pulled out Ringo. *When did I start using words like besmirched?*

Jillian took a deep breath herself. *Everything was so much easier when we weren't speaking.* She tapped her pen on her desk. He'd really looked shocked about the list. Outraged for a moment or two also. *Maybe he really didn't do all those things.* If that was true, then he wasn't who she thought he was. Of course, she'd made up her mind on very little evidence and never attempted to acquire any more, as they went along.

She looked at the flowers. *And he is still trying to take care of that situation for me.* That thought made her squirm a little. It was nice to have someone wanting to protect her. But it was also demeaning. So she'd been taken off guard yesterday, so what? That didn't mean she wasn't ready and able to deal with it today. And yet, it felt good to think if anything else happened that she wasn't ready to deal with, he was right next door.

She frowned. *That's emotional thinking, not logical. Logically, I can handle one man.* Opening a new document on her computer she started to write up a note to Cisco Grec. She tried to keep it short and simple, a thank you for the flowers but... she choked when she came to the *I never want to see you again* part.

Break ups were bad enough, but she'd always had that conversation in person. This wasn't even a break up, and she couldn't figure out the words. Then again, it was probably tough to write because she was trying to sound professional and detached so that it wouldn't come out nasty. The best version she'd come up with actually used the words *I never want to see you again.* She sighed and wrote and rewrote for a while.

Finally as she stared down the words on the screen she decided that she couldn't send it anyway. She deleted the document and stared at the flowers. Three dozen beautiful and perfectly formed red roses. If only they'd been from somebody else. She'd never been given three dozen roses before. A dozen, yes. But three?

Shaking her head before she became too wistful, Jillian tried to concentrate on work. She looked down at Irene's file, took out a note pad, and started to look at what all Irene had accomplished that year. It was impressive. And she was starting to really come into her own when it came to team leadership too, venturing opinions in front of the group. Jillian wished she'd been a fly on the wall for the meeting yesterday. It was evident that Irene had taken the wheel for much, if not all, of that meeting. Perhaps it was time to recommend Irene into the promotional pool.

Jillian looked up at the flowers again and sighed. She wasn't going to get anything done if she kept thinking about them. Finally she decided to try a different approach. She got up from her desk, walked over to the flowers, and took a very deep breath, inhaling their scent as deeply as she could. It made her smile. *Good. Who cares who sent them? They're mine now and I can enjoy them.*

She picked up the vase and brought them back to her desk. It took a bit to rearrange things to make room for them, but she did. *Much better.*

She opened up a new document to start typing up Irene's appraisal, but stared at the blank screen for a while. She looked back at the flowers again. *Mmm.* They were amazing. She started tapping her pen on her desk again; trying to imagine anyone she'd ever dated sending her three dozen of anything. Her first college boyfriend, Luke, might have, if he'd ever had the money. He was into romantic gestures. But they were both pretty broke and the romantic gestures were kept within a budget.

But the romance trail sort of ended there. The other men she'd dated seriously hadn't exactly been romantic. It was more like they did what they had to, reluctantly. Not that they hadn't shown the proper amount of interest in her, but none of them had felt the need to be particularly romantic from within, it was an obligation, a necessary part of the courting process they had to get through.

Maybe I just don't attract the right kind of men. That was a new thought. If she wanted this kind of thing, she needed to be sure that the men she dated were willing to provide it. *Correction,* wanted *to provide it.* Luke couldn't be the only man on the planet who had romantic thoughts. There had to be others. *As soon as this ridiculous mess at work is over, I'll actively start looking again.* "That's a plan."

She glanced down at her notepad and wrote 'Romantic.' She smiled. *What else am I looking for?* 'Kind,' came next, followed by, 'Honest,' 'Loyal,' and 'Interesting.' She'd been tempted to write smart, but she then she thought about what smart meant, it was a vague term anyway, and decided that she'd met plenty of people that were interesting and she had no idea where she'd classify them regarding smarts. She didn't necessarily need him to be college-educated, just interesting. Someone well-traveled perhaps. Or with other experiences. Or just someone who liked to read, so he'd have something to talk about.

What else? She glanced at her list. With a frown she added the next word to her list. 'Attractive.' *I'm not talking hunk of the year, but he does have to inspire me a little on a physical level.* It still seemed a little shallow, but she wanted to be realistic.

'Well-dressed.' Another quasi-shallow requirement. She didn't mean someone who wore suits, just someone who could catch her attention. Poorly-dressed wouldn't do it.

'Open.' She looked at it after she wrote it. *Open to what?* She shook her head. *This is ridiculous.*

Setting aside the list she opened her email and had the chance to shake her head again. George had sent out an email to both their teams about lunch, which was good. He planned to order from Mario's, which was bad.

Jillian dug in her desk and retrieved her menu stack. Choosing three, a nice number, she debated picking up her phone and instead took the menus next door.

"Well, hello again," George said, when Jillian knocked on his door. "We've had more face time in the last forty-eight hours than I think we've had in the last month. To what do I owe the pleasure of *this* visit?"

Jillian raised her eyebrows. "Okaaaay. It's about lunch."

"Sure," George said. "What about it?"

"Well, Mario's is a lovely place, great food…"

George leaned forward. "And…"

"Actually, it's a 'but.' But, it doesn't have anything for the vegetarians or the gluten free diets except one salad."

"Oh," George said, sitting back. "I guess I didn't think about… that."

Jillian walked to his desk and handed him three menus. "Dietary restrictions are a hassle for large groups," she said, nodding. He couldn't help but think that was meant to placate him in some way. "All three of these places have options for that. The last one even has vegan, though the only vegan you're feeding today is Ishi and she always brings her own food. So you're probably not feeding her."

"Ishi's vegan?" George asked, surprised.

"Mm-hmm."

"How do you know?"

Jillian seemed to pause a moment. "I've eaten lunch with her."

"Of course," George said. *And I haven't.* "Well, since we are buying for both teams, maybe I can just add one of these places as a choice and order from both."

"Excellent idea." Jillian said, and then quickly disappeared from his office.

George leaned back in his chair. *Vegans. Vegetarians. What do you call people who eat gluten free? The world has changed around me.* When he'd started, the cafeteria had always had one vegetarian dish, but as he thought about it, he knew that they'd added at least one more daily choice. And the gluten free thing.

He shook his head. "I suck at this." It was a bit of a revelation. *I don't pay any attention to anyone, do I? First Rachel, now everyone when it comes to something as basic as food.* How was it possible?

He picked up the third menu, the one Jillian had assured him included vegan meals, and shot off a follow-up email.

As he looked at the menu, he wondered how he'd managed to become so oblivious. It's not like it was necessary for him to know that Ishi was vegan, in order to be her manager. But it was probably necessary to at least allow for the possibility that some people are when you're looking at food.

He thought back to the few times over the last year that he'd brought in food for meetings and even as a reward for hard work. He brought in doughnuts; they weren't vegan or gluten free. Though that was probably okay for vegetarians. And, of course, pizza.

He picked up his phone and pressed speed dial six, the first time he'd ever used it.

"Uh, hi, George," Jillian said, clearly having looked at her caller-id.

"Hi. So, just out of curiosity. Do you happen to know who else on my team has dietary restrictions?"

When she answered and provided him with a small list, he thought he could hear her smiling. He wrote it down and thanked her and hung up. Staring at the list, he wondered what else he'd been missing.

No use thinking about that. Just start paying attention. He put the list in his schedule folder where he knew he could find it the next time he was trying to be boss of the year, and began looking through the menus Jillian had given him. One place made a gluten free pizza. He opened his contacts on his computer and copied in the relevant information. There was one mistake he wouldn't be making again.

Jillian hung up the phone with George and added a star and the words 'to new things' next to 'Open.' Being able to grow was definitely important.

People started knocking off just after 2 pm. Jillian couldn't blame them. It was only going to get worse from there as the weeks went by. So at 3 pm, she started walking around and encouraging everyone to keep the weekend days a little shorter.

No one from Sergei's, Taro's, or Neal's teams, including them, had come in. She wondered if they had all given up already. As the number of the people on the floor dwindled and it became less likely anyone would be looking for her, Jillian took a few minutes to look out the window. Fall was taking a stronger hold, more leaves were down, and the wind was whipping the trees mercilessly. It almost made her want to stay, just so she could avoid going outside, but she had shopping to do on the way home and it would be much worse when winter actually made an appearance.

On the return path to her office she walked by all the cubes, verifying that everyone had indeed gone home. She caught Faisal and told him she was shutting off the lights in five minutes and he should go home. He smiled when she said it, so she knew he'd taken it the way she'd meant it. Unless someone was hiding in the bathroom, the office had cleared and she could go.

She stopped by George's office, he was packing up. "Oh, good. I was just going to tell you nearly everybody's gone."

"All my people came by on their way out," he said. "Some of yours still here?"

"Just one and I threatened to turn out the lights on him, so I think he's going."

"Good. Get your stuff and I'll walk out with you."

Jillian nodded and quickly returned to her office to pack up her things. The flowers were an interesting question. She debated taking them home. A few minutes later, as she was putting on her coat, George appeared in the doorway, yo-yo in hand, his bag on his shoulder. "You about ready?"

"Just a moment," Jillian said, and buttoned up her coat, so she could shoulder her purse and bag. Out of the corner of her eye, she could see George throwing his yo-yo again. She managed not to shake her head but picked up a pen and quickly scratched 'no yo-yos' on her list. Then she picked up the vase and headed for the door.

"You're taking them home?" George asked, and flipped her light switch and closed her door for her.

"Yes," she said, and when she moved to set them down, he took them from her so she could lock her door. Taking them back she said, "It occurred to me that if he showed up in the building again, they'd be a conversation starter."

George walked alongside her to the elevator. "He can still ask if you got them."

"Mmm," she nodded as George pressed the down button. "And I can say yes and then nothing else."

"Planning on the freeze out method, then?"

"I'm hoping that I don't have to actually plan."

George walked over to the lighting panels and started flipping switches. There were a few that stayed on 24x7, so even if Faisal was still hanging around he wouldn't be in the dark. He shrugged as he walked back to her and the elevator doors opened. "I'm sure you can handle it."

"Well, that's nice of you to say," Jillian said, and stepped into the elevator. He shrugged again. "What?"

"I don't want to piss you off again," he said, and pressed the button for the main floor.

Jillian blinked and looked at him. "Okay. What?"

He sighed and looked at her. "I just… Just know you've got backup. If you actually need it."

"Fair enough," she said. "I don't think he's going to attack me, or anything, but thank you."

"You're welcome. The man's got great taste. You've got to give him that."

Jillian's eyes widened and she felt herself flush from head to toe.

"The flowers," George said, quickly and turned his head back toward the doors.

Jillian looked away, too, as she felt her skin warming again. She was going to be crayon red by the time they escaped from the elevator. "Of course, the flowers. What else?" The walls in the elevator seemed to be closing in on them a little. She could hardly believe her relief when the doors opened. The few seconds left of their trip down had been much too long. She didn't wait to see if George was going to let her out first, she just started moving. Although logically she knew she couldn't outrun her embarrassment, she tried anyway.

By the time she turned to bump the release on the main door with her back, George hadn't even made it halfway across the floor. She wasn't sure if he was embarrassed himself and walking slowly on purpose, or if she was just moving that fast, but either way, she was glad he wasn't right behind her as she escaped into the wind.

The walk to the train seemed a little shorter than usual, and the ride did too. George knew it had been because he'd lost himself in thought. He'd done it *again*. But at least he'd recovered really well. Possibly too well. She might have taken his comment about the flowers as an insult. But it was just a cover and he was pretty sure she knew it. She'd flown out of the elevator and out of the building, and he'd been glad she'd done so, because he wasn't sure what he could've said, had they actually walked together. And pregnant silence was not going to work for him.

How was it possible that he'd opened his mouth and done it again? He'd made it through the entire day not thinking about how she'd touched him and then he'd gone and said something stupid, and then it was all he could think about. And in the elevator, too. One of his top favorite fantasy locales. *God, I'm dumb.* After a quick stop by a grocery on his way home, he took the time to cook with the television turned up loud enough to distract him from thinking.

It didn't work as well as he'd have liked though. Standing at the stove, he started to fantasize that instead of covering his mistake and turning away, he looked at her, and she'd continued to look at him, and he'd held her eyes until she swallowed, and then he'd taken the flowers out her hands and pushed her up against the wall of the car and she'd kissed him. In his mind they were tearing at each other's clothes when he realized the chicken he was sautéing had started to burn.

Damn. He hadn't even gotten to the best part of the fantasy yet. He focused on the mess in front of him and took care of it before the smoke detector went off. *What a red letter day this turned out to be! I have got to stop thinking about her.*

He suddenly had the flash that it was Saturday Night and he was supposed to visit Orville before dinner. "What a mess." He picked up the phone to call Orville and apologize before he started on a fresh piece of chicken and thinking about what he was going to do with himself that night. He sure as hell wasn't going to sit around thinking about what was going on with him.

The swim at the rec center did exactly what Jillian had hoped. She felt alive and relaxed, and most importantly at peace. It wasn't until she'd entered her apartment and spied the roses on her dining room table that she lost a little of her peace of mind. George's words had lingered with her during the day. Surely, he was right; the flowers weren't the end of Cisco.

But by night, George's last words came back to her. *He has great taste.* That hadn't been about the flowers. It was obvious that it had been a compliment to her. Add that to his *unless* from the other day and she couldn't help but wonder.

So she sat for a few minutes, imagining a different reality. A reality where she'd met him somewhere else. A reality where the result of meeting him would have been different. But she only gave herself a few minutes. Although she loved fiction, she preferred not to live it. *And I didn't meet him somewhere else. And he's still my competition.*

She stood up and walked to her entertainment center and started looking for a movie to watch, anything to get her mind back off work and the people in it. Charlie slinked up from wherever he'd been sleeping and circled her legs. She reached down and picked him up and enjoyed the immediate purr. "Hi, baby."

Nothing was jumping out at her from her collection, so she grabbed her remote and started flipping through the on-demand movies.

She and Charlie were stretched out on the couch and close to halfway through *Sabrina* with Humphrey Bogart and Audrey Hepburn when Jillian's cell phone rang. Glancing at the caller-id, Jillian decided to answer. "Hi, Christy."

"Hi, Jillian. I'm sorry to bother you, but I just wanted to know if you gave my note to George?"

"I did," Jillian said, and had to force herself not to sigh. "I told you, I would." *I wish I felt better about it.*

"I know," Christy said. "I just wanted to know when I should start counting."

"Counting?"

"You know men," Christy replied.

Do I? "I don't follow."

"It takes them a while to call, even if they're interested. They have rules about that. This way, I'll know how long he's waited."

"I guess that makes sense," Jillian said. *I wonder how long he'll wait. A few days? Well, it's not really my business anyway. Who he goes out with is entirely his business.*

"So what are you doing tonight?"

"Hmm?" Jillian asked. "Oh, watching *Sabrina.* What are you doing? Don't you have a date? It's Saturday night."

The line was quiet for a moment and Jillian sat up.

"Christy?"

"Well, I don't know that I should tell you."

"Of course, you should," Jillian said.

"But, I'm afraid you won't approve."

Jillian tried to laugh. "You know I don't judge you."

"Then you have to promise not to tell Mal. Although, knowing her, she might just surprise me and be okay with it."

"What is it?" Jillian asked, finally deciding the conversation was worth pausing the movie.

"Well, I do have a date, but it's late."

"Uh-huh."

"I've seen him a few times."

"Uh-huh."

Christy sighed. "Well, you see, he's married."

"Married!" Jillian couldn't stop herself from exclaiming her surprise. But after that, she managed to collect herself and not say anything particularly negative. "Doesn't that make life a bit... complicated?"

"Depends on what you consider complicated. Perhaps it's complicated for him. For me, it's just fun. Not serious."

"Really? Well, that's good, I guess." Jillian stood up and went into the kitchen, thinking about the ice cream in the freezer. "But, you've seen him a few times. That sounds a little serious."

"Never," Christy said, with a laugh. "It's all right for me to see him as often as I like, because he isn't going to make demands on me. He's not in a position. And when I'm bored, it'll be easy to break off. But single men can be trouble. That's why I don't like to see them more than once or twice. Misunderstandings are a problem."

"Oh. I guess we've never talked philosophy before," Jillian said. "I'm mean, about dating."

Christy chuckled. "Do you even have a dating philosophy, Jills?"

Jillian plucked the Oreo ice cream out of the freezer and moved on to collect a bowl and spoon. "I suppose not much of one. Although, I don't think I could go out with a married man."

"No, you couldn't. You take the whole thing too seriously. Every man you date you hold onto for a while, trying him on again and again, hoping to make him fit. I can tell in the first five minutes if there's any chance that's he's Mr. Right. If there's no chance, then a little fun and goodbye."

"What if there's a chance?" Jillian asked.

"Well, that hasn't happened yet," Christy answered.

"So, how *will* you know?"

"Trust me, I'll know."

After spooning a little ice cream into the bowl, Jillian shifted the phone from her right ear to her left, and then put the ice cream carton back in the freezer. "I hope you're right. What if you missed out on someone terrific just because you missed whatever sign you're looking for?"

"I have confidence. What about you? How are you going to know, Jills?"

Jillian lowered the spoon from her mouth without taking a bite of ice cream. "I don't know. I was thinking about it earlier today. Once this latest work disaster is over, I think I'm going to actively start looking. I haven't been out with anyone for a couple of months."

"Oo, excellent. You can come out with me to a couple of places. It'll be fun."

"Are these places bars?" Jillian asked, and finally took a bite of her ice cream.

"Maybe," Christy said, her voice dropping a little. "You've got to come! We haven't been out in ages."

"Because you've been out with guys."

Christy was silent a moment. "You've got a point. You know, we haven't done anything just for fun in a while. Yoga doesn't count. We should have a girls' night. How about this week?"

Jillian took her ice cream bowl back to her couch. "Depends on how early it starts and how late it goes. I'm going to be working weekends for a while and I'd hate to fall asleep either there or with the 'Fab 5.'"

"Working weekends?"

"My team is working weekends on that ridiculous project."

"Your idea?"

"Theirs, actually," Jillian said, and took another bite of her ice cream.

"Well, que sera, sera, I suppose. How about a movie on Wednesday? I'll check with Kai, Mal, and Lacey and see if they make it. I think that's one of Mal's free nights."

"Sure. You could join me at The Blue Feather on Monday night, too."

"Um, no. Not my scene," Christy said.

"Right," Jillian replied. *That's something to add to my list. A wide variety of musical tastes.*

"So, Wednesday?"

"Sure, if it works for everybody. Sounds fun."

"Excellent," Christy said.

As Jillian hung up the phone and unpaused her movie, she leaned back into the couch cushions. *Married? Oh, geez, Christy. That's just a disaster waiting to happen. Or maybe a disaster already happening.* She shook her head and looked at Charlie. "You know, Charlie, I think I do have a good life, even if I don't have a man. I have you."

Charlie meowed and tried to put his nose into her ice cream bowl and Jillian laughed and pushed his head back. "Behave and I'll give you a little tuna in a bit."

Charlie meowed again and sat down.

CHAPTER SEVEN

It was almost a relief, his office was quiet and he hadn't said anything stupid in close to twenty-four hours. George stood in his office throwing Ringo out and back, while his lunch got cold, because it wasn't a relief at all.

Neither Taro, Neal, nor Sergei had turned up. But then it was Sunday and if they hadn't been there on Saturday, why would they be there on Sunday? But it left George alone in his office. He didn't want to bother anyone and cause a delay in progress. He'd walked around a little before lunch and decided that he hadn't accomplished anything but to disturb everyone in the vicinity.

He was trapped. The only person in the office he could possibly talk to was the one person he'd decided not to talk to. So Ringo went out and back.

Actually, it was worse than that. It was one thing to not talk to her, but it was an entirely different matter that she wasn't talking to him. He'd let it go the night before by getting on his computer and blowing stuff up in a virtual world.

I'm bored. He stopped throwing Ringo as the thought came completely into his consciousness. It was surprising. But it was true. He was bored out of his mind.

And lonely.

Enough, he pocketed Ringo, grabbed his Styrofoam container, drink, and napkin and walked next door. "Up for company?" He asked when Jillian looked up from her desk, her food mostly untouched on her desk.

And then she smiled, nodding her head. "Please." And George's feet barely touched the floor as he joined her at her desk, smiling involuntarily in response to hers.

The conversation was rather impersonal, focusing on work, specifically the project. But it was still better than nothing and George boarded the train that afternoon happy to have been in her company and pleased beyond measure that he hadn't said anything stupid.

Monday, on the other hand, brought everyone back to the office and Jillian knew that she and George couldn't possibly be seen talking more than once, at most, during the entire day. So rather than allow herself to miss his company, which she'd already found herself depending on after only a few days, she made a point to interact with as many other people as possible. She went downstairs and visited with some Hardware people for over an hour in the morning, ate lunch with a group of programmers, and managed to spend her early afternoon with a few of the Hardware Developers in their lab. In between, she worked on the appraisals and found herself making headway.

George sent out his emails in the morning and spent the afternoon fielding phone calls from clients who ranged from unhappy to nearly crazy with anger. He rolled his shoulders and neck, and tapped his fingers on his desk while he dealt with them. The phone had kept him occupied enough that he didn't think about keeping his distance from Jillian. As the calls trickled off to a stop, he couldn't help but think that he'd have handled them better if he wasn't so tense.

Thinking about trying to get another impromptu B-ball game together, he walked out of his office and across the floor toward Taro's office. Jillian walked passed him, going the opposite direction, not far from Rachel's desk, and she smiled. He smiled back and turned his head to watch her continue on her way, enjoying the view.

The moment he realized what he'd done, he looked around and was relieved not to see anyone else in the immediate vicinity. Thank god no one caught him leering at Jillian's ass. *Something must be done.*

He continued on, but instead of Taro's office, he went into Sergei's and closed the door. "You free tonight?"

"Sure. Basketball?" Sergei asked, as he motioned George to sit.

"Actually, I'm thinking more of a wingman thing." George said. "I know it's Monday, but I need to get laid."

Sergei grinned. "Excellent. I know just the place."

The walk from the train station was long and cold, but George kept faith that it was worth it. He'd let Sergei talk him into a bar that was frequented by banker types, so in order to fit in he'd worn a suit. Fairly certain he was finally in striking distance; he tried not to be annoyed when his phone rang. It was Sergei.

"Yep," he answered.

"I'm running late," Sergei said.

"Oh, *lovely*," George said. "It's fucking freezing out here."

"You almost there?"

"I should have badgered you into giving me a ride."

"Hindsight," Sergei said.

George frowned. "How late are you going to be?"

"Oh, maybe twenty minutes," Sergei said. "Give or take."

"*Fantastic.*"

"Order a beer and relax."

"Uh-huh. Where am I?" George looked at the line along the side of a building he was about to pass. It was long. The area was hopping for a Monday. Glancing at the sign to see what that particular line was for, he snorted. "What the Hell is 'The Blue Feather'? It's got a line to the back of the building. Sounds like a drag club. Or a strip club."

Sergei laughed. "It's a jazz and blues club. This is the third name it's had in the last, I don't know, five years. It's always got 'Blue' in the name. You're almost there. So order a beer and see if you can hit pay dirt and be ready to leave before I even get there."

"Right," George said. "See you in twenty?"

"Give or take."

George disconnected the call. *Serge is going to be a half an hour or more, I bet. The putz.* He glanced at the line for the jazz club again as he crossed the street. It was popular place, but not exactly his type of haunt. As he turned his focus back up the street toward his destination, something caught his eye and he turned back while his brain tried to register what he'd seen.

A woman had come running up alongside the line, but outside the rope, stopped at the bouncer, and as George watched, he could just make out her auburn hair swing as she leaned over and gave the bouncer/doorman a kiss on the cheek and disappeared into the club. He was lucky he wasn't still in the street when his mind sorted out the input. He stopped in his tracks and stared at the empty space that he was absolutely certain Jillian had been in just a moment before. He couldn't be wrong; the coat she was wearing had a belt that pulled it tight enough that he was sure it was Jillian's body underneath. And the way she moved, even with such a short flash. It *had* to be her.

Sergei was going to be late...

George walked over to the front of the line and asked the bouncer how long the wait was likely to be. Jillian had bypassed the line, assuming he was right and it was her. But if there was a chance he could still get in and figure out if it was really her... he quit thinking.

"Not too long. We open in less than five," the bouncer said, looking at him with raised eyebrows. "I expect everyone in line will get in in less than twenty."

George figured he didn't look like he quite fit in from the look he was getting. "Thanks," George said. "I'm meeting someone and I think she just went in," George said, by way of an explanation. He started to turn to head down to the end of the line. If it wasn't going to be long, then it was worth it.

"Who you meeting?" The bouncer asked, standing up from his stool.

George got a good look at just how much bigger the bouncer was than him. Probably outweighed him by fifty pounds. "Uh, her name's Jillian-"

The bouncer cut him off. "Jilli-vanilli? She should'a told me." He looked George up and down again. "Huh. How do you know her? She never meets anyone here."

"Work," George spat out, quickly, wondering if his little lie was about to become a big problem, then shrugging it off. *So Jillian's a regular. And she skips the line. Interesting.*

The bouncer leaned to the left a little, as though he was trying to see George's back. "Well, good for Jilly." The bouncer lifted his arm and gave directions like a flight attendant. "She'll be at the band table, far end and then right, up against the stage." He paused a moment. "Tell her she can add anyone to the list, will you?"

"Sure," George said, surprised as the bouncer opened the door for him. He didn't want to look a gift horse in the mouth, but he couldn't help himself. He looked at the bouncer and asked, "Jilli-vanilli?"

The bouncer gave him a grin. "She always smells like vanilla."

"Oh," George said.

"Not at work, huh?"

"Uh, no," George said, thinking about it. She didn't wear much perfume, as far as he'd noticed.

The bouncer chuckled and leaned over as if he were taking George into his confidence. "She used to remind me of cookies. Now cookies remind me of hot women."

George nodded and grinned back. *Better and better.* He walked in and took in the atmosphere. The place was pretty upscale, actually. Nice wood work everywhere and quite clean, no smoky smell lingering from the old days. The bar ran along the left hand wall from the entrance. To the right were at least thirty tables and a stage.

Hoping not to be noticed, he walked to the end of the bar and looked toward the stage. Jillian was standing right where the bouncer had told him, next to the stage, wearing a sleeveless black dress with a snug red belt at her waist, and a full skirt that didn't quite cover her knees when she was standing. Her hair was down, as he'd noticed outside, but that evening, it was in waves at the side of her face that made him think of a 40s movie star, like Lauren Bacall.

She was talking to a man holding a trumpet. When she laughed at something he said, he put the trumpet down on the stage, took her hands in his, and kissed her fingers. She laughed again.

Not quite sure what to make of that, George settled on a stool where he supposed she wouldn't notice him. The bartender wandered down to him as the doors opened and people started entering, affording George a much better cover. He ordered a scotch that he figured he could nurse for a few minutes while he tried to determine if Jillian was involved with the finger-kissing trumpet player before he left to meet up with Sergei.

But he was no closer to figuring it out when the band went on stage and started playing; Jillian sitting at the table, moving to the music. *Okay. Big jazz fan.*

The trumpet player wasn't playing the trumpet, surprisingly enough. He was at the piano and kept glancing over at Jillian. *Can't blame him there.* Even from his position mostly behind her with her sitting down, she was fun to look at.

After two songs, the trumpet player/pianist got up and brought a mic and stand forward. "For those of you who are regulars, you'll not be surprised at who is going to help out our little combo tonight. Sweet Jillian Olivia."

The crowd began to applaud.

No fucking way.

Jillian stood up and walked up on stage and nodded to the audience with a shy smile. There, under the lights of the stage, George was able to see that she had done much more with her makeup then she did for work, her eyes were outlined, which was okay. But her lips, oh, her lips. They sported bright red, shiny lipstick. He took a breath in response to the sight and felt just the slightest tightening in his groin. *Oh, sweet Jesus.* If she ever wore that red lipstick to the office he'd have to leave. As it was, he had a new fantasy. Those red lacquered lips on him. Anywhere. Better still, *everywhere.*

The trumpet player took her hands and kissed the fingers again. "Thank you for tickling those ivories for us."

She leaned over and kissed the trumpet players' cheek. "The pleasure is all mine, Freddy." George couldn't help but think that his life would have been immeasurably better if he'd been a musician.

He shifted on the stool and watched her move to the piano. Her walk clearly wasn't intended to be anything provocative, and yet it was sensual. Her hair bounced a little.

His phone vibrated. He glanced at it. Sergei had texted *Where R U?* George looked back at the stage as Freddy asked Jillian to choose the next song. She said something, but being away from the mic, he couldn't hear.

"For Jillian Olivia," Freddy said. She started up the song with a blues intro on the piano and then the drum and bass joined in with Freddy coming in on the lyrics a few bars later. George didn't really pay much attention to the music itself, and certainly not to the lyrics. He watched Jillian at the piano.

She clearly loved what she doing. From her attitude at work, he thought she'd be serious, but instead she was smiling and moving her head with the music. She leaned into the piano and back. She wasn't just a pianist, she was a performer.

When the song ended, he blinked and realized he'd been in a near trance watching her. He quickly thumbed a reply to Sergei. *Decided 2 check out the jazz. BRT.* Another lie, he wasn't going to Be Right There. He wasn't going anywhere yet. Leaving meant walking away from one hell of a fantasy.

"We're just taking a breather, so nobody blow," Freddy told the audience over their applause. Soon the conversations started.

Jillian was bone-tired *and* exhilarated. Thank goodness Freddy had needed her that night. She'd have enjoyed sitting and listening too, but playing was always so much better. As she left the stage for the set break, she tried to signal Judy, but she was looking the other way. And Leslie had her back turned. Lisa too. So, rather than wait, she ran up to the end of the bar where the waitresses put in their orders and waited for Brian to get to her.

"You're swinging, tonight," Brian said, and placed two bottles of water in front of her, not even having to ask what she wanted.

"The guys are really on," Jillian said, uncomfortable with the praise, but smiling at it too. She cracked the lid on one of the bottles.

Brian leaned over. "Hey. What happened with your friend?"

"Huh?" Jillian asked, and took a quick swallow.

"Huey let some guy in. Somebody you know from work. Said he was meeting you here."

"Some guy? What guy?" Jillian closed the lid on her water and picked up the second. "I think Huey was mistaken." She lifted the bottles in a thank you gesture and turned toward the stage, only to see George slightly behind the man nearest her. He was wearing a suit, with the coat unbuttoned, his tie loosened and his top shirt button unbuttoned, one hand in his pocket, the other holding a nearly empty lowball glass. He was looking right at her. "Hi, Jillian."

Oh, my word. Jillian heard plastic thud and bounce against the floor and realized she'd dropped her water bottles.

"Oh, geez," George said, and set down his glass. He walked closer, bent down, picked up the water bottles, and smiled grimly as he straightened and held them out to her. "Here. Sorry about that. I didn't mean to startle you."

Jillian blinked, trying to think. "What are you doing here?"

He took a breath and lowered the water bottles. "Listening."

Jillian crossed her arms. *Oh, my. What is he doing here?* "What are you doing here?"

George tilted his head toward the wall a few feet away and walked a short distance from the bar so it'd be easier to hear each other. Jillian joined him, her arms still crossed. "How did... Where did..." She shook her head. "What are you doing here?"

"It's not a big deal," George said, motioning for her to calm down, while still holding the water bottles. "Just a funny coincidence."

"The rec center was a coincidence, this is... unsettling. Did you follow me?" *I almost wish you did. Almost.*

"Of course, not. I was meeting Sergei a couple of doors down," he said, gesturing with just one of the water bottles in the general direction of where he was supposed to be. "He called and said he was going to be late just as I happened to be passing by."

"So you decided to drop in and *just happened* to tell Huey you were meeting me? How did you even know-?"

"I saw you, okay?" George said. "I caught sight of you running up to the door, out of the corner of my eye. And I saw you kiss the bouncer and come in. And I was sure it was you, but I wasn't. So I told him a story that I was meeting you here and some other tripe, so he'd confirm it was you, which he did, and then to my surprise he sent me in.

"I couldn't very well confess that I was lying at that point, could I? So I came in. And you were talking with the band, so I didn't want to disturb you, but I figured I'd hang out for a bit since Sergei was going to be late anyway.

"And it was fun, so I stayed."

Jillian loosened her arms. "But you did follow me." *Not in a creepy way, but in a...a...different way.*

"After a fashion, I suppose. Not after work or anything like that." George held up one of her water bottles and she accepted it from him. "It was just a coincidence. And a good one. I've had a much better time here then I would've down the street." *Of course, it'd be even better if you wanted me to be here. Good God, that lipstick is amazing.*

"You like jazz and blues?" Jillian asked, and took a small sip from her water, which allowed her a perfect cover to look him over again. *Oh, that suit does nice things for you, George. Hmm. Correction, you do nice things for that suit. What is it about a man with his tie loosened?*

George smiled again. "Yes. It's new to me, but I've enjoyed myself. You're good."

"No," Jillian shook her head. "I'm all right, not good." She looked over his shoulder at the stage. *Open to new things… Oh, no, you don't, girl!* "But I do get away with it."

George held up the second water bottle. "Are you trying to mega hydrate between sets?" *Give me a sign. Are you okay with me being here? Don't make me ask.*

"No, I'll take the spare up on stage." She accepted the bottle from him and looked him in the eye. "I can't believe that we'd just run into each other here. I've been coming here for years and I've never seen anyone from work."

"We've been missing out," he said. *I've been missing out. A whole year of avoiding…*

She nodded and said, "It's a great place." *And now you're in it. What am I supposed to do now? I can't talk for more than a few minutes. You're going to get bored. Do I want you to stay? If I do, how do I make that happen?*

"Sure is," George said. *Guess I'll have to ask.* "Will it throw you off, if I stick around for a while, yet? If it's a problem, I could, you know, blow."

Jillian laughed, partly in relief that he wanted to stay and she didn't have to ask, but mostly from his attempt to use the word 'blow.' "Blow? You can't carry off that word." *Hearing you attempt to fit in is just hilarious, George.*

"I suppose not."

"It sounds unnatural," she said, smiling. *Perhaps you shouldn't tease him too much, if you want him stay, dummy.*

"Okay," he said.

They were silent between for a moment. "So," George started again. "Do I need to leave?"

No! I missed you today. Hang around. Let me look at you. Maybe we could even talk some. We don't have to pretend here like we do at work. She tapped a water bottle with the nail of her index finger. *Why on Earth would you want to stick around?* "You're really having a good time?" Her eyes narrowed.

"Yes." *I can't imagine any place I'd rather be at this moment.*

Yes! "Then you should come down and sit at the band table." She started to walk around him toward the stage. *Brilliant. I can sneak looks at him while I'm playing.*

"Seriously?" He asked from behind her.

"Sure," she said, over her shoulder. "It's more comfortable than a stool or standing, and then I'll know when you decide to… *blow.*"

Man, is she sexy. The over-the-shoulder look and smile. He grinned and followed her to the table. But she didn't sit. "I have to be unladylike now. I don't have much time." She reopened her water bottle and chugged it. "Please excuse me," she said, putting the empty on the table. "Quick visit to the ladies."

He nodded and sat down after she left. Freddy appeared almost immediately and George stood back up for introductions and a handshake.

While Freddy was still gripping George's hand, he said to George, "You know, Jilly never has guests. I hope you realize what that means."

"Oh, yes," George said. Freddy obviously thought he'd been invited. Well, he almost was now.

"And we all like Jilly a lot." Freddy went on.

"Uh-huh," George said.

"So, don't be pulling any flimflam, or you'll be seeing the fish in the river from underneath. Permanently."

"Got it," George said, grateful to have his hand released. "No flimflam."

Freddy nodded and then smiled. "Now, you enjoy the music, and it was nice to have met ya."

"Likewise," George said, and sat down and was debating another scotch when Jillian returned. He started to rise and she motioned him back down, but he stood anyway.

"Don't bother," she said, and took a seat next to him. "You'll begin to look like a jack-in-the-box. I'm up and down a lot between sets."

"It's polite," he said. "And I've just been warned to be a gentleman with you, so you'll have to let me be."

"You've just- who said what to you?" Then she turned and looked at the stage. "Freddy! Did you just threaten him?"

"Why, no, Jilly," Freddy said. Jillian raised her eyebrows and Freddy looked very innocent. "I just told him his future, based on his actions. I'm like a fortune cookie. Or a one of those eight ball things. But significantly more reliable."

Jillian laughed and shook her head. "This isn't a date, Freddy. George and I aren't..." She looked back at George who was sitting close and looking... *Oh, but if we could be... No, that's alternate reality thinking. Just enjoy what you can.* "We work together."

"That's right," George said, and made a point to sit back in his chair so he was a further away from her, exactly the opposite of what he wanted. *I'm going to have to change my stance on this thing with her. Fighting it isn't working. Who am I kidding? I just blew off Sergei. I'm barely fighting it now. I'm going to have to do something. Later, after she's finished playing. Something.*

"Uh-huh," Freddy said, sarcastically and started doing something with his horn and a rag.

"He doesn't believe us," Jillian said.

"Oh, well," George said. *Random people can tell something's going on.* "If he saw us at work, he'd know."

Her smile faded just a little. *I'm probably obvious enough now. How pathetic am I going to be tomorrow at work?* "We're not as bad as we once were, though. We've had a conversation or two."

"Yeah," George said, "maybe we can keep that going."

Jillian leaned toward him, just a little, and dropped her voice. "But, we'll be found out."

He leaned forward again and lowered his voice too. "I'd ask if we really care, but I know you do-"

Jillian cut him off. "You don't?"

I'm starting to care less and less about anything that puts an arbitrary barrier between us. "Sure. But I don't think it'll be the end of the world if our little alliance is discovered. What'll Gardiner do? Fire us? I suppose he could, but then he'd be in even deeper. His best shot gone."

Jillian tilted her head and then nodded, slapping the table lightly with her hand. "I see your point. But even so, wouldn't the rest of the four musketeers come after you for the betrayal?"

George groaned. "Is that what you think of us as?"

"The four musketeers? Sure. That's what everyone…" Jillian trailed off. *Oops.* "It's not derogatory."

"I'm sure," he said.

"I bet you all call me something. Ice queen, perhaps? Just 'the girl'? Or something really nasty."

George leaned closer to her, placing his hand on the table just an inch from hers. "I think that it's time to drop all that stuff. Act like adults. Don't you?"

Jillian took a small breath when he moved closer and felt her pulse pick up just a little. "Sure. You're right. Act our ages. But are the rest of the musket- *the guys* - going to do the same? What'll they think?"

"I don't care," George said, looking steadily into her eyes, wondering if it was his imagination that she seemed to be breathing faster. Maybe he was breathing faster. *Screw waiting.* "I *really* don't care. We should-"

"Hey, Jilly!" Freddy called from the stage, kindly not into the mic.

Jillian looked at Freddy. "Just a moment."

"Don't be fiddling while Rome's burning," Freddy said.

"Just a moment," Jillian said, and looked back at George. *What were you about to say?*

"Jilly!"

She stood up, glaring at Freddy, and then looked back down at George, who hadn't stood up that time. "I have to play now. I said I would. But we can talk more afterwards. So, don't go anywhere, okay?"

George cursed fate's bad timing. He had his nerve up and here the door had slammed. Well, he'd get his nerve up again when the timing worked. "Nothing can tear me away."

Normally, the piano, the music, and the rest of the group would have held Jillian's attention as, while she was playing, she mostly forgot the audience.

But this time, as she bounced her fingers from key to key, she couldn't stop thinking about the man at the table nearest her.

The very idea that he'd shown up right then was just so unlikely, she couldn't help but wonder if he was lying about following her from work. Of course, he'd changed his clothes, so he couldn't have followed her from work.

She threw a glance at the band table and saw him smiling and tapping his hand in time to the rhythm. Since he was looking right at her, he knew when she looked at him and he winked at her. Feeling the blood in her face warming her skin, she quickly turned back to the piano, grinning despite herself.

It was the second time he'd winked at her. The first had been three days before, when she'd been leaning into his office and he'd scared her. The first one was in jest, she supposed. What was this one about? *Maybe the how and the why that he's here doesn't matter. Maybe it just matters that he's here.*

For the final song of the set, Freddy called for a song she'd played with him before, a medley of *Swing Lo' Sweet Chariot* and *When The Saints Come Marching In* called *Swingin' With the Saints*. Jillian wasn't surprised. Freddy's arrangement of the piece had a great trumpet part and the audience was familiar enough with the number to sing along since Freddy and his combo played it almost every gig. His arrangement also lasted almost nine minutes, not that anyone who was feeling it would notice how long it was and Jillian allowed herself to feel it. When the audience sang along, she broke her rule and sang too. No one would hear her over the rest of the audience.

As she released the final chord of the piece in unison with the final stroke of the drum and cymbals, the cutoff of the bass, and the cutoff of the trumpet, the whole room exploded with cheering and applause and Jillian jumped up from the piano bench and hugged Freddy over the upright, laughing with joy at the marvel she'd just been a part of.

Freddy kept hold of her as the hug ended and tugged her around the piano to pull her in front of the mic as he credited the players for the evening to a standing ovation. Jillian felt so light, she actually made a small curtsy when he mentioned her. She stayed on the stage to applaud for the other members of the combo and then to close the fall board over the keys of the piano.

When she turned away from the piano, George was standing by the table, grinning and shaking his head. She put her hands on her hips and mouthed, "What?"

He walked over to the stage and looked at her. "You're 'just all right,' huh, Jillian Olivia?" He held out a hand for her to take so he could help her off the stage. "Most people exaggerate their talents. You down play yours. False modesty."

Jillian hoped her momentary hesitation to take his hand wasn't obvious.

While she'd have accepted practically anyone's offer of assistance as something casual and nice normally, this was George. There was something about taking his hand that seemed…more than casual. Not that he was acting like it meant anything particularly special.

So after a slight hesitation, she took his hand and said, "I'll take that as a compliment." His hand was just like it had been when they'd shaken hands a lifetime ago, warm and strong, but not rough.

"It was."

She stepped off the stage, depending on George for balance, and then slid her hand from his. "What do you want to do now? They'll start up the jukebox in a few minutes for dancing. It isn't too loud, so we could sit and talk." Then she glanced into the hallway. The official bar time was on a digital clock above the pay phone. "Though it is getting late and we have a long week and a longer weekend in front of us."

"Are you hinting that you're tired and want to call it a night?" George asked.

"Yes and no," Jillian said. "I'm tired, but we were having a conversation, and I did ask you to stick around. I don't want to be rude and undo all the progress we've made at being decent to each other."

George chuckled and shook his head. "You're priceless. Nice job making me feel guilty about keeping you here. Fine, let's call it a night."

"That's not what I meant to do," Jillian said, her face darkening. "I was just observing that it was late and we have early days for the rest of the foreseeable future and-"

Holding up his hands in surrender, George said, "Okay, okay. Relax. I'm fine with calling it a night, all right?" When her face softened again, he put his hands in his pockets. "Can I ask that we walk out together? I'd prefer Huey not realize I lied to him."

"Sure," Jillian nodded. "Just let me get my things." She threaded around a few people and disappeared into one of the staff areas, returning swiftly with her coat and purse.

George walked over to her as she was about to put her coat on. "Hey. Allow me. Freddy might be watching." When Jillian exhaled a small laugh and smiled again, George let out a breath. *If I can just keep her smiling.*

She handed him her coat and he held it out for her and secured it onto her shoulders once she'd put her arms into the armholes. He let his fingers linger against her, until she lifted an arm to pull her hair out from under the collar and turned around. "Thank you," Jillian said, and began to work the buttons from the top down. "Where are you parked?"

"I took the train," George said.

"Where's the nearest station? Four blocks over? Five?"

George nodded.

"That's a bit of a hike. Don't you worry about making it home safe when you're out drinking?"

"We weren't going drinking like that. I wasn't planning on getting sloshed," George laughed and Jillian laughed with him.

"No?"

"Yeah, uh, no, no. Definitely not."

"Where're you heading now? Do you think Sergei's still waiting for you?"

George watched her tie the belt on her coat and then jammed his right hand in his pocket. "I'm only about, oh, two and half hours late, so…"

"Probably not, then."

"Probably not."

She nodded and then motioned him to follow her as she led the way out of The Blue Feather. There was a fairly sizable crowd still, and it took a bit to make their way through it to the door. As they walked out, Jillian leaned over and whispered something to Huey and he laughed. "G'night, Jilly."

"Night, Huey."

Taking a few steps away from the door, she started, "So, where are you heading?"

"At the moment," George said, and buttoned up his suit coat for the little good it would do him against the cold. "I'm seeing you to your car."

"You are?"

"Yes," he said, and took her right hand in his and then turned and lifted his left arm over top and around so that when he released her hand, it was natural for her to leave her arm through his. "This way, right?" He asked, and then set off.

"Mm-hmm," she nodded, letting her hand settle on his arm. "I'm just down there, in that lot on the left."

"Okay."

When they'd passed the end of the building, she asked, "Aren't you cold?"

"Yes."

"Why didn't you wear another coat?"

"Poor planning and decision making on my part."

"That doesn't sound like you," Jillian said.

"No?" He smiled at her even though she wasn't looking at him. "That may be the nicest thing you've ever said to me."

She took it the way he meant it and laughed again. "How about I do one better than that?"

"Make my night," George said.

"I'm going to offer you a ride."

"Really?"

Jillian nodded. "Yes."

"Then I'm going to accept. But, um, and I don't mean to make you change your mind because I'd really like that ride, but in the interest of fairness, I have to disclose that I live a little further than you might expect."

"I guess I'll just have to suffer. Is it far enough out that I'll get lost on my way back?"

"You? I sincerely doubt it. From what I've seen you have a stellar memory."

"And that may be the nicest thing you've ever said to me, except," she stopped as she pointed him toward her car in the lot. *...for the 'good taste' comment last night, if it was what I thought it was.*

"Except?" George asked, as they moved into the parking lot.

Jillian was silent for a few paces as they arrived at her car. She unlocked the doors and George opened the driver's side door for her. "Thank you," she said, and slid into the seat.

George shut the door, walked around to the passenger side, and entered the car. Jillian started the car and adjusted the heater controls. "It'll take a bit to warm up." She started to put on the gloves she'd left on her seat earlier.

"Except?" George repeated.

"Oh," she said, and looked at him in the dim light. "You were very kind about my musical skills." *I can't possibly bring up that comment. If I'm wrong...* She watched his face squinch up a little in disbelief.

"I'll have to remedy that, then."

"Oh? Go ahead."

"Not now. A good compliment should be spontaneous and in the moment."

Jillian shifted into drive. "There are additional things that can be nice, other than compliments. Where am I headed?"

George provided some directions and watched her pull out of the parking lot smoothly and efficiently, like most things she did. He could have said it then, but he wanted to wait. Although he wanted to finish what he'd started to say earlier, in her car just wasn't the right place.

Jillian did her best to focus on the road and the route despite her realization that something was happening. It wasn't her mind playing tricks on her. And it wasn't in an alternate reality. She thought of her first day and how they'd had a fun few minutes together, how ridiculously attracted to George she'd been. *Still am, if I'm honest.* If that hadn't all turned so bad so suddenly... where might it have led?

It didn't really matter. She'd been telling herself that for a long time. And it still didn't. What mattered was the present. In the present, something was happening and she was definitely encouraging it, asking him to stay, giving him a ride. She swallowed a little as she wondered if George was planning to make a move on her and if he did make a move what she would do. He was about to say something when she had to join Freddy back on stage. It certainly had the feeling…

It'll lead to disaster at work. She'd been having that thought for a few days and it was starting to wear on her a little. Work was an impending disaster anyway.

She glanced over at her passenger and let herself think about how unbelievable he looked in his suit and just how wonderful a champion he'd been with the whole Cisco mess. He was more than a little charming too.

Maybe it was because it was late. Maybe it was because she was feeling high from playing. Maybe it was neither of those things, but whatever the case Jillian made a decision. She wouldn't let it go any farther, but if George tried to kiss her, she was going to find out what that felt like, regardless of the consequences.

CHAPTER EIGHT

At least the conversation hasn't been completely inane. George had managed to ask Jillian a few questions about jazz music and received quite an education. But neither of them had strayed toward anything personal. George had a reason for that; he wasn't about to risk building up another opportunity while he was stuck inside a moving vehicle. He wanted her undivided attention the next time he attempted *and succeeded* in talking about the possibility of *them.*

Thankfully, they turned onto his street when he was about to run out of thoughts. He would have babbled about pretty much anything other than work, if it came to that. But work was off-limits too. He wasn't going to let either of them get their heads back there. Work may have been how they met, and that should have been good, but it wasn't, it was definitely one reason they hadn't already tried. He was still pretty sure that she'd been interested that first day. And just the other day, if he'd just done- said something different when he'd stumbled about the jerk having great taste, they might already be in a different place.

It was still entirely possible she would swat him like a fly. But he wasn't about to continue to wonder any longer. The trick was timing, well, that and location. He still didn't like the idea of the car, even if it was in park.

He was preoccupied with how to convince Jillian to come inside for a just a minute, when Jillian leaned toward him as she pulled up to the curb. No, not toward him, around him. "Wow. You live here? This is a really *nice* place. Is that original brick? It's beautiful."

"The original stone, yes. And thank you, it is beautiful," he said. *Perfect.*

"I bet it's amazing in daylight. I can see why you live a greater distance from work. This is fabulous." She'd turned off the engine and was leaning over farther, looking up at his house.

"Want to come in for a minute and see the inside?"

"I'd hate to disturb your neighbors," she said, still looking at the house.

"I don't think they'll be bothered." He pointed to the houses on either side. "They won't hear us unless we start shouting up the street."

"Not them," Jillian said, sitting back. "Your upstairs or downstairs neighbors. Which floor is yours?"

He chuckled. "All of them."

"All of them? You rent this whole place? Do you have a roommate or...?"

"I own it. Just me. Well, I've got a mortgage, of course." He smiled at her and watched her mouth drop open.

"You *own* it? How can you afford it? You must make twice as much as I do." Then she shook her head. "I'm sorry. That's none of my business."

"It's okay. Property out here is a little cheaper, that's how I can afford it. Also, I don't have a car."

"No car?" Jillian asked, incredulously.

"Nope," he started to open his car door. "Come on in and check it out."

"Oh, I don't know," Jillian said.

George shook his head and got of the car, quickly closed the door behind him, and circled the car to open Jillian's. "Come on," he said, as she looked up at him, still gripping the steering wheel. "It's even better on the inside." He held a hand out to her.

"I don't think... It's late."

"Just take five minutes for the ten cent tour and then I'll see you safely back in your car and you can go home and get plenty of sleep. Just five minutes."

"Well..." She took his hand, placing a gloved hand in his, and stepped out of the car. "I suppose if it's just five minutes." But she paused between the car door and the body. "Maybe, I'd better not..."

"You don't even need to take off your coat," George said, as her hand slipped out of his again.

"Okay," she said, and leaned back down a bit to grab her purse. He watched as she locked the doors and pocketed her keys, figuring that he'd best wait to say anything until after he'd shown her around.

While his motive to get her inside the house had nothing to do with showing it off, he found himself absurdly pleased as she admired it. He'd planned to keep the tour short, but she took her time walking around looking at everything. He decided to save the room to the right of the entry, passed the stairs, for last and escorted her to the left of the entry into an oddly shaped room with a bay window. He pointed out the molding he'd managed to save and showed her the original glass panels he'd hung.

"That's genius to use them like that. Was that the previous owner's idea?"

"Nope. Mine," he said, despite feeling slightly offended that she didn't ascribe the idea to him. But then she turned to him and said, "Brilliant. You should put your ideas on a website for other people who are renovating older houses like this," and he didn't need to forgive her.

"So, no furniture in here apart from the bookcases?"

"Since it's just me, I haven't thrown too much money at furnishing rooms I don't use. The previous owner had a piano in here, but I keep thinking library."

"It's a parlor, or perhaps a drawing room," Jillian said. "Meant for formal entertaining." He frowned into her back. "It'd be a lovely library. This faces south, doesn't it? Lots of natural light for reading." The frown quickly changed into a smile. "What color are you going to paint in here?" She asked, looking at the white walls.

"I haven't thought much about it. When I'm ready to furnish it, I'll consider my options."

The empty dining room made Jillian gasp when he turned on the chandelier. "Oh, my word," she said, as she walked the length of the room toward the fireplace at the far end. "This house is amazing. Look at that fireplace. This room is huge. My dining room table with both leaves wouldn't fill this up. You could seat twenty in here with plenty of room for a buffet against that wall." She gestured around the room. "Wow! I know I've said that before and I should come up with another word, but I can't. Wow!" She turned around looking at the room. "And you saved the molding in here too. This is incredible. It's practically a ballroom." She shook her head. "How did you luck into this place?"

"Timing was important," he answered.

"I know I haven't any right to say anything at all, but looking at the white mantel and surround and gray brick masonry... I just have to suggest you consider a blue in here. A dark... no, not dark blue, a deep blue. It'd be amazing with a large table and a white table cloth. Or you could go for a dark purple wine shade for the table cloth. And then all the silver shining... White dishes with blue patterning... It'd be breath taking."

He grinned. "Are you planning a dinner party in here?"

"It doesn't have to be dinner. It could be a party, maybe Christmas or New Year's. The table as a buffet. It could be so elegant." She stopped and looked at him. "Sorry. Empty rooms inspire me a little. And this is amazing." She glanced at her shoes and then back at him. "I'm repeating myself. Show me the rest."

"I don't know. What if you don't approve of the rooms I've actually done?"

She laughed and headed toward the doorway on the far end. "If you're worried, I'll show myself." He jogged to catch up to her in the butler's pantry and then followed on her heels into the kitchen. "This place is huge," she shook her head looking around the kitchen and over the table and through the living room toward the front of the house.

"They took down the wall here," he motioned to an archway that his kitchen table slightly projected under. "It wasn't a load bearing wall, so they could open it all the way across and that afforded..." He stopped as she walked out of his kitchen into the living room toward the fireplace that sat at the end of the staircase, so that the chimney ran up the center of the house.

"Another fireplace. I'd kill for one and you've got two," she said, as she turned around and looked at the giant entertainment center opposite the fireplace. The couch and recliner faced the entertainment center. She shook her head. *How can you have such a beautiful thing and not showcase it?*

"What?"

"Nothing."

He sighed. "What? Come on. Let's hear it."

"Well, having the walkway between the back of your sofa and the fireplace is a terrible waste. You could put your flat screen up above the fireplace. Check the space under the stairs. You might be able to make some cuts and build in for you're the rest of your electronics over here." She drew an imaginary box on the wall next to the fireplace. "Then you could turn all this around," she turned and gestured toward his sofa and recliner, "and have a usable fireplace *and* watch television.

"If there isn't room under the stairs, you could always get a small upright cabinet for the electronics and..." She put a hand to her head. *Oh my, God. Shut up. Shut up. Don't criticize. Don't even comment.* "I'm sorry. Really. I won't say another word. This place is lovely and this room looks comfortable and the last thing I should be doing is telling you how to live in your own home."

"It's okay to have opinions," he said. *I've thought about that exact rearrangement in here quite a few times myself.*

"No. Really. Zipped." She drew an imaginary zipper across her lips. Then she pointed to the stairs and raised her eyebrows.

"Go ahead," he said, with a chuckle. It was always interesting to see reactions to his house. Most of his friends focused on the question of why he'd bother to get such a big place when it was just him. That didn't bother him. It was an investment *and* a place to live *and* roots. Owning a place meant he was permanent, not temporary.

And why start small, when you didn't have to? Although he knew that some people would question the choice to give up a car. Finally, there was the obvious reality that he would never be lucky enough to find a place like this waiting for him in a few years when he was in a different place in his life. It only made sense to jump on the opportunity when it presented itself.

Unlike his friends, Jillian was reacting to the space itself. It was... interesting. She was a manager at work, a pianist on the side, and now a designer. *Who in the world are you?*

She peeked around the corner first and into the empty room on the other side that he'd been saving. "I've no idea what to do with that one," he said. She nodded and then took the stairs. He followed and said, "Go left, first."

She obeyed his direction and walked down to the end of the hall.

"Spare bedroom number one," he said, as she opened the door on a white bedroom. "The upstairs had a lot of work done too. They put in closets."

The walls were white, like most of the rooms downstairs, and it looked fresh, but empty and unlived-in. She nodded and then walked back into the hallway. He pointed at the doors heading back toward the stairs. "Spare bedroom number two. Spare bedroom number three."

Her eyes widened a little.

"You said it yourself, this house is huge." He continued. "Linen closet. Bath."

She raised her eyebrows and pointed at the door to the bath. "Sure, go ahead. And you can open your mouth."

She shook her head really hard and then stepped up to enter the bath. "Ohhhhh, look at that tub," she couldn't stop herself from saying as she saw the large clawfoot tub; it was more than deep enough for soaking. She looked around. "This is more genius." She took in the double sinks and the small shower stall that fit into the room without being squished. "How did they ever come up with this much room?"

"A fourth and fifth bedroom were taken out during the previous owner's renovation and made into this bath and the master's bath. A bit was left over to expand the master too."

"There's a master bath too? This place is a mansion."

He held out his arm toward the right and she stepped back down out of the bathroom and toward the final door on the upstairs hallway.

The master bedroom made an impression. *It's like a really expensive hotel. Gorgeous, but a little impersonal.* The room was painted in a lovely green, not white like the majority of the house, with a light not-quite-white carpet. The bed had a crisp white bedspread, with a matching green rectangle trimming out the edges. Even with what she supposed was a large closet; there was plenty of room for four chests of drawers and two chairs. The chairs flanked another fireplace, this one converted to gas.

The artwork was all nature scene photography rather than paintings. The only giveaways about the man who slept there were a few books on a bedside table whose titles she couldn't make out from the doorway, what looked like a family picture in a frame atop a chest of drawers, and the pocket watch that sat beside the photo frame.

As she started toward the open door that obviously led to the bath, he asked, "No comment?"

"On what?"

"The bedroom."

I'm not going to make that blunder again. I'm not going to say anything negative. "It's very well done. Very classy. Very... finished."

She stepped up into the bath quickly, hoping to avoid any more discussion.

"You don't like it," he said, following her into the bath. She stood gaping at the room.

Jillian tried to take in the huge bath, done in greens and blues. A large shower, plenty of room for more than one person, with several shower heads and a bench, in gray stone and glass. Another large tub, this one not a clawfoot, but a freestanding tub with jets. *I could live in that.* Separate room for the toilet. Double sinks again with mirrors all down the wall. The cabinets painted white. A fern near the frosted window at the back.

It was bright, light, clean, and airy. She wanted to stay. "I've never envied a man his bathroom before," she said, running her hand along what turned out to be a genuine marble counter top.

"It's okay, then?"

"It's glorious," she said, looking back at the tub and imagining soaking in warm water with the jets going.

"Heated flooring too," he said, and when she looked away from the tub toward him, he pointed to the controls on the wall. She winced. "Something wrong?"

"Jealousy. Severe, painful, and obnoxious jealousy. I almost wish I hadn't come in." She walked to the tub, but crossed her arms to keep from touching anything else.

"Well, now. That makes me feel guilty. Why don't you tell me what's wrong with the bedroom and even it out?"

"There's nothing wrong with it," she answered.

He nodded, smirked, and said, "Liar." Then he headed back out of the bath and she followed slowly, suddenly more aware of that fact that she was in his private domain then she'd been. When he walked out of the bedroom and into the hall, she quickly exited the bedroom behind him.

"All that's left," he said, as he started down the stairs, "is the room you peeked into down there. I haven't a clue what it is. Oh, and the room between it and the kitchen, that's the laundry."

"It's a morning room or a breakfast room," she answered. "It's on the east side of the house, right?"

"Yes," he said.

"It's intended for use in the morning hours."

"Okay," he said. At the bottom of the stairs he took a few steps back toward his family room.

"It has a lot of glass," Jillian said, looking into the room again. "But, it might make a nice den. Once the sun is high enough, it wouldn't interfere with a television screen."

"Okay," he repeated and took another couple of steps, hoping she'd follow him. Now that the tour was over, it was time to make his move.

When Jillian turned around again, George had ducked out of sight. She headed back passed the front door and looked around for a moment, wondering where he'd gone. Just a few more steps and she could see him in the family room, sort of perched on the back of his sofa. "Well," Jillian started. "Thank you for the tour. Your home is amazing-"

"You'll have to come back in the daylight hours. You missed the yard. It's a big part of why I bought it."

"Um, sure," she said. And it was clear to George that she wasn't sure at all. Then he saw her twist her hands together a moment and then quickly stick them in her pockets. *Thank God, she's nervous too.*

"We should talk about something, before you go." He said, sliding further away from her along the sofa back to make plenty of room and then leaning over and patting the end nearest her just once and then sitting up straight again.

Her stomach dropped and her heart picked up pace. There was that same something in his tone, despite the completely casual action. *Forget that decision to kiss him. That was a bad decision. Run like the wind.* "Can't it wait until tomorrow?"

"Jillian."

"It's really late now and the tour took more than five minutes." She motioned toward the door with her thumb. "I should go."

"Jillian." He tried not to sigh. "It can't wait. It's waited for far too long already." George stood up and walked over to stand in front her, pleased that she didn't move away. He watched her eyes; they focused straight ahead of her. "Jillian," he said, again, requesting her attention and focus.

She lifted her head a bit and raised her eyes to meet his.

He wanted to smile, but his face wouldn't reflect the lightness he didn't feel. *Just do it.* "I want to take you out, Jillian. For dinner. For lunch. For drinks, whatever." In his peripheral vision, he watched his hand reach out and touch her soft hair, slipping it between his fingers as he pushed it back over her shoulder, and he saw her swallow. "Whatever you'll give me. Will you come out with me?"

She reached up a hand to touch his and disappointed him by pulling his down and away from her. "George. You don't know me…"

"That's the point," he answered and twisted his hand against hers, balling a fist against her palm and then spreading his fingers against her hand, so that it opened for him and he could slip his fingers between hers. It was the first time he'd touched her with intent. Her hand fit with his exactly. "I want to know you."

"I don't know you either." Her mind traveled to her where their fingers were suddenly intertwined. His hand felt pleasantly warm against hers. She hadn't touched anyone or been touched by anyone for some months, but even that amount of time couldn't explain how right it felt to have her fingers next to his.

"Get to know me," he said, and lifted his other hand to her hair and then slid it along her cheek.

She almost closed her eyes at the soft caress. *So right. But so wrong.*

He could feel her tremble under his hand as he leaned closer to her.

"This is a bad idea." *Nothing but trouble can come from this.*

"No," he whispered as he brought his lips close to hers, still looking her in the eyes. "It's a beautiful idea. Just like you."

Oh, who cares? "George," she whispered. "I think… I think…"

"Me too," George said, and saw her eyes close just before he closed his and finally, gently, touched his lips to hers. Her lips were as soft as he expected, pliant, and they quivered a little against his. She removed her hand from his and reached up to lightly settle her palm against his cheek. A moment more and he felt a tremor come over him, a shiver that made his heart pound and his blood race.

At first, Jillian surrendered to the moment, and then as his lips moved against hers, she surrendered to him, letting herself open to him, letting herself accept him. Soon the need for him began a faint hum in her veins and she felt so dizzy she had to bring her free hand up to his shoulder just to hold on.

Holy… George tried to breathe as he left her lips and straightened. He wanted so much to go back for more, to take her in his arms and demand everything she had. Instead, he forced himself to give her space, though he couldn't drop his hand from her cheek and quit touching her quite that soon.

Her eyes fluttered open and she blinked at him, confused about where she was and a little worried about losing her balance. As it all sunk in, as *he* sunk in, she took a deep breath and found herself smiling.

George smiled back. "Dinner," he said.

"Okay," she said.

"Tomorrow night."

She nodded wordlessly. *Kiss me again.*

Thank God. "Good. You were concerned about the lateness of the hour."

"Was I?"

"Yes," he said, and took a breath. Then he leaned over and put his forehead against hers, noticing a delicate scent on her skin. "I'll see you at work and we'll finalize our plans."

"Okay," she said, again and dropped her hands from him.

"You know, Huey was right. You do smell like vanilla," George said, and she barked a laugh of nerves and excess energy.

"All right." She stepped back from him. "Goodnight."

"Goodnight," he said, and missed the feel of her cheek against his palm. He did accompany her to her car, though he tried not to get too close to her.

"Goodnight," Jillian said, again and he closed her door. "Tomorrow," she said to herself.

George stepped back to the sidewalk and watched her until the tail lights turned the corner. "Tomorrow."

Jillian arrived at the office a few minutes later than usual and, for once, it didn't bother her in the slightest. She'd tried on four outfits before deciding on her red sweater, brown and red and orange plaid skirt, and brown knee high boots. It was a perfect fall outfit, and it was partly red. Survey after survey told her that men notice women in red. Since they'd agreed to a dinner date, but not a time, she wanted to be sure that she could dress up what she was wearing if he wanted to go straight from the office.

She'd worn her regular work jewelry, a thin chain with a small pendant, small gold hoops, and her charm bracelet. She brought a long necklace with red sparkly beads and chunky stones, drop earrings, even a scarf if it felt right, and high heels if the boots weren't nice enough.

After finding the perfect outfit, she'd spent extra time on her hair, keeping it down, but curling it. He'd touched her hair the night before, so she wanted to be sure that it was convenient for him if he wanted to again. Her normal makeup routine wasn't altered, but she'd brought makeup with her for her possible quick change.

She took the stairs, careful of spilling her Starbucks splurge. Since she was late, she made a point to walk passed Rachel's desk and let her know that she was in. *Fine. Fine. Acting normal.*

She made a point not to walk to quickly, because she'd noticed a slight spring in her step when she was crossing the first floor, and she was focusing on taming it. As she approached her office, she saw George's door was open and his light was on. *Normal. Act normal.* She didn't pause or even look, she just headed straight to her office and followed the rest of her usual morning routine, settling in and checking messages.

She responded to a few emails and finished her Starbucks before going to the break room to get a cup of water. George was alone in the break room, pouring coffee when she entered. He looked especially nice that morning in a dress shirt, blue patterned tie, and what Jillian thought were suit pants. *That blue tie is fabulous on you.* He glanced up and then back to his coffee. "Morning," he said, flatly.

"Morning," Jillian said, just as flatly and took her mug to the water fountain. *Okay. That was not good. Why didn't he smile or anything? Did I do something wrong?*

She'd tossed and turned most of the night alternating between happily replaying the night in her head and trying to figure out why he'd called a halt to it after one, single, solitary kiss. The question of what she'd done wrong had come up over and over.

As she started to fill her mug, she glanced over her shoulder at him. All she saw was his back as he walked out of the break room and she stopped the fountain and set her mug down. *Ouch. Does that mean our date's cancelled? Probably.* She gripped the counter and blinked at a slight sting in her eyes. *He actually had promise. Ouch.*

She heard a sound outside the break room and took a breath to still herself because she really didn't want anyone to see her looking upset. George walked back in and set his coffee on the counter as he walked to her saying, "I checked the hallway." Then he took her face in his hands and kissed her quickly. "Good morning," he said, softly and then laughed and grabbed a napkin to wipe her lip gloss off his mouth. "I should have seen that coming. I suppose I deserve it for taking a liberty."

"Good morning," Jillian sighed.

"What?" George asked.

"What, what?" Jillian asked.

"You're looking at me funny."

"I am?"

"Yes."

Jillian glanced over his shoulder at the doorway, and then looked him in the eyes a moment before she took his face in her hands and kissed him, taking her time, working her lips against his as his hands found her back and he leaned into her. But before she was finished, George's hands moved and he gripped her arms and set back from him. "Okay," he said, taking a deep breath, "we can't be doing that here. Right?"

After a brief feeling of disappointment, Jillian smiled at George. He looked a little taken aback by her kiss, definitely in a good way. And he was sporting more of her lip gloss. She handed him another napkin and he shook his head.

"Come on. I want to hear you say it."

"What?"

He wiped his mouth again. "That we can't be doing that here. We need an agreement on this."

She shrugged and looked around the room a moment and then picked up her mug and turned to finish filling it. "Hmm. Do I feel agreeable this morning? I'm not sure." When she stopped the water and looked back at him, he had his hands on his hips and he was shaking his head again.

"And I thought last night was the hard part." He tossed the napkin away. Jillian opened her mouth to ask him what he meant, but he kept talking. "I realized this morning that I should double check something with you before I finalize plans for tonight." He picked up his coffee. "You do eat meat, right," he asked, and jammed his free hand into his pants pocket. "Any dietary restrictions?"

"What if I do? What if I don't? Do I have to tell you all the intimate details of my digestive system so early on?"

He rubbed a hand over his face. "Oh, you're even more trouble than I thought you were going to be. Fine. I guess I'll have to deal with that. Can I assume you're fine with any restaurant I choose?"

She shrugged again. "Hmm. You know what they say about assuming..."

George looked at the ceiling and lifted his arms in a 'why me' gesture a moment and then he looked at Jillian again. "If you have any preferences or concerns, now is the time."

"Why? It's Tuesday. I should think we won't need reservations. We could change our minds at the last minute."

"Nope," he said. "I already know where were going, unless you give me a reason not to."

"Where?"

George grinned, "I guess you'll find out when we get there."

"No," Jillian said, in a slight whine. "I need to be sure I'm dressed correctly. Where are we going?"

"You'll be fine," he said, and started to leave the break room.

Jillian followed with her water. "George," she said, in a loud whisper. "Tell me."

"Nah," George said, over his shoulder. "At least not now."

"George," Jillian repeated in a loud whisper. But they were near the cubes and she only had a moment or two left so she used it for another important question. "What time?"

He stopped walking and glanced around before he looked at her again. "I'll let you know." His mouth morphed into a mocking grin. "You must learn to develop some trust. Have a little faith. Let someone else do the planning."

"Oh, funny," she said.

"I'll let you know. Trust me," he said, softly and then turned and walked away again.

Jillian executed an about-face herself and walked around the cubes the opposite direction, grinning despite his being purposely difficult. Fighting with him had always been so exhausting before, but play fighting... *That's something else entirely.*

Not five minutes later, George found himself on his cell phone up on the roof of the building for a little privacy, pacing. "I need a favor, Orville. A couple actually."

"You didn't show up on Saturday and you want favors," Orville grumped.

"Yeah, well, I did call and apologize for that," George said. "Besides, this is an emergency."

"An emergency? What kind of emergency?"

George grabbed the back of his neck with his free hand. "A dating emergency. I've got a first date tonight and it needs to be something extraordinary."

Orville snorted. "Oh, yeah? Why?"

"Because she's extraordinary and I want to make an impression. I'm fairly certain she's seen all the usual stuff." He thought of the three dozen roses the jackass had sent. *Bastard had to ruin flowers.* "I had been thinking of taking her to a Moroccan place for dinner to be different, but that's not going to do it. I need something no one's ever done before."

"In the whole of human history? I think that's a tall order."

"No kidding," George laughed. "No, I was thinking something no one's done for *her* before. I want to be unique and memorable."

"You're unique, Kid. And if she's truly extraordinary, she's not gonna need a big production from you."

"I'm not talking about a big production, at all. Just different."

"Okay. I'll help if I can. So, who's so extraordinary that you're scrambling to put the perfect date together at the last minute?"

George stopped walking. "Well, uh, actually it's Jillian from work. Do you remem-?"

"Well, it's about time! She sounded interesting the first time you mentioned her, and that was how long ago? So, I'm guessing this is new since you started working together on that project. The one that supposedly kept you on Saturday."

Shaking his head, George said, "You could say that." *More like it's been a long time coming.*

"And the project wasn't actually what kept you on Saturday..."

"Orville," George said, "give me all the crap you want, but do some other things for me first."

Rachel knocked on Jillian's door just after lunch. "Special delivery," Rachel said, and walked in to set a pot with red flowers on Jillian's table. "So, now I know what's up with you today." Rachel said.

"What do you mean?" Jillian asked, trying to sound casual and normal, even though if Rachel was mentioning it, it was already too late, and she knew she was grinning like an idiot. She stood up and walked over to see the flowers.

There was no mistaking, even at a distance, that they weren't roses. They were about a foot tall and pretty, with wide open faces of six petals on each flower that reminded her a little of petunias. And, since they were in a pot and weren't dead or dying, they might be something she could keep in her office. *How sweet.*

Rachel sat on the corner of Jillian's desk. "Are you really going to pretend? You've been walking around in a fog all morning with a smile on your face. Now flowers." She lowered her voice. "Tell me about him."

"They're so pretty," Jillian said. "Was there a card?"

Rachel frowned and produced an envelope. "At least tell me who he is and where you met him."

The envelope had her name in bold block letters, no giveaway on the handwriting, as far as she could tell. *That's good.* Opening the envelope, Jillian took a step back to be certain that Rachel wouldn't be able to read the card, just in case.

More block lettering. It read, "+ 2.5."

Jillian flipped the card over. Nothing else. It was almost entirely blank except the puzzling math.

"What does it say?" Rachel asked, and Jillian held it up for her. "It makes me think of an optical prescription. What does it mean?"

"I'm stumped." Jillian said.

"Is he an eye doctor?"

"No," Jillian said.

"Well, so much for that. Do you think it's something to do with the whole 'average family being 2.5 kids?'?"

Jillian looked at Rachel. "No. I don't think so. Our first date is tonight." She looked back at the card. *George.* "No. He's being clever about something. Unfortunately, I think he's overestimated *my* cleverness. I don't get it."

"You can always call him."

"Give me a few minutes to figure it out first. I mean, I don't want him to think I didn't even try." *And I can't call him with you in the room.*

Rachel picked up the envelope from the desk where Jillian had dropped it. "Maybe there was a second card and the florist forgot it." She dialed the number on the envelope. "Yes. I just took a delivery for Jillian Braden..."

Jillian quit listening to Rachel and looked at the flowers. *They aren't roses.* She smiled widely and leaned over for a sniff. They weren't particularly fragrant. They weren't showy. There were a lot of things they weren't. But they were pretty. And they seemed... sincere. *They are so much better than roses.*

They had to be from George, of course. No one else would send her something like this with a cryptic note. He was being playful. *But, I want to play too. And I just don't get it.*

"Well, that was a dead end." Rachel said, as she hung up.

"Huh?" Jillian focused on Rachel.

Rachel smiled indulgently. "You weren't paying attention? No other card. Although, we made the florist's day. He was very concerned about this order."

"Oh?"

"Apparently the order was very specific and he was concerned that you'd be unhappy."

"Why?"

"Well, there were supposed to be at least thirty-seven flowers, more was fine, but no fewer than thirty-seven. And he had to take the last of these out of his hothouse to fill it. And, I guess they aren't going to last much longer now due to the season since they're out of the special lights, and they're annuals. He just went on and on."

"Oh. Poor guy. My flowers stressed him out."

"I told him you are very happy. He said not to forget to collect the seeds. 4 o'clocks are easy to grow, and you can plant them in the same pot next spring."

"4 o'clocks." Jillian laughed. "These are 4 o'clocks. That's what they're called?"

"Yeah." Rachel answered, her face scrunching a little in confusion. "Is that funny?"

"4 o'clock plus two and a half." Jillian lifted the card up. "That's when we're going out. 6:30."

Rachel tilted her head. "Ohhhhkay."

"No, you don't understand. He said he'd let me know when and this is him letting me know."

Rachel considered it a moment. "All right. Thirty-seven? Are you sure that it's 6:30?"

Jillian smiled again. "I don't know that I was supposed to know about or even notice the thirty-seven." *That thirty-seven was for George. I bet it was to top the three dozen roses.* She started counting blooms.

"So, are you going to tell me about him, or what?"

"I don't know," Jillian said.

"Why not?" Rachel asked.

Jillian paused. If it didn't work out, it'd be better if no one at work knew... But she was dying to talk about it to someone. "Shut the door." *Forty-two. I better remember, in case George wants to know.*

Rachel's eyes lit up and she quickly shut the door. "So, spill."

Jillian returned to her desk, put an elbow on her desk, and rested her head on her hand and sighed.

"Oo, that good, huh?" Rachel said, and pulled up a chair.

"I don't know," Jillian said. "It's still awfully early. I mean, it's just our first date is tonight. It's not like we've..."

"Well, I knew that," Rachel said, and Jillian furrowed her brow in confusion, so Rachel explained. "You don't have the 'morning after' glow. You've got the 'infatuated' glow."

Jillian felt the giggle coming and couldn't stop it. "I don't know about infatuated..."

Rachel raised her eyebrows.

"All right, fine. But-"

"Tell me about *him*," Rachel said.

"He's..." Jillian thought about all the words she could use to describe George and then told the truth. "I don't know. I mean, I don't know him yet. We've been, I guess the word is *acquainted* for forever, it seems, but I don't know him."

Rachel put her elbow on Jillian's desk and leaned her chin on her palm. "So what happened? One of those rare moments when you look at each other and suddenly everything changes? He isn't the guy next door anymore? He's suddenly *someone?*"

After a brief rush of adrenalin from the 'guy next door' analogy, Jillian had to work very hard to keep herself from glancing toward George's office. Rachel couldn't possibly have guessed so quickly. Focusing on the question, Jillian kept on. "No. He was always someone. I mean, I was attracted to him right off." *Don't say anything about not getting along, because that might give it away.* "It just didn't happen. Then last night, he said he wanted to take me out for dinner and then... he kissed me." Jillian heard the wistfulness in her own voice when she said it. "The most perfect first kiss ever. Soft and sweet and yet it set my head spinning. I wasn't sure where I was when it was over."

Rachel smiled broadly then. "I love those kinds of kisses."

"Hmm?"

"The ones that reach way down inside and make you feel all loopy. Not a 'let's have sex' kiss, but an 'I'm nuts about you' kiss."

"You think that's what it meant?"

"I don't know, what do you think?"

"Well, that's a good question. He kissed me just the once and then he said goodnight."

Rachel sighed. "Oh. How romantic. He must really like you."

"You think?"

"He kissed you, you *liked* it, and didn't make any kind of move for sex?"

"Right."

"He really likes you."

Jillian giggled again. "Oh, I hope so. I've been thinking about him for forever. It always seemed impossible, but now…" She looked back at her flowers and sighed again. "I hope so."

Once he'd made all the arrangements for the evening, George all but sequestered himself in his office. It was the only way to control the urge to pop into Jillian's office or look for her in other locations, around the building. He didn't want to spoil the fun.

It was also the only way to avoid Sergei. At some point, George was sure, Sergei was going to ask him what had happened the previous night, and he hadn't decided what the answer was going to be.

He and Jillian already had a secret at work and he was pretty sure that that secret was going to be next to impossible to keep. It would probably be even harder to keep the fact that they were dating under wraps. It was early and the added pressure, the scrutiny they'd be under, would make it uncomfortable at the very least. It seemed like he'd been fighting this thing forever and now that he'd given in, he didn't want to see it crumble simply from early exposure. Better to hide a little until there was something *worth* gossiping about.

So that left him with the question of what to tell Sergei, and the lack of an answer kept him imprisoned in his office staring at the walls. The only contact he had with the outside world for over an hour was the text from the florist when his delivery had been made. He'd watched through his open door for the delivery to make it to Jillian's office wishing he could hear the conversation when Rachel took the flowers inside. The voices had been barely detectable, let alone decipherable, but he did hear Jillian laugh and that made his shoulders drop a little.

But sitting and waiting for the second delivery was killing him. He definitely wanted to see her face. Of course, if he was there and she knew it, there was always the chance she'd look right at him after she opened it. That kind of thing was reflexive.

Before he knew it, Ringo was out trying to give him some relief. Poor Ringo was quickly pocketed, however, when George saw the mail guy pass by Rachel's desk. He jumped up and used the pretense that he was waiting on something important to rush over to Rachel's desk. His timing wasn't ideal, but it wasn't bad.

Rachel was on the phone and holding a large yellow envelope, clearly puffed out by the bubble wrap that lined it and the contents. "...bring it to you?" Pause. "Okay." She hung up and looked at George. "Yes?"

"Did a registered letter come for me?"

"I don't think so," Rachel said, and laid Jillian's envelope aside to look through the mail one extra time. "No. I don't see one."

"Hmm. Okay. Thanks," George said, as Jillian arrived at Rachel's desk. He gave her a polite nod and started back for his office. He stopped at the printer and pretended to look for something, while he snuck a look at Jillian.

She struggled to open the envelope and finally had to have Rachel use some scissors on the end. When she did, a white notecard fell out onto Rachel's desk.

"Oh, my," Rachel said, as she looked at the card and put one hand to her chest. George smirked.

Jillian took the card from Rachel and glanced down at the over-sized block lettering filling the notecard. "Don't wear anything," Jillian read in a hushed voice. Unlike Rachel, she immediately flipped it over. "That requires dry cleaning."

Both Jillian and Rachel laughed.

Rachel leaned over to see what else was in the envelope. Jillian slid the contents out and began to unfold what appeared to be red fabric and her brow furrowed. "Okay, this is mysterious." The fabric had opened into a large red bib apron with ties around both the neck and the waist. She pulled a sticky note off the bib. "Bring me."

"What's goin' on?" Ishi asked from her desk, and George debated how much longer he could get away with watching.

"Jillian's got a date," Rachel said, "with a mystery man."

"How's that work?" Ishi asked. "Blind date?"

"He's not a mystery to her. She just won't spill much of anything about him. I can't even get a first name."

"Oh, he's definitely a mystery to me," Jillian said, shaking her head and looking at the apron. But just as George started to worry a little that he'd made a mistake, he saw her mouth curve up in smile. "And a little unexpected." She threw a sideways glance in his direction and he quickly turned and headed for his office.

CHAPTER NINE

At 6:25 pm, Jillian was pacing back and forth in her apartment. Charlie sat on the back of the couch and watched her. She'd been trying to sit for ten minutes and she couldn't keep still, even with the television on, so she shut it off and paced. "I'm going to die before he gets here, Charlie," she said, gripping her hands together behind her back.

"I'm sure he'll find the place," she said. George had popped into her office for a minute around the time of her usual afternoon coffee break. He'd walked in with a notepad and placed it on her desk.

"May I have your home address, please?"

It had been so formal, that all she could think to say was, "Of course," and then she'd written down her address and handed the notepad back to him. "I'm a little curious…" She'd said, by way of an introduction to asking what exactly the plans were.

George had simply smiled and said, "Good," and then disappeared out of her office.

Still pacing, Jillian looked at Charlie. "I thought women were supposed to be mysterious, Charlie. Not men. He's made me so nervous; I'm going to act like an idiot tonight. I just know it."

Charlie meowed.

"You can say that, Charlie," Jillian said, "you're a cat. I have to actually construct sentences." It was then that Jillian spied the roses on her dining room table. She'd been in such a rush to put herself together that she hadn't thought anything about her apartment. She kept it clean and always cleaned up after meals, so it wasn't as though she had to tidy to make it presentable.

Looking at the roses, she wondered if she ought to get rid of them. They probably had a few days left in them which made it sad to throw them away. But the 4 o'clocks were still at work. She expected George to at least step inside for a few minutes, so… perhaps it would be best if he didn't see the roses.

She raced over to the dining room table, picked up the vase, and then grabbed her keys on her way to the front door. She could get to the trash chute and back in a minute. As long as he wasn't early. She threw the dead bolt, opened the door, and stepped into the hallway.

Hurry. Hurry. Hurry. The elevator bell dinged from the middle of the hallway *shoot!* and Jillian quickly turned and scurried back to her door. *Hurry. Hurry. Hurry.*

She was still twisting her key in the lock when she heard George's voice call up the hall. "Good evening."

"Ah, heh," she made a half-laugh sound and turned to watch him walk up the hallway. He looked casual, like he had over the weekend, in a blue dress shirt and black slacks, but no tie, under an unbuttoned winter coat. His shoes were buffed to a high shine.

Her right hand was still on her key and her left hand was still full of the vase and flowers when George arrived at her door. Jillian forced out, "Good evening."

"Am I early?"

"Um, maybe a minute. This is embarrassing." She quickly let go of the key and grabbed the doorknob. "I was just…" She opened the door. "Why don't you go in while I take care of these?"

"What are you doing?"

"I was just…" She looked at the flowers and then back at him. "I was going to throw these out."

"Oh? Why?" He took the vase from her.

Jillian felt her skin heat from head to toe. "Because I didn't want you to see them."

"I knew you took them home."

"Yes, but. After yesterday and then today…" She gave up on trying to say anymore on the subject, stepped into her apartment, and extended her arm. "Won't you come in?"

"Thank you." He walked in and set the vase on her kitchen island, the nearest flat surface, and turned to face her as she closed the door. "You look nice. Black again, huh?"

Jillian tugged at the waist of her washable sweater. She'd chosen all black, hoping that whatever he had in mind wouldn't show on the black. She'd gone a little more casual herself, pants instead of a skirt, flats, and the sweater. But she'd put on a little sparkle with her earrings, a pendant necklace, and a ring, skipping bracelets and a watch. Whatever they were doing, she figured she could put a ring in her pocket, her purse, or even on her necklace chain, but the bracelets and watch might get in the way. "Since *someone* wouldn't give me much by way of hints as to the agenda, it seemed the safest bet."

He grinned. "That is really bothering the daylights out of you, isn't it?"

She almost tried to lie. "Yes. I really wish it didn't, but yes. And you're just loving it, aren't you?"

"Maybe, just a tad." He held up his thumb and index finger and squished them together. "Okay. We've got about five minutes before we need to be enroute, so can I have the short tour?"

Jillian shook her head. "Right. Where are my manners? Can I take your coat?"

"Nah. We'll see if your five minute tour is shorter than mine."

She shrugged and waved her hand about the space. "Open floor plan. Kitchen, dining room, living space."

She watched him walk passed the kitchen and look around the dining room and living room. "You have a lot of space, for an apartment."

"It's a great place. There's a stackable laundry unit behind the bi-fold doors."

He nodded and looked around some more and Jillian felt a kettlebell weight in her stomach. He lived in a very old house. The decorating he'd done had been fairly traditional. Her space was not. She had batik fabric and musical instruments hung on the walls. A sculpture of found metal and piano keys hung above her entertainment center. A rainbow colored throw was on the back of her couch. Her framed print of Starry Night hung in the entryway. Apart from the neutral colors of her furniture, the place was rather eclectic.

George walked around a minute and Jillian realized Charlie had vanished. *Oh, dear. Where did he wander off to? With a stranger in the house, that could be bad.*

After a look around, George headed toward the open door she hadn't indicated. "Bedroom?"

"Uh, yes," Jillian followed him.

Her bedroom was large as well. Two dressers and a vanity filled the nearest wall, while the bed and the side tables covered the far wall. Her side tables were a bit cluttered with books, pictures, notepads and pens, and other odds and ends. Above her bed, she had hung a triptych of impressionist paintings of Japanese gardens. The fabric duvet cover was a peachy silk with white flowers that was used for kimonos, though she didn't expect George to know that.

The window coverings in the bedroom took up the entire exterior wall, more of the kimono fabric. And the remaining wall had a chair next to the door to her bathroom.

To make the scene even more interesting, Charlie sat in the middle of the bed, upright and blinking.

"I take it, this is Charlie," George said, and walked up to the cat, his hand outstretched, palm up and well below Charlie's head level. Charlie sniffed him and then nudged his hand.

"That is Charlie," Jillian said, as George petted Charlie. *Well, that's a good sign.*

"Hi, Charlie. He's a nice cat." Then he straightened and looked at her. "Shall we go?"

"No commentary?"

"I said he's a nice cat."

"On the apartment. I deserve something after my comments last night." She turned and headed back into the living room to get her coat.

"All right," George said, and followed her. "It's colorful. I can see why you were a little shocked by my white walls."

"So, you don't like it." She lifted her coat off the couch.

George held out his hand for the coat and helped her into it. "No. I didn't say that. It's actually really interesting. A complete juxtaposition to what I've seen of you at work. You dress fairly conservatively and although your management style is more contemporary, you still present yourself as a rather traditional person. Come to think of it, your suggestions for my dining room were traditional too. It's not exactly in keeping with the pianist from last night either."

When she turned around again, he left his fingers on the collar, so that the fabric slid under his fingers and he could hold her lapels. "I like your place just fine." He said, looking into her eyes as she noticed the spicy scent he was wearing again. "It makes me think that I'm going to find an even more interesting woman beneath the surface I've seen so far."

Jillian's breath caught. *Oh, God, kiss me. Please, kiss me.*

Then his hands left her coat. "Do you have your apron? We should get going."

"Mm-hmm," she murmured, swallowing, trying to get her breath back. Picking up the apron from the back of the couch along with her purse, she managed to inhale. *Okay. Date first. Then…whatever.*

"Well, well, well," the man in the chef's hat and coat said, looking at George and Jillian like they were new recruits and he was a drill instructor. "I looked at my contract, and I can't stop Mr. Greene from allowing you in here. It also appears that I also have to do this favor for him, instructing you. But I warn you both right now, this is my kitchen. Neither of you will do anything without instruction. You will touch nothing without permission. Do you understand?"

Jillian took a sidelong glance at George and George saw it. "Perfectly," George said.

"Sir! Yes, Sir!" Jillian said, and George had to bite his lip when the chef reddened a little.

"Funny," the chef said. He looked at George. "You date a comedienne, huh? How nice for you." He looked at Jillian. "You may make your jokes, but you will listen and follow instructions. This isn't Disneyland, this is a kitchen. The most dangerous place on Earth."

The moment the chef turned his head, Jillian looked at George with wide eyes and mouthed "Oooo." George bit back another laugh. This wasn't exactly what he had in mind when he asked Orville to ask Delaney to make arrangements for this special date at Delaney's restaurant. Of course, he hadn't known the chef would be quite so put out on a Tuesday night.

The chef turned back and said, "Hair nets and wash your hands in that sink." He pointed to the sink that had a big sign above it that read "For Washing Hands Only."

George put on his hair net and whispered to Jillian. "If this gets too intense, let me know, and we'll go. This guy isn't exactly what I had in mind."

Jillian whispered back. "Oh, no. I'm going to be a good little student."

"And that, 'sir, yes sir' bit?"

"Just couldn't help myself."

The chef started again. "Please notice the fire extinguishers…" Jillian and George exchanged a wide-eyed look.

An hour later, George held open the door for Jillian and they took only a few steps up the street before they stopped walking, looked at each other, and started laughing.

"That man is insane!" Jillian said.

"It's a good thing he can cook, if he had to deal with the customers he wouldn't last a shift."

"He really can cook though," Jillian said. "And other than the yelling and swearing, he wasn't a bad teacher. I've never done that flipping thing with a pan before."

"You looked terrified!" George said.

"Well, there was a big flame right there and he'd made such a production about the fire extinguishers," Jillian said, and laughed again. "You looked like you were going to faint when the sous chef was chopping the vegetables like a maniac."

"I did not! But, I did think he was just showing off and was going to lose a finger."

"You were worried they were going to ask you to do it like that!"

"Okay, that's true. *I* didn't want to lose a finger." George said. "Was it fun?"

"Definitely. *And* now I can say I've made a wine reduction."

"We should have asked him about dessert. Done something flambé."

Jillian shook her head. "I think I've had enough fire for one evening. That was intense." She laughed again. "Do you think he was really speaking French when he was muttering under his breath?"

"No. I'm thinking it sounded like French, but it was really stuff he made up that sounded like French. He did it to try to intimidate us. Did you see the look on the Sous Chef's face?"

"Several times. It was hysterical!"

"Thank you for having fun in there, it was really *not* what I had in mind," George said, and he looked at her full lips for a moment longer than he probably should have.

"No?" Jillian asked. "You didn't want to be screamed at by a lunatic?"

"What am I saying?" George lifted his hands up. "Of course, I did. No better way to get to know someone else then to study under a mad man together for an hour!"

"Oh, I don't know. I learned a lot about you." Jillian turned and started walking up the street to where he'd parked the 1965 Ford Falcon convertible he'd borrowed from Orville.

"Oh? And what did you learn?" He asked, as he caught up and would have put an arm around her shoulders, but they'd already made it to the car.

"Let's see. You're stubborn. Oh, but I knew that already. Of course. You can scrub a pot!"

He shook his head. "Right. I can scrub a pot. How *am* I single?" After unlocking the car door and opening it for her, he watched her slide into the car. She'd had fun, at least. Actually, he had too. Being yelled at by an insane chef had been surprisingly entertaining. And he had learned a few tricks for use in his own kitchen.

She stretched across the car and unlocked the driver's door for him, so he could open the door quickly. He slid in and he said, "Thanks."

As he started the car, she said, "Hey," and he looked at her. "I had a really good time."

"Excellent," he said, then quickly refocused on the car. It wasn't exactly the perfect moment. Okay, it could be the perfect moment, but if he kissed her now, he'd never get his head back for the rest of the date. "Now for part two." He shifted into first and pulled out onto the street.

"Part two? I didn't know there was more."

"Well, that's probably because I didn't tell you."

"You're really enjoying keeping things from me, aren't you?"

He shifted into second. "Yes, I am. Lately, at work, you're the one who knows all. It's only fair that I get to know more some of the time."

"You've known all day," she said, softly. "You could tell me now."

He laughed, but never looked away from the road. "Nice try. I don't think so."

"Oh, come on," she said, her soft tone a memory as she crossed her arms. "At least give me a hint. You've already had your fun. You really had me going with the flowers and the apron."

"I wanted to see your face for the flowers. Especially after I heard you laughing with Rachel. What was so funny?"

"The 4 o'clocks, of course. I had no idea that's what they were called. I'm standing there with a card in my hand that says '+ 2.5' trying to figure out what on Earth that means. If Rachel hadn't called the florist, I'd still be there staring at the card."

"I'd hope that you'd have gone home when the lights were turned off."

"Actually, you're lucky I figured it out. If it had been Rachel, she would've been expecting you at 7:07 and not been ready." One arm dropped back to her lap and the other rested on the door.

"Why?"

"The florist mentioned the minimum of thirty-seven blooms. I think she wanted to add that on. Although, that wouldn't have worked, because there were actually forty-two blooms. Which I suppose would have been 7:12."

The interior of the car fell silent and George debated turning on the radio, though he didn't even know if it worked. He tightened his grip on the steering wheel wondering if she'd picked up on the reasoning, the significance of the thirty-seven. She seemed to be the type of woman who might. Completely unexpected, even after all the time they'd worked together. New age management-type who plays jazz and blues and wears traditional clothes and has an unconventionally decorated apartment. She might.

"By the way, I really should tell you how much I liked the flowers, George. They're lovely and I love that they're alive instead of cut. Thank you."

Finally shifting into third, George tried not to think about his need to surpass a jackass that Jillian didn't even like. "You're welcome." *Forty-two.* He smiled. *Six better than the jackass. And the answer to the ultimate question.* Of course, he didn't expect Jillian to know *that*.

"What *are* you thinking?" Jillian asked.

"Huh?"

"That smirk. Something amusing."

Ah, what the hell. "Just about the number forty-two."

"Forty-two. The answer to the ultimate question of life, the universe, and everything," Jillian said, and George took his eyes of the road to look at her. "What?" She gave him a moment and then said, "Watch the road."

He looked back that road. "You know about the 'ultimate question'?"

"Doesn't everyone know *The Hitchhiker's Guide to the Galaxy*?"

She's just seen the movie. She hasn't read it, I'll bet. "Right. The movie."

"I was thinking more of the actual book. I mean, the movie was good and the acting was good, etc. Loved Alan Rickman voicing Marvin. But if you want to watch it rather than read it, the original TV series from the BBC in the 80s was sooo much better. It was cheesy, but better."

"You've seen that?!?"

"Mm-hmm. I don't remember where anymore, though. I don't remember who showed it to me."

That's it. George couldn't take it any longer. Her mouth was hard enough to resist when they were laughing about the chef. But now this. She'd actually read the book. He looked around for the nearest parking lot or parking space. He found a five minute parking spot in front of a dry cleaning store. *That'll do.*

Jillian was looking at him funny again when he pulled the parking brake. "I thought you said no dry cleaning."

He didn't bother to respond to her comment. Instead he quickly undid his seatbelt, leaned over, and reached for her. She seemed a little surprised, straightening when he moved, but as soon as his lips touched hers, she leaned into him and kissed him back with her mouth open.

He moved his hands through her hair, loving the slide of it between his fingers. Then the feel of her hands on his arms. Then one hand clutching at the back of his head, not letting go. She certainly seemed to enjoy kissing him as much as he enjoyed kissing her.

Why hadn't he done this before? Why hadn't he just shrugged off the threat he felt she was that first afternoon, walked into her office, apologized for the stupidity with the yo-yo, and asked her out then? Or any of the days that had followed? He could have been running his hands through her hair for nearly a year, if he'd just said to himself, 'to Hell with Hardware and Agile and everything else.'

He broke the kiss and moved just enough so that when he shifted his eyes he could see her entire face. He accepted that he hadn't said, 'to Hell with it.' He'd wasted all that time being petty, *no*, being panicked, about his *job*. He'd been so stupid.

At least he could forgive himself now. He could make it up to himself. This time, when her eyes opened, instead of giving her space after the kiss, he went back for more.

Jillian blinked her eyes open when she realized the sound she was hearing was someone rapping on the window next to her head and saw the startled look on George's face. *Oh, my God! We're making out in a car by a busy sidewalk!* She pulled back and slid down the seat, trying to hide. Even though she didn't want to know, didn't want to acknowledge the person at the window, she glanced up and could see the uniform and the badge and slid lower. *I can't believe this! Oh, my God!*

Thankfully, George didn't shrink into himself. "It's okay," he said, quietly and Jillian tried to believe him. He reached across her, not as far of a reach as it should have been, and cranked the handle to lower the window. "Good evening, Officer."

Jillian prayed that she would turn invisible and closed her eyes tightly to save herself. If not, it was entirely possible she'd die of embarrassment.

"Hello, folks," a new voice said, into the car from outside.

"How can we help you, Officer?" George's voice was clear and calm. *Oh, I wish I felt like he sounded.*

"I'm just making certain everything here is what it should be. You've been here a bit longer than the sign there allows. And we have laws regarding ages and indecent exposure and such. I don't see as there is a problem with indecent exposure, though the display might have been pushing the limit a bit. Ma'am?"

Jillian opened one eye and looked at the policeman. *Oh, please. Oh, please. Let this be a nightmare.* "Yes?"

"Please step out of the vehicle."

Jillian's other eye opened and she looked at the policeman. "Why?"

The policeman simply repeated, "Please step out of the vehicle."

She swallowed and looked at George. He nodded and scooched a little away from her and back to the driver's seat. She could almost feel him thinking, 'Just do as he says.' She sat back up in the seat and then looked back at the policeman. "Please don't make me," she said. *What if someone I know sees me?*

The policeman opened the door to the car. "Ma'am, I need you to exit the vehicle."

Still quite reluctant, she stepped out of the car and when the policeman motioned her to move to the building across the sidewalk, she did. He shut the door of the car and then joined her. "I know you're over eighteen, but I'm obligated to ask. Are you over eighteen?"

"Yes," Jillian said.

"Do you have identification on you to prove that?"

"It's in the car."

"Are you in the vehicle of your own free will?"

Jillian knew she was flushed beet red and she was fighting hanging her head in shameful embarrassment. "Certainly."

The policeman looked her up and down and frowned. "If you have any reservations about getting back in the vehicle, I can be of assistance to you."

"No reservations," she said.

"All right. Stay here please."

He walked back to the car and this time conversed with George through the driver's window. Jillian couldn't catch much with the policeman leaning down and talking into the car. He took George's license for a minute, but returned it to him without writing anything down. When he was through, he returned to Jillian. "I'll need you to produce that identification now, Ma'am."

Jillian nodded and walked back to the car, opening the door and turning to grab her purse from the back seat. George, however, had already grabbed it for her. She took it from him and stood up, going through her purse for her wallet. Her hands were shaking when she pulled her driver's license free and handed it to the policeman.

He looked at it and nodded, and then he handed it back to her. "Thank you, Ma'am."

"Certainly, Officer."

"You may re-enter the vehicle."

"Thank you," Jillian said, and all but fell into the car closing the door behind her with a slam. She returned to her previous position, most of the way down the seat, so she couldn't be seen.

The policeman leaned down to her still open window and said, "Ma'am, you'll want to buckle up."

She nodded and began to raise the window, struggling to sit up and stay below the dash at the same time, finally buckling her seatbelt under the watchful eye of the policeman.

George's window was already back up and his belt secure. He started the car the moment her belt snapped closed, pulling out of the parking space slowly.

Neither of them said anything for about a block, and then George spoke. "I jinxed us. It's my fault."

"What?"

"I wanted to give you a date that you'd never been on before, something memorable. Unique, even. And I found us an insane chef and a police officer. It's like a twisted version of a reality show crossed with high school."

"Well, you certainly hit the bull's-eye on memorable and unique," Jillian said.

She heard George taking a very deep breath. "How badly did that hurt me? Is this one of those things that we'll laugh about someday or is this something you'll make me suffer for or should I just take you home now, say goodnight, and never darken your doorway again?"

Wow, that's a direct question. She wasn't over her embarrassment that was for certain. But it wasn't exactly all his fault, if she was being fair. And although she didn't want to kiss him in front of an audience again, she couldn't say that she wouldn't ever want to kiss him again. *Make out. Be truthful with yourself, at least. No one's hands had wandered yet; no clothes had been tugged at. But that was definitely making out and if that cop hadn't come along…* She stopped herself from continuing on into that thought. They were in a car and she wouldn't have let it go too far. *Right?*

She hadn't actually been arrested or ticketed or anything like that. "I'm not sure exactly. But I'll lean more toward either laughing or making you pay." She watched him and he glanced at her, then back at the road, a slow smile creeping over his face.

"I'll pay, if that's what you want."

Jillian finally started to relax. "I guess we'll see."

"So, we're still on for part two?"

Jillian waited a moment and then nodded. "Yes. We're still on for part two."

George enjoyed the confusion on Jillian's face as he parked at Whistling Elms, a confusion that stayed while he signed them in and lead her to Orville's small apartment. She was polite and shook hands as he introduced his family friend, doing a much better job of hiding her confusion. But count on Orville…

After taking their coats, he took Jillian's hand and led her away from George toward his tight living room saying, "It's such a pleasure to meet you. Though what made you give a second look to the brat here, I'll never know."

"Brat?" Jillian asked, as she sat down on the sofa.

"He's yet to grow up, far as I'm concerned." Orville joined her.

George tried to defend himself. "Well, if it isn't the pot calling the kettle black. You like playing video games more than I do."

Orville looked around Jillian. "You know I'm not talking about video games. I'm talking about growing up." Then he smiled at Jillian. "I hope I get to see you around here again after tonight. I know George thinks what we're going to show you will just amaze you."

"What are you going to show me?" Jillian asked, and George detected a hint of concern in her voice.

"Nothing illegal, I assure you," George said.

"Illegal?" Orville asked.

"It's been an interesting evening," Jillian said.

"Was something going on a Delaney's?"

"Illegal? No." George said, quickly, hoping to fend off worry about that but not wanting to rehash it all. "Why don't we get started? Where are the boxes?"

Orville pointed. "Still in the closet. Javier left before I could get him. You'll have to drag them out."

George opened the closest and was confronted with twelve boxes, stacked in 4 rows across. At least they all had labels and the first one he was going for was on the top.

Jillian turned and watched over the back of the sofa as George hefted a box from a closet. "What's in the boxes?"

"You really didn't tell her?" Orville asked.

"No," Jillian said. "This whole evening is one surprise after another."

"What's with the face?" Orville asked.

George turned to see the face, but couldn't.

"One of the surprises wasn't what I would call great," Jillian said.

Hoping to change the subject, George lifted the first box. "Jesus, these are heavy." George could barely get out the words and he brought a box into the living room. Orville moved his coffee table.

"I'm thinking you should put it on the floor, if it's that heavy."

George managed to get the box to the floor without dropping it. "Geez, Orville. Couldn't you use smaller boxes so they don't weigh so much?"

"Get me the smaller boxes, George..." Orville said, and then popped the lid off the box and turned to Jillian again. "Go ahead. Let's see how he did."

Jillian leaned over and looked into the box. "They're LPs!" She lifted out the first vinyl record. "Oh, my. Miles Davis?"

She slid to the floor and started flipping through the jackets. "This is incredible." She looked at Orville. "You have a jazz collection on vinyl."

"Yep," Orville said. "If you want to listen to something, I checked the turntable in the common room today. It's working."

"Dizzy Gillespie. Thelonious Monk. Lena Horne. Billie Holiday. Fats Waller. Stan Getz. Etta James. And, of course, Ella. Jelly Roll Morton! This is from the 20s. How did you even get this?"

"It was a splurge for my birthday. I lucked into it at a swap meet," Orville answered.

Jillian kept going through the jackets until she was at that end of the box.

George grinned at Orville, who raised his eyebrows and nodded as if saying, 'You were right. How about that?'

Jillian sat back from the box and looked up at George. "I can't believe you'd do this to me two nights in a row."

"What?" George asked, as his stomach turned.

"Show me something to make me jealous."

Orville leaned in. "What were you jealous of last night?"

"His bathroom," Jillian answered, pulling a record out from the middle of the box. "He has a bathroom I could live in. That tub alone..."

Orville looked at George again. "His *tub*. I bet he'd let you use it."

"Not the point," Jillian said, and flipped over the record. "The point is, it's his." She looked side-long at Orville. "He has three fireplaces. Did you know that?"

"I've only seen the main floor."

"The one in the master is gas, but it's still amazing."

Orville looked up at George and raised his eyebrows and quickly slid his eyes toward Jillian and back. George shook his head. *No, we haven't had sex. Yet. I hope it's yet. I hope she hasn't already written me off.*

"Pick out a few records and let's go listen," Orville said, and George silently thanked him. "Oh, and there is a second box." George silently cursed him.

"No," George said. "I'll break my back."

Jillian stood up. "That's okay. I'll go to them." As she passed by George she patted his back. "Save your back."

George smiled at the light touch. He wasn't sure that she'd ever let go of the whole thing with the policeman, but it was a hopeful sign that she was touching him. He sat down next to Orville and lowered his voice. "What do you think?"

"She's pretty, has taste in music, and she likes you. Not a bad start."

"I'm not so sure I'm still in the 'like' category." He was about to start at the top and fill Orville in on the crazy chef when Jillian made a strange sound. "Everything okay?"

"Are all of these boxes filled with records?"

"Yes, my wife, May and I collected records. Instead of going to the movies we bought music. But just the one in here and the one that was under it in the closet are jazz. Do you see the labeling?"

"Mm-hmm. Can I look through another box?"

"Sure," Orville answered, a slight wonder in his voice.

Jillian made a grunting sound and George heard a thud. He jumped up and found Jillian had slid the other jazz box onto the floor. She looked all right. "Please tell me they aren't broken."

"Of course not. I controlled the drop. I wouldn't allow them to break."

"You could have asked for help."

"Your back," she said. Jillian pried the lid off the other jazz box and pulled out the record in front and the one in back and examined them. "These look fine." She slid them back in and checked one in the middle. "This one is fine too. I'll check them all in a minute. I just have to see what's in this box." She pointed to the box that George supposed was under the one she'd just pulled out.

He helped her slide the jazz box from in front of the closet and out of the way. "What are you looking at?"

She lifted the lid on the newly exposed box and started leafing through. "I'm going to die. This is incredible. Unbelievable."

Orville stood up. "Which box you in, honey?"

"One of the ones labeled Rock 'n' Roll. You've got 'Bill Haley & His Comets.' My favorite version of Shake, Rattle, and Roll is on this."

Orville joined her and they went through the box. She kept making excited sounds and George smiled a little from off to the side. *At least she's having fun for certain now.* This time he struggled with the box when Jillian wanted to see in the one below it. *How on Earth am I going to get these back in the closet?*

Jillian got down on her knees for the last box and she and Orville were talking groups and music. Suddenly she stopped flipping through and made a sound that made George think she was choking. "What?"

"Sam Cooke," she said, with a note of reverence in her voice. "Oh. My." She started flipping again. "You've got everything. His singles too?"

"May was a big fan," Orville said.

"Oh, me too," Jillian whispered as she pulled out a record. *Twistin' the Night Away. That's It, I Quit, I'm Movin' On.*" She pulled out another. "And his *My Kind of Blues* album." She kept going, shaking her head and murmuring words like *fantastic* and *amazing.*

She looked at Orville. "Are you really okay with listening to these?"

"Sure thing."

"Well, then let's take all of Sam and a few of your jazz albums."

Orville was grinning. "*Cupid* was our song, May and I."

Jillian touched his arm. "Then that one's first."

CHAPTER TEN

While Orville and Jillian picked out the records to take to the common room, George considered the problem of returning the boxes to the closet. If only he'd studied engineering at school. He was pretty sure he was going to need something like a ramp to slide the boxes up. There was no way he could just lift them. He was startled out of his reverie when Orville called him and he quit worrying about the boxes and joined Orville and Jillian.

Sitting on the softer of the couches in the common room was as unusual as not sitting with a game controller in his hand, but George adapted. Jillian sat on the end nearest the turntable and George sat beside her, throwing his arm across the back in her direction. Orville took up a position on a club chair that also flanked the turntable. George had fully expected Jillian's interest in the jazz albums, but not the rock 'n' roll. In a way, that was better. At least he recognized some of the music.

Although Jillian had suggested *Cupid* to start, Orville insisted on Fats Waller's *Ain't Misbehavin'*. George loved it. He wondered if Jillian ever played the song. He could picture her hands running over the keys for the introduction.

They listened to two more songs before Delaney wandered in and chatted a moment. George introduced him as the owner of the restaurant he and Jillian had had their lesson in earlier and couldn't help but feel relief when Jillian expressed her gratitude for the cooking lesson and kept the insanity from Delaney. Orville put on *Sh-boom Sh-boom* by the Crewcuts and Delaney said, "Now this isn't right. The prettiest girl in the room is sitting when the music is playing. Would you like to dance?"

"That's sweet, but I'm also the only girl in the room."

"Doesn't make you less pretty."

Jillian smiled at that. "Well, you'll have to ask my escort." Jillian waved a hand toward George.

"A proper lady, to be sure. I think he'll be okay with it," Delaney said, and grinned.

George looked at Jillian and smiled. "Do you want to dance with him?"

"Sure," Jillian said.

"Then it's all right by me."

Delaney could dance! George hadn't realized that until Delaney had taken hold of Jillian and maneuvered her around the floor, expertly avoiding furniture, but clearly he could. She smiled and then laughed at something Delaney said and George clutched a fist for a moment. *Don't laugh with him. Laugh with me.* It was almost funny, being jealous of an eighty-three year old man.

"You're up next," Orville said.

"What?" George looked away from Jillian to focus on Orville. "No."

"Yes."

"No. I can't dance like that."

"Then sway with her to the music."

"No."

"You have to. You know that."

George slumped back against the couch and sighed. "I haven't danced in a long time."

"Sarah?"

"Yeah."

"Well, she isn't here." He looked across the floor. "Jillian is. So, don't be stupid."

"Orville…"

Orville just looked at him.

"Okay," George said. "But I only know one dance and it isn't romantic. The cha cha."

"It's Latin. It'll do." He paused. "Sarah?"

"Yeah."

"Well then, for once, she goaded you into something that'll work for you. You'll never guess." Orville reached into the stack of records, slid out a forty-five, flipped it over, and handed it to George. "*Everybody Loves to Cha Cha Cha.*"

"A single," George said, with a laugh. "Of course, her favorite singer would have made a single that's a cha cha."

"You know, it's possible that Sarah was your June and Jillian could be your May."

George refocused on Orville. "But not my November? What are you talking about?"

Orville took the forty-five out of George's hands and stood up to put it on the turntable. "I'll have to tell you about June some other time. Before I started seeing May, there was June."

George sat up straight. "Before May? This is news."

"Old news," Orville said, and gestured toward Delaney and Jillian. "The present is right there."

"I'm not going to forget about the old news," George said, as Delaney brought Jillian back, smiling and sharing some kind of joke. Knowing that Orville was in his corner, but that he wouldn't mind giving him a blatant shove if necessary, George decided to ask her to dance before he was embarrassed into it. "May I have the next one? Orville's helped pick out something for us."

"Delighted," Jillian said, and then she looked at Delaney. "Thank you, Delaney. I really enjoyed myself."

"The pleasure was all mine," Delaney said, and then sat down as George took Jillian's hand and led her around the sofa to the more open section of floor.

As he took her right in his left preparing to move when the music started, he managed a smile. Although he couldn't help but worry that the dancing would be a disaster, he knew it couldn't be any worse than the cop. He'd have to trip her and cause her to break something before he could blow it that bad. So while it might be a little humbling if it went poorly, it wouldn't be the low of the evening.

The music started and Jillian placed her hand on his shoulder and waited for him to lead. When he started, her eyes widened. "George, you can cha-cha-cha?"

He quietly snorted a laugh. "Yes. But that's it. The only dance I know. Don't expect anything else."

"You must be joking. How did you ever learn to cha-cha-cha without learning any other dances?"

It was probably for the best to get the short, short version out of the way. After all, the name would come up again someday and it'd be better if it wasn't such a surprise. But all the same, he dreaded it, so George did his best to downplay the situation as it had been. "This girl I was seeing, Sarah, got it in her head that we should take dance lessons. She'd heard about this particular instructor and we couldn't afford his private lessons. Sarah badgered somebody into letting us join a group lesson in the middle of an eight week course he was teaching. We did okay, but then she didn't want to go back. So I learned one dance and that was it."

"Well, you certainly did get the basics down," Jillian said, and then made a surprised sound as he turned her under his arm. "Or, perhaps, more."

He took the praise with a grain of salt, he knew he wasn't particularly good, but he was managing and not tripping her or himself. She was an excellent follow, making it all much easier. And she was smiling, more broadly than she had all night, save when they were laughing together, and that meant a great deal more than any words. But words were next. He knew that. He hoped that he could just get her talking about jazz, while they were seated safely on a sofa, and it would all flow naturally.

"George?" Jillian asked. "Where are you from?" After a moment's pause she looked away and then back. "I'm sorry, that feels like such a tired question, but-"

"No. No, it's fine." He felt more relieved than anything else, something he didn't have to think about too hard. "I'm from Washington. I came here for school."

"And you loved it so much you decided to stay?"

"Sort of. I always knew I wasn't going home."

"Why?"

"I'm not from a major metropolitan area. Opportunities in software weren't exactly in abundance." *True, but not the whole story.*

"Ah," Jillian said. "Is it hard to be so far away?"

"Not really," George said. "My Great-Uncle knew Orville from way back and Orville... sort of adopted me when I came out here. You know I was pretty sure I was going to be fine on my own and didn't need some old guy hanging around, he was more mobile back then so he'd show up from time to time. But, you know, one day things are suddenly overwhelming and you need someone to listen and I... just found myself at his door. We've been close since then." He snorted a little. "I'd say surrogate family, but... that sort of minimizes it... so just... family." He nodded, mostly to himself. "And you? Where are you from?"

"Well, I was born in Atlanta, but we moved when I was four. My parents are only about seventy miles from here. So, I'm almost home."

George marveled at that. He couldn't stand being that close to his folks. But if she got along with her family better than he did with his, it might be nice, he supposed. "Do they ever come to see you play, Jillian Olivia?"

"At the Blue Feather? Oh, no. They paid for *classical* piano lessons."

"So, is playing the piano a secret?"

"No. I invite my friends all the time, but they don't enjoy it, so they rarely come. I don't advertise it at work, though. I consider it my private life."

"Uh-oh. Does that mean I'm an interloper?"

Jillian looked at her shoes a moment and then back at him. "I'm not sure. The lines are blurred a bit at the moment, aren't they?"

True enough. He nodded. "I'm glad," he said, as the song ended.

"Are you, George... What's your middle name?"

He could feel himself flush, so he quickly took her hand to lead her back to the sofa before he answered. "Harrison."

"So you're glad, are you George Har-" She stopped mid question and he knew she'd registered it. "George Harrison?"

Yep. She's got it. "Crewes. George Harrison Crewes."

"George Harrison?" She asked, as she sat on the sofa again. "As in the Beatle? Or is that a coincidence?"

George sighed and glanced at Orville for a moment. Orville moved to the turntable and started another record. "Well, I have a brother named Richard and another named John and another named James Paul."

"No!"

"Well, James goes by J.P. and John goes by Jack." This time when George sat, Jillian turned her body toward him.

"And Richard?"

"He goes by 'Richard.'"

"And you?"

"At home, I'm 'G.' But I like 'George' better."

Jillian nodded and he could see she wasn't laughing at him. "Mm-hmm. Just like I prefer Jillian to 'Jill.' I get you."

"But, even so, Mom got her Beatles."

"So, it was your Mom's idea?"

"Yep. I was the last one. Officially, I was named after my uncle. But the story goes that Dad figured it out *after* the birth certificate was signed and filed."

"Was there an argument?"

He shrugged. "I don't know. I was just born and my brothers were at home. They'd tell me, if they knew."

"So, you're close with your brothers?"

"Yeah," George nodded. "They were actually pretty great, growing up. I mean, I did get my share of grief, especially as the youngest. But when I competed and was still too young to drive, Richard took me to the competitions since Mom and Dad thought it was a waste of time."

"What competitions?"

He could feel his cheeks reddening again. "Yo-yo competitions."

"Yo-yo? I didn't realize that there was a competitive world for yo-yos."

"Oh, yeah. There's an international competition every year. I never did anything other than regional stuff."

"How long did you compete?"

"All of Middle and High School."

"That's a long time," Jillian observed as she put an elbow on the back of the sofa and linked her hands in front of her. "Should I take it to mean you did well?"

"Would it sound stupid if I told you I had a few first place trophies?"

"Not if it's true. Wow! I had no idea that you were serious with your yo-yo. I thought it was more of an affectation."

"I know," George said. "And then I was kind of a jerk to you with Ringo."

That statement rewarded George with a brilliant smile from Jillian.

"Ringo?"

"I always named my yo-yos. The one I carry at work is my looping practice yo-yo, Ringo."

"Named after your brother?"

"Nah. The Beatle. I have a blue competition yo-yo that's named John. Paul is the yellow one. And the green one is Marvin."

"Not a Beatle. Why Marvin?"

"No special reason. I just named him after Marvin the Martian, from the Looney Tunes cartoons."

"Okay. Why not name it George and have all the Beatles?"

George looked away for a moment, clearly biting back a laugh. "Just think about for a while."

"I don't get it."

"Just think about it. Think back to say, oh, Middle School, and how our brains worked at the time. Since I was competing regularly then, I was carrying it around all the time. And I do mean all the time. I always had a yo-yo in my pocket.

"My friends used to ask me to do tricks for 'em between classes, on lunch, whatever. And they'd say things like, 'whip out Marvin and show us something.' That's bad enough. But 'whip out George?'"

Jillian covered her mouth, trying not to laugh. "Oh, my."

"In the eighth grade, Josh nearly had me sent to the Principal when the Lang Arts teacher asked what I was doing and, trying to be funny, he said, 'He's playing with his Marvin.'"

Jillian's shoulders shook a little.

"She, of course, thought it was new slang of some kind."

Jillian laughed harder. "Oh, God."

"Yep," George nodded, and tried not to snicker himself. "After that I couldn't bring Marvin to school anymore, because Marvin did become new slang."

"That's hilarious," Jillian forced out.

"So that's the story of me and my yo-yos. Well, some of them."

"Great story," Jillian said, and wiped her eyes. "I love it. You're going to have to show me some tricks, sometime."

"I'd enjoy that." He waited for her to settle down a little more, before changing the subject a bit. "Do you have any other hobbies I don't know about?"

"Can you really call your yo-yo a hobby, when you competed?"

"It is now."

"What else do you do with your free time?"

"I just asked you that."

"So? You can answer it first."

"Uh, I don't know. I like to cook. I like to read. As you know, I play basketball with the guys from work."

"You *like* to cook?"

"I do."

Jillian touched his arm, much like she had touched his leg in the stairwell, a quick pat and then her hand was gone. "Well, you are much more interesting than I ever gave you credit for."

"I don't suppose that's saying much," George answered with a smirk.

"Oh, I don't know about that," Jillian answered.

"No? Tell me."

She shook her head, but then tilted her head like she was thinking about it. "You were always interesting. From when we first met."

"Was I?" He scooted just a little closer to her on the couch, not quite entering her personal space. "I thought you were pretty interesting right off, too."

"Did you? I kind of thought, but then..." Her tone dropped ominously at the end.

"Yeah, but then..." He mimicked. *I lost my temper and my apparently my mind.* "I'm glad we're finally past it."

"Me too."

They were both quiet for a few heartbeats, letting the music fill in the sound. Then Jillian asked him more about his family and he answered that he had the three brothers and no sisters. She had a younger sister, no brothers. They talked about their education. And shared their high level dating histories.

Jillian wasn't surprised to find out that Sarah was more than George had let on when he'd mentioned her earlier. They'd been together for two years and had actually started the house hunt with the intention of moving in together. But she'd dumped him to move to California, not asking him to join her, though not telling him not to either, before they'd found a place. George had decided not to follow, making it a borderline mutual dumping.

Then he'd called the realtor to tell him not to bother anymore, but the realtor said he'd found something that was listing the following day and George had to see it. It was so amazing; George made an offer before they left the property. He saw it as fate's consolation prize to a broken heart, back when it happened. But now he was pretty sure that it was actually a generous move on fate's part that she was gone before he found it. If they'd both signed the paperwork, they'd probably have had to sell it when they split up. Instead, it was his. And he loved it.

Jillian hadn't come that close to living with anybody before. She liked her space, so she'd never wanted to give that up. She did share the two bad breakups she had, one where she'd broken up and the other where she'd been dumped. The dumping had come when she'd turned down an offer to move in together. After that, she asked George to expand on the breakup he'd mentioned at work about the open door. He admitted to the relief that he'd felt with that breakup, saying, "We both knew it wasn't going anywhere. It wasn't as cold as it sounds; it was just pointless to go on. But I made it sound more dramatic."

"Ah," she said, and the speakers went silent. That's when they both realized that they'd been left alone in the Common Room. Jillian blushed. "We've been abandoned."

"I guess I would have gone too, in their places."

"Oh?"

"We've been ignoring them for most of that record. I'd say that's a hint."

"I suppose so." Her eyes dropped. "I wonder how long they've been gone."

"Let's not worry about it. Let's clean up and go."

"Now?"

"Yes," George said.

"But, it's not late yet. Is there somewhere else we're going?"

George exhaled. "No part three, if that's what you're asking. But, I don't think we should hang around here when we're not with any residents."

"Point well made," Jillian said, and helped him by taking the records off the turntable and returning them to their sleeves and jackets while George shut off the amp. He took the stack of records to Orville's apartment and exchanged them for his and Jillian's coats and a promise to put the boxes back in the closet the next evening when he came over to play video games.

Deciding not to take any risks, after signing them out, he simply offered Jillian his arm on the way to the car. She took it for a few paces and then slid her hand along his forearm to his hand and they interlaced their fingers. *I owe Orville big for this one.*

"I'm sorry we hardly listened to any of the records," George said. "I'm sure we'd be welcome back another time."

"It was lovely," Jillian said, holding George's hand as they walked across the parking lot. It *had* been lovely. Orville was a dear and Jillian was sad that they'd never listened to his and May's song. Then again, maybe that's how Orville wanted it. "I can hardly believe the size of Orville's collection. It was good of him to share them with us, even just a little." She'd also enjoyed meeting Delaney. He'd been charming and funny. She'd been hard pressed not to laugh when he'd declared himself a character reference for George. She'd thanked him, but had not asked for the actual reference.

"He's great, isn't he?" George said, still on the subject of Orville. "When I came out here for school, he jumped in to play the part of extended family immediately."

"Do you visit often?"

"I visit on Wednesdays and Saturdays. We play video games. Usually it's just me and Orville, but sometimes Delaney or someone else will sit with us while we play."

George was a dear too. She wasn't ready for the evening to be over. There was far too much left to know about him. "That's really nice." *He said he hadn't planned any more for our evening.* "Can we go somewhere for coffee or something?"

"Sure. That would be great," he answered. "I thought you might be tired after working all weekend and the late night last night, so I wasn't counting on it."

"Being tired is sort of a perpetual thing these days," Jillian said. "It's just a matter of how tired and then adjusting priorities."

"I think I'm flattered," George said, as he unlocked the car door and then released her hand to open it for her.

You should be. "I suppose that's up to you." She slid into the car.

"Being flattered?"

"It's sort of like beauty in the eye of the beholder, flattery in the ear of the recipient." She looked up at him and grinned.

He closed her door and walked around to the driver's side. She unlocked the door for him and he got in. "You never give an inch, do you?"

"You can't possibly believe that after this evening. I didn't just hand over control of the agenda; I even gave up *seeing* the agenda."

"That would be a fabulous argument, if you weren't using the word *agenda* like we're talking about a meeting."

"If you say so."

He put the key in the ignition but he didn't turn it. "You know, I'm still trying to make sense of you, of the layers I've discovered so far. Maybe it's not you, but me; falling back into the layer I thought I was most familiar with, the work layer. Though, the last few days have made that layer much less familiar. I'm starting to feel like I'm in a foreign country without a map." He glanced at her.

I know the feeling. And everyone knows that when you're in a foreign country you can't help but fall in love. Jillian shook her head to dislodge the thought. "We're in uncharted waters, that's for certain."

"Uncharted, eh? Does that mean we're in International waters? Or can the Coast Guard still rescue us?"

She laughed a little. "If we need help, I don't think I want to call the Coast Guard."

"Is it still a call if you use a radio? I've never been quite solid on that."

She laughed again. "I don't know. My nautical experience ends with knowing the word maritime."

"That's a pretty big word for someone who doesn't have nautical experience."

"Maritime? I'd have thought nautical was...more..." *Can I possibly converse with him without arguing every other thought? Even in jest.* She exhaled. *Probably not. It's probably not him at all, it's probably me.* "Just, ignore that. Shall we go?"

"Sure," he started the car. "Since you've cooperated with my *agenda*, even if it was reluctantly, how about you choose the place for coffee?"

Jillian almost said that she made a terrific cup of coffee, but her mouth was silent long enough for her brain to catch up. *That would probably lead to a misunderstanding.* Not that she wasn't interested. She'd already been interested, and the more they talked, the more she liked him. He had always been attractive and he was only improving upon further exposure. But reality kept intruding. She was going to have to face him at work tomorrow, and while she hoped she wouldn't color too much when the thought of the cop passed through her mind, she couldn't imagine facing him after *that*.

Actually, facing *him* wouldn't be a problem; it was the other people in the office. It wasn't as though he was the sort to make a sport of it. At least, she didn't think so. While she'd originally thought him the Casanova of the office, that idea had been proven quite false over the last year. She knew nothing of his conversations regarding women with his friends, of course. But she didn't think he'd go around the office announcing it, not after his careful concealment that morning. Then again, even with precautionary measures, kissing in the break room had been more than a little reckless.

No, it would be a mistake, a mistake with potentially devastating consequences, should the news come out at work. Before she could seriously consider *that* step, she had to be sure that he was serious enough, decent enough, to protect her from the consequences. She needed to be certain, that at work, at least, he'd treat such a thing as sacred and private. It was an entirely different level of trust then she was used to worrying about, evoking memories of high school, when girls' reputations were ruined and it haunted them for years. Now, it wouldn't necessarily hang on for years, but it would certainly ruin her chances at Gardiner D.

Good, God. What am I doing? Just this date, as it is, makes for trouble. I shouldn't be here, at all. I should never have come in the first place. And now coffee. But, I can't very well back out of it now without being rude. It was technically my idea. "There's a lovely place on Cherry Street. Not far from here. I think they're open late."

"Okay," George said, with a smiling glance after he started up the car and before he shifted into reverse.

His smile, she noticed, gave her the slightest, faintest, warming sensation in her chest. She was pleased then, knowing he was pleased. It was... surprising to feel that way, at the very least. Surprising to respond to his apparent emotion, like for like. Perhaps that was what had led them to be so disagreeable before, responding to one another, like for like. And suddenly... not so disagreeably.

What does an intelligent woman do when she knows every single thing she wants is in contradiction with every other thing she wants? Even not choosing was a choice. And what choice did she really have at that point? To lie? Tell him that their time together had been nice, but she saw no potential and then say goodbye. Oh, she could. She might even be able to do it convincingly. And then she could sit in the office next to him and never, ever think about anything *but* him for the rest of eternity.

She wanted her career, yes. But she wanted other things too. *I don't need to choose between conflicting desires. I need to delve into the conflict and resolve it so that I can have both. That is, assuming I'll even be interested in him once I've resolved it.* She let that thought bounce around a moment until she had to pinch herself to keep from laughing. *If a year of thinking bad thoughts about him and trying to date other people didn't get me over this, I'm not going to lose interest that quickly.*

The coffee was decent, the atmosphere adequate, and the company sublime. George escorted Jillian back to the car for the final time that evening with a smile on his face that he couldn't have banished for anything. Over coffee, she'd listened to him, just as she had all evening, really listened to him. Although she still kept up a bit of playful air, challenging him a little, he had no doubt that she had taken him seriously. The only question left in his mind was where he stood in the progression.

The incident with the cop had set him back a bit, he knew that. But she'd been gracious and he couldn't help but think that the records and the sentimentality of the visit with Orville had allowed him to gain some ground again. Coffee had gone well, though she hadn't shared quite as much as he'd have liked. He just hoped that it wasn't a sign. After all, she hadn't held back at Whistling Elms.

So, where did he stand? Were they friends? More than friends? Would she act like everything was fine and then turn him down for another date? ...Did she *like* him?

He hoped kissing her again wouldn't be out of the question. She did take his hand earlier which had been pleasantly surprising. It had felt so right, if he hadn't been nervous, he'd have done it himself. But she'd taken the lead there.

He thought back over the signals he picked up since, while they had coffee. She'd focused on him and looked him in the eye. The remainder of her body language hadn't seemed to contradict the impression. He just wished he could be certain that her smiles were as genuine as they seemed and not just nerves. Although, nerves might not be the worst sign either. *Nerves don't generally come into play when you couldn't care less.*

If he could just stop worrying about the cop!

The drive back to her building wasn't silent, but the topics were almost inconsequential. George found himself discussing the weather and the increasing traffic on various roads. It was polite chatter, more in keeping with what should have come at the beginning of the date.

Maybe she is nervous. God knows, I am.

He walked her to her door and waited while she unlocked it, still debating what he should do. When she opened the door, he decided he'd take his cue from her. If she didn't invite him in or give him any other positive sign, he'd play it conservative.

"Well," she started as she turned back to him. "It certainly has been an interesting evening. And you can rest assured that this was a completely unique and extremely memorable date."

He smiled, trying to take the comment with humor. She wasn't really meeting his eyes. The cop had definitely done him in. For that night, anyway. "It's good to know that I won't be forgotten."

She did meet his eyes then, briefly. "No," she said. "Definitely not." But then she looked away again and he took that as the sign he'd been waiting for.

"Well, then," he said. "Thank you for coming out with me and goodnight."

"Thank you for taking me out," she said, taking another glance at him. "Goodnight." He thought she paused for a moment, but then she walked inside and closed the door.

George ran his hands over his face. *One stupid screw-up.* He shook his head at himself and frowned. Then he walked a few paces down the hall. *No. This wasn't how the night should end.* He turned around and walked back up the hall, swallowed, and knocked on the door. "Jillian?"

CHAPTER ELEVEN

Jillian hadn't even taken off her coat or put down her purse, she'd just closed the door and stared toward the windows of her apartment, reviewing the evening in her head, trying to figure out how it had ended the way it had but not being able to think, not really. The apartment was in mixes of light and shadows from the street lamps coming through the open drapes, a moody look that she loved, but she didn't even notice at that moment.

The knock on the door brought her back to Earth and she turned toward the knock, blinking. "Jillian?" *His* voice came through the door.

She blinked again, still not quite able to think. Finally comprehending that George was still at her door and had knocked, she opened the door wide. The bright light from the hall behind him made her blink and for a moment he was just a dark mass of a silhouette. Then he moved a little and blocked the light behind him and she could mostly make out his features again. He looked strange, but that may have been the lighting. Or it might not have been.

She supposed she ought to say something, but she wasn't quite sure what. *Perhaps he should, he was the one who knocked.* But he didn't say anything. She realized that she was still holding the doorknob when her fingers began to hurt from the tight grip. She let go of the doorknob and took a step back, finally mustering up her voice. "Yes, George?"

George swallowed again. Jillian's face was a little incomprehensible, almost blank, and she was still wearing her coat and had her keys in one hand. Maybe he should just go. Everything felt a little... off. *Nope. It's off because we're doing this all wrong.* "I forgot something."

She knew what he was going to do before he did it and she felt so much relief when he stepped toward her that she jumped to her tiptoes, threw her arms around his neck, and pressed her lips to his. "Ouch," he muttered against her mouth when her keys smacked into the back of his neck, but then he looped his arms around her and kissed her back.

"Ouch?" She asked, after a moment, pulling back just a little.

He reached up and took the keys out of her hand. "Keys," he said.

"Oh," she said, as she heard the keys rattle when he slipped them into her coat pocket. "Sorry about that."

"Not a problem." He moved his hands inside of her coat and slid them around her again. "Such a small price to pay."

"That's right. I still have to make you pay."

"If you want," he said, smiling into her eyes, despite her face being caught in the shadow he was casting. "Got something in mind?"

"Not yet. But I will." She took a breath. "George, would you please get the door?"

He had trouble swallowing. *Does that mean...* "Sure," he said, and noticed the slight tremor in his voice, even in just that one word. The possibility alone put the tremor there.

While he closed the door, she put her coat in the closet, removing the keys from her pocket and placing them and her purse on a nearby table. He made a point to flip her extra deadbolt and then turned to her, immediately grateful that she was making some things easier by giving him the pretty obvious cue of holding an empty hanger in her hand. He took off his coat and had to forcibly keep himself still while he waited for her to hang it in the closet. And then she shut the closet door and it was just them in the artificial twilight.

"Jillian," he exhaled as she turned around.

"Hi," she said, softly. *Let's try this again.*

He smiled, stepping close again and reached for her face with both hands, brushing her hair back with his fingers. She closed her eyes at his touch. "Hi," he said, and leaned back down to kiss her again, running his hands down her back so that when she rose to her tiptoes to kiss him back, he could snug her against him.

Jillian inhaled as he leaned down to kiss her, feeling certain, before his lips even touched hers, that this time was going to be different. It was soft, just like the first kiss the night before, but he didn't stop when she started to feel *how did Rachel phrase it?* loopy. Instead, every time he paused to breathe, he immediately started again.

It didn't stay soft either. And unlike the few minutes in the car, he became increasingly more demanding. When he slipped his tongue between her lips, she moved quickly from loopy to lost and lightheaded in his arms. Even though she held onto him, she couldn't keep her balance and when she dropped down to her heels, she didn't quite manage to recover her balance and they both ended up falling against the closet door.

George felt a brief spurt of panic when Jillian fell backward and he went with her, smashing her between his body and the door. So much for the relief he'd felt after the dancing and not tripping and hurting her. But when he managed to put a hand on the door and lift himself just a few inches away, she laughed. He laughed too, for a moment. "Are you hurt?" George asked, as he maneuvered his right foot around her legs and then forward to find his own balance.

"God," she said, putting a hand to her head, still reeling from his kiss, her head spinning like she'd had too much to drink. *It's only going to get more challenging to keep my head and my feet.* "I'm not hurt." She paused. "I don't know which is more dangerous, me and my keys, or you and your kiss."

"How is my kiss dangerous?"

"You make me so dizzy. I'm not sure that I should have been driving after you kissed me last night."

"Really?" George asked. *I can make her dizzy.* "It shouldn't be dangerous now, should it?"

"Well," Jillian said, "only if we're vertical." She closed her eyes and felt her face burning crimson. *And if I needed proof that kissing him has turned my brain to mush, there it is.* "I can't believe I just said that."

George laughed again. "I can. Ever since we started talking to each other, I've been having trouble keeping it in too. In the elevator, my comment about great taste wasn't about the flowers. But, I think you knew that." Although he had his balance back, he continued to lean over her. "I've wanted you so much, for so long, I don't even remember what it felt like not to." He paused for a breath and her eyes snapped open. "Yes, I said it. Out loud. I want you. I'm crazy for you." He watched her eyes dart around his face for a moment and then she finally looked him in the eye. "Everything you say. Everything you do. It's mesmerizing to me. I don't want to just watch anymore. I want to be a part of it all."

His words echoed in her head. *I want you. I'm crazy for you. You mesmerize me.* Her heart was pounding in her ears. *I'm crazy for you, too.* "I'm crazy for you, too." She grabbed the front of his shirt and kissed him as hard as she could, closing her eyes as soon as she saw him do the same. Both of his hands flattened against the door above and on either side of her head. When she plunged her tongue into his mouth he groaned and took a step closer to her. Her right hand released his shirt and she wrapped her arm around his neck, trying to get as close as possible.

He shifted his weight around, moving his legs again, keeping his hands on the door while he stabilized himself in the new position. Once he was sure he was steady, he bent his knees a little and reached down to lift her off of her feet, grunting just slightly as he took her weight, propping her between him and the door, never breaking the kiss.

Jillian gasped against his mouth and opened her eyes as he lifted her and quickly wrapped her legs around his waist to secure herself as the heat started. But then her back was against the door and she was pressed so tightly against it by his chest that she didn't need to hold on to him at all, and she closed her eyes again to make the sensation of him stronger and felt the heat begin to build. She turned her head. "Oh." His mouth dropped down to her neck. "Ohhhh."

She still smells faintly like vanilla. He smiled into her neck and then kissed it again, enjoying another quiet moan from Jillian. She felt so delicate against him. Not at all the hard woman he'd believed he knew at work. Thank God he'd finally seen more than that. There was more still, too, so much more.

"G-G-George," Jillian said, in a shuddering breath, uncertain of what she was going to say to him, but she knew she couldn't take any more of the waiting.

He shifted a little again so he could lean back and see her. "Jillian."

She looked at him through the dizzying fog he'd given her again. He was so strong, so solid, just as she'd always known. He was also a warm man, deep and caring, as he showed her with his friends, Orville and Delaney. She'd seen so much, too much. She needed him. She needed him so much that she was lost for words.

He was meeting her eyes, waiting for her to speak. She took a centering breath. "You know, I have this really nice bed in the other room."

"Oh?" He said, smiling with his whole being.

"Mm-hmm. The mattress is firm and I've got flannel sheets on it. They're so soft. It's like reclining in a cloud."

"Sounds wonderful."

Another deep breath. "Care to try it out?"

An actual invitation. No implications or assumptions, but an actual invitation. "More than anything."

No questions or doubts left, George shifted again, working himself completely upright. He bounced her once to get a better hold and was rewarded not only with his intended grip, but another gasp from her and she leaned into him, helping him balance.

Oh, I hope Charlie doesn't wander into the path. She hadn't been carried before. It was thrilling, the thought that he wanted her too much to put her down, that he want to keep her against him. But if he tripped over Charlie…

George caught her light switch with his elbow and continued until he stopped at the bed and raised his knee up to the mattress, tilting as slowly as he could, holding her tight with one arm when the other had to connect with the comforter. It worked better than he'd even hoped. He poised himself just above her while her arms and legs gripped him, pulling him to her.

At last he lowered himself the remaining few inches and felt all of her, delicate and yielding, and he closed his eyes just a moment to relish it. The moment passed and he raised himself just enough to kiss her again, gently and slowly. One at a time, he reached for her arms, bringing them down from his neck to the bed so that he could put their hands together and intertwine their fingers.

His palms against hers, her arms against the bed, she let him set the pace as he teased her with a slow kiss. She wanted him immediately, had wanted him so fiercely since he'd lifted her up against the closet door that if they had been naked she'd have encouraged him to take her right there.

The thought made her shudder, him inside her. It didn't matter where they were, it just mattered that it happened. She had the urge to push him over and climb onto him, to take control, to take him into her fast. Only the competing idea of wanting to know what he was like, how he made love, kept her in check. *What's it like to be under George?*

That was the last chance she had to be contemplative. He kissed her harder again, invading her, taking her mouth thoroughly as he stretched her arms above her head. When she couldn't quite breathe, he lowered his mouth to her neck and made his way down. She arched under him as his lips planted a kiss at the bottom of the vee neck line of her sweater.

He released her hands to reach down to her waist, clutching the hem of her sweater as he moved back to his knees and she unlocked her legs to let him, kicking off her shoes and dropping her feet to the bed. His fingers slid the hem of her sweater up just a fraction of an inch and he leaned down to press his lips to the thin line of exposed skin.

Her breathing shortened and she arched again. He nudged the fabric just slightly higher and kissed her stomach again. She shuddered under him, beginning to really feel the heat. Her hands suddenly found themselves in his hair, tugging lightly, trying to urge him higher.

So it went on, Jillian with her back arched and barely able breathe, as George slowly made his way up her frame, chasing the tortoise of her hem with his lips, until he finally had the hem up to her bra. At the first glimpse of red lace he had to stifle a moan. He didn't know what she kept in her drawers, but he hadn't known many women who wore something as sexy as red lace on a daily basis. Something about itching, he'd been told. He was sure that she'd put it on with their date in mind, with *him* in mind.

Well, if she'd put it on for him, he was going to enjoy seeing it. Instead of continuing his leisurely path, he tugged the hem up and over her head with the speed of the hare. She had to release him and lift her arms. Unable to see for a moment, as soon as he had the sweater off, her eyes dashed to find his face. He glanced up from her lace covered breasts to her eyes, then he grinned and she shuddered again, wondering what was coming next.

George could hardly wait to taste the rest of her, but he kept a tight rein on his discipline. Patience was always rewarded. If he moved too fast he would miss something and he wanted to remember every curve of her body, every breath she took, every sound she made, every moment. *The more moments, the better.*

Dropping his mouth back to her stomach, his fingers went to work on the button of her pants and then the zipper and Jillian couldn't help but arch yet again, the heat in her moving lower. Her body wanted his touch almost as much as her mind wanted it. She found herself breathing little gasps that didn't satisfy her at all as he tortuously and deliberately moved down her body as the tortoise once again. She gripped his hair this time, not lightly, but hard, trying to push him lower.

She thought she heard him laugh for a moment, but if he had, she forgave him when his lips found the top of her panties and he groaned. "God. More red lace," he whispered.

Then it was like before. He moved fast and she found herself dizzy and surprisingly upright again, snugged against him for a moment by one of his arms, while the other whipped open the bed. She didn't recall her pants actually leaving her hips, but they were in a pool around her feet when she felt George raising and lowering himself next to her and she realized he was toeing off his shoes.

He picked her up in his arms and knelt onto the bed again, placing her in the middle. She couldn't hold back anymore and she scrambled to her knees in front of him and grabbed his belt with both hands and smiled into his eyes while she unbuckled it and began to work the button and zipper, enjoying how he'd sucked in his breath when she'd touched him and how his stomach muscles had tightened.

Meeting Jillian's eyes while she worked his belt and pants was easy for him, and seeing the desire there just made every moment sweeter. *Want me like I want you.* He put his hands on her cheeks and moved in tight to kiss her. *Need me like I need you.* He took her lips while she fumbled with the buttons on his shirt managing only two, finally giving up and pulling back from him. "Your shirt," she said, softly.

He moved back off the bed as he undid his cuffs and then pulled the shirt over his head by gripping the collar and tugging. The weight of his belt and wallet tugged at his pants, so he pushed those down too, tossing the wallet on the bedside table. He came back to her still in his undershirt and boxer-briefs, tugging off his socks with his fingertips as he moved.

She didn't mind the opportunity to help him with his undershirt, pulling it up and over his head like he'd removed her sweater, though she didn't remove it slowly like he had. Once it was off, she ran her hands over his chest, appreciating the masculinity of his muscles, the solidness of him and his frame. *He's beautiful.* He had such a great body; she wanted to touch all of it at once.

"You're so beautiful," George said, and Jillian remembered he was looking at her body too. She flushed a little, but then his lips were on hers and he lowered her back to the bed. He didn't linger at her mouth, though. "This red lace…" Then one of his hands was on her breast and his mouth was closing over the other, and through the lace she felt the tug, a pull that went straight down her body and made her hips move against him, searching for him, as the heat finally engulfed her entirely.

"Like it?" She asked, as her hands traveled over his head and his upper back, trying to get a sense of him.

"Oh, yeah," he answered as he reached behind her to unclasp her bra. "If you had on that red lipstick from last night too, it might just kill me."

She arched into him to help with the bra. "What about my lipstick?"

"It was a huge turn on. You look really hot in it."

She nodded. "Really?"

"Uh-huh," he answered as he succeeded in opening her bra. "The dress, the hair, the lipstick. Kissing you became a matter of life and death."

"Oh," she said. "So I was hotter last night?"

He snorted. "You're always hot. You're even hot in your work clothes. It's just a matter of degrees. Either you're so hot I'm fantasizing about you or so hot I'm ready to get on my knees. For the record, you look the hottest right now in your underwear."

Jillian relaxed into him at that. It was funny. If he'd said something like that earlier in the evening she'd have smacked him with all her might. But in his arms, she wanted him to want her so much he couldn't stand it. He removed her bra. "George, for the record, you're hotter out of your shirt then in it."

"You always have to top me, don't you?" She could feel the smile on his mouth as it closed around her again and she wove her fingers into to his hair to hold his head to her, letting out another stuttering moan. When she could speak again, she said, "That feels incredible." He increased the pull against her skin and she shut up and shuddered against him.

He moved to her other breast and reveled in her moans and the way her body was moving against him. But he wasn't aiming for incredible, he was aiming for transcendent. Taking his time was still the plan, so he tarried and added more sensations to his memory for playback later.

His mouth drove her to the brink of madness, her body pulsing and aching to be filled, and she was still in her underwear. "G-G-George. George, please."

Closer and closer. He started kissing his way down her ribs and stomach again to the sounds of her short breaths, an *mmm*, an *ohhhh*, and the shuddering of her muscles. When he reached the lace, instead of removing them right away, he slid a little lower and kissed her through the fabric.

The sound she made was something like a moan, but full of surprise, and her hips jerked. Up on his knees again, he slid her underwear down her legs, looking into her eyes, but taking in all the rest of her too. She was flushed and... "So beautiful," he murmured. She raised her arms toward him and he could see them tremble. "Not yet," he said, parting her legs again and lowering his head. "Patience."

Jillian threw her arms above her head to grip the headboard as she closed her eyes and arched her back yet again. *Oh, God.* She stopped breathing when his tongue touched her. *Oh, God.* Her pulse picked up, the heat spread into her blood, and her hips moved unconsciously. George's fingers gripped her hard, holding her still, as he caressed her. *OhGodOhGod.*

Heaven. That was the only word to describe George's experience of Jillian. He loved her moans. And then her voice had such an edge to it when she said his name. He moved faster against her, wishing he could see her face, only able to take his cues from her breathing.

When she sounded like she'd been for a run, he stopped for a moment and raised his head enough to see her closed eyes over her taut body. *More.* He lowered his head and started again.

"Oh, Go-" Jillian choked out. "Geor-" He'd built so much tension into her that she thought she'd die before he'd paused, then he'd started again and the tension grew and the heat in her blood slammed through her and she couldn't think at all anymore.

He paused one more time during his quest, needing to see all of her again, wishing he could see her face when the pleasure took her. One last time, he pushed her toward bliss, harder and faster this time, struggling to keep her still and enjoying the work all the more for it.

There wasn't anything left to her but straining muscles and heat. No Earth beneath her, no air above or around. Just him pushing her up. *OhGodOhGodOhGodOhGod.* And finally he pushed her over, as the tension sharpened into a point and exploded outward, tearing her apart, shattering her in pieces, while her body spasmed in ecstasy.

Blinking into the light, she had the fleeting thought that she really had died; no one could live through that. Every nerve in her body was pulsing blissfully, worshipping George. *George?!* Yes, her eyes came into focus again and she moved her head just enough to see he was still with her, lying next to her then, his head propped up on one hand and the other hand resting on her stomach, smiling broader than she'd ever seen.

She inhaled her first ragged breath after her death and brought her arms back down from where they'd dropped onto the pillow above her head when she'd let go of headboard, just barely able to get one hand to stop against his cheek. She still couldn't speak.

"I really wish I could have watched that," George said.

You wish you could have experienced it.

He leaned over her and kissed her softly, giving her more time to recover before she needed to attempt speech, although it seemed pointless to try, since there weren't words worth saying after that. After a few moments, she was able to kiss him back. The hand on her stomach slipped around her then, splaying on her back and turning her against him.

When she felt his firm chest next to hers, she raised one shaking arm to his back, rolled into him, and her hips found the hardness they'd been searching for. She broke the gentle kiss and tried for her voice. What came out was a faint whisper of his name, but she knew he could hear it when he smiled and then kissed her again in response, finally rolling her onto her back again.

It felt like hours had passed since he'd first been pressed onto all that softness, not because he hadn't enjoyed every moment, but because he'd missed it so much, having had so little time to savor it. Jillian's shaking hands found the waistband of his shorts and began to tug on them and he closed his eyes at the exquisite gratification of her still wanting him after already having had her pleasure.

He reached down and pushed off the shorts and shifted himself so that they were aligned. Jillian shuddered under him again, whispering, "Oh, George, I need you." He looked down into her eyes again, seeing how they'd softened after her release. A hand reached up hesitantly to touch his face, her fingers lightly touching his cheek. He had to kiss her softly again, she seemed so delicate, so fragile.

An involuntary swallow preceded his voice. "I need you, too, Jillian." Another swallow. "Put your legs around me again. I've waited my whole life to feel you wrapped around me."

"I need you inside me," she answered.

George shuddered as she lifted her legs around him and he pressed against her. *Oh, fuck!* He had to stop then. "Sorry. Hold on. Almost forgot something."

"What?" She watched him stretch to her nightstand to grab his wallet. *Oh. Right.* She lowered her legs again. *I'm on the pill.* It was a good thought *not* to have shared. There were a million reasons to still have him use a condom, and she was always a stickler about that. Until now. She'd completely forgotten about it. Well, he didn't. *He's such a good man.*

He had to kneel to put it on. She struggled to her elbows to watch, and then decided it wasn't enough. "Let me do that." He handed her the packet and then groaned as she rolled it onto him, hoping he wouldn't finish right then in her hands.

Finally, they were able to settle back onto the mattress. Jillian smiled and touched his face again. "You know, I thought this was going to be sort of a crazed dash to the finish after you lifted me against that door."

"Not disappointed, I hope," he said, and wished he could call the words back. It was so stupid to setup her up to tell him she was disappointed.

"No," she said, with conviction and shook her head as she put her legs around him. "I just need you so much. Now. Please."

"Your wish," he said, and leaned down for a quick kiss, "is my command, milady." He never took his eyes from hers as he reached between them to touch her again, to be sure that she was ready for him, nor when he finally slid inside of her. He let out a shaky breath as she wrapped him in her tight heat, fighting the natural need to close his eyes at the intense pleasure.

He was rewarded for his efforts by the sight of Jillian's face, the shudder of her entire body as he filled her. She was his then. All the months and months of foreplay in the guise of fighting and posturing and even ignoring each other, while the electricity charged up higher and higher between them, was over. She was *finally* his. He moved and her eyes widened and her lips parted.

Even though he'd been more than reasonably slow and gentle entering her, it was still a shock to feel him hard inside her. But more than that, she shook from the mere knowledge that it was George. George who had driven her nuts with his not-quite-so-stupid-anymore yo-yo. George who had bristled at every little success she had. George who had never given her the slightest break. George who made her so crazy with anger that she sometimes found she couldn't even speak to tell him off.

George who turned her on like nobody turned her on.

This was inevitable. The thought felt so sudden, so surprising. *We couldn't have stopped it no matter how hard we tried.*

She'd never considered that they'd been fighting it, though George had said something like it not long before in the other room, something about keeping it in. That was the silence that they'd fallen into. The inability to say anything kind or even decent because then they'd break and say what needed to be said. That was exactly how it had happened. The moment they'd turned down the anger, the fate they'd been holding at bay had come roaring up and they'd been helpless.

And she still felt helplessly out of control. Not that she'd realized it until then. She'd honestly thought she was making choices. But as George started to move, stroking inside of her, taking her body all the while looking into her eyes, she knew that none of the choices had been hers, that saying no would have been impossible. The best she could ever have hoped to have done would have been to continue to delay it.

In her peripheral vision, she could make out the tension in George's jaw and the tight flexing of the muscles in his shoulders. Under her hands, the muscles in his back surged with his every movement. She saw a slight wince and he shifted a little, and then started to move again.

She inhaled and closed her eyes at an unexpected intense sensation.

"Look at me," George said, and she opened her eyes again.

He hit something good again and she closed her eyes and bit her lip.

"Look at me," George said, again. Jillian quickly met his eyes.

He moved again and she inhaled sharply and fought to keep her eyes open, but failed.

"Look at me," George said, and she opened her eyes. He was still then. "Something good, I'm hoping?"

She sort of nodded her head a little and then he moved hard and she arched with a gasp and closed her eyes.

"Look at me."

Jillian opened her eyes and struggled to bring her chin down to look at him again. She realized she was shaking.

George's face was a hard, but his voice was soft. "Think you might make it again?"

"Ma-ay-be," she stuttered.

"Okay," he said, and she could hear the slight edge in it. "I don't know if I can hold off long enough. I'm sure as hell going to try. But you have to look at me."

"Wh-y-y?"

"Because all of this means nothing if you're holding back."

That time, she shuddered at his words. *Don't hold back.* She nodded, not trusting her voice.

George started to move again, watching the myriad of expressions that played across Jillian's face. She was biting her lip, which was sexy as hell. And he could see her fight the urge to close her eyes each time he moved as she blinked several times really fast. God, that was sexy too, that she was trying so hard to do as he asked and keep her eyes on him while feeling so much pleasure that she needed to escape it.

He was sure he'd never last long enough for her to make it a second time, but that didn't mean he'd go down without a fight, so times tables it was. He stared into Jillian's eyes, trying to be as present in the moment as he was asking her to be, and still disconnected enough that he could start with the sevens. *Seven. Fourteen. Twenty-one. Twenty-eight.* "Huhhh," he let a breath with a shudder of his own. *Never going to last. Uh. Next. Next. Uh. Thirty-fi-i-i-ive.*

Even his thoughts were stuttering at the intense feel of her around him as he stroked into her and her body squeezed him just perfectly, as nature intended, to make him let go. *Okay, okay. Get somewhere near one hundred before you lose it. Come on! Uh. Forty-something. Forty... Forty... Ha, oh, God. Mmm. Forty-forty-forty... two! Forty-two.*

Her lips parted and she let out the tiniest breath of a sigh. He was lost. Thought stopped and he moved helplessly in her for a while, caught in her eyes, until her eyes closed again and she made a wonderful throaty sound and he knew. *Jillian.* He dropped his weight onto one arm so he could grab her chin and demand, "Look at me!"

Jillian's eyes lifted and as she focused into George's eyes, she could see the need in him, how exposed he was, how he was reaching for her, asking her to meet him. The sudden reciprocating need for him made her reach for him too across the void. *George.*

For just that instant something new crackled to life between them but then the physical overwhelmed the infinite. George closed his eyes and groaned with his release, shaking and struggling not to collapse on her, while Jillian arched under him and shook around him and cried out.

"Good Lord," George said, next to her ear as he attempted to get back onto his elbows. The words were totally inadequate, but he had to say something, do something, to make it all real. Every moment up until the last were perfectly believable, intense and wonderful and certainly believable. But that last moment, *God*, that wasn't believable... but it *was* perfect.

He lifted himself up again and looked at Jillian. Her eyes were closed and her lips were just slightly parted. She looked even more beautiful than he'd ever thought before. And she was his, *all* his. He wanted to laugh out loud, she was so wonderful, so full of everything good, and she'd given it all to him in that precious moment when they'd both had their souls opened and then they'd filled each other. He was about to say 'look at me' again, just to be sort of funny, but he noticed what looked like a tear roll down her cheek from the outside of her eye, cutting all the joy to shreds. "Jillian? Are you okay?"

She tilted her head to the side and he could see her squeezing her eyes tightly shut.

"Did I hurt you?" He pulled back a little and then realized he needed to take care of the condom. "Jillian?" She shook her head, still keeping her face turned away when she'd finished.

She dropped her arms and legs from him when he started to move away. He returned to her as quickly as possible, lying on his side next to her, sliding an arm under her, trying to encourage her to roll toward him. "Jillian? Talk to me. Please."

Jillian rolled over, buried her face in his chest, and let out a sob. He tightened his arms around her and dropped his chin on her head. "Please, please, talk to me. I don't know what to do."

"Why didn't you warn me?"

"Warn you?" He stroked her hair with his left hand. "I'm sorry, I don't understand."

"How could you do that, knowing what was coming, and not warn me? I feel so..." She couldn't finish because she couldn't even identify all the emotions that were rolling over her. *I was willing to give you my body. But the rest... I didn't agree to that. I didn't expect that. I don't know what to do with that.*

George held her tightly and kissed the top of head. "I didn't know," he said, as he realized what she meant. "It's never been like that before. Ever."

She pulled back from his chest and looked at him with red rimmed eyes. "Really? You've never... had *that*, with anyone else?"

He kept his right arm tight around her, but with his left, he touched her cheek. "Are you kidding? No. I've never had anything like that. Honestly. Whatever happened at the end was completely new to me. I didn't even know it could happen."

"Then how can you be so composed? I feel... I feel so much I don't even know what I feel." She took a normal breath and another tear slid down her cheek.

He was able to smile again, feeling a little of the joy start to return. She wasn't hurt and she was calming down. He hated that she'd been crying, but this time he was going to comfort her and make it better. Somehow he was going to find the right words. "I'm composed because I'm happy. As unexpected as that was, it was wonderful too. *You're* wonderful. I'm happy. Although, I'm still more than a little concerned about you at the moment."

"You're happy?"

"Let's see. Just made love to a wonderful woman. It included an intense cosmic experience never before seen or felt. Yep. I'm happy. Though I'd probably achieve something a great deal more than happy if the wonderful woman wasn't crying in my arms." He smoothed her hair again. "What can I say, Sweetheart? How do I make this better?"

Jillian took a breath and put her face against him again. "I don't know. I don't know. I just wasn't expecting... *that*."

"Would it help if I said I was particularly glad I experienced it with you?"

Jillian leaned back again. "Why?"

He took a minute searching for the best way to describe what he was thinking. "Because you're filled with all this... light. I don't think I've known anyone else who was like that. And now it's part of me."

She blinked. "I'm filled with light?"

"Yes," he said, "and you can deny it all you want, if you want, but I've seen it and I've touched it and I know better."

"Oh," she said, and curled back into him. After a little while, she exhaled really loudly. "I'm sorry."

"For what?"

"For ruining it."

He laughed lightly. "Oh, Sweetheart. You didn't ruin it. And next time we'll know, so there won't be any more tears. No surprises, right?"

She leaned back again and looked into his eyes. "Unbelievable."

"What?"

She grinned at him and wiped the last of the tears from her face. "The moment I've found even a little calm, you begin laying the groundwork for a repeat performance."

"Well," he said, and brushed her cheek with his hand again. "You know, I like to plan." She laughed shakily and he leaned over and kissed her softly and she sighed against his mouth and he could feel her starting to relax into him again. "You cold?" He asked, and sat up to grab the covers, ready to snuggle with her. *We're so great together. I wish...*

"No," she said, and sat up with him and wiped her face again. "No, actually, I'm hungry. Are you?"

"Uh, yeah," George said, wondering what she had in mind. "I could eat. Why? You want to go out?" *That could be bad. Go out and then when we come back, say goodnight at the car. No. That won't work. Not after this. No.*

"Ha, no," Jillian said, and started crawling out of the bed. "Let's see what's in the refrigerator."

Well, that ought to be interesting. George managed to keep the sarcasm internal and he slowly followed her out of the bed. "Where are you getting all this energy?" He asked, as she opened her closet and pulled out a shiny green robe.

She tied the belt on her favorite satin robe. "Well, I suppose, realistically," she paused and walked over to where he was on the edge of the bed, putting his legs into his shorts. "You pretty much did all the work."

He stood up and pulled up his shorts. "Gee, you're right. That doesn't seem fair, does it?" She shrugged and started out of the bedroom. "Should I pull up the covers, you know, because of Charlie?"

"That would be nice," she called from the other room.

He pulled up the covers, grabbed his shirt, and then went to join her in the kitchen. She was in the living room though, closing the drapes. "That's better," she said, and then turned on a light.

Since she was in the living room, George flipped on the kitchen light, walked over to the fridge, and opened the door to take a look. "Well, this is a pleasant surprise."

"What?" She said, walking up behind him.

He looked over his shoulder at her. "You actually keep food in your fridge."

Jillian looked at him quizzically.

"It's just... I guess I'm used to opening a woman's fridge and seeing light yogurt and a bottle of wine. Kathy had eggs too, but no butter." He stood up. "You actually have food in there. I see meat and vegetables, even fruit and dairy products."

"Who is Kathy?"

"Kathy *was* 'we're done' and the open door."

"Oh," Jillian said, nodding thoughtfully, and then circling around him to the pantry. "Not sure what I want." *At least I have that step up on Kathy.*

He shut the door to the fridge and looked over her shoulder, then reached around her and pulled out a box of pancake mix. "Well, I found breakfast." He set it on the counter and returned to the fridge.

"Oh. Breakfast. You want breakfast?" She realized she was tapping the fingernails of her left hand on the door of the pantry and stopped.

"Not now. In the morning."

She shut the door and turned around.

George looked up from the fridge. "What?"

"So, does that mean you're staying?"

He stood up and shut the fridge door. *I hope so.* "I was planning on it, unless you want me to go."

I wonder if the relief shows on my face. Jillian felt her shoulders drop; she didn't even know she'd tensed them. "No. I don't. I just didn't want to assume... since we didn't talk about it. And everything."

He quirked a grin at her. *No. We didn't. But we should.* "No. We didn't. Let's talk about it over a snack. Is that okay?"

"Talk about what? You just said you were going to stay."

"Oh, man. Can we just do this over the food? Is that so much to ask?" *How am I going to say this?*

Jillian felt her throat tighten a little. "Sure." *Oh, no. Keep calm. Don't panic. Don't think about it.*

"How hungry are you?" George asked, and opened the fridge again. "I'm reconsidering the pancake breakfast idea. How about some French toast now? We can go classic bacon and eggs in the morning."

"Sure, okay." Jillian worked her way around him and put away the pancake mix and grabbed the syrup. While he getting the bread, eggs, and milk out of the fridge, she found her large skillet.

They fell into a rhythm, working around each other, her ducking under his arm to get a bowl, him reaching around her for the milk, never once getting in each other's way, and never more than a few feet apart.

"Butter?" She asked, as the skillet was warming and he smiled and opened the fridge again.

"Good God, yes."

"Wow," she laughed. "I had no idea butter was such a turn on for you."

He raised his eyebrows and looked like he was thinking about it. "Well," he started and then she laughed and elbowed him. "It's just I've eaten about as much diet food as I can stand. Not that cooking sprays and everything don't have a place in the world, but once in a while it's nice to have the real thing."

"Ah," she nodded and accepted the butter dish from him and dropped a pat into the skillet. He walked up behind her.

"I need a whisk," he said, quietly against her ear and watched with pleasure as she shivered.

"Uh, um, sure." She pointed toward a caddy sitting on the counter.

"Thank you." He stood next to her by the stove, whipping the eggs and milk together in the bowl she'd brought out, and looking at her while she pushed her melting pat of butter around the skillet with a spatula. He set down the bowl and said, "Why don't I do that and you get out the plates? I don't know where they are."

Right. The plates. Jillian nodded and stepped aside. *What am I going to do about the plates? I guess I don't have much of a choice now, do I?* She opened up her cabinets and started pulling out her fall/winter plates. *If only two of them matched.*

The plates were waiting next to the stove when George had the first two slices done. "How many do you want?" He asked.

"Oh, two slices is plenty for me." *He doesn't seem to have noticed the plates.*

"Okay," he said, and handed her the green plate with hot slices. "You can start, if you want. This won't take long." And he was focused back on the stove.

Jillian set the plate on the kitchen island where it was relatively safe from Charlie. "What would you like to drink?"

"Hmm, I think just water," he answered without turning around.

"Big glass or little?"

This time he glanced over his shoulder and saw the two sizes of glassware she had in her hands. "Big."

"Okay." She filled the glasses and took them to the table. *At least these match.*

"You know what we forgot? Do you have any powdered sugar?"

"Yes."

When they sat down, Jillian at the head of the table and George at her right, she tried not to think about her mismatched plates. It wasn't as difficult a task as she'd feared, since George was sitting right there in his shorts with his shirt unbuttoned. It was much more fun to think about him, or not to think much at all and just look. At least, it was fun for now. How much longer she'd be able to do it was the question. Jillian took another bite and looked at him, trying to enjoy it as much as she could for however long it would last.

George ate another bite. The food was good. But it wasn't really food he wanted. The food was a nice distraction from what he knew he had to do.

The night had turned so unexpectedly on him. The day had been hope and planning, but then it had been up and down the whole night. Finally, it had peaked and everything had felt so right. It needed to stay that way. It needed to stay right. There was only one way to ensure that it stayed right. *You can do this. What's the worst that can happen?* He reached for the glass.

Complete and total rejection. That would be the worst. I could wait. He lifted the glass. *But if I wait... I don't want to wait. We're adults. Why should we wait?*

About halfway through the French toast, George put down his fork, took a very big drink, and then looked at her when he set the glass down. *It's coming. I don't think I can take it.* Jillian glanced around for something to talk about instead. *Right there on the table.*

"Jillian," he said, and placed a hand on the table near her.

"You know, it's funny, I didn't think about this before," she picked up her glass, turning it in the light, its' blue tint obvious, "this is the shade of blue I was thinking of last night for your dining room." She held it out toward him. "But, as I look at it, maybe it is a little dark. You know, I'm starting to think that you had the right idea to wait until you're ready to furnish."

She had to stop to take a breath and he repeated himself, "Jillian," as he touched her empty hand.

"Then again, when a room has a character of its' own, it makes sense to worry about-"

"Hey!" George hadn't said it loudly or very sharply, but he'd had to cut her off. Although it might have been interesting to see just how long she could go on the train of thought she boarded, he didn't want to put it off any longer. He needed to settle things before they finished the food and tried to sleep because some subjects just didn't belong in bed. "I'm sorry for interrupting, but can we talk now?"

"I thought we were," she replied. He lifted his eyebrows. "Right. Sure. I know what you mean. Go ahead." *Brace for impact.*

CHAPTER TWELVE

George took a deep breath, clutched her hand in his, and looked into her eyes again. *Here goes nothing.* "Jillian... I really..." He cleared his throat. *How do I even start?* "Look, are you seeing anybody else?"

She blinked. "No," she said, and shook her head. She could see his shoulders drop then. *Oh! He was worried about that.*

"Good. I want... shit." He exhaled. "Oh, sorry."

Jillian started to smile. "Are you seeing anybody else?" She asked, hoping to confirm her new hypothesis. Maybe this wasn't going to be a 'this is nice, but I'm not really looking for anything too serious' talk after all.

"No, I'm not." George said, and exhaled again. "Definitely not."

When he didn't go on right away, she decided to just force his hand. In the end, she'd be doing him a favor anyway. He was already struggling and since he'd started it, it was best to just get it over with. "What are you trying to say, George? Do you want to keep seeing each other? Or not? Or is it something else?"

"Of course, I want to keep seeing each other," he said, angry that she'd asked the question, angry that she wouldn't already know the answer. *How can you not know? Oh, no. Please don't tell me*, fearful that she didn't feel the same. "Don't you?"

She nodded. "Yes. I want to keep seeing you."

He sighed and smiled, all the anger gone and forgotten. *It's okay. It's okay.* "Okay. Good." He nodded in response to his internal dialogue, telling himself to just get on with it. "Look. What I want to say..." He glanced at his plate and then back at her. He leaned forward. "Look, I don't want to see anybody else. And, I'm hoping you don't want to see anybody else. And if that's true, then maybe we can agree to not see other people. And then we won't just be seeing each other, and we won't just be involved, but we'll be," he paused for not just another breath, but to squeeze her hand as well, "together."

Jillian blinked and blinked again. *That was so not the impact I thought I was bracing for. Oh, George. You are unbelievable.* Words felt inadequate yet again, so she leaned over and kissed him.

Afterward, his forehead dropped against hers and he laced their fingers together. "You're fabulous. But I'd still like to actually hear the words."

"I don't want to see anybody else."

"Good start."

"We're together."

He sighed. "That's made my night."

She laughed. "That did? What about earlier?"

"This makes earlier even better." As he was sat back, he asked, "So when the inevitable happens tomorrow, because that's how these things work, and somebody asks you out, will you say 'sorry, I've got a boyfriend'?" She raised her eyebrows. "That is the usual title to go with an exclusive relationship, like the one we just agreed to."

"Are you seriously asking me to call you my 'boyfriend'?"

"Well, it would be weird for me to call you my 'girlfriend' and for you *not* to call me your 'boyfriend.'"

"George," she said, shaking her head, "are you sure about this? I mean, are you really *sure*? After one date?"

"After a year," he said. "Yes." He took a bite of his French toast. "Look, if it blows up in our faces, it blows up. But if I don't want anybody else and you don't want anybody else and we're together, then why wait for the labels? We're already lovers. I don't see any reason to play around anymore, do you? Waiting for no reason?"

"No," Jillian said, wistfully. "No, I suppose not." The next bite of French toast seemed to taste much sweeter and Jillian looked forward to the next.

George made a point to do as much of the cleanup as possible, enjoying the moments of closeness to her as they again maneuvered around each other and shared the tasks. He also secretly hoped that his help would garner that much more of her good opinion. His relief after their conversation would likely carry him into an exhilarated sleep, but he knew he could become complacent far too soon. Though she'd agreed so readily to his suggestion, they still had a long road ahead. All he'd really secured was her assurance that he'd have no active competition.

As they returned to the bedroom, George stopped at the closet and retrieved his phone from the pocket of his coat. Jillian saw the phone and immediately went looking for a spare charger for him. He felt a slight warming in his chest at her thoughtfulness. She perceived a need and thought of nothing beyond filling it.

Thinking of her simple concern, he wondered how much easier the last year could have been if he'd tried to be even just pleasant colleagues. She took care of everyone around her, not like a mother hen or anything, but with a genuine concern. She'd likely have done the same for him. He wondered what the next meeting with Hardware would look like.

As he plugged in his phone, he sat down on the edge of the bed and realized that he was short an important piece of information. He looked over his shoulder and saw Jillian brushing her hair. "I've just realized I don't have your phone number. Your personal one, that is."

"No?" She said, as she brushed another lock of her hair. "I suppose I don't have yours either. Send me a text." She rattled off her phone number and he thumbed it into his contacts, then he bounced his phone once. After everything that had happened, he still felt like he'd won a prize getting that sequence of numbers. Her *personal* number. He gave himself a second to think about what he should send her. Something that would make her smile. Maybe something that would make her think of him the next day.

He unplugged his phone and walked over to her. "Hey," he said, and lifted up his phone with the camera app ready. "Can I take a picture of the two of us?"

Her head snapped toward him. "I look terrible."

"No, you don't," he said, laughing. "Come on." He held up the phone and put his head next to hers.

"Oh," she said, and turned to look at him. "Please don't."

He looked at her and took the photo. She squealed "You didn't!" when she heard the phone make the fake shutter noise. He looked at the picture and grinned. The angle was a little off, but it was a lovely profile of them looking at each other. Well, she was lovely. And despite her asking him not to take the picture, there was a smile on her face. He was smiling too, laughing to himself as he planned to take the picture. "Look at that," he said, and turned the phone toward her.

"Well," she said, but left it at that. Of course, he could see her mouth twitching toward a smile again.

"Come here," he said, taking her hand and pulling her over to the bed. He wrapped an arm around her and dropped backwards, taking her with him. He held up the phone and she covered her face. He took the picture anyway.

"I can't believe you," Jillian said, and lowered her arms. He snapped another.

"If you want something different, just look at the phone and smile."

"Oh, fine," she said, and put her head next to his and looked up at the phone. "Just give me a sec to push my hair back."

George watched her fussing with her hair in the phone's screen. He humored her for a moment, then realized how focused she was on her hair and quickly slid his thumb across a selection on the side of the screen to make the camera take a succession of pictures with a single tap of the shutter button.

When she said, "Ok," he moved his thumb again and the phone made the shutter sound, and then it repeated as she moved. "What?"

The camera snapped again as he turned his head toward her. "Just a few more." She turned toward him and the camera snapped and then he kissed her and the camera snapped the last time.

"Blackmail pictures," Jillian mumbled and snatched the phone away from him.

"Do *not* delete any of those. And they're all rated G, so I wouldn't exactly call them blackmail."

"I'm not deleting them," she said, and swiped through them, smiling. "Not bad."

George took his phone back, dropped it behind him on the mattress, and slipped his arms around her. "Are you ready to sleep? Or?"

She raised her eyebrows. "Or?"

He grinned.

"Sleep," Jillian said, with a laugh. "Definitely sleep."

He let go of her so they could climb into bed, dropping his shirt back on the floor. Jillian walked around the room, collected the clothes, both hers and his, including the shirt, and laid them out on her chair so they wouldn't wrinkle, then disappeared into the bathroom. He plugged in his phone and sent her all of the pictures that he'd taken, hoping to find out what she would do with them, hoping even harder that she'd save them and maybe use one like he intended. He set the first one he'd taken as his wallpaper so he could see it anytime he used the phone. He also cropped it and used the profile shot as her contact picture.

When she reemerged from the bathroom, she told him that she'd put out some things for him, if he wanted them. He wandered in to make himself a little more comfortable for sleep and found a toothbrush package on the counter atop a few towels and, to his amusement, a comb. If the comb wasn't new, it had been cleaned so well it looked new. Interesting. There was also a glass right next to pile, a different size from the ones she'd had in the kitchen, but that same blue tinted stuff. He could see the one she used regularly on the counter on the opposite side of the sink.

He liked that she used real glass, for some reason. Not paper, of course. But also not a mug. A pretty glass.

Also on the counter, he noticed a tube of lotion with "vanilla scented" on it. He popped the top and took a sniff. That was probably the scent that was on her skin. He smiled again.

George found Jillian lying on her side, facing the bathroom, having turned out the light next to her. The light on the opposite side of the bed was still casting a glow from behind her. Her shoulders were exposed and he could see straps in a shiny fabric, so he knew she'd put on a nightgown. "Is that your side?"

"Mm-hmm. Unless you want to fight me for it."

"As much fun as that could potentially be, I sleep on the other side, so it works out." He flicked off the light switch and climbed in beside her, wondering if it would take much to get comfortable and work out how to sleep together. It would have been easier if they'd gone to sleep earlier, when he was exhausted enough not to think about it. But after she turned the switch on her bedside light, which didn't come back on since he'd flipped the master switch, and then rolled over, wrapped her arms around him, and pulled him close, he didn't have any trouble feeling relaxed. After a few shifts, they fell asleep with him on his back, one arm out so she could tuck into his side with her head against his shoulder and an arm across his chest, his free hand on her arm and his other arm curved down her back, holding her close.

When the alarm woke them, earlier than usual for either of them, Jillian stretched and felt strong muscles flexing against her. "Mmm. Good morning."

"Morning," George's voice answered and she could feel his voice rumbling in his chest against hers.

I could stay here for years. If only this was a weekend and we could spend the entire day in bed. If only…

But since it wasn't a weekend, they both crawled out of the bed and began to put themselves together, disturbing Charlie who'd curled up next to George at some point during the night. Since George needed clean clothes and his work bag anyway, it was decided that he'd shower at home before work. While Jillian showered and dressed, George put together breakfast. He even cleaned up alone, since he had nothing to do while she finished drying her hair and putting on her makeup.

She wondered if he knew just how big a deal it had been for her to face him over breakfast with wet hair and no makeup, but he'd been adamant about the food getting cold, so she'd swallowed her pride and gone for it, her courage spurred on by the extra toothbrush perched across a second glass in her bathroom. So long as that toothbrush had a purpose, an owner, a reason to sit there, everything was all right.

It wasn't until she was ready to go that she realized that he had a car and wondered how that would work and why he'd stayed to clean up breakfast. He told her that Orville didn't need the car; he was supposed to put it back in storage when he was finished with it. It was up to them when the car was returned. So after the tiniest of debates, Orville's car remained at Jillian's and she drove them both to George's where she spent her time nosing through his things, while he finished getting ready.

Not that she was too nosy. At first, she poked around downstairs, finding very little to amuse her, save the books on the shelves in the library. After a few minutes, she decided to explore his bedroom a little. She looked at the books on his bedside table, two were about golf and one was something about American History, but she didn't get a chance to delve beyond a glance, as he emerged from the bathroom, towel about his waist with wet hair, looking for underwear and she found herself focusing on the man rather than his interests.

It was a fun game, him catching her looking at him and then going about his routine, only to look over and find her still looking at him. He played while he got dressed then disappeared to comb his hair. After he finished up, he looked in the mirror and sighed. He didn't want to go in to the office. He wanted to walk back out to his bedroom and climb under the covers with his *girlfriend*.

At that thought, he smiled broadly at himself in the mirror. As badly as he'd expressed himself over the French toast, she'd said, 'yes.' That she wanted to be with him. That she didn't want anybody else. And then she'd slept all curled into him, breathing so deeply he could feel it throughout his whole body. And he'd been at such peace. Relaxed and satisfied and secure.

The memory of the *whatever it was* moment came back to him in a shining, sparkly Technicolor and he leaned over and gripped the edge of the counter. It wasn't the right time to think about that, not if he was going to work. But he did want to talk about it. And soon. If nothing else, he wanted to know what she'd seen and felt. He'd have talked about it last night too, if it hadn't unglued her.

He'd never had anything like it before and he wanted to celebrate. She'd never had anything like it before and she cried. Was that a fundamental difference between men and women, or just him and her?

Well, they'd talk about it eventually. Maybe even later in the evening. But not right then. He took a deep breath to help him push all the errant thoughts back out of his mind. *Gotta go to work.*

When he walked back into the bedroom, Jillian was still sitting on his bed. He watched her mouth curve into a smile when he made eye contact and he sighed again.

"Work," he said.

"Uh-huh."

Jillian felt ridiculous driving passed the building and stopping the car a block away from the building and letting him out, but he'd suggested it would make it less obvious they were coming in together, if he at least appeared to be coming from the train. Then she had to loop around to get back to the parking lot. It was ridiculous.

But that didn't come close to the ridiculous of walking up to the doors from the opposite directions at exactly the same time. As soon as she'd seen it coming, she'd slowed her pace and, naturally, he'd seen the same thing and slowed his. So then she'd picked up her pace and so had he.

The excruciating moment was made worse by the smirk he kept fighting that she then also had to fight. *Who'd have thought that it took the same amount of time to walk a block as it did for me to circle around and park and walk up to the door?*

He opened the door for her and followed her inside. They were silent all the way to the stairs, which they both took. They were silent up the stairs, her in the lead. They were silent walking to their offices. And finally, they were silent as Jillian unlocked her office and went in as he unlocked his.

Oh, my God. What on Earth am I going to do? Jillian followed her morning routine to hang up her coat and put away her things. She looked at her sweet, Darling, sincere 4 o'clocks and sighed as the ridiculous faded and she smiled at her memories. *I am never going to pull this off. We should just accept the consequences and go public.*

She sat down at her desk and put her head in her hands for just a moment and then pushed her hair back. *Okay. I can do this. We're being smart. If we go public, then we'll have to deal with all sorts of nonsense. And who knows what Gardiner will do about the promotion.*

After she logged into her computer, she went looking for the personnel files she'd attempted to start working on at some point in the recent past. The recent past that was so full of all kinds of strange and other nonsensical things that she hadn't the slightest idea when that part of the past had been. Yesterday? The day before? The day before that?

Ping.

She looked up from the stack of folders she'd just laid on her desk. Her IM had popped up. It was George.

Hi

Despite the message not even being a true sentence since he hadn't tacked on the period, she could already feel herself grinning. She tried to smooth out her face.

Hi. With a period. Enter key. Too late, she saw the wisdom of the lack of punctuation. The period made it seem like she wasn't particularly excited to hear from him. But an exclamation point would have seemed over the top. *Oh, God.* She dropped her head onto her desk. *Two words and one punctuation mark and this is already a disaster.*

Ping.

She raised her head to look at her screen.

I've been thinking about you all morning.

She grinned again.

By "all morning," do you mean the last five minutes since we started work? Gee. I feel so special. Enter key.

Ping.

I suppose you shouldn't feel special over a measly five minutes. My powers of concentration are legenda- Look, a squirrel!

She giggled.

Ping.

So, then… you've not thought of me, not once, since we parted? :(

"Ha," she sputtered, sat back in her chair, and bit her thumb, trying to wrap her brain around the slightly poetic phrasing and the frowning emoticon. *So not like him.* Or so she'd thought. Who was the man in the next office? For an ignorant moment the previous night, she'd thought she knew, at least a little. Then she remembered the playful few minutes they'd shared on her first day and she was fighting the grin again as she realized she knew more than she thought she did.

Not once. I have self-control. Enter key.

Ping.

So do I. I'm actually sitting at my desk while you're in the next office."

Her eyebrows raised.

You mean it takes self-control… to sit? Enter key.

Ping.

Ha-ha. You know I meant it's taking all my self-control not to be in your office.

She propped an elbow on her desk and dropped her chin into her hand for a moment, then sat up to reply.

You're not missing anything. My office is dreadfully dull. Enter key.

Ping.

Dull, huh? I wonder if there's any way to make it more exciting.

Jillian sat back and swiveled her chair back and forth for a minute then leaned back up to her desk.

I can think of plenty of ways, but none that are actually going to happen. Enter key.

Ping.

Pick one and tell me. I'll MAKE it happen.

More giggling.

No you won't. You're going to use that amazing power of concentration and be a good little manager and get some work done. Besides, where are you going to find a lion, an elephant, and a seal on such short notice? And fit them in my office? Enter key.

The delay for a response was long enough that Jillian picked up her files again and resumed going through them. Once she'd found what she was looking for, she opened her drawer and slid the files back off her desk. A loose piece of paper fluttered to the floor and she eventually picked it up.

Oh, the list. She glanced over the list and found herself giggling again. She didn't have the foggiest idea how George was going to hold up in the long term to some of the items on the list, but there were a few that he definitely made.

She placed the list on her desk and glanced at her screen. She'd clearly gone too far with that last one. Returning to her list, Jillian picked up a pen and placed check marks next to attractive, well-dressed, open to new things, interesting, and a wide variety of musical tastes. She smiled again at the musical tastes one because that might actually have been a fib on his part, just providing an excuse to stay on Monday night. Things had gone in quite a different direction after that. But, no, she believed him. Then, after another moment of reflection, she checked off kind too. *Why not? This is my opinion and I think he's kind. Certainly is good to Orville.* She ran her finger across the word "romantic." *Perhaps.* She drew what turned out to be a little flower next to it.

She wasn't ready to check off honest or loyal yet, either. Time would tell. She sighed. *Those are probably the most important ones too, aside from kind.* Then her eyes traveled to the "no yo-yos" she'd scratched. She drew a line through it and smiled. Then wrote the word "exception" next to it.

Ping.

Perhaps I did over-promise a bit. So far, all I've been able to find is a tap dancing penguin. Disney has scads of them. I can have one here next week.

Jillian laughed and then smacked her hand over her mouth to silence herself, glancing at her open door to see if anyone heard. She looked at her list, added 'sense of humor' and checked it off.

I'm sorry, but the tap dancing penguin simply won't do. I want a traditional three ring circus or no circus at all. Enter key.

Ping.

I had no idea you were so spoiled.

Jillian pursed her lips.

I'm not spoiled. I just know what I want. Enter key.

Ping.

So do I.

Jillian bit her lip. *How far will he take this?*

What do you want? Enter key.

Ping.

To relive the last 18 hours over and over.

Ping.

However, I'll settle for seeing your beautiful face.

Ping.

Meet me, accidentally, in the break room in five minutes?

Jillian bit her thumb again. *Oh, boy. Here's where it starts to get complicated.* She sat back in her chair and spun it around once, considering. *T-r-o-u-b-l-e.*

That's not really a good idea, is it? Enter key.

Ping.

Of course it's a good idea.

Ping.

But if that doesn't work for you... how about lunch?

Jillian shook her head.

Let's see if I have this correct. Enter key.

I had to drive passed the building this morning, drop you off a block away, and then circle back to park, in an attempt to hide that we were coming in together. Enter key.

And now you want to just toss that effort out the window and have lunch together? Enter key.

Ping.

When you put it that way...

Ping.

I still want to have lunch with you.

Jillian laughed again and then followed it with a sigh.

It's a bad idea. Enter key.

Ping.

Okay. Compromise.

Ping.

Let's sneak out and go to the Art Museum. Or the Zoo.

Ping.

Let's go somewhere, anywhere, so we can walk around holding hands and talk.

Jillian closed her eyes for a moment, visualizing strolling with George, holding hands and laughing. It was so good that she deliberated it a moment.

What are you trying to do to me? We have to WORK. Enter key.

Ping.

I'm not trying to do anything TO you. I just want to be WITH you.

Jillian closed her eyes again thinking that he was demonstrating one of the many reasons why it's a bad idea to be involved with someone from work... even if it wasn't a reason she'd considered.

Ping.

You won't sneak out with me or even just bump into me casually in the break room. You've got to give me something here.

Ping.

Something to hold me...

Ping.

until I can hold you again.

"Oh," she sighed.

Ping.

Please

"Oh," she whispered.

What do you want? Enter key.

Ping.

Something to make me feel close to you.

Jillian swallowed. *Not asking much are you?* She pushed her hair back from her face, regretting leaving it down again. She should have put it up and out of her way, but no, she'd left it down for no intelligent reason.

She shook her head trying to reengage her brain. It was all fuzzy and obstructed with memories and more than a few fantasies. As one particular memory pushed its way forward, Jillian had a brief flash of an idea.

Okay. Just a minute. Enter key.

She dug her personal phone out of the purse. Normally, she left it in her purse and checked it a few times during the day, just in case. Anyone who'd call her with an emergency had her work number too, so she didn't worry about it much, especially since she hadn't been dating anybody and nobody contacted her during the day very often.

It didn't take long to go through her music and then she paused a moment as she opened her messaging app. She'd been so distracted, she'd all but forgotten that she'd told George to text her so she'd have his number.

He hadn't just sent her a text; he'd sent her all the pictures he'd taken the previous night. Swiping through them made her smile yet again. She downloaded them to her phone before she did anything else to guarantee she wouldn't accidentally delete any of them. Then she glanced at the text he'd sent her before the pictures.

You are Some Kind of Wonderful.

She sighed at the romantic thought. *He must have meant the song. I hope he did.* Trying to get her head back together, she attached the song she'd been looking for to a message and sent it to him.

George's right leg was bouncing and his fingers were tapping on his desk, wondering what she was thinking, what she was doing. He didn't need much, not really. It seemed like nothing. If he could just sit in her office and watch her working, that would be enough. *Just being in the same room.*

For an instant, the thought of putting a hole in their common wall flashed through his mind. *A door would be even better. Or maybe tear down the entire wall. A tiny bit of remodeling.*

But the instant full of sledgehammers passed and he stood up. Sitting still wasn't really an option. He knew better. Being in the office was pointless too. He might as well log into Steam and play a video game for all the work he was going to get done.

He took out Ringo and made a few inside loops. What he really needed was to go to the gym and work off some of his energy. Of course, there were better ways to work off energy. If they could have both called in sick…

Ringo smacked him in the shoulder.

"You okay?"

George was in such shock from having actually hit himself with Ringo that he almost didn't register Taro at his door. "Oh. Hey."

"Hey. Didn't see you yesterday. Hiding?"

"Nah," George said, and started winding Ringo back up.

"Getting coffee," Taro said.

"Right behind you," George said, stuffing Ringo in his pocket. He walked back to his computer and glanced at the IM conversation. Nothing new had popped up since her message to hold on. He locked his computer and looked up. Taro had waited. Not only that, Taro's eyes were narrowed just slightly. He was inspecting George.

Rather than address it, George just headed toward the doorway. Thankfully, Taro moved and they walked to the break room. Sergei and Neal were already there, talking about the game they had coming up the following night.

Geez. I'd forgotten about that. He was pretty sure he had a reminder on his phone. The game was in the evening, after dinner. That would pretty much ruin seeing Jillian on Thursday. *Dammit. Come to think of it, we need to make plans for tonight.*

George poured himself a cup of coffee, nodding to Sergei and Neal when they glanced at him as they kept talking. It didn't last long though. Neal stopped talking mid-sentence and both he and Sergei stared at George for a moment.

"What?" George glanced over at Taro who was scowling. "What?"

Neal spoke first. "Does she have a sister?"

Thank God no one else is in here. George snorted. "That obvious, huh?"

"Oh, yeah," Sergei said. "By any chance did you happen to find her at The Blue Feather on Monday? I might just forgive you for bailing on me."

Neal looked at Sergei. "What the hell is the Blue Feather? A strip club?"

Taro chimed in. "Sounds like a drag club."

George leaned against the counter. "Yes, actually," he said to Sergei, figuring the more truth he told the less likely he'd be caught in a lie. Then he looked at Neal. "Jazz club. And her sister is married and lives in Atlanta."

Neal grinned. "Shame. A stripper would probably be… interesting."

"She's plenty interesting without adding something like *that* to her CV,"

George said, noticing Taro was still scowling. *What the hell is his problem?*

"And what is her name?" Sergei asked.

"Olivia," George said, before he had time to think. *Okay. That's not bad. That'll work. Her middle name. Okay. Just got to remember that's what I told 'em.*

Taro rolled his eyes and George frowned at him. "What?" Taro shook his head.

George's personal phone chirped. He had a text message. *Shit. Can't look at it with them here. They might grab the phone.*

Neal pointed to George's hip. "Is that her?"

"Possibly," George answered and took a sip of his coffee.

"Aren't you going to look?" Sergei asked.

"In a few minutes."

Neal looked at Sergei. "He's hiding it from us."

"Yep," Sergei answered and looked at George sidelong. "Wonder why?"

"He must be embarrassed."

"Mm-hmm," Sergei nodded and looked at George. "What do we think? Is he texting romantic shit to her?

"Could be, could be." Neal said. "Or maybe she's sexting him."

Sergei puckered his lips for just a moment imagining something pornographic, and then he grinned and lifted his chin. "Nah. Look at him. Pathetic puppy dog. It's romantic shit."

Neal nodded. "Yep."

Sergei sighed. "It's so sad, what some men have to do just to get a little pussy."

Neal made a choked sound and George realized it wasn't so much what Sergei had said as it was who'd just walked into the break room and overheard it. *Of course.* And to make matters worse, she looked like... herself. Composed and controlled, nothing could break her concentration, cold and still, like a frozen lake, giving nothing away. If she'd heard what Sergei had said, and George didn't doubt she had, it didn't show. No seething beneath the surface, no disgust, nothing showed.

The group parted like the Red Sea for Jillian and she took her mug to the water fountain. For once, George didn't have to force himself to stand still, he was mortified and more than a little worried. She'd overheard it and God only knew what that was going to do to her feelings about him. He could only imagine what she would imagine *he'd* been saying.

She filled her mug, turned back around, and started to walk out of the room. "Children," she said, as if she had just called them gentlemen. George watched her go, suddenly certain that she had put a little more sway in her hips on purpose and he forgot about Sergei completely and started to wonder what kind of underwear she was wearing. He'd missed seeing her get dressed because he'd cooked breakfast.

Neal smacked Sergei on the back of the head. "You are so fired. She is definitely going to report that to HR."

Taro walked around Sergei and Neal and looked right at George who had taken way too long watching Jillian leave. "No, she won't. Will she, George?" Then he continued on out of the break room.

That caught Neal's attention. "Do you have something on Jillian?" He asked George.

"Nope," George said. "I've no idea what he meant by that." He looked at Sergei. "You are an ass." Then he left the break room as quickly as he could, not entirely certain of his destination. He wanted to go straight to Jillian's office. But that was probably a mistake. He also wanted to know what Taro was getting at. But, then, he didn't want to know either.

He took his coffee to his own office and found Taro standing inside waiting for him, arms crossed and frowning.

"Hello, again," George said.

Taro uncrossed his arms to shut the door. "I hope you know what the fuck you're doing."

"What?" George said, and sat on the edge of his desk.

"Jillian."

"Jillian, what?"

"Really?" Taro re-crossed his arms and motioned toward the coat rack with his head. "You know, I can smell Jillian's perfume on your coat."

"Jillian doesn't wear perfume. She has a vanilla-scented lo-" He stopped.

Taro nodded. "Yep."

George exhaled.

"Gonna deny it anymore?"

George crossed his arms. "I'd hoped, *we'd* hoped, to keep it quiet."

"I would too, if it were me. What's the plan here? When Gardiner promotes one of you, where's the other one going? There aren't any open management positions in any other departments. No way in hell HR will let anyone work for someone they're involved with, or were previously. No way in hell. So what's the plan?"

"Well..." George didn't know what to say.

"No plan. Great," Taro said. "So one of you will be the Director, the other is out the door, and we'll be short not one, but two managers. Fantastic."

"Couldn't possibly be happy for me," George said.

"Couldn't possibly put anything above your own pathetic wants," Taro said. "If she gets the promotion, we lose you. You get that, right? We lose you and you lose everything here. Eight years. How can you not give a shit about that?"

"Maybe being with her is more important."

Taro's face opened in surprise and his arms dropped. He tried to speak several times, opening and closing his mouth. George looked away. He was surprised too.

He stood up and started pacing his office.

Taro found his voice first. "Already? Are you sure?"

"No," George said, still pacing. "No. But..." *Yes. And I'm sure. Oh, fuck! Oh, fuck! I can't be. Not already. It's way too soon... too fast... That kind of thing doesn't happen that quickly. Certainly not to me.* He collected himself and tried a different tack. Logic. "You know, that promotion may never happen anyway. Who knows? We may all be looking for new jobs."

Taro, eyes still wide, said, "You say that like it's a good thing."

George inhaled and walked faster.

"Does she know?"

George stopped walking and closed his eyes. "Stay out of it, Taro."

"George," Taro said. "If you're seriously willing to give up everything you've worked for since you started here, just for her..."

"Taro, stay out of it," George warned.

"You've got to ask yourself if she's willing to do the same."

George imagined Jillian being let go if he was promoted. "Oh, fuck," he muttered and collapsed into his desk chair.

CHAPTER THIRTEEN

So much for accidentally meeting George in the break room. Jillian didn't bother to walk passed her office; she headed straight for the elevator. She'd needed a little distance for a moment. The safest place she could think of was Melissa's desk. Apart from Taro, who she knew was making a point not to be seen there too much; none of the rest of the Musketeers would be wandering by HR. Especially after what she'd just heard.

It had taken *all* her willpower not to say something to Sergei about how rough it must be on him to absolutely *never* get any. But it didn't take a genius to know that no matter how she phrased it, whether she dropped into the gutter or tried to keep it lofty, she couldn't really win anything. Odds were she'd just lose. And she didn't know if they knew where George had 'gotten it.'

Her cheeks flushed as she thought about everyone knowing. How could she find out if people knew? Did she just have to wait for the looks? The conversations grinding to a halt when she walked up? If that was the case, then she was doomed to more moments like the break room.

"Hi?" Melissa said, as more of a question. "Did you need something?"

Jillian tried to smile. "I'm having a strange morning." *That's one way to put it.* "And since we haven't chatted in a while, I thought I'd come down and ask how the wedding prep is going."

Melissa smiled and launched into the latest problem she was having. *Easy as pie.* Jillian set her mug on Melissa's desk and did her best to absorb what Melissa was saying. It was astounding how a supposed elopement could still take as much planning as it apparently did. Of course, the elopement sounded less and less like an elopement and more and more like a venue choice of City Hall and a clever way to keep the guest list small.

Jillian was able to give Melissa about half of her attention, which really wasn't bad considering. Despite the scene she'd walked in on, or maybe because of it, she kept thinking that George really ought to be texting her back, or something. Unless he'd just been messing with her. He'd asked for something, she'd sent it, shouldn't he be responding in some way?

"Earth to Jillian," Melissa said.

"Oh," Jillian muttered shaking her head. "I'm so sorry. I zoned out on you." She looked at Melissa. "I'm sorry. What did I miss?"

Melissa sighed. "Nothing. I'm repeating myself, just to a different audience. What's up with you?"

Jillian looked at the floor for a moment and then back at Melissa. "I don't know." Then she laughed at herself. "New guy. I'm trying to figure it all out. It's messy."

"Relationships always are," Melissa said, as though her engagement ring had made her a sage to all single women. "If you don't want messy, you'll have to give them up completely."

True enough. Maybe her engagement ring does make her a sage. "Is it messy with you and Taro?"

Melissa looked like someone had placed a bomb on her desk. "Everything's fine."

"I didn't mean to imply it isn't fine," Jillian said. "I just wondered if it's messy."

"It's fine! We're fine!"

Oh, my word, what did I just step in? Jillian sat forward and grabbed Melissa's hands. "Of course, you are. It's just stress from the wedding."

"Right," Melissa said, nodding. "Just stress from the wedding."

"Everything's fine."

"Yes, everything's fine."

"Okay, good." Jillian sat back. "I didn't mean to-" Christy's ringtone cut her off. She looked at the phone for a moment and then sent the call to voice mail. *Oh, goodie. There's another little mess. I get to tell Christy I'm seeing George. She's going to take that ever so well. I'm not sure I'm even taking it well. He should have responded by now. Why hasn't he responded by now? I thought we had this clearly defined relationship.*

Don't you respond to your girlfriend, George?

She looked at Melissa. "I'm sorry to have bothered you."

"Jill?" Melissa said, into Jillian's back as she dashed away.

I shouldn't have to be dealing with this shit. Taro had finally left George's office some minutes later when he'd sucked George completely dry of every positive emotion he had. Even remembering Jillian in her red lace wasn't giving him the sort of pleasure it should, since he was pretty sure that they were headed for a break-up at record-breaking speed.

He went up to the roof and felt the cold biting into him immediately, which was somehow totally appropriate and almost comforting. It took him a few minutes of walking around to decide to check his phone; he was so sure it was all about to go to hell.

Punching in his passcode, he tried, actively tried, to bring back all the heat and light he'd felt. There was no way he should have lost it all, already, no matter what Taro had said.

Everyone had been right, even though they hadn't known the specifics; the chirp was a message from Jillian.

We need our own, but I don't think that Orville will mind sharing his and May's until we figure it out. Hold onto this. xxxx

George looked at the attachment. She'd sent him a Sam Cooke song, *Cupid*, Orville's and May's song. It was such a beautifully sappy, romantic kind of thing to do. She'd given him the song from a couple that had been together for over sixty years. Sixty years.

Apparently, he hadn't been cleaned out of every good emotion, after all. He was halfway down the stairs, moving at a reckless clip, before he remembered that he couldn't just run into her office and slowed his pace. *Calm down, calm down. You'd think you were eighteen.*

He walked, still a little fast, but more reasonable, to his office, looking to see if her light was on. One good thing about her habits after all the practical jokes, it was always easy to tell if she was there. Unfortunately, her light was off. Then again, perhaps it was fortunate, less temptation to go in and give it all away.

Stepping into his office, he started the phone dialing. Not bothering with turning on the light, he paced around again, waiting until the sound of the connection and the phone ringing on the other end finally reverberated through the speaker, to perch on the edge of his desk.

"George?" Her voice came through the speaker and spread through him like a ripple on a pond, moving outward from in his chest to every extremity bringing with it all the light he'd been given the night before. He was so overwhelmed by the feeling that he couldn't speak for a moment. But eventually he pushed it out.

"I love the song," he said. *I love you.* "That- it, it's perfect. The perfect thing."

"Oh, well... good."

"Where are you?"

"Outside."

"Outside? Why?"

He could detect the slight pause; it made him a little nervous. *Why don't you want to answer such a simple question?*

"I, uh, I needed some air," Jillian said.

Oh, of course. Sergei. George shut the door to his office and turned on the light. "Sergei's an ass. I didn't say anything about you. I mean, he and

Neal and Taro guessed that I'd..."

"Had a good night?" Jillian supplied.

George couldn't stop the nervous chuckle. "Ha, um, yeah. And then the crap started. But I never said anything-"

"It's fine!"

She wasn't loud, but George could hear the tightness in her lips. *That's it. This is stupid. This is beyond stupid. And it's beyond torture too.* "Where are you?!"

"I'm out front, freezing, about thirty feet upwind of the smokers."

"Why?" He asked, as he opened his door and shut off the light again.

"I already told you, I needed some air."

"Stay there." He took the stairs, once again at reckless speed, made especially more so by the one hand holding his phone to his ear.

"Why?"

"Because I want to talk to you. In person. I'm joining you outside."

"No! We had an *agreement.* No acting out of the ordinary. Keep things quiet."

"Stay there!"

"Act like an adult." She hung up.

"Right," he muttered to himself as he shoved his phone back in the holster on the way down the second flight of stairs, figuring if she could act like an adult by hanging up on him, he could act like an adult by running out of a building. By the time he actually hit the door release to leave the stairwell, he'd calmed down enough to just sort of jog across the first floor, not entirely oblivious to a few people watching him curiously as he went.

Once out the front door, he glanced to his left and then his right to see which way happened to be upwind of the smokers, then a few more strides and he was sort of face to face with Jillian. She was standing on the sidewalk, phone in one hand, mug in the other, arms kind of crossed around her to block out the cold, but clearly struggling to do so and keep the mug upright. Her face wasn't disguised this time, not like in the break room. He couldn't quite make out what was playing over it when she looked at him, other than it wasn't good. "It's good to know that you don't listen," she said.

It was nearly impossible to refrain from touching her in some small way, but he'd managed to keep a reasonable distance between them when he jogged up to her. "If you're worried about acting normal, being out here in the cold without a coat isn't doing you any favors either."

"I told you not to come out here."

"Well, I had to," George answered, jamming his hands in his pockets and trying to keep his cool around her for once. "That song."

Jillian shook her head. "I can't do this, George."

"Do what?" *Not us. Because it's a little late for that.*

"I can't *be* this."

"What do you mean?"

"*This*," she said. "This person. This isn't me. I don't act like this. I don't..."

"Act like what? Stand outside in the cold?"

She sighed and closed her eyes. "After I sent you that song, I started counting the seconds while waiting for a reply. Well, not immediately, but I noticed how long it had been without a reply." She opened her eyes and looked at her feet. "I don't do this. I don't get distracted like this." She looked up at him. "I *can't do* this. I can't sit in my office staring at a computer screen doing absolutely no work while I hang on your every IM and then start having a fit because you haven't texted in twenty minutes. I am *not* this girl."

He fought the grin as much as he could. "Well, apparently you are. And I'm this guy. Because you were killing me over the IM." He lost the fight with the grin, but still managed to keep his hands in his pockets. "I'm sorry I didn't respond fast enough to the text. I'll do better. I hadn't thought to set a ringtone for you yet, but I will, and then I'll know for sure it's you and I'll do better."

She shook her head again. "I'm not asking you to do better."

"Sure you are," George said. "Would you be out here right now, if I'd responded faster?"

Jillian looked over his shoulder. "Well, maybe not. I don't know. Those twenty minutes weren't entirely empty. Things happened."

George frowned at the thought. "Serge is not to be taken seriously. Not on any subject. Ever."

Jillian rolled her eyes. "I don't take him seriously."

"But he did offend you, didn't he?" George took his right hand out of his pocket to rub her upper arm, but managed to stop himself and lifted his hand to rub the back of his neck. "I swear I didn't say anything to get him going like that. He's no idea that we're together. And I never thought of you... like that."

"I believe you," Jillian said, looking him in the eye.

George dropped his hand from his neck, but didn't put it in his pocket. "Um, along those lines, there is something I do have to tell you." He exhaled, realizing it best to do it quickly, say it quickly. "Taro figured it out. And worse, he caught me in really simple trap, so he... well, he *knows*."

Jillian dropped her arms and the water started to spill out of her mug and it splashed her a little as it hit the sidewalk. "Oh, shoot!" She righted the mug and made a fake laughing sound. "Taro knows. How excellent. We kept the secret nearly an hour. We're master spies."

"He's not going to-"

"How did he figure it out?" Jillian asked.

George pondered a moment. "I don't know. He didn't tell me and I didn't ask. But it was like he knew just by looking at me."

"If the whole building doesn't know by close of business today, it'll be a miracle."

"You're right. Let's get it over with and just go public so we can go to lunch together."

The water started to pour out of Jillian's mug again. "Oh!"

George took the mug from her, tossed the remaining water into a bush near them, and then handed it back to her.

She looked at the mug and then at him. "A simple and elegant solution."

"To which problem, us or the water?"

She smiled and then sighed. "I don't know what to do. Do you know what I really want right now?"

George attempted to be funny. "Coffee? No, ice cream. No, chocolate. Chocolate, right?"

It worked and Jillian laughed. "No. What I want is to sit next to you and for you to put your arm around me and let me lean on your shoulder."

"Sounds nice. I can give you that. Easy. All you have to do is let me."

"I thought we agreed that it was better to keep this quiet. In fact, I think you brought it up initially," Jillian said.

George's mouth quirked. "Yes. But there was one thing I didn't take into consideration when I first suggested keeping this quiet."

"What?"

"That I don't actually want to."

Jillian made a frustrated sound and spun on her heel once in a full circle. "Now, *you're* killing *me*."

"All right," George said, as he stepped closer, threw his arm around her shoulders and started walking them back toward the building. "It's time to be brave." For him, walking into the building together was more an act of authenticity then an act of bravery. Touching her, on the other hand, when she hadn't actually agreed to it, was either extremely brave or extremely stupid.

But she leaned into him and said, "I am definitely going to regret this."

"Just relax and think about the fact that we won't have to try to hide. I can bring my laptop into your office and we can actually get something done."

Jillian raised her arm to hold him about the waist as they walked and leaned further into him for a moment. "That's not what people are going to think, you know."

He grinned and dropped a kiss on her hair; she squeezed him just a little in response. "We'll leave the door open and the blinds too." As they arrived at the front doors, he glanced over at the smokers. Vidar was there, clearly staring at them, his mouth hanging open. George whispered to Jillian, "And it's as good as done. Vidar is over there."

Jillian pulled back from him and he opened the door for her. She glanced over and waved at Vidar.

George smiled. *Classy.* Back in the building was a different story. It was one thing to have a public display of affection outside, but inside, they were still attempting to be professionals. Suddenly they were back to not touching. Next to him, Jillian spoke in a low voice as they headed for the stairs. "We're going to actually have to tell people. Otherwise, it'll just be a rumor, assuming Vidar tells anybody and they believe him or at least decide to spread it."

"Yeah, I suppose so. Who are you going to tell?"

"I'm thinking about Rachel. You?"

George opened the door to the stairwell and exhaled really hard. "I'm thinking it'll have to be both Neal and Sergei."

"Will you do me a favor?" Jillian asked.

"Probably," George said.

She stopped and looked at the door and waited for it to shut, and then she looked back at George. "Please be very clear with them about... this, us. That we're serious and not just goofing around. I know you can't control anybody else's behavior, but if I overhear Sergei calling me your 'piece of ass' or something like that, I swear, I'll kill him."

George blinked and then covered his mouth with his fist to try to turn the laugh into a cough. "Did you seriously just say 'piece of ass' or did I hallucinate that?"

"I'm not kidding. I'm not really a violent person, but if he starts calling me something nasty..."

"Dear God, this day is just going to keep getting better and better. I can't believe you said, 'piec-'"

"It's not funny," Jillian said.

"Oh, yes it is. Maybe you should be there when I tell them."

"I don't think so," Jillian said, and started for the stairs.

George followed and quickly changed the subject. "Have I told you how beautiful you look this morning?"

"You said something about it when we woke up," she said, not looking back at him.

"Good. You look beautiful now too."

"Thank you," she said, still not looking back at him.

Since she wasn't looking, George didn't bother to fight his instincts and watched her backside as they climbed the stairs, wondering again about what underwear she was wearing and if he could find out personally. "Can I see you tonight or were you already busy?"

"I'm not sure. I have to call Christy back. We were supposed to see a movie tonight with the girls. She was arranging it. If it happened, then I have to go. Don't you have plans with Orville?"

"Yeah," George said. "But I leave when he goes to dinner. So, I'm free after that."

"Oh," Jillian sounded a little surprised. "Okay, then. I'll let you know." She glanced over her shoulder. He noticed peripherally that she'd looked back, but it was too late to do anything about it, she saw him looking at her backside.

When they reached the top of the stairs, she stopped for a moment and took a deep breath. "Okay. I'm going to tell Rachel right away. You?"

"Yeah, I'll get this done."

"Why am I hesitating?" She asked, clearly rhetorically, but George grinned.

"Because you think your life's about to change."

"Oh," she said, and thought about it for a moment. "That's very insightful."

"But, you're wrong."

"I'm wrong?"

"Yeah." He leaned over and kissed her on the cheek very close to her ear, whispering, "It already has." Then he opened the door and held it for her.

Jillian headed toward Rachel's desk, but detoured before she got there. *What on Earth am I going to say? 'Good morning, you'll never guess who I did last night.'* Jillian laughed bitterly to herself. *That's how Sergei would put it. How do I do this?*

Instead of trying any harder, she returned to her office. When she sat at her desk, she sighed and checked her phone. Christy's voice mail had only been a 'call me' so Jillian steeled herself and did just that. At first the conversation was exactly as Jillian would have expected, with Christy confirming the plans for the evening, dinner and a movie, everyone was available.

Jillian attempted to hide her disappointment that she wouldn't be able to spend her evening with George, but she failed.

"You don't sound very thrilled, Jills. Don't you want to come with us?"

"Of course, I do." She paused a moment to formulate her words. "But, since we last spoke, something's happened."

"And that is...?"

"Well... I've got a boyfriend. And I've gone all junior high and want to spend every minute with him."

Christy laughed. "Funny."

"No, really."

"Okay. Who is this 'dreamy' guy you want to let come between you and your friends?"

Jillian closed her eyes while she spoke, hiding from Christy's face, which wasn't even there. "Actually. It's... um, George."

The silence over the connection made Jillian fidget. When she finally couldn't take it anymore, she said, "Christy?"

"One day, I'll learn. Mal's always right."

"What's that mean?"

"She told me you wanted him. I believed you when you said you didn't. Then she told me you wanted him and that nothing was going to stop you and I didn't believe her."

"I didn't go after him, Christy. I gave him your note. I didn't-"

"I don't care about that. I doubt he's *the one* since he went for you, though I'd have given him his five minutes," Christy said. "But it sure would have been nice if you'd been honest with me."

"Christy," Jillian said.

"I'm supposed to be one of your best friends, right? I asked you, Jills. Directly. You could have just told me 'hands off.' I certainly would have respected it. And I wouldn't have thought any less about you for wanting him. I mean, I *asked*. You didn't have to lie."

"I didn't lie," Jillian said, and put her free hand to her head. "Okay. Fine. I did. I did lie. I wanted him but I didn't think I could have him, so I tried to leave it alone. You have no idea what had happened that day. It was crazy and I wasn't really myself. And when you asked, I couldn't face it. I lied to myself more than I lied to you."

"Jillian, that's such-"

"I'm sorry, Christy. I'm so sorry. Please, forgive me."

"I'm so beyond disappointed in you," Christy said. "You could have trusted me."

"I know, but-"

"Just tell me one thing," Christy said.

"What?"

"Were we ever actually friends?" Christy disconnected the call.

Jillian laid her phone on her desk and swiveled her desk chair to face the wall, taking a few deep breaths. She swiveled back, grabbed her phone, and swung around again.

She dialed Malvinia and waited, finally leaving a short and simple message, "Vi, when you have a minute, I need you."

It's funny how the world seems more colorful when you're happy. The building had looked brighter when he'd first come in that morning. Taro had dimmed it; something awful, he'd dimmed it. But Jillian had put her arm about his waist and leaned into him and they were going to tell everybody and now that different lighting was back.

George caught up with Neal by the printer. "Hey," he said. "Got a minute?" Neal nodded a little absently, as he looked through the papers. "Uh, in private."

Neal's head snapped up. "Sure," he answered and then walked to the nearest conference room.

George made sure the door was closed and then tried to get himself in the proper frame of mind for the confession. He decided on the band-aid method again. Just rip it off and get it over with. Of course, that was easier thought than done. "I, uh," he almost started.

"What's up?" Neal leaned against the conference table.

"It's about earlier, in the break room. When you asked about... stuff. It was Jillian. I'm with Jillian. Olivia's her middle name."

"You're with..." Neal trailed off. He didn't really move, apart from his eyebrows coming together. "Jillian? As in Jillian? Not another Jillian, a different Jillian?"

"As in Jillian." *Here it comes.*

"So the woman who put that look on your face this morning... was Jillian?"

And there it is. "Er, yes."

"*Jesus.*" Neal said, and then his face released. "You and Jillian." He shook his head. "I don't know how you ever had the nerve. She scares the shit out of me. I don't think I could even get it up... *Jesus.* Well... I guess you're proof she doesn't kill her mates, after all."

"Ha-ha," George said. "Look. I'm telling you this because it's serious. I mean, this isn't just some kind of fling or whatever. It's serious. We're going to be doing the kind of stuff you do when you're with someone, we'll be having lunch together, maybe leaving together, taking breaks together. That kind of thing. It's serious. So when the rumors start going around, well, you know the truth."

"Okay," Neal said.

"All right," George said, and he opened the door.

From behind him, Neal asked, "You tell Sergei and Taro yet?"

"I'm going to talk to Sergei now." George said.

"Ah," Neal said, and headed for his office, shaking his head and mumbling something about black widows.

Rachel knocked on Jillian's open door, "Jillian?" Jillian swung back around and grabbed a tissue. "Oh, my! Are you all right?" Rachel ran up to Jillian's desk and dropped whatever she was carrying onto it.

"I'm sorry. I'm fine," Jillian choked out.

"What's wrong?" Rachel asked, as Jillian wiped her eyes.

Jillian shook her head. "I should go to the bathroom. Clean up."

Rachel quickly shut Jillian's door and turned the blinds. "People will see you walking to the bathroom. You can put yourself together here. I'll get you a mirror, if you don't have one." She walked back to Jillian. "What's happened?"

"Too much. I'm on overload," Jillian replied, as a few fresh tears welled up in her eyes, but she managed to wipe them away and put an embarrassed smile on her face. "I haven't been myself for the last few days. I can hardly believe myself. The things I've done, the things I've said."

Rachel smiled sympathetically. "Was the date that bad?"

"Oh, no. It was wonderful. But now everything is a mess. And the fallout, it's not finished yet." Jillian looked away and cleared her throat. "I'm supposed to tell you something."

"Me?" Rachel asked.

"Yes. We decided to just get it out in the open. And I promised to tell you." Jillian shook her head. "I was so happy just an hour ago."

Rachel leaned over. "What's happened?"

Jillian sat up straight and looked up at Rachel. "I've lost my mind." She took more breath and forced it out. "The guy from last night, my date, was…" She pointed toward the wall the separated her office from George's and watched Rachel's eyebrows knit together. "George."

"What?" Rachel asked. Then her eyes went wide and she dropped onto Jillian's desk. "What?! You mean, George asked you out? Oh, my God!" Rachel stood back up. "Oh, my God! I don't believe it."

Jillian twisted the tissue in her hands waiting for the other shoe to drop. She didn't wait long. Rachel dropped back onto her desk.

"So the kiss? That was George?!" Jillian nodded with a faint smile starting to play about her mouth. "And he sent the 4 o'clocks?" Jillian nodded again. "And the whole apron and the 'don't wear anything' bit?"

Jillian nodded again. "That required dry cleaning," she made a point to add.

"Oh, my God!" Rachel exclaimed again, and then she seemed to settle. "So, wait. You said the date was wonderful. Was it really wonderful?" As Jillian tried to think of the best way to answer the question and a few choice moments flashed through her mind, a flush entered her cheeks, and Rachel pounced. "*That* good?"

Jillian's smile widened a bit more, but she kept the best to herself. "Actually, that's what I'm supposed to tell you. We, George and I, we're actually a couple now."

Rachel stood up again. "What does that mean exactly? You're a *couple* couple?"

"Uh-huh. As in we're seeing each other and *just* each other."

"Oh, my God, that must have been some date."

"It was," Jillian said. "It really was."

Rachel sat down again and grinned. "So, you must've... Right?"

"Rachel!" Jillian tossed the tissue in the trash, as she felt her ears heat.

"Oh, come on. You can tell me."

"Rachel." Jillian sat back and tried not to look like she was hiding something. "Look, I told you about George and me because people are probably going to start talking about us and everybody is going to be asking you. So, now you know what you need to know to answer them, and that's it."

"Jillian," Rachel said, and leaned toward her. "I won't go around announcing anything."

"Sure, but it'll be easier for you to be able to say you don't know, if you don't know."

"Oh, please. Who's going to ask me about you and George having sex?"

Jillian crossed her arms. "Once this gets out, who knows? You work for both of us. Someone might even ask you if we do it in the office."

"Do you?" Rachel asked, her eyes widening again.

"Rachel!" Jillian shook her head. "First, no one is doing anything in the office. Second, we just got together last night, so we couldn't have anyway. Third, I'm neither confirming nor denying anything outside of the office either. This way you can honestly say you have no idea."

"I repeat, no one is going to ask me that."

"Well, they certainly aren't going to ask me," Jillian said.

There was a knock on the door and Ishi opened the door and leaned in without waiting for an invitation and looked at Jillian. "Hey. So, Vidar is telling everybody that while he was on his smoke break he saw you and George walking outside with, like, your arms around each other, and that George kissed your hair or nuzzled it or something. Are you guys, like, together or what?"

Jillian looked at Rachel and then back at Ishi. *I guess we didn't need Rachel for this after all.* "Well, yes, actually. We're a couple."

"Cool," Ishi said, and started to close the door, but then swung it back open. "FYI, everybody is talking about whether you've, you know, 'done it,' in your office."

Rachel started laughing. "Oh, my God," Jillian murmured and brought her hand to her forehead.

"What should I tell them?" Ishi asked.

"No!" Jillian answered. "You should tell them a big, fat, emphatic, 'No!'"

"Ohhhhkay," Ishi said, and closed the door.

Rachel was still laughing. "I guess you were sort of right!"

Jillian slid down in her chair. "I'm going to die, right here."

Sergei was in his office on the computer, but not the phone, so George figured he'd just get it over with and walked in, shut the door, and sat down.

"'S'up?" Sergei muttered and looked away from his computer screen. "Looks like some of the euphoria has worn off. Good. I'm still pissed at you. Did you want to hear about how my Monday night went?"

"Oh, sure," George said, and listened to Sergei detail several very disappointing moments that could have gone better, possibly, had George been there.

Sergei finished off with, "but you didn't even bother to let me know."

"Yeah," George said. "I should've texted you. But, you know..."

"Whatever," Sergei said. "See what kind of response you get next time you're looking for a wingman."

George sighed. "Well, that's just it. I hopefully won't be."

"What the hell does that mean?" Sergei asked.

"It means," George took a breath, "that I'm serious about this woman."

Sergei sat back and picked up the baseball he kept on his desk and started toss it back and forth between his hands. "What does she do that the rest of womankind doesn't, that she can convince you to get serious in less than forty-eight hours? It had better be goddamn impressive. Something beyond basic gymnastics or just a decent blow job, I hope. There's no need to tie yourself down for anything less tha-"

"Serge," George interrupted. "Shut up a second."

Sergei raised his eyebrows. "You about to tell me about all of Olivia's fabulous qualities? Spare me. I don't give a shit. Just don't-"

"It's Jillian," George said.

"What's Jillian?" Sergei asked, and then his eyes went wide and he sat forward and put his baseball on his desk. "What do you mean, it's Jillian?"

"I mean, when you guys asked, I said Olivia because we hadn't been planning on telling anybody and I was cornered. But since then, Jillian and I talked and decided that keeping this a secret isn't going to be possible. So, we're not trying to keep it a secret. There it is, the woman I'm seeing is Jillian."

Sergei blinked once. "You fucked Jillian?!?"

George frowned and exhaled. "Can we not-"

"Holy shit! You are my idol!" Sergei said, and then leaned over his desk.

"Serge-"

"I mean, she's got herself laced up so tight, she must have so much bottled up sexual energy. God! To have all that loosed."

"Serge-"

"And she's got such a sweet ass and perfect tits too." Sergei held his hands out mimicking gripping a perfect sized pair of breasts.

"Serge-"

"What was it like? Did you do that sugar hole from behind?"

Without thinking, George reached over the desk and grabbed Sergei by his shirt, pulling him nearly nose to nose over the desk and spoke through clenched teeth. "Don't. Ever. Talk. About. Jillian. Like. That." He jerked Sergei's shirt one more time. "*Ever.*"

"Okay, man," Sergei said. "Okay." When George released Sergei's shirt, they both stood up very slowly, eyeing each other warily. Sergei brushed the front of his shirt to try to dislodge the wrinkles. George realized how fast he was breathing and that both his hands were balled into fists and took a breath to calm down. He was shaking just a little.

"I'm sorry, man," Sergei said, and George flexed his fingers. "Take a step back. I didn't mean anything."

"You didn't mean anything?" George half-asked, half-repeated. "I don't want to hear of you ever 'not meant anything' again. Ever. Whether I'm there or not. Never say anything about her again. Am I in any way not clear?"

"No," Sergei said. "You're crystal."

"Okay," George said, and flexed his fingers again.

"Okay," Sergei said.

George took another breath and started to realize what he'd just done. "Shit," George muttered.

"Are we good?" Sergei asked.

"Yeah," George said, and then rubbed his face with his hands. Then he exhaled again. "*Are* we good?" He forced himself to meet Sergei's gaze.

"Yeah," Sergei answered.

"Okay," George said. *Now what do I do? I just threatened one of my best friends. In his office. Jillian knew he was going to be a prick, told me, and I still lost it. Shit.* He took another deep breath and started for the door.

"Hey, George," Sergei called and George reluctantly turned around and looked at Sergei, hoping whatever came out Sergei's mouth wouldn't make him want to punch him. "Good luck. I hope it turns out to be, you know, everything you want."

And now I'm the prick. "Thanks, Serge." He left the door open and headed for the roof again.

CHAPTER FOURTEEN

Jillian had shut her office door behind Rachel, who was laughing like a hyena as she left, and leaned against it. Her assumption that Christy would be unhappy had been a gross underestimate and her assumption that no one was going to have the nerve to say anything to her face had also been wrong. She looked at her desk and started to consider the likely impacts if she just left the building right then and there. Based on how well she'd done predicting things so far, clearly she wasn't the corporate chess player she'd previously imagined herself to be. *On the upside, it can't get worse than this.*

She heard faint laughter outside her office. *Please don't let that have anything to do with me. Please don't let that have anything to do with me. Plea-*

Her personal phone rang and she walked back to her desk to pick it up.

"How did things go for you?" George asked.

"Oh, I want to melt into the floor. You?"

"Just swell. Why do you want to melt into the floor?"

"Humiliation."

"From Rachel?"

Jillian shook her head. "No, the whole world. It's not important. Why are you calling on your mobile?"

George was silent a moment, just long enough for Jillian to wonder why he wasn't telling her. "I'm on the roof."

"The roof? Why?"

She must've had a little tension or something in her voice, because George laughed and said, "Well, I'm not going to jump, if that's what you're thinking. I come up here to think. To get away. Why don't you come up?"

"To the roof," Jillian said.

"Yep. It's just as cold as it was in front of the building but without the smokers, or anybody else for that matter. Quiet."

Jillian thought about it for a moment. Not being on the floor sounded great. Not being in her office sounded great. Being near George sounded even better. But leaving her office and going up the stairs meant... leaving her office and walking across the floor to get to the stairs.

George's voice reverberated through the speaker again. "Private."

Private. Oh, my. Not that he'd said it like that. *It is the* roof *for goodness sake. But a minute or two, without anybody else around. That might be just what the doctor ordered.* "Do you just take the stairs up?"

"Yep. It's not locked from the inside. Fire escape route without an alarm. But it is locked from the outside. I put a rock in as a doorstop when I come out here. I figure, so long as I'm here, it's not a security risk. Are you coming up?"

Jillian almost said that she was thinking about it, and then she opened her mouth. "Yes. Be right there."

"Good. Watch the rock. We don't want to have to go over the side and down the fire escape."

"Definitely not," Jillian said, and looked down at her high heels. "That would be bad."

George couldn't help but smile when the door creaked. Just to be safe, he did move to be within range if she made a mistake regarding the rock doorstop. She didn't, she focused on the rock and the door and made certain that everything was in place before she even looked up at him. That moment made his life worth every bad moment he'd ever lived through. Jillian was still mostly facing the door, but she turned her head ahead of her body and saw him standing there, and he watched as her mouth turned up and her eyes lit up and she smiled as bright as the sun with all of her face.

Another time, another place, he would have kissed her, just for that smile. But he hadn't invited her to his private sanctuary to take advantage of the solitude and be physical with her.

"Hi," she said.

"Hi. Welcome to my sanctuary." He wrapped his arm around her shoulders and walked her a little way toward the edge so that they could both take in the view. "What do you think?"

"You were wrong," Jillian said, and she crossed her arms around herself, but still leaned into him a little. "It's much colder up here than down on the sidewalk."

He chuckled. "Yeah. I suppose it is."

"But this view..."

"Yeah," he said, looking down at her. "The view is fantastic."

"I didn't know this was accessible." She looked up at him again. "So you come up here to think, huh?"

"Yes. Do you realize I've just given away a secret I've had since I started at this place?"

"None of the muske- *guys* know?"

"Nope," he said. "So, why do you want to melt into the floor?"

Jillian stepped away from him and covered her face a moment and then re-crossed her arms. She told him about her conversation with Rachel and then Ishi, omitting nothing. He laughed, not nearly as hard as Rachel, but he laughed.

"I don't think it's funny." Jillian said.

"Oh, come on. It's just people being people. Amusing themselves with a little harmless fantasy. Anyone with a brain cell knows you'd never do anything inappropriate in the office."

He watched her eyebrows rise. "And you would?"

They both laughed then. "Uh, no. Getting fired for misconduct isn't on the top of my list either." He turned toward the view again.

After a few minutes of silence, Jillian spoke again. "Why are you up here, thinking? Didn't it go well with Sergei and Neal? Were they... disapproving, or something? I know they hate me."

George chuckled wryly and reached for her again. "That's not exactly true." He nearly sighed when she put her arm around his waist again. "But, uh, Sergei was Sergei, as expected." He could see her looking up at him out of the corner of his eye. Waiting. "And, well, then I was a jerk. But, uh, he wished us luck."

"Really? Sergei? He wished us luck?"

"Yep," George said. "I think he meant it, too."

"Wow," Jillian said. "That may be the most unbelievable thing to happen in the last few days."

"Oh, I don't know. I can think of a few other moments that top the unbelievable scale."

Jillian exhaled a light laugh and squeezed him. "I so don't want to be here."

"Then go back to your office," George said, grinning.

"That's not what I meant."

"I know," he said, and squeezed her. Then he looked down at her. "Let's go to lunch early."

"It wouldn't be an early lunch, it's practically still breakfast. You know what people will think..."

George started for the door. "You know what I think? I think that you shouldn't be taking any of them seriously." When she didn't follow, he walked back to her and reached out a hand for her to take.

"Oh, no? I should be laughing it all off?"

He looked down at his hand and then back at her, raising his eyebrows questioningly. "Yes. Because as soon as you start laughing, they'll stop.

And as soon as they get used to us, they'll get bored. We won't be interesting for long."

"So you want to walk back downstairs and leave together? At this hour? In full view of everyone?"

"Yes," he said, and shook his hand just a little to bring her attention to it again. "If you'd rather, we could attempt to work some more instead. But hiding isn't doing us any good."

She finally uncrossed her arms and took his hand. "Then why'd you come up here? And invite me up?"

"Even now, you won't give me an inch, will you?" He led her back to the door and then stopped alongside it, changing his mind about one thing. "Because," he said, with a really warm grin, "a minute alone with you is a minute alone with you. And I'll never get away with this again, back on the floor."

He tugged her hand toward his back and raised his other to her cheek. To his surprise, she didn't even move to stop him, so he leaned over and kissed her. He'd meant to keep it brief and light, but he fell into her all over again and found both his hands in her hair before he even realized he'd moved. Her hands stole around him as she kissed him back. It was when he slid his hands down her back, with the intention of drawing her tight against him, that he regained his senses, and instead he pulled back a little.

Jillian looked at him through blurry eyes, feeling dizzy again and confused. "Oh," she whispered. "I didn't think you'd still be able to do that."

"Do what?" He whispered back.

"Make me dizzy. Make me forget where I am." As her vision cleared, she looked into his eyes. "I thought that would pass after we... were together. But you just did it again. How do you do that?"

"I don't know," he answered softly. "I don't think I ever made anyone dizzy like that before." He lifted a hand to her face, rubbing his thumb very lightly across her lips and she closed her eyes. "But then, maybe it's not me."

She spoke faintly against his skin. "It's definitely you. I know it's you. Because I've never felt anything, anything at all, that's quite like..." She had to stop talking as a lump formed in her throat. *The way I feel with you. Nothing ever.*

"I mean, it's not *just* me." He took a breath. "It's *us.*" He moved his thumb aside and he brushed his lips against hers so lightly he almost couldn't feel it, but he knew she felt it as she quickly drew in a breath. "I may not be dizzy, but I've never felt anything like this either." Another soft kiss and she trembled; it took his breath away.

"George," she whispered against his lips. *I've never felt like this* about *anyone, either. And certainly not this fast. Oh, God. Oh, God.* "George, please."

When she didn't say anything further, George asked, "What is it, Jillian?"

Oh, I can't think. This has to stop. Say something. Anything. Quick. "I thought we agreed not to do this here."

He let out a breath that sounded something like a laugh. "I don't remember you actually agreeing. In fact... I think you were *disagreeable* on this subject..." His thumb ran across her cheek. She still hadn't opened her eyes. Without lowering his hand, he dropped his forehead against hers and closed his eyes again at the intense rightness of something so simple and his next words just tumbled out of him. "I'm in so far over my head here."

"Oh?" It was all she could manage to say.

"We're necking on the roof at work. Yeah, I'd say so."

She laughed a little.

"Seriously? That's all I get? No response."

She slid her hands around to his chest and then up to his cheeks as she collected herself. *No more of this.* Pushing back from him just enough to be able to see him, holding his face gently, she opened her eyes and he opened his. "You've had enough responses from me. Now, I'm going back to work," Jillian said, and took a single step back. "And so are you."

It was another few breaths with George looking into her eyes before he finally nodded and said, "Okay. You're right. We should work. But, um, are you exiling me back to my office?"

Jillian shook her head. "Actually, I have an idea." Then she swiped her thumb across George's mouth to wipe off her lip gloss before they went back downstairs and separated for their respective offices.

They met up again a few minutes later in the smaller of the conference rooms on the floor; one that had blinds floor-to-ceiling which Jillian opened completely. Both she and George set up their laptops and brought in a few personnel files.

Although neither claimed to have accomplished much, their IMs being more active on their computers than any other typing, by the time they agreed to leave for lunch Jillian felt a little less self-conscious. People had walked passed the conference room and looked, in some cases pointedly, so the looks had been hard to miss, but no one had stopped and stared.

After putting her computer and files back in her office, Jillian stopped in the restroom and was freshening her makeup when Rachel came in. Spying Jillian, Rachel walked up to the sinks, stood next to her, and smiled at her in the mirror. She waited a few moments, leaned over, and said, "You guys are so cute!"

Jillian met Rachel's eyes in the mirror for an instant before she returned to her face and applied a fresh coat of lip gloss. "We're cute?" She asked.

"Mm-hmm. Sitting just far enough apart for professional appearances, but only just that far. Trying not to smile. Sneaking looks at each other. Or not even bothering to sneak the looks, at all. That was him, by the way, one time I was at the printer. I saw him just looking at you and smiling."

Jillian noticed her face warming but tried to pretend it wasn't happening by looking for her eye shadow.

"I thought it would be weird to see you together, but it's just so adorable. You're so adorable together."

"Thanks. That's nice of you," Jillian said, as she put her makeup back in her bag, giving up on her face, knowing her ears were red by then.

"Oh, don't be embarrassed this time," Rachel continued. "Really. I've worked for George for well over three years and I've *never* seen him look like that. I've seen him smile, I've seen him pleased, but that was more. He's... really, really happy. It's sweet."

"Thanks," Jillian said, nodded, making her escape as quickly as possible. From behind Jillian, as she opened the door, Rachel said, "Now, we just need to see *you* look at *him*..."

George stood by her office door, already in his coat and glancing at his watch, when she returned from the bathroom. As he looked up and saw her, his face lit up and her stomach flipped over, her knees weakened, and she grinned back just at the sight, the embarrassment with Rachel forgotten.

"Ready?" He asked.

"Nearly," she answered and unlocked her door to retrieve her coat.

He cleared his throat. "What would you say to the idea of having lunch with the musketeers?"

"What?" She turned around.

Well, I suppose that's an answer in and of itself. Her face said it all. The idea was horrifying. "It was just an idea. I thought perhaps it might help... to integrate..." Her face didn't soften. "A bad idea. I understand. Too soon? Or too awful to consider ever?"

She tightened her grip on the door knob for support. "I don't know. I suppose... they are your friends, right? Close friends."

"Taro asked me to be his Best Man."

"Then... I guess at some point... but, now?"

He stepped into her office, though he didn't close the door. "They don't know you," he said. "And you don't know them. Just how you and I were. Now you're in my life. If you're in my life, you're going to be in theirs. And visa-versa. It doesn't have to be today. It was just a thought. But-"

"Have you ever dated anyone at work?" Jillian asked, cutting him off.

"Not here, no," he said.

"Then this is different. Your work life and your private life have been separate. Asking them to get used to us as a couple is different from asking them to accept me at lunch when they're used to having just you, their work buddy. Conversation would be awkward, at best. Just give it a little time," she said. *Like a lifetime.* "This is too much all at once."

He exhaled sharply. "Okay. Okay. Not lunch today." *But, if you are my girlfriend...* He took her coat from her and held it up. "What are you doing tomorrow night?"

"I promised Mrs. Kerchner, she lives next door, that I'd take her grocery shopping. Her daughter is out of town. But nothing after that." She slid her arms into the sleeves of her coat and looked over her shoulder to see his face.

"Good. I have a basketball game. How about coming?" As she turned around, he tried to smile again. "Melissa comes to most of the games, if that's any help."

Jillian swallowed. "Don't you think I might be a bit of a distraction?"

"No," George said, shaking his head. "But, if you are a distraction, well, that's too bad. Taro invited Melissa, his girlfriend. I'm inviting you, my girlfriend."

"She's his fiancée," Jillian said.

"Not when she first attended a game." He took a breath. *Please.* "I want you there. Please."

Her lips were a little tight, but they turned up. *He really wants me around. All the time.* "All right. If you want me there, I'll be there." She motioned him toward the door, followed him out, and locked it behind her.

"Good," he said, grinning again. As they started for the stairs, he reached for her hand, but pulled back his hand at the last moment, realizing where he was and what he was doing. "What's tonight looking like?"

"Not sure yet," she said, and hoped he couldn't tell that thinking about it was upsetting. At least he was only looking at her from the side. She hadn't heard back from Mal. After the *lovely* chat with Christy, she wasn't sure if the dinner was still on or not. *And if it is on, am I still invited?* "I'll let you know." She forced a smile onto her face. "If we work in the conference room all afternoon, you'll know as soon as I do." He opened the door to the stairwell for her. "Of course," she said, as she went through, "we need to get more done."

As the door shut behind him, he said, "I still think we should take time off. This afternoon. Let's not come back."

Jillian laughed as her stomach turned over again at several thoughts of what they could do with an afternoon and she smiled for real. "We have to come back. Our laptops are here."

"We could go back up and get them now."

She laughed again and stopped on the stairs. "You know, I had no idea you were such a bad influence."

"I'm not a bad influence," he said, as he stopped on the stairs next to her and put his arm around her shoulders. "I'm *trying* to be a bad influence."

She laughed again. "Let's go to lunch and not talk about anything to do with work."

"Perfect," he said, and they started down the stairs again.

Lunch and two coffee breaks later, Ishi knocked on the conference room door and waited while George and Jillian exchanged confused looks until George motioned her to enter. Still, she didn't really enter; she leaned in, keeping her feet firmly on the outside of the threshold. "Uh, hey guys."

"Everything all right?" George asked.

After the embarrassing confrontation earlier, Jillian almost enjoyed how uncomfortable Ishi looked as she shifted her weight and didn't look either of them in the eye, but not quite. Apart from Ishi being a friendly acquaintance, Jillian also felt there was a lot wrong with the possibility of anyone being uncomfortable because of her. "What's up, Ishi?" She asked, trying to smooth out whatever was rough.

"Well, a few of the guys were planning on heading out soon. They wanted to make their daily reports but they weren't sure if they should... interrupt."

George sighed. "You have got to be kidding me. What does anyone think they'd be interrupting?"

Ishi tilted her head, raised her eyebrows, and blinked. "Yeah, right," she said, with sarcasm thick in her voice as she leaned out and shut the door.

George rolled his eyes. Jillian glanced at him and saw the eye roll. "Time, remember? People need to get used to us. *You* said that." When George looked at her, she continued, "Why don't we go back to our own offices and *look* a little more approachable?"

He had to concentrate to keep his face from turning to a pout. *But I don't want to. I want to be with you.* He sighed again. "You're right." And he closed the folder in front of him. When her face turned up in a smile, he smiled back. "But keep your IM open."

"Mm-hmm," she murmured and nodded. She closed the folder in front of her as her phone chirped. She flipped it over. *Sorry. Super busy. See you at dinner. —Mal*

"Everything, ok?" George asked, and Jillian realized she was frowning.

She put the phone down again and looked back at him. That made smiling again easy. "Mostly. But it looks like I have plans with the girls."

"Oh," he said, trying not to sound too disappointed. "Will you call me, after?"

It was all she could do not to sigh at the disappointment in his voice, how much he wanted to be with her. *God, you're dreamy. I want to see you too.*

"Sure. We're doing dinner and a movie, so it'll be a few hours."

"I'll look forward to it, regardless of the hour. So if you and girls decide on drinks afterward, still call me." He paused a moment. "Please."

This time she didn't quite catch herself before the sigh. "Definitely."

His mouth quirked a little. "I'll be thinking about you."

"Me too," she said, before she could stop herself. She blushed and looked down at her folders. "About you, that is."

If the blinds weren't open, I'd kiss you right now. "Good," George said, as he gathered up his laptop and papers. "Keep thinking about me," he said, as he looked back at her and smiled broadly again. "All the time."

"Tell me you brought something new," Orville said, as a greeting when George walked in. He'd already setup the console. George tossed him a box and watched him grin. "Good job, my boy," Orville said, as he opened it.

George sat down and picked up a controller. "Let's shoot 'em up."

Orville put the disc in the console and then turned and shuffled back to the couch.

"Knees bad today?" George asked.

"Mmm," Orville murmured with a frown. "It's going to rain tomorrow morning."

"Oh, yeah? I hadn't watched the weather."

"The weather man may or may not know anything. I assure you, it'll rain tomorrow morning." Orville sat slowly and picked up a controller. "So, you gonna tell me or do I have to ask?"

Knowing full well what Orville meant, George smiled at just the thought of Jillian.

"Well, that certainly looks like good news. I take it the rest of the date went well?"

George fought the natural impulse to tell Orville just *how well* and said, "She's really amazing, Orville. I mean really. There's nobody out there like her."

"I could have told you that after two minutes," Orville said. "The important part is if you two fit together and whether or not she's in your future. Well, you look happy, so I guess at least you didn't goof it up yet."

"God, I hope not," George said. "Everything was going great when I left work. And thank you, for the vote of confidence."

"I didn't mean it was inevitable. I just worry for you. I don't like seeing you alone."

"Well, I'm not alone now," George started flicking through the games settings with his controller. "In fact, we decided to be exclusive." He didn't turn his head, but he shifted his eyes to try to see Orville's expression.

Orville leaned forward a little to better see George's face. "Really? Don't think you're hurrying things a bit?"

George thought of Jillian's face when he'd kissed her at lunch. "Not in the slightest." *She's mine. I'm not going to lose her.*

"So, then…" Orville sat back. "I suppose you've told her all about Sarah."

"Er," George mumbled, "mostly."

"Uh-huh." Orville said. "She should know, you know."

"Oh, who cares? The past is the past. You said something like that last night. Jillian's the present. No point in getting bogged down in the old garbage."

"I thought the term these days was baggage."

"Whatever! Let's play." George started the game and he and Orville played for nearly a minute before their characters were shot and they had to start the level again.

"This one might last us a while," Orville muttered.

"Yeah."

As the level began to load, Orville took a deep breath and George knew something was coming. He even guessed what it was.

"I think you ought to tell her about Sarah. Soon."

"I heard you the first time, Orville."

"It would be good for you too, you know. I know you didn't tell me the half of it. If this one's the right one, then she'd be the one to understand and maybe help you close up the remaining wounds. May helped me with June."

George looked away from the game as he pushed pause. "Now, that's a story I'd like to hear."

Orville focused back on the game and started it up again. The second attempt they kept their characters alive for just over a minute. "I'm thinking this might last us forever. Are you having trouble aiming, like I am?"

"I don't think my aim is the problem. It's the fact that we can't get under cover while they all shoot at us. Then again, I don't think I took out more than two guys, so maybe my aim is an issue."

They tried one more time, managing less than a minute again.

George groaned. "I'm going to look up a walk-through on this one and find out if we need to be going in a different direction or something."

"We may need cheats to get through this."

"That's desperate talk. Let's give it a few more tries before we're desperate. How about we start by turning around and going the other way?"

"You think they'd design it like that?"

"Well," George said, as he thought a moment. "Okay, so it would be strange, but then the target audience for this game has seen and played a lot of others that are just like it. Maybe the designers laid it out with some odd twists so it would different."

"Really?"

"Well, I wouldn't. But that doesn't mean someone else wouldn't."

"What would you do, if you were laying this out?" Orville asked, as the shooting started again.

"I would combine the strategy games with the shooters. I don't think this one has much strategy, so I don't know." George tried sending his character in the opposite direction and watched him go down even quicker. "Well, the opposite direction isn't the solution."

Orville snorted. "Why don't you?"

"Why don't I what?"

"Why don't you make your own game?"

It was George's turn to snort. "I moved on from that idea ages ago. I'm doing what I should be."

Orville nodded next to him.

One more try and they both set down the controllers. "What was this about a walk through?" Orville asked.

"I'll find one. There has to be a way out of there." George sat forward a little. "Since we aren't making progress on this... why don't you tell me about June?"

Orville struggled to his feet and went to the console to swap games. "It's a long story. And you may not find it as fascinating as you think."

"It's come up twice in less than twenty-four hours. Tell me."

"Okay," Orville said, as he put a disc in the console. "I put in the racing one with the motorcycles."

George picked up his controller again. They could talk and race at the same time. He waited for Orville to sit and pick up his controller. "Tell you what. Let's skip the motorcycles and go for the muscle cars. I'll let you drive the Mustang if you tell me about June."

Orville was silent a moment. "Deal."

The first race was into its third lap before Orville started.

"So May and I were in the same class in school. I wouldn't say we knew each other so much as knew of each other. But it was a smaller town, so everybody knew everybody a little. May was smart and serious, pretty too, but serious. She started working for the bank when she was sixteen. After graduation they promoted her. By the time she was twenty, she was head teller.

"By then, I had been promoted to head of my line at the factory. I was holding out hope, not completely unwarranted, that I might be promoted off the line.

"Now, June. She was younger than us. She was five years behind us in school. When she turned sixteen, she took a job in the dress shop. She was," Orville paused a moment, and not for the game. George stayed quiet and waited for him to go on.

"Okay. Have you seen the movie *It's A Wonderful Life?*"

"Sure," George answered.

"So, one of the side characters in the movie is this girl Violet. And she's beautiful and all the men in town wish they could be with her. Right? And she wears these unbelievable clothes that show off all the reasons they want to be with her, apart from her pretty face.

"Well, that was June. At sixteen, Miss Millicent hired her and put her in some of the clothes she wanted to sell. June would wear the dress around town a few times, and then, back to the store. And once that happened, sure enough, a couple of women would buy a dress just like it. Hoping they'd get the same looks June got.

"I would've thought that it would work the other way. Because nobody got the looks that June got. When she would help with the windows in the shop, the guys who worked the hardware store across the street would eat their lunches on the sidewalk, just to watch. Traffic stopped for June. That's the kind of amazing she was."

Orville paused again, and George glanced over, worried that Orville was reliving a painful memory. But Orville just laughed when he over took George's car in the game. "You're too nice a kid, sometimes."

George accelerated and said, "Oh, yeah? We'll see."

After another lap, Orville went on. "So, I suppose the story actually starts three days before I turned twenty-three. I was promoted to shift supervisor, which was huge. I was finally bringing in enough money to start really saving. I was planning on college, you know. And my folks had been really good about it. They were letting me live at home so I could save up.

"The day after I was promoted, I was supposed to stop at Croft's Bakery on the way home from work and pick up some cupcakes for my mother. When I walked in, June was there ordering a birthday cake for her father. I don't know that I ever stood in a line that took as long as that, and I was next! You'd have thought that I would have been patient waiting for her. She was leaning over the counter, so I had a lovely view. I mean," he made an mmm sound, "a *lovely* view. Her dress was so tight along her frame, flaring out at her hips, she was absolutely breathtaking."

George thought a moment about the way Jillian had taken his breath away that first day, and how just thinking of her warmed him from head to toe.

"But I wasn't patient," Orville continued. "I never felt like pacing so much in my life, though I did keep control. I'm pretty sure that I sniffed once or twice, and I coughed once, trying to hint to hurry up. By the time she'd finished, there were two more people in line behind me. I wouldn't say that was outrageous by any standard, it wasn't even unusual, but it stood out in my mind. I was standing there and felt the weight of my own impatience and the eyes of the people behind me.

"I was so tense and so irritable inside my own head. I think I must have known what was coming somehow. I couldn't bear to wait. Couldn't take it. But I don't know how I could have known.

"Anyway, she *finally* finished with her order and when she turned to leave, she did the thing that all pretty girls do when they know they've inconvenienced you. She looked at my shoes, smiling sheepishly, and then brought up her eyes and looked into mine and very softly and sweetly said, 'I'm terribly sorry for making you wait. I hope I've caused you no inconvenience.' And I knew she wasn't sorry in the slightest and yet I smiled back and said, 'No trouble at all, Miss.' And then I swore at myself in my head for being so taken by a pretty face, knowing that it wasn't manners that made me reply like that.

"I suppose I would have quickly forgotten the encounter, but as I left the shop with the boxes, she was lingering outside, looking in the window of the milliner's next door. When I came out, she turned and called out. I was so startled that she even knew my name, I was at a loss to speak.

"She walked up to me and apologized again and then asked me why I was picking up something from the bakery when my mother was such a talented and gifted baker. It was true, I must brag. My mother's pies and cakes always went for the highest bids at the church fundraisers. And she took home more than one blue ribbon from the county fair.

"I thanked June for her generous compliment, agreed with her, and then replied that I hadn't the slightest idea why she wanted the cupcakes. She said something about me being a dutiful son and then asked how tall I was. I answered, not even in a complete sentence. And she muttered an um-hmm and then said, 'perfect' and started walking along the sidewalk. She glanced at me and made it clear I was expected to walk with her.

"After a short distance, she asked that if it wasn't asking too much, and I wouldn't be too late, would I mind terribly giving her the tiniest of bit assistance? Her father wanted a box in from the garage, and she'd said she'd bring it in, but she'd need a ladder. She thought I was just tall enough to not need one.

Orville stopped his story to sigh, a very long, very wistful sigh. "When I didn't answer right away, she started on about how close her house was, which of course, I knew. It was just two streets over and three houses up from the corner. I let her go on a few moments, distracted by my own curiosity at her request, and then I agreed to help her.

"June led me into the garage via the side door and showed me the box up on the top shelf. She held onto the cupcakes while I got it down. It was ridiculously heavy, not unlike my record boxes. I struggled to get the thing onto the bench. Once I had it there, I asked her if her father really needed the whole thing in the house, or if there was something in the box that he wanted and we could just take that in.

"She didn't answer. She tilted her head and looked me up and down and then turned and walked into the house, taking the cupcake boxes with her. Naturally, I followed her. And I asked where her dad was. He should have been off work by that time. She said he was at his weekly bowling league.

"I was smart enough not to ask about her mom. She'd passed, oh, around two years prior. It could have slipped out, though. The stupid runs deep in front of a beautiful girl like that.

"We were in the kitchen and she offered me a drink. I started to wonder what was actually going on. There were a lot of thoughts flashing through my head. Like the rumor she'd given it up to Ed Jones on their prom night, though he wasn't bragging around town about it, so that made it less likely. But why was I in her kitchen? I'd never been in her house before. I'd never said more than a polite hello to her in all my life. I was going to be late getting home. But, of course, June was standing in front of me, offering me a drink, so what was I going to do? What any man would've done."

George lowered his hands to his lap and looked at Orville. "You're not saying that you got it on with her? Right then?"

Orville didn't stop the game. "I am. We had a drink of her father's whiskey and she took me upstairs to her room and that was the beginning."

"Geez," George muttered. "How long did it last? A week? A month?"

"Actually, it was over a year. We were inseparable. And we kept it looking proper for the neighbors. On Fridays I'd deposit my check at the bank and take a little in cash so I could take her out with the gang for sodas and dancing over the weekend, brought her home at a decent hour, chaste kiss on the cheek, then drove down the block to park and walked up the alley and came in the back door. Her dad had taken to drinking after her mom died and he usually passed out by eleven. So we'd spend a little time in her room before saying our real goodnight."

"Orville! Holy... I can't believe you. With her father in the house? Oh, my God."

"I know, Kid. I know. There are times I think back and can't hardly believe it either. But you never saw this girl. You'd understand if you did. And her dad. Well, he was in mighty sorry shape. He'd come home and start drinking at dinner.

"June used to say that he didn't really care what she did as long as she had dinner on the table when he got home, breakfast on the table in the morning, and a lunch packed for him to take to work. She told me that she washed his sheets on the regular schedule, but that he hadn't slept in the bed since a few months after her mom died. He'd just pass out in his easy chair.

"It was a sad state of affairs. I suppose a gentleman wouldn't have contributed to the mess by getting involved with her like that, but I couldn't help myself. And it was worse than that. I was in love with her after the first kiss, so stopping it wasn't an option.

"I counted the minutes until I could see her. And I'm talking about all the time. Innocently, too. When she'd have a day off during the week, I'd leave my keys so she could bring my car up to the factory and we'd have lunch. When she worked Saturdays, I'd bring her lunch and we'd eat out back of the store. Just sitting next to her felt like heaven."

George shook his head. "I can't believe I hadn't heard this until now."

"May was the love of my life, kid. I was crazy in love with June, really, but if it'd never happened with her, I wouldn't have lost out. May, on the other hand... not having May would have been a real tragedy."

"Alright," George said. "So this crazy thing went on for a year with the hottest girl in town. What happened? Why'd it go south?"

Orville nodded and exhaled a few times. "That was the ten thousand dollar question. It took me a long time to figure it out. The obvious answer was that she had aspirations that I couldn't be a part of. I was staring down the prospect of being factory foreman. He was retiring and though I'd only been off the line a year, well, the boss liked me. So, decision time was coming. I could take the job and a hefty raise or I could stay where I was and keep saving for college.

"Everybody at the factory knew I was looking at college and the boss wasn't dumb. He and I had a few informal chats and he made it pretty clear that he was going to make me sign a contract to keep me in the job for a few years, if I took it. It was a weird time. He didn't offer it to me right then, but he pretty much told me that those were his terms. I took that to mean that I should decide and tell him if I was willing to sign the contract.

"Anyway, I sat on the idea for a few days. Didn't tell anybody, except to float it to my folks. They were... well, they surprised me. They wouldn't advise me. Wouldn't even give me any pros and cons. Just nothing, until my dad asked me if I'd talked it over with June.

"Now, you have to understand. We really did do things right, apart from the obvious. She had dinner at my house with my folks every few weeks. I had dinner with her and her dad every few weeks. The families were well aware that we were together. So I suppose it shouldn't have been a surprise when dad mentioned her, but it was.

"See, the real problem was that June and I never talked about the future. Ever. I just assumed that she was looking for the happy ever after that the rest of the town was looking for. A house and kids. I had the choice to

216

take the foreman job and then I'd be able to afford a house immediately and marry her. Or I had the college dream and that would have meant putting it all off.

"So, the time had come, after a year, to talk about the future. And I didn't realize that I was wrong about what she wanted until she told me. I started laying everything out and she stopped me, not even midway through, with this confused look on her face.

"She told me her father had finally decided to sell the house and that he was giving her enough money to go to New York. And she was going to go there and become a model, just like she'd always wanted. And she figured I had enough money saved that we could go together.

"But I said that I didn't have enough for school yet. And she looked at me like she'd no idea what I was talking about. And I said that I was planning on going to college for engineering and asked if she didn't know that. And she said no, she had no idea. She figured I could get work in New York. I was a supervisor now, so that should make it easy.

"I didn't even bother to mention that one year's experience was nothing. Or that the factories probably wouldn't be in New York City proper. And I didn't bother to ask her how she expected to become a model overnight. Nope. We just sat there, staring at each other as we realized that we didn't really know each other after all.

"I knew who her first crush was. And what her punishment was when her mom caught her putting on her lipstick. And who her best friend was in kindergarten. All kinds of stuff about her mom and her mom's passing away and how she had been getting through it. But nothing about what she actually wanted in her life.

"And it was the same for her about me. For some reason she'd assumed I wanted to get out of that town too. And why not New York? And she was sort of right. Getting out of the small town was an eventual goal. But I was going to get out with an education, not a starry-eyed dream.

"We must have been silent, sitting on the porch swing outside her house for over an hour, just looking at each other and then out across the street. Staring out at the future that so obviously didn't have the two of us together."

George swallowed painfully. If Orville had been talking about anything else, he'd have given him a hard time about sounding poetic again. But he couldn't imagine making a joke just then. "That's awful," he said, and then mentally kicked himself for being so trite. Of course it was awful. Saying it didn't help at all.

"Yeah, kiddo, it was." Orville sighed. "And then it got worse."

"Worse?" George asked, and then felt his stomach drop. "She wasn't pregnant, was she?"

"What? No. No." Orville laughed bitterly again. "That would have changed things alright. But, no. No, the worse was that we both knew it was over, but we had the disentangling of our lives to go yet. She wasn't leaving right away. Not until the actual sale of the house went through and she had the money. But it was over. So we weren't *seeing* each other anymore but we *saw* each other around town plenty.

"And after a year together, we had a lot of the same friends, went to the same places. So, in the beginning, or should I say the ending, we ran into each other a lot. I'd go somewhere and she'd be there already. Or I'd spot her coming in the door while I was trying to laugh with my friends. And we'd see each other and whatever smile might have been on our faces just fell.

"Not that I was smiling much anyway. I fell pretty low. My friends were great. They kept trying to bring me out of it. All I wanted to do was go sit with her dad and drink myself into oblivion. Of course, any chance of that went with the wind. He hadn't done a thing while we were seeing each other, but after we split, he wanted to cut me in two.

"I guess it was a good thing that her dad already had a buyer for the house and they closed the sale in a little over a month. I don't know how long I could have stood it, continually seeing her and not being able to touch her or even speak to her. That's when I learned why it's called a break up. I figured it was *breaking apart* but really it's just plain *breaking*.

"My folks were good on that count, like my friends. They didn't say anything except to invite me to participate in activities they were attending. Tried to help get my mind off of it. It didn't work.

"You know, I still wonder about one thing. No one ever asked me why we split up. I wonder if everybody else knew it wasn't going to last."

He shook his head and mumbled. "I guess that's neither here nor there. You know the real bottom was actually the night before she left. She showed up at my house, just after dinner, standing there at the door. Mom answered and called for me. We looked at each other for a minute or two and then I gestured toward the street and we sat in my car for a while not saying anything. Then she asked me to go with her. She said everything would work out. That she loved me.

"I told her that I loved her too, but I wasn't interested in a lifetime of resenting her for not going to school. That's when I said she could change her mind and stay and we could get married. I won't burden you with the words that came after that. It was a long conversation that went nowhere. Then I drove her to her friend's house, where she'd been staying the last two days, and then said I'd take her to the station the next day.

"And the following morning I helped her get on the train, kissed her on the cheek, wished her good luck, and walked away. Well, that's what she saw anyway. I went into the station, but when the train pulled out I went back on the platform and watched it go. And then she was gone. For real.

Forever."

George put a hand on Orville's shoulder. "I'm sorry."

Orville reached across his torso and patted George's hand twice. "Thanks, Kid." Then he shrugged off George's hand. "I lived, you know."

"Right," George said, dropping his hand into his lap.

"And so did you," Orville said.

Sarah. "Right," George said, again. He slumped a moment and then looked at Orville.

Orville's lips pulled together into a tight line, but curved up a little. "And you know that phrase, 'it's always darkest just before the dawn'? Well, although it wasn't really the beginning in the proper sense, it was sort of when things started with May."

"Oh, yeah?"

CHAPTER FIFTEEN

Jillian would have slammed the door to the restaurant, had it not had a door closer that kept it from closing too quickly. As her shoes clicked on the sidewalk, she muttered to herself rhythmically to the sound. She was close to having composed something that resembled a very angry three verse limerick with only one bad rhyme in the middle, when Malvinia nearly caught up to her.

"Jills! Slow down!"

"Unh-uh," Jillian said, as loudly as she could manage. *If time stops for no man, I'm not stopping for any woman. Okay. That didn't come together quite right. Whatever. Forget it. Go home.*

"Jillian," Malvinia called again, getting closer. "I told Christy to go... well, actually that isn't important." She was puffing a little and her footfalls were much faster than Jillian's. "But I told her off. You were very poised. I'm impressed."

Jillian let out an unladylike snort and kept walking. For all the steam she was puffing, her heels were clearly slowing her down. Malvinia was wearing lower wedges and had made excellent time.

"Oh, honestly, Jillian. Give us both a break! One of us will fall and break an ankle or a wrist."

At that thought, Jillian slowed her pace and Malvinia was next to her nearly instantly. "I'm walking off the anger."

"I know that," Malvinia said. "Let's do it together." After a slight pause she continued. "You know that she's just really jealous. That's all it is. She can dress it up anyway she wants but you and I and probably Lacey and Kai know that it's just jealousy. She'll get over it and then she'll apologize."

"I'm not entirely sure I'll want her apology. If she was going to be like that, why didn't she just cancel tonight?"

Malvinia sighed. "Who amongst us doesn't like to make a fool of ourselves now and then? She probably couldn't help herself. She wanted to take a few shots at you and she did. And she made herself look bad. When she comes to her senses, she'll be embarrassed."

"Maybe," Jillian said, and looked over at Malvinia. "I understand that she's disappointed. I just thought that everyone could... I don't know... be happy for me."

Her mouth curving up into a smile, Malvinia chuckled. "Oh, my poor, dear, Jillian. I'm happy for you."

"You are?" Jillian asked, astonished at the thought.

"Of course," Malvinia said. "You got what you wanted. He just better turn out to be wonderful, or I'll have to hurt to him."

A small strangled laugh escaped Jillian's mouth. "You'll hurt him?"

"Oh, yes. I'm not putting up with another Sam-like fiasco."

"No worries there. George is nothing like Sam."

Malvinia's eyebrows rose. "He's good-looking, smart, and successful. He's very much like Sam. How's the sex?"

Jillian closed her eyes a moment and opened them just in time to miss sideswiping a bush. *How do I even begin to put words around that?* "You know when I use words like amazing, intense, life-altering... they still feel like they fall short."

"Wow! I'd ask what he does, but since I'm not with anybody right now, it'd probably just depress me."

"Let's just say, even though we only did it once last night, I made it twice."

Malvinia made a sound that made Jillian think of a sigh and a groan all at once. "The first time you were together? Wow! That man has skills. I need to get myself one of those. Oh, well, someday. Maybe." She paused and grinned. "After Christy pulls herself together, do *not* tell her he's that good in bed. She might regress. Of course, if she could look at it logically, she'd see that he was never going to go for her."

Surprised, Jillian looked a Malvinia. "No?"

"Pfft. I could tell he was into you from those few minutes the other night. He didn't give even one of us a second glance. He had his eyes on you the whole time."

Jillian could feel her cheeks warming.

"Do yourself a favor, though, please? Figure out if there are any obvious signs that this isn't going to work out, really soon. Before you've had so many orgasms that you're in love with the guy."

"Mal!" Jillian slapped her shoulder. There were people on the street and Malvinia was saying the word 'orgasm' as if no one could hear her.

"I'm not kidding," Malvinia said. "A good orgasm is a hormonal brain wash. They make you fall in love. You don't want to be in too deep, too soon. Poke and prod and look for the big flags. Snoop if you have to.

There's no way to be sure it'll work out, but there are certainly ways to know it *won't*." When Jillian didn't say anything right away, Malvinia spoke again. "I assume he doesn't smoke weed, or anything like that."

"He's not like Sam," Jillian said.

"And he better like you just like you are. If I find out he's trying to change you…"

Jillian shook her head. "No. He won't. He definitely likes me as I am."

"Oh, yeah?"

"Yes," Jillian said, firmly. "Last night he told me I mesmerize him."

Malvinia stopped walking and grabbed Jillian's arm. "Okay, this I want to focus on. What did he say?"

"He said that I mesmerize him. Everything I say and everything I do. And that he didn't want to just watch anymore. He wanted to be a part of it."

This time Malvinia did sigh. "Oh, my. Does he have a brother?"

Jillian grinned. "Three of them. But they're all in Washington."

"DC?" Malvinia asked, in a hopeful tone.

"State."

"Oh, well. What are the odds of more than one like that in the family, anyway?" She shook her head. "That is the best line I've ever heard."

"I don't believe it was a line," Jillian said. *It wasn't some ridiculous slush that he shovels at every woman he meets. No one has ever heard that from him, but me.* She swallowed. *I hope.*

Malvinia helped solidify Jillian's assertion as quickly as she'd made her question it. "After the way he was looking at you, I don't think it was either. I wonder how everyone in your office has been able to stand the sexual tension all this time. Or did it just start recently?"

Jillian took a breath, slid her arms through Malvinia's, started walking again, and finally told her everything. It was a relief to admit to her immediate attraction to George and how she'd felt when they'd first met. It was an even bigger relief to admit to just how much she'd secretly wished for things to happen between them, despite feeling foolish about wishing such a thing after all the stupid things they'd done to each other and even more foolish about just how deep she had buried that secret, so deep that she only saw it when her subconscious brought it up in her dreams.

Since no one from work was around, she also told Malivinia how everything had turned two nights earlier when he'd shown up at The Blue Feather, the startling kiss, his clues about their date, the highlights of the night before, and how he'd still managed to scramble her mind, again, with a kiss earlier that day.

When she'd finished, she waited impatiently for Malvinia's thoughts. Malvinia never stopped smiling. "I like hearing that tone in your voice," Malvinia said.

"What tone?"

"Excited. Happy." When Jillian grinned, Malvinia nodded. "And you're right. I don't think he's like Sam. But, um," she paused a moment, "do check him out. And be sure to let me check him out too. For real. And soon."

Jillian shook her head. "If you're serious, you'd better open up your schedule."

"All right," Malvinia said. "Can you arrange something for tomorrow? I'd say you're about a short train ride away from hopelessly in love. A speeding train too."

Malvinia and Jillian shared a looked and burst out laughing.

"Thank you for not using the word 'doomed,'" Jillian said. "I would have thought you'd be less supportive... You're the best." She squeezed Malvinia's arm.

"I'm in favor of love," Malvinia said, suddenly serious. "I'm just not in favor of seeing anyone's insides kicked around over it."

"I'll be fine. You know, even if it doesn't work out, I'd rather risk it and feel something, then not and feel nothing."

Malvinia nodded then cleared her throat. "So, not to be awful..."

"Uh-oh."

"What are you planning to do about the job?"

Jillian had been *not* thinking about it since two nights prior. How could it possibly do her any good *to* think about it? "I don't know, Mal. Right now, the promotion has to be on hold. The money trouble... the investor... this weird competition thing. I'm not even sure my current job will be there by next year."

Malvinia nodded again. "In other words, you're not thinking about it."

"Pretty much," Jillian said.

"Well," Malvinia said, with a sigh, "I suppose I shouldn't be surprised. You've got all the early relationship hormones to deal with, so you're probably only thinking about him and being with him. Why let a pesky little thing like employment bother you?"

"Mal!"

Malvinia laughed. "Oh, sweetie. You know I don't mean that in a mean way. I just wanted to bring it to your attention so that it *might* pass through your thoughts once in a while. Especially in case the situation changes and *if* the promotion possibility reemerges, you're going to be in an interesting position. I don't want you making career decisions while on Oxytocin and Vassopresin."

"Um... what?"

"They're the pair-bonding hormones released during orgasm."

"Oh, God, Mal! Could you not say that so loud?" Jillian was sure she was flushed from head to toe.

"I'm just trying to make sure that you have all the information you need *prior* to any significant decision-making moments. *If* you're on a mind trip from all those great orgasms, you may make a mistake and not know it."

"Please, Mal, I'm begging you. Don't say 'orgasm' again. People can hear you."

Malvinia laughed. "All the women in ear shot should be listening to everything I'm saying. For that matter, so should the men. We both get a dose of each, each time we," Malvinia lowered her voice to a whisper, "orgasm." Then she spoke normally again. "And they cloud your judgment by causing pair-bonding. That's a good thing, from a perspective of family and child-rearing. Perhaps even from a perspective that marriage and permanent relationships appear to increase overall happiness from a statistical perspective. But no one, and I mean *no one*, should ever make important decisions while under the influence.

"Even the cocktail you're on right this very minute, the rush of new love, with all the dopamine, adrenaline, and serotonin, is keeping you from thinking clearly. The levels we're talking about are similar to those when you're taking cocaine. And there are studies that show a brain in the new love stages has a chemistry that's like low grade OCD. That's why you think about your partner all the time."

"Okay, Doctor. Can we end the biochemistry lesson?" Jillian asked.

"I'm only telling you so that you know what's going on in your head. You might have to make a choice between a man and a job. And while I can say that if he's really 'the one' that it isn't much of a contest and I won't blame you if you make the less logical choice in favor of the emotional choice, if he isn't 'the one' and you choose him, you'll be kicking yourself for a very long time."

Jillian swallowed as the buildings seemed to close in on her. It wasn't that Malvinia was being cruel. She was right. It was all Jillian could do not to hate her for it. There was a chance, maybe not much of one with the way things were at the moment at Gardiner D, but a chance all the same that she might find herself in a position where she really did have to choose. It was a depressing thought. But much less depressing than the ones that followed it.

If she *was* actually *forced* to choose, what would she do? She could only hope that if it really came to that, they'd have a few months, or maybe a lot of months, under their belts and she'd be able to feel confident about whether or not they'd last. Would the decision be based on how the relationship was doing that week? Would she take the job and hope that he'd forgive her and stay with her? Would she give it up and hope that she wouldn't end up resenting him for it? *I think I hope that Gardiner D folds.*

Malvinia shook Jillian's arm. "You gotta breathe, Jillian."

Lack of oxygen might explain the feeling that the buildings were all caving in, Jillian thought as she took a deep breath.

"I didn't mean to upset you," Malvinia said. "Really. I'm sorry." She steered Jillian to a bench and made her put her head between her legs. "Breathe. I'm so sorry, Jills. I wasn't trying to freak you out. I'm so sorry.

"I bet it all works out just great. He's going to continue being wonderful and if the job thing comes up, you'll talk it out between you and work it out together."

When she finally sat back up, Jillian looked at Malvinia. She was surprised to see her looking close to tears.

"I'm so sorry," Malvinia said, quietly.

Jillian hugged her. "It's okay, Vi. I know you are just concerned for me."

Malvinia hugged her back tightly. "I want all the best for you." She released Jillian and sat back. "I don't want you to have to choose. I want you to have everything."

Jillian hugged her again. "Thank you. I want you to have everything too."

When they stood again, Malvinia wiped a tear from her cheek. "Okay, I didn't realize how hormonal *I* am, right now. Can you stand a little more of me and we'll get dinner?"

"Oh, I suppose so," Jillian said. "I'll choose you over my new hormonally influential lover for another hour."

Malvinia laughed, it was a bit forced, but not entirely. "Do you think you should be saying the word 'lover' so loud?"

Looping her arm through Malvinia's again, Jillian laughed sincerely. "Yes. And you should feel honored that I'm choosing you over him, since he'd probably be giving me another mind-altering orgasm, if I chose him."

A passing woman gave them a wide-eyed look and they leaned their heads together like teenagers and giggled.

"So how did June leaving start things with May?" George asked.

"She was there with her family, seeing off an Aunt. I didn't notice her in the slightest until she walked up to me and said something about how melodramatic I looked, watching the train go. I was too shocked to respond. She said I looked like I needed a drink. Which I did. And she," Orville paused to laugh, "she took me into the station and got us each a coke. Not quite the drink I needed.

"But we sat down and after a bit she looked me straight in the eyes and said, 'I know you think you're the only person in the whole world who has ever felt like you do. I won't pretend to know exactly how you feel, but I know it hurts. Would it help to talk about it?' I sort of chuckled for a moment, wondering why she'd think I'd want to talk about it. Then it felt serious. Nobody was offering to talk about it, not in so many words. I suppose I could've talked to a lot of people, if I'd wanted. But they weren't so straightforward about it.

"It was a pointless gesture, though. I couldn't have said anything at that point. Not like that. And certainly not to a woman that I sort of knew. A stranger I'd never see again... maybe. But not someone from town. No matter how much it might have helped. So I shook my head.

"She said that was alright and she looked away and we drank our cokes. Then she said she'd see me at the bank and left."

"And that was the beginning?"

"Well, you see, even though I had quite a few months ahead of me that were mostly about misery and grieving for June, May had captured my attention. Not even really thinking about what I doing, I started flirting with her every Friday when I was cashing my check. Frequently asking her when she was going to go out with me. She never acknowledged any of the attempts at flirting or anything else. She just did her job and thanked me for my business in her polite teller voice and with her polite teller smile.

"Annoyed me to no end. So, naturally, I behaved worse. And every now and then I'd see her out with her friends and I always made a point to talk to her and ask her when she was going to go out with me. When she wasn't at the bank, she wasn't as restrained. She'd give me these horrible looks and would tell me things like 'not even if I was the last man on Earth.' Which just made me more determined. I was such an ass. It was like we were back in grade school and I was pulling her pigtails. The only excuse I had was the broken heart I was nursing."

George ran his hand across his mouth, wondering if any of the pranks that he had pulled on Jillian had actually been motivated by a desire to get her to think of him. He certainly hadn't done what he had with that thought in mind, but subconsciously? Maybe. "So you made her angry with you? How did you wind up together?"

"Well, now, let's see. I kept it up for, oh, I suppose it was the better half of a year. I didn't date anyone else. Didn't really want to. I was still thinking about June most of the time. Then, eventually, a couple of my friends started asking me if I was really into May. I denied it, of course. Didn't really think anything much about it. But I kept up the poor behavior.

"It all turned the Friday that she slipped a note into my cash. We'd had a perfectly normal exchange. I was an ass. She was polite. But as I was putting my cash in my wallet, I noticed a piece of paper in with the bills. I read it and looked back at her. She glanced at me and I knew that she knew I'd read it.

"May had asked me to wait for her across the street at the lunch counter. I was surprised. Really surprised. She still had nearly a half hour of work until the bank closed so I spent most of the time vacillating between meeting her at the lunch counter and taking off. I wasn't sure what she meant to do.

"In the end, I did park myself on a stool and waited the remaining minutes for her. She came through the door with an impressive air of cool and calm; it was very bank-like of her. She was dressed in a sort of brown wool suit and a matching hat, with gloves and sensible shoes, of course. And she walked up to the counter and perched on a stool next to me. I waited to see what she would do; I hadn't any of my usual nerve.

"She ordered a coke and I paid Jimmy for it and she exhaled and I could just see the fury in her. It was only time I'd ever been genuinely worried that I was going to end up in a physical confrontation with a woman. And I hadn't the slightest idea what I would do if she hit me. I certainly couldn't hit her back. But if she started to pound on me, I couldn't just take it.

"Whether she'd planned it or not, I don't know, I never asked her. But the way she kept me waiting on whatever was coming was clever on her part, if it was intentional. I got more and more nervous and tense and unsure of myself. By the time she finished her coke and turned to look at me, I probably would have just let her hit me all she wanted, if she'd wanted.

"Thankfully, she didn't hit me. I can tell you from later years that May, even at her angriest, never hit anyone, but I didn't know that then. Anyway, she'd apparently composed herself a bit. She looked at me with what I'd call quiet determination on her face. Well, at first, anyway. She asked me to please quit bothering her.

"I must have smirked or something, because I could see her getting angry again. She took some change out of her bag and slapped it on the counter, to pay for her own coke, and stood up. I opened my mouth to say something, I'm not sure what, but she spoke again first. She said that she wasn't going to put up with my shenanigans any longer and stomped out the door.

"Naturally, I couldn't just let that go. I jumped up, pocketing her money, and followed her out to the street so that we could make a *really good* public scene." Orville shook his head and snorted. "And we outdid ourselves."

"Oh, yeah?" George asked.

"She crossed the street and I shouted at her, and she shouted back at me, it was that bad."

"What were you shouting?"

"Well, at first I followed her out asking what she was talking about, you know, a little righteous indignation. Not that I had any reason to feel righteous or indignant. And, of course, she said I knew exactly what she was talking about and she'd had enough of being treated that way.

"I said, 'What way?'

"She scowled and said that she'd never done anything to me, except to be nice that one time, and if she'd known that trying to show me a little kindness would have brought her such ill-mannered attention, she'd have left me to stew on the platform. That's when she crossed the street.

"I raised my voice a little while she was walking and asked her since when was asking somebody out ill-mannered. She turned once she'd crossed the street and shouted back that I hadn't been asking her out like a gentlemen. She said I'd been behaving like cad.

"Now, the fact that I *had* been behaving badly was entirely beside the point for me, by that time. I was enjoying the argument. So I shouted back, asking her how *gentlemen* behave. And she shouted that a proper invitation included a date, a time, and a description of the activity planned. What I'd been doing was insulting.

"She started walking up the street, so I walked parallel to her on the side I was on and shouted back at her that she should be flattered I was paying her attention. Even across the street I could see her face reddening. She shouted back at me that that she wasn't my type, so why didn't I just leave her alone?

"I yelled back asking her what she meant by *not being my type*. And she shouted back that she knew she wasn't pretty, certainly not as pretty as June. I was a little taken aback by that.

"But she wasn't finished there. She yelled that even if her looks didn't make a difference, then at the very least her moral character wasn't what I was looking for."

Orville sighed and sat back. "I thought that seemed a little over the top. Her taking a swipe at me and my relationship with June like that. I wouldn't admit it to anybody but you, Kid, but um… that shot hurt. Suddenly, I wasn't having fun anymore, I was angry. So I shot back that if she took that kind of attitude toward men who were interested in her she'd be an old maid. That was a nasty thing to say, back then. Don't know about now. But it didn't work the way I'd hoped."

"No?" George asked. He'd never heard any of the story before. All Orville had ever told him was that he'd known May since they were kids. Not friends, but acquaintances. And that she'd worked at the bank. That Orville had adored her, well… that had been evident in other ways. But the antagonism at the beginning was unexpected. *This is almost like me and Jillian, with the fighting. Almost.*

"Oh, no. I should have realized. May was practical. Terribly practical. So when she stopped walking and turned with her fists on her hips, she yelled at me that that was her plan, to be an old maid. But, she shouted, she intended to be a *respectable* old maid. I'll never forget the way she said that. 'I intend to be a *respectable* old maid. And that means I want nothing to do with you, in anyway, ever!'

"I know that by then, people were watching, but I was seeing red. I marched across the street shouting that I was perfectly respectable. And she shouted that I obviously had no idea what folks in town thought of me. And I marched up to her, still shouting even though we were no more than few feet apart, asking what people thought of me.

"She shouted that she was too much of a lady to say. I yelled that she must not be much of lady if she brought it up. She shouted that I wouldn't know a lady if God himself put a halo around her head. I laughed and shouted that if she thought she deserved a halo she ought to be a nun.

"She shouted that if I didn't leave her alone, she'd take the matter to a higher power. I was still on the nun thing and asked if she was going to ask God to strike me down. She shouted, 'No, I'll go to your mother!'"

"You're kidding!" George said, and leaned forward. "*Your mother?*"

"Yes, sir. I was floored too. The next thing she said was that she knew my mother from church and wouldn't hesitate, if I made it necessary."

"Oh, geez. What did you do?"

"I yelled at her that if she really needed to tattle on me to my mother, she should go ahead. She shouted 'Fine!' and took off as quickly as I'd ever seen, the other way along the street, in the general direction of my house."

"Oh, boy. What'd you do then?"

"Why, I took off after her, of course. Grabbed her arm and pulled her to a stop and shouted that she was making a scene and the last thing in the world she really wanted to do was make it worse by embarrassing herself in front of my mother.

"She shouted that if anyone was causing a scene it was me and that I had best let her go immediately. I yelled, 'What if I don't?' She pulled back an arm and for a moment I thought she was going to slap me. But she dropped it backwards and called me a philistine."

George leaned back and let out a low whistle. "She was pushing you as hard as she could, wasn't she?"

Orville chuckled again. "Mm-hmm. Both of us. Pushing and pushing."

"Did you crack? Or did she?"

"I suppose that's a matter of opinion. I didn't take the philistine comment well and I grabbed her other arm, intending to shake her, I think. I had her by her upper arms. But even at that, I guess I had some sense. You know that domestic violence is a big deal now, well, it was then too. Just in a different way. Not a legal thing, a moral thing. Making a public spectacle was bad enough. But once I grabbed hold of her, it was only a matter of time until somebody was going to come break it up, because grabbing a woman like that, it just wasn't done."

"But nobody did?" George asked.

"Nobody had to. I gritted my teeth and asked how she'd dare call me that. But her face wasn't fury anymore. She looked so sad, so hurt. For a moment I thought I was gripping her too hard, but then I knew it wasn't that. You know, one of those moments where you just know things you didn't before?"

George nodded.

"I realized that for all her huff and puff, she wasn't so much mad at me, as she was hurt. I hadn't been irritating her with my weekly rudeness. I'd hurt her feelings. I've never felt quite the same kind of shame as I did at that moment. But it was more than that too. The shame was for myself, but there was empathy, too. Just the look on her face made my heart hurt.

Orville looked down at his hands. "Had I not been in the middle of it all, I might have had time to think about what it meant. But all I knew then was that I had to stop her pain.

"I don't remember exactly what I said. The words just started tumbling out. Something like, 'Oh, gosh, May. I'm so sorry. I didn't mean to...'"

Orville sniffed. "And suddenly she was crying and I was choked up." Orville swallowed hard and George nearly looked away, feeling like he was trespassing in a very private memory, but the need to know, held him motionless. He waited for Orville to continue.

After a few swallows, Orville looked up again, but not at George. He looked straight ahead toward the wall. "I did something pretty unthinkable then. Not as bad putting my hands on her, exactly. But bad enough in its own way. I wrapped my arms around her and hugged her to me, repeating over and over that I was sorry.

"She had her hands at her sides and she kept them there. I remember thinking that I wished she'd either push me or hug me back. Either be affronted or allow me to comfort her. Something other than just crying. When she finally spoke, she was hard to understand, but I made out that she was saying that I was cruel. I loathed myself then, really loathed myself. What could I say or do? Nothing."

"But you did or said something, eventually," George prompted.

Shaking his head slowly, Orville looked back at George again. "I kept saying I was sorry over and over until she finally moved back a step, her head still down so I couldn't see her face, and said, 'I could have really liked you.' My arms fell so fast, they were like lead at my sides. And I knew I'd lost something. Even though it was just a possibility, I'd lost it."

"But you didn't. It worked out," George said.

Orville exhaled slowly. "She was still crying. When she said that, she opened her bag and took out a handkerchief and started to wipe her eyes. I repeated myself with another, 'I'm sorry' and she finally looked up at me. Her eyes were all red and puffy. She said she was going home." Orville fell silent again.

"You let her? You let her just walk away?" George asked.

"I'd already gone over the line," Orville said. "Twice."

"So, what did you do, then? Start groveling the next time you were at the bank?"

"No, Kid. Since I'd already made a scene and gone over the line, I had nothing left to lose. I groveled right then and there, on the sidewalk. I don't recall the exact words I said then, either. Except that I know I said that if she'd give me a chance I'd do it right. If she'd let me, I'd show her that I knew she was a lady. And I begged her to let me take her home."

"What did she do?"

The sides of Orville's mouth twitched up a little. "Well, May said no, but she started walking really slowly and this time it was in the direction of my car. So I walked with her and kept up the groveling. I wish I could remember what I said that made her laugh, but by the time we got to the car, she was laughing. And I drove her home and went in and met her parents."

"Wow," George said. "How did that go?"

"Oh, it wasn't a great experience. She was right about what other people thought of me. All that time I thought June and I had been real successful with hiding the unsavory, I'd been wrong. But I stuck it out. And then we did the most proper thing we possibly could. We dated… at her house. The way people used to, I'm told. I called on her twice a week. I'd go over and we'd sit on the porch and talk, in front of the whole town, it felt like. Then as the weather cooled off even more, I had the thrill of sitting in her parlor with her family for most of the winter. The outside evenings were the ones where we were able to share the most about ourselves.

"That's when she explained her plans at the bank. The manager was supposed to retire in about a year and she'd been working hard, taking classes, and so on to be the most qualified so she'd be promoted to assistant manager. She hoped to be the manager in about fifteen years."

George nodded. "Pretty ambitious back then, wasn't it?"

Orville smiled broadly. "If you'd met May back then, and actually gotten to know her, you'd know that she was very driven. And she was driven in everything she attempted. Before I knew it, I was helping her at the church fundraisers, same committee as my mother, no less. It was impossible to say no when May had something in her head.

"Finally, after almost five months of calling on her, she decided to accept my invitation, made properly with date and time and an actual plan, to actually go out." Orville grinned then. "That was one of the best days of my life, the day I asked her to dinner and she said yes."

Smiling, George said, "Five months of penance."

Orville chuckled. "Yep, five long months. But dinner with her was everything that I could have hoped. The conversation was terrific. And she was sweet and shy and absolutely beautiful.

"After that I found myself sitting in her pew at church, next to her on one side and her father on the other. I should have been on the outside of the group, of course, but he wasn't about to let me that far out of sight. Although I can't imagine what he thought would happen in church. He'd let me take her to dinner, in my car, I'd have thought that would have been much more...

"But, there we were. And that went on for a while. Dinner out Saturday night. Church Sunday morning. Sunday lunch every other week with her family. Sunday dinner every other week with mine."

"And all perfectly innocent," George said.

"Mmm. She'd let me kiss her on the cheek when we said goodbye. And once in a while, she'd kiss me on the cheek. I remember remarking one evening after I took her home from Sunday dinner, that I looked forward to every time that she'd surprise me like that.

"She blushed so... charmingly. I asked her if she'd ever been kissed before. On the lips. She told me it was just the once. Prom night. And she'd slapped him immediately, so it almost didn't count. She was twenty-four and she'd never been properly kissed."

"So," George said, leaning his elbows onto his knees. "Did you kiss her?"

"Not then. I wanted it to be right, you understand. I'd already spent about seven months doing things right. I didn't want to make a mistake at that point. But she surprised me again when I walked her to the door and said goodnight, I leaned over to peck her on the cheek, and she turned and pecked me on the lips. It wasn't much of a kiss, with her tightly puckered lips and the contact only lasting a moment, but my heart pounded in my ears, all the same. It was like I was a boy again, experiencing first love."

"You'd been seeing her for seven months and you'd never kissed?" George asked, and fell back against the sofa. "Seven months?"

Orville shrugged. "She was a nice girl from a nice family and I had a bad reputation. I had to earn my way in."

George shook his head.

"I know it's different now," Orville said. "But, let me tell you there is one thing that the old and proper way has over the new and fast way."

"Ok," George said. "What?"

"May knew I was serious about her. She didn't have to rely on promises that could easily be lies. I demonstrated that she was important to me every time I was in her company. Especially, when I was in her company *and* her family's." Orville leaned forward a little. "Actions speak louder than words, you know."

George nodded. *He's right.* "So what happened, after that?"

"After that, we started negotiating *our* future. She still thought she had a pretty good chance at the assistant manager position. I had over two years left on my contract at the factory as foreman. She encouraged me to start some night classes. It was only a half hour train ride to get to a junior college. That's where she had taken her accounting and business classes. So we both went up on Wednesday nights. I also went up on Thursdays.

"I was taking the basics, so I could transfer some credits and get a jump on the four year degree. She was taking some kind of macroeconomics course. We kept going back and forth on what we'd do after I finished out my contract. I figured I might cut a year off of the time it took to get my degree with the night courses. She still wanted the bank job.

"We were looking at the possibility of some pretty extensive time apart, even if I went to the state college, it was almost four hours away by train so I couldn't live at home and go to school. I was afraid it was going to end up just like things had with June. So, I decided to do the only reasonable thing."

"You didn't break it off, did you?" George asked.

"No, of course not. Losing May was unfathomable. I proposed and told her that I was giving up the school plan. I'd stay on at the factory and she could stay on at the bank."

George sat forward again. "You gave up the school plan?" Orville nodded. "How did you propose and say all this to her?"

"On the train coming home one Wednesday, about nine months since we'd started seeing each other, I told her that I'd been giving it all a lot of thought and that of all the things I wanted, she was the most important. I said that I'd decided I could live without everything else, except her, so I was letting go of any plans that interfered with being near her. And that I hoped she'd do me the honor of being my wife."

"That's pretty good," George said.

Orville chuckled. "It wasn't bad. It could have been better."

"I don't see how."

"I do," Orville said. "But that's water under the bridge."

"Can I assume she said yes?" George asked.

"Actually, she said she needed to think about it. And she wanted me to think about it. She was concerned that perhaps I was making a mistake to give up on school." Orville frowned. "And then June came back to haunt me. May said that if I couldn't give up school for June, it didn't make sense for me to give it up for her.

"That's when I learned she had a real complex about June. I had no idea that the ghost of that relationship was even in her mind at that point, but apparently she was constantly comparing herself to June. That was even the reason she kissed me on the lips that one time. She felt she had too." Orville shook his head. "She assured me that she'd wanted to kiss me too. But, apparently, it was the specter of June that made her do it. She was certain I was going to get tired of her because she wasn't exciting and definitely not pretty.

"That made me angry. It was one thing to be aware that I'd been involved with someone else, the whole town knew, but to compare herself like that and to find herself as wanting? It was ridiculous. She was pretty, you know that, you saw her. At eighty-four she was beautiful.

"And she was smart and selfless and definitely interesting, and well, I don't know what she meant by exciting, because she was exciting to me. So we had another discussion about how I'd never have kept up seeing her so long if she wasn't everything I wanted. I asked her if she was just putting me off because I wasn't everything she was looking for. And I asked if she could forgive me my relationship with June."

Orville grinned again. "She said she'd try, if I'd convince her that it was really her that I wanted. She didn't want to be my second choice. She said, 'Kiss me, Orville, if you really mean it.' I could see what trouble that would be. So, I said that as soon as she agreed to marry me and her father gave us his blessing, I'd kiss her until she was so dizzy she couldn't see straight."

"Dizzy?" George asked, sitting up straight. "You kissed her and made her dizzy?"

"Yep. Why?" Orville asked.

"Never mind," George said, shaking his head. "Finish the story. I won't interrupt again."

"She said she still had to think about it. We drove back from the station in silence. I walked her to her door and she said goodnight and went in with no kiss at all. Not even my usual cheek kiss. I sat in my car for a few minutes trying to figure things out. There was something I'd missed.

"Felt like a real heel when I realized what it was. She'd just turned on the light in her room. So I jumped out the car and grabbed a few pebbles from her neighbors' yard and started throwing them at her window, until she opened it up and asked me what I was doing.

"I called up, in a hushed tone, that I had forgotten to say something, something important. And she asked me what I could possibly have forgotten that couldn't wait until Saturday. I said, 'I love you, May.' I felt lighter than air after that.

"She shook her head and told me to go home. I shouted at her that I loved her and I'd go when she either told me she loved me too or told me she didn't love me at all. And I mean, I shouted. It was as ridiculous as that day in the street. Out of the corner of my eye, I saw a light come on in a neighbors' window.

"She repeated that I should go home. So I shouted louder. 'I love you, May. I asked you to marry me. Give an answer.' Instead, the front door opened and her father came out."

"Oh, boy," George said.

"No, it was fine. He calmly asked me if I'd really proposed to her. I said yes, and that I'd planned to ask his permission once I knew her answer. He said that usually it was done the other way 'round, permission first. I started to apologize, but he held up his hand and then said that we had his permission, so it was close enough. Then he brought me into the house and called May downstairs. He told us to sit at the kitchen table and talk it out. Her mother came in for a moment and made sure we each had a cup of coffee and then they both disappeared upstairs.

"May turned on the radio, low, but enough to cover our voices a little. The first thing she said to me was to ask why I'd made such a scene outside. I told her that she was special and that I was willing to make a complete fool of myself for her, because I loved her madly. And she looked down into her coffee. For a moment I really thought she was going to tell me that it wasn't going to work, or something. But she looked back at me and said that she loved me too and that she'd be proud to be my wife.

"I'm pretty sure I cried a little at that point. I took her in arms, which I hadn't done since that day nearly a year before, and held her for a while. That time, she held me too. The Platters, *Only You*, started playing on the radio and *that's* when I kissed her, for real, for the first time. And it was… glorious.

"We were married about three months later and never looked back."

George shook his head. "But, you went to school."

"Yep, May made me. We discussed, she called it a renegotiation, the future again after we were engaged and she told me that it wasn't okay for me to give up my dream of being an engineer. I told her she couldn't give up her dream at the bank. That's when she said that the bank wasn't a dream as much as it was a plan. She'd made the plan when she came to the conclusion that boys weren't interested in her. She'd had three dates in high school, including the huge disappointment prom night, and nothing after graduation.

"She'd decided that although she wasn't pretty or interesting, she was smart, so she could take care of herself. She'd planned to buy a small house when she became the assistant manager and take in single girls as lodgers. But since it turned out that she wasn't going to be all alone after all, she could work wherever I went to school.

"So I went and she came with me. After I earned my degree, I got a really good job, we settled, and she didn't work anymore to stay home and be a mother."

"And you lived happily ever after," George said, not entirely sarcastically.

Orville laughed and said, "We never went to bed angry. There were a few late nights, working things out. But we always worked everything out."

"That's beautiful," George said, and thought about the song Jillian had sent him. "So why wasn't *Only You* your song?"

"It was for a few years, until May went crazy over Sam. We picked *Cupid* because," Orville paused, "well, for a private reason, actually."

George cocked his head. "Oh, come on. What could possibly be private after all you've told me?"

Orville leaned toward George and lowered his voice. "Okay. But you asked. We conceived our first child to *Cupid*."

George shook his head and started to laugh as his personal cell phone rang.

CHAPTER SIXTEEN

Thank God, I'm home. Just the *ding* of the elevator as it reached her floor made Jillian feel better. Despite the overall support from Malvinia, the day had certainly taken its toll. Jillian actually took off her shoes before exiting the elevator. *Mental note to self. Never start a relationship during the middle of a work crisis, with a man that one of your friends wants, ever again. Too much at once!* And she hadn't even begun to deal with *his* friends yet.

She sighed as she stepped into the hall. *Far too much.* She was starting to mentally compose her to do list when she looked toward her door and came to a stop as she blinked to convince herself she wasn't seeing things. "George?"

Oh, shit. This was a bad idea. George scrambled to his feet from his position on the hallway floor leaning against her door. "Hi." As Jillian walked up to the hallway, George thought he saw a mix of confusion and a little pleasure, maybe. Her mouth was tipped up at the edges.

"Hi," Jillian said. "I thought I was supposed to call you..."

George closed his eyes a second and fought the embarrassment. "That was the plan, yes. But..." He opened his eyes and watched her walk the last few paces.

"But..." Jillian said.

"But, I just..." George trailed off as he saw her looking over his face. *I must look like I've been hit by truck.*

"What's wrong?" Jillian said, quickly transferring her keys to her left hand with her coat and shoes, so she could touch his face with her right. *You look like you've been run over by a bus.* "What happened?"

George closed his eyes at her touch and tried to verbalize for a moment and then shrugged as he opened his eyes. "Tonight turned out to be a really bad night. I just wanted to see you. If you'd like, I can go. I know just showing up here was... inappropriate."

Jillian nodded and George thought she was telling him to go, but she said, "I've had a rough night too. You're just what the doctor ordered." She grinned just a little thinking about Malvinia's orgasm commentary. "Come in." She dropped her hand and transferred her keys back to her right hand, but she continued to look at George and watched his face relax a little. She bit her lip and then told him the whole truth. "I'm glad you're here." She heard him respond with an exhale in a rush.

"Thank God," he mumbled to himself.

Jillian unlocked her door and started to walk in, but stopped as her foot kicked something on the floor. Both she and George looked down at two bags that had been hidden behind him. Jillian recognized one of them as his work bag. The other looked like... "An overnight bag?" Jillian asked, and looked up at George.

George felt his face warm a little. "That is... purely precautionary." He shrugged again. "To save time in the morning... you know, if... if I can stay."

Jillian stepped over the bag and said, "Come in, give me five minutes to change my clothes, and then you're going to tell me exactly what's happened."

He brought in his bags and set them next to the sofa, while Jillian locked the door behind them and set her things in their usual places, hanging up her coat and then walking over to George with a hanger. He took off his coat and handed it to her. She draped the coat over the arm of the sofa and dropped the hanger, then reached up and lifted her arms around him. "It's going to be okay," she said, quietly. "Whatever it is."

He rapidly exhaled through his nose, leaned his head down to touch hers, and put his arms around her. "You're an angel," he said, as he closed his eyes.

She squeezed tightly, wondering what could possibly have happened since she'd last seen him. After a minute, she released him a little and said, "All right. Have a seat or help yourself to a drink. I'll just be a few minutes." She hung up his coat and as she walked into her bedroom, she called over her shoulder, "I don't have any beer, but there's wine in the fridge and the hard liquor, if you want it, is in an upper cabinet at the end, next to the one with the glasses."

George watched her walk into the bedroom and chose... *Neither.* He could get a drink anytime, but watching her change her clothes was not an every moment opportunity. *And a much better distraction than a drink any day, any hour, any minute...*

Jillian had her skirt off and was sitting on the bed removing a stocking when she noticed George in the doorway. She gasped and put a hand to her heart. "You startled me."

"I'm sorry. You didn't close the door," George said.

She went back to removing her stocking and said, "So you decided to be a voyeur."

"No, you're just far more appealing than a drink."

She laughed. "Very nice. Are you going to stay in the doorway or come in?"

"Oh, I'd planned on staying in the doorway," George said, as she removed her remaining stocking. "But I can come in, if you'd like."

Jillian stood up and took her skirt into her closet. "No. Stay there. You're going to tell me what's wrong, once I've changed."

"Can I ask one favor?" George said, running his hand over the door frame. The wood had a nice finish and was cool to the touch. A nice solid sensation to keep him rooted in the reality of her apartment as opposed the reality outside it that he was trying so desperately to avoid.

"Perhaps," Jillian said.

"It's not bad, just a curiosity I've had all day."

"Well?"

"Can I see your underwear?"

Jillian leaned her head out of the closet to look at him. "Are you kidding me?"

"I've been wondering what was under your clothes all day," George said, with a wide grin.

"You've been…" Jillian said. "All day?"

George shrugged. "I didn't see you get dressed. I was busy with breakfast."

Jillian ducked back into the closet and called out, "Just because it's been implied that you can stay the night again, doesn't mean anything more than that. And I want to hear what's wrong."

"Agreed," George said. "But I don't see how that's in conflict with seeing your underwear." When Jillian's laughter floated out of the closet, George laughed too, but he still said, "Since you asked, I'm not kidding."

Leaning just her head out of the closet again, Jillian gave him a quizzical look. "So… does that mean sex is your drug of choice?"

"What?" George asked.

She leaned back in and said, "It's obvious you're upset. Alcohol is a socially acceptable drug that many people use to relax when they're upset, but when I suggested you get a drink, you didn't. And while you look awful, you don't appear high or crashing after being high. Instead you're asking to see my underwear. Are you hoping to use sex to distract yourself?"

"I guess, in addition to being an MBA and a jazz pianist, you're an amateur psychologist?"

"Answer the question, please," Jillian said.

George crossed his arms. "I'll make you a deal. Show me the

underwear and you can ask me anything you want."

"Make that *answer* anything I want and you have a deal. I'm fairly certain I already have the right to ask."

"I'm not that tricky. I meant that I'd answer. But fine. It's a deal," George said.

Jillian stepped out of her closet barefoot, wearing her jeans and a near nude color satin bra with white lace trim, carrying what George assumed was a t-shirt. She lifted her arms out from her sides with a shrug. "Good enough?"

George tilted his head. *Lord, are you hot… and in satin, not lace. Evidence that you wore that lace last night for me.* "Very nice, but um…" He lifted a hand and motioned to her jeans.

"Seriously?"

"Anything you want to know," George said. "I'll tell you anything you want to know."

"Why Grandmother, what big eyes you have!" Jillian said.

"What?"

Jillian unzipped her jeans. "Little Red Riding Hood. The wolf tricked her into coming too close." She slid her jeans down just enough that he could see that her panties matched. "So, is this enough?"

"Yes," George said. "That answers that question." Jillian zipped her jeans and pulled her t-shirt over her head and George started laughing as he read her shirt. "*It's not a bug. It's a feature.* Very nice."

Walking toward him with enough speed that George knew to get out of the way, Jillian smiled and said, "I thought you'd like it. I also have *If at first you don't succeed, call it version 1.0.* And *Programmers do it in Java.*" She passed by him and through the door and into the kitchen. "Sit down. I'm fixing us a drink. What do you want?"

He shrugged again. "What do you have?"

Jillian laughed. "Well, I guess you don't want wine, then. Hard liquor, it is." George sat down on the sofa and waited for Jillian to bring him a glass and he took a sip of what turned out to be a really smooth scotch.

When she'd seated herself next to him with a glass in her hand, he turned to face his body toward her. He looked into her eyes for a few moments and then shook his head. "I don't know where to begin."

Jillian was tempted to quote *Disney's Alice in Wonderland* to him, telling him to start at the beginning and stop at the end. But he still looked awful, even after the strange underwear request, so she hadn't the heart to be glib. "Start anywhere, back track in the middle if you have too. It really doesn't matter."

He let out a really long breath and Jillian felt as though she'd taken in whatever he'd just exhaled as her chest and throat tightened and she had to blink to stop a tear. *A bit overly empathetic, there girl, just relax. And relax him while you're at it.* "Okay," Jillian set down her glass and reached for his shoulders. "Come here." A little shifting, twisting, and turning was all it took to get Jillian to the end of the sofa and George lying back into her, with his head resting against her chest. She started to run her fingers through his hair and then massaged his scalp. "You're safe here," she said, quietly. "Whatever is going on, it's outside that door. You don't need to worry about anything. Not the right choice of words or the wrong ones. It's all good. Start anywhere. Just tell me anything and everything."

He took another sip of the scotch and then put his glass down on the coffee table. "God, that feels good," George said, delaying talking again with a moment of a little honesty. "You've got magic fingers."

"Thank you," Jillian said, but stopped there in hopes that the silence would propel him forward.

"Okay," George said, with a sigh and closed his eyes. "There's big stuff and little stuff. The little stuff includes the fact that I agreed to be Taro's Best Man, which means that I need to organize a Bachelor Party in the next few weeks. I know that probably sounds stupid, but I've never done it before and it's just not something I need to deal with right now. I could be lazy and just plan something at a strip club, I suppose. But, Taro deserves something more."

Behind him, Jillian chuckled. "You should ask him. He might be plenty happy with a strip club."

"Yeah," he said. "And then there's the list you gave me."

"The list?" Jillian quit rubbing his head for a moment while she thought of her list in or on her desk. He hadn't seen that, had he?

"I'm still no closer to figuring out who did all that stuff then when you gave it to me." He stopped a moment and Jillian, having realized he was talking about the prank list, started rubbing his scalp again. "It's really bothering me that people think that I... I would do some of those things. I didn't."

Jillian rubbed a little harder. "I believe you," she said, quietly.

"Do you?" George asked.

"Of course, I do."

He reached for and clasped one of her hands in his and brought it down to his mouth to kiss it. "Thank you," he said, softly.

As soon as he released her fingers, she flattened her palm to his cheek and smiled at the slight roughness. "You've got a bit of stubble here."

Taking her hand again, he massaged her fingers. "I guess I was in such a rush to get here that I forgot to clean up. I'll take care of it later."

She smiled wider and slid her hand back to continue his scalp massage. "Are you going to tell me about the *big stuff*?"

"Yes," George said, and exhaled again, then reached over and collected his glass. He took a much bigger sip than he had before, hoping it would be mentally bracing. It wasn't, but he managed to start all the same. "My uncle is really, really sick," he pushed out quickly. "Really, really sick."

"Oh?" Jillian asked, as she rubbed behind his ears and he sighed in response. "I'm so sorry to hear that."

"It gets worse. My mother keeps calling and calling and calling. She wants me to come home for Thanksgiving because he may not make it until Christmas."

"That's not a problem," Jillian said. "I'll figure out how to work with your group and still keep everything quiet. I'll cover whatever needs covering. You've nothing to worry about."

"You're sweet, Angel," George said, as he took one of her hands in his again. "I'm not worried about getting away. Not really. For a family emergency, I'm sure I could work it out.

"But I don't know that I can stand it, I mean, to go and see Uncle George is one thing. But sitting down with my family while he's dying is entirely different. I hate visiting enough normally and this time everything will just be magnified."

With her free hand, Jillian gently massaged George's temple. She assumed that it must feel good because he let go of her other hand and sighed loudly. Lifting her other hand to his temple she began to rub. It was tempting to prod him, to ask why he hated visiting home so much that he'd be tempted to ignore that his uncle was dying. She refrained, though, hoping that he'd share on his own. She'd seen his face. *The last thing I want to be is more pressure.* "Does that feel good?"

"God, yes. Where did you learn this?"

"Actually, I had a hairstylist who used to do scalp massage on all her clients. The level of pressure I use, though, is a guess."

"The temple rub you're doing now is marvelous."

Smiling, Jillian managed to drop a kiss a top his head. "Good."

"I knew I wanted to be with you tonight. But I didn't imagine it would be quite like this," George said.

"How was it supposed to be?" Jillian asked.

George tilted his head back, sliding down her stomach, so that he could see her inverted smiling face. "I don't know. But I didn't expect you to make me feel this relaxed with so little effort on your part."

"I'm glad I could help." *I wish he'd tell me more. At least about his parents. Talk it out.*

"Now," George said, sat up, and twisted a little to see her face. "What's been so awful for you?"

Jillian wanted to reach out to touch him again, but she didn't. "Just a bunch of foolishness. My friend Christy, I gave you a note from her, she was quite interested in you. She didn't take it well that we're together."

"You have got to be joking," George said, and reached a hand to her cheek. "I was never going to call her."

"No?" Jillian asked. *Oh, I want so much to believe it.*

"No," George said. "How could I? If I did, no matter how it turned out, you'd never have gone out with me later. Calling her would have meant giving up on the possibility of us."

"Oh, really? You thought about that when I gave you the note?"

Running his hand up her cheek to push her hair back, George weighed his answer. "Not in so many conscious thoughts, no. But I can tell you that I haven't seen that slip of paper since you gave it to me. I don't know if I dropped it or if it's still in my pants or I threw it away, because I never noticed it was missing until you mentioned her. I never once thought about calling her."

Just a few quick movements and Jillian was on her knees, leaning down. "George," she whispered.

He still had his hand in her hair and he guided her head toward his. Softly, just letting their lips brush together, George kissed her and felt the remaining weight lift from his shoulders as he gave all of himself to the task of loving her.

"I've really scratched you," George said, as he gently ran a hand down Jillian's neck. "You should have asked me to shave."

Jillian laughed and let her fingers run along his ribs. "I can live with a little beard burn." She moved from her pillow to drop her cheek against his chest.

He began to draw little circles on her back. "You asked me earlier about sex being my drug of choice." He waited for her to make a little mmm-hmm sound. "I still say no, because I think *you* are. I feel... so amazing right now."

Giggling again, Jillian kissed his chest. "Mmm. Me t-" A sudden appearance by Charlie interrupted Jillian.

"Meow!"

"Oh, dear. He's hungry," Jillian said, and started to move.

"Now, wait a minute," George said, as he quickly slid his arms around her. "You aren't getting up are you? That'll be twice we didn't enjoy the afterglow."

Jillian kissed him again, despite the stubble, and then moved away.

"Meow!"

She sighed. "He's only going to get louder. If I'd been thinking, I'd have fed him when we came in. But I suppose, there we are."

"Meow!"

George sat up and frowned as Jillian grabbed her t-shirt. "Tell me something. Why do you have programming joke t-shirts? Did your team give them to you for being such a great boss?"

Jillian twisted from her spot at the edge of the bed to look at him. She ignored the loud meow at her feet for a moment. "No. You really don't know? My undergraduate degree?"

"Yes?" George asked, shaking his head a little.

Jillian turned around again and found her panties. When she'd slid them on, she stood and looked at George, covered to his waist in her sheets, leaning up on his elbow, looking marvelously rumpled, and grinned at him. "I have a Bachelor's in Computer Science with a minor in Business."

"No!" He sat up.

"Meow!"

"Yes, Charlie, Darling." Jillian started out of the bedroom but called back to George. "I'll just be a minute. If you want me to bring you anything, just say so."

"Oh, I don't need anything. Just you, Sweetheart," George muttered to himself as he wrapped as arm around a knee to give himself a little support. "I can't believe you. Have you actually programmed as a job?"

"Yep!"

"My word. You're a geek, you know," he said.

She walked back into the room, grinning. "I know."

"I can't believe I didn't catch it when you were talking about *Hitchhiker's Guide To The Galaxy* last night. I made love to a geek."

Jillian crawled onto the bed and up toward George so that he lay back down for her to hover over him. "You poor thing. Deceived and used. You must be so disappointed."

He reached up to slip his hands into her hair again. "You mistake my meaning. Deceived? Yes. Disappointed? Never. More like incredibly turned on. A woman who can code. How hot is that?"

Giggling, Jillian leaned lower and whispered in his ear. "Should I warn Ishi and Irene?"

George rolled and knocked Jillian onto her side, their faces just a few inches apart. "Who?" He asked, with a grin.

"Good answer," Jillian said, and closed the distance to kiss him, but then pulled back. "You realize you're a geek too."

An unbidden snort erupted from George. "I'm not a geek. I'm a jock."

"Oh, right. Sure," Jillian said, with no restraint on the sarcasm.

"No, I am. I played basketball in school. Jock." He slid his hand down her back to pull her closer, although with the sheet between them and still under her pulled taut, so she still wasn't quite against him.

"I played basketball in high school. That didn't make me any less of a geek."

"Hmm," George said. "I guess *that* explains the three point shot that was all net. I wondered if that was luck or talent or skill."

Jillian placed a quick kiss on his lips. "A little of all three. I haven't played in a while. Did you play in college?"

"Sort of. I had the partial scholarship, but I didn't see much court time, mostly bench. Trained with the team, of course, but I just couldn't make starting line-up. I like to blame it mostly on my height. I was never going to make it as a pro, just for that alone. But the scholarship mostly paid for tuition. So I did what was necessary for the scholarship and started playing in the rec leagues."

"What's your position?"

George's mouth quirked a little, but he stayed on topic instead of making the easy joke. "Small Forward."

Jillian didn't resist playing blue. "I *definitely* wouldn't say *small*."

George laughed. "Thank you."

"But *forward*, well…"

"Uh-huh. What was your position?" George asked.

With a little hesitation, Jillian answered, "Point Guard."

"Yep," George said, nodding. "I can see that. Coach on the floor. Focused on seeing the plays rather than making the scores yourself."

"My three point shot helped me hold the position. That was the when-all-else-fails backup play."

"You are something. We have to play sometime. If you whip me, I'll start calling you a jock instead of a geek."

Jillian moved her arm up under her head. "I don't want to be a jock. I'm happy to be me."

"Good for you," George said, as he shifted under the sheet to snug up against her. "I like you just the way you are."

"Say that aga-" Jillian's phone rang with a light chirp and her eyes slid to the side. "Oh, no."

"What?"

Rolling away from George to grab her cell, Jillian took a deep breath. Instead of answering George, she answered the phone. "Hi, Mom."

"Oh," George said, quietly.

"Hello, Jillian." Her mother's voice came through the handset with the usual familiarity. "Is everything all right?"

"Of course, Mom," Jillian said, as she sat up. "Why would something be wrong?"

"Did anything… happen yesterday?"

"Mom, what do you think happened?" George sat up next to her and Jillian looked over at him. His presence really improved her bed. It was going to be hard to converse with her mother if she looked at George. She turned away and tried to focus.

"Leslie came by today."

"Okay," Jillian said, and waited.

"She said," Jillian's mother paused. "She said that she saw you last evening. Downtown. There was a police man."

Oh, no, no, no, no, no, no. "Right. Right, last night."

"Were you drinking?"

Jillian got up from the bed and started pacing. *Oh, no. What do I say?*

"That wasn't a sobriety test, was it?"

"No. No, of course not."

"Well?"

Jillian stopped walking and pushed her hair back from her face with her free hand. *Well... oh, just Hell.* "I was the passenger."

The silence couldn't have lasted more than a few seconds, but the absence said as much, if not more than the words that followed. "Then why, exactly, were you outside the car? Don't the police usually ask drivers to exit vehicles?"

"I don't know." *That's certainly true enough.*

From a few feet away, George whispered, "Your mother knows about the cop?"

Jillian glanced at George and nodded with a frown on her face followed by a shrug of her shoulders, while her mother went on. "What exactly happened?"

Tilting the phone away from her head, Jillian closed her eyes and tried to think of a satisfactory explanation. *If I'd any brains, I'd have lied right away. But, noooo!* "I, um, well..."

"Jillian?" The tone had dropped just enough to be discernible. Her mother was about to lose her patience.

"Alright, Mom. If you really want to know..." Jillian glanced at George again; he'd raised his eyebrows and was waiting expectantly. She held back the sigh. "If you really must know, I was on a date and the officer had concerns about a display of public affection."

Again, silence. And this time it continued until Jillian couldn't take it anymore. "Mom?" She started pacing the room again.

"What kind of *display*?"

Oh, Heaven help me. This is awful, just awful. Even though the conversation was over the phone, Jillian couldn't help but hang her head and she felt herself begin to blush with embarrassment. "We were just kissing, Mom. I don't know why he bothered us."

"Just kissing? And a police officer asked you to step out of the car?"

Jillian glanced at George again. His face appeared a mixture of concern and curiosity. And he was still in her bed, propped up against a pillow, with the sheet just covering his lap. "Yes. Just kissing." *It was another two hours, at least, before we were naked.*

"Who? Who were you kissing?"

Shit. I can't say just 'some guy' because she'd flip and so will he. Oh! This is soooo not the right way for her to find out about us. "George Crewes, my, um, my boyfriend."

This time, instead of silence, she could hear her mother talking in the background to her father. But George smiled at her, and rather broadly, at that. Yes, he was pleased. She smiled back at him. Maybe it wasn't the right way for her parents to find out, but she supposed it was good that she'd told them.

Waiting for her mother to speak to her again, Jillian moved back to the bed. George put his arm around her as she leaned her back against his side, and kissed her just above her ear and whispered, "Thank you."

She sighed lightly and tilted her head to rest against him. There was no way he could know the true gravity of what she'd just done, but he apparently had some idea about it.

"Jillian?" Her father's voice emerged from the phone speaker.

She sat up straight as her heart started to pound. "Dad!"

"We want to meet him, your… friend. On Saturday. We'll drive in and have dinner at six."

"Oh, no," Jillian shook her head. "I'm sorry. That won't be possible. There is this project at work and everyone is working weekends. Maybe in a few weeks or-"

"And you can't get away for a six o'clock meal? What is the project?"

"No, Dad, it's just… he has plans on Saturday. It just won't-"

George had leaned forward. "We should go," he whispered.

"Hold on, Dad." Jillian turned toward George and tilted the phone away from her mouth. "What!?" She whispered.

"Your folks want to have dinner, right?"

"Yes," Jillian said. "This Saturday at six. You have plans with Orville…"

"Ask them if seven is too late."

"George, I don't think…"

He raised his eyebrows and cocked his head. "They know I exist because of the cop. I don't think we're going to get away with putting this off for very long."

She closed her eyes and leaned forward to put her head against his chest, lowering her phone to the bed. "You really don't know what you're getting into. You really don't."

He kissed the top of her head. "I'd rather plan it than have your dad track me down and show up at my door at 2 am with a shotgun or something."

That did it. The shame of how she'd been caught, the panic at the thought of introducing a man she barely knew to her parents, and then the unbelievable absurdity that he *wanted* to meet them. She started laughing.

He put his arms around her and inhaled the scent of her hair. "Your dad's waiting."

"Ugh," she said, and lifted the phone to her ear without moving away from him. "Ok, Dad. If we can move it to seven, then we're on for Saturday."

Her father harrumphed and then said, "I'll try and get a reservation at a decent restaurant and I or your mother will call you. We'll see you and… what is his name?"

"George Crewes."

"We'll see you and George on Saturday, promptly at seven."

"Yes, Dad."

"Goodnight, Jillian."

"Goodnight." She dropped the phone next to her and still didn't move away from George. "Oh, what have we done?"

"Well, I suppose we've made plans for Saturday," George said, lightly.

"No," Jillian said. "We've sentenced *us* to a premature death."

George moved his hands to her shoulders and pushed her back. "Oh, gee. Thanks," he said when she looked up at him. "You know, I may not be the guy your parents envisioned for you, but I will try."

"No, no," she said, and shook her head. "It's not you, it's them. They haven't liked anyone I've dated since high school. And I think they only liked those guys because they knew those relationships weren't going to last. I hate to think what they're going to say, especially about the cop and everything.

"Don't take it personally when they don't approve of you."

George's eyes widened a little. "They won't approve of me? Not at all?"

Jillian shook her head.

"Oh, come on," George said. "Apart from our being caught necking in a car, what's wrong with me? I have a house and an education and a job."

"There's nothing wrong with you," Jillian replied, rubbing a hand on his neck. "The house will be in your favor, for certain. But when they find out you don't have a car… they'll think you're a bit eccentric. And your job won't win you any points."

"You have the same job," he pointed out as he ran his fingers through her hair.

"Yes, and they don't approve of it for me, either."

George frowned. "And what do they expect of you?"

"My mother wanted a concert pianist."

"And your father?"

"Something in the Arts. Something lady-like. He'd have preferred an operatic singer, I think. Or maybe a poet."

"They really don't approve you? You're successful in your field."

Jillian nodded. "I'm still a bit of a disappointment to them, I'm afraid."

"I can't believe that," George said.

"It's true."

"But you live close to them. And you sounded happy about it when you told me."

"I am happy to live near them. I love them very much. And I enjoy seeing them most of the time. Hopefully, they'll be on their best behavior and you'll see why. They're really quite wonderful people. Most of the time." *When I'm not the topic of conversation.*

"You sure don't sell them that way."

"You're right," Jillian said, and covered her face with her hands. "I'm being terrible. I really shouldn't."

George pulled her hands down from her face. "Okay, so... Let's deal with all this on Saturday. And I'll surprise you by making a dazzling impression and they'll surprise you by liking me and all will be right with the Universe."

"Goodness, all?"

"Well, close," George said, suddenly grinning. "But we're going to have to actually have a nice, relaxed afterglow, before we can say that. So far, we're zero for two."

"I'd still say it's nice," Jillian said, putting a pout on her face.

"Tell you what," George said. "Take off your clothes and come back under the covers with me and I'll give you half credit for this one."

"You'll give me...?" Jillian started. "Oh, very funny," she finally grinned back at him. "You know, if you have such a desperate need for a relaxing afterglow, you could have been the one rubbing my temples."

"You're right. It never occurred to me that rubbing your temples would keep you from jumping out of bed, the minute we've finished, to feed Charlie and chit-chat with your folks. My bad. You'll just have to teach me how to best meet your... needs, that way." He sighed. "But, in the meantime..." He grabbed the hem of her t-shirt and tugged just a little. "What do we think?"

She raised her arms over her head. "You tell me..."

CHAPTER SEVENTEEN

Thursday began with a nice, happy buzz for Jillian. Although she was dreading dinner with her parents, there had been something freeing about telling them about George, and she'd slept deeply and woken refreshed before the alarm chimed. George had stirred next to her when she woke and they'd made love again.

After she'd been in her office for a few minutes, put her things away, and retrieved the files she intended to work on, she looked up to see Sergei in her doorway and she realized that she'd been humming and moving a little to the song in her head.

She blinked, wondering if her eyes were playing tricks on her and then felt herself flushing, just slightly.

"Good morning," Sergei said, through a slightly quirked mouth.

"Er, yes, good morning." Jillian stumbled over her words, and then she recovered from her surprise and embarrassment enough to form a coherent thought. "Is there anything I can help you with?"

Sergei had his hands in his pockets and he shrugged, his face going serious. "I was going to... but, now." He shrugged again. "Are you planning to...? Did George invite you to our game tonight?"

Jillian's mind raced as she tried to figure out why Sergei would ask. But for all the reasons she could think up, she still wouldn't know unless she asked. "Yes. He did. May I ask why you're asking?"

Sergei tapped his foot and answered. "I wanted to be sure that you were coming." His lips formed a reluctant smile. "I think he really wants you there. And we've all had a... sort of... well; we haven't all gotten on very well. But, I hope you'll come. For George."

"I'm probably going to be a few minutes late, but I'm coming." Jillian said.

"Good," Sergei said, and walked up to her, taking his right out of his pocket to produce a folded sheet of paper. "That's where we're playing, in case he didn't give you the address, yet."

She took the paper. "Thank you."

Sergei nodded. "Yep." Then he turned and left her office.

"Did that just happen?" Jillian asked herself, in a low mumble. She opened the paper. It was the same address that George had given her, so it wasn't a mean joke. Sergei was genuinely making certain she was coming to the game. *Wow.*

George's Thursday was a mix of emotion and exhaustion. While early on the previous evening Jillian had relaxed him and relieved more than just his stress, she'd also hidden from him while they'd made love. Although he wasn't certain that it was intentional, it sure seemed that way because she'd closed her eyes, kissed him, and at times even tucked her head against him, blocking any chance for *the whatever* to happen again.

So instead of sleeping well, he'd lain awake wondering why she wouldn't open up to him again and worse, why he'd been unable to broach the topic of *the whatever* with her. Since he hadn't brought it up, essentially, it was his fault. He'd seen something beautiful and amazing in her the night before, maybe what she'd seen wasn't beautiful, maybe it was frightening. But he had trouble believing that; if he was frightening, why would she have kept on seeing him at all, let alone get into a bed with him again? It just didn't make sense. It was up to him to talk to her about it. But he wasn't about to wake her up to talk about it. It would just have to wait.

Why did she hide? Why wasn't she willing to open up to me like that again? He couldn't stop thinking about it. *Maybe she wasn't really hiding. Maybe it was just how she felt at the time.* He hadn't wanted to demand that she look at him. He'd wanted her to give it freely.

It was all he could do to lie still and all the while Jillian slept soundly.

He'd dozed off in the wee hours, only to waken when she'd stirred and they'd made love again, this time in the dark with the lights off, denying him yet again of any possibility of the special connection and leaving him feeling irritated and cheated. While he'd showered, he'd pondered how quickly he'd become so dissatisfied when everything was so good, with the minor exception that he wanted *the whatever* again. He decided to blame his dissatisfaction on the rest of the excitement in his life. After all, he was looking at the prospect of losing his job, meeting her parents in a few days, and losing his uncle. *Things aren't really good.*

All the same, he did his best to keep his dissatisfaction from Jillian. *Thirty-six hours into a relationship is a bit early to be griping. Especially about sex. Particularly when we're having it frequently. God, I cannot screw this up, not this fast. I need to figure this out.*

But hiding anything meant subterfuge and he was too tired to be any good at it in person. After a putting his coat on the rack in his office, he picked up his office phone and called Jillian, telling her that he was going to work in his office rather than the conference room which had seemed to be the unspoken plan. She'd said, 'ok' in a soft, questioning tone leaving him remorseful, but uncertain how to take it back without making a bigger deal of it.

Shit! I'm screwing it up.

He picked up the receiver again and then put it down, unsure of what he'd say. Maybe he could work for an hour, get his mind on something else, and then ask if she wanted to sit in the conference room again.

He dropped into his desk chair. *This is not good.* He rubbed his hands over his face, then setup his laptop and started it booting. At least that was a normal thing to do. Once everything was up and running he stood up, stretched, and headed to the break room for coffee. *Maybe that'll help, even though the two cups I had at Jillian's didn't.*

Ishi was in the break room with Faisal chattering about a television show that apparently came close to accurately portraying cybersecurity and hacking. She didn't stop talking when George entered; though he saw her eyes move toward him and stay there for more than a moment.

He filled a cup with the marginally intolerable coffee and added sugar and creamer to make it marginally tolerable. At least it smelled good and it would help his synapses fire periodically.

As George turned to leave the break room, Ishi stopped talking to Faisal mid-sentence and raised her voice to George's back. "You look like shit."

He pivoted to face Ishi and Faisal.

"Everything okay?" Ishi asked, before George could say anything.

He shook his head and smiled faintly, shocked by her bluntness, but warmed a little by her concern. "No, Ishi, it's not. But thank you for asking."

"You didn't look like this when you came in," Ishi said. "Just tired. Maybe a little constipated. What changed? Is it bad news? Should we be worried?"

Geez, Ishi! You have the opposite problem, verbal diarrhea. It wasn't the first time he'd seen proof she had no filter. Although it was one of the more interesting verbal dumps she'd ever laid on him. The worst had been when she hadn't been happy with an appraisal. The only reasons she was still at Gardiner D were that when she'd let loose the door had been closed and she'd kept her voice down. George knew what an amazing programmer she was and that she often spoke up about things that needed to be addressed, so he basically let her get away with it, within certain bounds.

"Everything that's bothering me is personal." *Mostly.*

"You and Jillian have a fight?" Ishi continued.

"No," George said, firmly. "Do you recall the conversation about boundaries?"

Ishi put her hand on her hip. "This is one of *those* times, is it?"

"Yes," George said, and left the break room. He purposely walked passed Jillian's office on the way back to his, Ishi's question about them having a fight in the forefront of his mind. She was typing on her computer and appeared lost in thought. *To disturb or not to disturb? That is the question. Actually, no. It's more like 'what do I say if I do disturb?'*

George didn't stop.

He returned to his office and tried to work. For all the distraction he'd had the day before in the conference room flirting with Jillian, he'd had fun with the appraisals. With the prospect of writing appraisals alone staring him down, it was just work.

"Suck it up," he muttered to himself. He opened Vidar's file, picked up a pen, and began to make notes.

By lunch, Jillian had shifted from confused about George's behavior to upset. She was ready to climb the walls with her teeth. All morning, she'd waited and waited for any kind of communication from George. She'd even kept her personal phone on her desk, just in case. But there hadn't been a single blip, beep, ping, or bong. Absolutely nothing. Not even an invite to coffee.

"Well, this isn't who we are, is it?" She asked herself, and pushed back from her desk. *We can allow him to set appropriate limits for himself in the office. But now it's lunch time. Now, we negotiate.*

Knocking softly on his open door, she watched him drop his pen and look up at her. His eyes were drooping and although his mouth turned up a little at her, it wasn't as big a smile as she'd become accustomed to seeing the past two days. *George, you don't look so good.* She walked into his office, stopping at the edge of his desk. "I was thinking about lunch…"

"Right," George said, as his eyes moved back to his desk. "Luuuunch." He strung out the word in an attempt to give himself a moment to think. Perhaps at lunch could be a good time to actually talk. Then again, he didn't want her upset for the rest of the day when he wouldn't be able to do anything about it.

Jillian took his hesitation straight into her stomach, then up to her heart, and even squeezing around her lungs. "I see," she choked out and turned quickly.

Screwing it up! "No, wait," George said, and popped out of his chair. "I didn't mean it like that. I was just thinking about a million things and about time." *And apparently how best to lie.* "I'd like to have lunch with you." *I need to keep the status quo for now. Talk tonight. Unless I can convince her to take the afternoon off. Then we could really talk. But if she says no, then I... Oh, just hell.* "Can I talk you into a long lunch?"

It was Jillian's turn to hesitate. "George, we really can't be away too much. Not even worrying about people talking, our absence wouldn't be good for morale. We're at the early stages of this nightmare project and that's when we need good attitudes and a big effort. You and I can't just disappear for hours-"

"Right," George said. "I get it. I do." He sighed and then leaned over to lock his computer. "Just a regular length lunch, then?"

Jillian nodded. "In or out?"

"Definitely out," George said. *I have got to get outta here. Even if only for a few minutes.*

There was no awkward need to be cautious about touching as they left the office. Neither of them reached for the other.

Just as Orville had predicted, rain had been coming down most of the morning. But the sky was starting to break and George suggested they get sandwiches and eat in the car. It was the best he could do for privacy.

Jillian didn't know he was looking to have a private talk and she asked for a sit down restaurant instead, if he didn't mind.

They compromised on a diner with fast service and that found them back in Jillian's car in the Gardiner D parking lot with a few minutes to spare. When Jillian reached for the door handle, George put his hand on her other arm. "Jillian, can we talk a minute? Before we go in?"

She turned toward him and nodded. "Yes," she said. Her voice wavered a little as she found herself both relieved and nervous. *I hope he tells me whatever is bothering him.*

George cleared his throat and Jillian slid her hand to where he'd dropped his when she'd turned. She didn't quite touch him, but the near gesture helped spur George forward. He slid his hand until their little fingers brushed. "I didn't sleep well last night."

She nodded again. *Not surprising with everything going on.*

"It wasn't just the stuff I told you about last night, though."

"No?"

He shook his head, exhaled, and then looked her in the eyes, not measuring his words at all. "You held back on me last night and then this morning was in the dark."

"Oh," Jillian said, and her eyes darted away from his. *Oh.*

She must've known what he was talking about. "I know I shouldn't be complaining. I'm not. We're having a great time and the frequency is great and everything. And more importantly, I really like us." He covered her hand with his.

"Uh-huh." She wanted to pull her hand away and get out of the car. Somehow, she managed to stay put and tried to focus on what he was saying despite the dim buzz in her head repeating that he was unhappy with her and the sting in her eyes. *Do* not *cry. Do* not *cry.*

"But, I still want you to look at me, *need* you to look at me, at least a little. So I know that it's *me* that you want. When you close your eyes, I could be anybody."

Her lungs burned so much that she realized she'd quit breathing. She managed to inhale. "Is this an ultimatum?"

"What?" George gripped her hand. "No! No, this is me telling you what I *need*, hoping that you'll *want* to give it to me. If I'm really asking that much, too much, then this is meant to open a dialogue."

"A dialogue?" Jillian asked, and snatched her hand away to dig in her purse for a tissue.

"Am I asking so much?"

She let out a tight laugh and shook her head, still looking in her purse. "You've no idea."

He threw his arm around the back of her seat, shifted so he was angled toward her, and leaned closer. "Obviously not. Though you were fine with it the first time. What changed? Is it me?"

"Last night you said, you like me just the way I am." She finally produced a tissue and dabbed at her eyes.

George frowned. "Yes. I do. And I want you to like me the way I am too. But I'm starting to see a pattern. And if I add in the fact that you climb out of bed the minute we're done... I'm not so sure you like me at all."

Jillian's mouth dropped open and she looked at him.

He didn't like that he'd shocked or offended her, but he was glad she was finally looking at him again. "Well?"

"How can... honestly!"

"Honesty would be good right about now," he said. *You're just delaying and dancing. Come on.* "Give it to me straight."

Her jaw tensed, he could see the slight puff at the backs of her cheeks. But after a few seconds, she opened her mouth again. "It was frightening, okay? I mean, you have this beautiful moment with white light. I had this encounter with... I don't even know how to verbalize it."

"Just say it. Am I like a black hole or something? Soulless?"

"No!" She looked up at the ceiling of the car and dropped her head against the seat rest. "You're... I don't know... volcanic, fiery, red, molten maybe?" She tilted her head toward him and looked at him again. "I don't know how to say it. I guess *fire* is the best word. *Heat* too." She exhaled softly. "I'm afraid of burning."

"Okay," George said, in an attempt to stall and buy himself time. *That wasn't quite what I was expecting. Of course, I don't know what I was expecting either.* "Did you burn then? Our first time?"

"Not exactly." She looked back at the ceiling and sighed again. "I don't know how to explain it any better. And I'm more than a little lost with why we're talking about this here and now."

"Because I want *us*! And if we can't talk about the most basic of things now, when we're new, then what will it be like down the road when we've gotten used to not talking?" He turned and looked out through the windshield, though he wasn't really looking at anything. *That's part of what I need to be sure about. Not repeating the past.* "I'm not interested in making the same mistakes over and over again. I've played this round before. Not the same subject, but it's the same problem." He ran his hands through his hair and then dropped them in his lap. "I'm not doing it again."

Jillian rolled her head to peer at him, grateful to be out of the spotlight and more than a little curious too. "Again, huh? Who was this?"

Orville told you to tell her. But, now? He turned his head. "Maybe now isn't the right time."

"Now isn't the right time? What about the rest of this conversation? No, you're not getting out of it that easily. You started this."

"I started this to talk about us, not the past."

Jillian had to fight to keep her face smooth. "And who are we, but the sum of our experiences? Tell me."

Shit. "Sarah."

Jillian sat up straight. "The woman who moved to California?"

"Uh, yeah."

"She just keeps becoming more and more important, doesn't she? Ok, so... do I get to hear the rest of the story, or not?"

"Now?" George looked forward and ran his hands through his hair again. Even Orville didn't know it all. He could probably tell the whole nightmare in ten minutes, but was that really the way to do this? Blurt it out and then have no more time to say anything... *Actually, that sounds perfect.* "Ok, now."

Looking mostly at Jillian again, he swallowed once. "I thought I'd done my soul-searching after she left. You know, 'what did I do wrong?' and all that. All I'd come up with was a classic, 'we want different things.' That worked, for the most part. About five months later I was doing better and had started dating again. Then I got a call from one of our old friends. I'd figured I'd lost custody of the couple in the *divorce* so it really surprised me when she called and suggested we have lunch.

"At first, I truly thought it was two old friends getting together and catching up, but by the time the check came, I knew something was up. She kept asking these tiny, little probing questions about my love life. It had to be something about Sarah, so I asked her point blank. She got all flustered and said that Sarah had asked her for a favor and she was trying to be subtle, but she didn't know how. Finally, I got it out of her. 'Sarah's getting married. She's not sure whether she should invite you or not.'"

"After *five months?!*" Jillian burst out.

"Thank you for that," George said. "That's what went through my mind, but I kept my mouth shut for a moment as I realized that I was probably about to get the answers to some questions. I managed to say something like, 'Of course, she should. We're still friends.' And the next thing I know, I'm being handed an envelope."

"She sent her friend to invite you?"

"Yes. I guess I played it cool because she didn't try to take it back. I managed to wait until I was home to open it and find out who she was marrying. He was on the invitation as 'Doctor' so-and-so. I looked him up, he's a pediatrician in California, who had, *surprise, surprise*, moved his practice there five months before."

"No!" Jillian said. "Oh, no."

"It gets better, or should I say, worse. I thought I recognized the last name, so I started searching. His family has money. His father's a semi-retired lawyer with family money and sits on over a half a dozen charity boards. His mother comes from money too. She heads up charity events and has some kind of charity with the hospital. They're all over the society blogs, pictures of them and the doctor everywhere. And starting about four months before Sarah left... she started appearing in pictures with them as a 'friend.' No way to know how long she'd been seeing him before that."

"Oh, George," Jillian whispered, dropping a hand on his leg and patting it gently. "Oh, I'm so sorry." She twisted and leaned over to put her head against his neck and shoulder. "That's so... awful." She took his hand in hers, squeezing it gently.

"She was in pictures at fundraisers for the ballet and the symphony and some theatre. I had no idea she was interested in any of that. So I figure, that's where it really went wrong. We didn't talk enough. Maybe, if I'd known and had taken her to performances... Maybe it wouldn't have mattered.

"My take away from the whole thing, aside from the panicked visit to my doctor to be tested for every sexually transmitted disease known to man which, thank God, turned out fine, was that it was a mutual problem. There were things I wanted to do that I never said anything to her about either. A lot of things. Most of them, I don't think they really mattered. I don't think I ever told her about my old dreams and plans either. But the difference was I didn't do things behind her back.

"I'll never know if she was physically cheating on me. I'll never know if I could have saved the relationship. I'm not even totally sure when it started to fall apart. I'm pretty sure it was before we were planning to move in together, so I've no idea what she was thinking, agreeing to that."

George shifted and moved Jillian so that they could meet each other's gaze. "What I do know, is that I'm not making the mistake of keeping stuff in again. Especially, if it's important. I suppose the little stuff builds up too, and I should be careful there, as well. But the big stuff, that's obvious. Even if it doesn't resolve the way I want it to, I'm not going to make the mistake of not talking. I hope this is another thing we can agree on."

His eyes were darting around her face after he finished, sizing up her reaction, she guessed. Even though he hadn't actually asked a question at the end, he was waiting for an answer. She sat back and wet her lips, searching for words, finally venturing a rhetorical question. "What am I supposed to do with you?"

"What do you mean?"

Jillian shook her head slightly. "I hardly know. George, you completely overwhelm me."

"That's not an answer, Jillian," George replied, before he could stop himself.

"No," Jillian said, and then sighed. "I don't suppose it is. But what do you expect? You catch me off-guard and tell me that I'm not satisfying you, and then-"

"Whoa," George said, and leaned toward her. "That's *not* what I said."

"Oh, yes, it is. And then you follow it up with this story to make me feel guilty, like it's my fault we're not communicating! How can we be having problems communicating? We've been a couple for less than two days! Our first date was less than forty-eight hours ago. What do you expect from me?"

"Hold up," George said. "I *didn't* say you weren't satisfying me. I just want you to look at me. And you *asked* me to tell you about Sarah and I certainly wasn't trying to make you feel guilty." Without looking away, he gestured toward the windshield. "That was me laying my heart open on the damn dashboard!"

"Geor-"

"Nobody else knows what happened with Sarah. Nobody in my life knows that she left me for somebody else. Nobody. But now I've told you because I'm trying to do this right. Because this is important to me. *You're* important to me. You've been important for a long time. Longer than forty-eight hours. Now, I'm not asking for any more from you than what we've already agreed to and what we've already done. All I want is for you to be *with me*. Is *that* too much to ask?"

Jillian swallowed and glanced down at her lap. *He's just so overwhelming. What can I even say to that?* "God, George."

"Jill-" George started to say, but stopped when she looked back up at him, her eyes glistening. He extended his hand to touch her cheek and felt a stillness inside, even though he was unsure whether the tears were a reaction to a pleasant emotion or an unpleasant one. *I'm going to have to make a point to hold onto her during any difficult conversation.* He slid his hand down toward her jaw and then back up again. *Just touching her is wonderful.* "Jillian," he whispered.

She was having a little trouble breathing because her nose beginning to run and she knew the tears would fall any moment, so she reached for his face too, trying to the summon words as quickly as possible. *True words. Kind words.* Sigh. *The right words.* "I don't know if I can be what you need," Jillian said, "but I'll try." She followed it up with a watery smile.

"You're already everything I need," George said, and kissed her to keep himself from saying anything more, what he was really thinking. *I love you.* Because it was just too soon for that. Even if he could have been sure that she wouldn't panic if he said it, it was too soon. Even if he was starting to feel fairly sure about it, it was too soon. It was just too soon. And he was dancing on the edge even then.

Jillian tried not to cry all over herself or George. It was all too much. Too much had happened. She hadn't had enough sleep either; making love all night was wonderful, but exhausting. And there was *everything else*, including her *parents*.

And, of course, there was George, who, contrary to his words, seemed to want more and more from her and she wasn't sure she could give it to him. *If only we'd gone slowly.* But that wasn't in the cards. She'd run toward this as surely as she breathed, and she couldn't turn and run away any more than she could stop breathing.

So she threw herself into the kiss. It was warm and comforting, at first. The kind of kiss that comes at the end of a fight, a 'Let's make up' kiss. And like kisses at the end of a fight, it began to spiral outward toward a more passionate connection. Jillian felt her heart quicken as she let herself stop thinking and just be in the moment.

It was then that George sensed the change in her and his body echoed it. At that, he backed off fairly quickly and dropped his forehead to hers, grasping tightly on his control. They were in the Gardiner D parking lot, after all. He seemed to find his control, in that position, though it had never had quite the allure before as it did with Jillian. There was something about putting their heads together. It was... comforting in the closeness, and intimate without being inappropriate. "I want to be what you need, too," he said, before he could think it through.

"Oh, George," she whispered and gripped the front of his jacket. *There isn't another man in the Universe who's as much what I need as you are.*

"Just tell me what you need," he whispered. "Please, just always tell me. Don't let this end without giving me the chance to be what you need."

She nodded against his forehead and they both laughed quietly at the awkward motion.

"What do you need?" he asked, softly. "How can I be what you need?"

What do I need? She sat back a few inches, still gripping his jacket, and looked into his eyes. Around her arms, he reached for her face and wiped the tears away with his thumbs. *What do I need?* "Right now, just keep being you," she whispered back, starting to tear up again.

"That, I can do," George said. "But, is that really... everything?"

"Just give me a little time," Jillian said. "Okay?"

George took a breath. "Yeah, okay." But it wasn't. Not really. *Just so long as she starts talking before it's too late.*

Jillian had no idea how she'd managed to pull herself together enough to go back into the building, but she did. She wasn't sure how she'd managed to calmly tell George that it would be best to work separately in their respective offices again, especially with how his face fell when she said it, but she'd done that, too. Trying to make amends in a small way, she'd opened her IM and tried to have a conversation. It wasn't a great conversation, it wasn't cute or flirty, but she made the effort. It seemed they'd struck a new, hopefully temporary, rather uncomfortable, stasis.

All of the afternoon, though, her mind kept turning to the basketball game that night, a purely social event which, unfortunately, had the weight of the world on it. For all the trepidation she felt about her relationship with George, if they weren't breaking up, it was time to attempt to get along with his friends. *The weight of the world.* Only the fact that Sergei had made a point to re-invite her in the morning saved her from heaving up her lunch. Every time she felt queasy, she told herself that the men were going to make an effort too. Maybe it wouldn't be a complete disaster.

After work, she kept her appointment with Mrs. Kerchner, taking her grocery shopping and helping her put the groceries away. It was when they were emptying the bags that Mrs. Kerchner brought up the subject that Jillian hadn't been able to avoid thinking about and was even less interested in talking about.

"You know, dear," Mrs. Kerchner started, "you seem quite preoccupied."

"Oh? Mmm." Jillian said, as she put the flour away. "I suppose a little."

"Anything to do with the gentleman you've *entertained through breakfast* two days in a row?"

Jillian turned toward Mrs. Kerchner. "Why, Mrs. K!"

Mrs. Kerchner chuckled. "Nobody thinks that I pay any attention. But at my age, what else do I have to do?" She placed a bag of bread on the counter. "He looks nice. Tell me about him."

When Jillian didn't reply quickly, Mrs. Kerchner continued. "That's a nice classic car he had parked here for a few days. And I like the graying hair at the temples. It isn't fair how men get more attractive with age.

What's his name? It's a shame I've never seen him straight on, just a profile or from above."

Jillian found her phone and showed Mrs. Kerchner their pictures. "George."

"Oh! That's a good name! Strong. Solid. Is he as he's named?"

"Strong and solid?" Jillian asked, swiping through to the picture of their profiles. "Yes. Yes, he is. And brave." She paused, to think for a moment. "And kind. And sweet. And wonderful." She smiled at the picture. "And brave."

"You already said that."

"What?" Jillian said, looking back up at Mrs. Kerchner.

"Brave, Dear. You said, 'brave' twice."

"Did I?" Jillian asked herself, as she looked back at the picture. "Well, he is. So very, very brave."

"How so?"

Jillian looked at Mrs. Kerchner again. "When he wants something, he asks for it. And he's not afraid of exposing himself. Not at all." She bit her lip and looked at the floor. "Today, he tried to talk to me about something and I didn't want to hear it. He was unhappy with me because... because I was a coward about something. Thinking back now, I wish I'd been prepared. I should have told him everything. *Really* explained myself.

"But I didn't want to. I didn't even consider it. So I turned it around on him." She returned her gaze to Mrs. Kerchner. "And do you know what he did?" She swallowed. "He opened himself up even more. He told me about a private, deep wound. And I... I don't know how to deal with that. I admire him for it, his bravery. But it also makes me feel cowardly and inadequate. So, I, um," she swallowed again. "I rewarded his openness by hiding in my office the rest of the day. I said just enough to get him to let me alone and then I hid. And now things are really awkward. I don't know how to change that."

"You know," Mrs. Kerchner said, "relationships aren't easy. Even the best of them come at varying degrees of difficulty. And there is only one solution."

Jillian tried to smile. "And what is that?"

"To give it your all."

"That's what he wants. All of me. Right now."

"If he's willing to match that, what's the problem?"

"I don't want him to see the mess I am until I'm sure that it will work. It hurts too much to let someone know you like that and then have him leave."

"If you don't let him in, then you'll never know it'll work." Mrs. Kerchner said.

Jillian blinked a few times.

Mrs. Kerchner shook her head. "You know what you should do? Tell him exactly what you told me."

Jillian looked back at her phone. "It won't be enough."

"Let him decide that. You might be pleasantly surprised. At the very least, if you apologize for how you handled the situation that would allow for more discussion. And tell him you're scared. If he's half as wonderful as you think, you can work through it together." When Jillian didn't answer right away, Mrs. Kerchner continued. "I expect you're braver than you think."

"I am?" Jillian asked.

"Mm-hmm. Just quit thinking about it and do what you have to do. Now, let's get you in the right frame of mind."

"What do you mean?"

Mrs. Kerchner took the phone from Jillian, held it up, and turned it toward her. "I want you to list all the things you like about George. Every one of them. And if you feel that some of thoughts are too personal to share, share them anyway. I could use a little vicarious living."

Jillian smiled at the thought of Mrs. Kerchner living vicariously through her. Well, maybe that wasn't the worst thing that could happen. She looked back at the picture. "Every single thing?"

"Every one."

They'd played just over a quarter of the game when George noticed Jillian was sitting next to Melissa in the three rows of bleachers off to the side of the court, during Chris's two foul shots. She waved at him and he waved back, hardly believing the relief he felt, although if he'd had more time to reflect on it, it wouldn't have been surprising. They'd worked in their individual offices during the afternoon, just like the morning, and though there had been a few IMs, it just wasn't the same as it had been. He couldn't help but think they were in the middle of something, not a fight exactly, but *something*, and he didn't know how to end it. Something was off, just like it was a few nights back, only he couldn't fix it by knocking on her door.

But she'd shown up to the game, so at least they were still spending time together and keeping promises. She looked cute, too, in a sweater and jeans with Keds. After Chris sank his second foul shot, George did his best to get his head back in the game until the break at the half. He managed better than he expected.

At the half, one of the guys on the other team wanted to talk about a disputed foul and George found himself in the discussion. By the time he turned around to see Jillian, Chris and Sergei were over at the bleachers.

Apparently, Sergei had taken care of introductions because Jillian and Chris were shaking hands. He started to walk over and watched curiously as neither Chris nor Jillian released the handshake.

He picked up his pace to a jog, wondering if Sergei had introduced her as his girlfriend or not. Seeing her smiling at Chris was *not* something he'd been prepared for that night. Chris wasn't in bad shape, either. *Might even be her type. Fuck! I'm going to rip his head off if he doesn't let go of her right now!*

Jillian turned her head and smiled at George. It wasn't the same smile she'd been giving Chris. Her mouth widened and her eyes lit up. At the same moment, she let go of Chris, not saying a thing to him, and jumped to her feet, stepping down the one tier that was in her way and to the floor. She even took a step toward George to meet him, tossing her arms around his neck for a brief kiss on the lips. "Hi! You look great out there!"

"Hi back! And thanks," George said, as the new tension drained away, leaving him a little shaky from the adrenalin rush. He tried to play it cool, hoping no one had any idea that he'd just had a terrific bout of jealousy. Not entirely confident that the shaking wouldn't be evident, but unwilling to wait long enough to be sure, he raised his arms around her. "I'm so glad you could make it."

"Had to see my man in action," Jillian said, her arms still about his neck.

"Oh, yeah?" He said, smiling into her eyes. "Even though he's a sweaty, disgusting mess?"

"One of the hazards of having a jock boyfriend." She giggled a little.

George tightened his grip. "Your mood sure has turned."

"Oh," Jillian said. She looked to the side a moment and then back at George. "Well, yes. I had a lovely time with Mrs. Kerchner and it put me in a better frame of mind."

"Remind me to thank Mrs. Kerchner."

"I already did," Jillian replied, and leaned up to kiss him again.

George leaned over and kissed her softly. "I still owe her."

"Hey, hey, hey!" Sergei said, with a slightly raised voice, even though he was only a few steps away. "None of *that* until after the game."

George continued to look at Jillian while he tilted his head in Sergei's general direction. "He thinks I care about the game."

"And... you don't?"

"Not at this moment."

"You better, or the musk- *guys* will *really* hate me."

"I've got a few minutes before we start the second half."

"Okay." Jillian pushed out a breath and whispered. "May I have just one of those?"

"You can have them all," George said, softly.

She slid her arms down from his neck, taking one of his hands in hers, and leading him a few feet away. Once they'd achieved some semblance of privacy considering they were in gymnasium, she turned and faced him and pushed out another breath. "Okay."

"Okay?" George asked, trying to contain himself, trying to stay neutral. The welcome had been fantastic, so hopefully whatever she wanted next wasn't bad. But after the disaster at lunch, he wasn't counting on anything.

She bit her lip and then exhaled again. "So... I'm really sorry. I'm sorry about how things went earlier. You tried to talk to me about something important to you and I... I just... I didn't handle it well. I'm really very, very sorry about it. So... um..."

George was starting to feel like smiling again. "So?"

"So, can I get a do-over? I know it's not really sportsman-like, but we're not playing a game, right? Maybe I can use my credit from the mess with the cop? Talk about us, again, after your game? I'll do it better this time. I promise. So... what do you think? Do-over?"

"Yeah," George said, nodding and grinning. "Yeah, we can definitely talk again."

"Yeah?" Jillian said, as she started smiling back at him.

"Yeah. Absolutely." George reached up and touched her cheek. She closed her eyes and leaned into his hand. After a few heartbeats, George leaned over and kissed her on the forehead and her lips parted and she let out a soft sigh.

I want this. I want this more than anything. I've got to get myself together. She pulled back slightly and her eyes fluttered open and focused on him. The affectionate look in his eyes shored up her nerves. "You've been important for more than forty-eight hours, too. I wish I'd said that earlier." His eyes crinkled a bit as his smile broadened. "And I'll look at you. I will. I promise." She reached up and clutched his arm. "But, I want you to know that, even with my eyes closed, I knew I was with you. There's nobody else I want. Not in my imagination, not in my dreams, and certainly not in reality when I can be with you."

"Jillian." It was all he could manage to say as he was interrupted by Sergei who shouted that George was needed to talk strategy before the break was over. He turned his head toward Sergei and nodded, then looked back at Jillian. "I want you to know that I really want to blow-off the rest of the game and continue this right now, but..."

"No," Jillian said, shaking her head slightly. "I completely understand. I hadn't planned to say any of this now. I was planning on saving it for after. It all just kind of came out. So, don't worry. Get back to your game. I'll be here when you're finished."

"You better be," he said, kissing her quick and hard on the lips, before he began to walk toward the team, but he turned and walked backwards, looking at her. "If you're not, I'll find you. Hunt you down."

"Oh? And what'll you do with me?" She asked, with a flirty smirk on her face.

"Oh, marvelous, incredible things, I assure you. But it'll be even more marvelous and incredible if I don't have to waste time and energy tracking you."

"Then I suppose I'll just have to wait here."

"Darn straight."

Jillian tossed her hair back over her shoulders and started to walk back toward the bleachers. "Be a groupie."

"Only for me."

"Your own, personal... fan."

"Exactly." He wiggled his eyebrows.

Sergei caught George before he walked into Taro. "What the frig was that?" He asked.

"What?" George asked, turning.

"He thinks he's in love," Taro said, with distain in his voice and an eye roll.

Chris, apparently as confused as George, asked, "And that's a problem?"

"Yeah, pot," Sergei said, as he elbowed Taro. "You're as black as the kettle. Engaged to that woman, right over there, aren't ya?"

Taro just rolled his eyes again. "'Here's to plain speaking and clear understanding.'"

"*The Maltese Falcon*," Neal said, easily identifying the movie quote. "But I don't get the connection to the reference."

"Perhaps," George said, also confused, "we should just play ball."

"I think we need to change up our defense," Chris said. George nodded and resumed his focus on basketball.

Jillian retook her seat next to Melissa who nudged her and smiled. "That looked interesting."

"Oh, I'm sure," Jillian said, and leaned back with her elbows on the tier behind her. "I hadn't meant to make a spectacle, but I guess that's how it went."

"I wouldn't call it 'spectacle.' But it was a bit of a show."

"Of course, it was," Jillian said, and then let out a sigh. "If I'm going to make an idiot of myself, it has to be in front of the guys from work.

Melissa leaned back like Jillian. "That didn't look embarrassing. It looked romantic."

Jillian couldn't help but grin. "I'm absolutely nuts about him."

"I'd say he's absolutely nuts about you, too."

"Do you really think so?" Jillian asked, as the guys returned to the court and George looked over at them, caught Jillian's eyes and wiggled his eyebrows again. Melissa nudged Jillian. Jillian nudged her back.

"Yeah." Melissa said. "Absolutely nuts."

They both giggled.

For the remainder of the game they periodically yelled encouragements from the bleachers, making a point to yell for all the team's players, not just George and Taro. But when Jillian noticed a displeased look on George's face after she yelled *Way to go, Chris!* when Chris sank a three point shot, she cut back a little on the cheering.

Melissa must have seen it too, because she looked at Jillian and said, "I wouldn't have thought George was the jealous type."

It may be a learned response to a very painful experience. I just hope it isn't a tell-tale sign of a possessiveness problem, instead. "I'm looking at it as sweet." *And apparently modifying my behavior accordingly... oh, this might not be so good. Well, let's just not assume it's any more than it appears. Relax.*

After the game, Jillian waited with Melissa, while the guys quickly showered and changed, planning to join the team for *the usual post-game beer.* Not wanting to create any additional jealousy issues, Jillian stuck with Melissa for the drink too. They sat next to each other and their respective partners. Jillian also made a point to speak to everyone, but favor only George with large amounts of attention. They were at the pizza place for a mere fifteen minutes, so it was easy enough to focus and not slip.

And then they were alone again. And Jillian knew he would expect to talk, and she had promised him that she would. She couldn't very well back track and disappoint him; not for a second time in one day. So when he suggested they go to his place, and it was certainly a lot closer than hers, she agreed.

As she was dropping her purse onto his couch, he slipped his arms around her waist from behind and hugged her. "I'm so glad you came tonight." He dropped a kiss on her hair. "And you look great, by the way."

She crossed her arms over his, gripped his forearms, and leaned back into him. "Oh? In jeans and a sweater?"

"Well, I was hoping for your java programmer's t-shirt... but, this works for you too."

"Thank you," she said.

"Want anything?" He asked, and released her to head to the kitchen.

"No," she answered. "I'm good." She followed him into the kitchen and watched him get himself a glass of water, feeling pleased he wasn't choosing more alcohol. She'd never seen him take more than one drink. That was another positive sign. *Why can't I just believe he's as great as I feel he is? I had all these thoughts on Tuesday and then threw caution to wind. Why can't I just stay in that place? Why do I keep questioning him? Anyone can tell he isn't another Sam. I don't need to keep looking for signs. I need to trust him and myself.*

Sigh.

What about this jealousy thing?

She waited until George had lowered his glass from his lips to ask, "Did I upset you when I was talking to Chris?"

George set the glass on the counter and leaned back. "And here I was hoping you didn't notice that."

"I got a bad feeling about cheering for him too."

It was George's turn to sigh and cross his arms. He nodded his head twice and then unwound himself, walked over to her, tossed his arm around her shoulders, and led her back into the family room. They settled onto the couch as he said, "I'm sorry. I'm not usually like that. I didn't think..." George snorted a nervous laugh. "I wasn't thinking much of anything except that that handshake was going on way too long. After that... well, it was just more of the same thoughts."

"Oh." *I hadn't thought anything of that handshake.*

"Irrational, I know."

"Right," Jillian said.

He exhaled. "It's not that I don't trust you. I mean, you came to the game for me."

Jillian stopped him with a touch on his arm. "Look, it's only a big deal if you start telling me who I can and can't talk to."

"I'd never-"

"No," Jillian said. "I don't think you would." *We're going to figure out how to make this work.* "However, in the future, I'll be more restrained-"

"Don't," George said. "You don't have to change yourself. I didn't think you were flirting with him or anything like that. I just didn't want him touching you."

Jillian fought the smile that threatened her smooth countenance. His jealousy really was sweet. "Neither do I. Certainly not in *that* way."

George didn't fight his smile as he took her hand in his, interlacing their fingers. "That's good to hear. A few other things you said tonight were also good to hear."

Jillian leaned into him. "Thanks for the do-over."

"I'm not even going to charge you the credit from the cop." George wrapped his other hand around their already joined hands.

Jillian grinned and tilted her head. "Why not?"

"Because this way, you'll still have a credit if you ever need another do-over. I'd rather you ask than let a change of heart, or a misunderstanding, come between us."

Her heart started to pound again. *He says the most amazing things.*

"What's that look?" George asked.

"I'm just trying to get my head around some of the things you've said. I've never known anybody who says things like you do."

"Oh? Like what?"

Jillian shook her head and looked at their hands. "Like... I mesmerize you. That is the best line I've ever heard."

"Come on," George said, and leaned down a little, trying to see her face. "That wasn't a line and you know it. I'd been watching you for a year. Believe me; I was mesmerized by what I saw. I still am, actually."

"Oh, George," Jillian said, tugged her hand from his, and reached for his face with both hands. "You know, it's not that I've never known anyone who says things like you do…"

"No?" He asked, as he slipped his arms around her.

"No. It's that I've never known anyone who's *anything* at all like you." She kissed him and he kissed her back as he ran his hands up her back, into her hair, and back down again, before pulling her closer.

She thought he stopped to breathe, but when he pulled back, he quietly said, "So, about your do-over…"

"Yeah?" She asked.

"You said you would look at me."

"I did," Jillian said.

George cleared his throat. "I just want to be clear. Are you sure about that? Because you seemed pretty sure before that that wasn't going to work for you. And… as much as I want it, I only want what you'll give me willingly, not under pressure."

She closed her eyes for a moment. *Where was this man a few years ago? And why couldn't I have met him then?* She opened her eyes and smiled. It was time to let go, even if it was ridiculously fast and reckless. "You can have as much from me as you're willing to give in return."

George could feel his throat tighten slightly. *I love you.* "You can have everything," George said. *I love you so much.* "Absolutely everything."

"Then so can you," Jillian said. *Please don't break my heart.*

They kissed again, this time with more passion, and they shifted and twisted on the couch, trying to get as close as they could. He slipped his hands under her sweater just to touch the skin of her back.

He was breathing so fast, George found he almost couldn't speak when he quietly asked Jillian if she'd like to go upstairs. She replied with a nod and an inaudible whisper that he could easily enough guess was a yes. He was fighting with himself to take his hands off of her, the reward would be moving somewhere that would eventually allow them to be much more comfortable, but he just didn't want to release her. The thought of trying to carry her any significant distance, especially one that included stairs, made him nervous. An emergency room visit would not be an improvement to the evening. He was just going to have to release her… eventually.

He lowered his head to kiss her neck and she shivered and tightened her arms around him, whispering his name.

"I want you so much," George said, and lifted the hem of her sweater.

"I thought you wanted to go upstairs," Jillian breathed out.

George kissed her ear. "Yes. But I want to teleport there, so I don't have to let go of you."

She giggled. "You're inner geek is showing. Teleporting…" Then she took his face in her hands again and kissed him; he fell back against the couch cushions and took her with him.

He was trying to convince himself to get off the couch and race up the stairs to his bed, possibly carrying her after all, when the phone rang in the kitchen. He ignored it until the third ring when Jillian broke the kiss and asked him, "Should you answer that?"

"Now?" He asked, with a laugh. "No. There's voice mail."

"Okay," Jillian said, and pushed off from him to get to her feet. "Then let's go upstairs."

George scrambled to his feet next to her, taking her hand in his, and heading toward the stairs before he even replied with, "Let's."

The phone started to ring again as they climbed the stairs, George first with Jillian in tow. He stopped on the landing to grab her by the waist when she finally reached the top, and lift her off of her feet to kiss her again. He set her back down and walked her backwards, ever so slowly, toward his bedroom, capturing her eyes with his gaze.

It didn't surprise him at all that she matched his gaze and it pleased him tremendously to see the look in her eyes. She didn't look at him with her usual bold strength or even lust; instead her eyes were soft, like they were *after* making love. Her feelings were starting to show more and more. She was beginning to let down her guard. He was going to be able to touch her in a different way, eventually. Maybe it would even be that night.

The phone rang for the fourth time and went to voice mail again.

George paused at the doorway to kiss her again. She felt so good, every touch felt so good, he wished he never had to stop touching her. He slid his hands under her sweater again, just to feel the soft skin of her back.

She turned them around and started to walk him backwards toward the bed. When he felt the bed behind him, he sat and pulled her close, edging up her sweater to kiss her stomach. He loved the way her muscles moved and the gasp she made. He loved everything about her.

The phone rang again. "Blast," he mumbled against her skin.

"Perhaps, you should answer that." Jillian said.

George groaned and dropped backwards on the bed, taking her with him, and she squealed as she landed sprawled over him. "No," George said. "If it's my mother, she'll give up after the third try. If it's anyone else, I don't want to talk to them anymore than I want to talk to my mother right now."

Jillian smiled down at him and said, "Okay." They both kicked off their shoes, ignoring the phone, and George started tugging on Jillian's sweater.

When the phone finally went to voice mail again, Jillian moved away from George. "We could take this off the hook, you know." She pointed at the phone.

"Okay," George said, and got from the bed. "Take that off the hook and take off your sweater, while I get something from the bathroom."

"Excuse me?!" Jillian said, and George walked backwards toward the bathroom. "Just take off my sweater?"

"Yeah," George said, wiggling his eyebrows and then turned just before the step into the bathroom, disappearing without tripping.

I better make sure we leave a light on in there, or I may trip later. She picked up the handset on George's night table. It rang just as she pushed the talk button. *Oh, crap!*

"Uh, hello?" Jillian said, unable to think of anything else to do. *Please don't be George's mom. Please don't be George's mom.*

George walked back out of the bathroom with a box of condoms, trying to remember why he'd thought it made sense to put them in a drawer in the bathroom as opposed to next to his bed, when he heard the short half-ring of the phone and then Jillian's tentative hello.

He stepped back into the bedroom and saw Jillian sitting up, clutching the phone, white as a sheet. "What? Who is it?"

Jillian held the phone out toward him, covering the mouthpiece with her hand. "Sarah."

Oh, shit...

CHAPTER EIGHTEEN

Jillian handed George the phone and started to get up from the bed. He wrapped his free arm around her waist and tugged her back to the bed with him, dropping her on her back next to him, as he lay down. "George," she whispered. "Let go."

He shook his head and said, "Hello," into the phone.

She stared up at the ceiling, willing herself to be someplace else. In fact, pretty much *anywhere* else. She'd even take being at the dentist.

"Uh, yeah," George said, beside her. "As a matter of-"

Oh, my God. I don't want to hear this. She started to move again and he gripped her tighter.

"Well, yeah, it's been..."

Jillian tried not to listen.

"Oh, really?" And after a short pause, "Tomorrow?"

Jillian struggled to sit up.

"Well, I don't know. Let me see..." He lowered the phone and placed the mouthpiece next to his hip. "Jillian," he said, quietly.

"Sure, go out with Sarah." She crossed her arms over her chest and debated kicking him to make him let go of her. *Or maybe an elbow in the stomach, if I can just move a little to the right...*

George squeezed her. "Don't be mad. The invitation is for both of us. Tomorrow night. Drinks with her and the doctor."

"Oh," Jillian said, and looked at George. His face wasn't exactly smiling. "Why?"

"I have no idea. She said, she wants to talk to me and they're leaving on Saturday, so tomorrow is the only time. What do you think?"

"What do I think?" *I think that one thing I want to do on a Friday night is to go out for drinks with your ex-girlfriend. Oh, yeah. That's definitely the best thing that could happen.*

271

She looked back at the ceiling. *Now I have to choose between being myself and being the perfect girlfriend.* "Fine. Let's go see what she wants." *Okay, that's not exactly the attitude of the perfect girlfriend. But, that's the best I can do right now.*

George squeezed her again. "Come on. I haven't seen her in years."

Jillian looked at him again. "Is she pretty?" She wanted to clamp a hand over her mouth. *How mortifying! I can't believe I just said that.*

"She'll be with her husband," George said.

"So, she's *really* beautiful," Jillian said. This time she *did* clamp her hand over her mouth.

George snickered and lifted the phone back to his mouth. "We'll see you then. Thanks for the invitation." He disconnected and dropped the phone. "Now, about you."

It doesn't matter how jealous you are of this woman. You need to be here for him now. "Don't worry about me." Jillian twisted under his arm to roll onto her side. "Are you all right?"

"I think I'm in shock right now. Apart from the wedding invitation, I haven't had a single word from her." He sighed. "I don't want to think about it. Whatever it is that she wants, I'll find out tomorrow." He tightened his arm around her. "I'd rather think about you."

Oh, boy. I just can't right now. All I'll think about is you with her. For all I know she looks like... Angelina Jolie. I can't compete with that. I'm no super model. No movie star. And she's beautiful. It's obvious.

George sighed again. "Great. Not one word for years and then poof. It would have been nice if she'd called last week and this would have been over before you and I ever got together. Instead, she manages to mess up our evening."

"What?"

"The look on your face," George said. "You're not in the mood anymore, are you?"

Jillian grimaced. "No. I'm sorry. I can try to ignore it, but..."

"Yeah." George rolled onto his back, his arm still under and around her. "All right."

I am the worst girlfriend ever. Jillian struggled up onto her arm and leaned over him. After a few moments he looked at her and she smiled at him. "Oh, my dear, George." She lifted her free hand to his face. "Please forgive me for being human."

He smiled back. "In a way, I like that you're jealous this time."

She looked away for just a moment out of embarrassment. "Um..."

"And if you start calling me 'dear' and other things like that, well, that will certainly help." He took her hand in his and lifted it to his lips for a quick kiss. "I don't want her. Not at all. Not even a little. I want you. Just you." *I'm not even sure I'd go find out what Sarah wants if I didn't have you.*

She looked at him again. "You sure know how to make a girl melt."

"It's all true," he said. He reached up and pushed her hair back behind her ear, his smile quirking a little. "Can I ask you a question?"

"Of course."

"You didn't used to wear your hair down much. I think I've only seen it down twice at work until Tuesday. Then the last three days in a row."

"I didn't hear a question in there," Jillian said, then laughed shyly. "Yes. I've been wearing it down because I thought I noticed you liked it on Monday evening. Does that stroke your masculine pride?"

George laughed. "Yes. That does it, really nicely. And you're right, of course. I like it."

They looked at each other quietly for a minute.

"It's not fair," Jillian said, "that things suddenly feel so awkward." She sighed. "Again."

George rubbed her arm. "Yeah." He paused a moment, then his mouth quirked in a faint smile. "Stay with me tonight."

"Stay here?" Jillian asked.

"Yes," George said. "I want to be with you tonight. No pressure to do anything other than sleep. Keep all your clothes on, if you want."

"Now there's a line I haven't heard in years."

"You know me better than that." He said. "No lines. I'm serious. I just want you here with me. Set any conditions you like. I'll abide by them."

"I can't stay," Jillian said, biting her lip.

"Can't you have someone else feed Charlie?" George asked.

"It's not just Charlie." *Oh, boy. I guess it's time to tell him.*

George's brow had wrinkled a bit. "Then, what?"

"I didn't plan ahead for this. I don't have my pills," Jillian said.

"Pills?" George shifted and then raised himself up on his elbow. "What pills? I don't remember you taking anything the last two days. What are they?"

And, here it comes. Jillian took a breath and forced it out. "Birth control pills. I take one every morning at the same time."

"Oh," he said. "So… you're on the pill."

"Uh-huh," Jillian said, and nodded slowly.

"Well, this is interesting information," George said, and then sat up and Jillian's hands fell from him.

It's coming. I can see it in his face. "Not really," Jillian said. "It doesn't change anything."

George's brow furrowed just a little. "It could. Couldn't it? We're in a committed relationship. And I promise you that I'm clean. I haven't had sex without a condom since Sarah. And you know I was tested after that."

Jillian bit her lip. *No.* "I'm sorry, but no."

His eyes narrowing were almost unnoticeable. "Mind telling me why? I really won't cheat on you. Ever. I've never run around on anybody. That's *not* one of my failings. You could ask around, if you wanted. Nobody has any stories about me."

"I'm sorry," Jillian repeated. "No."

"Why?"

Jillian couldn't look at him anymore. His face had changed to confused and hurt. What was she going to say to him? That it didn't matter what he said or did? That she wasn't going to change her mind?

There were some mistakes that were unredeemable. And this could be one of them.

If I tell him even a part of this, he'll want to know everything.

She felt her shoulders tense. *And I just told him that if he'd give me everything, I'd do the same. If I don't...*

Steel yourself.

She turned back to him. "Okay. Here's the situation. I've *never* had sex without a..." She couldn't bring herself to say the word. She didn't even bother to think about why, since she was waiting to see what he'd say.

It was hard to tell how long he sat without saying anything, but based on the number of blinks, it was probably close to minute.

"Never?"

"Never," she said, as she shook her head.

He ran a hand through this hair. "What about the college boyfriend? You were together for what? Three years?"

"Nope," Jillian said.

"And the guy who wanted you to move in?"

Jillian shook her head again.

"Did they know you were taking the pill?"

"Luke, the college boyfriend, did."

This time George's tone was incredulous. "And there weren't any arguments about it? After three years?"

Jillian shook her head.

"And the more recent guy? He *didn't* know?"

Jillian didn't even bother to respond. The question had already been answered.

"How long were you with this guy?"

"I was with Sam just over nine months."

"Nine months and he didn't know you were taking birth control pills," George said. "Are you sure he didn't know? How is that possible?"

Jillian covered her face with her hands for a moment and then dropped them in her lap. She wasn't going to be able to duck the Sam story for much longer. But she could at least hold out for a few more days. Maybe she could get through the Friday night drinks and Saturday dinner nightmares first. If they were actually still together after all that, well, that would mean there was hope for them. And if that was true, then talking about the Sam debacle might be worth it.

Just tell him enough so that he can understand this, but don't add any details to make him inquire further.

"You didn't notice either, in the last two days." She paused long enough to take a breath. "Listen, Sam was oblivious to many things about me. It isn't important. What's important is that I told you. And I've told you how I feel about the subject."

"Why didn't you tell him?"

"I don't know, exactly. I just never felt like I could, or should even. And when it ended, I certainly didn't regret the decision."

She stopped when she realized she'd gone too far. She was sure of it. And then George confirmed it.

"Couldn't it be that *not* telling him things was why you broke up?" *That's got to be what destroyed me and Sarah.*

At least she could respond to that with the truth. "We *both* kept things from each other. It was not a healthy relationship on many levels, which is why I'm no longer in it. That's why I was available to get into this, with you."

George took her hand in his. "You really don't trust very easily, do you?"

It was the first time anyone had ever said that to her which meant that it wasn't true, or that it had become true recently, or that no one in her life had noticed. It was true, that much sank into her stomach like lead and she turned her head so she wouldn't have to face George.

What a lovely revelation! To make matters worse, it was possible that he had another point too, about her relationships. Had she kept herself too closed off? Was that what doomed her and Luke? It certainly wouldn't have saved her and Sam. But there had been a few others. Others that had had possibilities. At least at the beginning.

Were they all her fault? Every last one of them?

No. She wouldn't take the blame for her and Luke. She'd been open with him. Completely. It hadn't worked out for all the same reasons that other college relationships she'd seen fall apart, had fallen apart. She and Luke had grown apart. And that was that.

But it had hurt when he left. Even though he was heading off to save the world. It still hurt. Had it started then? The need to protect herself and keep more things private? She wasn't sure. But it was true. She had been holding back as much of herself as she could.

And *no one* had said anything! Not a single friend.

So, it was either a recent development or she had that many oblivious people in her life. Or they didn't care. In a way, she wanted it to be really recent. So it wouldn't be her fault she'd been alone. She felt tremendous relief when another thought occurred. Maybe people noticed but didn't have the nerve to say anything about it.

Not having the nerve to say something certainly wasn't one of George's faults. "And you're never afraid to say anything, are you? No matter what it is? No matter how much it hurts?"

"I didn't-" he started to say that he didn't mean to hurt her, but Jillian wasn't finished.

"I suppose you're right." She swallowed hard as her head drooped. "That's why it hurts. Because it's true."

"I didn't mean to…" He stopped as he gripped her hand a little tighter and with the other touched her shoulder. "Jillian, I'm sorry."

She shook her head, fighting the urge to shake his hands off of her. Putting up more walls wasn't going to help resolve a trust problem. *That's basic logic.* "It's not your fault. It's me." The lead in her stomach began to ache. *I'm really broken, aren't I?*

"You're not broken," George said, and Jillian's head turned sharply toward him.

"Did I say that out loud?"

George nodded, his face tight. "We've all got baggage. Some of mine called tonight and wants to have drinks." He took a breath. "I didn't realize that trust was such a touchy subject."

I didn't either. Jillian realized her fingernails were digging in to her palm.

"Want to tell me about it?" When she didn't answer right away, but bit her lip instead, he tried again. "Was this all Sam? Or is there more? Did he cheat on you?"

"It's not about that. It's not about cheating. I don't know," Jillian said, quietly. "I never thought about it." *If I had, maybe I'd be… different. More open. And ready for somebody like you.* "And it's not like I don't trust you at all. I believe you when you say you've been safe." She forced herself to keep looking at him as her throat tightened. "Obviously, I trust you about a lot of things…"

George moved his hand from her shoulder to touch her cheek. Even then, when he meant it to feel comforting to her, he felt a small amount of warmth spread through him, calming him from the inside. *Just touching her is like Valium. No, much better than Valium, it's a natural relaxer. But that's not the topic here.*

He swallowed again, and leaned over to touch his forehead to hers, feeling the soothing contact seep into him. *You're just not ready, are you? You're not in the same place I am. But, it's already too late for me. I love you. Despite how much I don't know about you and having to dig so hard to try to find out what it is, I love you. Maybe I even love you because there's so much I don't know and want to know.*

"One day," he said. "One day you'll be ready to let go with me. And I'll be here." *And I will be. I don't have a choice. I can't just stop feeling like this about you. I just hope you're ready sooner rather than later. I don't know how much longer I can keep from saying exactly how I feel about you and when I do, I don't want you to run.*

She closed her eyes. "I don't mean to hurt you. I don't want to hurt you. I'm really trying here. I'll give you what you want, as much as I can. This is just one little thing, for me. Is it too much for me to ask you to use one? I've heard that it feels better for you without, but it's not *that* big a deal, is it?"

George laughed. It was so hard to control the impulse to laugh that he had to sit back from her to avoid smacking his head against hers. The conversation had moved so far beyond condoms that her turning it back then was beyond absurd. "No, it's not a big deal," he said, when he'd stopped laughing. Then he sighed. "How did we get here?" It was rhetorical, and probably shouldn't have been said out loud any more than he should have laughed, but it summed up his thoughts pretty well.

"Well," Jillian said, with a light air, but a tight smile. "We came here after your game, got affectionate, and you took a phone call from your ex."

"So, it's my fault." George let go of her and dropped back on the bed. "If only you hadn't answered the phone..."

"I didn't answer it. It rang as I took it off the hook. What was I supposed to do?"

George made a slight shrug of his shoulders and made a grunting sound that had the feel of 'I don't know.' *We should have unplugged it.*

"And to think," Jillian said, and crossed her arms, "I was worried it was your mother."

George snorted then. "*That* would have been interesting." *Well, that made it final. No way in Hell we are making love tonight.* Between Jillian's walls going up, the question mark of a phone call, and the mention of his mother, his mood was as shot as hers.

Jillian got up and grabbed one of her shoes.

George sat up and reached for her, but she was already too far away and his arm dropped. "Hey. Wait. You aren't leaving?"

She picked up her other shoe, then straightened and tilted her head. "What's the point in staying?" She walked back to the bed. "We're both in miserable moods. I still need my pills. That hasn't changed." She put on a shoe and started tying the laces.

"But," George started, and then he stopped, as his mind raced. "Was that a fight? It didn't sound like a fight. Are you mad?"

"I'm not mad." Jillian began lacing up her other shoe. "It wasn't a fight."

"Then don't go."

She shook her head. "And do what here?"

George blinked. "Did you only come over for sex?"

Jillian leaned back. "What?! Of course not."

"Then why not stay?"

"George, I'm tired. I want to go home and go to bed."

That left him three choices. One, try to wear her down and get her to reluctantly stay. Two, watch her go. Three, go with her. *Option three.* "Okay. Give me ten minutes to get some stuff together."

"What?" Jillian asked, and rose from the bed.

"I'll need stuff." George stood and walked toward the door, still in his stocking feet. "My bag is downstairs." He decided to ignore the surprise on Jillian's face. So long as she didn't actually refuse to let him go along, it was okay. Not great. But, okay. Just because they weren't making love didn't mean he didn't want to hold her all night.

Jillian followed him downstairs, not saying anything. She was at a loss. While George took his bag upstairs, she dropped on the sofa and tried to figure out why he wanted it all, right away. No time to spare. They had to go from zero to the speed of light in no time flat. *We're a couple. We've told people. It's a commitment, of sorts. Why can't that be enough for a while? Take more time to get comfortable with each other. To build more trust.*

She got up from the sofa and wandered into the kitchen to look in his fridge. There wasn't anything in it that she wanted. Honestly, there wasn't anything she wanted at all. It was a distraction, plain and simple. *I'm not going to start stress eating.*

Her phone chirped and she checked her messages to find a message from her mother about their dinner plans on Saturday. *Perhaps some ice cream and a glass of wine, after all.* How were they going to get through dinner? Maybe they'd break up after drinks with the ex and she'd be able to get out of the dinner. *Maybe we'll break up tonight.*

She stopped herself from continuing that unpleasant train of thought as she heard him coming back down the stairs. He'd just invited himself to stay at her place. She should be furious. But instead, she felt... relieved. He was right. The weirdness upstairs had been a fight of sorts. She didn't want to fight. She wanted it to be easy, like love is supposed to be. *Oh, Lord. Love! Seriously...*

A carton *of ice cream and a bottle of wine.* Maybe that would take her mind off of the 'L' word. Thinking like that wasn't going to get her anywhere. He might be all in for sharing dark secrets and sex, but the 'L' word would drive him away faster than she could snap her fingers. *And if you make the mistake of thinking it, eventually it will come out.* Since it hadn't gone that far yet, it would be so stupid to say something without thinking and scare him off.

She closed her eyes for a moment as the anticipation of the feelings she'd experience if he dumped her poured over her. Her stomach clenched, her throat constricted, and her chest tightened. *Maybe Mal was right about the orgasms. Maybe it's already too late.* It was going to hurt so much when they broke up. Work consequences no longer mattered. She didn't care if she'd be the talk of office for the rest of her life. *I can't lose him. Not so soon. Not because I'm… afraid. Not because I'm broken and can't trust. I can. I can trust. I can do better. I can. I can tell him the stuff he wants to know.*

She picked up her purse and said, "Let's stop for a bottle of wine on our way." His eyebrows drew slightly together. "I want something special I don't have at home."

George nodded slowly. "Okay."

She managed to swallow and to breathe. *Just a little liquid courage.*

George had driven her car back to her place. That in and of itself would have told him something, if he'd known her longer. She didn't let people drive her car. Not because the car was particularly special. It was just something she didn't do. It was her car and she was a good driver.

But when she'd dropped her keys, he'd picked them up and held onto them. Not that she felt she couldn't have asked for them back. Initially, he'd just unlocked the doors and put his bags in the trunk. But then he'd walked to the passenger door and held it open for her and she'd entered the car.

Thirty-five minutes later, having decided to skip the special wine at the last moment, they were taking off their coats in her apartment. George was quiet. Jillian told herself it was because he was lost in thought, not that he was upset, and she quickly fed Charlie and got ready for bed. When she emerged from the bathroom, George took his turn, and she slid under the covers, trying to decide what to do.

At his house, she'd almost been resolute about telling him all about Sam. Almost. The wine had seemed like a good idea to help move it along. But they were both tired and she didn't want a hangover, so she'd backed away in favor of sleep. *Apparently any excuse will do. Chicken!*

The light in the bathroom switched off and George walked back into her room wearing pajama bottoms. Jillian looked at them and wondered if there was a hidden message in them. He'd been sleeping in his underwear the last few nights. *If there's a message, I probably deserve it. If not, I still probably deserve it.*

He shut off the lights in the bedroom with the switch on the wall and climbed into the bed, pulling the covers up to his chest and lying on his back with his arms over the covers. He made no move to touch her.

She lay on her back for a while, too, staring at the ceiling through the shadows. *You've reached an impasse. Either go back or go on. You can't stay here.*

George tried to convince himself to go to sleep. But he couldn't stop the churning of his mind. Every time he thought he'd made progress with

Jillian, he found himself thrown back again. This time he wasn't sure if it was really just her, or if it was Sarah. But it didn't really matter, because the walls were up again. And they weren't coming down, at least not right then. And they weren't coming down if he laid a siege, any more than if he begged and pleaded at the gate, so there wasn't any point in doing either. And he couldn't sleep.

He wanted to at least roll over and place an arm around her, but even that seemed out of the question at the moment. Maybe he was wrong. Maybe it wouldn't be a problem. Maybe she'd welcome the affection despite the current distance between them.

Jillian tilted her head and looked at the clock. Ten minutes had disappeared slowly. Another ten would eventually go by just as slowly. And then another and another until the dawn, unless she did something.

"With Sam, I was a fool," she said. It seemed like the best place to start. She heard George's head turn toward her on the pillow. "I fell for his charm so quickly. He was always complimentary, always concerned about my comfort. At least at first. I don't even remember when it changed, exactly, because it was so subtle. The compliments when I dressed as he liked, acted as he liked, and so on, were accompanied by the most subtle comments when I didn't. It made me feel like I'd failed him.

"Just a month in, he invited me to accompany him to gatherings with his friends and also his business functions. He was in banking and there were two, sometimes three, gatherings for drinks and appetizers nearly every week. Sometimes there were dinners. I should have noticed how he managed to manipulate me into wearing clothes that he wanted, jewelry he wanted, and even wearing my hair the way he wanted.

"But I never noticed, not really. Not until we'd been together eight months and it was Thanksgiving and he wanted us to have dinner with his parents. I assumed that it meant he was getting serious. Despite the nerves, I pushed to act as hostess here, in my own apartment. I seldom asked for anything, so I felt okay to push. Finally, he relented. Instead of a restaurant or a catered dinner in his apartment, I would cook and serve in mine.

"I thought it went very well. But the next day he didn't call. Or the next. It was nearly a week when I decided to call him. He said he needed time to calm down. When I asked him why, he tore into me and the apartment. He said, he couldn't believe that after all the time we'd spent together, attending all those functions, that I couldn't manage a dinner with his parents.

"He went on to criticize my boho-thrift store decorating. My place settings. How I could not know to use white dishes for a formal dinner with his parents... but to use mis-matched plates? And the blue glassware. He asked why I couldn't have at least bought some clear glass, if not some decent crystal. Except it wasn't asking, by then he'd raised his voice. It was the first time ever. How could I not know that people listen to light classical music during a formal dinner? Soft harps and woodwinds. Not light jazz with brass. And his voice was so nasty when he yelled that I hadn't enough sense to wear black and pearls either, I cringed at the tone. I'd worn red, my God, red with sparkly earrings. What was I, some kind of harlot?

"Yes, he actually used the word 'harlot.' I tried to defend myself. The plates were in fall colors, the way I like them. And I loved the blue glass. And the dress. I wanted to feel confident meeting his parents.

"But I couldn't defend myself to him. No matter how much I said or how I said it. He just kept on about how embarrassed he was, both for himself and for me. Never mind the food, or the conversation. It was a disaster. He said, we'd talk later when he'd calmed down.

"I cried. I cried and cried. Because I loved him. I really did. And I still didn't see it. Couldn't see it. How I was never myself anymore. Two weeks later, we had been speaking again, and he invited me to accompany him to a party.

"On the way to the party, he asked me to move in with him. I said, 'no.' He said, I needed to think about it. He said, we'd go to the party and talk about it later. But that's where I finally saw things as they were. For one thing, he wasn't who I thought he was, any more than I was who he wanted. I found him, not that he saw me, smoking grass on a balcony with his best friend. And the things he was saying, they were horrible. Beyond horrible.

"He was talking about how he'd fixed me up. Or thought he had. Trained me to dress and act the way I was supposed to. How he'd methodically complimented and coerced me to change my wardrobe. How he'd tricked me into putting highlights in my hair by suggesting I'd look wonderful with short hair and when I balked, he said, perhaps highlights then.

"He went on and on. How many times he'd attended events he didn't even want to go to, just to keep me from my eccentricity of playing jazz piano at that 'trashy club.' Finally, he finished with a last thought that I'd disappointed him something awful with his parents. But that he'd give me another chance around Christmas, and if I could pull myself together, he would propose. In the meantime, he'd asked me to move in.

"And he had a plan worked out where we'd move all my clothes, and important personal things, like photo albums. And then he was going to see to it that something happened while the movers moved the rest of my things. He'd see to it that my plates and glasses never entered his apartment. My hideous furniture would be a thing of the past. And my music and movies that he was so sick of, he'd never have to put up with those again. If he never saw another picture of Humphrey Bogart, let alone a movie, it'd be too soon. The one thing he wanted was my dining room table. He figured he'd hire a second truck for that. That would work.

"All that was left was to come up with an accident to get rid of the clothes he hated. That would take much more planning. And, of course, the 'damn' cat. But he'd just deal with 'that' for the time being.

"Everything that I was, I realized, he hated. And I'd fallen in love with him and let him do exactly what he'd said. He cut me up and shaped me. And I hated it. It may not have been in my consciousness. But I knew it, somewhere deep down. I'd let him do it. I hadn't ever said no. But, I hated it.

"I don't think the dinner was a rebellion. It was simply an assertion of myself because I'd been buried too deep for too long.

"But I'm just so grateful that I did it. And then that I overheard him. He wasn't who I thought he was. I still can't believe I caught him smoking grass. I had no idea. For all his desires for my image, I guess he hadn't thought much about his own.

"Still, the problem was, I loved him. All I could do was break it off and stay away from him. It was months before I even considered thinking about dating, let alone trying. One thing I'm sure about now is that I don't want anyone who isn't right for me. I mean, I don't want someone who has to change himself to be right. I haven't the slightest idea what makes someone right. But, what makes someone wrong; I suppose that's easier. But only when you know them, see them. Aren't being a fool.

"So there it is," Jillian said. "That's Sam."

George had been silent and still through the whole thing. She hadn't moved much either, just looked up at the ceiling. He wanted to say the right thing. *But what is the right thing?* He moved his hand across the gap between them over the covers and let the back of it touch her arm. "What a tool," he murmured.

She let out a snort-like laugh. "Something like that," she said, and rolled onto her side toward him. She'd actually done it. Not that she'd done the best job of explaining it, but it was accurate enough. She'd actually told George.

He rolled toward her and tossed his arm over her, then held on while he scooted the distance between them, so he could hold her against him. "Come here." Jillian hesitated, but only a moment, and then snuggled up against him and he kissed her hair. "*He's* the fool. Is he anywhere in the picture anymore? Mutual friends? Stuff like that?"

"No," she answered. "Thankfully, we didn't have a group in common, so cutting him out was easy in that sense."

"Good. I don't want to run into him."

"Why not?"

George sighed. "I might just lose my temper and punch the guy."

Jillian smiled. She wasn't able to help herself. "You would not," Jillian said. "That's not you, at all. Jealous, maybe. But punching someone for a wrong in the past like that. No. The first thing Mal said to me when I told her about us was to be sure you weren't another Sam. And you aren't like him. But you're not like that either."

"That was the first thing Mal said?" George asked.

"Well, after she told Christy off and did say she was happy for us."

"Oh. That's nice," George said, hesitantly. "Is she your best friend? I just realized that I don't know…"

Jillian smiled a little broader. "If forced to choose, then yes. Mal and I usually see things eye to eye. Although, lately she's been a little aggressive in the work arena."

"You're not aggressive at work, huh?"

"Uh, not like Mal is."

George nodded against her head. "Okay." He paused a moment and then said, "Well, thanks for telling me about the tool. I didn't think it was such a big deal. I get it now."

Jillian nodded against his chest.

"And for the record, I agree completely. Either a person is right for you or they aren't. Changing people is impossible."

Jillian nodded again.

"I like you the way you are."

Jillian smiled. "I like you too. The way you are."

"So far, so good, then." He lifted his arm and slipped it under the covers, so he could slide down a little and be closer to her face. "How're you doing?"

"Ok," Jillian said, pleased when he took her in his arms again.

"Ready to sleep?"

Even without the tears that sometimes still came when her thoughts turned to Sam, just telling George everything had been draining. She nodded. "I think so. I'm tired enough. But I may still have trouble falling asleep. Thinking about Sam has that rather annoying effect on me. Once I start thinking about it, I have trouble stopping."

"Mm-hmm," George said. "Well, let's try." At least she was in his arms again. And while on an average day he'd take sex over just about anything, that night he was willing to give it up for the way she'd opened up to him. Nothing was ever going to be quite the same after that. Some of the barriers, he figured, had come down.

When Sergei waved to George as he was heading back from the breakroom with his first cup of coffee, George nodded at him and changed his direction. He and Sergei talked a little about the game and then Sergei asked George into his office.

"Everything all right on the, uh, romantic front?" Sergei asked, after pushing his office door against the door jam.

"Yeah," George said. "Why?"

Sergei raised an eyebrow and then shrugged. "I thought you two looked all cozy last night. But you're, uh, you're not looking like you did on Wednesday. I *had* figured it'd be a good night…"

George exhaled through his nose. "It was a good night, Serge."

"Sure," Sergei said. "But she didn't wax your pole. Did she?"

"Oh, Christ, Serge," George said, as he stuffed his free hand in his pocket. "After the game we went back to my place and Sarah happened."

Sergei took a step back. "Sarah? What's Sarah got to do with this?"

"She called, if you can believe it, after all this time. She wants to have drinks."

"I assume you made the mistake of telling Jillian."

"She was there when Sarah called," George said, not adding that she'd been the one to answer the phone. He rubbed his forehead with his free hand. "And she's invited."

Sergei let out a low whistle. "Oh, there's a recipe for disaster. You're going?"

George took a step back and leaned against Sergei's office wall. "I know its nuts, but one day I'll go crazy wondering what she wanted, if I don't."

"And Jillian's going too? When is this?"

"Tonight."

"Shit. How are you so calm?"

"Mostly, I'm trying not to think about it."

"Denial, the non-prescription solution for millions," Sergei said, as he sat on the edge of his desk. "Well, on the plus side, you've got proof Jillian's really into you."

George's eyebrows pulled together. "Huh?"

"Would you go meet her ex for drinks under the same circumstances?"

Before George could even think about an answer, his phone chirruped a short series of sounds that made him smile. As he took out his phone, Sergei asked, with a smirk, "That her?" George, still smiling since he'd set both a special ringtone and a message tone for her so that he knew without looking, glanced at Sergei for a moment in affirmation and then looked at his phone to read Jillian's message.

I've changed my mind. The tap dancing penguin will do nicely.

George smiled wider. "Yep," he said, in answer to Sergei then thumbed a one-handed reply to Jillian. *Now you tell me. I've been working on a seal for 24 hours.* That was a good sign. The flirting was back.

He holstered his phone and glanced back at Sergei, who nodded and then said, "Okay. I'll lay off. I can see that she's making you happy. Despite…"

George gave him a friendly smack on the arm. "See ya later."

"Yeah," Sergei said.

Halfway across the floor, heading back to his office, George's phone chirruped again. He lifted it out and read. *You need to start anticipating my whims…*

He walked straight to Jillian's office, just rapping the door as he walked in. He was grinning from ear to ear, so when he crossed his arms like he was angry, he couldn't even begin to carry it off. "I'm supposed to anticipate your *whims*, am I?"

Jillian looked up from her computer and blinked at him with an innocent look on her face. Then she batted her eyes at him and her voice came out a bit like Scarlett O'Hara. "Why, of course."

He laughed and uncrossed his arms. "I guess I'll get on the phone then."

"You just do that little thing," she said, sounding even more like Vivien Leigh.

George sat on the edge of her desk. "I'm not very good at anticipating whims. I'll need to learn that skill. Tell me what you might be thinking about in terms of lunch and give me a head start, hmm?"

Still channeling Scarlett, Jillian batted her eyelashes again. "Well, now, I'm afraid I won't be able to join you for lunch today."

"What? Why?" George asked.

Dropping the sweet, southern simper, Jillian exhaled. "I'm going shopping. I need a dress for tonight."

George leaned forward. "What do mean? You have dresses."

"Nothing that will work for tonight," Jillian said, and pushed her back from her desk. "This isn't just any occasion."

"I'm sure there's something-"

"Nothing. I donated the dresses I bought to look appropriate for Sam. That leaves my work clothes, formal wear which is too formal, and my…um…weird stuff. Well, anyway, nothing that you'd like me wearing tonight." She crossed her arms.

George tilted his head a bit. "Wear the dress you had on Monday night. You looked fantastic in that."

"I haven't washed it. Besides, that's not a cocktail dress either." Jillian lifted a hand to her mouth and bit her thumbnail.

It's not? That's not what this is about, is it? George leaned over further, trying to make himself more level with her eyes. "Hey, now. You're not supposed to be nervous about tonight. That's for me."

Jillian dropped her hands into her lap and looked at them. "I'll be on your arm when you meet your ex and her husband. Whether I'm nervous or not, I'm sure that my appearance will matter to you then."

"Just the way you are," George said. "Remember?" He paused for Jillian to look up at him again. "Forget about who we're meeting tonight. Dress however you'd dress if we were going for drinks, just us."

Jillian crossed her arms again. "You sure about that? You still haven't seen much of my wardrobe."

He grinned. "You're right. But, I'm not afraid."

"Okay. You win." She stood up and stepped next to him, careful not to touch, but close. "I'll go home and change after work. You do the same and I'll pick you up."

"All right," George said, as he slid his hand along the top of the desk, blocked from the view outside the office by his body, to touch her skirt with the tip of his finger. "Now about lunch…"

"I'm thinking we eat in today," Jillian said.

George let out a soft sigh. "Yeah. I figured it would be something like that."

George had been calm all afternoon. He even managed to not think much about the evening while he changed his clothes. But in the moments before Jillian arrived, he sat on his couch and then his mind wandered. In only a few short minutes, he found himself up and pacing the room. *There are only so many things she could possibly want. She invited Jillian, so logically it could just be something as simple as catching up. Not necessarily anything big.* But as Jillian had been earlier, he was now quite concerned about his appearance. *Sergei was right about being in denial.*

By the time Jillian arrived, he'd picked up Ringo and been practicing a few simple loops while he waited outside on the porch. He chose the simple loops because his hands were shaking and he began to worry he'd give himself a black eye if he tried anything more complicated.

He didn't let Jillian stop the engine. He rushed down the steps and slid into her car. She had a coat on, wise in the cold, so he couldn't see her dress. But he could see that she'd done her hair and make-up like she had at the blue feather on Monday night, even down to the red lipstick and 40s hair.

When she turned her head and said, "Hi!" he lost his train of thought for a moment, watching her lips move, even just that little bit.

"Hi," he said. "You look fantastic."

She swallowed noticeably. "So do you. I forgot to tell you how great you look in a suit." She reached toward him and grabbed his hand for a quick squeeze. "Buckle up," she said, and put her hand back on the wheel. "Safety first."

He laughed softly. "Yes, ma'am."

As she pulled away from the curb, she glanced at him again. "How's it going getting my tap dancing penguin?"

He really laughed. "Um, tricky. Disney has a lot of paperwork. But we shall triumph."

"I never doubted," Jillian said. After a few minutes of silence, she switched on the radio.

Sarah had picked the bar of a nice hotel for their rendezvous, making it all the better Jillian had come with him, to George's way of thinking. He wouldn't touch Sarah, not for anything, but that didn't mean that Jillian would believe it, when it was important. And if she didn't come along, he wouldn't have proof the doctor had come along.

The bar was nice enough, with a pianist and a singer entertaining, and a small dance floor next to the long bar and the tables. Although initially Jillian's arm had been through his as they walked into the hotel, when they entered the bar, he'd taken her hand in his instead, squeezing lightly. It seemed ridiculous, but he had an ominous feeling.

They moved to the coat check room, and George finally had a look at Jillian's complete outfit. Why she'd been worried was beyond him. She looked beautiful in a blue dress, with a v-neckline, that hugged her fairly tightly until the hips where the skirt flared out just a bit. *There isn't another woman in the world that I'd want with me at this moment.* "You really look great. Thank you for coming."

Jillian smiled at him with tight lips. "I'm glad you wanted me here." It was true. She was glad he wanted her there, no matter how awkward it was going to be.

He took her hand again, instead of offering his arm. He needed to hold on to her. Her smile broadened a little. Even if nothing good came of the evening otherwise, with the way he kept holding onto her, she knew that he wanted her there and found her presence comforting.

So rather than on his arm, Jillian followed George's lead holding onto his hand. She could tell the moment he spotted his ex as his body seemed to stiffen a bit and he squeezed her tighter. She gave his hand a squeeze back and he looked back at her. She managed a real smile for him, thinking about how much he seemed to be depending on her.

George smiled back at Jillian and then turned back to face whatever was coming.

CHAPTER NINETEEN

Introductions didn't take very long and George found it quite ironic that he was actually shaking the hand of the man that had come between him and Sarah. *Not that it matters anymore. A few years back I might have considered plunging a utensil into the man's gut. Maybe that's why she suggested drinks...*

The doctor wasn't at all what Jillian expected, although she hadn't thought consciously about what she did expect. *I guess for some reason I thought he'd be something like George.* He was short with thinning hair, and gave Jillian the impression that he put in a lot of time on his appearance, though it may have mostly been the expensive suit and cologne. He seemed fit enough, but again, not like George.

At least he didn't come off as if he believed he knew everything or was rude in the first five minutes. The man clearly had been raised to have manners. In fact, he led the conversation at first, making the necessary small talk, asking Jillian what she did for a living.

Sarah wasn't quite what Jillian had expected either. She was pretty, but not on the super model/movie star level that Jillian had been worrying about. Much like her doctor, Sarah seemed mostly fit, and also clearly spent a lot of her time under the California sun. She also had taste in clothes, elegant and expensive.

Jillian wondered what Sarah thought of her. She'd followed George's directive to dress like herself. It was just a shame that herself wanted to wear her hair and makeup like a 40s movie starlet, or she could look like everybody else. At least she'd had a dress that wasn't from the last century in her closet. Glancing around the bar, she saw mostly business travelers in suits. The majority of the women wear in blacks, grays, and beiges, even Sarah had worn all black, so Jillian really stood out.

Jillian had been considering her mood when Sarah ordered a glass of the house red. Since a white wine was Jillian's usual drink, she'd been thinking ordering the house white. Suddenly that seemed like a bad move, as if she was making some kind of statement about Sarah. She ordered a soda. While alcohol would have probably helped her nerves, she couldn't shake the feeling that she needed to be able to think very clearly, and since this meeting was supposed to be just drinks, she wouldn't have a meal to help cut the alcohol before she drove again.

While the atmosphere was a bit awkward, it seemed benign enough until George ordered and Sarah commented that George's drink was still a scotch neat and Jillian realized she was gritting her teeth. She had a past too, so she couldn't expect George not to, but she didn't want anyone else to have a claim on him, even in memory.

The conversation tripped along for a nearly ten minutes, mostly with George and Sarah catching up, while avoiding the topic of her and the doctor. After those ten minutes and a few sips of their drinks, George could feel the tension in the air increase when the doctor gave Sarah a look and she seemed to nod. The doctor turned to George and asked if there was any objection to a dance with Jillian. *And here it comes...* He looked at Jillian, she winked at him with her left eye so neither Sarah or the doctor could see it. "No objections," he said.

Jillian stood up and walked behind George's chair on her way to the clear section of floor. She dropped her hand on George's shoulder and squeezed. He reached up and caught her hand as she was just letting go, and she turned to see his face. He smiled at her and gave her hand a brief squeeze.

"Everything all right?" The doctor asked Jillian, and she realized she'd mostly been watching the conversation back at the table.

She wasn't a lip reader, but she could tell from the way Sarah kept hunching over and looking down that she was saying things that she didn't particularly want to. *Is she confessing to him? Telling him when she started seeing the doctor?*

Focusing for a moment on her current dance partner, Jillian answered. "I suppose I'm more than a little interested in what's going on over there."

The doctor nodded. "I can imagine." He glanced over there. "I'm worried about her, too."

The bomb was coming, that much was obvious, he just wished she'd drop it and get it over with. Sarah was clearly dancing around whatever it was she wanted to tell him. Her doctor had taken Jillian away so she could say whatever it was, and she was stalling.

When George ran out of patience, he said, "What do you want, Sarah?

Why did you want to see me?"

She stared at her wine glass and let out a deep breath. "Truthfully, I don't. It's an assignment for my therapy."

"Therapy?" George snorted a bit. "I didn't realize it was still in vogue for everyone in California to be in therapy."

"It isn't. Mark asked me to go... it's a long story." She looked at him. "I figure the past is the past, but my therapist thinks I have some guilt issues causing me trouble in the present. So I'm supposed to confess my wrongs and ask forgiveness."

"That's very ten steps, isn't it?" George said, with a slight laugh.

"George, please," she said. "This isn't easy for me."

"Do you think this is easy for me?" He crossed his arms. "And you still haven't told me whatever it is-"

"I was pregnant," she blurted out.

George blinked slowly. The light dimmed a bit. He could hear the ice clinking in Jillian's soda glass. He could smell the scotch in his own all the way on the table. There was a fly buzzing somewhere in the room. And apparently someone had opened a window and all the oxygen had been sucked out of the bar. *Pregnant?* He finally managed to refocus his eyes. "Whatwhenhow?" It all spilled out as one word. *God, do I have a kid? Was she pregnant when she left me? Have she and the doctor been raising my kid? Oh, fuck, fuck, fuck... WAS pregnant? Wait. Did she... terminate it?*

"I miscarried about a month before you asked me if I wanted to move in."

George swallowed and said nothing to stop her from continuing. *Miscarried.* He listened to her tell him how she'd been in denial about being pregnant. How she'd put off telling him for a few weeks until she was sure, and then a few more weeks, and a few more weeks. She admitted to putting off telling him because she wasn't sure what she wanted to do about it. Then she'd miscarried before she'd made any kind of decision. She'd felt so awful about not telling him that she couldn't bring herself to do it later.

She then told him that she'd met the doctor in some kind of support group. A support group that George didn't know she belonged too, of course. The doctor had been at a few meetings as a sort of guest speaker, answering questions about the clinical aspects of miscarriage. George was grateful that she didn't go into much detail about how the relationship had developed from there. He didn't want to know. It was enough to know that their relationship had been disintegrating as early as he suspected, maybe even a little earlier. He didn't even care if she'd physically cheated on him anymore.

It was more than enough to know that about half of the time they were together, they hadn't been. She'd already checked out. And that she'd kept one of the most important things that can happen in a relationship from him. And he hadn't even noticed. Was that his fault? Or was she just that good at acting?

While she kept on talking, he took a drink. There wasn't much else to do apart from asking her to be quiet. There couldn't be much else to say. But Jillian wasn't back yet. So, what did it matter? He didn't realize he'd downed the entire drink until he set the glass on the table. "Hmmph." *Maybe another scotch…*

He glanced back up at Sarah. She was still talking. *What could she possibly have left to say?* He didn't listen. He glanced toward the dance floor. Jillian and the doctor were still there. Must not have taken as long as he thought it had to suddenly have such a life altering revelation, the responsibility of a kid and the loss of it. Couldn't have taken a minute. There and gone.

He turned his whole head toward Jillian. *I want to get out of here.*

Even though Jillian was trying to be polite and pay attention to what Sarah's doctor was saying, she was still much more attune to what was happening back at the table. She didn't even see the motion, but she knew the instant that George turned to look at her and she turned toward him. *Ohhhh, noooo.* The look on his face was pure misery. *What did that woman do to you?*

She didn't even look back at the doctor. "I think it's time for me to go."

He followed her gaze. "Oh. Yes. I see." He quit moving, but he held onto Jillian's hand. "Give me a second, please." He released her and pulled out his wallet and retrieved a card. He passed it to Jillian. "That didn't take long, so I'm guessing he isn't responding or asking questions… If he decides he needs… something, please call."

Jillian frowned and smacked the card against her other hand. "I don't know what she just told him, but the look on his face… I don't think he wants this."

"And that's why I gave it to *you*," the doctor said.

Jillian didn't bother to answer. *You* knew *she was going to do something just awful to George and you* let *her*. She walked away from the doctor neither knowing nor caring whether or not he was following behind her. She took the quickest route back to the table.

George jumped up as soon as he saw her coming and fumbled with his wallet. He didn't look to see what he pulled out; he just dropped some bills on the table.

"Ready?" Jillian asked, from two tables away.

"Oh, yeah," George answered, stuffing his wallet into his back pocket. Jillian spared only a the briefest glance at Sarah, who looked surprised at the movement, and grabbed her purse from the table with one hand, George's hand with the other, and then led the way out of the bar.

Jillian struggled into her coat on the way out of the hotel, trying to keep pace with George. She didn't think he was leaving her behind, but he wasn't exactly taking into account the difference his stride and her high heels created either. In a way, she supposed it was convenient that they couldn't hold hands at that point; he might just drag her along.

He hadn't said a word since they'd left the table. Of course, she didn't expect him to, not right then, anyway. As they were nearing the car, he seemed to realize that he'd been moving a bit faster than she could manage, because he actually turned and looked for her.

George would never have claimed to have been actually thinking at that point, not about where he was or what he was doing, at any rate. He was mostly moving because he needed to move. And walking fast was all he really had at that moment. Matching his stride to the repetitive chant that kept echoing through his head. *What the fuck? What the fuck?*

When he saw the rear bumper of Jillian's car he flashed back to the outside world. *Jillian. Christ.* After he'd retrieved her coat, he'd gone on auto-pilot. He quickly looked over his shoulder to see if she was still with him. He took a breath when he saw she was there and then, although still not slowing down, he reached out for her hand again.

She took his hand and he slowed his pace just a little, hesitant of his next move. He still felt like moving, perhaps running. But he had a responsibility. "Sorry," he said, over his shoulder.

"It's okay," Jillian said.

He figured it wasn't, but if she was going to be understanding, he wasn't going to argue. He slowed a little more.

When they arrived at her car, she let go of him and unlocked her door. He paced back and forth at the rear bumper. "What do you want to do?"

He'd gone back into his head again. Her voice pulled him out. "Huh? Oh." He didn't have much of an answer. "I don't know. I'm thinking I need a walk."

"Okay." She relocked her car door. "Let's go."

He stopped walking and looked at her, really looked at her. "You're not in walking shoes."

"Well, that's beside the point." She walked over to him, reached out a hand to his arm, and squeezed lightly. "I'm not leaving you alone."

"I'm not going to be good company," George said, shaking his head.

"I'm not expecting good company. I don't know what she said to you, I can only tell it was terrible. You're too upset; there's no way I'm leaving you alone."

He pulled his lips into a tight smile and covered her hand with his. "You're great, but, really, I'm no good to you right now."

She shook her head and exhaled. "Right now, it's about you. Not me. Come on." She turned her body away from the car. "Pick a direction."

"No," George said. "No, your shoes. Look-"

"Argue all you like; I'm not leaving you alone. Do you have your yo-yo?"

"My yo-yo isn't up to the challenge."

"All right. Where do you want to go? Would you like to get some food?"

He shook his head.

"Change clothes and shoot some hoops?"

He shook his head again.

"Have angry sex?"

"What?!"

"I guess you are listening," Jillian said. "I was beginning to wonder if you were just saying no. Come on." She took a step away from the car and her hand slid down his arm. "Walking is good for you."

"Now, look. I need…" *I can't do what I need to do around you. I need to shout. I need to swear. I need to pound something. I need to…* "I need to talk to Orville."

Jillian turned back. "Okay. Get in the car."

"I can get there on my own."

"Of course, you can." Jillian nodded, then she cocked her head to the left and her lips curved up into a tight smile. "Now get in the car."

George stood his ground a moment. He didn't need Jillian to start bossing him around. He'd had enough. She wasn't-

"Get in the car."

Her soft, but commanding, voice snapped him back again. She'd unlocked her door and was standing there, between the door and car.

"George. Let's go."

He didn't want to get into a confined space. As it was, he was breathing a bit hard and feeling short of oxygen. He already felt claustrophobic just thinking about the car.

She shut the car door and walked back to him. "You know it wasn't very long ago that I was really upset and you told me it was going to be okay." She put her arms around him and squeezed him. "Eventually, this will be too."

He closed his eyes and hugged her back for a moment. "I can't believe you're not asking me what happened."

"You'll tell me when you're ready. And I'll be here when you are."

George recognized his own words again and shook his head. "You're amazing."

"Thank you," she said, and then stepped back from him. "Now, if you still want to see Orville…"

"…then get in the car. Right."

Half-way down the hall from the rec room, George stopped and leaned against the wall. Jillian was turning out to be just as stubborn as could be in their private life. She wouldn't listen to him. She refused to leave him alone. She wouldn't drop him off at Whistling Elms. It was all he could do to get her to wait in the rec room, rather than follow him to Orville's door. She'd promised she'd leave him at Orville's door, but he didn't want her to go even that far.

So, there he stood, leaning against the wall, trying to get a grip on why he suddenly felt like he was making some kind of mistake. Everything he was doing made sense. He didn't want, couldn't allow, Jillian to see the kind of anger he was experiencing at that moment. It would scare the crap out of her. And she'd be gone. No chance left in hell that she'd ever fall in love with him.

He needed to talk it out, correction, scream and curse it out, with someone who could understand. He needed to get through this. Deal with it. *Then I can go back to Jillian.*

His eyes closed and he sagged against the wall. That was it. He'd calmed down enough, just enough, to see it.

Jillian had selected a hard sofa, rather than a squishy one, figuring she would be there a while and needed the back support. She folded her coat and set it next to her, atop her purse, thinking how she should have pushed harder to get him to eat. *I doubt I would have succeeded. But I should have tried harder.*

The question of what to do while she waited for who knows how long sprang up. She supposed she could fool around with her phone. At some point she'd downloaded a few books to it. Maybe one of them would keep her occupied.

But she didn't bother to dig out her phone. Wondering about what *that woman* had said to George was going to distract her from a book. It wasn't hard to imagine a few things that could get such a reaction, and although she was dying to know, she'd resisted asking. He'd made it even more challenging when he mentioned that she wasn't asking.

She'd bit her tongue, knowing that pushing wasn't going to help. She couldn't force her way in. Well, she could try. But if he didn't open up when she'd pushed, it was going to take them right back to the stalemate from the previous night. Only this time, it wouldn't be a proper stalemate, it'd be a fight. She didn't want to fight.

So, what did the miserable cow say? What did she do? Was it a confession?

Probably. But what did she confess to? He already knew that she'd been seeing that doctor, in some way. Whether it was an emotional thing or if it had become physical before she'd left didn't really matter, he knew.

Would he react that strongly to something he already knew? I don't know. Maybe. It was probably something he didn't know. More men? A kid? Or something else?

The possibilities were overwhelming, really. There was no way she could narrow it down herself. If only she could, she'd be more prepared... *Why did she ever call him? She could have left him alone. She could have just left well enough alone.* She took a breath. *Unless, of course, it's about a kid. That's it isn't it? There isn't any other reason-"*

She looked up as she heard the footsteps. *George? I thought you wanted to talk to Orville. Am I imagining this?* But he wasn't a hallucination. He hurried up to her and dropped to his haunches in front of her.

"I'm sorry," George said, half-hanging his head. "I know I *should* be talking to you. I just... I just..." He exhaled really hard and raised his eyes to meet hers. "I... really don't want you to see this. To see *me* like this."

Jillian almost asked him what he didn't want her to see, but it was obvious enough that that wasn't the point at all. She sat forward a little and opened her arms.

The cover of his anger fell in the face of her blind acceptance and the beginnings of the aching that he'd tried to hold at bay with that anger welled up behind it. He tried to focus on her instead. "Ah, God, Jillian," he mumbled and then dropped to his knees, plopped his head into her lap, and wrapped his arms around her waist.

She gently laid her hands on his head, running her fingers over his hair, trying to soothe him. He closed his eyes. "George," she said, continuing to rub his head. "Oh, George. I'm so sorry."

"You don't even *know*," he said.

"I don't have to," she answered. *Maybe it's better I don't. If I did I'd probably say something to try to make you feel better and make it worse instead.*

The trouble he was having breathing changed from his lungs to his nose as his eyes watered. "I thought I had a handle on what had happened between us, me and Sarah. I thought I was done with it. I thought it was dead and buried. I thought I'd taken my lessons and crawled away. But I had no idea when things had actually fallen apart. I had no idea how messed up it was. I didn't know, until just now."

Her hands were still on him. "I'm sorry."

He didn't deserve it, her sympathy. "You don't know what *I did*."

Jillian slid her fingers through his hair, feeling an ache in her chest for him. "No. I don't." She lowered one hand her along his neck and rubbed his back through his suit coat. "But I do know you." He made a snorting sound. "Not as well as I will. But I know you didn't do anything to deserve-"

"She was pregnant!" It would have been a loud shout had it not been muffled by her lap. "She carried my child. And I was such a great partner, such a terrific potential father, that she never told me."

Jillian caught her breath. *A child.*

George started to choke. "And she lost it."

Jillian didn't stop rubbing him but she closed her eyes as his words squeezed her inside. *Lost.* She bent more at the waist, wanting to hug him or find some way to blot out the pain, cover and defend him. She whispered. "I'm so sorry."

"All the time she was saying she loved me to my face, it must have been a lie. I thought we'd fallen apart, but we never were together."

"Oh, George," Jillian said.

"But the worst is," he stopped to swallow and then realized he couldn't say it. If he confessed that now, it was the definitely the end of them. No woman in her right mind would want to be with him after he told her that. And she was rubbing his head like a mother too…

The seconds ticked away and Jillian kept on rubbing him, sliding her hand up his back, then back down under the collar of his jacket. Eventually, she prompted him to continue, saying, "But the worst…"

He squeezed his eyes tighter. Why hadn't he stopped before saying that?

"But the worst…" Jillian prompted again.

He wanted to say that it was nothing. That he was rambling. But he couldn't quite manage the lie. "I shouldn't have said that," George choked out.

Jillian leaned over further and dropped a kiss on his head. "You can say anything. Tell me anything."

In his need to believe her, he opened his mouth, but couldn't quite let out the words. That was when Jillian moved her hands to lift him up a bit, and he sat back and looked up her.

She moved her hands to the sides of his face. "It *will* be all right, someday. I promise you."

He blinked, still fighting the moisture in his eyes, and reached up for her hands. It was only as he realized that she was leaning over, in what he thought was likely a move to kiss him, that he panicked for her. *You deserve better than me.* "I'm glad!" It was the only thing to do, the only way to save her from him. He had to confess, after all.

"What?" She froze. "Glad of what?"

"That's the worst of it. I'm glad she lost it."

Oh, the baby. "I see," she said.

He pulled back from her, taking her hands down from his face. "Do you understand me? I'm glad. I'm grateful."

"Yes," Jillian said. "I understand."

"I don't think you do. I'm *glad*. It's as bad as asking her to get rid of it. Don't you think?"

"To be grateful that a woman who hurt you this much, who kept so much a secret from you, didn't have your child?" Jillian leaned just a little closer and turned her hands in his so she could squeeze them. "To be glad you're not tied to her for the rest of your life? The same as asking her to get rid of it? No. I don't think it's the same at all."

He closed his eyes and exhaled through his nose, though it was still a little tough to breathe through it. He next opened his eyes when she tugged her hands free and placed them about his neck. George raised himself onto his knees and leaned forward. She scooted a little closer to the edge of the sofa so she could give him a real hug. He held onto her tightly, trying to comprehend how she could be okay with him feeling as he did, but failing in that, simply began to repeat to himself, *Thank God, thank God, thank God.*

"Everything alright?" Orville's voice penetrated the private zone that George hadn't even noticed had been created around them until the spell was broken.

"Hello, Orville," Jillian said, and slid away from both George and the sofa to shake Orville's hand, affording George a moment to collect himself.

He had to actually wipe his eyes before he struggled to his feet.

Jillian was talking to Orville, making polite conversation, when he'd finally decided he could turn around. "Hey, Orville," he said.

Orville wasn't fooled, that was obvious. But he didn't pry either. "I wasn't expecting you two tonight."

"Yeah, um," George faltered and Jillian picked up the conversation. "It really wasn't planned and we didn't mean to disturb you. I think we're just going to go now." She took George's hand and looked up at him. "You're still planning to come by for your regular Saturday night, tomorrow, aren't you?"

He nodded, and mumbled something agreeable.

Orville nodded back. "Okay. You two kids have a good night, then."

As Jillian grabbed her coat, Orville dropped his voice to speak to George. "Sorry. The desk called. I didn't mean to interrupt anything."

George shook his head. "Nah. It's okay. My fault. Long story." Then as Jillian rejoined them he forced a smile. "See you tomorrow, Orville."

Although he'd much rather have taken the day off, George couldn't argue his way out of sitting in his office on Saturday. Unlike Jillian, he wasn't worried about the dinner with her parents. After the Hell of Friday night, he figured it couldn't get much worse unless there was violence. Although anything was possible, he didn't think her father *knew* they were having sex, so the likelihood of violence was pretty low.

Another night had come and gone and he hadn't had much sleep. So, while he kept vacillating between asking himself over and over why Sarah had done that to him and gratefully marveling at Jillian's response to it all, he was officially useless. He sat at his desk, trying to stay awake by drinking caffeine, and trying to distract his thoughts by surfing the web. *I'm really only here as moral support for my people, so it's okay.* Of course, he didn't believe it, but he couldn't concentrate either.

Since Jillian had been adamant about getting her nails done over lunch, he didn't even have lunch to look forward to. He tried to convince her that she looked wonderful and didn't need to worry about anything, but she wouldn't listen, and he gave up, certain that it was just nerves and he knew better than to be logical about feelings. It was his turn to be a rock for her, and he figured from her tight lips when he'd spoken, she needed a strong, but silent, rock.

Whether he was right about what she needed or not, at least he did better with the lunch order, making a point to cover all the needs he was aware of. *A lot has changed in the last week. Much of it, for the better.*

Somethings, however, hadn't changed. He had a text from Taro just after lunch about shooting hoops, which he had to decline without explanation, not comfortable lying to his friends at the moment. The team up with Jillian was still a secret and he wasn't willing to blow that.

Taro hadn't replied. Sergei did a few minutes later though, texting something just a little crass about what George was finding more important than basketball. George made a point to delete it immediately, just in case. He'd never seen Jillian glance at his phone when it was out, but since she'd been clear that she didn't want Sergei saying anything about her, it was certainly better not to risk her ever stumbling on it.

Despite her apparent nerves, or perhaps to give her more of a feeling of control, Jillian had offered to drop George at Whistling Elms after work, and then pick him up there to go to dinner. While he usually enjoyed the walk, George accepted. It gave him more time with Orville and made it easier for him to bring a suit along.

Even though he'd set a reminder on his phone to give him time to change, George kept glancing at his watch. Orville noticed.

"What's up with you tonight? You're as unfocused on the game as I've ever seen you."

George didn't look away from the game to answer; Orville had used this kind of distraction before. "Meeting Jillian's parents tonight."

Orville looked at George. "Yeah. That'll do it. And it explains the suit you brought with you." After a few seconds, Orville's simulated car crashed into a simulated embankment. He continued, "That's a little fast these days isn't it?"

"What? Meeting her parents? Yes and no," George said, keeping his eyes on the screen so he could finish the race and get the prize money to upgrade his car. "I told you we decided to be exclusive."

"Yeah," Orville said. "I remember. I also remember that your first date was Tuesday. And she's already pushing you to meet her parents?"

"Actually, she isn't too sure about it. But they called. Some busybody they know saw us together. They want to meet me."

Orville sat back and crossed his arms. "She isn't too sure about it? Why?"

"She seems to think that it's not going to go well. She's really nervous. She had to have her nails done today." He laughed. "As if a fresh manicure will make some kind of difference."

"Can I give you fifty cents worth of free advice?"

"Sure," George said, and he steered around a barrier. *You will anyway.*

"Never underestimate the power of a woman who thinks she looks good. Something about that helps them channel their inner strength. You think she had a manicure or had her hair done or something and in reality she just got a booster dose of cosmic rays."

George laughed. "Cosmic rays?"

"Yeah. You know. Super hero stuff. Or super villain, depending." Orville chuckled too.

"And me without my kryptonite. What'll I do?" George, suddenly thinking of his most recent villain/archenemy, took the final turn too fast and rolled the car. "Dammit!"

Orville shushed him and George apologized, and then glanced at his watch. Orville grinned. "If you'd rather put on your suit and pace, I think I'd understand."

George frowned at him. "I'm not worried. I just don't want to be late. Jillian's picking me up and we're going straight there."

"Uh-huh." He patted George on the shoulder. "We should race again, if you have time. I might win with you being this distracted."

"We have time," George said. "And I'm not distracted."

Orville picked up his controller. "If I were you, I'd be on pins and needles."

"Yeah, well, I'm fine."

"Good." Orville started the game. "Then when I win, I'll be able to claim it."

After a few minutes, Orville leaned toward the game, not looking at George. "How is it you're able to sit, Kid? You know her father's going to ask you about your intentions and all."

George didn't let Orville's question distract him. He'd had plenty of time to think about it in between bouts of self-pity and anger the previous night, as he and Jillian had lain in each other's arms. "Because I know my intentions," he said, with emphasis.

Orville let out a heavy breath. "So it's come to that already, has it? She's the one?"

George nodded, though he kept his eyes on the game. "If there really is such a thing, she's it."

"And if there isn't?"

In the darkest black of the night, when I saw myself as evil and dirty and undeserving of forgiveness, let alone affection, and she knew all about why, she still chose me. "Then she's still it."

"How do you know?" Orville asked.

George paused the game and turned toward Orville. "Because," he exhaled another breath, "if I lose her, I've really lost something. I need to be next to her, all the time. And when I touch her, there's everything, fireworks and music and also stillness and peace. It's the most confusing thing I've ever experienced, when I think about it. When I don't think… it's the easiest, most wonderful thing I've ever experienced."

Orville's eyebrows twitched up and he said nothing.

"Yeah," George said, and smiled. "I love her." He nodded a few times.

Orville nodded back. "Your May, then?"

"Nope. My Jillian."

Under normal circumstances, Jillian wouldn't have texted from the drive, considering it rude not to come in and see Orville, but because George had told her to and they *were* in a bit of a hurry, she did. When he came out, she stepped out of the car and tossed him the keys. She didn't realize at first that she meant anything other than giving him access to the trunk, but the idea of him driving was suddenly very appealing.

She wouldn't have given him the keys the previous night for anything, but he seemed to have come back enough to trust behind the wheel. After stopping at Whistling Elms, they'd spent the remainder of the night picking out of her fridge and watching garbage on television, or more accurately, not watching. It was on, but they sat on her couch not really watching it. Well, then again, maybe that was just her. They hadn't talked much either, just sort of held onto each other, which was better than not.

She was at a loss for what she was supposed to do to make him feel better. With Sam it wouldn't have mattered. Whatever was wrong with him, it could be cured by sex, or if it was really bad, drunken sex.

But George was different. And George wasn't just upset; he'd been wounded, wounded in a very odd way. A way that had made him hurt not so much because of what had happened, but from how he felt about it. And she was more than a little worried that she'd say or do the wrong thing. It was even worse when they'd decided to go to bed. He couldn't sleep.

And since he couldn't sleep, she couldn't sleep.

As she got back into her car on the passenger side, she thought about how much she'd wished that they'd made love. She'd need that kind of warmth to carry her through the evening. But she'd been unable to make a move, knowing that *that* was how he'd been hurt; terrified that he'd say no. Instead, they'd lain there in silence, holding each other. She hoped that she'd been of some comfort to him.

She hoped it more at that moment, waiting for him to get in the car, than she had even the night before. He'd been so hurt, so cut up, and she'd felt so powerless. The lowest moment was sometime in the wee hours when he'd gotten out of bed and gone into the bathroom. She hadn't the heart to let him know, but she was sure she'd heard him crying for a minute.

And he was still hurt, of course. Even though he was doing his best to move around and shake it off. And now she was taking him to meet her parents. It was the worst timing she could imagine. *And here I am, worrying about myself. I have got to get it together.*

Jillian was distracting. As he drove, he could see her raising her right hand to her mouth, clamping down with her teeth like she was going to bite her nails, and then stopping herself and putting her hand back in her lap. *Maybe she should have driven. It would've given her something to do with her hands.*

And she was also really, really, really uptight. Even her hair. She had it up in a twist and it wasn't a hairstyle like she wore at work, loose and soft, it was tight and exacting. And her makeup was... different, subdued and yet heavy. Not like her at all.

"Hey," George said, as they were nearing the restaurant and she started and stopped biting her nails again.

"Hmm?" She looked at him.

"Look, if anyone should be nervous, it's me."

Jillian let out a nervous titter. "Oh, yeah. You'd think that, wouldn't you? Well, we'll see."

When they entered the restaurant and checked their coats, George had a chance to look at the rest of Jillian's outfit. Like her hair, she looked expensive and uptight. Her dress was all black, with a high neckline, and tailored to fit, and she was wearing pearls.

At the time they first met, he'd not have been surprised to see her like that. But after getting to know her, it was bizarre. She looked lifeless and cold whereas the real Jillian was warm and very much alive. At least she wasn't looking nervous anymore. She was taking on the work persona she had when she was dealing with him and the rest of the musketeers, aloof.

The maître d' brought them to the table, where her parents were already seated. Her father rose and gave Jillian a brief hug and kiss. Then Jillian leaned over and she and her mother exchanged a quick cheek kiss. George couldn't see much of her mother's outfit, but from the top half, he'd say it was a near clone of Jillian's. Or more likely, Jillian's was a clone of her mother's.

Jillian's father held out his hand and introduced himself. "Jack Braden."

George took his hand and shook it with a nod. "George Crewes." *So far so good.*

Jillian tried not to bristle when her father pulled out her chair for her, taking the responsibility away from George. She just hoped George didn't notice. If he did, he ignored it and took his seat when her father sat.

"You look nice, Jillian," her mother started up the conversation.

"Thank you, Mom," Jillian said. "So do you. Lovely dress."

And the conversation came to an immediate halt and everyone perused their menus. George looked at Jillian and she shared the look with him. He expected some kind of smile, but it didn't happen. She dropped her cover for the briefest flash of a moment, but George couldn't make out anything other than tension.

Jillian picked up her water glass and took a swallow, trying to settle herself. George looked at his menu and realized there weren't any prices. *Oh, Hell.*

CHAPTER TWENTY

From George's perspective, the evening went on with at least a polite veneer. Jillian didn't see the polite, at all. Her father took the reins at every opportunity, even to the point of placing the orders for both her and her mother. She hadn't thought to prepare George for the restaurant, so she'd attempted to telepathically tell him not to worry about the missing prices. It was her father's favorite restaurant in the city and he'd known what he was doing, getting reservations there, although Jillian was still a little perplexed wondering *how* he'd done it at such a late date.

She's much tenser than necessary. George kept trying to figure out why. The talk over drinks and appetizers was a little stiff, focusing on the weather at first. But by the time the salads arrived, George and Jack had found a common interest in basketball, though not a common team, and had had a well-mannered and lively debate about the abilities of their teams and the likelihood of a championship title. Jillian had even chimed in a few times and George saw her mother frown. *Maybe the tension is more appropriate than I thought.*

He didn't even think about how nothing had been said about work, until her father finally asked the typical, "What is it you do, George?" in the middle of the entrée.

"Actually, Jillian and I work together at Gardiner D. We do the same thing, manage a team of programmers," he answered.

Jillian's mother and father set down their forks in unison. "Oh?" Her mother asked.

George saw Jillian close her eyes for a moment as if he'd just made a serious blunder. *Ohhhhkay.* "Yes." He looked at her father. *Wow, this man does not look pleased.*

"So you met at work, then?" Jack asked, to confirm.

"Yes, sir," George said. *She did say they weren't happy with her career choice...*

"You'd be proud too, if you saw her in action. She's brilliant at it. And, she's on the short list for a promotion." *That ought to help.*

"Really?" Jillian's mother asked, looking straight across the table at Jillian. "This is the first we've heard of it."

Jillian picked up her water glass and took a sip, looking over the glass at her mother.

Jack chimed in. "And what would this promotion be? What would you be doing?"

Jillian had to unclench her jaw. "The promotion is to director."

"The Director is over all the Software Teams," George said, still trying to understand why Jillian was clearly unhappy about sharing this information. *Even if they want her to do something different, if she's a success at what she does...*

Her mother's eyes narrowed a little. "I suppose this promotion will make it all worthwhile. Everything you gave up..."

When no one spoke for a bit, George couldn't help but ask, "Gave up?"

Jack spoke first. "So, he doesn't know, hmm?"

"Dad, please."

Jillian's mother looked at George. "She had a scholarship to a prestigious music school," she looked at Jillian, "and she passed it up for programming and management."

Jillian sat back. "It's not like it was Juilliard, Mom."

"Would that have made a difference? If you want to boss people around, you could always have moved into conducting and been responsible for the entire orchestra." Her mother picked up her glass and looked at George. "We're a little disappointed that Jillian has chosen to deny her gift."

Jillian was so stunned that her mother had actually spoken aloud of her disappointment, rather than the usual alluding to it, that she almost didn't feel the thick cloud of doom that had gathered in the air. Almost. George looked at her, his brows knit together and a look of... defiance?... on his face, and Jillian realized too late that she needed to stop him. "She isn't denying it. I've heard her play. Just the other night."

"The other night? Where?" Jack asked.

"At The Blue Feather."

"Oh, good Lord," Jack said.

Jillian's mother's eyes widened. "You're not still pretending to be some kind of *entertainer* at that... *establishment.*"

Well, that could have been worse. Of course, her mother had said the word 'entertainer' as if she was saying the word 'whore,' and the 'establishment' was clearly the likes of an 'opium den.' It was time to cut off the conversation. It wasn't going to go anywhere productive from here. "Yes, Mom. I have to live my own life."

"Oh, don't start that again, Jillian." Jack shook his head.

"I love you both, but I have to live my own life."

Jack and her mother exchanged a look. Jack cleared his throat. "You know, Jillian, it's not too late. You could audition to be a substitute. Your mother spoke to Alan just the other night. They're accepting applications."

"I love you both, but I have to live my own life," Jillian said, again.

Jillian's mother slid her chair back. "Jillian, why don't we powder our noses before dessert?"

"I'm not quite finished with the entrée."

"Now, dear," Jillian's mother said, quietly.

Jillian put down her water glass and began to rise from the table. Both George and her father stood as she and her mother left the table.

George sat when Jack did and tried to figure out what exactly was going on. It was clear enough that he'd opened up a rather unpleasant issue between Jillian and her folks. The logical move was to change the subject.

"How long have you and Jillian being seeing each other?" Jack asked, before George could come up with a safe topic. *Apparently, it's time for the quiz portion of the evening.*

"Not very long," George said.

"That's a bit vague."

"It is," George said, figuring the actual answer wouldn't give him any points. "Jillian and I have known each other since her first day at Gardiner D, so it's a little hard to start counting accurately."

"Well, it hasn't been a year, has it?"

"No," George said, thinking it was best not to lie. He didn't figure that Jack would understand how recent they really were, but he also didn't know what else to say. "The thing is… we've been a long time coming." When Jack raised an eyebrow, George went on. "Due to complications with work, we didn't get together as soon as we would have, had we met in a purely social context." *At least, I'd like to believe that.*

"Oh? What are the complications?"

George started contemplating the remaining scotch in his glass. "Well, as it turns out, we're both up for the promotion I mentioned."

Jack's face lightened a little. "Then you've been competing for it?"

"Yes."

Jack nodded. "Well, that would make for interesting pillow talk." George wasn't sure what to say in response, so he let it fall without one. "So, what changed? You're still both up for it, you said."

"That's right." George had figured he'd get the *what are your intentions* question. He felt ready for that. But this line of questioning was a little different. *May as well just plunge in.* He used words similar to those he'd used with Taro. "Nothing actually changed. It just became obvious that being together was more important than the job."

Jack sat back a bit, his face opened in what George read as surprise. "I see." Then he grinned just a little. "She and her sister always did attract the boys." He leaned forward again. "She's calling you her boyfriend. Is that accurate?"

"Yes, sir." *For as long as she'll have me or, hopefully, until I can get a more permanent title.*

"So, then what? You just jumped in? No dating to feel it out? Or have you been seeing each other longer than I'm guessing?"

George wasn't sure what exactly Mr. Braden was hoping to figure out with this line of questioning. He took his own guess. "Sir, I didn't rush her into it, if that's what's worrying you." Which was true. At that point, that first night, all he'd done was ask. That wasn't rushing. She could have said, 'no.'

"More like the other way around," Jack said. "When she was young, she always took every date seriously. In fact, I would say that she didn't date. She had boyfriends. With her it was very much all or nothing."

George picked up his water glass and took a sip. *That was interesting to hear. I'm the one doing all the pushing now.* He hid the grimace. *More evidence of the hurt she'd taken since then, perhaps? Or evidence that nobody understood her. Or, I'm rushing things.* "I'm happy with the way things are going," George said. "I enjoy every minute with her."

"Right," Jack said, his voice thick.

George took a breath. *That's not what I meant.*

Jack and George passed a look between them. It was time to dance around the topic of sex.

I'm not going to ask, because I don't want to know.

Good, because I don't want to answer that.

"All right, then," Jack said, "before the women come back…"

And, here it comes. Finally.

"What exactly are your intentions toward my daughter?"

Classic. Down to each and every single word. Classic. Which made it all the easier to answer.

"He's very attractive," Jillian's mother observed.

Jillian refreshed her lip gloss. "That, he most definitely is."

"And he seems intelligent."

"He is that too. We have wonderful conversation." Jillian put her lip gloss in her purse.

Her mother ran a comb atop her hair to smooth any strays, as if a hair on her head would dare to move out of place. "How's he in bed?"

Jillian didn't even blink. *So like Mom to be like this when she's mad. Trying to get a rise out of me.* "Magnificent."

"Hmm," her mother said. "Good for you. So, how serious is this?"

It almost doesn't matter what I say. She's going to hear whatever she wants to hear now. "Well, it's serious enough that when you asked to meet him, we agreed." *Deflect and dodge.* "What do you think of him?"

Her mother's lips lifted just slightly. "I like that he speaks so well of you."

Well, that's something. Jillian zipped her purse shut.

"And he makes an excellent first impression."

At that, Jillian looked at her mother, not in the glass, but directly. "Is that a little approval?"

"Jillian, I don't expect that my opinion will affect your choices. I so seldom have any effect on you, anymore."

That's what you think.

"Although, at times I think you still do things simply to rebel. I'm almost afraid to say what I think because you'll make a choice to oppose it."

Jillian shook her head. "No, Mom. I don't-"

"That said," her mother said, while holding up a hand to quiet her, "and with only a first impression to go on, I'd say that he's the nicest man you've allowed us to meet. Not as driven as some. Or as able to offer you as generous a lifestyle as others."

Oh, God, Mother. Are you serious?

"But, I think he sincerely cares for you. How deeply? Only time will tell."

Even the compliments come with a backhanded hit. "Of course."

Her mother turned back to the mirror to watch herself as she smoothed her hair with just her hand this time. "So, you, Jillian?" She looked at Jillian in the mirror. "Answer me this time, please. How serious is it for you?"

Jillian's heart began to beat just a little faster and she could hear the blood rushing in her ears. She held her breath for a bit to slow her heart. *I don't know if I can safely be honest here, or not.* She'd had plenty of time to think about this very question the previous night, despite everything else on her mind. And while she wouldn't say she was sure of much, life had taught her to know better than to think she was sure, there *was* one thing that she was sure of. *I'm going to do everything in my power to make it work. Talk about things I don't want to talk about. Confront things I don't want to confront. Because everything is better with him. I'm better with him.* "To me, it's serious. But, like you said, time will tell."

Her mother looked back at her own reflection. "Hmm," her mother murmured a little as she patted her hair one last time and then closed up her purse. She focused directly on Jillian. "If that's the case, you should bring him to Thanksgiving dinner."

"Thank you, Mom," Jillian said, softly. It was as close to approval as she could hope for.

"Rachel Robbins phoned yesterday and she isn't going to join us, after all, so there will be plenty of room."

Walking from the restaurant to the car, George took Jillian's hand. It was ice cold, not unlike her demeanor since the visit to the ladies' room. She'd spent the remaining minutes of the dinner hardly saying anything, though she seemed able enough to meet the gaze of both her parents. However, she only looked at any of them, including him, when they spoke. He could count the number of words she'd said until the end of dinner on one hand, though she was slightly more vocal at the goodbyes.

When they arrived at the car, Jillian released him and held out her hand, palm up. George snorted. "I don't think you should drive."

"It'll be easier this way. I can drop you off and not have to change seats."

"Yeah, that's not the plan," George said, as he opened the passenger door for Jillian. She gave him a very pained look, but she got in the car, buckled her seat belt, and placed her hands in her lap.

George entered the driver's side and, after closing the door, covered her hands with one of his. "Okay. Deep breath. You're going to be fine."

Jillian stared out of the windshield. "I'm so... so... mortified. And sorry. So very sorry. I hope that you weren't insulted to your face while I was gone." She turned her face toward him. "I'm so sorry."

"It's okay. Really."

"No, it's not. I should have warned you. I should've told you... about everything. They were in... such rare form tonight. Top of their game. I can't believe I allowed this to happen."

George squeezed her hands. "Alright, now. Take that deep breath."

"Please, don't," Jillian said, and pulled her hands out from under his. "Please, don't sound understanding. I can only imagine what you're thinking right now. Let's just make this as short as possible, not drag it out. Start the car and drive to your house. I'll check my apartment tonight and if you've left anything, I'll bring it to the office tomorrow."

"What?" George bit back a surprised yelp. "You'll bring... Are you breaking up with me?"

"No," Jillian said. "I'm making it easy for you."

George barked a laugh. "You must be joking. I'm not going to break up with you because of this dinner!"

"Now, you're joking." Jillian finally blinked. "You met them. I mean even though this was even more impressive than usual, the choice of restaurant and the choice of insults were over the top even for them, it's still them. Those are my parents and if we're seeing each other you'll be subjected to them from time to time even though they're so... them. Nobody could want that."

George took a breath and squeezed her leg that was still under his hand. "Jillian, please breathe. I'm not breaking up with you. You're not breaking up with me. It's all going to be fine."

She blinked. *Are you crazy? You must be crazy! Who would want to be involved with anyone descending from that family tree? Even for a few hours, it would be risky. I might turn out to be a fatal attraction type. Or at the very least a version of my mother.*

"You're not your mother," George said.

Jillian sat back, startled. "Oh, God. Did I say that out loud?"

"Jillian, Sweetheart, you've got to calm down. You're not your mother." He leaned toward her, reached for her head, and brought her forehead to his. As always, he felt the calm seep into him the moment his skin touched hers. *It's so right.* He only hoped that she got the same feeling from him, that tonight he could be a rock for her, just like she'd been for him the previous night. "And you'll feel much better when you stop looking like her." He started to fumble with her hair.

She finally made an amused sound, lifted her hands to hair, and fought his hands a little to pull out the pins. His fingers ran through her hair, making it spill down over her shoulders. She sat back just a little to shake out the hair herself and he smiled at her. "That's much better." She smiled back. "And now, with that smile, you look like you." He sat back and started the car. "Well, mostly. Where did that dress come from? I thought you said you got rid of all the Stepford clothes."

"Oh," she said, trying to think about anything other than how humiliated she was and how grateful she was that he wasn't gone. Yet. "Um." She looked at herself. "I keep this for the occasions with my parents."

"Ah. Parent clothes. You know, my college roommate had some of those." He buckled his seat belt. *Time to begin the recovery process.* "Okay. So, I was thinking... it's a little after nine on a Saturday night. I think we should stay out for a bit yet. Cheer you up."

"Oh, no," Jillian said. "I'm not up for anything right now. I just want to go home, curl up into a ball, and try to sleep."

I get that. But I don't think that's really you. "I could be very wrong, but I think I'm starting to actually *get* you. I know the perfect place. Will you trust me on this, just for a little? If I'm wrong, we'll leave."

"What do you mean *trust you on this*?"

"Just come along, no arguments, and see how I do."

Jillian started to cross her arms, but stopped herself. "Like Tuesday night, you mean?"

George nodded. "Yeah. Just like Tuesday. What do you say? Trust me? Think there's any chance that I might be right?"

"I don't know. I feel like someone wound me up like a spring."

"Exactly. Let's unwind."

Jillian looked at her nails for a moment and then back at him. "If I'm miserable, you'll be okay leaving?"

"Yes," he said.

"Okay, then." Jillian said. *It certainly can't get much worse.* Jillian answered, not even realizing she was borrowing Orville's phrase. "Let's see how you do."

George leaned over and kissed her cheek. "Excellent." Then he sat back and shifted the car into drive.

Jillian spent much of the drive sunk back in her seat trying to become invisible rather than paying attention, making it easy for George to get them close to their destination before she realized what he had in mind. "The Blue Feather?"

"Mm-hmm," he mumbled and nodded, keeping his eyes on the road.

"It's Saturday night, we'll never get in," Jillian said.

He glanced at her sideways for a moment. "Oh, I don't know. We've got friends there."

By the time George unlocked the door to Jillian's apartment, she was starting to feel only mildly glazed. She didn't think she'd quite gotten drunk at The Blue Feather, but she'd definitely seen the bottom of more than one glass. They'd danced and laughed, mostly at things that weren't really funny, but seemed funny at the time.

"I just realized," Jillian said, as he opened her door and she saw through her remaining fog just how unglazed he looked, "that you didn't have more than a swallow since dinner."

"What?" He asked, grabbing her arm as she entered the apartment.

"Alcohol. You've been loading me up. All the while, you've completely dried out." He closed the door and she threw her arms around his neck, knocking him back into the door. "Are you going to take advantage of me?"

After a grunt from the contact with the door, he laughed, his hands already on her waist. "Nope. Just getting you to relax. I think it worked a bit too well."

"No?" She stopped talking and stepped back from him laughing nervously, avoiding his eyes, and pushing her hair back from her face. "I'm more drunk than I thought."

More drunk? "Let's get you out of your coat before we worry about anything else, including your current state of drunkenness." He helped her unbutton her coat. "You can still walk in your high heels, so you can't be that bad off."

"High heels are a reflex," Jillian said, and leaned against the wall.

"Okay." George hung up her coat, but didn't take his off.

"George," Jillian said, as she realized what he had and hadn't done, "you're not going are you?"

"Wel-"

"You said, we weren't breaking up," Jillian said, and started unbuttoning his coat. "If we're not breaking up, then you're staying."

"Are you sure you want me to?" George asked, an odd expression on his face that she couldn't make out. "I seem to recall you wanting to curl up into a ball. That sentiment implied wanting to be alone."

"Oh, don't," she said, and pushed his coat off his shoulders. "I was feeling sorry for myself, yes. Please don't throw that back in my face now."

"Okay, then." George pushed her hands away. "Just let me get my stuff from the trunk of your car."

"Ohhhhh," Jillian said, realizing why he hadn't taken off his coat. "You wanted to get your things, so you kept your coat on. Were you always planning to stay?"

He grinned. "Assuming you let me. Yes."

Jillian flushed red and covered her face. "Oh, how embarrassing."

George took her hands in his and pulled them down from her face. "I don't know. It's nice to know that I'm wanted." He kissed her softly, then whispered, "I'll be right back," and let go of her hands to move back to the door.

As soon as the door closed behind him, warmed more than she expected by the soft kiss, Jillian took off her shoes and moved, as quickly as she felt comfortable going, into the bedroom. She tossed the shoes into her closet and fumbled with the pearl necklace. Finally free of the pearls, she stripped off her nylons, tossed them into the closet as well, and headed into the bathroom. She didn't think she had time to brush her teeth so she opted for a quick gargle and rinse with mouthwash.

She was struggling with the zipper on her dress when George returned. She kept trying, hoping to be in her underwear and looking sexy when he next saw her, rather than drunk and pathetic, so he'd be overcome and quickly take charge. She heard him open the coat closet door and tried switching hands. She had lowered the zipper to the hard to reach spot in the middle of her back and was still trying to reach it by the time that George walked into the room.

"What are you doing?" He asked, sounding amused.

Jillian frowned. "What does it look like? I'm trying to get this *thing* off and I just…"

George walked over, turned her around, and unzipped the dress. "There. No problem."

Jillian hoped for a moment that he'd put his arms around her from behind, the way he had at his house the other night, but he didn't, which left her with the choice to make a move or not. It was outrageously unfair. *Men are supposed to be the pursuers, not women. For goodness sake, they like it. All he has to do is take me in his arms, and I'm his. This shouldn't be complicated. He must not be in the mood. Again.*

George took off his tie while Jillian ran to the closet. *I wouldn't think she's drunk. She's moving awfully fast.* But something was off. He couldn't quite put his finger on it, so maybe she was drunk. She wanted him to stay and he wanted to stay, so that shouldn't be it. She was trying to get undressed, and when she'd needed it, he'd helped. *Everything ought to be okay.* Maybe it was still the dinner with her folks. He sat down on the bed to unlace his shoes and tried to make a peace offering. "What do you want to do now? Watch part of a movie? Or are you ready to go to sleep? Or…" He stopped mid-thought as Jillian stepped out of the closet, in nothing but violet-colored lace underwear, and walked to her dresser.

She picked up her hair brush and started to brush her hair. "I don't know. What do you want to do?"

She'd walked to the dresser as quickly as she could, not looking directly at George. *I don't have the slightest idea how to seduce a man.* All she could think of in the confined space of the closet was to walk back out wearing as little as possible and hope he took it from there. She knew that if she was naked, it would have been more obvious, but she just didn't have the nerve.

Brushing her hair, she didn't look at him in the mirror. If he wasn't interested, the only way she could deal with it would be to pretend it wasn't happening. She didn't hear him for quite a few brush strokes and started to think that when she was finished with her hair, she'd go back to her closet and put on her nightgown. *He'll never know what I was thinking about. It's okay.*

George cleared his throat before he spoke. "Jillian, how, um, drunk are you?" *Christ, her and lace. Her in lace.*

"What?" She asked, and turned to look at him.

"How drunk are you?" He asked, again, still on the bed, frozen with one shoe off and the laces of the other in his hands.

"Why?" She asked, feeling a little more warmth come over her from the intensity of the look he was giving her. *This might just have worked.*

"Because," George said, then he yanked off his remaining shoe, dropped it on the floor, and stood up to stand very close to her, but not touch her. Another throat clearing. "If you're too drunk to consent, I'm going to fetch you something to cover up that lace before I have a stroke."

The room wasn't spinning or anything along those lines. "I'm definitely not that drunk," Jillian said, and reached out to run a finger along his chest, finally comfortable enough to provide him a stronger cue.

"Thank God," George said, before taking her in his arms and proceeding to make the room spin for her all by himself.

Sometime in the night, George rolled over and found Jillian awake too. "Hey," he whispered.

"Hey," she replied.

"Something the matter?"

"No," she cuddled up against him again. "At least, not with me. I just woke up and remembered that you had a pretty bad day yesterday. How are you doing with that?"

His tightened his grip on her. "Mostly, I'm not thinking about it."

"Oh. Sure." Jillian nodded into his chest. "Um, you know, if you want to talk about it, I'm here to listen."

"Thanks, Sweetheart," George said, and kissed the top of her head. "I know you are."

"I think I may have been a little selfish tonight. Focusing on myself and my parents and all."

"It was a rough night for you," George said.

Jillian nodded again. "And for you too. I hope to make it up to you sometime."

George slid down the bed a little to be face to face, even though he could hardly see in the dark. "There's nothing to make up for." *I love you.*

She ran a hand through his hair. "You're amazing." Then she kissed him and they lost another hour of sleep.

Sunday morning came and went in a pleasant blur. George and Jillian had decided to work in a conference room again. Despite the constant IMing, Jillian began to feel she was making headway on her appraisals. George felt like he was making headway breaking through Jillian's defenses.

Although they hadn't experienced another *whatever* the previous night, she hadn't hidden from him and that morning in the conference room she laughed out loud more than he'd ever heard her laugh in the office in the past year. And she kept glancing at him with that same mirth in her eyes. Something had changed in the way she related to him at the office and it was making him giddy. He followed her to the break room and back, telling jokes and making smart comments. The only time he left her alone was when she went to the ladies' room.

Ishi was at the mirror doing something with her eye make-up when

Jillian took a brief break before lunch. Jillian said, a simple, "Hi."

Ishi stopped what she was doing and called after Jillian. "Good to see the two of you can function outside of each other's air space. Or is George dying back there now?"

Jillian turned and grinned at Ishi. "We can only be apart for about five minutes before the effects become noticeable, so I have to hurry."

Ishi snorted and went back to the mirror. She was still there when Jillian washed her hands. "Are you trying something new?" Jillian asked, looking at Ishi's broad sweep of liquid eyeliner. It had created a sort of cat's eye effect.

"Always," Ishi muttered. "Can't attract attention no matter what I do. Tomorrow, it'll be Cleopatra style. Maybe he'll notice."

Jillian dried her hands and said, "I know it's none of my business-"

"It definitely isn't!" Ishi said.

"Fair enough," Jillian said. "But, um, you know, it might work better if you stop trying to get his attention. Maybe ignore him, if you're at all friendly now. For some insane reason, men want you more when you don't want them."

"Is that how it worked with you and George? You ignored him?"

Jillian smiled and leaned against the counter. "Oh, no." She crossed her arms. "Neither of us was chasing after the other." *We were just suddenly together.*

Taking a step back Ishi looked Jillian up and down. "What did happen? Really? I mean, you were totally cold shoulder with the four musketeers and then suddenly one day you and George are all gooey looks and giggling."

Jillian uncrossed her arms and stood back up. She still wasn't sure how to characterize what had happened apart from saying that they'd quit fighting it, which didn't seem quite the thing to share with Ishi. Then she thought about his turning up at The Blue Feather. "Fate happened," she said, and opened the door.

"Oh, well, good luck with *that*." Ishi called after her.

Jillian wondered who Ishi was interested in, but only for the short walk back to the conference room. Once she entered and George looked up and smiled at her, everything else seemed to fade away. She didn't make any more progress on the appraisals before lunch.

For lunch, Jillian suggested that they encourage everyone to actually eat together in the large conference room. She told the naysayers that just wanted to eat at their desks that if they were working seven days a week, they needed to at least take solid breaks and rest. She didn't push the thought she had that it would be good for them all as a team too, to be just a little social. Although Gardiner D was small enough that everybody recognized everybody else, the Software Teams were still made up of mostly introverted types that didn't socialize much. Over half the staff didn't even attend the holiday party.

Nodding along, George let Jillian lead the way on her idea. There were a few who refused her, still taking their lunch to their desks. But most of them responded to her argument about taking a break to recharge. The conversation, however, Jillian couldn't control all by herself, and it did drift quickly back to the project, causing several more programmers to jump up from their seats to return to their desks to make notes about something.

"Lunch turned into a brainstorming session," Jillian said, disappointed.

George smirked, began to reach for her, and had to check himself. It was getting harder and harder to keep his hands off of her at work, not that he'd made that mistake since Tuesday. But even thinking about touching her or kissing her would only lead to more involved fantasies which had an entirely new unpleasantness, as there was the slightest chance now, though only slight, that they might come true. So he put his hand in his pocket and said, "I think that's actually a good sign. And for anyone who wasn't certain they wanted to eat with everyone, you proved it was worth the time."

"I wasn't looking to prove anything," Jillian said, wiggling her mouse to bring the computer back to life. "I was hoping for a little social interaction."

"I know," George said. "But that's a lot to expect out of a group of programmers brought together solely by the need of employment."

Jillian laughed again. "Right you are." She felt like kissing him on the cheek and had to restrain herself. She shook her head. "How did we get here?"

"By car, if you're being literal," George said, and Jillian laughed again. "If you're being more metaphorical…"

She sat down and propped her chin on her hand. "We should definitely call it a day at two, today. I have an idea on how to spend the afternoon."

George took a breath at the totally inappropriate look on her face. It wasn't often he felt like Little Red Riding Hood staring down the Wolf. He remembered they were in a conference with lots of glass. *Good thing it's the weekend and so few people are around that might see this.* "I have a few ideas too." Then his mind tripped. "Ah, shoot! It's Sunday. I've got basketball practice at two."

"Oh," Jillian said, and her face returned to normal. "So you need to leave earlier than two." She sat back in her chair. "You'll need to go home and get changed, right? Well, I can wrap things up here. So, blow whenever you have to."

There is something truly unique about you. "Alright, then. I'll plan on taking off a bit early. Do I get to see you after?"

Jillian tapped her finger a moment. *I could do with some time to do laundry and clean up around home.* "Maybe we could do with a few hours to ourselves. I know I have chores I've been neglecting."

"But only a few hours," George said, and Jillian smiled at the determined look on his face. "What?"

"You look like you're ready to have an argument."

"I don't want to have an argument," George said, confused.

"No," Jillian said, as her smile softened. "I mean, you look like you're ready to argue if I don't agree. Of course, I'll see you." She tapped her finger again. "But I really could do with a little time to clean and do laundry. So, can we make it after dinner?"

George shook his head immediately. "After dinner? No, how about a late dinner? My place? I'll cook so you can take every last second at home and join me when it's ready."

Jillian paused at the thought. He wanted to stay at his place. He'd asked before. If she said yes to a late dinner at his place, she would also be saying yes to staying over. *On a Sunday Night. With work in the morning.* "What are you making for dinner?" She asked.

George grinned and she wished they weren't at work, because, when it was appropriate, that grin usually came with a kiss attached. "Dare I surprise you?"

Jillian grinned back. "I don't know, dare you?"

The sun had set before Jillian and George sat down to dinner and it was a distant memory when Jillian found herself in George's bathtub, luxuriating in hot water with the jets going. The evening was almost too much. He'd cooked, nothing particularly fancy, but extremely tasty and satisfying. Then he'd disappeared for a few minutes after dessert and had eventually returned with the promise of a surprise. The surprise had been a candlelit bathroom with a fully drawn bath, soft music playing, and a glass of wine. A sweet kiss and a gentle wish that she enjoy the bath and he was off to clean up the kitchen. Jillian looked at the glass and understood why he hadn't served wine with the dinner.

Soon after, staring off into space, feeling so relaxed that she might just melt, she began to imagine what it would be like to wake up in the house, to eat breakfast in the morning room, which, of course, wasn't going to happen since there wasn't a table in it. *A small table, but rectangular rather than round like his kitchen table...* She could almost see it. The room, like nearly every room in the house, needed color. *Maybe yellow?* Switch out the blinds for some drapes. *Sitting down to start a late morning with toast, eggs, add coffee with George in a lovely yellow room. Oh, stop. Stop decorating his house.*

She laughed out loud at herself. It was easy to see why the place had called out to him, it resonated with her too. It was even easier to imagine living there. *So much space to move around in. Too much space for one person. Practically too much space for two people. The house really did scream out for a family.*

Some of the thoughts she'd been having started swirling in her mind again, but with new twists. She tried to figure out how a man with a yo-yo could be such a grown-up. The house's décor mostly screamed bachelor, but the house didn't. And he cooked. And he cleaned. And he played basketball, and kept fit. And he drew her a bath... *My, God, where does a man like this come from? Manly and yet able to treat me like a queen.*

Another laugh as she realized that she now felt a little sorry for Sarah. *Idiot didn't know what she had when she had it.* But then the somber took over again. *Oh, my poor, dear, sweet George. Why on Earth did that woman come back to hurt you like that?* It was easy to go from sad to a lather again on his behalf. She wouldn't mind the opportunity to rip out Sarah's hair.

She sighed and took another sip of the wine. *That kind of thinking is counter-productive. I'll get myself so wound up, I won't even enjoy the rest of the night with George. And that would be unfair to him. After all this, he deserves some quality attention.*

Perhaps a little massage? Jillian thought that she'd seemed to have had a pretty nice effect on him the other night, just rubbing his temples. Maybe a back rub would be a good way to reciprocate. It just didn't seem like enough.

Stop thinking!

She tried to quiet her mind again and enjoy the special treatment like she had when she first settled into the tub. She didn't get that kind of opportunity every day.

But, maybe I could... the thought jumped out again, this time in full form. Living there, with *him*. It was too decadent a thought to play with for long. Especially since she'd always been so opposed to the idea of losing her own space before.

She closed her eyes and tried to push the thought aside again. *It isn't like we're at that point in our relationship. It isn't like he asked. And it's his house. Not even a rental, but a mortgage. I'm putting the cart before the horse, thinking like this. Stop it! It's a dangerous fantasy. It's as bad as thinking I love him.*

A light knock on the door made her open her eyes again. "Hi!" She called out.

"May I come in?" His voice came through the door, still rich despite the muffle.

"Yes," she answered and felt a bit of anticipation as the doorknob turned and the door swung open. He didn't completely come in, just stood in the doorway, holding the doorknob.

"How are you doing?" He asked, a soft smile about his lips.

"Wonderful," Jillian answered.

His deep voice echoed a bit in the bathroom. "Need anything? Or, want anything?"

"No, you've thought of everything," Jillian said. "I feel so spoiled right now."

He let go of the doorknob, stepped up to the tub, and dropped to his haunches to cross his arms on the side of the tub and rest his chin on his arms. "Good. I wanted to spoil you. Are you sure there isn't anything else you want?"

She shifted in the tub so that she could bring her face close to his. "Not while I'm in here."

"Not while you're in there. How about when you come out?" He asked.

"Hmm," she lifted her eyes to the ceiling to think a moment. "I suppose, if you absolutely insist on doing something more, you could bring in my bag. I'll want some of my lotion."

"That's not really necessary." He grinned again and then leaned away from the tub to open a cabinet at the sinks. He returned holding a tube of her vanilla scented lotion. "I picked this up this afternoon. Thought you might like not having to bring one along. Then I couldn't figure out how to mention it without sounding strange."

Jillian shifted again to she could kiss him. "Thank you, for thinking of everything. For thinking of me."

"This one," he said, "was as much for me, as for you. I really like the scent on you."

"Oh? You do, do you?" She bit her lip.

"Yeah," he said, and his eyebrows rose a little then dropped.

That time she lifted her hand from the water and held his head while she kissed him and he set the lotion down so that he could do the same. Her pulse raced and she forgot to breathe, and when they separated just enough to see each other's eyes, she saw he was as open as ever, wanting nothing more than her. She found it easier to channel the emotion into the physical, so she kissed him again, and before long his shirt was soaking.

"Either you come out or I'm coming in," he said, breathlessly and she couldn't stop herself from giggling.

CHAPTER TWENTY-ONE

Well over an hour later, they were wrapped together in his bed and laughing at the state of his sheets. "The vanilla smells great, but it makes a mess," George observed.

"I think the solution is not to put on so much that you can't rub it in," Jillian answered and he could hear not only the laughter but the drowsy in her voice.

Rubbing his hand along her slick back, George said, "I'll remember that for next time. Are you falling asleep?"

"Mmm," she mumbled against his ear. "Just a little tired. Aren't you?"

"Yes," he said, as his fingers found the small of her back. "I am tired. But I'm still contemplating changing these sheets."

She laughed against his skin and he felt a slight shiver.

"Then again, this is pretty comfortable. I'd hate to ask you to move."

"Mm-hmm," she said, and he enjoyed the rumble against his skin. "Then it'd be your fault for ruining the afterglow."

"Ah, fighting words," he laughed. "I'd say that's proof you're awake, but you might just argue with me in your sleep."

Jillian sighed. "Not anymore." She kissed his earlobe.

"No?" George had been trying to bring up a tricky subject all evening. He'd figured the bath would make a great apology, if she flipped out. Then he'd wimped out and just used the idea as a treat. But it was back in his mind again and since everybody knows that after great sex was a terrific time for sharing personal stuff, maybe he could do it right then. But he wasn't sure where they stood on personal stuff anymore. *Go for it? Or not?*

"Hey, Jillian," he started and took a breath before he pushed ahead, "I was just wondering…"

"Hmm?"

"And you're under no obligation to tell me, of course…"

"Hmm?"

"Was your childhood happy, at all?"

She giggled again, making him think she was either in a really good mood or high off of the smell of vanilla scented lotion.

"It was happy. I mean, it was a little strange in some aspects. But it was happy."

"What was strange?" He took one of her hands in his and interlaced their fingers.

Jillian moved their joined hands to rest on his hip. "Maybe strange isn't the word. I grew up in a nice little house, smaller than this one by quite a bit, but I had my own room. Even back then, Mom was all about status. She liked her furnishings to be high quality and expensive.

"The couches weren't overly comfortable. When Beth and I watched television, we brought our bean bag chairs down from our bedrooms. And when we were finished, they had to be put away. Our bedrooms were our own to decorate, to be ourselves in, but the rest of the house was Mom's.

"Dinnertime was almost always the whole family. We didn't fight or argue much. It was almost a Stepford family, really. Or maybe a Donna Reed thing. The family sits down and enjoys a meal and shares their day."

George slid his hand free from hers and let it glide up her arm. "Sounds pretty nice."

"Yep. Then Dad started making a little more money and Mom quit teaching and began to start aspiring to things. Do you recall how you described the doctor's parents? Well, that's what my mom wants to be.

"At first, she was volunteering with a few charities, trying to move up to be someone *important*. After she made President of one of them, she was looking for the next thing. Something bigger and more... I think she's looking for high society glamor.

"Right now, she's, obsessed is too strong a word, let's say she's focused on being some kind of Board Member or something for the local Symphony. She's been on the committee that organizes three fundraisers each year, for five years this coming Christmas. Each year, she hopes that she'll be the Chairperson, because that will have her making reports to the Board at actual Board meetings, which increases her chances. So far, no.

"Anyway, when those dreams started popping up, Beth and I were part of her... identity, her presentation. So, we dressed up and attended a few important gatherings and smiled and said all the right things. At least, we were always thanked for being terrific, so I think we said all the right things.

"It was... silly, but fine, until Mom suddenly had this vision of me as her brilliant musician daughter. I'd been studying piano since I could remember, I loved it, and then suddenly there was this huge push to get me into music school. I never wanted music school and that put a damper on loving the piano.

"I tried. I really did try. In addition to practicing, I used to play for them every Sunday night after dinner. Mom and Dad invited friends over on Sunday nights, just to hear me. We kept it up when I visited or was on break from school.

"But it all came apart when I started working. I didn't have much time to practice, or access to a piano for that matter. And the little jibes about work were starting to get to me anyway, so I quit playing after dinner, excusing myself early due to early work days, or whatever I could come up with at the time.

"I found my way back into playing when my girlfriends decided to check out The Blue Feather on a lark one night. I'd always loved jazz, but I'd never tried to play it. Even without asking, I knew Mom and Dad would have freaked out. Anyway, it was a sort of awakening, just listening to it live. I came back the next evening. Alone. Introduced myself to the piano player and kept returning. It evolved from there. Friendships and music. Eventually, I was invited to practice just before the band rehearsed.

"As you heard, my parents still want me to be part of some prestigious music group. I say that prestige isn't the same as satisfying. And, of course, I don't have time to do something like that with a regular job. Usually, we don't talk about it. It's easier that way. The one time they accepted my invitation to come and hear me play, they made it as far as driving by the building. I couldn't even get them through the door."

Jillian paused for a moment, then she slid her hand from his, tracing up his arm. "Is that what you wanted to know?"

"Yep," George said, overcome with how much information she'd shared off of his little question that he'd meant to use as a starter. She definitely wasn't hiding from him anymore. *A little shared pain, or in our case a lot of shared pain, gives way to a bond, I guess.* "I'm glad to hear it was pretty rosy when you were young."

Jillian slid her arm behind him and shifted her body closer. "Now you don't have to worry that I'm fundamentally damaged. There might be hope for me."

"I never thought you were fundamentally damaged," George said, with a laugh, hoping she was still being a little silly. "Though now I'm curious what your bedroom looked like at home. Was it like your apartment?"

Jillian nuzzled his ear. "No. I had a princess bed. You know, all pink and lace, with a canopy."

"Ah. Do you miss it?"

"No. I grew into silk, instead."

"Right," he said, thinking of her bedroom and trying to form an observation or comment that would keep the conversation going. "That's an interesting pattern on your bedspread and curtains. Not the same as the pictures above your bed, but similar. Has an oriental feel."

Jillian leaned back from him. "It is oriental. It's Kimono fabric."

"Really?" George asked.

"I don't think anyone's ever noticed that before."

"I notice everything about you."

Jillian snuggled back into him. "You sure do. Just tonight you surprised me with the lotion and now my curtains."

"Yeah," George said. "About the lotion... I don't think we should sleep in these sheets."

Jillian giggled into his neck. "Probably not. Just a few more minutes, okay? I don't want to move yet."

"Neither do I, but if we stay here too long, we'll fall asleep."

"No, we won't," Jillian said.

George sighed. "Fine, a few more minutes." His mind was still on other things anyway. "So, you never wanted to play piano as a career? Not even jazz piano?"

"No," Jillian said. "I'm not interested in the musician lifestyle. A lot of late nights. And I like my job. Most of the time."

"Right. What did you want to be when you were a kid?"

Jillian giggled. "A majorette."

"What's that?"

"The girl who twirls the baton with the marching band."

"That's a job?" George asked.

"Not really."

"Oh."

"What did you want to do?" Her hand was gliding over the skin of his shoulders.

"I always wanted software. As a kid, I wanted to make video games."

"And that changed because?"

George chuckled. "I decided food and shelter were also good things."

"I see," Jillian said.

Another sigh. He really didn't want to get out of bed, but the sheets were really disgusting. "I need to change these sheets soon."

"Does it really matter?"

"Yes," George said. If she was going to be difficult...

"Ok," Jillian said, and started scooching away from him.

"Hey! What are you doing?"

"You're right. I'm going to fall asleep, if we don't move now," Jillian replied, and struggled to her feet. She rubbed her hands on her arms and then her stomach and laughed. "I need a shower to get this excess lotion off. I feel like I've been covered in grease."

George immediately rolled out of bed. "Good idea. I'll join you."

Staring at her office wall, Jillian was contemplating doing and saying something that she didn't want to say or do. She was thinking very seriously about not seeing George that evening so that she could get some sleep. *That's the problem with actually moving around again after sex, you end up awake and not sleeping.* The idea of being in the same bed and *not* making love had occurred to her, of course. But she knew herself better than that. She'd want him. So, unless they had another horrible day or he said no, they'd make love and she'd be shy at least an hour of sleep again, if not two, or even three.

Actually, she wanted him right then too. Even though he was in his office and she was in hers. Their IM conversation had been flirty, clean of course, but flirty. And from that alone, she wanted him. *This is insane.*

She decided to give herself a few minutes of sanity by using the ladies' room. *I must be on a hormone overload.* It wasn't like she hadn't had a healthy sex drive in the past. But this twice a night thing was outside of her usual experience. If it ramped up to once during the day too... no, that wouldn't happen. *We're here during the day.*

She walked in to hear Rachel talking to Irene in a hushed tone. "...exhausted. You could propose a day off."

"Hi, ladies," Jillian said, as a way of announcing her presence.

"Hi." "Morning."

"Sorry to interrupt," Jillian said.

"No problem," Irene said.

Rachel nudged Irene. "Come on," she whispered.

Jillian paused. "Is there something I should know?"

Rachel looked at Irene and eventually nudged her again. Irene said, "No."

"Okay, then," Jillian said. But Rachel and Irene didn't leave and they started whispering. Jillian gave them a few minutes. After she'd dried her hands, she turned to them. "Can I help?"

"Oh, come on," Rachel said to Irene.

"No," Irene said. "Everybody's tired. It's not like it matters."

It was then that Jillian noticed the circles under Irene's eyes. "Do you need a day off?"

"I couldn't possibly take one. We've made such an aggressive schedule. I'll fall behind, and I don't want to be the one who blows it for everybody else."

Jillian looked at Rachel. "How's everyone else doing?"

Rachel shrugged. "Nobody else said anything, but I'd say everybody looks tired."

"Mm-hmm," Jillian said. "We don't need people burning out." She looked back at Irene. "We're all worried about losing our jobs. That's taking its toll too. If you need a day, you should take one."

"One won't help."

Rachel gave her another nudge. "Come on."

Irene sighed. "I'm pregnant."

"Congratulations!" Jillian said, and couldn't help herself, she gave Irene a quick hug.

Irene didn't look particularly thrilled. "I wasn't planning on telling anyone at work for a bit yet. It's still the first trimester. But I'm so tired. And I've been getting sick every time I eat."

"Oh, I'm sorry," Jillian said. "Is there anything we can do?"

"Not really. The doctor says I just have to get through it. Make sure I'm not dehydrated. But other than that..."

Rachel chimed in. "I think she should take a day off and rest."

Jillian wanted a day to lounge around too. Thanksgiving was too far off. *Oh, well.* "Irene, you need to look after yourself. If you don't want to take a whole day off, why don't you leave early today? Don't say anything, just go. If anyone asks, it's a doctor's appointment or something. I'd be okay if you just want to leave at lunch. That's only a half day."

"Thanks," Irene said. "I don't know. I'd just hate to be responsible..."

Rachel made a grunting sound.

Looking at Rachel for a moment, Jillian said, "You win." She focused on Irene again. "And so do you. You've no choice. Boss's order. Go home at lunch. Rest. You'll work better after you rest anyway."

Irene looked close to tears. "I really shouldn't..."

"No choice," Jillian repeated. "Say yes, or I'll send you home now."

"Okay," Irene said, and Rachel started to maneuver her toward the door.

"Good," Jillian said, "and I don't want to see the half day on your timesheet. You worked all weekend."

"Okay," Irene said, again. "Thank you."

Rachel looked over her shoulder and mouthed *thank you* to Jillian also.

Jillian smiled and nodded. It was the least she could do.

"Shut up, Serge," George said, though he couldn't stop grinning.

"Sure," Sergei laughed as sipped his coffee. "I'm just glad to see the lady is tending to your needs. That's all."

"Shut up, Serge," George said, again as Taro and Neal walked into Sergei's office.

"What's that about?" Neal asked Sergei.

Sergei moved to sit on his desk. "Nothing at all. Just observing that our friend here is looking like he hasn't been getting enough sleep."

Taro snorted. "Yeah, yeah. Whatever. We all know what he's getting."

"Does it smell like cookies in here?" Neal asked, and Sergei laughed.

George ground his teeth and put his free hand in his pocket, ignoring Neal and Sergei. Taro needed to quit being such an asshole about Jillian. And soon. Well, he was offering an olive branch. Maybe that would help. "On the subject of not getting enough sleep… there's a bachelor party that needs planning."

"Yes!" Neal said.

"And not much time to do it," Sergei observed.

"Exactly," George said. "So, man," he addressed Taro, "what do you think? Are we doing the old, traditional night before the wedding?"

Taro thought for a moment. "Actually, there's no one coming in from out of town for this. So it doesn't need to wait. And, it'd be nice not to be hungover for the wedding. Can we do it sooner? A week from Friday?"

George was a bit taken aback. "Um, sure. I can try. I don't think that would be too tough. As long as we can get everybody you want to invite."

"Great. Do we have a plan?"

"I have two excellent choices for you. An evening traveling from strip club to strip club getting a look at as many women as possible. Or, the gang at my place with a keg, porn, and one stripper up close."

"Could we have two strippers?" Neal asked.

George blinked and then looked at Neal. "Sure, buddy. I'll need you to chip in a bit more."

Neal nodded, "Yeah. Sure."

"That is, if that's what the groom-to-be wants…" George looked back at Taro, who suddenly had the oddest look on his face. "If you want something different, I can revise the plan. Just say the word, man. Whatever you want to do. We could keep it cleaner. Booze and cards."

Taro shook his head like he was angry. "Sounds great. Two strippers. Plan it." He walked out of Sergei's office with a huff.

George frowned. "Okay, guys, tell me it isn't just me. He's acting really weird, right?"

"Uh-huh," Sergei said, nodding. "Really weird."

"Do you think it's cold feet?" Neal asked.

George gave the idea some thought. "Maybe."

"Could be the employment situation," Sergei said.

"Yeah," Neal said, with a sigh. "How are things going for you guys?"

George snorted. "It could be worse. I think."

"But not much," Sergei said.

"Yeah," Neal said, sighing again. "Not much. I need to start looking for a new job."

"Alright," George said, "let's not go too far, here."

Sergei tapped his desk with his fingers. "May as well be calm. You'll interview better."

"Come on guys," George said. "It may still work out. We've got weeks

325

yet."

Neal shook his head. "Yeah, sure. Later." He turned and left.

George looked at Sergei again. "That's two leaving the room irritated, or whatever. Is it me?"

Sergei laughed. "Could be. The *aroma* of your *satisfaction* might be getting to them." As George began to open his mouth, Sergei said, "Shut up, Serge."

George couldn't help it, he finally chuckled. "I'm not telling you about it."

"Come on," Sergei said. "It must be good."

"Noooo," George said, and left Sergei's office, nearly running into Ishi as she passed by. He apologized and went on.

He heard Ishi from behind him. "Why does it smell like cookies here?" And Sergei's laugh floated behind him down the hall.

George went straight to Jillian's office. She looked up from her computer and smiled when he walked in. He sat on the edge of her desk and kept his voice low. "Why didn't you tell me I smell like your lotion, this morning?"

"I didn't realize... it's awfully strong on me. Overwhelmed the olfactory senses."

"Okay, well, just know that it's a great source of amusement to the people who've noticed."

"Oh," Jillian said, and flushed bright red. "People have noticed?"

"Mm-hmm," George said.

Jillian grinned. "Well, at least if you have another girl, she'll know you've been with me."

"Oh-ho," George said, grinning back at her. "So that was your plan. Get me in trouble with my other girl."

Her smile broadened. "In trouble? Oh, no. Perish the thought." She leaned just slightly closer. "It's more of a warning to her. Hands off. He's taken."

George stilled. *He's taken? She's putting in an actual claim on me.* Not that one hadn't been in place since they'd gotten together, but she'd never said anything like that. Even her spurt of jealousy over Sarah hadn't been quite the same. *This is good. This is really good.* "I'll tell you what, Sweetheart. I'm all yours." Then he decided to keep it light. "And apparently, so are my clothes." He sniffed his shirt.

Jillian giggled.

Even though the news had been out for over a week, George had figured that Hardware had buried their collective heads in the sand, since they weren't reacting. Late Monday afternoon, they dug out, and Jillian and

George found themselves taking call after call, and meetings began to fill up their calendars for the rest of the week. Everything Hardware had ever had on their development list was under discussion, not just their current new product. Suddenly the long days of goofing around on IM, while they took their time working on appraisals, were gone.

Monday night, Jillian didn't tell George that she didn't want to see him. By the time they left the building, she'd missed him as much that afternoon as if they'd been apart for a week. They spent a short portion of the evening at The Blue Feather and then the rest at her apartment.

Tuesday work came and went. That evening they visited Delaney's restaurant. Jillian had found the idea plenty romantic as it was, but when they had their wine, George lifted his glass and said, "To the best week of my life."

Jillian felt a lump form in her throat. *Despite everything else. Or maybe because of it.* She managed to keep her voice level when she replied, with the truth, "The best week of my life, too."

On Wednesday, Orville hadn't said anything more than hello to George then he asked about Jillian. George smiled and said, "Terrific."

Orville grunted an okay type of sound and started the game. A few minutes and a few dozen dead simulated soldiers later, Orville asked, "So have you *professed* your love?"

George didn't lose his concentration on the game. "Not as yet."

"Why not?"

"One of the drawbacks of the modern age." George gunned down another simulated soldier.

"Which is?"

George took his character into a tank and the glanced at Orville. "Gotta be sure she'll say it back. If not..." The character began to fire the tank's main gun. "... generally, not always, but in most cases, you break up."

"I don't think I understand that. You tell her what women are always claiming they most want to hear, and then you break up?"

"If you really mean it and she isn't ready, then yeah. Absolutely. Too *awkward*."

Orville tilted his head a bit, and then shrugged. "I thought you were already burning up the sheets, from the way you two were touching on Saturday night."

George chuckled. "That is one way to put it."

"But not sure about love."

"Exactly."

"The modern age really *is* Hell, isn't it?"

George laughed again. "It's the same game you played. Patience and persistence. I just get the bonus of not having to wait nine months for a kiss. Only half-Hell."

"I don't know," Orville said. "It's hard enough to lose someone you love. But to lose them after you've actually experienced just how good you can be together? And clearly, you're good together. It might be double."

George thought for a moment about *the whatever* that hadn't happened again. It was another thing that he was ignoring as best he could. He was sure in his bones that it *could* happen again, that it wasn't a one-time only kind of experience. But wherever they had been that first time, the unique set of circumstances that had allowed them that experience, he'd been unable to duplicate it, even with her looking at him again. Maybe it was just time and patience. Maybe it was something else. Maybe he'd never have her like that again. Maybe it was Hell.

Thursday, Jillian and Melissa cheered on the team, and Jillian didn't hold back cheering for the whole team. She knew she was okay when she cheered for Chris on his first foul shot and George looked right at her and, even across the court, she could see his wink.

Melissa nudged her. "So, how's everything going?"

"Fine," Jillian said, with a smile.

"Just fine?" Melissa said, with a teasing tone.

"Okay. Terrific, then."

"You don't sound so sure," Melissa said, that time her tone was serious. "Is there anything wrong?"

Jillian looked at George on the court. He was marvelous. And she loved it there. She loved the way he'd look at her when he had a moment where he needn't completely concentrate on the game. It felt almost like high school again. She loved being his girl and that he was her guy. There was just the one problem. It wasn't high school anymore.

"Nothing's wrong," Jillian said. He made a layup and she cheered. *Nothing's wrong. But...* She didn't want high school or even college. She wanted the grown up version. And she wanted it to be real. And she wanted it with George. It didn't matter whether or not he ever surprised her with a luxurious bath again. No one else in the whole world would ever do.

She looked at Melissa. "How did you and Taro get together?"

Melissa tore her eyes from the court. "He asked me out."

"But, how? Exactly?"

"Exactly?" Melissa repeated. "Well, he showed up at my desk just before quitting time and asked if I had a minute before I left. I thought it was a work concern, we'd been dealing with something I can't elaborate on for quite some time, and then he asked for privacy. I didn't think anything in particular about it, because we'd had some professional contact about the thing I can't elaborate on. I'd thought he was nice and cute and everything, but I really didn't see it coming. He'd never seemed to pay any attention to me in *that* way.

"He surprised me. We went into a conference room and he said, oh, I wish I could remember the exact words, but it was something like, 'I want to get to know you away from the office. Can I buy you dinner, tonight?'"

Jillian put her feet up on the bleacher in front of her, rested her elbows on her knees, and her chin on her hands. "That doesn't sound like him. Although, it is blunt and to the point, which is somewhat like him."

"No," Melissa said, smiling and shaking her head. "It was like he was reading it from a cue card, it was so dry and without inflection. I think he'd practiced it, too. I hated to turn him down."

"Wait," Jillian said. "You turned him down.?"

"I did. I told him that it was inappropriate."

"But-" Jillian waved her finger from Melissa to Taro. "So, what happened?"

Melissa looked down at her shoes and her smile turned a bit embarrassed. "Actually, it was *completely* inappropriate." She twisted the toe of her shoes on a spot on the bleacher. "He should have taken my no and left it alone. I could have pressed a complaint on him."

Jillian dropped her arms and leaned down to see Melissa's grinning face. "So?"

"So," Melissa kept on twisting the toe of her shoe, "he said, and this I do remember, he said, 'Don't be stupid. I like you and you like me.' Which was true."

"He said, you were being stupid?" Jillian half-laughed.

Melissa's face was starting to pink a bit. "Yeah. And I told him that if he asked again, he'd be the one being stupid, implying I'd get him in trouble. And then," Melissa paused, sucked in her lips and wet them.

"Yeah?"

"He pulled a total caveman," Melissa said. "He grabbed the string on the blinds to shut them, took me by my shoulders, and laid one on me."

"What?!" Jillian could hardly picture Taro kissing anyone, let alone being aggressive and grabby. "Taro?"

"Mm-hmm," Melissa nodded, still eyeing her shoes. "It was like in the movies, when the hero just claims the heroine, no doubt in his mind that she's his. I mean, he had me by the shoulders and there was this kiss, right? And then he pushes us apart and looks at me, it couldn't have been for more than a second, but it was an eternity. And then his arms were around me and he was really kissing me... kissing me right out of my mind."

"Wow," Jillian said, quietly.

"I didn't want him to ever stop. But when he did, we were both breathing really hard and he said to me, 'Now, you aren't going to be stupid anymore, are you?'" She glanced up at Jillian. "And I said, 'no.'

And he said, 'good.' And after I took a few minutes to pull myself together, we went to dinner and the rest is history."

Jillian shook her head. "I can't quite visualize Taro manhandling someone, let alone someone from HR and *at work*."

"You and me, both," Melissa said. "What a turn on!"

"Really?" Jillian thought about her first day of work fantasy of George backing her into her office wall and kissing her stupid. "Yes, I guess so."

"All that passion from a guy who's nice too. He treats me right. What more could you ask for?"

"Well, love…" Jillian said, and then wished she could take it back. *That was so rude.*

Thankfully, Melissa didn't take it that way. She laughed. "And that too. All rolled into one."

Jillian sighed in relief. *Okay. That's good.* "When was that?"

"When was what?"

"The first 'I love you.'" *How did you make him fall in love with you, not just lust with fantastically good manners, like I've got?*

Melissa nudged Jillian again. "Is that on your mind?"

Jillian's mind started racing. She had to be careful. If she said something to Melissa, and Melissa said it to Taro… well, of course, George would hear about it. The last thing she needed to do was give him cause to run. "No, we've only been seeing each other a little over a week. I just love romantic stories. 'I love you' stories tend to be romantic."

"But you are still nuts about him," Melissa said.

"Oh, yes," Jillian answered. "Do I get to hear the rest of your story?"

"Sure," Melissa said, and proceeded to describe a sweet scene where Taro, not in a fit of caveman-esk passion, had stopped her while they were walking one evening, and simply said, "Melissa, I love you."

Jillian sighed. "And you said it, too."

"Of course. I'd been waiting a while to hear it."

Jillian and Melissa both said, "Men," in unison and began to laugh.

"What about the proposal?" Jillian asked, after a minute.

Melissa turned a bit shy again. "I hadn't actually expected it, right then. But I knew something was up when the dinner turned out to be such a production."

"So, he did it big, hmm?" Jillian asked.

"Yes. It was lovely. Nice restaurant. Flowers at the table. Ridiculously expensive wine. He got down on one knee before dessert arrived. I never thought I needed the old fashioned stuff. But I did feel so… not just loved, but adored, and appreciated. It was lovely."

Jillian nudged Melissa that time. "It sounds lovely."

"A story to tell the grandchildren, someday." After a few minutes, Melissa looked at Jillian. "Half-time soon. Quickly. How did you and

George… happen? Did he act like a caveman in a conference room?"

Jillian laughed and flushed. "No. He'd never do that. It was a coincidence where we ran into each other outside of work and things just happened from there."

"No fireworks?"

"Of course, fireworks. Why do you think I'm so nuts about him?" Melissa giggled and Jillian continued. "But, um, no manhandling. It was very… respectful, when he asked me out."

"So, what? Just a 'let's go out?'"

Jillian glanced at the court, then back at Melissa. "No. He said, he wanted to take me out and I told him it wasn't a good idea and then…" She glanced at the court again. "He kissed me. And my head swam. And when I still couldn't think he said, it again. 'Dinner. Tomorrow.'"

"Hmm. Sounds a bit caveman to me."

"No," Jillian said, shaking her head and looking at George moving around the court. "I could've stopped him at any moment. There was no grabbing." She thought about it a moment. "It was just time. We'd waited so long."

"Oh?"

Jillian felt her skin continuing to warm. There certainly couldn't be any harm in sharing things he already knew. "I was into him the first minute I saw him. He's told me he felt the same."

Melissa nodded. "That would explain a lot." Jillian looked at Melissa and raised her eyebrows. "The sudden seriousness for you two. I mean, Taro and I dated for a bit. We didn't know each other."

We didn't either.

Melissa went on with a slight nervous titter in her speech. "Not that that always matters. My best friend was completely and totally in love in one afternoon. They've been married about five years now."

"That's nice." Jillian looked back at the court. There was only a minute left before the half. She lowered her voice even further. "Sometimes it doesn't even take that long." *How long have I been in love with him? Since the nightmare dinner with my parents? Since the nightmare drinks with the witch? Since the first time he touched me? Since that first kiss? Since… forever?*

Friday was a tough schedule, but George was handling it until Taro hit him just before lunch. It was just a brief moment in passing, but he snagged him and said, "Tough luck."

"About what?" George asked, noting how incredibly chipper Taro seemed about something that was supposed to be bad.

"Melissa and Jillian are getting to be thick as thieves."

"And…?"

"And... last night, Jillian told Melissa that she's *not* in love with you."

George blinked. *She what?*

"I guess you've got skills and all that are keeping her around. But, um, tough luck, man." Taro patted him on the shoulder and walked on while George tried to remember how to breathe. Then he forced himself back to his office, dropped into his chair, and leaned a little forward to stare at his desk.

"Hey!" Jillian said, from his office doorway.

George looked up from desk and the papers he was staring at but not reading, with no idea how long he'd been sitting there. "Hey."

"Lunch?"

"Yeah, uh, no. Not today. I gotta work through lunch." He watched her face fall, but only a little. *What am I to you? Am I even a possibility? Or just a good fuck?*

"Um, sure. Okay." She nodded a little. "See you later, then?"

"Of course," he forced a smile on his face. "Later." His cell phone rang and Jillian left, so he answered it. "This is George."

"G, it's J.P. You need to get the next flight home. Mom just called. It's Uncle."

George sat back in his chair and closed his eyes. *Fuck! Fuck! Fuck!*

"You still there, G?"

"Yep." He still had his eyes closed. "I'm still here. But I'll be *there* just as soon as I can."

"Let me know when you'll be here. Come to Mom and Dad's."

George hung up with his brother and hopped on-line, getting a stand-by ticket that required him to get to the airport as quickly as possible. He packed up his things, including his laptop and started looking for Jillian. *Of course, she's nowhere to be found.* Her coat was in her office, but she wasn't in any of the conference rooms on the floor. He asked Rachel if she'd seen her. He begged Ishi to check the ladies' room for him. When he'd exhausted the options on the floor, he headed down to the cafeteria and couldn't find her.

One more trip around the third floor. Nothing. *Well, not in person then.* He thumbed her a short message that he had to catch a flight and he'd call her later.

He stopped at Rachel's desk and gave her the run down, asking her to send a message to his team to report to Jillian while he was gone. *God, please, no disasters here while I'm gone.* He was heading for the stairs when Sergei saw him and asked what was up. Sergei ran back to his office for his coat and then gave George a lift home so he could pack.

Jillian's phone bleeped with George's text message, but she couldn't look at

332

right away, since she found herself cornered in the HR cubicles by Gardiner who felt the sudden need to ask how her team was doing. His manner was odd and he seemed uncomfortable. A few sentences should have done the trick, but Gardiner led her to the reception area for his office.

Gardiner babbled for another minute or two until his wife appeared. He looked at his watch and said, "Oh, dear." Then he kissed his wife on the cheek and asked Jillian if they'd met before. When Jillian confirmed they'd been introduced at the holiday party, Gardiner nodded and said, "Good. Good." Then he turned to his wife. "I'm sorry, Darling. I can't get away for lunch today, like we'd planned."

"Oh, that's too bad. Maybe one of the up-and-comers would be interested in joining me," Mrs. Dabney said, and then she turned to Jillian. "How about it? My treat."

"Me?" Jillian said, the text message forgotten.

Mrs. Dabney smiled genially. "Unless you have other plans…"

Well, I thought I did, but I don't. "No, actually," Jillian said, laughing nervously. *It's a good opportunity. Lunch with the boss's wife. … I think.*

"Great. Are you free now?"

Jillian smiled at Mrs. Dabney. "Yes. Yes, I am."

"All right then," Mrs. Dabney said. "Let's go get your things." She led the way to the elevator. "I'm taking you to my favorite spot for lunch. It's a bit of a drive. I hope you can spare the time."

Jillian felt like shaking her head to clear it. "Of course, I can."

The trite chit chat that Mrs. Dabney made in the elevator and then on the way to Jillian's office made Jillian think that lunch was going to be a painfully dull experience. The small talk continued the entire forty minutes to the restaurant and through the ordering. Jillian had begun to wonder how anyone could come up with so much to say regarding the weather and clothes. The restaurant was lovely though. It reminded Jillian of the restaurants her father loved but could only afford once in a while, very upscale.

When the salads arrived, Mrs. Dabney suddenly leaned a little toward Jillian. "How long is it that you've been with us, Dear?"

Dear? You're not that much older than me. "A little over a year," Jillian said, and set down her fork.

"How do you like it?"

Jillian picked up her water glass. "I like it a lot, Mrs. Dabney," Jillian said, and grimaced inwardly for the lie. She took a drink and replaced the glass.

Mrs. Dabney smiled. "You must call me Patty," she said.

"All right," Jillian said. "Patty."

Mrs. Dabney continued. "I understand that you're being considered for a promotion."

Jillian smoothed her face the moment she realized her brow had furled. *So that's what this is about!* "I believe so. Yes. For the Director position over Software."

Mrs. Dabney nodded. "That's good. It's about time Gardiner started looking at female talent for the technical side of things."

"Are you involved with the management of the company, Mrs. Da-Patty?" Jillian asked. Seeing Mrs. Dabney in the building wasn't unheard of, but usually it was to see her husband or being social on the first floor or in the cafeteria. She attended other social activities too, like the holiday party and the company picnic. She was even known to attend the odd promotion celebration or retirement party, from time to time. But Jillian had never heard of her being involved in the company in a non-social capacity.

"Not officially, of course," Mrs. Dabney replied. "It's Gardiner's business." Jillian saw a strange look pass quickly over of Mrs. Dabney's face, but she couldn't make it out, it was gone so suddenly. "But, we talk things over. He likes to get my impressions of people."

Ah! Now we're getting somewhere. "Is that what this lunch is about? To form an impression of me?"

"No, Dear," Mrs. Dabney said, and took a drink from her water glass. "No. I already have my impression of you. It's about...something a little delicate."

Jillian started to twist her napkin in her lap. *Delicate?*

Mrs. Dabney leaned back and looked away for a moment. When she looked back at Jillian, she sighed. "It's about Mr. Grec."

Jillian stared at Mrs. Dabney and didn't move a muscle, not even to blink. *Oh. My. God.*

"I know you don't like him," Mrs. Dabney went on. "I suppose when one considers his...initial overture...one can certainly understand why. But he's actually quite a charming man. Not at all hard to look at. And he's quite wealthy."

Oh. My. God. Jillian finally blinked, but she didn't move otherwise.

"You know the company is in financial trouble."

Oh. My. God. Jillian blinked again.

"We could all use your help."

Unbelievable. Jillian blinked again. Then it became a staring contest. Jillian let Mrs. Dabney have the win by going back to eating her salad. She wasn't about to respond. There wasn't a single thing she could say that was worth saying.

Mrs. Dabney didn't say anything for a while either. The entrées came and they continued to eat in silence. When Jillian had finished and placed her silverware in position for the plate to be cleared, Mrs. Dabney sighed. "I'm sorry to have offended you, dear."

Jillian let out a soft, but undignified snort and took a sip from her water glass.

"I didn't mean what you thought I meant."

Jillian looked at Mrs. Dabney and raised her eyebrows and curled her lips in a mocking smile. *Oh, really?*

Mrs. Dabney tapped her water glass with the nail of her index finger. She looked up and signaled the waiter, handing him her credit card without even asking for the check, then she stood up and said, "Shall we go?"

Jillian glanced toward the quickly moving waiter who had only just taken Mrs. Dabney's credit card. "Um, sure."

The waiter met them at the coat check and Mrs. Dabney signed the receipt and took back her card. Jillian debated calling a cab for the ride back to work, but Mrs. Dabney looked at her silently over the car when the valet brought it up and Jillian got in the passenger side.

Mrs. Dabney drove two blocks and then pulled into a parking lot where she parked, shut off the engine, and stared straight ahead. After a very deep breath, she spoke again. "I'm a desperate woman, Miss Braden."

Jillian swallowed. *Oh, my.*

"In fact, desperate is hardly the word. I believe that Gardiner told everyone the situation the company is in, knowing him, he downplayed it a little. I doubt he told anyone that he's been pouring our money into it too. We're broke, in debt up to our ears. If the company goes under, we'll have to declare bankruptcy. Of course, everyone at the company will be out of work. The shame Gardiner feels…"

Jillian swallowed again and looked at Mrs. Dabney's profile.

"I would never ask another woman to…" Mrs. Dabney closed her eyes. "Just dinner." She opened her eyes and looked at Jillian. "Please."

Jillian exhaled at the twisted face before her. Mrs. Dabney looked as though she was in acute pain.

"He'd agree to any terms you want, I'm sure of that. You could pick the restaurant. Provide your own transportation. Never be in a situation that makes you uncomfortable. Just laugh at a few of his jokes and smile a few times."

Mrs. Dabney tightened her grip on the steering wheel. "Please. He tells very funny stories. And he's been all over the world. I'm sure he could entertain you a little. You wouldn't have to humor him beyond that. He does have the European cheek kiss habit, but I'm certain he wouldn't try anything." When Jillian didn't respond, her voice dropped. "Bring a chaperone."

Jillian turned her head to look out the windshield. "Do you have any idea what he said to me?"

"Well, not exactly," Mrs. Dabney said. "But he seemed quite contrite. I'm sure you'll have no trouble at all communicating with him that it's just dinner. He knows that you're not…"

Jillian looked back at Mrs. Dabney. "Not what, Patty? Not interested or not for sale?"

Mrs. Dabney closed her eyes again and then turned back to the windshield and let go of the steering wheel. "Don't think that this is easy for me."

Jillian leaned her elbow on the car door and rested her head on her hand. "Why should I care if this is easy for you or not?"

Out of the corner of her eye, Jillian saw Mrs. Dabney shake her head. "You're right, of course. You shouldn't. I can hardly believe I'm doing it. But, as I said, I'm desperate. And he talks about you every time we see him. Every time. And we've seen him nearly every day this last week." She paused a moment. "Gardiner is at his wits end. And he couldn't bring himself to talk to you about it."

"He's afraid I'll sue," Jillian said.

"Maybe," Mrs. Dabney responded. "I also think he's as disgusted as you are."

"Oh, I doubt that."

Mrs. Dabney nodded. "No. I'm sure you're right. At the moment, though, I doubt you're as disgusted as I am. I feel like I need a shower."

Jillian snorted at that. "I can't believe this," she muttered.

"Neither can I," Mrs. Dabney said, and started the car. "Of all the things I've done for Gardiner and the company over the years, nothing comes close to this." Mrs. Dabney slid the gear shift into reverse. "I'll take you back."

CHAPTER TWENTY-TWO

It was Rachel who roused Jillian from her post-lunch trance. She had apparently walked into Jillian's office and cleared her throat several times before she finally poked Jillian with her finger. "Oh!" Jillian turned from her computer, the screen was dark anyway, and looked at Rachel.

"Okay," Rachel said. "I've seen you happy, sad, tired, stressed, and probably a few other things, but this one, I can't identify. What's up with you?"

If there was one rule Jillian had learned from spending time with Kai and Melissa, it was that when you're dealing with something actionable, if you're not going to take action, you keep your mouth shut. Jillian didn't know if she was going to take action or not. She wasn't sure if she actually could, since technically Patty Dabney had no authority over her and hadn't really threatened her with anything. But even if she could, she wasn't sure she wanted to. Then her name would be associated with the mess and, whether it made the papers or not, it was sure to turn up on a background check. If she said anything, she'd need to commit to doing something and deal with it.

Rachel tilted her head. "I'm going to go with shock. Are you in shock?"

Yes. That's probably it. "Perceptive," she said, but didn't elaborate. "What do you need?"

"Well, since you're covering for George-"

"Covering?" Jillian interrupted. It was then that she remembered the text message and flipped her phone.

Family emergency - Uncle. Taking first flight out. Call you later.

"Oh." Jillian looked back up at Rachel. "It's been a rough day for a lot of people, I guess. What can I do for you?"

George glanced at his phone as he stood in line to board the airplane. For all the bad luck he was having everywhere else, getting the flight had actually been easy. But as he looked at his phone, he couldn't help but wonder why she hadn't even texted back. Even if she didn't feel the same about him as he did about her, she was his girlfriend. *I shouldn't have left the building 'til I found her.* His moody reaction to Jillian's lunch invitation after Taro's news meant that his last in person interaction with her had been negative. *That was a stupid thing to do. The right move would have been to work harder at selling her, not being a pissy baby. Crap!* He moved forward in the line and tried to decide if he could place a quick call to her before the attendants made him shut off his phone.

It wasn't that he didn't have time, but the things he wanted to say probably shouldn't be said, surrounded by strangers. He quickly thumbed her another message. *About to board. Miss you already.* Then he looked at the message. Was that miss you comment too much? He didn't want to scare her off. *Nah. It's okay.* He sent the text.

Not having succeeded in shaking off the lunch, Jillian barely managed to keep pace with the afternoon. Between two meetings with Hardware in the afternoon, she ran up the stairs intending to stop by her office and pick up her personal cell phone. Rachel waved her down with a message from one of George's clients, asking whether to leave the message for George or if she'd return it.

Jillian figured she'd be next to useless about whatever the client wanted, but that she'd at least return the call and find out. That shaved another few minutes off of her brief break, but at least the client had been exceptionally understanding about George's family emergency and had been willing to wait until Monday to see if George would be available.

She locked her office again and ran to the ladies' room, certain she'd be late to the Hardware meeting and trying to come up with excuses that didn't sound like excuses. On her way back, planning to grab her notepad, pen, and personal phone, she nearly collided with Taro.

"Whoa, there, girl," he said. "Slow down."

Jillian must have given him quite the look because he turned and followed her to her office.

"Hey. You okay?"

Jillian simply said, "I'm just in a real hurry. Trying to cover all these meetings and with George gone…"

"Right," Taro said. "I wasn't even thinking about that when he blew out of here. How much he was dumping on you. Pretty selfish of him."

"He didn't dump anything on me," Jillian replied, too stressed to be anything but irritated. *He's your friend, Taro. Lay off.*

"Oh, of course," Taro said. "I'm sure he asked nicely. And you were only too happy to help."

Well, no. Not at all. But I am happy to help. But since she wasn't actually in a happy state of mind, Jillian didn't look at him.

She gathered up her things and moved toward her door.

"Oh, now don't tell me there's trouble in paradise," Taro said.

When Jillian looked at him he was almost sneering at her as he blocked the doorway. "I'm too busy for whatever this is about. Excuse me."

"Then he's expressed his undying gratitude. Good. I'd hate to see you feeling put out by your *boyfriend.*"

"I'm sorry. I'm going to be late. Would you like to either say what's on your mind or kindly exit my office please?" It was as polite as she could manage.

"Ah," he said, his mouth turning to a grin and his hand mimed brushing away. "I was just messing with you. I guess I should ease up since you're so busy. I just figured you were much more laid back than I had originally sized you up. That you'd at least have a sense of humor. Most girls would have to, if they were in your situation."

"What are you talking about?"

He took a step back, but didn't quite clear the door. "What am I talking about? About you and George and your little... I assume you know all about it."

She knew somewhere deep down that she shouldn't respond, that she should physically move him out of the door. But sense gave way to exhaustion and irritation. "All about what?"

"About this supposed *relationship.* What George was doing... the night you two... started."

"Taro," Jillian said.

Taro stepped back out of the doorway and kept talking, though he dropped his voice to nearly a whisper. "He was supposed to meet Sergei that night. He'd asked Sergei to meet him, in fact. He told him he needed a wingman because he needed to get laid."

Jillian twisted her key in the lock of her door. *He did not.*

"And low and behold, who does he track down and pick up, but the hottie from work that he's wanted to lay since he first set eyes on her. That's our George."

Jillian turned toward the stairwell and started walking as quickly as she could. *Shut up!*

"Don't believe me? Ask Sergei," Taro said, from behind her. "Gotta give him credit for keeping it going too. A nice regular schedule for him. Pretty much every night, right?"

She picked up her pace and Taro quit following her. By the time Jillian staggered into the stairwell, she could hardly see through the blur. *That's a lie. That's a lie. That's a damn lie.* She recited to herself over and over as she made her way as carefully as she could down the stairs.

But, what was he doing there? He said, he was meeting Sergei. So was that part true? He said, it was a coincidence. But was it a coincidence or an opportunity? She couldn't think about it anymore. She wiped her eyes and exited the stairwell on the second floor for her meeting. *I'll think about this later.*

She was all the way to the conference room door when the thought popped up before she could squash it. *He didn't even care enough to say good-bye.*

One of the Hardware Managers asked her if she was okay and she forced a smile on her face and told him she'd grazed a filing cabinet with her shoe and hurt her little toe something awful. It was an effective lie and Jillian shoved all the misery to back of her mind to focus on the meeting.

After the meeting, Jillian stayed in the conference room and flipped over her phone. She took a deep breath when she saw the new message from George. At the words *miss you already* she sagged back in the chair. *See that, Taro? You're full of it.*

She started swiping her finger across the screen. *I miss you too. You've no idea how much.* Then she blanched. *Okay. That was* way *too strong.* She spent a minute trying to recraft her message.

Her next swipe didn't yield any improvement. *Sorry about your Uncle. I'll be thinking of you.* She bit her thumb nail, added *Call when you can.*, and then put down her phone. "This is worse than the IM."

Another attempt yielded a message that she almost sent. *Miss you too. Hoping for the best for your family.* It was then that she realized she'd never replied to his first message. *Oh, no. Not good. Should I apologize?*

People were arriving for the next time slot on the conference room, so she deleted her text, picked up her things, and headed up, all the way up, to the roof. She had a half-hour before her next meeting and she was certain that she'd get caught up with something if she went back to her office.

After securing the door with the rock, Jillian set everything down but her phone and took a few deep breaths of cold, fresh air. *Okay. I can do this. It's just a text message.* She exhaled. It wasn't just a text message.

She glanced at her phone and then gave herself another minute to walk a little closer to the edge and take in the view. The view was nice, despite the cold, but it was obvious enough that what had made the roof wonderful the other day wasn't the view, it was the company. Jillian looked at her phone again, swiping through her pictures, stopping on the one of the two of them looking at each other. It moved her the most, they both looked happy just to be together. *We don't just look it, we are. We are happy just to be together.*

That thought finally did it.

Missing you too! Had to escape to your sanctuary to get a moment's peace. So sorry about your Uncle. Call whenever. I'll keep my phone with me the rest of the day.

It wasn't great literature, or even a greeting card, but at least it was honest. She hadn't apologized for not replying, but she'd hinted at why, so she could offer the actual apology whenever he called. She sent the text and tried not to worry about it.

Damn you, Taro!

By the time George's flight landed, he was famished from having missed lunch, but he put off the thought of food for a few more important matters. While he focused on making his way through baggage claim and on to the car rentals, hoping beyond hope that he'd be able to get something drivable without a reservation, he was also thinking of Jillian.

He'd switched on his phone as soon as the seat belt sign went off, and checked it a couple of times while waiting to disembark. Her message came through just as the line was moving, but he'd been able to take it in, and it had fortified him a little.

The quick call he'd made had fortified him a lot more. It improved his mood just hearing her voice when she answered, "George? How are you? Are you in Washington already?"

Not even a hello. He smiled. "Yes. I'm at the terminal and heading out to try to get a car."

"I'm so sorry I missed you earlier. I was in the middle of- You know, it doesn't matter. I'm just sorry. And I'm so sorry about your Uncle. I hope he's doing all right. And I hope you're doing all right."

His smile widened. These little moments Jillian had where everything she was thinking just poured out of her were wonderful. She'd done it at the basketball game, then in bed the previous Sunday night, and again right then. Since these outbursts seemed to be uncensored, he couldn't help but think it was another sign of her letting her guard down. *Maybe it isn't love yet, but it was going in the right direction.* "Thank you. I'm holding up, so far. Gotta get a car and some food and drive a long way tonight."

"Oh, right. So I should let you go, so you can go do…"

"If you like, but I do have a few minutes' walk here. You could tell me about your day."

Even across the connection, he could hear Jillian inhale. "I don't know what to say other than busy and awful. But it's better now. How was the flight?"

Okay. Not entirely letting her guard down. But still. "Fine. Minimal turbulence."

Then came a few moments of silence. George was about to ask her what she was going to do with her evening, just to keep the conversation going, when she burst again.

"I miss you. I don't mean to put any extra pressure on you, or anything. I know you need to be there and I don't want you to feel at all bad about it. But I need you to know that I miss you."

It was George's turn to inhale. "I miss you, too." *God, I miss you. I wish you were here now.* "I don't know how long I'm going to be here. I'll keep you posted. Since I'm not there, what are you going to do tonight?"

"Well, since you're not here, I thought I'd take a swim and then watch a movie with Charlie."

"Sounds nice."

After a few moments of silence, she said, "It'll be okay. It's what I used to do... Would you call me when you get to your parents' house? Just to ease my mind."

"Sure," he said. "Just FYI, my folks are a little way outside of town and the town is a little way outside of the metropolitan areas and there isn't cell signal there yet. Supposed to be a tower going in soon that will reach the house. But for now it's a landline and satellite phones. I'll get signal at the hotel, I don't know which one yet. And I'll get signal around town and the hospital. So, if my cell goes straight to voice mail, I'm in the boonies. Leave a message and I'll call back the minute I get it. Okay?"

"The very minute?" Jillian asked, her voice lighter, and then it turned serious again. "Do you want me to get you a reservation somewhere?"

"Really?"

"Sure. I could do that."

George gave her the name of the town, the three small hotels, and gave her his preference, in case it worked out. She told him once she'd taken care of the reservation, she'd call and if she didn't get an answer, she'd leave him a voice mail and text him. He thanked her and wondered at how she could be that generous and not care about him. The answer was obvious, she did care. She may have said something negative to Melissa, but she cared. He was going to have to figure out how to sweep her off her feet when he got home, and that was that.

Jillian was ready to hang up, since she had something to do for him, but he stopped her for a moment after she said goodbye, saying, "I'll be thinking of you."

"If you're not, I think I'll understand. You've got-"

"No. I'll be thinking of you."

"Me too," Jillian said, softly and George reflexively closed his eyes at her tone. He wanted to be in her arms more than anything. He opened his eyes to look where he was going again.

"I'll call you."

"Okay."

They finally exchanged good-byes, or as George thought, they unfortunately exchanged good-byes and he found himself thinking of her as he as he moved on through the airport. Jillian didn't respond to extravagance, based on her apartment and the dinner with her folks. She'd be moved by something thoughtful, like the bath, more so than dropping a lot of money on an evening out. What would move Jillian?

Just in case he would be tied up until late, George checked into the hotel before he headed out to his parents' house. Although he knew logically that Jillian calling a few hours before probably hadn't made a difference in the occupancy rate of the hotel, he was still smiling that she'd taken care of it for him. She'd even used her credit card to hold the room for him. He'd used his own when he actually checked in, of course, but it was sweet.

On the way out of town, he drove passed a locally owned store that boasted one-of-a-kind gifts. Another fifteen minutes wouldn't likely make much difference and by the time he was heading back to the hotel, the local shops would probably be closed, though the few chain stores wouldn't be, so he turned and took a few minutes to look around.

They had one-of-a-kind things all right. At least, he had trouble imagining anyone making more than one of some of the odd stuff. *No accounting for taste.* Just as he laughed to himself at some weird leather goth-like bracelet thing with all kinds of evil-looking metal demons on it, his eyes landed on several somethings that weren't funny at all. Animal bracelets, which could have been funny, except they had one with a lion's head on it and one that was elephants, trunk to tail, in a circle. He asked, but they didn't have a seal. *That's what the internet is for.*

He purchased the two bracelets, figuring it was better to have them, than not, and paid to have them gift wrapped in individual boxes. *Two rings down, one to go.*

One less thing to think about, George headed out of town to deal with his family.

Jillian was curled up on the couch with Charlie watching *Casablanca* when her landline rang. She expected it to be either Malvinia or Kai, but when she said hello and heard a male voice with an accent start with, "Good evening. Is this Miss Braden?"

It was easy enough to guess who the caller was. Her heart started to pound in her ears. *Oh, my God. What do I do? Play dumb for a minute and buy yourself time.* "Yes. Who is this?"

"Miss Braden, this is Cisco Grec."

Should have pretended to be my sister or a roommate or something.

343

"I'm calling this evening to express my sincerest apologies for the other day."

"Well, I already received your note," she said, cutting in before he said anything else. *Calm down. Try to sound detached. Don't say anything about the flowers.* "I don't see how anything more is required. I consider the issue closed."

"Miss Braden, I'm afraid that we had a misunderstanding."

Jillian almost laughed at the thought of it all being a misunderstanding, but she shuddered at the memory instead. "I think you were quite clear, Mr. Grec."

"Yes and, er, no. I think that I inadvertently gave the impression that-"

"Mr. Grec," Jillian interrupted him, "I don't believe that there is any more to say on this subject. At the very least, there is nothing I'd like to hear. Please don't call me again. Goodnight." She clicked the hook instead of slamming the phone down and said to Charlie, "Tonight would have been a good night to be at George's." She leaned back against the sofa, realizing that she'd had another rush of adrenaline. "Oh, Charlie. Can you believe he had the nerve?"

Charlie nudged the remote with his nose.

"More *Casablanca*, eh? Okay. You're the boss. Anything to shut my brain off." She picked up the remote with a shaky hand and pushed play, but she looked away from the screen and through her windows, wondering exactly where George was and what he was doing, trying to push the errant phone call out of her mind. It would have been much easier if George had been there.

She wondered what he would have done. Letting her imagination go, she pictured him taking the phone from her and telling Mr. Grec that she wasn't available, then or for the rest of life, and slamming the phone down. As her fantasy continued, she crossed her arms and asked, "For the rest of my life, hmm?" And George had nodded and then taken her into his arms and said, "That's what I want. You and me. For the rest of our lives. What do you say, Jillian?"

I think this sounds like the script from a bad movie. Jillian stood up from the sofa, disturbing Charlie and getting a faint meow from him. "Sorry, baby," she mumbled and walked over to the windows to look out at the dark streets. *I'd take it, though. If he said that, I'd say 'yes.'* "But how likely is it he'll *ever* say anything like that?"

She thought of Mr. Grec again and felt her stomach churn. *Ugh.* The bottle of wine in the fridge called and she settled back next to Charlie with a glass to try not to think about men, while watching *Casablanca*. "Charlie, we need to put on something else. I've got men trouble."

Charlie looked up at her for a moment and then back at the screen.

"Compromise? I'll fast forward to the song you like and then we'll get a different movie."

Charlie seemed contented enough, since he didn't meow at her after she took the disc out of the player and put in a different one. But he looked at her again once the movie had started.

"Don't give me that look," she said. "I want to watch a movie where the girl kicks everybody's butt. And Lara Croft does it."

Charlie got up from the sofa and wandered off, apparently uninterested in *Tomb Raider*.

Jillian put her feet up on the coffee table. "Go, Lara."

"This can't be good," George said to himself, as he pulled into the long drive and the headlights picked up his three brothers rising from the chairs on the deck and walking down the stairs. He parked and as he exited the car he shouted a greeting to his brothers, hoping to get a hint. *Must be bad news. Maybe I missed him.*

They all returned his greeting, but didn't move from their position in front of the stairs. *Or I'm in trouble.* When he got closer, he could make out that all of them had their hands in their pockets and their shoulders were raised a little. "What's going on?" He asked.

Richard looked at J.P. and then at Jack. Then J.P. and Jack exchanged a look.

"Am I too late?" George asked.

J.P. took his right hand out of his pocket and pointed at Richard. Richard shook his head at J.P.

George's brow furled. "All right, what's up?" He looked around at all of them in turn. Jack actually looked down and kicked at a rock. "Well, this is pointless." He nodded toward Richard. "Talk."

Richard sighed and raised a hand to rub the back of his neck. "All right. But… just don't lose your temper. Okay?"

"What's going on?!"

Richard took a step toward George and put his hand on his shoulder. "We all raced out here this afternoon, when we got word. And then," he cleared his throat and looked back at J.P. and Jack. They both nodded slowly. "Then we found out that Mom had, um, exaggerated the situation a bit."

George's eyebrows flew up and he blinked. "What does that mean, exaggerated?"

"Uncle went to the hospital today, but he wasn't admitted. He's doing chemo. And apparently, the prognosis is actually really good. There are no guarantees, but they caught it early and it's likely he'll beat it."

Shaking off Richard's hand and rubbing his hands over his face, George tried to think. "So, there's no emergency."

"Nope," J.P. said.

"Then, what?" George dropped his hands to his sides.

Richard let out a long breath. "Mom misses you. Dad too, I guess."

George took a step back. "So they just told us all that Uncle was about to die?! Or did you guys know what was going on?"

Looking up from the rock, Jack said, "No. Like Richard said. We had no idea. J.P. brought Melanie and the kids. And Sue came with me. We all thought…"

Richard jammed his hand back in his pocket. "Mom's laid out a feast in there, like it's Thanksgiving. She wants a family dinner."

"So, she lied to all of us, to get us all here at once," George said, shaking his head in disbelief.

"Looks like it," J.P. said.

"*Holy fu-*" George started but J.P. cut him off.

"My kids! My kids are in there! Anything you can do to *not* swear would be appreciated." J.P. started at a shout and then quieted back to conversational tone. "We all stuck around because it was too late to stop you from coming and we figured you'd want the… support."

George snorted. "You're rewarding really bad behavior, *Dad*, that's what you're doing."

Jack sat down on the stairs. "That may be, but we're here for *you*. We all know that you're the one that they wanted. We all visit at least once a month."

Crossing his arms, George tried to unlock his tense jaw. "So, it's my fault. I don't visit enough, so this trick gets played on all of us."

Richard stepped forward again. "That's not what he meant and you know it. Now, what are you going to do?"

"Do?"

"Yes, do. Are you going in? Or are you turning around and going home?"

"Oh, I'm definitely going in," George said, and took a step toward the stairs. Jack jumped back up and he and J.P. and Richard formed a small blockade.

"Then you're going to be calm, right?" Richard told him, though he'd phrased it like a question.

"Sure," George said. "I'll be calm." He looked at J.P. "The kids are in the house."

The other three exchanged looks, but then stepped aside and let George head into the house. Rather than looking for his parents, George looked for his niece and nephews in the rec room, deciding to play Wii with them. He figured one of his brothers would announce that he'd arrived.

He must have been right because some twenty minutes later, Melanie came to bring everyone in to dinner. She gave him a tight smile that he took to be a measure of support mixed with worry. *Why does everyone expect me to blow up?* He laughed to himself. *Because they'd all understand why, if I did.*

Once grace was over and the passing of the platters and bowls started, George could feel the tension. Almost no one was speaking and the kids were squirming more than usual. *I guess it's up to me...*

He looked at his dad. "I'm glad Uncle is doing well." The whole table went silent and everyone froze, save for turning to look at him. "What?" He asked, looking around. "I *am* glad. Oh, come on. What were we going to do, eat and not talk?" He looked at Richard.

"G's right," Richard said, "We're all glad." He turned his attention to Sue and asked her about work. George looked at his mom and said, "This all smells delicious."

"Thank you, George."

The tension wasn't completely broken, but at least conversation started up. By the time dessert arrived, the family was laughing and telling stories. It almost was Thanksgiving.

Jillian tossed and turned in her bed. She couldn't get comfortable and she was wide awake despite the hour. Lara Croft hadn't settled her, she'd wound her up. At least the movie had been distracting while it was playing.

When she finally decided to get up for a while, she opened up her personal laptop and surfed the internet until the idea struck her to do a little holiday shopping. Patting herself on the back for having had a practical idea, she started with her parents and her sister and her sister's family. They were easy since her parents seldom reacted to the gifts and Beth always loved hers. The kids were getting easier to shop for too. They were old enough to want gift cards. So she bought them fun things to do as a family, a board game, and then the gift cards.

Taro's awful lie hadn't quite doused her hopes. She decided to shop a bit for George, telling herself that they'd still be together at Christmas. She started on eBay looking at yo-yos. It seemed a little obvious, but then again, he loved yo-yos, so what was the harm in looking.

"Unbelievable," she said to Charlie, who'd been disturbed by her change in sleep patterns and had come by to see what she was doing. "Did you know they made sterling silver yo-yos in the 1940's? I didn't. I wonder if they even work. They're probably a collector item as opposed to something you use. They certainly cost a lot."

She looked on. "I like these wooden ones, for some reason." A nice one caught her eye as she scrolled though. "Oh, I thought it said Marvin. It says Martin." It read 'Martin' with a logo of a bunny on it. The description read 'Bunny Martin' yo-yo.

"Okay, Charlie. Who do you suppose Bunny Martin is?" She googled

Bunny who turned out to be a guy and a yo-yo champ who won the world tournament at the age of 16 back in the 1970's. "Charlie-boy. I think was may have found a winner."

She wanted something more, much more. But this gift was a start. She bought it outright and shut down the computer. "Time for bed. Again."

As she drifted off, she thought about George. *Maybe I should get one of the wooden yo-yos and get someone to paint the green cosmic cutie from the cover of the Hitchhiker's Guide to the Galaxy on it. No! A picture of Marvin from the 80's BBC version.* Well, it was an idea anyway.

CHAPTER TWENTY-THREE

While the dinner discussion had been pretty typical, mostly funny, some serious, a crack from his dad about how nice it was to have the whole family at dinner made all of George's brothers glance at him. The next comment was from his mom about a house that was for sale in town and because it was small, it was perfect for a single man. George just smiled and let it roll off his back. Two weeks ago he'd have lost it with his parents for pulling such a stunt and then making remarks about him moving home. He was still mad, in all fairness he was furious, but now he had the benefit of insight.

When everyone started clearing the table and the kids had run off to play the Wii again, George asked his mom and dad to stay in the room. They did, a little reluctantly, but they did. The near silence in the kitchen made it clear that everyone was eavesdropping. *Well, let 'em. This isn't a secret anyway.*

He walked over to his mom and gave her a huge bear hug. "I love you, Mom."

"I love you too, honey," his mom said.

Then he turned to his dad and hugged him too. "I love you, Dad."

His dad grunted a "Me too."

When they didn't say anything more, he guessed they were stunned.

"Ok," George said, "let's sit down." Before they'd re-seated themselves, he started talking to beat his dad to it. "I have some things to say and you're going to listen. I'll be brief. I'm disappointed that you chose to do something like this-"

"Now, George," his mom started. "We had to do something."

"Not this." He took a deep breath. "It's time we cleared the air. You keep on after me to visit and I don't. Well, the reason I don't visit much isn't because I don't love you or miss you. I do." He leaned toward the kitchen and shouted, "All of you!" Then he leaned back. "I don't visit because when I come here all I hear about is moving back. For that matter, when we talk on the phone, it's all about what I miss not being here, not about sharing what's happening. It's all just guilt."

"Well, I'm not moving back. And if you want me around more, you'll stop making me feel bad about it when I'm here."

His mom bit her lip. "Honey, we miss you so much."

"Then show me that. Be glad to see me, not angry with me. And by the way, it goes both ways. How often have you been out to visit me since I got out of school? Not once.

"I have a house. I've had a house for two years. You don't even need to stay at a hotel." He looked at his dad. "And before you say you can't get away from the business, we all know that you take a long weekend sometimes. Fly out Friday and come back Monday. That'd give us two days."

His dad shifted a little. "We don't like to travel much."

"I know. But you'd think you'd make the sacrifice if you wanted to see me badly enough to lie to all your kids."

His mom looked on the verge of tears.

"Don't start crying, Mom. I was at dinner last week with a family that can't communicate with each other and they'd dug in their heels and weren't moving an inch for each other. I thought of them tonight and I realized that we can have a better relationship, if we can learn how to talk to each other. No more of this guilt stuff. Not from you. Not from me, either.

"You've a standing invitation to visit. Use it or don't. I won't mention it. From now on, when we talk on the phone, you can tell me about what's been happening, but no more saying 'you should have been there,' not even as an expression.

"And when I'm here, I don't want to hear any more about moving back. I want to hear that it's good to see me." He reached over and took his mom's hand. "Because it's sure good to see you."

His mom looked at the down at the table. "You only come maybe twice a year."

"I might be able to see to more than that, but it's got to be more pleasant to visit."

George's dad stood up. "I can't believe that we're so unbearable that you want to live across the country, rather than live here."

George shook his head then looked up at his dad. "Dad, it's not like I ran away from home. I don't want to live there just to not live here. I want to live there because I like it there. I have a job, a home, friends, a life… " He looked at his mom. "I can't live my life for you. I have to live my life for me. I'm not doing it to hurt you. It's what I want and what makes me happy. And if you can start being happy for me, then we can have conversations that don't make me angry or sad, and I'll *want* to visit."

Everyone fell silent.

His mom spoke first. "I suppose a short trip wouldn't be out of the question. Maybe right after the new year."

His dad frowned. "The weather can be terrible then."

Sue walked in from the kitchen and picked up two plates. "I'll drive you to the airport and pick you up." She looked at George and winked.

Well, an ally in the sister-in-law. Who'd have guessed?

George's mom stood up. "Then it's settled. We'll get tickets for the second Friday in January." She picked up George's plate. "Excuse me. There's washing up."

George stood up and faced his father. "Well, sir?"

"I don't suppose there's much more to say. You've got your mother on your side."

"My side?" George asked. "What side is that?"

His dad started to move around the table. "It's not important. Sounds like you won."

George rubbed his face with his hands. "This. This is the problem, Dad. There's no communication. How can we ever do anything but fight, if we don't even say what we're thinking?"

His dad stopped and put his hands on the back of a chair. "Alright. I think you abandoned this family. You should be here. Working the business. That's what I think."

George shook his head and put his hands behind his back, so his dad wouldn't see the fists he was making. "Doing what, dad? There isn't anything for me here."

"You could do IT for us."

"You don't need any IT. You've already got a LAN and all the software you need. You want me to update or upgrade you. I can do it in a weekend. That isn't a job. And we both know I'm not a logger."

"Well, I don't like it!" His dad snapped. "I don't like you living all the way out there."

George exhaled. "On that point, we're not going to agree. Can we call a truce?"

His dad crossed his arms. "I don't see how. I don't like you out there all alone."

George closed his eyes for a moment, then opened them and shook his head. "Dad, I'm not alone. Even if I was, it's not like I'm a kid anymore. I've been out of school for over eight years. If you could just keep an open mind and come out and see my life."

"The life you made without us," his dad said.

"How do I get through to you?" George asked. "How can I phrase this so that you'll hear me? I didn't leave *you*, I left the *town*. I didn't quit calling because I didn't miss you. I quit calling because the calls are upsetting. I didn't quit visiting because I didn't miss you. I quit visiting because the visits are upsetting. I've been working my tail off for over a year to get a promotion just to impress you. To show you that I have something of value out there."

George stopped talking, pulled out a chair, and sat down. *I've been working my tail off to get a promotion just to impress my parents?* He leaned back and dropped his head back so he could see the ceiling. *Oh, God. I don't want to be a director! Orville said it and I didn't listen. I don't want the stupid job for me, I want it for them. To prove something.*

I don't even want to be a manager. What I want is to quit this management crap and go back to programming. Hell, I want to make games, not productivity software.

His dad walked a few chairs closer. "George? You doing okay?"

He didn't look at his dad, he let out a snort. "I just realized that the last four years of my life, I've been working a job I hate because I thought it would show you that my life had value. And the four years before that I worked a job I didn't like because I gave up on what I wanted to do a lot sooner than I should have, for the same reason." He lifted his head then. "Eight years of not doing what I wanted, because, like an idiot, I wanted to make you proud of me. And I failed."

George's dad swallowed so hard George could see the lump go down his throat. "I am proud of you. I just want to be proud in closer proximity."

"You're proud of me?"

George's dad pulled out the chair he was standing behind, two apart from George, and he sat down. He clasped his hands together and looked at them. "Of course, I'm proud. You're out there, making you're way in the world, don't need any help from us. What's not to be proud of?"

"Well, geez, Dad. I didn't know you felt-"

George's dad's head snapped up and he cut George off. "But we're not going to get mushy. I'm a logger, even if I'm in the office these days, and we don't do that. You want mushy, go see your mom in the kitchen."

"Right," George said, and he stood up, figuring that was as much a breakthrough as he could ever hope for. "No mushy stuff."

His dad stood up too. "Let's grab a beer and put on ESPN." George nodded. As he looked at, but didn't watch, ESPN with his dad, he thought about the stupid job that he didn't even want and tried to figure out what he was going to do.

Later that night, as he walked into his hotel room, exhausted from the events of the day, the jet lag, and the lateness of the hour due in part to the time zone change, he accepted that there was only one thing to do. *I have to tell Gardiner I don't want the job and start looking for one I do want.* But in the shower, as he tried to wash off the airplane, another realization came to him. *If I withdraw, then when Jillian gets it, some might say she got it by default.* He could start looking for a new job, but he should stay in the running until Gardiner told them it was Jillian. For her sake.

Shit! Jillian! It's way too late to call. He looked at the clock again as he opened the bed and groaned. After everything that had happened, he'd forgotten to call her from his parent's house. He didn't want to add waking her up to his list of screw-ups, so he sent a text message instead.

I know I forgot to call. I made it safely. Turns out my Uncle is doing better than I thought. Tell you about it in the morning.

Before anything else, he needed to book a return flight. He looked at the flights the following day and stopped himself. *I am here, after all.* He could visit some people, including his Uncle, the next day, and then go home. After securing a seat on a late flight Sunday evening, getting in just after nine, he was able to get some sleep.

"Wow," Ishi said, walking into Jillian's office. "I'd say you look tired, but you look like you're going through withdrawal. Is my boss really that addictive?"

Jillian smiled weakly at the jab. She wasn't tired anymore, exhausted was the proper word. She'd tossed and turned, and then finally fallen asleep before George's text came in. At least she'd had that to wake up to. But then, it wasn't exactly a very moving text, either. She'd replied with, *I'll be in the office. Call anytime.* She'd been tempted to add something about missing him again, but since he hadn't said it and she didn't want to start coming off needy or clingy, she didn't add it. "These weekends are rough," Jillian said to Ishi, ignoring the rest of her comment. "What can I do for you?"

Ishi's problem solved, Jillian decided to put a sign on her door saying to knock and come in, then shut off her lights, and put her head down. She'd downed some ibuprofen that morning, but it couldn't make up for the lost sleep and was only slightly dulling her headache.

Her phone rang and she heard herself groan. She must've actually dozed off. As soon as she realized it was her personal cell and it was George's ring tone, she grabbed her phone and sat up. "Hello?"

"Good morning." His lovely bass rumbled over the connection.

"Hi," she said, with a sigh, glad her office door was closed.

"I'm sorry I forgot to call you. You'll never believe what happened."

"Do tell," she said, and listened while George described his evening. He finished with a comment, "I owe you, you know. I heard what you said to your parents about loving them but having to live your own life. I used that. I think I may have gotten through to them. A little, at least."

"It's more than I've ever been able to do. I'm glad it worked for you."

Jillian said.

"So, how did your evening go?"

Jillian bit her thumb nail. She didn't want to tell him about Grec, not over the phone with him so far away, but she needed him. He'd told her he'd have her back. She was just so tired of it all and tired in general and her head hurt. She blurted it out.

George was silent for a moment. "You did good, Sweetheart. Telling him not to call you again. Straight forward and completely clear. Unmistakable." He went quiet again.

"Thanks, I tried."

"You did good. Listen. I'm not back until late tomorrow. Do you think you need somebody around? I'm pretty sure I can ask a favor of someone." She heard him snap his fingers. "You know who'd be great for this, Sergei."

"Um, what?!" Jillian thought she must've misheard.

"I know you don't know him like I do. He says a lot of crude stuff and you've heard some of it. But there are things you don't know about him. He actually doesn't put up with guys harassing women. I've watched him get into it with guys on the street that were following a woman and making rude comments and whistling at her. He tells them to shut up, the other guy says 'what are you going to do about it?' and Sergei says he'll knock the guy's teeth out. The guy shuts up.

"It's almost funny, Sergei isn't that big. But he certainly looks it when he's toe to toe with somebody and not blinking."

"Sergei?" Jillian asked. "The guy who said how sad it was what some men have to do to get a lit-"

"That," George said, cutting her off, "was between us guys. He actually does respect women, when he's dealing with one."

"I've never felt like I had any respect from him." Then she thought about it. "Although, he did make sure I knew where your basketball game was the other week."

"You see," George said. "And anything else you think he's ever done is work crap. I'm going to ask him if he'll be on call for you, if something goes on with Grec."

"That's... sweet," Jillian said. *It's sweet in a really uncomfortable and weird sort of way.* "But I can call one of my girlfriends. I can handle it."

"I'm going to ask him anyway. Just in case. Let me give you his cell number."

Reluctantly and with an eye roll, Jillian wrote down Sergei's phone number.

"Please promise me if anything gets out of hand, you'll call him."

"George, that's really awkward."

"He'll be there. I'm sure of it. I'll ask him now and text you. Okay?"

George asked.

Jillian, still with her phone to her ear, put her forehead back on her desk. "George…"

"I don't want you to have to deal with that guy again." She could hear the tension in his voice that time.

Jillian sighed. "Okay. Fine."

"Thank you," George said, with a sigh. "I wish I could be there. If I'd known… I'd have tried for a flight tonight."

"It's okay, George. I'm a grown woman."

"…who shouldn't have to deal with this *alone*."

She felt a twist in her chest. He wanted her supported, not necessarily defended as some weak woman who couldn't take care of herself. *I love you, George.* "Thank you."

He was quiet for a moment. "I'll call Sergei now. Right now. And I'll be home tomorrow night."

"Okay," she said.

"Okay," he said. "Um, I guess I'll talk to you later. I'll remember, tonight, to call and make sure you're doing all right."

"Okay. Good-bye, George."

"Bye, Jillian."

Jillian left her forehead on her desk as she hung up and set her phone next to her ear. "Oh, God. Please let it work out with George! Please."

The day went fast for George. After talking to Sergei, who had, verbally at least, leapt at the chance to stand-in for George as Jillian's backup, he'd texted her and then began to make the rounds. His Uncle was home, so he visited him and Aunt Louise. Then Aunt Veronica and Uncle Mark. Next there were a few cousins that he managed to catch. And then it was back to the homestead to see his parents and whichever of his brothers might have decided to be there.

When he pulled up, he discovered that word had gone around that he'd stayed in town. All his brothers were back and he got to enjoy a competitive game of football on the Xbox. Had he been dressed for it, he'd have gone for a live game, two on two. Richard told him, somewhat confidentially, that he preferred the Xbox anyway; he was getting old and couldn't take the beating anymore. George had laughed at that.

Even though the game was good, he had trouble focusing. Jillian and the rat bastard were on his mind. The only thing that allowed him to keep going and not just head straight for the airport was Sergei. He knew Sergei would stand-in, if needed. It was Jack who pulled him aside before dinner and asked if he was having second thoughts about hanging around. George decided to partly confess and told Jack about his new girlfriend.

At dinner, under protest, George's phone had gone around the table so everyone could see his pictures. It was Richard who, finishing swiping through the pictures, asked, "Is it if just me, or does this look like the real thing?"

George felt himself flush beet red. Why his brothers could embarrass him like he was still a kid, he didn't know. But he was fairly certain it also had something to do with Richard being right.

"Well, er," he started, trying to figure out what to say. "It's fairly new," he said, neutrally. Then J.P. started laughing and he flushed even brighter and turned to his mom. "You can meet her when you come out in January."

There was more laughter and poking fun until George finally said, "Yes! Okay! You've got me! I'm mad about her!"

And Richard asked, "Mad about or in love with?"

And George laughed to cover up whatever might show on his face as the realization completely formed in his mind, no longer a vague notion playing around at the sides of his consciousness or a thought popping up at inconvenient times to be pushed back down again, but a solid, clear certainty that he couldn't ignore anymore. *I love her* and *I have to tell her.* "At least let me tell *her* first."

Then there was some cheering and Jack slapped George on the back. "About time you brought in a sister-in-law."

"Give me time on that one," George said.

"Don't take too long," Richard said, quietly. "The good ones get away, if you do."

Mrs. Kerchner had left Jillian a voice mail about accepting a delivery for her, so she headed over, planning to visit for a few moments until she saw the delivery. A giant box with, Jillian estimated, at least four dozen red roses peeking out over the top. *Oh, no.*

She couldn't quite seem to find the words to explain her disappointment to Mrs. Kerchner, so she didn't even try. She just took the over-sized box to her apartment, thinking about what she should do with the blooms and the vase. She had to rip the box to get it open and she only did that in case there was chance the George had actually sent them. She didn't believe he would, he'd know what she'd think. But since she thought there were more roses then before, maybe he did do it and thought it would be a joke or something.

As she pulled down the last side, her eyes landed on a large white envelope. She shook her head and then plucked it from the box. Beneath the envelope, wedged in against the vase, was a long, rectangular, velvet covered box. *No. NoNoNoNoNoNoNoNo.* She dropped the envelope and took a step back.

She picked up her phone and pressed her speed dial for Malvinia. Mal's phone went straight to voice mail. *That's right, she's got a double shift.* She dialed Kai, but cutoff the call before it went through. Kai had something that night too, Jillian was sure. She and Christy weren't speaking. That left Lacey, who was out of town, like George.

He won't be available. But Jillian pressed her speed dial for George anyway. The call went straight to voice mail and she disconnected. *Probably for the best. He'd just get mad.*

She stared at the envelope and the velvet covered box behind it for a few minutes. Finally, she had to know. But first, she poured herself a glass of wine, figuring she'd need something to calm her down. *A little anti-anxiety medication would be great about now.*

She took a sip of the wine and walked up to the box and slid the envelope aside with her fingernail. *And there it is.* She took a bigger sip of wine and set down her glass. She nudged the box with her fingernail. The box, itself, was docile.

Okay. You're just going to look. She picked up the box with just her fingertips, like it had been soaked in something foul. After a bit, she tilted it from side to side. *It isn't a bomb.* She laughed to herself. *That's it.* She started opening the box and the hinges snapped wide.

It wasn't until she'd snapped it shut again, that she realized her mouth was hanging open. The clear, sparkling rocks attached to the metal were so big it was ludicrous. She dropped the thing back on the counter, picked up her phone, and dialed.

"Hello?" The male voice on the other was just familiar enough to assume she'd dialed correctly.

"Sergei? It's Jillian. I'm, um…" Her wits failed her as her throat tightened. "George said, that if… I could…"

"Something going on?"

Jillian started to cry.

"I'll be right there. Gimme the address."

CHAPTER TWENTY-FOUR

Sergei opened the velvet covered box and swore. Several times. With a great deal of creativity. Then he rubbed one hand over his mouth. "What do you want to do?" He looked at Jillian.

She shook her head, which still hurt a little from crying. "I don't know. I need to give it back, but I don't know how to do it." She thought a moment. "Actually, throwing it at his head would be better. But then I'd need to be in the same room as him."

Sergei exhaled. "No idea which messenger service it was?"

Jillian shook her head again.

"Dammit." He snapped the box shut and set it on the counter. "George is going to be pissed."

"Oh, *that* helps," Jillian said, sarcastically.

"Well, I gotta tell you, I don't exactly know what to do here." Sergei crossed his arms.

"Me neither," Jillian said.

Sergei nodded toward the counter. "You gonna open the note?"

Jillian bit her lip. "I keep thinking it's only going to upset me, so why should I?"

"I see your point," Sergei said. "But I'd still want to know."

Jillian shook her head. "Not worth it. I just have to figure out how to get this back to him. The unopened note will say something too."

"Yeah, that's true," Sergei said, thoughtfully, and then he looked at Jillian. "You know, you could just keep it."

Jillian crossed her arms and stared at him.

"Okay, you're right, you can't. It would just be easier than trying to figure this out. Sorry." He looked at the stuff on the counter again and swore again. "You're gonna have to open the note."

"No."

"He's gonna be expecting a response from you and the way to respond is probably in that note."

It was Jillian's turn to swear, though her choice was more sedate then Sergei's had been.

Sergei walked into her living room space and dropped onto the arm of her couch. "I don't see a lot of choices here."

Jillian dropped her arms and her shoulders sagged and she let out the whine she'd been holding in. "Why can't this guy just leave me alone?"

Sergei snorted. "Like you don't know."

"I don't," Jillian said.

"Oh, *please*. Do you need your ego fed so badly that I have to say it too?"

"No," Jillian said. "I just don't get why he's still bothering me after I made myself clear last evening on the phone-"

"Because you're hot. And he's rich. He's probably used to women dropping their panties without him even suggesting. So you're interesting on multiple levels."

Jillian shuddered and felt her stomach turn again. "I think I may be sick," she said, and covered her mouth.

"You asked," Sergei said.

Her stomach lurched again. "Oh, God. I really think-" Jillian rushed to her bathroom and vomited.

Sergei followed her to the doorway of her bathroom. "You aren't pregnant are you?"

"No," she said, when she could speak again. "Why is that the default assumption for women of a given age?"

"Well, I wouldn't have assumed except you're sleeping with my friend, so there's a chance." Sergei frowned. "If it weren't for that, I'd still think you're frigid."

Jillian struggled to her feet. "Why did George think you were going to be some kind of help to me?"

Sergei bobbed his head a bit. "Okay. Okay. I'm sorry." He watched her as she flushed the toilet, washed her hands, and then gargled with some mouthwash. "I gotta admit, even now I don't have the slightest idea how to talk to you."

"Well, if you've given up on my problem, you can just go. You're under no obligation here."

Sergei turned and walked back to her living room. "Oh, I don't know about that. You're no damsel in distress, but this is bad all the same."

"No damsel in distress?" Jillian asked.

Sergei picked up the envelope and turned it over a couple of times. "I've seen you at work. You're like a juggernaut. Unstoppable. I'd pick you against just about anybody in a fight. You'd kick their ass. It's actually a little unnerving to see you unnerved." He held the envelope out to her. "Sorta messes up my world view."

She took the envelope. "I've seen you at work too. I've been waiting for you to suggest I just sleep with the guy."

"Hey! I'm *trying* here. I'd never suggest that."

Jillian raised her eyebrows. "Never? Even if I wasn't with George?"

Sergei looked a little sheepish. "I don't know. But you are with George. So that's pretty much that."

She nodded at him. "Yeah. That is pretty much that." She felt a twinge of guilt, which was much better than a stomach turn. "I'm sorry. I appreciate you coming here to help me with this." She held up the envelope. "I'm a little out of my element here."

He nodded. "Me too. I've pursued women before, but this is not something I'd ever have a chance to do, even if I wanted. Apart from the obvious, I got no idea what he's thinking."

"The obvious?"

Sergei rolled his eyes.

"Oh, the obvious," Jillian flushed. "Right." She pushed on in the conversation. "So you don't think you'd do this, even if you had the money."

Sergei shook his head. "I've yet to meet a woman who wants to think she's been bought. It's one thing to drop money on a date. It's okay to bring small gifts. But something like that," he pointed at the counter. "That sends a pretty clear message, and it isn't 'I'd like to get to know you as a person.'" He looked back at Jillian. "I'm sorry you've been insulted."

"Well... thank you, Sergei."

He nodded a little again. "Okay, steel magnolia. Brace yourself and open that note. Then we'll make our move and we can go back to our own lives."

She couldn't help but smile a little. "Steel magnolia?"

"You prefer ice queen? Come on." He motioned to the envelope. "You're made of stalwart stuff. Just do it."

Jillian looked at the envelope and said, a quiet, "Okay." A minute later she shoved the opened note at Sergei, saying, "You're right, there's a phone number."

Sergei glanced at the note. "Is that a Shakespeare sonnet?"

"I don't know. Shakespeare isn't my thing."

"No?" He asked. "I would've thought..."

"What?" Jillian asked. "The ice queen has to be into highbrow stuff?" Then she crossed her arms and nodded at the note. "So, what do you think our move is? Do I actually have to call him?"

"Well," Sergei tried to delay, but he couldn't. "I see only so many options. One, you call him and tell him to send someone to fetch this stuff and that the answer is 'no' now and forever."

Jillian cringed a little. "Two?"

"Two. Two is basically the same, but with some profanity."

"That doesn't appeal. Is that all you've got?"

Sergei lifted his eyes to the ceiling. "Um." He looked back at her. "I suppose you could call and then put me on the phone and I'll tell him what to do with himself."

Jillian blew out her breath and twisted her hands. "You're right. I have to do this." She walked over to the side table and picked up the phone, and then she turned to Sergei. "Maybe he'll listen to you..."

Sergei handed her the note and smirked. "Woman up and shred the guy. I know you've got it in you."

"Okay." Jillian started to think out loud. "I need to tell him that I'm not interested and that he needs to send someone to get this stuff. And I need to be extremely clear."

"Don't let a little polite get in the way. Be rude," Sergei said.

"Really?"

Sergei shrugged. "Some guys don't get it unless you're rude. You'd think he should have gotten it by now. Yet, he's making a play like this."

"Okay. So be rude."

"Yeah. Be rude."

Jillian nodded her head a couple of times and then started punching the numbers into the phone, muttering "be rude, be rude," to herself. She heard Sergei chuckle and looked at him with a frown.

He whispered, "Channel your inner bitch."

She rolled her eyes as the phone started ringing on the other end. As soon as a feminine voice answered with the words "Good evening, how may I direct your call?" Jillian reached out for support and Sergei caught her hand, squeezing it a little harder than necessary.

She cleared her throat. "I need to speak to Cisco." She glanced at Sergei. "Now." Sergei nodded.

"And who is calling please?" The voice asked.

"Miss Braden," she answered as clipped as she could manage.

"He's expecting your call, Miss. I'll put you right through. One moment, please."

Jillian looked at Sergei again. "He's got an answering service that is so polite."

Sergei whispered, "Don't fall for it. Be strong."

Jillian nodded as the line starting ringing again.

"Okay," Sergei said, "not so hard."

Jillian looked at him and realized she was squeezing his hand awfully hard. She consciously relaxed her muscles and muttered, "You'd think I was a kid. Acting like this."

"You're fine," Sergei said. "Destroy him and be done with it."

The other end of line clicked and that accented voice answered with a syrupy, "Ah, Miss Braden. I'm so glad you called."

"Well, you shouldn't be." She tried to breathe, her stomach was turning again. "I'm…" she felt Sergei give her hand squeeze. "I'm calling to tell you that I want nothing to do with you-"

"Now, now. Settle down. Didn't you like the gift?"

"Absolutely not! You send somebody over here to fetch that thing right now! I don't ever want to see or hear from you ever again, after that!" She slammed down the phone and her stomach moved again. "Oh, no!"

She ran to her bathroom again. When she came back out, Sergei was still sitting on the arm of the couch, now with his hands on his knees. "Sure you don't have a little bun in the oven?"

"I'm quite sure," Jillian said, but with less enthusiasm. She was worn out from the drop in adrenaline and the physical wear and tear of her stomach problem. "I'm so glad that's over."

"I'm a bit disappointed," Sergei said.

"Huh?" Jillian said, as she ungracefully dropped onto her couch.

"I know you've got it in you to be a lot nastier than that. The slamming the phone was good, but you needed to call him a name or something."

"Well, at least I did it. It's over. Thank you for being here."

Sergei slid off the arm and onto the sofa. "Yeah."

"Aren't you leaving?"

"Yeeee- no." He crossed his arms and rolled his head toward her. "I heard the conversation. That wasn't tough enough. You said, 'I don't want to see or hear from you *after that*.'"

Jillian slid down in her seat on the couch. "You mean, you think he's coming here?"

"I think anyone with enough nerve to send that bracelet, may just show up on your doorstep."

Jillian groaned.

"I may be wrong. Maybe he'll send a lackey. But if he does show up, access that bitch I know is in there."

Jillian said, "Maybe I don't have one."

Sergei let out a loud, "Ha! Now, we need to kill some time here. I wouldn't expect it'll be that long, but who knows. So, what do you want to do?"

"Watch television?"

Sergei shrugged. "Okay." He leaned forward and grabbed up the remote. "What's on?"

Jillian climbed back to her feet. "I'm going to change out of my work clothes."

"'K," Sergei mumbled.

Although Sergei appeared to already be lost in the television, Jillian locked her bedroom door behind her so she could change into jeans and a sweater. Once that was done she brushed her teeth. Finally, she dropped onto her bed. Sergei would be fine out in the living room for at least a few minutes. She thought she'd leave George a message, but she'd left her phone in the other room, so she closed her eyes for a few minutes instead.

She awoke to a soft rapping on her bedroom door. "Hey. You okay?" Looking at the clock, she realized she'd been asleep for at least a half an hour. She rolled over and sat up. Her head hurt a little.

"Yeah," she called out and got to her feet, trudged to her bathroom, and got an ibuprofen. When she opened her bedroom door, she apologized to Sergei and told him she'd fallen asleep. He told her it was no problem, and then asked if she had anything to eat and any beer.

She sniffed. *Classic.* "No beer. Sorry."

Sergei was flipping channels. "No beer? I'll have to bring that up with George. He needs to stock your fridge."

"Uh-huh," Jillian said, with an eye roll. "How about tacos?" She knew she had the ingredients.

"Great," Sergei said.

Jillian shook her head, regretted it, and went into the kitchen. Twenty minutes later she had to use her bossy mama's voice to make Sergei eat at the table. "Come on, they're tacos. That's a perfect couch food," Sergei whined.

So, he is *a bit of a Neanderthal.* Jillian couldn't say she was surprised. "Table or starve." She didn't ask him to turn off the television.

After a bite, he bobbed his head and said, "Good." That was the extent of the dinner conversation, as his attention turned back to the television, which worked fine for Jillian.

She was putting the plates in the dishwasher when the knock came at the door. Straightening quickly, she turned toward Sergei and saw he'd snapped up too. He nodded at her and then rose.

Jillian walked to the door and looked through the peephole. Her stomach sank again, but at least it didn't lurch. She was quite grateful Sergei had stayed; Cisco had a man with him, behind him. That man gave off the distinct impression of a body guard, but all the same, Jillian would never have opened the door to the two of them by herself.

Glancing over her shoulder, she whispered, "It's him. And he's got someone with him."

Sergei sort of sneered. "I'll answer it then. Anything interesting happens, call the police." Jillian wasn't sure what to make of that, but she got her phone, just in case. Sergei had been right so far.

He started to unlock the door, and then motioned her to get behind it. *Okay.* She stepped behind the door.

The door swung wide. "Señor Grec, I presume."

"Er, yes. Where is Miss Braden?" The accented voice made Jillian shudder. Again.

Jillian could see Sergei pretty clearly. He put one hand against the edge of the door. "She left and asked me to be here to point you to *that* and to give you a message. So let's make this quick."

"All right," Grec said. "May we come in and take *that* off your hands?"

"Be my guest," Sergei said, and stepped back. He didn't move to close the door; he actually opened it a little wider and then stood in front of it, keeping Jillian hidden, which was comforting, except she couldn't see what was going on.

"So, who are you?"

Sergei slapped his thigh. "I'm nobody. There's your *present*, this is the door." He slapped the door. "And Miss Braden would like-"

"Nobody? Are you sure?" She could hear Grec moving around a little. She guessed he'd walked over to the counter. His company had only just come over the threshold. "Not, perhaps, a potential suitor? Or even her boyfriend?"

"Heh, no. I don't think so." Sergei said. "Have him pick that up."

The shoes of the second man moved into the apartment and Jillian hoped that meant that he would carry the package.

"No? Surprising."

Sergei shifted a little. "My only concern is to get you and *that* out of here, with a message."

"Oh, yes. The message. Perhaps you can give her one from me."

"Not getting paid for that," Sergei said.

"I see. Well, just for your edification then. I'm not taking the bracelet back. It was purchased for her and no one else."

"Ah, no. It's not up for negotiation. She doesn't accept it."

"And if you'd simply give her a message, then she'd accept it. We had a misunderstanding and the bracelet is an apology."

An apology!?! Jillian almost laughed aloud, but she clapped her hand over her mouth.

Sergei shifted again. "She knows exactly what that bracelet is. Take all of that and go. Now. Before this becomes antagonistic."

Grec laughed. "*Becomes* antagonistic. Very good. Well, I'm not leaving until I have established some level of clarity. I believe there's a cultural difference that's confusing Miss Braden."

It was Sergei's turn to laugh. "I'm pretty sure that there's no cultural difference that could confuse anyone when it comes to matters like this."

Go, Sergei! Jillian tried to breathe as quietly as possible.

"Are you quite certain Miss Braden isn't available for just a minute? I assure you that she's mistaken in my intentions."

"Oh, I'm quite sure. Take it and get out."

There was a little bit of movement and Jillian bit her lip. She'd expected this to go much quicker. *Why won't he just take it and go?*

Sergei spoke again. "No. You're not leaving your little 'fuck me' bracelet. Pick it up too. And get the hell out. Her message is to never come near her again. Don't write. Don't call. And definitely don't show up in person. She'll fuck you when hell freezes over. Personally, I don't know your cash situation, but I pretty much doubt even *you* can pay for that much air-conditioning."

There was a loud sigh. "On second thought," Grec said, "I think we shall leave all of this. She can return it in person. Then we'll clear this up."

"No!" Jillian heard herself say. *Oh, no. Stupid mouth!* They'd heard her. She couldn't hide any longer. She slowly pushed the door toward the doorway.

"Ah, Miss Braden!" Grec said, and clapped his hands together. "I knew you wouldn't disappoint. You're here. Please, come, sit down, and allow me to explain."

No! I've had enough. I want you to disappear at the bottom of a lake and never come back! I hate that you've made me feel like this. I hate that I've let you make me feel like this. I hope you die! She hesitated only a moment until Sergei mouthed at her what looked like 'be rude.' That time it wasn't her stomach that surged, instead her fists balled and she found she didn't need Sergei's suggestion anymore.

"You. You cheap, lowlife. You not only have the nerve to send me something like that," Jillian pointed toward the box that was still on the counter, "but you come to my home, invite yourself in, and tell me that *I'm* the one who's misunderstanding. Well, it sounds to me like *you're* the one who's misunderstanding." She took a step toward him, careful to keep her hands at her sides.

"I don't care what you think or what you say. You disgust me." She started to circle toward the interior of her apartment, but still facing Grec. "Just because you have money, you think you can have anything you want. Well, here's a flash for you." She arrived at the counter. "My friend here was sugar coating things. I wouldn't be caught *dead* in the same room with you even if hell froze over, just in case you're into necrophilia!"

She grabbed the vase and shoved it at the bodyguard. "You, take this and get moving!" Then she turned to Grec. "And you," she picked up the jewelry box and waved it at him. "You are so low the slime beneath the rocks looks down on you. You have until the count of three to get out of my home or I'll take a knife and cutoff whatever pathetic little excuse for a dick you're hiding behind this monster bracelet and feed it to my cat!" Grec was finally backing out of the door. "And here's the message I left for you." She threw the jewelry box at him. "Take that bracelet and shove it up your backside, so the next time you're spouting crap out of your mouth, you can shit diamonds out your ass too! Go to Hell, you bastard!"

Jillian slammed the door in his face, locked it, and turned toward Sergei, breathing so fast and so hard she thought she might hyperventilate. Sergei's mouth was open, but with a smile around the edges, and he had his arms raised just a little at the elbows.

"Holy shit! That was fantastic! How do you feel?"

She started laughing hysterically. "I feel amazing!" She ran over to him and he gave her a brief spin hug while they both laughed.

After he put her down, he asked, "Where did you get that? My God, I was worried you were going to be so polite that you'd actually... you know... with him... But then..."

She could feel her nose crinkle with the smile she was sort of fighting. "But then..." She laughed again and spun herself once in a mock pirouette.

"Yeah!" He nodded. "You knocked that out of the park! I don't what my favorite moment was. The little dick part. Or the shitting diamonds. Hell, I even liked the necrophilia. You were freaking amazing."

Jillian started blushing, covered her mouth with her hands, and then spoke through her fingers. "I can't believe I said any of that!"

Sergei gripped her shoulders and shook her, gently, a few times. "Believe it. That was a championship game winning rejection. If he doesn't get it now, I'll help you get the restraining order. But I wouldn't worry. He got it. I saw his face!"

Jillian couldn't help herself, she did a little dance in a circle again. Sergei nodded and smiled, and then crossed his arms. "You're a freaking jaguar or something. You totally shredded him."

"Yeah! I'm a mountain lion!"

"Okay! A mountain lion, it is."

She was still laughing a little. "I feel like I need to celebrate."

"How about a quick... very small and very quick, drink? D'ya have anything, at all?"

"I've got..." Jillian danced into the kitchen and opened her cabinet. "Scotch, vodka, whiskey, ooh, I've got Kahlua. Almost forgot Kahlua. I love White Russians! My friend Mal made me try hers once. I generally just stick to wine. But this is a cause for a celebration! What would you like?"

She mixed her White Russian, using milk rather than cream, since she didn't have any. Sergei opted for a slug of whiskey.

They toasted each other.

"To my moral support and the best second for my boyfriend, in the world!"

"To the most surprisingly foulmouthed wildcat one of my friends has ever gotten himself involved with!"

After a swallow, Sergei started laughing again. "Okay. I need a pen and paper. I gotta write all that down while it's fresh in my mind. If only I'd videoed it. George is never gonna believe it."

Jillian shook her head. "No way I'm letting you write it down."

"Okay," Sergei said, setting down his glass and taking his phone out of his back pocket. "Dictation." He wiggled his eyebrows and started swiping around his screen.

"No!" Jillian said, putting her glass down and trying to get the phone away from him. He turned, the phone beeped, and he started to talk into it. "Let's see. How did it start? I can't remember exactly. I do remember, 'I'll give you three seconds to get out my-"

"No!" Jillian squealed and tried to reach around him.

"-house or I'll cut your," Sergei looked over his shoulder while she tried to reach around him. "I can't remember now. Was it 'pathetic little dick?'" He turned back and Jillian squealed again and jumped on his back, reaching over his shoulder and grabbing his phone.

"Ha!" She yelled. "Got it!" And she jumped down and ran into the kitchen. "How do I stop this?"

He chased her into the kitchen and they sort of half-chased, half-danced around the island, until Sergei snatched his phone back out of her hands. He turned off the recording. "Okay. I gotta go."

"Sure," Jillian said, picking up her glass again.

Sergei found his glass and brought into the kitchen, finished the last swallow, and set the glass in the sink. "So, you're good now?"

"I'm fantastic."

He laughed. "Yes, you are... No more stomach upset?"

"Nope. Cast iron." She whacked her stomach with her palm.

"No freak outs coming later? Nothing I need to worry about?"

Jillian shook her head. "No. I'm great."

"Good." He scooped up his jacket and headed for the door. "If you really, really, really need something, you can call me. Otherwise, please leave me alone for the rest of the night, Miss not-a-damsel."

Jillian giggled. "Not-a-damsel."

Sergei looked at her. "No more booze for you tonight, either, alright? You're already high enough."

"No booze." Jillian repeated, nodding a little bit more vigorously than necessary.

It was then that Sergei frowned for a moment.

"What?" Jillian asked.

"Nothing," Sergei said, and then sighed. "I guess I just get it, a little bit, now. I've been trying to figure out this thing with you and George. I mean, a onetime deal, I understood. But a real thing? You two were just such an unlikely combination, as far as I could tell. But you're not as...

cold, as I thought. I told you to access your inner bitch, but that's not what happened. You accessed... well, there's a bit of fire in you. Like George."

"Yeah?"

"Yeah." He snorted softly. "I, uh, look forward to getting to know you, over the next however long. God-willing, a long while, I think."

"Well, thank you, Sergei. I guess I look forward to getting to know you too. I'll tell you though, the white knight bit, you can keep it in the future."

"I know. You don't need it."

They stood there another few moments until Jillian said, "Okay. This just got weird. What do we do? Hit each other on the shoulder?"

Sergei chuckled. "How about a friendly hug?"

They gave each other a short hug and then Jillian opened the door and showed Sergei out. *I guess we're friends now?* She thought about the four musketeers. If there was one that she'd figured would be the hardest to win over, it was Sergei. Having him like, or at the very least tolerate, her was a big step forward.

With the time difference, George was feeling guilty about calling Jillian, but he'd already been letting her down when it came to communication during his trip, and he wanted to hear her voice more than ever. So, even though she hadn't complained, he called anyway. When her sleepy, soft hello came over the line, he almost felt like he was next to her in bed. That would have so much better than the empty bed in the hotel room; he closed his eyes just to imagine it.

"Hi, Sweetheart," he said.

"Mmm. Hi," she said, and again he thought about her lying next to him, just waking up.

"I'm sorry it's so late."

"Mmm," she mumbled again. "I was having a crazy dream. It was raining diamonds. Big ones. And they hurt when they fell on me."

"Wow, painful diamonds. That's some dream."

"Yeaaaaah," she slurred a little. "How was your day?"

He smiled. "Actually, it was good. I visited with a lot of family. How about you? Was work okay?"

"Work," Jillian said, "was work. It was nice, in a way, being in the building without the Hardware people, after Friday's crazy. I did some stuff instead of sitting in meetings. For the most part, our folks are holding their own. But they're all losing steam."

"I guess that's to be expected."

"We're going to have to do something to help reenergize them. I'm starting to worry about flu season. If they're all run down..."

"Oh," George said. "Yeah. That could be a problem. I'll think about it. You too."

"I am," Jillian said.

"Right, you brought it up." George swallowed. "So, on the subject of thinking… I thought of you more than a few times today." He stopped at that thought. *Not over the phone. Everything and anything else, but that.*

"You did?" Jillian asked, and he thought he could hear a smile in her voice.

"Yep," he said. "I'll be glad to be home tomorrow."

Jillian was quiet a moment and then asked, "Do you need someone to pick you up at the airport?"

"It's going to be late, I figured on a cab."

"If you're sure," Jillian said, then after a moment added, "I've been thinking about you too, you know. I'm… glad to hear your voice."

George closed his eyes. "I'm glad to hear your voice too. I just plain miss you."

Jillian let out a sound that was like a whimper. "I miss you too. Are you sure you don't want me to meet you at the airport?"

George wished he could have booked an earlier flight. "Sold," he said.

"Great! Would you text me your flight information as soon as we hang up? I don't remember where I wrote it down. I'm losing my mind."

"Sure. I'll text before I board the plane too. And maybe from onboard, before they make us turn off our phones."

"Text me anytime. Since I won't have meetings tomorrow, we might even be able to have a conversation. But, no pressure! I know you're with your family and-"

"And missing you like crazy. It's worse now, when I'm not surrounded by a bunch of people," George said, "but it's there when I'm surrounded, too."

He heard Jillian inhale. "I'll park at the airport and be waiting just outside security."

He smiled. "I'll be looking for you."

"I'll be wearing bright red, in case you've forgotten what I look like." Jillian's voice had a teasing lilt to it.

"Just make sure you've applied your lotion in last few hours and I'll be able to track you, no visual hints needed."

Jillian laughed. "Okay. I'll see you then."

"Yep, see you then." George had to force himself to hang up before he said something stupid, like 'I love you.' He was just glad that the 'I miss you' sentiments kept getting returned in kind.

It was late. She needed sleep. He needed sleep, especially since he was going to be fighting jet lag the next night. He nodded off imagining lying next to her.

Until Sergei texted Jillian around noon, she hadn't thought once that morning about Grec. It was a simple, straightforward message. *You haven't heard anymore from the asshole, have you?*

More than a little surprised to have him checking on her, Jillian kept her reply brief. *No. It's all fine here.* Then she went to check on Irene, who had looked a little better earlier that morning.

She took her phone with her, still hoping for a text or two from George. He'd texted the flight details to her and she'd googled his drive. If she didn't hear from him shortly, she wouldn't hear from him before he arrived at the airport, the drive was that long. *He's going to be so tired, travelling most of the day. I better bring a bag and stay at his place tonight.* Assuming he wanted her to stay, at any rate. *He'll want me to stay, right? He may be too exhausted to make love, but he'll want me to stay, anyway. Won't he? We're more than just sex, no matter what Taro said.* He'd called every day.

Looking pale, Irene was sitting at her desk, propping her head up on one of her hands. Shaking her head, Jillian sat on Irene's desk and asked her if she needed to go home. After some back and forth, Jillian told Irene to go home after lunch. "Almost everyone leaves between two and three anyway on the weekend. You'll only be an hour or two short."

The argument hadn't actually won her over, but Irene clearly felt awful and she decided to go home.

Jillian's phone chirped as she was heading back to her desk. It was Sergei again. *Good. If you do, let me know immediately.*

Okay. Thanks. Jillian sent the message and gave a moment's pause to wonder about Sergei texting her. It was nice, him checking on her, wasn't it? She decided that was all it was. Sergei was checking on his best friend's girl. It was nice.

She set down her phone and started gathering up all the folders and papers that had managed to wind up in piles atop her desk. It was a little out of control. As she sorted through them, making fresh piles of papers, one to file, one to keep out, and even one for recycling, she came across the slip of paper with her list of qualities for a man. That gave her a smile.

She sorted the rest of the papers and then looked at the list again. She found a marker and wrote *George* across the top. The two qualities left were tricky, honest and loyal. *There's no way to prove you're honest or loyal, you either are or aren't. The only way to be sure would be to have them disproven. And I'm definitely* not *looking to disprove them.*

I may have been wrong about Sam, but I'm not wrong about George. Maybe he was out looking for something else that night, like Taro said, but that isn't what he wants now. Heck, I'm not even sure what I was thinking on our first date. It was mostly chemistry. I can't blame him for feeling the same thing.

She placed checkmarks next to honest and loyal, but didn't feel the pleasure at checking off the entire list as she'd expected. Having the perfect man measure up to her ideal should have been pleasing, but there was something else. She wasn't sure what it was. There was something missing. She smacked her forehead when she realized what it was. It was so obvious. She'd been thinking about it for days.

At the top of the list, between George's name and the first entry, she wrote in all caps block text *LOVES ME* followed by a little heart. That was easily the most important thing on the list.

Sam hadn't loved her. If he did, he loved what he wanted her to be, not what she was.

Her eyes were starting to water before she even let the thought surface. *I need to be loved as I am. The nightmare mess that I am. By George. He's the one. And he's seen the nightmare mess I am.*

She laid the marker on her desk and quickly rose and shut her door. Tears were coming before she quite had it shut. Not a lot of tears, just enough to cause a sniffle and the need to wipe her eyes. Maybe it wasn't as bad as she feared. He really had seen the mess and he hadn't dumped her yet.

Then again, she hadn't been particularly demanding on him. If she started pushing him, demanding things, maybe he'd get tired of her. In reality, he was the one always asking to be together. *That should say something shouldn't it?* He wanted to be with her all the time. And it definitely wasn't always about sex. They'd spent a lot more time talking or eating or going places or watching movies, than making love.

It's more than just sex!

She picked up her list and looked at it one more time, then opened her drawer and stuffed it in her purse. She needed to get it together. Relax. They'd only been together for what, ten days? Even though she was sure, it was ridiculous to expect him to be there too. *Give it time.* Of course, while past experience had taught her not to put emotion on a timeline, it was hard not to.

Luke *had* really loved her, and he'd told her that on what she loosely called their second date. They'd gone to a party and when he'd taken her back to the dorm, he'd just said it. Someone more skeptical wouldn't have believed him. Back then, she wasn't so skeptical. And it had been wonderful for years.

Holding George up to the romantic standard set by someone else wasn't just unfair, it was illogical. She sat down, dropped her recycling pile in the bin beside her desk, and started working on filing papers. When she'd finished with the filing, she wiggled her mouse, brought up Google, and started a search *how to know if someone loves you.*

CHAPTER TWENTY-FIVE

The good-byes were easily the worst part of the trip. *At least this time everyone was kind enough to not say anything to make me feel guilty about leaving.* He drove away from the house and fairly close to town before he pulled over, set his phone into hands-free mode, and called Jillian.

She answered just the way he'd have wanted if he'd thought about it, a little bit of a breathy edge to her voice. "Hi, George."

"Hi. I'm on my way to the airport."

Jillian let out an exasperate sound. "Don't call me and drive at the same time. That's dangerous. I want you back in one piece."

George smiled. "Okay, Sweetheart. I figured a text would be worse."

"Oh! It would! Don't *do* that!"

"Never," he said. "I'll be safe."

"Good. But this isn't safe. Let's hang up and you can call or text or whatever from the airport."

"But I wanted to hear your voice. And it'll make the drive go faster."

Another exasperated sound. "I like hearing your voice too, but I want to hear it, in person, later tonight. I don't want the last time I hear from you to include the sound of a crash."

"Okay. Okay." George felt a mix of pleasure at her worry and a bit of irritation. "I'm not holding the phone, you know. I've got two hands on the wheel."

"George, I'm not arguing with you about this. Call me from the airport. Please?"

"Fine," George said, shortly. "I'll call you later."

"Good. Thank you. Bye, George."

"Bye, Jillian." He frowned as the call ended from her end and started muttering to himself. "You'd think I was committing a crime. Geez. Just wanted to hear your voice."

By the time George reached the airport he wasn't grumbling anymore, it was hard to even grumble when all he wanted to do was sleep. *There's always hope for the airplane.*

Security was slow, which ended up working out for him as he arrived at the gate with about ten minutes to spare before boarding. *Not too long a wait. Not stressing about being late.* He thought about texting but called Jillian instead. "Hi," she answered softly.

I'm beginning to like the way she answers my calls. "Hi," he said, getting close to a wall. *The one problem with calls in airports, no privacy.* "I'm at the airport, alive, and in one piece."

"Then, I forgive you," she joked.

"Good, because if you're mad and aren't meeting me at the airport, I'd like to know now."

"I'd meet you at the gate, if I could get through security."

He took a deep breath. "Oh, man, I'm going to be so happy to see you."

"Me too. I'll be watching your flight on the internet. Anything you want me to bring for you? A snack for the car or anything like that? Are you eating on the plane?"

"Don't go to any more trouble. Just being there… that's plenty."

"That's sweet," she said, her voice dropping again. "I… um… I can hardly wait. To see you." She took a breath and then exhaled her next words, "In person."

"Oh, Lord," he mumbled, thinking of touching her. "I can't wait either. I'm going to hang up now. They'll be boarding us soon. I hope. I don't know how I'm going to sit still for this flight. Geez. Five hours."

"I'll see you then."

"Good, I'll see you then."

He looked at his phone as he was putting it away. *I love this woman. And I have to tell her. Shit.*

Jillian hung up the phone. She didn't want to hang up, but the conversation was going nowhere fast. Repetitions of 'I miss you' could only go on so long. Once she'd changed, packed an overnight bag, packed some snacks for the car, and taken care of Charlie, telling him how sorry she was she wouldn't be home that night, she paced. Nothing eased her guilty conscience about Charlie, but the thought of being with George was overriding nearly every other thought in her mind.

She finally gave up on the waiting and drove out earlier than necessary, planning to kill time at the airport, rather than her apartment. By the time she'd found a parking space, she was twitching inside, wanting to move. She double checked that the flight was still on time, and then headed into the airport. *One good thing about airports: shopping.*

Having tried, and failed, to sleep on the plane, George could feel the fatigue creeping over him. But instead of slogging off the plane from exhaustion, he had to keep himself from pushing his way forward. He'd survived the flight, waiting an extra couple of minutes in order not to be rude wasn't out of the question. Once out of the gate, however, he raced like a thoroughbred most of the way down the terminal.

As he cleared the security area, he started to look around. True to her word, Jillian was there in a red sweater, waving at him, and even bouncing a little, just a few feet back. He made his way through the people who were milling. There weren't many, but he had to cut around a few. Jillian moved toward him too.

He dropped his bag and coat at his feet to free up his right hand and wrap his arms around her, and she threw her arms around his neck and pressed tightly against him, the coat over her arm bouncing into him. A moment later he kissed her, slightly more vigorously than was probably appropriate in public, but she kissed him back and he couldn't help himself.

Then her head was against his neck, tucked into him, as they caught their breath. "I missed you," he said, for what was probably the millionth time. At least it was the millionth time he'd thought it.

Jillian laughed against his skin. "I missed you, too." Reluctantly, she pulled back from him, though not entirely out of his arms. "Let's go home."

"Yes, let's," George said, letting go of her and picking up his bag and coat. As they turned to walk, she moved her arm around his waist, and he looked down at her. He threw his arm over her shoulder and snugged her against his side. "I missed you." *A million and one.*

Jillian laughed and reached up with her hand to touch his hand on her shoulder. "I missed you, too." After a few steps, she looked up at him. "Do you need to go to baggage claim?"

"Unfortunately."

At the baggage claim, they found a spot not too far back, but not front and center, to stand together, still holding onto each other. She asked all the usual inane questions about his flight, the other passengers, and even the service. He answered and asked a few inane questions about work. By the time the bags started coming out, he was ready to move on to more serious topics.

Jillian waited with his carry-on and both their coats, while he picked up his checked bag. The walk to the car was filled by a few anecdotes from

George's trip. At the car, Jillian unlocked the trunk and lifted the hatch; George noticed Jillian's overnight bag. He looked at her. "Does that mean what I think it means?"

She smoothed the smile off of her face, trying to look serious. "That is… purely precautionary."

He grabbed her waist with his left hand, pulled her closer, and kissed her briefly. "I do love a practical woman."

Do you? Jillian made herself get into the driver's seat and tried to relax and breathe. *Calm down. You are* not *going to put any pressure on him. You're going to shut up and be patient.* She jumped when the trunk slammed shut.

Then George was next to her in the car. She retrieved the bag of snacks from the backseat and handed it to him, hoping it would keep them both a little distracted on the ride to his place.

She thought of everything. George ripped into a granola bar. While a real meal would be helpful, the granola would tide him over for a bit. He didn't think he needed the energy boost, just being home with her was enough to keep him going; he just needed to keep his stomach from rumbling.

As soon as Jillian had cleared the area around the airport and felt comfortable enough, she reached her hand across the car and dropped it on George's shoulder. She could see him looking at her out of the corner of her eye. He finished the granola bar, dealt with the wrapper, and then took her hand from his shoulder, brought it to his lips, and kissed it.

The rest of the drive, Jillian was mostly one-handed. George thought of pointing out how dangerous it was, just to be funny, but he was afraid she'd take her hand back, and he wanted to hold it. *Even touching her hand is a luxury.*

The bags were just a minor distraction; he carried all of them up the stairs, into the house, and then straight up the stairs to the bedroom, calling to Jillian to lock up behind them. She took his keys out of the door and locked up, laughing a bit as she did, enjoying his impatience.

Unlike George, she took the time to take off her coat and hang it up, and then proceeded to the kitchen with the snacks she'd brought. She was putting the bottles of water in the fridge when she heard George quickly pounding down the stairs. "What'cha doing down here?" he asked.

"Just putting things away," Jillian said.

"So good of you to be neat and tidy," George said, and wrapped his arms around her from behind. "But I'd rather worry about that later, tomorrow, maybe never, hmm?" He leaned over and kissed her hair, nudged the hair aside with his nose and kissed her ear.

Her arms crossed and grabbed his, as she tilted her head to give him better access. He didn't disappoint, nuzzling behind her ear, below it, kissing her neck and making her knees go a little weak. She reached back with one hand to grab his head. "Mmm. You should miss me more often."

His kisses stopped and he stood up straight. "I don't want to ever miss you like that again."

She tried to turn her head far enough to see his face, but couldn't. "Are you okay?" she asked, quietly.

He turned her in his arms. "I am now." Then his lips were on hers and he didn't have any public displays to worry about.

A few minutes later, Jillian leaned just slightly away from him and whispered against his lips, "You're making me dizzy again."

"Does that mean you want me to stop or that you want to do something about our being vertical?" He tried to slow his breathing and dropped his forehead to hers. As always, the wave of calm washed over him and he closed his eyes.

The weight of his forehead against hers was soothing, and she closed her eyes just to feel it more deeply. "I don't remember ever wanting you to stop."

"No? Never?"

"Unh-uh. Not since the first one." Jillian thought about the first kiss and what she'd heard from Taro. She couldn't stand to think about it anymore. She had to know.

He moved a hand to touch her face. "I've worried about rushing you. Even after we got together."

"George," Jillian started. "What were you thinking that Monday night?"

"Thinking?" George asked, confused.

"I mean, we were standing just over there, nearer the door, and you asked me out and I said it was a bad idea and then you kissed me, and it was… amazing, and I was surprised that you stopped…"

"You were surprised?" George asked, with a smile. "I was trying to show you some respect."

"Oh!" Jillian exclaimed, embarrassed.

George chuckled. "What did you think?"

"I don't know. It was confusing. I just didn't understand," she said. "I mean, it was such a good kiss and I was surprised you didn't want another one."

"Of course, I wanted another one. I just wanted there to be more than just a few. It may make for good fiction, but how many times has a one-night stand turned into something more?"

Jillian let out a sigh. "So, you always wanted more?" *Oh, thank you. Thank you, George.*

"Didn't you?"

She opened her eyes and saw him looking at her, so close it made her swallow. "I didn't think I could have it. I didn't think I could have you, at all, even for a minute, let alone…"

"More?"

She nodded her head against his. "I'm just so crazy about you." *Come on, girl.* "And I want to be with you, for real." *Chicken! Well, better than nothing. At least it implies… something. Maybe that wasn't a good thing to say…*

George jerked back. "This is for real, isn't it?"

"It is! If it is to you. Because it is to me. But, I wasn't sure that you felt-" *Please, George. Please just love me.*

George kissed her not only because he wanted to, the same way he always wanted to, but also because he wanted to shut her up. Hearing her say that she wasn't sure how he felt, when all the while he'd been worried about how she felt, it was punch to his stomach and a relief at the same time. *Is she ready for the words? Will she say them back?* "It's definitely real for me," he heard himself say. *Not quite what I wanted to say. Try again? Yeah. Try again.* "Stay here, just a moment."

George turned away as he realized the bracelets were still in his bag upstairs. "On second thought, come with me." He took her hand and looked at her again. The look on her face froze him in his tracks. He still wasn't quite used to seeing her with her shields down. Usually when she was showing how she felt, he liked it. But just then, she looked so vulnerable, and maybe even in pain. *Forget the props. And I guess the atmosphere and setting, too.*

He turned back to completely face her. "Jillian, Sweetheart." He slid his hand to her waist and with the other touched her face again, running his thumb over her lips. Her hands went to his waist without hesitation, but he could feel it, then, a distance between them and the weight of the something that filled that distance. And he wished that it was already over. That they'd both said, it and they were free of the barrier, through the gate, beyond it… whatever. "I'm sick of being afraid of this," he said to himself.

"What?" Jillian asked, against his thumb as her brow crinkled.

"Jillian," he tried to form the words, but they wouldn't quite come. If she wasn't ready, it was all over. And he had reason to believe she wasn't ready. Though he now had reason to believe that she was. *Oh, God. Don't let me mess this up.*

She watched him stumbling with something, while she felt an ache all throughout her being, it was easy enough to identify. It started in her chest and pulled everything inward, like a black hole. The light touch he placed on her face and lips only made it worse, because soon enough it would be gone and she'd still be aching and collapsing in on herself. She hated that she was so dependent on him. But she was, so that was that. She hated Taro for making her doubt. She hated herself for letting the doubts hold her back. She hated that she couldn't force herself to take any more steps forward. She hated… "George?"

He swallowed, so hard it hurt. "Jillian…"

"What is it?" She asked, pulled out of herself by the sight of his pain.

"Whatever it is, it'll be okay." She lifted a hand to his face and used it to brush back his hair, then returned her eyes to his.

"I love you," George blurted out and Jillian's eyes widened and then she blinked. It could only have been a second, but it felt like a year until she blinked again and his heart started to pound in his ears. *Oh, shit. Oh, shit.* "I know that was a little sud-" She dropped her hand from his hair to cover his mouth. *Oh, shit. Oh, shit.*

"I love you, too," she whispered, hardly able to breathe in enough to get the words out, she was so surprised.

"You do?" He asked, against her fingers. She lowered her hand to his chin, and then she dropped her eyes a moment and smiled shyly, letting out a strangled laugh.

"Of course, I do," Jillian said, and lifted her eyes back to his. "I love you, George."

"Ha!" George exclaimed and dropped his hands to then encircle her waist and lift her up. She wrapped her arms around his neck and squealed a little as her feet left the floor. "Oh, thank God." He started to laugh. "Thank God."

Jillian laughed too. "Are you that surprised?"

"Just so relieved," he said, and put her back on the floor. "Say it again."

"Ha!" Jillian barked. "You'd think it was the first time anyone ever told you they loved you."

"It's the first time you did," George said. "Say it again."

Jillian shook her head and said, "I love you, you lunatic."

He took her face in his hands. "And I love you." He kissed her softly, just barely touching her lips, making her lean into him to complete it; and lean into him, she did.

Another few soft kisses then George nuzzled her ear again, and she shivered. "Let's go upstairs."

"Okay," Jillian said. "Did you get that transporter working yet?"

"'Fraid not." George said, with a chuckle. "We'll have to take the stairs."

"I don't mind the stairs," Jillian replied. "I just don't want you to move away from me."

He laughed. "All right, then. Race you!" He moved quickly, though he did grab her hand in the process.

She stumbled after him and made a comment about the heels on her boots. He stopped and dropped to his knees and unzipped her boots, saying, "Take 'em off, then. They're coming off anyway, aren't they?"

"Yes," she said, with a laugh and stepped out of them. He clutched the boots together in one hand, stood up, and claimed her hand again.

"You set, now?" He asked, and rushed to the stairs again without waiting for an answer. She raced along behind him, actually overtaking him on the stairs, and finally leading him into his bedroom. Not stopping until she reached the bed, she towed him along with her, hearing him drop her boots by the door.

When she stopped, she turned and his hands were on her body and his lips were on her lips and then her back bounced on the bed, and he bounced atop her and they both laughed. He rolled them onto their sides and kissed her and whispered that he loved her and kissed her and whispered it again.

She ran her hands over the back of his shirt and whispered that she loved him too. Had always loved him, perhaps from the first moment she'd laid eyes on him. She moved her hands back to his chest and started working on the buttons of his shirt.

Kicking off his shoes, George slid his hands under Jillian's sweater, grateful as always for the feel of her soft skin. "We were made for each other," he said, and began to slide her sweater up. "I don't want to ever quit touching you."

She finished with the buttons on his shirt and started to pull it free from his pants. "Then don't." She kissed his chest and pushed the shirt down his arms. He sat up to get the shirt off, and started off another round of laughter when he was caught in the cuffs and she had to help pull the shirt back up his arms so he could unbutton the cuffs and loose himself.

He stayed sitting for a moment and looked at her, lying in his bed. "I love you," he said, again.

"I love you," she said, it back.

"Okay, come here." He grabbed her hands and brought her up to him, and they both got on their knees. He didn't slowly creep the hem of her sweater up her body; she didn't let him. She clutched the hem herself and whipped it over her head. "Green lace," he breathed.

She smiled. "What do we think of green?"

"If you're in it, it's frigging fantastic," he answered and went to work on the zipper of her skirt. "Wear lace in any color and I'm yours."

"I thought you were mine already." Jillian pushed her skirt and half-slip down to her knees and then shifted her weight to slip one leg out at a time.

"Oh, I am."

George's hands were all over her, making it tough to get out of the skirt, but finally, both it and the slip were tossed off the bed.

"Tell me you're mine," George said, as his hands grabbed her hips and pulled her against him.

"Take off your pants," Jillian ordered and when George looked startled, she continued the thought. "Your belt buckle's cold and your pants are scratchy…" She laughed up into his face.

"If you're going to be difficult," George said, "you're going to pay." His fingers ran up and down her sides so lightly that it tickled, and she laughed again and he tickled her with greater intent and she fell over and he kept on tickling her.

"Please!" She gasped. "Stop!" She laughed.

"Tell me you're mine," he said, laughing too as he straddled her body.

"Sto-o-o-o-o-op!"

"Tell me you're mine."

"I'm," she got out, between laughs and gasps. "I'm…"

He stopped moving his fingers, but kept his hands on her skin. "Say it, like you mean it, or there's more."

She looked up at him through a veil of her hair while he watched her chest rise and fall quickly. She swooped her hair from her face and left her arm above her head, while her other hand reached for his face. Jillian whispered, "I'm so, so, so, so, very much yours."

George let out a breath he didn't realize he'd been holding and shook his head. "You can't say that too much. I'll never get sick of hearing it." He put his hands on the bed on either side of her and leaned down.

She smiled into his eyes, put both her hands on his cheeks, and lifted herself a little from the bed by her waist, to kiss him softly. Then she dropped back to the bed, keeping her hands on his face. "I think I was born yours."

He had to kiss her again for that. There was no other way to react when taking in something like that. And, although the thought was sweet and tender, the kiss had to show just how it made him feel, tender at first and then more involved and powerful, as he tried to overwhelm her the way she did him.

It wasn't long before her head was spinning again and she turned her head just a little to the side and said, "That's it. You're a drug. I'm feeling dizzy lying down. How do you *do* that?"

He laughed against her neck and felt her shiver against him, under him. "I don't know. But you do things to me too."

"Like what?" She asked, and reached between them to unbuckle his belt.

He moved away from her to get rid of his pants and socks, then he tugged the covers down behind her head, and she giggled and moved like a worm, so he could pulled the covers completely down without her moving off the bed.

When he was next to her again, the covers over them, he took her in his arms and said, "All I can think about is you. I have little bursts where I can completely concentrate on something else, and then it's gone and I'm just thinking about you again.

"I thought about you while I was playing xbox with my brothers. It didn't help my game any."

She smiled, but didn't say anything.

"And," George searched for the words, "you touch me, somewhere inside, where nobody else ever has."

Jillian's lip part slightly in a small gasp. "Oh, George," she whispered, her eyes roved over his face. "I love you. Make love to me. Please. I need you in every way possible."

In contrast to all the laughter before, they became quiet and serious, kissing each other gently and long periods of time. They both moved slowly, touching each other everywhere.

Jillian slid down the bed and kissed her way down George's chest, running her hands down his back to his legs and back again, listening to his breath stutter and feeling his muscles flutter at her touch. For all the times they'd made love, Jillian realized that after the clothes were off, she hadn't focused much on his body.

So she helped him slide off his underwear and stayed to touch him, everywhere, just like he always did for her, letting her hands and her mouth revere him while he touched her head and her hair, unable to lie completely passive and receptive.

He groaned when her mouth enclosed him, and then he moaned her name. She couldn't see his face, but his breathing changed and she continued to show him she loved him.

"Okay, okay, okay," he suddenly said, and reached down to clutch her arms and drag her back up his body. "You gotta stop now."

Jillian blinked, "Why?"

He settled her on top of him so she could feel him where she'd feel it the most, and he could feel her too. "I want to be inside you and it'll take me to long to recover."

His words made her shudder. Thinking of him, inside, still made her heart race and her body shake. *How many times will we be together before it stops feeling like it's the first time?*

And then it became hard to think. His mouth was on hers with passion again, then on her neck, while his hands roamed over her, removing her bra to leave just one remaining wisp of lace between them. He kept her on top of him, and when she couldn't hold still any longer and squirmed just a little from the pleasure of his touch, he grabbed her hips and moved under her.

"Ohhhhh," she didn't even realize she'd opened her mouth until she heard herself echoing in her ears.

"Let's have a little fun this way, tonight," George said, then he moved under her again and she groaned again. He gripped her hips and encouraged her to move in counterpoint and soon they were both breathing faster.

And then faster.

And he didn't stop.

And he moved his left hand to push her hair over her shoulder and then to hold her neck while he moved his mouth there again and provided just the lightest amount of suction.

And Jillian started to feel the buildup. And she didn't want to stop.

And he *didn't* stop.

He moved both his hands to her shoulders and lifted her up, so that she placed her hands on the bed to hold herself, and she looked down at him.

"I love you," George said, and then lifted his hands to touch her breasts. "God, you are so beautiful." He lifted his head to take her into his mouth, and the pull from his mouth shot straight down her body to where they were moving together.

"Oh, God, George." She pressed harder against him. "Oh, God, that feels so good."

When he released her from his mouth, he said, "Good. Tell me when it feels great." Then his mouth was on her other breast and she lifted one of her hands from the bed to hold his head against her.

"Don't stop."

And he *didn't stop.*

It all felt so good that Jillian wanted it to last forever. She wanted him to go on touching her and making her pulse pound in her ears until the world ended. "It…" One of his hands dropped to her hip again and he moved just slightly faster. *Oh, God, George.* "It feels…" The twisting was starting. *Oh, God, George!* The twist sharpened. "It feels…"

He dropped his head back to the bed and pushed some of her damp hair out of her face, all the while still moving with her. The hand on her hip moved to squeeze her a little and the twisting grew stronger. *OhGodOhGod.*

She was fighting for air, trapped in the heat, lost in rhythm and the twist and-

And *he didn't stop.*

OhGodOhGodOhGod! He pulled her harder against him, gripping her so hard it almost hurt, and he lifted his head to her breast again, took her in his mouth, and the twist became a torrent and she exploded on top of him, screaming.

And he didn't stop!

He moved under her until the cascade had ended and the very last spasm had finished playing out and she had collapsed on his chest.

Her face was against his neck, so he pulled her hair to the side again, allowing her to breathe. His other hand running lightly up and down her back. He twisted his head and dropped a kiss on her forehead. "You okay, Sweetheart?"

"Ohhhhh, God," she murmured into his neck. "I've never… not like that." She let out a groan. "That was amazing."

He laughed lightly and she bounced against his chest. "Amazing, huh?"

"You should teach," Jillian said, and sighed.

George laughed harder. "Teach?"

"Uh-huh."

"Okay, I'll have to look into that."

Jillian's eyes opened as she realized what she'd said, and what he'd said. "On second thought, no teaching. I'm just going to be selfish and keep you all to myself."

Another laugh from George. "No worries, Sweetheart. You're it." He drew a circle on her back and she quivered a little.

They were still for a few minutes then, apart from him rubbing her back. Jillian smiled into his neck. "You're too good to me, George."

"You deserve it." He couldn't imagine a more perfect moment with the woman he loved. Stillness and quiet and...

Jillian stirred against him and moved a hand to his chest. "So do you. Give me another minute to recover."

"It's not all give and take. Sometimes you're allowed to just take. And I can just give."

"But not tonight," Jillian said. She struggled to prop herself up. "You deserve everything too." She finally pushed herself off of him and he immediately rolled to his side to face her.

"Really, baby. You don't have to..."

She smiled at him. And then the smile turned just a little wicked. "It's really good for me too, you know." Her underwear dropped to the floor. "Now. Where were we?"

"Where-" He stopped talking as she slid along his body again, kissing and touching and reigniting all the fires that had simmered and enraging the ones hadn't yet tempered.

"Oh, Jillian," he whispered as she disappeared beneath the covers to reinvigorate him.

When he was shuddering and could feel his whole body pulsing with his heartbeat, she slid back up. "I can finish... or..."

He quickly slid his arms around her and rolled her onto her back. "Definitely 'or.'" He needed to touch her, all of her. Again. And he did, teasing her until she was gasping and shuddering, just like he was.

The tension was so high, that when he stopped to get a condom, she almost screamed at him. She did say, "Hurry," in a low, breathy voice she didn't even recognize and he laughed.

Finally, he filled her and she wrapped herself around him.

So hot. George could feel her pulsing around him. *So damn hot.* And she moaned as he moved. *So damn sexy.* And she took all of him, wanted all of him.

And she was looking in his eyes, just like he wanted, and moving with him, just like he wanted. And she started to shake in his arms. She'd actually gotten ahead of him. He picked up speed, hoping they'd finish together.

"Oh, God! Oh, George!" And her eyes closed as the pleasure took her, and her fingernails dug into his back, and her legs tightened about his waist, and he felt the contractions around him and came so hard he didn't even remember collapsing onto her.

When his brain was functioning, he knew all his weight was on her. *Move. Man. Move. Before you crush her. Start with one arm and go from there.* He struggled to move an arm.

But he didn't want to move. He could still feel her pulsing around him. Everything was better inside her. *Oh Hell.* He remembered the condom and moved quickly to dispose of it.

Jillian actually fought him as he moved, trying to keep him with her.

He frowned when he turned away from her. She was the one who wanted him to use it. If she would give that up, he could stay with her as long as she wanted. *Well, maybe not that long. But still.* He let go of the issue when he'd climbed back in bed with her and she'd kissed him so softly he almost couldn't feel it and said, "I love you, so, so, very much, George. I've never loved anyone or anything like I love you." And he *knew* she meant it.

"I love you, Jillian," he said, as he looked into her sated and already defocusing eyes. She was exhausted, fighting it, but exhausted. *Heck, I'm exhausted.* "Go to sleep, Sweetheart. I'll still love you in the morning. And I'll tell you again, then, too."

She wrapped herself around him again and fell asleep almost immediately. George held onto her, staring at his ceiling. *This is about as perfect as anything could possibly get. There can't be anything better than this. I want this all the time. Every day and every night.*

It would be two weeks on Tuesday. *What's the minimum time limit for inviting someone to live with you?* He'd thought he was pushing it with 'I love you' and maybe he had been. But it'd turned out all right.

Then again, living together was one area she'd been pretty clear about. She'd never gone for it before. It made sense when she was young, parental disapproval can be powerful, whether the parents or the kids think so or not. The more recent guy she'd claimed she'd been in love with, she'd turned him down. But then again, that relationship was unhealthy and maybe she just sensed it was coming to an end.

If he asked, and she decided to say no, could she say no and not break it off? If he did it in a real casual way, maybe. Maybe he could give her a key, to start. Not make a big deal out of it. *Just give her one in the morning with a simple, "Here. In case." Nothing more. Then, maybe she'd feel comfortable leaving some things. Because she could always get anything she need, whether I'm home or not.*

Well, not if I said, "In case." That implies only in emergency circumstances. Maybe something like, "Here. Use it if you want..." No, that isn't going to work. I need something straightforward. Maybe just, "Hey. Here's a key." Nothing more, nothing less. See what happens...

Good Lord, I'm an idiot. None of that is going to work. It all needs to happen naturally. Let it go.

He thought about how they were playing ping pong with their nights, one at hers, one at his. *Well, not quite ping pong. More at hers. Of course, she's got the cat.*

Hmm.

I wonder if I bought a cat bed. Maybe that'd be a hint.

He rolled his eyes, rather than shaking his head and risk waking her up. It was time for sleep. It was not time to be wondering about things like that. He could live with the ping pong beds for a while, so long as she was in them with him.

Around 3 am, Jillian woke up to use the restroom and found herself wide awake. George, on the other hand, was out cold. Not wanting to wake him, *he needs the sleep so badly between the jet lag and the time changes*, she decided to slip downstairs and get a snack. *Maybe that will help me sleep again.*

She forgot to bring a robe in her overnight bag; she usually didn't get out of bed much when she was with him, at least not in the wee hours, which gave her reason to sneak quietly into George's closet to look for a temporary replacement.

Why she wasn't comfortable borrowing the actual robe she found, she couldn't say. Instead she found a big, flannel shirt, clearly oversized even for George, making it more than huge on her, and used it. The only thing wrong with it was that it was laundered so it didn't smell like him. At that moment, she wished it did.

Shuffling through George's kitchen gave her pause. The pantry was certainly not a bachelor's pantry. There were some mixes and pre-packaged things, of course, but he mainly stocked ingredients to prepare food. *Honestly, this is much better than I do. I may have to ask him to teach me to cook.*

Thankfully, there were snacks and as Jillian nibbled on a pretzel, feeling more awake than ever, she had a thought. *I could make breakfast now.*

That would save them both a little time in the morning, or George at the very least, since he always cooked while she showered. If she cooked now, he could sleep later. She opened the pantry again and decided to use one of the few mixes he had on hand, pancakes. She assembled the rest of the ingredients and added bacon and eggs. Before long, she was covering the food and placing it in the fridge for a quick microwave after dawn.

She filled the coffee maker and set the timer, then got busy with the cleanup. She was scrubbing his frying pan when a voice from the general direction of the family room asked her what she was doing.

"Ah!" Her heart was pounding and she'd whipped around holding a spatula in one hand like a sword and the other wet hand to her chest. She didn't scream loud enough to wake the neighbors, but she would have roused anyone else in the house, he'd scare her so badly. "Oh, God! You scared me half to death!"

"So I gathered," George said, and wandered in. "Guess I should be glad you didn't have a knife in your hand." He pointed at the spatula. "Nice defense."

"Oh!" Jillian exclaimed and turned back to the sink. "No criticism at this hour."

"It's not a criticism. What are you up to?"

"Cleanup," Jillian said.

George walked up behind her and bent over to drop his head on her shoulder. "I see that. What are you cleaning up, exactly?"

She motioned toward the fridge. "I made breakfast."

"That's what I smell! I thought I was hallucinating due to hunger."

Jillian turned her head slightly toward him. "I didn't wake you, did I? I woke up and you were out cold. I didn't want to disturb you."

"It wasn't you," he said, sliding his arms around her waist. "But it might have been the delicious smells. I really am starving."

"Then eat," Jillian said. "You can eat early. The food's fresh enough, you may not even need to reheat it."

George released her and padded over to the fridge. She glanced at him. He wasn't wearing his robe either, he'd just put on his underwear and his shirt. *Mmm, he looks so tasty.* She took a moment to admire tousled George, who looked like he'd been doing *exactly* what he'd been doing before he'd passed out from exhaustion.

He couldn't help but grin a little in embarrassment as he tucked into her breakfast. The word starved didn't really cover the ravenous need he was experiencing. The hardest part was not eating too fast, because it was definitely the kind of time when he could overeat.

Finished washing and drying, Jillian joined him at the table, but only had another pretzel. She was only peckish.

Between bites he thanked her for cooking, which seemed ridiculous to Jillian since he was a much better cook than she was. But she managed to nod and accept his thanks. Even if it wasn't quite the surprise or treat she'd envisioned for the morning, he appreciated it.

Well, maybe he just appreciated that it was hot and edible. He certainly was putting it away.

When he finished, the plate and silverware went into the dishwasher, which happened to be right next to the drawer that George had his spare house keys stored. He shut the dishwasher and looked over his shoulder to see what had become of Jillian. She was still in the kitchen, putting the pretzels back in the pantry. "Hey, Jillian," George called and opened the drawer.

"Hmm?" Jillian answered from inside the pantry.

They're in here somewhere. He fished around the drawer. "Is your purse down here?"

"Sure. I put it on the couch, I think. Or the coffee table. Why?" She came out of the pantry and closed the door.

He found the keys. "Just a second." After some twisting, he took the extra spare off the ring, dropped the ring back in the drawer, shut the drawer, and turned to her. *Casual.*

CHAPTER TWENTY-SIX

"Here," George said, and held out the house key. "Put it on your key ring. It opens the front door, the back door, and the side door on the garage."

Jillian took the key he held out to her, trying to act as though nothing out of the ordinary was happening until she could think it through. Her thinking was limited to *what is this* and *what does it mean* and *am I making a big deal out of nothing or am I making nothing out of a big deal*.

Slowly, she headed into the family room toward her purse. *He's given me a key. Oh. My. Oh. My. OhMyOhMyOhMyOhMy.*

Just as George was thinking that it might have gone well, he wasn't sure because she hadn't actually said anything, she returned to the kitchen. "Okay. Um," she said.

Not a good sign. Not a good sign at all.

"I'm not sure what to make of this," Jillian said to the key in her hand. *OhMyOhMyOhMyOhMy.*

It wasn't lost on George that she wasn't looking at him. "Well, it's a key." He wasn't sure what to make of it either. He knew what he wanted to make of it, but that wasn't necessarily what it was.

"To this house," Jillian said, with a questioning lift to her voice, but not as an actual question. *OhMyOhMyOhMyOhMy.*

"Yep," George said. *So, do I say something now? Or do I shut up?*

Jillian looked up from the key. *OhMyOhMyOhMyOhMy.*

George took a breath. *It's definitely my turn.* "I like it when you're here. Now, you can choose to be here, whenever." When she didn't answer right away, George panicked and made a joke. "You can show up and take a bath, or hide out from the law…"

"So this doesn't mean anything," Jillian said, trying to decide if she was relieved or upset.

George's face scrunched up at his gaff, and then he kind of groaned as if he'd heard a really bad joke, bent his knees, and rolled his head to the side. After a moment, he straightened back up. "Look, it isn't nothing. But, I don't want this to be such a big deal that you won't take it. I just want you to take it, use it when you want. That's all."

"That's all?" *Why does it feel like way more than that?*

"Well, like I said, I like you here, so I hope you'll use it a lot. Maybe, some night when I have basketball and you're doing something with the girls, but we're planning to meet up, you could use if it you're early. I don't know. Stuff like that." He paused a moment. "It's like an open invitation, if that makes sense."

An open invitation… I think I can wrap my head around that. "Well, yes," she closed her hand around the key. "That makes sense."

He sighed and then shook his head. "I did this all wrong, didn't I?"

"I don't know," Jillian said. "I just didn't expect a key." She smiled a little. "But then, I didn't expect 'I love you' either. And that was pretty fantastic." Jillian closed the distance between them and he put his arms around her while she did the same about him.

"Yeah," George said. "Having you say it too, was pretty fantastic."

Jillian's smile broadened across her face. "We've been moving pretty fast."

"Too fast?" George asked, just managing to hope rather than worry.

"I don't know. I mean, it feels good. Being together feels great. But when I think about this-" *I'm still out of control. Just like our first date. Completely out of control.*

"Don't think, then. Let's just be whatever makes us happy. No time tables but our own. No comparisons to anyone else. If it's right for us, it's right." *And it's right. It's perfect.*

"That sooounds good. But-"

"But, nothing," he said, and dropped a kiss on the tip of her nose. "I love you. Now that key doesn't come with any strings or obligations, so you can put it on your key ring and it'll be there whenever. Fair?"

"Fair." Jillian said, with a small laugh. *But, I don't know if I believe that 'no strings' bit. Are you going to be waiting for me to reciprocate? I'm not so sure that I'm ready for that.*

Still, she took the key and put it on her keyring. George said he'd see her upstairs and headed up and she smiled and said, "Be right there."

As she put her keyring back in her purse, she noticed her list again. Looking at it, she decided it needed to go in a scrapbook, along with one of her 4 o'clocks and the cards he'd sent for their first date. The apron was a little big for a scrapbook, but maybe she could convince him to put his on while she wore hers, and take a picture, and that could go in the scrapbook.

She had a second before George wondered what she was doing. There were several pens in her purse. She found one and doodled a few more hearts next to the *LOVES ME* she'd written and then wrote *Like I love him* and followed it with the previous days' date.

Smiling, she thought of her goofy, permanent record. *I'll have to make sure to make note of other things. We still need a song.*

(I Love You) For Sentimental Reasons suddenly sprang to mind. The repetition of 'I love you, I love you, I love you' reminded her of them earlier, saying it over and over. And then thinking of Sam Cooke brought another song to mind. *You Send Me.* She wrote it both down on the back. She'd have to play them for him sometime. Find out what he thought.

Glancing in her bag as she put everything away, she looked at the new key. *Oh, George. You definitely send me.*

"Every Monday has its up and downs," George said to himself, as he hung up with the client whom Jillian had stalled for him on Friday. The sentiment was intended to soothe. So far, the only up he'd had was at 3 am. The rest of the day had been accelerating downhill and the end wasn't in sight. Trying to make up for lost time, George had eaten at his desk. Taking advantage of his unavailability, Jillian had done the same. The Hardware people were driving them both crazy, so every minute really counted.

Around two in the afternoon, Taro stopped by to see if George could make a practice that night, right after work. "Chris is available, too. So we can totally make up for Sunday." He dropped onto the corner of George's desk. "Unless, of course, you've got to see Jillian every spare moment."

George had to think. He and Jillian hadn't actually talked about the evening. It was Jillian's Blue Feather night, so he could practice after work and meet her for dinner first, or even meet her there, if the timing was a problem. "I can make practice," George said, and shooed Taro away.

He turned to his IM and let Jillian know he'd been asked to make up the basketball practice. She replied that meeting at the Blue Feather would work for her, if he really wanted to come. Otherwise, she'd be okay with meeting up later. *Or we could just see each other tomorrow.*

Sitting back, George stared at his IM. "Just see each other tomorrow?" *We just said, 'I love you' and she doesn't want to see me tonight? No, no. That's not it. She's just giving me space to be myself. Do what I do. And she's probably wanting to do laundry again.*

If he was going to meet her at The Blue Feather, he was going to have to shrink down his overnight bag to look more casual, since he'd be bringing it in. *Dinner would definitely be better. Easier to transfer stuff into the trunk of her car.* And he was going to miss eating together, if they didn't.

He wrote back that he wanted to work out eating together. And they made plans to meet up early enough for dinner before Jazz.

Taro gave George a ride home after practice. As they were turning onto his street, Taro asked George how Jillian was doing. George answered that she was fine and Taro nodded. "Good. I know Sergei's been a bit worried."

George had to pause for a moment there. "Why has Sergei been worried?"

"Well, after the whole thing with that guy showing up at her apartment."

That guy? The rat bastard! It has to be. Who else would he be talking about? But, Jillian never mentioned him showing up at her apartment. Shit. "She's fine," he said, again, as if he knew all about it. "No worries."

"That's good. I guess now that you're home, Sergei can step back. He's been texting her. Making sure she was okay."

"I asked him to watch out for her, if that guy came around," George said, and crossed his arms. *She didn't mention any of this.*

"Well, he took it to heart," Taro said. "You couldn't have asked for a more conscientious protector."

Nodding, George said, "That's why I asked him."

"Okay, then," Taro said, as he pulled over to the sidewalk.

"Thanks for the ride," George said, as he exited the car and tried not to think about the fact that Jillian *hadn't* told him anything about it. Not the rat bastard. Not Sergei. Nothing.

It was obvious that something was wrong. George's body language was closed and possibly angry, even though he kept saying everything was fine. Dinner wasn't as... warm, as it usually was. Of course, since they ate out, the displays of affection would have been kept to a minimum anyway.

All the way to The Blue Feather, Jillian wondered what was wrong and if she could do anything about it. But he didn't want to talk about it. *That's as uncharacteristic of George as I've ever seen. He talks about everything. He's even comfortable talking about our relationship! More comfortable than me!* So, instead of even slightly meaningful conversation in the car, there was mostly silence.

Huey picked up on it too, he held onto Jillian a second as he was showing her in and asked her if everything was okay. She shrugged and said, "I'm sure it's fine."

But it clearly wasn't fine. George sat at the band table with his arms crossed and eyes glaring through the whole first set. He wasn't entirely wrapped in himself though, Jillian thought gratefully, when George ordered her two bottles of water before the set came to a close. *He's still treating me well, at least as far as that goes.*

And she needed the treatment. Actually she needed the full queen treatment. Her head hurt and her abdomen too. She'd started cramping at work, right on schedule, and was in her full monthly misery by the time the day had ended.

Of all the nights she could have used George's attention *that* was the night. Even her back was sore. She thought longingly of a gentle rub down, even just a few minutes of light pressure on her back. The idea of taking a bath had come up, but she didn't think she'd be able to explain it to George. And she didn't want to have to wipe out his tub.

There were certain things that were hard enough to talk about. She'd been dreading telling him that they were on hiatus from making love for at least four days. The timing could have been worse, but not by much.

Sitting on stage at the piano, one of her favorite places and experiences in the whole of the world, she was anything but happy. It was hard to concentrate on her fingers. She glanced down at the band table again. *What is going on with George?*

After the performance. That's when George planned to ask Jillian about what had gone on while he was away over the weekend. Not before, in case it upset her. He wanted answers, but not badly enough to ruin her performance. Of course, she'd made it difficult, asking him what was wrong. *Obviously, I'm not too good at the subterfuge.*

He put her off though. Then she was up on the stage playing and making beautiful music. And her purse was sitting right in front of him, with her phone in the pocket.

Sergei was texting her.

It was so close he could feel the electromagnetic radiation. All he had to do was slip the phone out of the side pocket and look through it. Then he'd know exactly what had been going on.

The phone called to him throughout the first three songs. *That's not the right thing to do.* So he crossed his arms, he felt like it anyway, and kept his hands to himself.

A song he recognized started up, Freddy was at the mic again, and he couldn't even enjoy it. *Sergei was texting Jillian… what exactly? What could he possibly be sending her?*

Until Taro had said something, George hadn't even realized he'd barely seen Sergei that entire day. Once, maybe twice, in passing. Of course, he'd been at practice, but he wasn't quite himself there. He'd been a little bit quiet. Not enough to bring attention to himself on its own merits. But with this additional information, George was wondering if Sergei wasn't avoiding him.

He ordered Jillian some water, polished off a scotch, but didn't get another, and looked at her purse out of the corner of his eye. Just one peek. That's all it would take.

She'd be furious though. He would be, if she started snooping through his phone, right in front of him. When he wasn't in a position to say or do anything about it. *Just calm down. Wait. Ask her when it's over, like you planned. For all you know, it's nothing. Taro was wrong about how she felt about you. But if he said Sergei was texting Jillian... that would be true. And if he said that guy showed up at her apartment... that would also be true. So why don't I know one single solitary thing about any of this?*

He glanced at her purse again. *Shit.*

At the set break, even Freddy asked what was up. Jillian answered the same way she'd answered Huey, a shrug and "I'm sure it's fine." But she wasn't sure at all. She cracked open a water bottle and went digging through her purse for some ibuprofen. She decided on a double dose. It would mean she'd have to skip a dose later, but that was going to have to be fine. At least at home she could get out the heating pad and relieve her symptoms more naturally.

Her attempt at small talk with George failed and she took her purse into the restroom and tried not to cry and then, after a moment, tried not to fume. *It's bad enough being I'm at my emotional time. I don't need this from George... whatever it is that's bunching up his shorts!*

She took her purse with her. Of frigging course, she did. He could have checked her phone, so she took it with her. Or worse than that, she was using the bathroom where he couldn't see what she was doing. She could be texting right then. *Dammit.*

Okay. He looks like he's going to break something into pieces. "What is the *matter* with you?" Jillian whispered-yelled at George as she sat down next to him. She couldn't stand it anymore and with the set break nearly over, she didn't have time to mess around.

George frowned at her. He actually frowned. "Let's talk about it when you're done."

"I don't want to talk about it when I've finished. You're bothering me now. And the whole place can see that something's the matter with you. I've been asked twice. So just talk." She glanced toward the stage and then back. "And do it fast. I haven't much time left."

Well, well, well. Here's Jillian the boss. Interesting to finally see her. "Look we don't have time now. Just finish the second set and we'll talk then."

Stubborn! "Don't be ridiculous. Today isn't the day for it. Just tell me what's going on!"

George clenched his teeth. "I'm trying really damn hard here, Jillian."

"Oh, you're succeeding in being trying, that's for sure!" Jillian crossed her arms. Freddy hopped down off the stage and marched up to the table.

"Pipe down. D'ya want the whole joint staring? Geez, the static is buzzing all over me." He looked at Jillian. "What's eating you two?"

Jillian stood up. "If only I knew, Freddy." She headed for the stage.

Freddy put his foot on her vacated chair and leaned over toward George. "I believe I gave you a warning. Jillian Olivia is not just another skirt around here, she's family. You better turn out to have the goods, or the band and I will take you for a ride. Not a one of us likes seeing her upset like that."

George sat forward. "Mind your own beeswax, Freddy."

Freddy raised his eyebrows. "I out number you." He tipped his head toward the stage.

She may be cheating on me and the band is going to beat me up. Yup. That makes sense. "Go toot your horn."

Freddy snorted, but he stepped off the chair and then returned to the stage and was talking in Jillian's ear. George ground his teeth, but it wasn't making any difference. Just as the set was beginning he went to the bar for his second round.

He came back to the table and her purse was sitting there, still, calling to him. Even with the second scotch to help nullify a few guilt riddled brain cells, he kept his hands to himself.

There had been much doubt towards the middle of the set, but Jillian had finished. All she wanted was to curl into a ball with heat all over her, but instead she had to deal with *the boyfriend* who was acting more and more childish every second and *didn't want to talk about it*. It was ridiculous.

She snatched up her purse for another visit to the ladies' room. "I'll be right back."

"I'll be here."

"Fine."

"Good."

She took her time, hoping for her physical discomfort to subside, not surprised when it didn't. The pain was getting worse and she was so tired. Returning to the table, she declined a chair. "George, I'm not feeling very well. I need to go home."

George could see it was true on her face. She looked sick. "Of course." He rose and picked up their coats. "What can I do?"

She shook her head, the pain pulled at her insides, begging her to bend over to ease it. "Just get me home." He helped her into her coat. "Please."

Had he known how bad the pain was, he'd have offered to carry her to the car, but she didn't tell him. Instead, she walked slowly, holding herself upright, and a bit stiff. At the car, he helped her into the passenger seat and asked her about buckling up. She took care of the seatbelt herself while he raced around the car and joined her in the driver's seat, his other concerns forgotten for the moment. He closed the door behind him but didn't start the car.

Turning to Jillian, he touched her forehead. "No fever."

"No," Jillian said. "No fever." It was too much. She bent over a little, her arms around her stomach. "Can you please…"

"I'll take you home," George said, turning the key in the ignition. "Unless you need a hospital."

She shook her head. "Home. Please."

"Okay," he said. When she lifted her legs up onto the seat, he looked at her. "What's wrong? Your stomach?"

I must be flushed from head to toe. She was so embarrassed by his question, she didn't want to answer. But it was only fair. Even if they were fighting, he was taking her home. "It's just really bad… cramps."

"Oh?" And then it sunk in. "Oh. Really bad?"

She nodded slightly.

"Did you take anything?"

"Of course, I did," she mumbled. In her mind, she felt like snapping at him, but she hurt too much to yell.

"I didn't know."

"Duh," the word was out before she could stop it. "I'm sorry."

He accelerated a little bit, speeding slightly, hoping to get her home faster. "How long has… when did it… the pain, I mean, start?"

"This afternoon." Then she mumbled again, "Right on schedule." She tried to breathe through it, but it wasn't an ebb and flow of pain, it was constant. Her back was hurting even more and she had to shift around in her seat, but it didn't ease the pain.

"What do you usually do? Is it usually this bad?"

"Don't worry about it. I'll deal with it."

"Jill-"

"Please, just get me home!"

On the way up in the elevator, Jillian reiterated that George could just go home, *should* just go home. "It's not like I'm going to be good company."

"We'll see," George said. She was in too much pain to leave alone. *And we haven't talked about what in the hell went on here while I was gone either.*

"I'm just going to lie down and try to sleep."

"We'll see," George repeated.

The first thing Jillian did upon entering her apartment was to take off her shoes. The second was to start into the kitchen to get Charlie's dinner. George set down his things and offered to take care of Charlie. It was a sweet thought, but Jillian didn't let him. Charlie was her responsibility. George asked her why she couldn't let him give her a hand. "I take care of Charlie. He's always here for me, so I should be here for him."

George shook his head and watched Jillian take some acetaminophen. She was walking around slightly bent over. It was absurd.

"Go, lie down. Whatever needs to be done, I'll take care of it."

About ten minutes later, Jillian was wearing sweatpants and a t-shirt, and curled up on her bed with the heating pad. She'd finished her chores with regard to Charlie, but after that, she'd given up. She hurt so much she wished George would just go. *I don't want him to see me like this.*

But, there was George, who'd acted like a big baby all evening, in her kitchen, putting away her clean dishes from the dishwasher. *I just don't get him!*

I've never felt so helpless in my life. Jillian wouldn't let him take care of anything, even though she was walking around like she'd just had abdominal surgery, and with each step, he could see her slowing down. *If you want to lie down, lie down!*

Finally, she was on her bed, not in it, lying atop the covers, twisted around her heating pad with her knees up to her chest and he had to admit she'd had a point in the elevator. There was nothing he could do for her. He was just there, taking up space and making noise.

Her dishwasher was clean, he noticed. So he emptied it. That took up maybe five minutes, even with the challenge of a few items he hadn't seen before and having to guess their proper storage location.

That task complete, he wandered into Jillian's bedroom, knelt down next to her, and asked, "Is that helping?"

"Not really," Jillian replied, not opening her eyes.

"Are you sure there isn't anything I can do for you?"

"Pretty sure," Jillian said, and then inhaled sharply as her back twinged again. Her hand flew to her back and pressed.

"Back's hurting too, Sweetheart?"

She exhaled like she'd run out of patience. "Look. You're being very thoughtful, but I'm not going to feel better until tomorrow. You don't have to sit around here, staring at the walls, and asking me what you can do to help. I know you've got to be bored already. Go home and relax."

George reached out a hand to lightly brush her hair out of her face and behind her shoulder. "You're in pain. I can't just go."

She opened her eyes. "You may actually be more stubborn than I am. How that's even possible, I don't know, but..." Her back spasmed, not just a twinge that time, but a full spasm, and she blinked at the pain and quit breathing until the spasm passed, then she closed her eyes and let out some air.

"What was that?" George asked, softly.

"Just my back," Jillian said. *It is a little worse than usual.*

"You're putting pressure on it."

"Yes."

"Would it help if I did that?" George asked.

Jillian's eyes flew open. *Are you kidding me? This has got to be the most embarrassing thing that's ever happened.* She'd worked hard to keep her monthly issues away from others in the past. "I don't know. More heat would probably feel good."

"Got it," George disappeared.

Jillian closed her eyes. *I shouldn't have taken anything. If the pain gets bad enough, maybe I'll pass out.* She found it hard to imagine it much worse than it was though.

George spent a few minutes searching for supplies. Heat was harder than cold. Frozen peas worked great as an ice pack. But heat was trickier. He finally found some washcloths in her linens and soaked them in water, wrung them out so they were just moist, then put them on a plate in the microwave. When they came out too hot to touch, he wrapped them in a hand towel. A second towel with him, just in case it was still too hot, George returned to Jillian, climbing on the bed opposite her.

"What are you doing?" Jillian asked, when George moved her hand.

"Tell me if this is too hot." He placed his makeshift heating pad against her shirt where her hand had been.

Jillian inhaled like she'd been startled, then she let it out slowly. "Ohhhhh. That's good." Her hand flew back to press it harder against her. George moved her hand again and pressed harder.

"Just tell me if it's too much," he said.

"Nuh-uh. Harder."

He pressed harder and Jillian made another pained sound, but then he could see her shoulders drop a little and her back curved downward, just a little, into the mattress.

"Thank you," she said, just above a whisper.

He leaned way over and kissed her temple. "I'm sorry you're hurting." He sat back up. *This is going to be a tough position to maintain for very long.*

Jillian closed her eyes as they started watering.

George held up for about fifteen minutes which nicely coincided with the cooling of his makeshift heating pad. "I'll go heat this up some," he said, climbing back off the bed and wincing at his own sore back. He needed to figure out a better position to sit in.

I want to die. Jillian's back didn't feel like it had twinged or spasmed, it felt like a disc ruptured or something. And then her abdomen answered her back with a squeeze that took her breath away. The tears were getting harder to fight.

George returned and walked around the bed to talk to her. "Okay. So I was thinking-" He dropped down next to her again. "Wow. Is it getting worse?"

She managed a nod. "You should go," she whispered.

"How about distraction?"

"What?" Jillian's face scrunched up.

"I was just thinking that laying here thinking about it, probably makes it worse. Why don't we move you out to the couch, put on a movie, and maybe it'll help take your mind off it, just a little. And a little is better than nothing."

"I don't want to move," she whispered.

"If you could transport there, would you want to do it?"

Jillian smiled just a little at the thought. "Sure."

"Okay, then."

Her pillow disappeared from under her head, and her heating pad slipped out from grip with a little whining on her part. Figuring George meant to risk his back carrying her to the sofa, she forced herself to sit up and, by the time he'd returned, mostly stood up.

"Oh, now, Sweetheart." He put an arm around her waist and grabbed her hand to take whatever weight she'd give him, which turned out to be next to nothing.

But he'd made a nice little nest for her on the couch. He'd brought down the throw, set up her pillow, and plugged in the heating pad. After he settled her onto the couch, he asked her what she wanted to watch.

She tried to think of something she had that he might like. She must have been thinking a long time, because he said, "This isn't a quiz with a right answer. What'll distract you?"

Jillian almost laughed, but she knew *that* wouldn't help. "Um, why don't we let Charlie choose? Charlie, baby." She called Charlie a few times and he came out, from wherever he'd been hiding, to slink over to Jillian. He sniffed at her. "I know this is weird, baby, me lying here. But mama's not doing too well. Wanna pick a movie?"

Charlie meowed and ran over to the entertainment center.

George looked back from Charlie to Jillian.

"He's learned the word 'movie,'" Jillian said.

George sort of shrugged and returned his attention to Charlie who was sniffing DVD cases with his front legs and paws up on the entertainment center. It would have been like watching a dog fetch somebody's slippers, except he was clearly taking his time. After a bit, he jumped up onto the next shelf up and started sniffing there. Finally, he knocked down a few cases.

"Okay, *that* is *funny*," George said. "You ought to record that."

"I have," Jillian said, as George bent over to pick up the movies. "What'd he knock over?"

Smiling to himself that the plan was working already, she was definitely speaking a little louder indicating less pain, George looked. "Let's see, *Gambit* and-"

"Stop! Have you ever seen that?"

"No," George said, and studied the front of the case.

"That's the one. Put the others down. You have to see this movie. It's a caper film with Shirley MacLaine and Michael Caine."

"Okay," he said, and returned the other movies to the shelf. Once he had the player cued up for the movie, he turned to pick a chair and saw that she had her hand on her back again. "Give me another moment."

He nuked the hot pack for just a few seconds and then came back to the sofa. "How about I sit at this end, you put your head in my lap, and I'll hold this on your back?"

Jillian thought about it a moment and then said, "We can try it." She worried that it wouldn't be comfortable. She laughed just a little and he looked quizzically at her. "I was just thinking how that might not be comfortable. Like anything *is* comfortable right now."

Once he was seated and Jillian's pillow and her head were in his lap, he started up the movie and pressed the hot pack into the small of her back. She tensed at the touch, and then relaxed against the heat.

He had to heat up the pack a few times during the movie, but he didn't mind. By the end, he suspected she might actually be feeling a little better, though certainly not well, but at least a little improved. And, he had to admit the film was super entertaining. A perfect 60's caper flick, absurdly funny and with a great twist / punchline at the end. He looked at Charlie, who'd been watching the movie from a chair. "You've got good taste in movies, Charlie."

Charlie looked at him and meowed, then turned back to the screen for the credits.

"You've got quite the cat," George observed to Jillian.

"He's so smart," Jillian said, as she tried to sit up. She tried to keep the wincing to a minimum, but George saw it.

"I thought you were feeling a bit better," he said.

She shook her head. "Not by much."

"Do you want to watch another one?"

She shook her head again. "I need to try to sleep."

"All right." He helped move her back to the bedroom, but when she did her hunchback walk to the bathroom, he started to wonder if she was going to let him sleep in the bed with her. She was still pretty miserable.

She came back out and crawled into bed, taking her heating pad with her.

"You can't do that," George said, walking around the bed and unplugging the heating pad. "You could burn while you sleep."

She groaned. "As if I'm going to sleep."

"You have to try," he said, and she dropped the heating pad out from under the covers to the floor with a whiney groan.

He used the bathroom and then checked on her, making sure she hadn't smuggled the heating pad back in. She hadn't, so he stripped to his shorts and slid into the bed next to her.

"I still think you'd be happier at home," she said, not rolling over to face him like she normally did.

"No, I wouldn't," he said, and rolled to his side and scooted up against her. "I don't think so."

"I don't really want to be touched right now," Jillian said, a little reluctantly.

"Not at all?" He asked. "You could roll over and let me put my arms around you, and put some pressure on your back."

He's trying so hard. Jillian started crying again and then his hand was on her shoulder.

"Oh, Sweetheart, what's wrong? Did the pain get worse again?"

"I just… want to be… alone."

He tugged on her shoulder, trying to roll her over. "Why?"

She took a minute to answer, wiping her eyes and trying not to sniffle. "I don't want to be seen like this."

He couldn't help but smile. *The ice queen is still in there. She doesn't want to be seen as weak.* He kissed her shoulder through the t-shirt. "Let me help," he said, quietly. "Let me be here for you."

"You've already helped. You've already done enough."

"Jillian," he said, and slid his hand down her back to where it hurt and began to rub in a small circle. "I love you. Just let me help you."

That's the first time you've said it all day. The tears came harder and faster and she rolled over and buried her face in his chest, although it was tough on her because she couldn't pull up her knees. "I love you, too," she said, against his skin.

The clock showed twelve something when George rolled over. He didn't bother to identify the remaining digits, they weren't important. Light was coming out from under the door to the bathroom and he thought he heard a soft whimper. *She must still feel awful.*

Awake enough that he didn't think he could just roll over and go back to sleep, George got out of bed and knocked on the bathroom door. "Hey,

Sweetheart. Are you doing all right? Can I get you anything?"

The replying voice was a little shaky. "No, thank you. I'm feeling a little better."

George nodded. "Good. Glad to hear it. I'm going to grab a glass of water." Her quiet 'okay' followed him into the living room. As he stood at the sink, he glanced around the room at all the colorful things she owned. His eyes settled on Jillian's purse. *Her phone is still in there.* They'd never plugged in their phones for charging, so hers had to be sitting in her purse. And she was in the bathroom.

He passed her purse and returned to the bedroom, calling out, "I'm getting our phones. We forgot to plug them in."

"Thank you," her muffled voice answered. He noted it sounded a little less shaky. *Probably not much time then.* He picked up his phone first, then opened her purse pocket and slid hers out. He held his breath. *Answers.* He pushed the button on the side and the lock screen lit up.

CHAPTER TWENTY-SEVEN

Crap! Of course she's got a lock code on it. What'd you expect, you idiot?

He shook his head and walked back into the bedroom. *What would she use as a lock code? She's a programmer, so she probably knows not to use her birthday or anything else that's easily found on-line.* Plugging in his phone, he thought through the likeliest possibilities.

Charlie? He typed and didn't gain entry. *What else? Probably only so many tries before the phone wipes. Best not take too many uncertain guesses. Good, solid, logical ones. That's what's called for. Maybe a piece of music. Maybe a composer. Maybe it's 'Sam Cooke.'*

He'd just sat back down on the bed and was holding her phone with his thumb poised to type if only he could decide on his next guess, when she reemerged from the bathroom. *Shit.*

She walked over to the bed and he tried to tuck the phone into the sheets.

"What's up?" Jillian asked, in response to his motion, the exhaustion in her voice coming through.

He almost shook his head, but instead flushed a bit and looked away. "Nothing." If he could have kicked himself, he would have. He looked at her again.

Jillian sat next to him and reached for his buried treasure. "What are you up to?" She asked, in a light tone, a near smile on her face. A near smile until her hand found the phone and slid it out to discover it was hers. "George?" She asked, as she flipped it over.

George's thoughts danced in a panicked fueled haze that looked for a defense for what he'd done. *I can't believe she caught me. Turn it around.* "Was Sergei here while I was away?"

"What?" Jillian asked, trying to wrap her head around the point of the question. "What does that have to do with my phone?"

George got up from the bed. "Was *anyone* here while I was away this weekend?"

"Yes," Jillian answered, still confused. "Yes, Sergei came over when Grec sent me stuff."

"You *needed* him, then?"

Jillian shook her head. "What? Yes. I needed him. You weren't here. I called Mal first. You said to call Sergei, so I called Sergei."

"Why didn't you tell me?" George asked.

"About what? About Grec?"

"Yes, Grec and Sergei. Why didn't you tell me?"

Jillian shifted and winced at the pain, but stayed focused on the conversation. "I didn't tell you because there was nothing you could do. The next time we talked, you were still in Washington, so what would have been the point? You'd just be mad. And then you were home, and I missed you so much and you'd missed me and it just didn't matter."

"You think I'd have been mad. Why?" George asked. "What happened that would make me mad?"

"Just Grec."

"Just Grec," George repeated. "But nothing to do with Sergei."

"No," Jillian said. "What are you driving at?"

George took a breath. "Nothing happened with Sergei?"

It wasn't a light bulb that went on in Jillian's head, it was hydrogen bomb. "Oh! You have got to be kidding me! You're not seriously standing there accusing me of cheating on you with Sergei!"

"And yet, I'm not hearing you deny it." George said.

"You honestly think that I'd do that?" Jillian closed her eyes and shook her head. "That's what's been bothering you all night." Jillian opened her eyes and then narrowed them at George. "I need you to leave. Right now."

"Are you going to deny it?" George asked.

"I'm so offended, I don't even want to talk to you."

"Then show me your phone," George said, and held out his hand.

"What? Why? No!"

"Just let me see it and show me that you and Sergei aren't..." *Lovers.*

"Have you lost your mind? Sergei and I are nothing. You *know* that. I would never do that to you." *How can you stand there and just accuse me of something like that?*

"Show me your phone."

"Why?"

"I know he's been texting you."

Oh. My. God. This irrational jealousy... I can't fight this! "You're insane!" Jillian struggled to her feet. "Leave."

"You can bet I'm leaving." George started to put on his clothes. "This is the last place I want to be. But I want to see what you two have been talking about." *Prove me right or prove me wrong. At least give me something. Deny it!*

"No," Jillian said. "This is nuts. I can't believe you've been here all night, taking care of me, and then this."

George tied his right shoe. "I can't believe you won't even deny it. If it's true, then admit it. If it's not, then deny it."

"George, if you can't tell that I'm denying it, you need your head examined!"

He tied his left shoe and stood up, pulling on his shirt. "Show me your phone!"

"No!"

He was buttoning his shirt and trying to think through the red haze that seemed to cover everything. It wasn't working. "If there's nothing to hide, then show it to me."

"Leave! Now!"

"Fine," George snapped and started shoving his things in his pockets. "Can't believe I'm still here."

"Neither can I," Jillian snapped back.

George picked up his bags and turned to Jillian. "One last chance, here, Jillian. Deny it and let me see your phone. We can put this behind us, if you just-"

"No! I am *not* going to show you my phone!" She followed him to the door. "But I will say this, George. I would *never* have cheated you. Ever!" She pushed him aside. After throwing the deadbolt open and yanking open the door, she gave him a bit of a shove as he walked out. "And when you get your head out of your, ahem, and realize what you've done and what you've said, don't bother calling me!" She slammed the door behind him and threw the deadbolt back to the locked position.

The reality of the fight hit Jillian when she woke with the alarm that was set early, so that, had George been there, they'd have had time for both of them to shower. It had been one thing to tell him to leave, but it was another entirely to wake up alone, even though her first thought after that brief, soulful one, was an angry one, which she clung to tightly.

The entire time she was in the shower, she repeated a question over and over to herself. "What did I *ever* do that he'd *dare* to think such a thing?"

All the same, breakfast was quiet. She called Charlie in to make it less lonely, grateful for him even more than usual. After breakfast, back in the bathroom, she brushed her teeth while she stared at George's toothbrush. When she finished, she picked up the spare and tossed it in the trash. "Gone." The spare glass found its way into the dishwasher.

"What else?" She asked herself, as she looked around the apartment. She'd wash her sheets that night to get rid of any scent he might have left on her pillow. There didn't seem to be much else. He was gone as easily as shutting the door. "Thank goodness."

The one thing left, of course, was the key. She'd have to take care of that at work. Carefully and quietly.

George's first brush with reality hit later. He stayed angry and awake all night, cursing at whatever he could come up with. He avoided her at the office as skillfully as he had weeks ago, until the meeting just before lunch, with Hardware. She walked into the room and sat quietly. For just a moment, he expected her to look at him and smile. And when she didn't, when her gaze passed over him the way it always had in the past, as if he were just wallpaper, he felt a sharp stab in his chest. *We're done.*

But the righteous indignation covered that up throughout the meeting. He was entirely in the right, after all.

As the participants filed out, he debated if he ought to say anything, try to forge some sort of truce. But Jillian cleared it up for him. She slipped him an envelope and disappeared, and with her went all the air in his lungs. He stuffed the envelope in his pocket, not bothering to open it, he knew what was inside. There was the odd chance that there was a note with it, but if there was, he didn't want to read it anyway.

He marched back to his office, passing Sergei and Neal on the way. He didn't dare stop because he knew that at some point he was going to hit Sergei, and doing so at work was probably not the wisest course of action. When Sergei yelled something after him about lunch, he just waved and kept going.

Back in his office, he opened his work bag and started looking for Ringo. Realizing quite suddenly that he hadn't been using the yo-yo hardly at all since he'd been seeing Jillian, gave him pause. The thought presented him with the question of why seeing Jillian would have caused such a change, but he shoved it aside as he finally found Ringo.

Out and back. Out and back. Loop it once and out and back. He felt better already. After a few more reps, he took the envelope out of his pocket and stuffed it in his bag. He'd put the key away tonight and try to get his life back to normal. Or, at least, as back to normal as it could be now that he had lost his girl and one of his best friends.

He shut his door and continued his yo-yo reps, determined not to think about anything. The thought occurred that he should just leave. Call it a half day and not be near any of the people he was trying not to think about.

The worst thoughts were the images of Sergei and Jillian together. They made him sick to his stomach and so angry he wanted to punch the wall.

And they just wouldn't stop.

Deciding the yo-yo wasn't helping, George tried to distract himself with work again. He sat down at his desk and opened his email. A knock sounded on his door and he screamed out, "What!?"

Rachel opened the door just a little. "Um, this came for you?" She held a fax in her hand.

"Well, bring it in," George said, with a frown. "What's the hesitation?"

"Oh, nothing," Rachel said, shaking her head over and over as she raced in, dropped the fax on his desk, and disappeared.

Jillian had been praising herself for acting normal until Irene, Ishi, and Rachel cornered her in the bathroom.

"What's going on?"

"Did something happen?"

"Are you and George in a fight?"

Jillian crossed her arms while she searched for the right words. As always, the simplest seemed to be the best. "We broke up." She pushed through the group only to be grabbed by several hands and pulled back.

"What happened?" "Why?" "You two were so happy."

"Ladies!" Jillian called. "Look. You all either work for me or work for him, so it's completely inappropriate to discuss this. We broke up. That's it. That's all."

Ishi snapped her gum. "Nope. What'd he do?"

"Oh, Ishi," Jillian started.

"Oh, nothing," Irene said, looking better then she had in days, flushed a little from the excitement. "You two were perfect together. Like you were made for each other."

Jillian shook her head. "Have you ever known two people who were made for each other? You know what happens? If two people stay together for their whole lives, then we say it was true. If they break up, then we suppose they weren't made for each other after all. It's like history... written after it's all over."

"Oh, dear. What *did* he do?" Rachel asked.

"Nothing," Jillian said, swallowing hard. "We broke up." *We broke up and that's it. Forever. It's done. We're done. Always and forever. Never again to...* She made a dash for the door, her heart pounding in her ears. *Hurry. Hurry. Hurry.* She raced to her office, grabbed her purse, work bag and laptop, coat, and shut off the lights and locked up. *Hurry. Hurry. Hurry.*

Down the stairs, quickly, quickly. She knew it was too late, but she moved through the first floor, doing her best to avoid anyone and started wiping her face only after she exited the building. She let herself cry for a few minutes in her car, finally stopping when she started to feel like she might choke and then did a little.

It was lunchtime, so she started the car and headed for the only place she could think to go.

By late afternoon, George figured the word must have gone around the way people were looking at him. *Well, what does it matter?* It didn't matter at all until Taro showed up. "Let's get a drink tonight. You look like you could use one."

George shook his head. "I could use about a hundred."

"Well, then, we better drink at your house. So all you have to do is crawl onto the couch to sleep."

George had already downed more scotch than he could calculate, and on an empty stomach, when the doorbell rang and Taro, who was significantly less impaired, went to answer it. George closed his eyes and leaned his head back on the couch, half-listening to whatever was on the television and half-listening to Taro.

"I don't think it's a good idea. You better go."

"You don't think it's a good idea? He's in bad shape, we're here to help."

It was Sergei. Probably Neal too, but Neal was uninteresting. Sergei on the other hand... Sergei *was* interesting. George got to his feet and started for the door, shouting, "Serge! Serge, is that you?"

"George!" Sergei shouted back. "Yep, it's me and Neal. We're here to cheer you up man."

"Excellent," George said, as he tripped but caught himself getting close to the door. "You are going to cheer me up. Cheer me up but good." George staggered closer and took a swing at Sergei.

Sergei didn't even have to move, George missed by so much. His momentum also took him off balance and he ended up on the floor.

"Oh, crap!" Taro shouted and moved to help George.

"What the fuck?" Sergei asked.

Neal set down the six pack, he'd brought with him, next to George and gave Taro a hand getting George into a sitting position on the floor.

"When I sober up," George said, pointing at Sergei, "I'm going to..." He stopped talking, swallowed really hard, and Taro grabbed a trash can.

"What in the fuck is going on?" Sergei asked Taro.

"He's a little loaded." Taro said.

"No shit," Neal said. "But why does he want to hit Sergei?"

Taro didn't answer; he took the nasty trashcan into the kitchen to clean it out. Neal took George's arm and helped him to his feet. "I hope that was worth it."

"I need to sit down," George said, wishing he'd known Sergei was going to show up so he could have been sober enough not to miss, but that was far from his only wish.

Neal got George to the sofa, Sergei following at a respectable distance.

The world was spinning, awfully fast. George put his hands over his eyes. "I haven't drunk like that since college."

"I bet you didn't drink like that in college, more than once, anyway," Neal said.

"Oh, fuck," George said, and attempted to get to the kitchen.

Taro sighed. "I'll get the mop. Shit, George. I thought you could hold your liquor better than this."

Neal moved George to the kitchen, positioning a chair next to the sink and putting George on it. "We'll get some food in you soon. How much did you drink?"

George had closed his eyes, when he opened them, the world spun again. "Too much." He leaned his head against the counter and debated asking for a bucket. The being drunk part was fine until the sick part. He'd had a few minutes were he hadn't thought about her at all, or the key that he'd thrown back in the drawer, or emptiness he'd felt in the house when he'd come home. He hadn't thought about how her laughter made the house feel even more like home or how hearing her moving around had made him feel so light inside he smiled. He hadn't thought about how she could make him feel calm, just by standing next to him and letting him rest his forehead against hers. He hadn't thought about how she slept or how she hummed to herself or the way she moved when she walked. He hadn't thought about the hole in his chest that should have caused him to bleed out by then.

But if it was going to happen, then it was for the best to have it happen sooner rather than later, and he could work on forgetting her. He had done his best to forget, and Taro had been helping, and then Sergei showed up and spoiled even that.

In the family room, Neal was talking, an awful lot for Neal. George tried to focus on what he was saying.

"You what?!" Neal's raised voice was much easier to hear in the kitchen.

"It was for his own good," Taro answered.

"How in the fuck was that for his own good?!" Sergei shouted. "What were you thinking?!"

There wasn't an answer, so George focused for a minute on getting up from the chair and getting a glass of water, planning to rinse out his mouth.

Neal walked into the kitchen and dug through George's pantry for some crackers. Then he pulled a chair around to face George. "How ya feeling?"

"The world is still spinning. Unfortunately, my brain isn't completely fogged in anymore." He debated trying a cracker. *Maybe not the worst idea.* He tried getting the saltine down.

"So, um, what happened with you and Jillian?" Neal asked.

George tried to quantify it and finally settled on, "She cheated on me, so we broke up." *Why? Why did she...? How could she...?*

Neal looked away from George and said, "I told you so," toward the family room. "Why'd you go after Serge?"

His stomach was turning again, so George gave up on the cracker. *May as well give it a few more minutes.* "Ask him. We're all *such good friends* here. I'm sure he'll tell you."

Sergei pushed Taro into the room. "We all want to hear it from the horse's mouth."

"What you all *still* seem to be missing is that he's much better off," Taro said.

George focused a little. "What is going on? I thought we were all getting wasted. Except for Serge, who's already a complete waste." *Not bad.* He snorted a laugh.

Neal sighed. "Taro, you tell him. Tell him *now.*"

"Maybe now isn't-"

Sergei gave Taro another shove. "Oh, I think now is just perfect." Taro didn't open his mouth again.

Neal shook his head and looked back at George. "Jillian didn't cheat on you, man. At least, she sure as anything didn't with Serge."

Yeah, right! George put his head on his hand and propped it up at the counter. After a shift and a twist, he looked at Sergei. "You were at her place. You've been texting her. You both kept it a secret. She wouldn't deny it. And she wouldn't let me see the texts. I don't think I'm far off the mark here."

Sergei moved a little closer, but not within arms' reach. "I don't know what went down between you and Jillian, what she did or didn't say. But I swear to you on my mother's life, I never touched her. I was over there as support, like you asked me to be, and that's it."

"Uh-huh," George said, and crossed his arms. "I suppose she needs more support and that's why you're texting her?"

Sergei looked at Neal and then Taro. Then he sighed and looked back at George. "Look, man. I know what it must look like, and the truth..." He looked at Neal again and then shook his head. "The truth is, after the other day, I've got a little bit of a crush on Jillian."

"Whoa!" "Oh, Hell!"

"What!?" George demanded, sat forward, wished he hadn't, and used the sink. Breathing heavily and slumped back in the chair, he pointed a wobbling finger at Sergei. "So, you never touched her, but you've got a crush on her?"

"It was never going anywhere, man. She's not sending out any signals that would give anybody the impression she's available. It was just... watching her tear into the guy. She was amazing. When she's not the frigging ice queen, she's... well, *you* know. Right?"

George managed to raise his eyebrows and Sergei launched into his story about helping out Jillian. "She was upset. She came home and her neighbor had taken a delivery of flowers for her."

"Flowers," George said. "The end of the world. She must have really *needed* you to deal with flowers."

Sergei snarled. "And when she opened them up, there was a diamond bracelet inside."

Nobody said anything that time.

"A big, damn diamond bracelet. And the neighbor didn't know the messenger service, so she couldn't just send it back. She had to *call* the asshole. And she needed somebody to support her through it.

"I held her hand then. Literally. She was so upset she got sick. In fact, she was sick twice while I was there. She isn't... knocked up, is she?"

"No," George said. "Definitely not." At least he could be grateful for that part, the clean break. No lingering worries in that department *this time*.

"Are you really sure? The timing-"

"She isn't!" George yelled and then sat back in the chair, wishing he hadn't exerted himself. The exhaustion from not sleeping and then being ill wasn't just catching up with him, it had overtaken him and he could barely see it off in the distance.

"Okay," Sergei said, holding up his hands. "She isn't. Whatever. So, anyway, the guy comes over and-"

"He came over?" George sat forward again. "To her apartment? He was there?"

"Yes," Sergei said. "So it was probably a good thing I was there too. She didn't enjoy the confrontation at all. He kept trying to tell her she was misunderstanding him."

Neal snorted. "Like there was anything to misconstrue!"

Sergei nodded. "I tried to be the delivery man for her. I told him to take the bracelet and get out. But he wouldn't hear me. Finally, Jillian snapped and started yelling at him. She was like a dragon, breathing fire everywhere. And after she backed him out the door, she threw the bracelet at him and told him to stuff it up his ass so the next time he was spewing crap out of his mouth he could shit diamonds too! Fucking brilliant!"

Neal was laughing lightly. George, not so much. "So then what happened?"

"We had a celebratory drink and I left."

"With a crush on *my girlfriend!*"

Sergei looked sheepish. "It's not like anything happened. Or was ever going to. I said it before. She didn't give off any signals that made me think I even had a prayer. It was just, seeing her like that, the real her, not the ice queen. I mean, George, I get it now. I get why you look at her like that. She's... the word amazing seems to fall short."

"I think we're getting off track here," Neal said, and George turned what he could of his focus to Neal.

"Huh?"

"Look, it was worth a few minutes for you to hear Sergei out. He says he didn't touch Jillian. He also vouches for her, which is more than he had to do. But it's time to look at the big picture. This paltry stuff doesn't matter. You need to sober up, call Jillian, apologize, and get back together."

George started laughing. "No. I don't think so."

"She makes you happy. Happier than I ever seen you. And that includes what's-her-name." He put his hand on George's shoulder. "I know Taro doesn't want to see this, but it's the real thing. I think you know it. You can't just let it go. Not when a few weeks from now, when it's too late, you'll be kicking yourself."

George shook his head. *The whole thing was a disaster from start to finish. Loss of sanity. Loss of control. Loss of dignity. Loss of... everything.*

"You're already drinking like a fish. Not acting like the George I know, at all." Neal patted his shoulder. "It may not be the most common thing between the four of us, but I know real heartbreak when I see it. This isn't just a matter of a break up. I know what you do when you're disappointed. That's basketball. This is over the top. It must be love."

"Ha!" George shouted. "Love! My three best friends are here to talk to me about love. Where's the ice cream? Let's share our feelings." He crossed his arms. "I don't love Jillian." *It's impossible to love someone who can do that to you.* "It was never going to work out, anyway."

Neal looked at Taro. "If you don't tell him, I will."

Taro looked at his shoes.

"What now?" George asked.

Neal got up and pushed Taro into the chair. "Speak."

Taro looked at Neal. "You heard him. He doesn't love her. It's all for the best. It was never going to work out, anyway."

Sergei placed a heavy hand on Taro's shoulder and pushed down. "You know, you didn't just do it to *him*. If you want any hope of avoiding a hospital tonight, you'll tell him."

"What!?" George shouted.

When Taro didn't speak, Neal did it for him. "He's been against you and Jillian from day one. After Sergei snagged your yo-yo and Jillian's keys, that first day-"

"You!" George moved toward Sergei, but Neal leaned over and pushed him back.

"It was just a joke," Sergei said, moving back a little. "I thought it would be funny. And, who knew? Maybe you'd both end up at Rachel's desk at the same time, and you'd look at each other, and the music would swell, and you'd be... I thought it would be funny."

Neal smacked Taro on the back. "But it wasn't. And somebody noticed just how badly you both took the prank."

George turned back to Taro. "Is he telling me that you're the one who played all those pranks on me and Jillian?"

Taro swallowed and looked away.

"The missing items, the *explosives*, the greased door knobs? You kept us apart for months, thinking the other... Why? Why would you do that? To hear this, everybody knew how I felt about her. Why?"

Taro spoke, but didn't meet George's eyes. "Because I knew she was trouble." He turned toward George. "And I was right. Look at you. You're a mess. And it's all because of her."

Neal put his hand on Taro's shoulder. "I think you pouring the drinks had something to do with the state he's in."

George was trying to focus. "You kept us apart. And then when we got together, you told me that she'd told Melissa she didn't love me. And then you told me about Sergei." *Oh, Hell.* "You were trying to break us up." *Oh, shiiiiit.*

"I was trying to show you the truth," Taro said. "She's not right for you. She's a nightmare. And look what's happened. You're going to lose your job. And she's gone anyway."

George leaned back again and closed his eyes. *Gone because I thought she...and then I said it. God. One friend trying to break up the best thing that ever happened to me and another wanting to be in my place. Fuuuuuck.* He opened his eyes toward the ceiling.

And one succeeded. I let him. I let him put all that crap in my head, so that even when she said she loved me, I didn't believe her... enough. So, the question is, did she mean it? Was it real? Did I just fuck up the best thing that ever happened to me? Am I sober enough to even know what the hell I'm thinking about?

Neal nudged him. "George." He handed George a small sheet of paper that he'd found sticking out between the couch cushions. "Whatever anybody said or didn't say, she loves you. You can work this out."

It was hard to focus on the slip of paper Neal had given him, but George put everything he had into deciphering what he was sure was Jillian's handwriting, just for a moment. *Loves me like I love him.* He swallowed. Whatever lingering doubt there might have been were erased. She hadn't been with anybody else. She didn't want anybody else. The proof was in his very hand. She loved him. Or at least, she *had* loved him.

"She didn't... and I..." George knew then he was still pretty drunk because he leaned forward, hunching over, and he started to cry.

"Oh, fuck," Sergei said, and jumped up. "Just relax, man." He slapped George on the back. "Sober up and then call her. Apologize. If she's tough, beg. Ask her to forgive you and take you back. It'll be okay."

The next morning, George was grateful for having been sick, since he wasn't dealing with a hangover. But that was about all he was grateful for. He tried to call Jillian once the night before, had gotten her voice mail, and left a message, "It's George. You were right. I'm an idiot and I'm sorry. Please call me and let me tell you just how sorry I am."

It wasn't particularly surprising that she didn't call him back. He figured she was pretty angry. She'd also told him *not* to call when he figured out what he'd done, but he'd had to try.

So he waited for her to come to work. It was unprofessional at best, but Neal kept telling him that an ambush was his best move and it had to happen somewhere and soon, and sooner was better.

But she didn't show.

She actually wasn't in the office at 9 am.

By 9:15 he went to Rachel's desk and asked if Jillian had called in. He smiled despite the scathing look Rachel gave him. Word had definitely gone around. He glanced down the row at Ishi who was looking at him with a scowl until he looked at her and she promptly turned her chair around. The women had certainly taken sides.

Rachel said, "I haven't heard from Jillian since yesterday. It's possible she called in to HR and they haven't notified me yet."

"Okay," George said. *Fuck!* "If she calls in, would you please tell her that I have a work related issue to discuss with her? It's rather urgent."

At 9:27, Rachel called George's work cell because he was on the roof, pacing, and not answering his desk phone. "Jillian is working from home today. She said to tell you to email her about any urgent matters."

"Okay, good. That'll work. She's at home," he said, mostly to himself, though it was out loud.

"I wouldn't bother," Rachel said.

"Wouldn't bother?" George asked, as if he didn't know what she was talking about, which was about half true.

"She said that she's not actually at home. She's elsewhere. But since she's off-site, 'working from home' was as good a description as any."

George sighed loudly. "Is it safe to assume this has to do with me?"

"She didn't share her state of mind, so I couldn't say," Rachel said.

"Right." George kicked at a chunk of roofing material. "Thank you."

"Of course," Rachel said, tightly and disconnected.

Just because she says she isn't at home, doesn't mean she isn't at home...

Thinking Jillian might anticipate him showing up at her door, he took lunch nearly an hour early, stopped for a sunny-looking, fall flower bouquet, and arrived at her apartment before the lunch hour would normally begin. If she planned to slip out to dodge him, she'd have to have anticipated his early arrival to make it work.

He knocked.

After a minute, he knocked again.

After another minute, he knocked again and called, "Jillian."

After another minute, he knocked and continued to knock while calling, "Jillian. I know you're mad. You deserve to be mad. I was an idiot. Please just allow me to beg for your forgiveness." Then he waited.

The door didn't open, but the one just down the hall did. Mrs. Kerchner stepped just slightly out of her door. "She isn't home. She took her cat with her this morning. She didn't say when she'd be back."

George took in a deep breath, let it out along with the drop of his head, and looked at his shoes. *She left. Okay, genius. What now?* He looked up at Mrs. Kerchner. "Hi. We haven't met. I'm George, the idiot that had a very big fight with Jillian on Monday night." He walked down the hall and held out his hand.

"I've seen you two together," she said, in a cautious tone, but then shook his hand.

"I suppose since you know her and not me, it'd be pointless my giving you my number and asking you to call if Jillian turns up."

"Well," Mrs. Kerchner stalled. "I think it would be a bit unfair for me to let you know without warning her. If she's gone because of this *big fight* then she probably wouldn't be too happy with me."

"Of course." George looked at the flowers and then held them out to her. "Please, enjoy these. If you see her, would let her know I came by?"

Mrs. Kerchner took the flowers. "Would you like to come in and talk?"

"No, thank you. That's very kind. I have to get back to work."

"Okay. Thank you for the flowers."

"My pleasure."

Neal saw George as he walked back in and joined him in his office. "Didn't go well?"

"Didn't go at all. She wasn't home." He dropped into his chair. "The neighbor lady says she left this morning and took the cat with her."

"And she's not answering her phone?"

"I only left the one message. Haven't called since. I've been trying not to make her think I'm stalking her or whatever."

Neal leaned against George's wall. "Last night, right? I think you could risk another call."

"I was figuring on waiting twenty-four hours."

Neal shrugged.

"I'm still hoping she'll calm down a little, miss me, and decide to call me back."

"How about a text?" Neal suggested. "Maybe just 'I'm sorry' and nothing else. Let her know you're thinking about her, but not demanding any kind of answer."

George tilted his head and thought about it. "Maybe. I just don't want her closing herself off further because I'm pushing too hard."

Neal crossed his arms. "For a man who was drunk and crying last night, you're being awfully calm."

"I'm not calm," George said. *I am so far from calm, it's ridiculous.* "I just don't think that showing everybody around here how *not calm* I am will help. If she talks to anybody and they report that I'm acting like a monster, she'll stay away."

"She might like it, if you're upset," Neal said.

"That's a good point. Upset, but not too upset." He leaned forward and rested his chin on his hands with his elbows wide on his desk. "I have to get her back, Neal." He dropped his forehead to his hands. "God. I miss her so fricking much. I miss just being near her. I have to get her back."

"I know."

"I wanted her back even when I thought..." *I didn't think it, but I felt it. I need her.*

"I know," Neal said.

"I just didn't think. I was so angry. And so... stupid."

Neal walked over to George and patted him on the shoulder. "I know."

George sat back up and took a breath. "I just have to..."

"You will," Neal said. "Think about the text. She might appreciate the irony."

That was an interesting point. Neal left and George started thinking about a text message.

Well, home, sweet home, I guess. Jillian turned the key in her lock and brought Charlie's carrier and her bags into her apartment with very little grace, grabbing the note taped to her door. The impromptu running away hadn't worked out, at all. She'd changed her mind with about five minutes left on the drive to her parents' house, realizing that she'd just have to explain. But by then, Charlie was very upset and she'd needed to work out a stop for him, so despite her then better judgment, she'd gone for a visit.

She'd been smart enough not to bring in her bags, just the necessities for Charlie. Not that her mom hadn't worked out that something was going on immediately, which Jillian confirmed by bursting into tears. They'd ended up eating ice cream in the kitchen while Jillian tried, and failed, not to cry anymore. Within an hour, Charlie was unhappy again and Jillian was ready to run back home after her mom started talking about auditions for the symphony.

After she closed the door and let Charlie loose, she opened the note in Mrs. Kerchner's writing and learned that George had been there around lunch time. Wadding up the note into a ball and tossing it into the kitchen trash, she started talking to Charlie to distract herself. "Need a treat, baby? I know I shouldn't have taken you to the sterile house. I know you hate it there. I'm so sorry."

A small portion of a can of tuna fish on a plate and Jillian knew she was forgiven. Knowing she couldn't avoid it, she set up her laptop and started checking her email. Most of it was either something she needn't reply to or something that simply needed acknowledgement. George had forwarded a few things to her, none of it urgent.

Between that, the phone message, and the lunch time near-visit, it was obvious that he'd lied to Rachel. Not surprising really. *He's actually not a bad liar.* Of course, she had him beat. She'd lied to herself for a year about him. *Hard to beat that.*

Then again, she supposed she'd done a bang up job over the last two weeks also. *Is it really lying when I didn't realize how bad a match we were? Chemistry, yes, amazing chemistry. But the rest…*

Malvinia's ring tone sounded out of her phone. *Thank God, she's finally available.* She grabbed the phone and answered it with, "Hi, Mal. George and I broke up."

The delay at the other end made Jillian wonder if Malvinia was surprised and looking of the right words, or just suppressing an 'I told you so.'

"Oh, Jills. I'm sorry," Malvinia finally said. "When? Why?"

"Two days ago and because it didn't work out."

"Two days and I'm just hearing about it? Oh, Jills. How are you doing?"

"Well," Jillian considered her answer. "I spent last night getting him completely out of my apartment. Then, I ran away from home today and went to my parents.'"

"Is that where you are now?"

"Nope. I ran away from there too and ended up back where I started." She moved into the living room, flipping on the television to make some noise in the apartment. The apartment was feeling a little … *cold? Charlie's here, so it isn't lonely.* Besides, she'd done lonely. He'd been gone for a few days and she *missed* him. That was *lonely*. She needed to get on with the grieving so it would be over with sooner.

"Do you need company?"

"Need it? No. Welcome it? Definitely." She changed the channel to the classic movies.

"Okay. I can't be there for... probably another two hours." Jillian pictured Mal looking at her watch. "I have to revisit some charts before I sign out."

"No biggie. I'm not going anywhere. And, don't feel obligated."

Mal let out a strangled laugh. "Yeah. No worries, Jills. It's not obligation. Just don't do anything rash before I get there. I'll bring ice cream, so don't go cleaning out your freezer."

"I've already had ice cream with my Mom. It was very cathartic until she changed the subject to the symphony."

"Ah, your mom. One track mind, that woman. Oh, well, then, since you're over your limit, the ice cream is for me. See you as soon as I can make it."

"Thanks, Mal. See you later."

And then it was her in the empty apartment again. She corrected herself that Charlie was there, so it wasn't empty. After pouring herself a glass of wine, she walked around her apartment reminding herself of all the things she loved about it. *Maybe it doesn't have a tub with jets. But, it's still great. Maybe it doesn't have a dozen rooms. But, it's just the right size for Charlie and me. Maybe it doesn't sit on a lovely, little street. But, it's close to work. Maybe...*

She sat down on her bed. *Who cares about the where, it's about who isn't here.* No. No. NO. "Maybe I don't miss him. Maybe I just got used to having him around. Maybe... Maybe..." She dropped back on the bed and looked at her ceiling. "I know I'm better off without him. Much better off. He doesn't trust me at all. Maybe..."

Her phone chirped a text message with George's ringtone. She debated a moment and then looked at it. *I'm sorry.*

The phone's messenger was setup so that to read the text, it opened the screen so it was ready for a reply. It also showed contact pictures. She'd cropped one of the pictures he'd taken and made it George's image. Looking at the picture, she could almost hear him saying it. *I'm sorry.*

Well... she certainly was sorry. She thumbed back. *Me too.*

Her phone rang and she closed her eyes. "No." She slid her thumb to reject the call and put the phone down. "That would be a bad idea. I never should have answered him in the first place."

A new text made her phone chirp. *A wise woman would ignore it, just like she ignored the phone call.*

Jillian decided that between being wise and being curious, she hadn't a prayer, and picked up her phone.

Please take my call.

"Ugh," she said, and sat back up. "No, George." She thought a bit and then thumbed the most concise reply she could think of. *We broke up.*

She dropped the phone on the bed and stared at her ceiling. It was nice ceiling. A little blah, but nice. No cracks or anything. And it didn't have that awful popcorn stuff to hide the imperfections either. It was the same ceiling she'd been looking at for, how many years? She actually wasn't sure. *Maybe it's time to move. And go where? To another apartment? To another city? Somewhere I don't think of him no matter where I look including when I stare at the ceiling. Somewhere I don't think 'he was sitting there, in that very spot, just a few days ago.'*

Her phone chirped and she closed her eyes. *Go away, George! I'm not playing this game with you.* Charlie hopped up on the bed and plopped down where George had been sleeping. *That's better. The bed isn't empty.* "Hi, Charlie baby." She reached over and scratched behind his ears.

The phone chirped again and Charlie's head whipped around to stare at it.

"That's nothing but trouble, baby. Ignore it. Want me to shut it off?"

Charlie looked at her for a moment, then away and closed his eyes, as he started to purr. The phone chirped again and he looked at it with disdain.

"I'll shut it off."

She picked up her phone and tried not to glance at the texts, but she couldn't stop herself.

We had a fight. That doesn't have to mean we broke up.

Even if we did break up, does that mean we can't talk? Make-up maybe?

As she pressed the button to shut off the phone, the last text started a repeating loop in her head and instead of shutting off the phone she pulled it tight against her chest.

Please talk to me. I love you.

"Oh, stop," she said to herself, and the words echoed in her head. *I love you. I love you. I love you.* And she knew his voice, knew his voice saying those words, over and over like he had so many times just a few nights before. She heard them echoing in *his* voice.

"Oh, George, I love you, too. But this just isn't going to work. I can't be with anyone who thinks I'm capable of such a betrayal." *Even if he doesn't think so anymore. Even if he's sorry. He believed it. He truly believed it.* Her chest started to throb again, and she pulled in her knees and felt the lump in her throat start to grow and her eyes start to water. *Oh, why do I have to love you?* She fought the tears just like she fought the tightness in her chest. *Why does it have to hurt so much?*

Jillian's phone rang again, Malvinia's ringtone. Jillian picked up the phone with a shaky hand. "Ha-ha-ha-hi."

"Oh, boy. You crying, Jills?"

"Na-na-na-no."

"I'm sorry, but I need you to pull yourself together. Lacey was in a car accident."

CHAPTER TWENTY-EIGHT

"Wha-a-a-t?" Jillian asked.

"Lacey's hurt. She's here. I don't know anything much yet, except she went into a trauma room and the staff is top-notch. But, you should come down here. I was just about to call Kai and Christy. Maybe you should call Kai and get a ride with her, since you're upset."

"Oh-ho-ho-okay."

"Jillian, you're going to be okay. Come down here and once we know Lacey is going to be okay, we can talk about the situation with George."

"I-I-I-I don't wa-a-a-ant to talk abo-ou-out Geo-or-orge. I-I-I-I'll call Kai."

Malvinia said goodbye and they disconnected. Jillian dialed Kai and wiped her eyes, hoping to be able to speak a little. She managed to get out the important information and while Kai agreed to pick her up, she was still at the office which was close to hospital. Jillian told Kai to go straight there and that she'd get a cab.

She went into her bathroom to try to fix her face and only ended up sitting on the floor crying for a few minutes. *Nowhere in this apartment is safe. He's in here too. Even when he's not. Even with the stuff gone. He's here.* Giving up on looking better, she grabbed the sink to haul herself up and went around her apartment grabbing her purse and phone. She started dialing for a cab on her way out the door.

The early experience at the hospital was much like the few other experiences Jillian had had, lots of waiting and wondering and worrying, followed by more waiting and wondering and worrying. But Jillian's day did improve in a way. When Christy arrived, there were hugs, all around. A few minutes later she whispered to Malvinia, "I think Christy and I are friends again."

Malvinia whispered back, "Forgiveness does more for the soul than any doctor can do for the body." Then she left Jillian to go make more inquiries into how Lacey was doing.

Jillian took a seat and closed her eyes, trying not to think. She didn't want to think about Lacey. She didn't want to think about George. And both of them were vying for her attention, though on different levels. She was even trying not to think about Christy because, of course, that brought up George.

Kai had reacted to Lacey's situation in a way that Jillian couldn't have, but probably should have, anticipated, she had only been off her phone for a few minutes since she'd arrived, whenever Malvinia had a report. Otherwise, she was on her phone with the police and with insurance and obviously others, using her attorney's status to get answers and make things happen. An hour or so in, she had announced that the police had taken the other driver into custody. She was speaking all kinds of lawyer-ese that Jillian couldn't follow but it was evident that she was on top of whatever was going on and planning to see the man punished to the fullest extent the law allowed.

Jillian kept waiting for Malvinia to do the same, but apparently there were reasons for her not to. Other doctors were more qualified and there were some ethical concerns about Lacey being a friend also. But that didn't keep her from pestering and, in some cases, badgering the staff. She was also the one communicating with Lacey's parents, who were on their way.

That left Christy and Jillian doing nothing but sitting and thinking. Jillian debated telling Christy about the breakup. She couldn't convince herself to, though, afraid that it would re-open their sore spot and perhaps cause a rift again. The old one wasn't even completely closed up yet. But, at least, they sat together, worrying together, and even grasping each other's hands whenever Malvinia came back and might have been bringing news.

George knew he was driving Orville nuts, but he couldn't quite get himself in the game. Orville held out a lot longer than George would have expected, probably sensing that whatever was wrong wasn't something George wanted to talk about.

Orville won the fourth race and he set down his controller. "Alright. What's wrong?"

George held onto his controller, but leaned back on the couch. He delayed a bit, trying to figure out what to say and how to say it. Finally, he summed it up and said with a sigh, "I messed up and Jillian broke up with me."

"*She* broke up with *you*," Orville repeated. "After what I saw the other night, you must've messed up pretty bad."

"Yeah," George said, and slid down the sofa a little. "Really bad."

"So..."

"So, what?"

"So, is it really done?" Orville asked.

"I don't know," George said. "I've been trying to talk to her, but she won't take my calls, she wasn't home when I tried to do it in person. She answered two texts, but not exactly positively. Then nothing."

Orville tapped his hand on his thigh a few times. "You want her back?"

"*Yes.*"

"What'd you do wrong?"

George slid further down the couch and crossed his arms. "I, uh..." He looked at Orville and then looked away. "I thought she'd..."

"What?" Orville asked.

"I thought she cheated on me, and I, uh, didn't exactly handle it well."

Orville took a really deep breath. "You *thought* she cheated on you?"

"I had what seemed like a good reason, at the time." *The middle of the night when I do all my best thinking.* George forced himself to meet Orville's eyes. "I was wrong. And I handled it wrong. And we had a fight. And it was bad. And it turned into a break up."

"So, she'd didn't break up with you. You broke up with each other."

"Does it matter?" George asked, looking away.

"It might," Orville said. "If it was a mutual decision, in the heat of the moment, then maybe she regrets it too."

"Well, she isn't talking to me. And one of her two reply texts said specifically that we broke up. I don't think she's regretting it."

Orville patted George's leg. "Give me five minutes, Kid." He stood up and started shuffling out of the room. A few minutes later he returned with Delaney, Sully, Martin, and Mac. George had met them all before, but had only spoken often with Delaney.

"Okay, kid. You've got over two hundred years' experience dealing with women here. Tell us what happened, in detail, and we'll see if we can't help."

"The trauma team has downgraded her from critical to serious but stable. It looks like she needs more surgery."

Jillian took a breath. "*More* surgery? I thought she was in a trauma room."

"She's stable enough to move to an OR. Technically, she's had surgery," Malvinia said. "But even with the critical status, her prognosis is good if they can-"

"Stop!" Christy said. "Please. I don't think I can take the details. Just tell me this, at the moment is she in good hands? And when will we know something?"

Malvinia put her hands on hips with her mouth open, but then sighed and dropped her hands. "She's got excellent doctors and we'll probably know something in about two hours."

"Two hours?!" Kai nearly shouted. "How can it take so long to know something?"

"Because, it's bad," Jillian said. "There's no point in telling us anything until it's either better or worse." She stood up. "Now, there's no use thinking about the worse, let's just calm down and think about the better. If it's going to be a while until we know something, why don't we all go to the cafeteria and get coffee."

Christy nodded. "Honestly, I could do with some walking, more than anything. But, I can try coffee."

"They have my pager," Malvinia said. "Let's go across the street and get Starbucks."

"Are you sure that's a good idea?" Kai asked. "Shouldn't we be here?"

Malvinia sighed again. "There's nothing I can do here Kai, so there's certainly nothing you can do. Her parents can reach us. The team on her case can reach us. We won't go far."

After a few seconds, Kai nodded and they all grabbed their things and took a walk to the Starbucks.

George's message tone chirped on Jillian's phone while they were in line. *Now is not a good time.*

When they sat down with their drinks, the phone chirped again. *Not now.*

It was Christy who asked her why she wasn't checking her text messages and suddenly the conversation went from worrying about Lacey, whom they could do nothing about, to dissecting Jillian's life, which apparently, they all felt they *could* do something about.

Perhaps it was her trial experience, or perhaps it was her natural demeanor and that had pushed her into the career, but Kai did a wonderful job pulling information out of Jillian. Several times Jillian plead the fifth, but her friends didn't stand for it. More poking and prodding, direct questioning, and cajoling and soon they knew Jillian's story.

"I don't understand," Kai said. "If you love him, why aren't you talking to him? I mean, I understand his offense. And I certainly see that punishment is appealing and even justified. But, aren't you just punishing yourself?"

"We broke up," Jillian said.

"There's no law that says you can't get back together," Kai said.

Malvinia shook her head. "That's true, but if he's got a severe jealousy problem, then maybe she's right."

"Why do you do that?" Jillian asked Malvinia.

"What?"

"Talk about me in the third person, like I'm not here. I..." *I hate that.* "I really don't like it."

"Oh," Malvinia said. "I didn't realize I was. I'm sorry."

"Thank you," Jillian said. "Now, anyone who wants to give me their two cents, go ahead. But *I* don't want to talk about this right now."

Christy set down her cup. "At least check his messages."

Jillian looked at Christy and raised her eyebrows.

"Oh, come on." Christy shook her head. "You're crazy about him. And it sounds like he's crazy about you. Kai's right, you're punishing yourself. What do you blame yourself for, that you're keeping him away when he's apologizing? Why can't you talk to him? Why *won't* you talk to him?"

Jillian didn't have an answer she wanted to share beyond, "I don't want to get back together with him. Isn't that enough?"

"No," Kai said.

Christy shook her head. "Not if there isn't a reason. That is, beyond the obvious reason."

"And what's the obvious reason?" Jillian asked.

"You're scared," Christy said. "He hurt you and now you're retreating into your shell, so he can't ever do it again."

Jillian looked at Malvinia. "You're on my side, aren't you?"

"There are sides?" Malvinia asked.

Jillian looked around the table. "I'm finished with him. How hard is that to understand? And, no, my reasons beyond his accusing me of cheating on him, aren't any of your business."

Christy picked up her coffee. "So, does that mean I *could* give him a call?"

"Don't even think about it!" Jillian slammed down her cup.

Christy looked smug. "You've got a jealousy problem too."

Jillian crossed her arms and glared at Christy.

"Oh, please. Like I'd ever do that! But, clearly you've still got possession. In your heart, if not your mind. And frankly, I'd say it's in your mind too." Christy poked Jillian's bag. "Read the texts. One of them may well say whatever it is you want to hear, allow you to change your mind, and be happy again."

Kai chimed in again. "You know, if you're really finished with him then there's no reason *not* to read the texts. They won't change anything."

Jillian looked at Malvinia. "Oh, Jills. Don't look at me. I'm behind you completely with whatever you do. But, I agree that there can't be any harm in reading some texts."

"If I do, will you all let this go? And *not* ask me what they say?" Jillian asked.

Kai took a sip of her latte and looked away. Tapping her fingers on the table, Christy slowly nodded her head. "If it'll make you read them, I can *try* to not bother you."

"Fine," Jillian took out her phone and set it on the table. "You know..."

Malvinia picked up the phone. "Enough. I'm going to guess your lock code." She pushed the button and Jillian made a grab for the phone. Malvinia handed it to Kai. "Look at that."

Kai sighed. "Really, Jillian. This is what you're giving up?" She turned the phone around and Christy was able to get a peek at the lock picture too.

"Actually, *he* gave it up first," Jillian said. *How can you all be on* his *side?*

"Wow. You guys definitely look like you're in love. That is a really sweet picture," Christy said. "When was that taken?"

Jillian snagged her phone back from Kai. "On our first date. That's why we look happy. Neither of us knew just how bad it was going to get."

"Look at the texts!" Kai said.

"Fine," Jillian said, and typed in her passcode. That was something she'd forgotten about that needed changing, her passcode. Her message app was already open and all she had to do was look.

You are the best thing that ever happened to me. You don't have to forgive me. Just, please, let me apologize.

The lump in Jillian's throat was back. She re-locked her phone. "I can't do this, especially right now. Lacey..."

"Lacey," Malvinia said, "is getting the best possible care. She's not an excuse right now. What did he say?"

"Just asking me to talk to him again. He says I don't have to forgive him, but he wants to apologize."

"Call him," Kai said.

"Now?" Jillian asked. "We could get a page about Lacey-"

"Call him," Christy said.

Malvinia leaned over and said, in a hushed tone, "You don't have to hear him out this minute. Call him and make a date to talk. Maybe tomorrow, after all of this settles."

"I can't believe you all," Jillian stood up and gathered her things. "You're really, truly on his side. He accused me of sleeping with his best friend! I can't believe you. I'll see you back in the waiting room."

Malvinia sent a text to Jillian's phone. It was unfair and irritating. But Jillian unlocked her phone and quickly exited her app so she could re-open it and see Malvinia's text without reading the other one that George had sent. Malvinia's text was short and simple and a little rude, telling her to go up to the fourth floor surgical waiting room when she'd calmed down.

She took a short walk around the block, hoping for something, anything, to change. *Of course, they're right.* She could let George apologize, if that gave him the closure he needed. The problem with that was then they'd be in the same room. And she'd have to fight with herself, between her sense and her idiotic emotions, not to get back together with him.

Taking a second lap seemed to help and then she walked faster for a third. After that, she decided to go up to the surgical waiting room. None of the girls were there yet. That gave her another minute to think on her own. She looked at the remaining text from George.

Just five minutes and then I'll leave you alone.

Jillian locked her phone and looked at the picture of the two of them that she still hadn't replaced. *Five minutes, five hours, five seconds, any amount of time with him is dangerous.*

George turned his bedroom upside-down, then his laundry room. He still couldn't seem to find the slip of paper. It was a desperate move, and probably a bad one, that he was hoping to make. It was Delaney's idea, though it had been seconded by everybody, but Orville.

Orville's reticence had made George wonder if it was actually a mistake or not, but the one thing all the men agreed on was that George was in need of a co-conspirator. And the co-conspirator needed to be on the inside of Jillian's circle. The first suggestion had been her parents, but since her relationship with them was tenuous, George hadn't leapt at the idea.

He began looking through his family room, hoping the piece of paper would be somewhere. He didn't know, or at least, didn't remember, the last names of Jillian's friends. Finding Christy's note was his best shot.

It turned up at the very bottom of his work bag and George sat down on his sofa with the paper in his hand and worked on his script. He had little doubt it was going to be tense and awkward. He shifted to take his phone out of his holster and picked up another slip of paper he'd placed on the coffee table.

For extra courage, George read the list again. He even liked the lettering she'd used to write his name at the top. Even just the one additional read through made him choke. *Loves me like I love him. Honest. Loyal.* The exception for yo-yos would have given him a smile, if he hadn't screwed up so bad.

I have to get her back.

He looked at his phone and then the slip of paper. *Fuck it.*

He dialed the phone and when the female voice answered he just launched into it. "Christy, please don't hang up. This is George Crewes, Jillian's..." He didn't know what to say other than 'ex' and he couldn't bring himself to say it. *I suppose Jillian's is an adequate description all by itself.*

"Well," she answered, "this is a surprise."

"Thank you for not hanging up. I assume you know about Jillian and I and our fight."

"Yes, I do."

George cleared his throat. "All right, then. I'll be brief. I've been trying to get in touch with her, to apologize." *And, maybe, possibly, hopefully, get back together.* "She's rightfully very angry with me. I messed up. I really messed up. And she won't take my calls."

"Uh-huh," Christy said.

"So, I, um… I'm calling to ask for help. Nothing too big! Just… All I want is five minutes, in person. Just to apologize. If, after that, she wants nothing to do with me, then I'll accept it. I'll leave her alone. But, I can't find her. Will you help me? Please?" He looked at Jillian's checklist and the hearts drawn on it. *We can work this out. She really loves me and I love her.*

There was a delay, but not too long.

"Now isn't really a good time. One of my friends was in a really bad car accident and I'm at the hospital with our other friends, waiting for her to come out of surgery. And after that, if all goes well, we'll probably all be waiting in the ICU area."

George had to fight for breath, so much information had been imparted in those few words, both bad and good. He focused on the bad first. "I'm so sorry. Who's hurt?"

"My friend, Lacey."

"I'm sorry to hear that," George said, exhaling in relief but also in sadness.

"Thank you."

"May I assume Jillian is there?" George asked, focusing on the good.

"Yes," Christy answered.

"And, she'll probably be there, with you all, for a while."

"I should think so."

George took another breath. "Obviously, now is a bad time for me to talk to her."

"Probably," Christy said.

"But, she's there."

"Correct."

It was time to be grateful. "Thank you, so much. I really can't thank you enough."

"Of course. Goodbye." Christy disconnected.

It didn't matter that she'd been somewhat abrupt, Christy had been immeasurably helpful and now he owed her. He'd finally caught a break.

"They've moved her to the ICU," Malvinia was telling Lacey's parents on her phone when Jillian looked up, expecting to see a doctor or perhaps a nurse entering the waiting area. She did a double take.

"Neal?" And it *was* Neal.

"Hi, Jillian," Neal said, and walked over to her, carrying a bag and holding out some flowers. "These are for your friend, though I expect you can't take them into the ICU."

"Well," Jillian said, trying to buy a little time as her mind tried to make sense of his presence. "That's very thoughtful. I don't... quite understand what you're doing here." She took the flowers and put them on a table.

"I'm an emissary," Neal said to Jillian's back, and Jillian closed her eyes a moment.

"Of course, you are," she said, and then turned back to face Neal. "I can't say I'm not surprised. How did...?"

"Word got around. I want you to know that, personally, I'm very sorry to hear about your friend. How is she?"

Jillian looked over Neal's shoulder at Malvinia, who answered, "All things considered, it's actually looking pretty good right now."

"I sincerely hope that she fully recovers," Neal said to the entire room. Returning his attention to Jillian, Neal went on. "Now, I know this isn't the time, and more importantly, *he* knows it isn't the time, so don't worry. He's not going to show up here."

Jillian nodded and crossed her arms. *Funny how we all know who we're talking about without using any names. Oh! I almost wish he would show up. I could use a shoulder to cry on. But half the reason I want to cry has to do with him, so thank goodness.*

"But he did send this," Neal held out an envelope. It wasn't anything like the envelope Grec's messages had come in. It was a simple, plain letter envelope, not stationery. Its simplicity was appealing all by itself. "He asked me to give it to you in person, and, if you weren't in so much distress about your friend that it was asking too much, to see if you'd read it and perhaps give a reply. I'm promised that it doesn't contain a plea to take him back." Neal looked at the envelope and then back at Jillian. "Though, I think it should. But he said that would upset you and he didn't want to be a burden to you."

"But he's sent you to guilt me into reading this," Jillian said, and released one arm to take the envelope.

"No," Neal said, with more certainty than she'd ever heard from him. "He sent me because he was worried that just the sight of him would be upsetting and you've had enough to upset you. He sent me because he cares. I've secondary instructions, that if you refuse to read it, I'm not to push you or prod you at all. I'm to go quietly and not make you feel any worse."

"Oh," Jillian said. "I see."

"That's sort of sweet," Christy said.

"Sort of?" Neal asked, and turned toward her.

"Well, he's still pushing his way in," she said. "He's trying to claim to be polite about it."

Neal put his hands on his hips. "People do lots of things when they're in love."

"I suppose that's an excuse," Christy said.

Neal took a step toward her and then back. "Don't get your undies in a twist; I'll go if that's what she wants." He looked at Jillian again. "I think he means it. That I'm not to be a pest." He opened the bag and pulled out a small stuffed penguin. "Sorry, I almost forgot this goes with the note."

"A penguin?" Kai asked.

"Don't ask me," Neal said to Kai. "He said, she'd know." He returned his attention to Jillian. "Should I go? Or wait to see if there's a reply?"

Jillian turned the penguin over once. "Give a minute to think, would you, Neal?"

"Sure. I'll wait in the hall."

"What's the story?" Kai asked, walking over to look at the penguin.

"I don't know. But, I probably should." It had all the hallmarks of a George mystery, just like the note cards. Something she should understand, but didn't. Maybe it was meant to arouse her curiosity?

Malvinia joined them. "Oh! It's Happy Feet!" When Kai and Jillian looked at her. "What? I've got nieces. That was a cute movie about a tap dancing penguin."

Jillian smiled. "A tap dancing penguin. I *should* have known."

Christy meandered over to the group. "So, what's the story, Jillian?"

"It was silly. An IM conversation that got out of hand. Some flirting about him wanting to be in my office and I told him my office was boring and he said, he could make it interesting and asked what I wanted. A bit of... innuendo about it."

"And you wanted a tap dancing penguin?"

"No," Jillian said, and lightly petted the stuffed penguin. "I told him I wanted a three ring circus. He didn't reply for a bit. I thought I'd been too weird or something for him. Then suddenly he's telling me that he may have overpromised and that the best he'd been able to do was a tap dancing penguin. That Disney has loads of them."

Kai grinned and Malvinia did too.

"Okay," Christy said. "Now *that's* sweet."

"It is, isn't it?" Jillian started fighting the smile. "But that's neither here nor there." She held up the envelope in her other hand. "I suppose you all want me to read this."

"How bad can it be?" Kai asked.

Christy nodded. "He did go to a bit of trouble... Found the perfect little stuffed animal..."

Jillian looked at Malvinia. "Mal?"

"Whatever you want, Jills. I think Kai's right. It can't be that bad. We know he's contrite, so it isn't going to be putting anything more onto *you*. And it sounds like he really did tell his friend to leave, if you refused."

She petted the little penguin one more time, then set it on the table near the flowers, freeing up her hands. "All right, then," she said to herself. *How bad can it be?*

Jillian opened the envelope and extracted a letter. As she opened it, two small sheets of paper fell out and onto the floor. She retrieved them quickly, not wanting to give her friends a chance to see before she'd had a chance herself. The first, she recognized. Her list! She must have dropped it somewhere and he'd found it.

The second, another list, but in George's handwriting. Her name was at the top. Some of her thoughts were echoed in this list and some weren't. He'd traded her 'Romantic' for 'Loving' and 'Wide variety of musical tastes' for 'Courageous,' both of which made her eyes water. He'd also swapped her 'no yo-yos' line for 'Patient, especially about my eccentric hobbies.'

Next to 'Loyal' he'd written in bold letters, 'Truer than the day is long' and placed an asterisk next to it.

She scanned down the paper again looking for another asterisk, and then flipped it over. The asterisk was on the back with *Silhouettes by The Rays* next to it. Uncertain what it meant, she pulled out her phone and googled it. She clicked on the link for the song lyrics and read through them, recognizing the song made popular by a doo wop group in the late 50's. It was a story of a man who was passing by his girlfriend's home and saw silhouettes on the curtains that appeared to be her with another man. He embarrasses himself at the door as he finds out it's not even her house. Then he rushes to her side, hoping for the rest of their days to be together as two silhouettes on the curtains.

Thinking that, if nothing else, he really knew her heart strings, she slipped the lists back into the envelope and then opened the letter.

My Dearest Jillian,

I know I haven't any right to make any demands on you. I gave up any rights I might have had when I accused you of something that we both know isn't in your character. But my heart refuses to listen to reason. And it aches for so many reasons that I can't begin to list them all. Perhaps that's a good thing, as these are my burden and not yours and it would be beneath either of us if I were to parade them in front of you.

But there is one that I can't let go unaddressed. It's the worst one and I'll carry it with me forever. I've hurt you.

Now is certainly not the right time to discuss this, which is I why I've asked Neal to act as a go-between, afraid that I'd lose my resolve to be patient the moment I saw you, like you did that night at the basketball game. So I've taken pen to paper to plead that you will give me just five minutes to allow me to properly apologize in person. If, after that, you should tell me you never want to see or hear from me again, I'll abide by your wishes.

Again, I know that right now is not the time, so I'll hope that you'll agree to see me and name the time that is appropriate and place and that it is soon. Of course, if you can't stomach the idea of five minutes, then it's my own fault and I'll understand. Simply tell Neal your answer and consider the matter tabled temporarily or closed, as you see fit.

Thank you for reading this. You truly are an amazing person and I'm grateful to have had the opportunity to get to know you and to fall in love with you. I'll always remember you as a bright light warming my heart.

Yours, with all my love, always,

George

Jillian slowly refolded the letter and began to slide it back in the envelope.

"Well?" Malvinia asked.

"It's a beautiful letter," Jillian said, and tried to contain herself. *Beautiful was hardly the word. It was poetic and sweet and charming and... so... amazing... by George.* She stood up and took a blurry walk to the doorway. There really wasn't any choice. Not after that. "Neal?"

"Yes?" He returned to the doorway.

"No reply," Jillian started.

Neal cut her off, "No?! Are you sure?"

Jillian smiled slightly, just the very corners of her mouth turning up. "I meant to say, I'll handle it myself."

Neal reached out, but just stopped short of grabbing her arms, and said, "You're going to call him? Or text him? Or something?"

"Mm-hmm," Jillian said, and nodded.

"Oh, bless you," Neal said, with a broad smile and dropped his arms. "Okay, then. I'm off." He leaned to see around her and into the waiting room. "I hope your friend is in for a speedy recovery. Good-bye, ladies."

They all waved and said good-bye. Jillian re-entered the room with a nurse on her heels who took Malvinia out of the room to talk more medical terms.

"I just can't believe..." Jillian wasn't even sure what she meant to say. She tucked the envelope into her purse and pulled out her phone.

"So, that wasn't really much news," Malvinia said, as she returned. "She's still stable. Hopefully healing. I think her parents are due in about two hours."

There was a chorus of positive sentiment and then they all took a chair near them. "I hate waiting," Christy said. "When will they know something new to tell us?"

"Well," Malvinia said, "by morning, they'll probably know more."

"Morning?" Christy asked.

Malvinia sat forward. "The human body is remarkable, but it doesn't heal that fast. I'm hoping she's out of the ICU tomorrow."

Jillian rubbed her face. "That would be a relief."

"Yes," Malvinia said. "Now, I'm thinking we should eat in shifts. Just in case her parents are early. Or, if there's news." She shifted in her chair. "Who wants to eat?"

"I think you should, Mal," Christy said. "You'd already put in a full day when Lacey came in. Take a break. And take Jillian with you. She needs to catch her breath and then make a phone call. Or the other way around, if she can manage it."

Jillian smiled at Christy and mouthed 'thank you' to her. Christy returned the smile and held up her hand, her thumb to her ear and pinky to her mouth, with her remaining fingers curled up and then mouthed 'call him.' Jillian nodded.

Having chosen a somewhat noisy sandwich shop nearby for their dinner, Jillian debated texting George, rather than calling, but Malvinia balked and told Jillian to find a quiet place and she'd order for them. *That will be better.*

Jillian stepped back outside and pulled her coat tight around her. Just a few hours ago, she'd rejected his call. A few steadying breaths and she pulled up George's contact and selected the call button.

CHAPTER TWENTY-NINE

He answered before the second ring. "Jillian."

"Hi," she said, quietly, uncertain of what to say.

"Hi," he said. "I'm so glad you called."

Jillian started pacing. "The letter... *your* letter... was pretty moving."

"I meant every word."

"Good," Jillian said, and tried to figure out what should come next.

"So, how is Lacey?"

"I don't know, really. Mal got Lacey's parents to have the hospital release information to her, but it's all pretty technical. I followed the part about a broken leg. But the other internal stuff is over my head. And Christy's pretty squeamish, so nobody has asked Mal to dumb it down. But, she thinks she might be out of the ICU tomorrow. That sounds good."

"It does sound good. I'm glad to hear it," George said. After a few seconds of silence, he went on. "So, I'm given to think that this call means I can have five minutes of your time, in person. I hope?"

"Yes, George. You can have five minutes." She bit her lip and then committed to a decision. "You can have more than five minutes."

"I can? That's fantastic. Not to pressure you, but when do you think the more than five minutes might be able to happen? Tomorrow?"

"I don't know about tomorrow. I need to be here for Lacey and her family. And you have a game, don't you?"

"Right. Right. Of course. But, um, *if* she's out of ICU, then maybe you'd have a little time. Maybe after the game, if not before. I'll come to you, of course. Or we can meet somewhere public. Whatever you want."

Jillian sighed. "Look, I don't want to make a plan and then have to disappoint you if I can't make it."

"We could say it's a soft plan. And you could let me know if it's working out or not."

"Wouldn't it be easier to just say that we'll do this on Friday?"

George was quiet again. "If that's what you want."

Jillian closed her eyes. "It's not that I want to put this off." *Or maybe I do. Maybe Christy was right that I'm scared. What will happen here? He'll say he's sorry and then we'll be back together and I'll be right back where I was, except I'll be more intensely aware of how much it hurts when... Deep breath. You're not committed to anything but talking to him.* "Fine, I'll let you know tomorrow, when I know, if I can see you."

"Wait," George said. "If it's a big deal, then no. No worries. It's all on your schedule. I don't want-"

"George," Jillian cut in. "Please." She shook her head. "Please. Just..."

"Just?"

"Just stop." She exhaled. "Just stop. I can't think. I can't..."

"I'm sorry."

"Don't..." *be sorry.* She pushed her hair back. "Look, I can't right now. Okay? I just... I just..." She was fighting the tears again from missing him and loving the sound of his voice, even as she didn't want to hear it and yet so desperately wanting to. She wanted this. She wanted him to come back. She sniffled.

"Please, don't cry," George said. "I can't stand that you're crying and I'm not able to do anything."

"You want to get back together," Jillian said, as steadily as she could manage. "Right? That's what your texts said. That's what that letter really meant. Despite 'I only want to apologize' and 'I'll respect your wishes.'"

"Yes," George said. "Yes, that's definitely what I want. But I *will* respect your wishes. If you say that we're really done, then I'll leave you alone. I just want to have the conversation, because everything I said the other night was jealous, angry, stupid, heat of the moment stuff. And I'm not going to try to justify it. It was wrong. I was wrong. There were reasons, but I don't have any excuses. I just want-"

"Do you want to do this over the phone?" She interrupted and sniffled again.

"No," George sighed. "No, Sweetheart. But, I want to do it soon. Actually, I want to do it now. I don't want to have to go another minute without you. Or, if we can't work this out, then, I guess, I'd rather know.

"I swore to myself that I wasn't going to push you again. But, this is really hard. Especially, because I think we *can* work this out."

"You're still calling me 'Sweetheart,'" Jillian said.

"Because I love you. You know that. Even if I didn't show it when it mattered. Even if I was being jealous and-"

"Stop, George!" Jillian crossed her free arm around herself, trying to physically hold herself together. "I thought we were doing this in person."

"Jillian, please. Please! I know I hurt you. I know I hurt you really badly. I know that. But, please, see me. Let me get down on my knees and tell you how sorry I am. I need to tell you how sorry I am. And I need to promise you that I won't ever to do it again. I need to promise I won't ever let you down again.

"Don't make me wait. I know I deserve to wait. I know I do. But, you love me. I know that too. And I love you. And our being apart isn't fixing anything.

"Please, just… just see me, Jillian. If not now, say when and where and I'll be there."

"George," Jillian said.

"I love you." His voice broke a little on the v in love. "Please."

"Oh, God, George," Jillian choked out. "Why does everything have to be *right now* with you?"

"It's not everything. Just you. Just us. I've waited my whole damn life for you, and then an extra stupid year because of Taro, and I didn't even realize it. But I'm sick of waiting and holding back and watching the world move on while I'm stuck. And I finally got it through my thick head that I have to ask for what I want or be content not to get it.

"Well, what I want is you. And I'll do anything, absolutely anything, to get you back. Ask anything you want of me. I'll walk through fire for you. Because without you, I'm a worthless, empty shell. But with you-"

"George!" Jillian shouted. *You're so impossible.*

"Shit. I'm sorry. I just got carried away and-"

"George!" Jillian shouted again. *You're driving me crazy.*

"I love you," he said, and Jillian closed her eyes again. "Shutting up now."

She opened her eyes. *Oh, Lord, I love you, too. I want to see you and talk to you and hide in your arms and be safe and happy again.* She tried to clear her throat without actually clearing it and not give in completely over the phone without even hearing what he had to say about everything. "All right. All right. If you want to come down here now, then come. If things are happening with Lacey, you'll have to wait. That's all there is to it. But, if you really can't stand to wait until Friday, or even tomorrow, then come. Mal and I are getting dinner; we'll be back up in the waiting area within an hour."

"I'm there. I'm so there," George said. "Is there anything you need? You said, you're getting dinner. Do you, I don't know, want snacks? Kleenex?"

"No, George. Thank you. I have to hang up now and go eat." *And maybe find my self-respect around here somewhere.*

"Right. Of course. Okay. So, I'll see you in about an hour."

"Until then," Jillian said. "Goodbye."

"Good- I love you, Jillian. Goodbye."

She disconnected, found a little bit of calm, and joined Malvinia.

"Well, *that* took a while," Malvinia observed and slid Jillian's coffee cup closer to her. "You look a bit chilled." When Jillian took a sip and didn't say anything, Malvinia leaned a little closer. "Don't hold out on your dearest friend. What happened? What'd he say? What did you say?"

Jillian thought a moment and then said, "Well, you wanted a chance to really meet him. You're going to get it." Malvinia lifted an eyebrow to give Jillian a quizzical look. *I wish I could do that.* "I told him I'd see him on Friday and we could talk. But he's as impossible as my mother, just on different subjects. He wants to see me *now*. Even though he says he knows that *now* isn't appropriate and yada yada, he wants to see me *now*. So…" *And thank God, really. Oh, you're just pitiful.*

"So, what? You're leaving after dinner?"

Jillian shook her head and took another sip, then said, "Nope. He's coming here. With a promise to get down on his knees to apologize to me."

The server appeared with their order, so Malvinia waited on the current conversation to thank the server, and then focused back on Jillian. "That man must have some hold on you. And vice versa." It was Jillian's turn to raise an eyebrow, in her case it was both. "May I see that letter?"

Jillian debated for only a moment. "Sure."

Malvinia wiped her hands several times before taking it from Jillian. Then she read it several times before handing it back.

"Well?" Jillian asked, after returning the letter to the envelope and the envelope to her purse. *Am I an idiot for taking him back?*

Malvinia smiled. "Well, it's not the most amazing thing ever written, but it's got to be the best I've ever read where I knew the people involved. The end was the best part." Malvinia put her hand to her heart. "*Yours, with all my love, always.*" Malvinia sighed dramatically and then dropped her hand. "Can't wait to see him on his knees."

"You think I should really make him do that?"

Malvinia shrugged. "Depends. If you're going to take him back regardless, you could do it just for fun. On the other hand, if you're going to take him back regardless, you could spare his dignity. I guess you have to decide how much he needs to pay for his crimes. I wonder if Kai would say to throw the book at him."

Jillian knew it was pointless to even think about it. She couldn't even keep her resolve over the phone to wait until Friday to talk. The minute he showed his face, she was going to be out of control all over again, wanting nothing more than be with him. They'd end up back together that night, if that's what he wanted, which was what he was saying. If she didn't want it, it wouldn't matter; she didn't really think she had much choice. The thought was both perplexing and comforting. "Vi?"

"Hmm?"

"Have you ever been out of control in love?"

"What do you mean?" Malvinia asked.

Jillian took a drink, trying to put her thoughts into order. "Ever since the first time he kissed me, I haven't been able to... No, that's not right, it started before then. If I'd been in control, I'd never have kissed him in the first place. I'm not sure how to say this." She couldn't come up with any other words. "Vi, I've been out of control since I let him anywhere near my life. And, I don't know... if it's good or bad."

Malvinia raised just the one eye brow again. "Out of control, how?"

"I can't say no to him, Vi. He touches me and I get weak. He kisses me and I get dizzy. Literally. He says he doesn't mean to push me, and yet he just keeps on and on, demanding..."

"Demanding, what?"

That's a good question. "I'm not... sure I know, anymore. I thought... Parts of it are so easy. But... he wants everything." She realized she was repeating herself. It was almost exactly what she'd said to Mrs. Kerchner. But one thing had changed. "And, just now, I've realized, I don't know what that is. Everything, I mean. I thought it was love and fidelity. But, there must be more. Because I do love him. And, fidelity, well, that was the fight, but I've *been* that. I just don't know what more he could want. But there must be something else, otherwise, he'd know. He wouldn't have thought that I'd... He'd be... satisfied." *Maybe I can't be what he needs. And we'll just fall apart again.*

Putting her chin on her hand, Malvinia sighed. "I can't believe this. You, so crazy in love and yet so pensive. I remember you with Luke. You were so carefree."

Looking down at her plate, Jillian cringed. "I think I'm broken or something. I've told him the ugly stuff. And he's met my parents and still..." She shook her head and looked at Malvinia. "There must be something wrong with me or it wouldn't be like this."

"Jills, you can't go blaming yourself. He's the one who accused you... That's all on him."

No. At least part of it is *me. There's something wrong with me. But what's left?* She nodded and asked Malvinia about her day before Lacey was admitted.

"Keep calm. No more pushing. Just relax." George had a litany he was repeating to himself as he walked the halls of the hospital. He managed to keep silent in the elevator when other people were around. But he talked to himself in the hallways. As he approached the ICU area, his stomach knotted and his litany changed. "She loves me. She'll forgive me. She loves me. She'll forgive me."

The room was quiet, only Jillian and one of her friends were there. He knocked on the wall as he entered and they both looked up at him. "Hello," was all he could think of to say, as it was certainly not a 'good evening' with their friend injured.

Jillian smiled with what he was sure was hesitation, but it was still a smile, and then she said, "Hello."

Her friend stood up saying, "I'll give you some privacy." But Jillian stopped her and said, "No, we'll walk and talk. You stay here. Text if there's news."

As they started down the hallway, George tried to think of his opening. He wasn't sure what to say. He could just launch into it with 'I'm sorry.' But he just felt like it should be bigger than that. His mistake sure was.

"Thank you for seeing me, tonight," George said, the moment the thought struck him, wishing he could touch her, just hold her hand, because that alone would help him get back to normal and make it all work out.

Jillian had her hands stuffed in her pockets. She also hadn't touched up her face since she'd last cried. *And those tears were probably my fault.*

"I don't know that I had much of a choice," Jillian said. "I seem to have a great deal of trouble saying no to you."

"Oh! Well, that'll work out great for me. Wanna get back together?" George asked, and as Jillian's head whipped toward him with her eyes wide, he quickly followed it with, "That's a joke. Well, no, not a joke. Not at all. But, I didn't mean... Oh, crap." He put his hands behind his neck.

Jillian started laughing.

"Something funny?" He asked, attempting to look like he was a bit peeved that she was laughing at him, instead of experiencing the overwhelming gratitude he actually felt. Even if it was at his expense, a laugh was a laugh.

"No," she said, and shook her head. "But, you've been very gifted in the world of words today. It's nice to see you..."

"Make an ass of myself?" George asked, before he could think.

"No. A bit more human. And unsure of yourself." Jillian said, and looked where they were going again. "Reminds me of our first night, when you said you wanted us to be together over french toast. You seemed nervous and worried."

"I was," George said. "I'd wanted to be with you for so long. And then I couldn't keep," he paused and look around. "Is it wise to be walking around talking about this?"

"Yes," Jillian said, with such firmness in her tone that George just shrugged.

"Okay, then. Well, anyway, I knew I should have settled things first.

Taken lots of time and been sure we were on the same page, but I just wanted you so bad. And when you wanted me, I just couldn't keep my hands off of you."

Jillian was blushing a little and George felt a smile coming on, despite his nerves. *It's going to be okay. Somehow. It's going to be okay.* "Jillian, I'm sorry."

She looked at him again briefly. "I know." *I know you're sorry.*

Right. The rest of it. "I was just so crazy with jealousy. I know you'd never. But when Taro told me about Serge texting you and you hadn't said a word about it, I just went nuts. Just the thought of somebody else touching you..."

"It didn't happen," Jillian said, flatly. *How could you think that it did? That it might, even? Why would I ever want anybody else, when I had you?*

"I know that. I knew it then, I think, inside, somewhere. I was just so... so..." He stopped walking and Jillian took one more step, and then realized he'd stopped, and she stopped and turned. "Insecure."

Jillian blinked. "Insecure?" *What do you have to be insecure about? I've never wanted to be with anyone the way I want to be with you.*

"I'd been dealing with my own stuff all weekend and being a crappy boyfriend by not calling or texting you, when I said I would and I just... thought you deserved better and maybe you were lonely... basically, I lost my mind. I was just crazed." *And hurt.*

"Yeah, I noticed that part," Jillian said.

"But, I kept telling myself that I needed to give you a chance to explain why you hadn't told me about Grec and Ser-"

"And yet, you never asked. You announced it and told me to deny it. You just *assumed* that something had gone on. The reason I didn't tell you about Grec and Sergei was because I didn't want to burden you with it!" Jillian shook her head. "You had all that stuff going on with your family. You weren't here. I didn't want to burden you with it.

"And then, when you came home, I just wanted to be with you. Not relive a miserable time. Not get you worked up about Grec. Why would I want to talk about anybody else, when I had you home and telling me you loved me for the first time?" She turned around and started walking.

George caught up as quickly as he could. "Yes. I know. I get that. It wasn't you. It was me. I was just so afraid that you were going to hurt me, had already hurt me and I just didn't know, that I didn't think or trust or..."

"Why? Why? Why would I hurt you?" Jillian had picked up the pace and slightly raised the volume of her words to match.

"Because I don't deserve you!" George nearly shouted and Jillian came to a halt.

"What?!"

"I don't deserve you. You're too good for me. You make me so happy it should be illegal. Do you know I haven't used my yo-yo to calm me down in weeks? I pulled it out yesterday because I felt like I had nothing else. And sadly, it was completely useless to me. It's been my crutch since I was kid and I haven't even thought of it for weeks, because even when stuff was bad, like with my folks, I was still high on you.

"So, how could I possibly be enough for you, when you're too good for me?"

"Oh," Jillian rubbed her face with her hands. "You're mad, in the clinical sense of the word, you know, crazy. That makes no sense. If I'm too good, then I'm a better person than to cheat on you." *Excuses! He said, he wasn't going to give me excuses.*

"I never said it made sense. Of course, it didn't make sense. I was jealous. Of someone you hate. And of a friend of mine. I mean, you and Serge are about the only thing I can imagine that's worse than Sarah and her doctor."

"Ugh," Jillian muttered. "Miserable, stupid cow."

"What?" George asked.

"I can't believe that woman felt the need to show back up in your life. All she did was make it harder for you to be happy. And make you even more cynical and distrustful. Lucky you. Hmmph. Lucky us." *Bitch.* It was one of the most uncharitable thoughts she could ever remember having. She didn't want to think about Sarah. She didn't want to think about anyone hurting George. But she did want to hurt Sarah on his behalf, for the misery she'd brought.

"Yes. I suppose that's true. Although, the cynical part... But, to make it worse, you were wonderful to me about that. You saw some ugly parts of me. And damaged parts of me. And you still wanted to be with me. *That* makes you too good for me."

Jillian started walking again, trying to walk instead of seethe. "That's ridiculous. Everybody feels that way. Do you know how hard it's been for me to let you see all the awful stuff I hide from everybody else? Any idea how hard it was for me to even face you after my parents? You may have noticed I never asked you about the conversation that happened between you and my dad, because I don't know if I could even survive hearing about it. And, ugh, talking about Sam.

"I didn't ever want to talk about Sam again, but I thought to myself, he's let me see him bleed. I have to give him that same honesty, even when I don't want to. Even when we barely know each other. So I did. I trusted you and cut myself open for you. And you come home and tell me you love me and then in practically the next breath accuse me-"

"I know. I know I messed up. Bad. Really bad. But, I'm sorry. I didn't mean it."

"Yes," Jillian said, unable to contain herself. "Yes, you did. If you hadn't, you wouldn't have said it and gone on and asked for my phone. You really thought I would cheat on you."

George gently took Jillian's arm in his hand to make her stop walking as he did. "It was temporary insanity. *Temporary.* I'm sane now. I'll stay sane. Forgive me. Come back to me. Please. I love you so much."

"And what's going to be different now?" Jillian asked, as her logical side took complete charge for an instant. "How are you going to stay sane? You were jealous of a handshake, George. And then of something you *imagined.* I can't fight this irrational jealousy. I *won't* fight it."

"You won't have to. I have it figured out."

"Oh, really? You aren't going to be jealous anymore."

"No, actually, I probably will be," George said. "I never was before, so I haven't a clue if this is a parting gift from her-who-shall-not-be-named, or if it's some crazy thing that's just about you. But since it was new, I didn't know how to handle it. Now, I do. I have a plan."

Jillian crossed her arms. "Well, let's hear it."

"Jealousy is an emotion. Emotions come and go. How I handle the emotion, that's another matter.

"I promise you that I will never again let myself stew about anything. I think that was a big part of the crazy outburst. I stewed about it all night.

"I promise I will always *ask* you, directly, if I ever have a reason to think something is going on.

"I promise you that I will remember who you are before I let myself react to any feelings of jealousy. And, I'm never, ever listening to Taro ever again."

"What did Taro say, exactly?" Her voice sounded very suspicious and George wondered a moment if there was more that he *hadn't* heard about. Then he forcibly banished the thought. If there was, surely she'd tell him right then. What point was there to keeping anything secret anymore?

He disclosed what he'd learned about Taro the previous night, playing the pranks on them and then what he'd said about Sergei. Jillian's face grew stormier as he talked and her hands dropped and balled at her sides. "I. Can't. Believe. Him." Jillian said, through clenched teeth. She took a breath and shuddered as she let it out. "He really has been trying to break us up. He told me after you left Friday, that that Monday night we met at the Blue Feather, you were just there looking to get laid." She shook her head and looked at him. "I can't..." She stopped mid-thought and looked at him strangely then.

"What?" George asked.

"It was true, wasn't it? I could see it in your face. It was fleeting, but I saw it. You were..." *Oh, no. Oh, no.*

"Out looking to get laid?" George took a breath. *Oh, shit. Now what do I do? Oh, shit.* He decided to just tell the truth and hope, because if he lied and she caught him in the lie… "Yes and no. Mostly no, but a little yes. I'd had a weird day, and you were driving me crazy just existing. You smiled at me in the walkway when we passed each other, going opposite directions, and I turned around and stared at your ass." He grimaced. "Sorry, but it's true. Anyway, I did it right there in the open, in the office, just stood there staring at you, like some kind of perv, and I figured if I did it again, I'd get caught and end up dealing with HR. I thought if I took the edge off, maybe I wouldn't catch myself doing it again.

"So, technically, yes. I was meeting Serge for that purpose, but it wasn't what I really wanted. What I really wanted, of course, was you. And not just to get laid. You *know* that. We've talked about that. I wanted more from you from the beginning. And that night was perfect, because he was late, and you were miraculously there. I totally blew off Serge. Didn't even text him that I wasn't joining him. Nothing else mattered except being with you."

Jillian shook her head again. "What a fine pair we are. The man in heat and the ice queen. Amazing we got this far." She started walking again. *How are we supposed to be anything but a disaster with this kind of history. Two broken and mangled peop-*

"Stop it," George said, walking with her.

"Stop what?"

"Everything," George said. "You know, we're a bit of a mess, yes. Of course, we are. We're people and people are a mess. But that doesn't mean that we aren't right for each other. Come on. There's nothing wrong with us that can't be fixed. I know I'm better just being near you."

When she didn't stop walking, he huffed a little, and then asked, "Do you love me?"

"What?"

"I said, 'do you love me?' Be honest."

Jillian stopped walking and faced him again, sighing. "Yes," she said, shaking her head. "Yes, I love you." *Of course I love you. I wouldn't have said it the first time if I hadn't meant it.*

"And I love you," he swallowed and then reached out toward her hand. "Let's be a mess together. We're good together. And now that we've talked, we'll be even better. We know it all now. There's nothing left to be misunderstood. Even if someone *did* come up with something to feed the other behind our backs, it won't matter, because we know we can talk. We will talk. And we know how we feel about each other."

She looked up at him, her lips taut and her shoulders tense. *She isn't going for it, is she?* Unable to refrain any longer, he grasped her hand. "I'll always be yours, Jillian. Always. Be mine again."

Her jaw trembled. *How do I know this won't happen again? Really? How can*

I possibly just turn my heart back over to you and let you do with it as you please? "I hate you for hurting me."

He closed his eyes as if he'd been slapped, then he looked back at her again. "I'm so sorry."

Her face crumbled and he knew she was about to cry. *That was a terrible lie, Jillian. A terrible, fear-based lie. You don't hate him. You can't hate him. …You love him.* "That's not true. I don't hate you. I want to hate you." *You can't have it both ways. Either you're safe without him, or risking it all with him.*

"Jillian…" George tried to breathe.

"Don't ever do it again." She gripped his hand tightly.

"Never."

"*Never.*"

"No. Never." He shook his head. "Never."

"*Never.*" She got to her toes and threw her free arm around his neck and he let go of her hand to put his arms around her. He buried his face in her hair, inhaling the comfort and warmth and passion and everything else that was her. She made a sobbing sound.

"Forgive me?" He asked, just to hear her answer.

"I forgive you." And then her other arm was around him. And she was back.

"Never again," he whispered, lifting a hand to touch her hair and smooth it down her back. "We'll never be apart again. I love you so much."

"I love you, too," she said. "And I'm sorry. I didn't mean it when I said, I hate you. And I'm sorry I fought with you."

"It's okay," he said, and smoothed her hair again. "I forgive you, too. I'll always love you."

They clung to each other in the hallway for a while and several people in scrubs passed them. When someone actually said, 'excuse me,' Jillian dropped down from her tiptoes and he had the opportunity to see her face again. She'd cried more, in his arms, so the tears were fresh and he wiped them away with his thumbs. "Oh, Sweetheart," he said. "Sweetheart, please don't cry. It's going to be even better from now on."

He kissed her, briefly, wishing they were somewhere private, so that he could make her his again, make her tremble, and he could lose himself in her and she could lose herself too. Then they'd put everything behind them.

But they weren't in private. And they weren't going to be soon. So, he dropped his forehead to hers and unexpectedly relaxed, for the first time since they fought, he relaxed. He'd known he was tense, but the comfort and pleasure and hope and even a sense of home welled up and his whole body went slack with relief. He didn't need to physically make her his again to be okay. Just being there together, forehead to forehead, with the calm that always came from that contact, was enough for him to know that all was right between them once again. They belonged to each other and nothing could take that away. Never again.

"We should probably go... somewhere," Jillian said. "Somewhere not a hallway."

"Yeah," he said. "Probably. You want to go back to the waiting area?"

"Okay. Yeah."

They walked hand in hand back down the hallway for a few paces, and then George transferred her hand to his other hand, so he could put his arm around her shoulders and hold her closer. As they neared the waiting area, he kissed her hair. "Do you want me to hang around or do you want me to go?"

"Well, I'd love it if you stayed, but if you need to go..." *Please stay. Please stay.*

"No way. I've got nothing better to do then be with you. I just want to be sure I'm wanted, you know, not in the way. You've got your friends..."

Jillian leaned further into him. *Thank you, George. Thank you for coming back. Thank you for fighting for this, for us. Thank you for being you.* "Please stay."

"Done."

Christy and Kai hadn't yet returned, so it was just Malvinia who witnessed Jillian and George walk in together and she smiled and stood up. "I take it we've made up."

"We have," Jillian said, and George lifted up the hand he'd been holding and kissed it. Jillian turned her head toward him. "George, you remember my friend, Malvinia."

He nodded and then let go of her hand to extend his to Malvinia. "Sure. I'm sorry to be meeting again under such unpleasant circumstances."

Malvinia shook his hand. "Well, at least there was one bright spot today." She winked at Jillian. "So, George, what did you study in school? English?"

Jillian's eyes narrowed at Malvinia. George sort of laughed. "Uh, no. Programming. Why?"

"You write a half-decent letter," Malvinia said, and took a seat.

George nodded. "Ah, yes." He led Jillian to a chair. "I assume everyone's read it."

"No," Jillian said. "Just Vi."

"Did you actually write it?" Malvinia asked George.

"Vi!" Jillian shot her a 'shut up' look.

George sat next to Jillian. As her took her hand, she felt a slight warmth spread from her fingers into her arm. "No. It's cool, Sweetheart." He looked deep into her eyes. "She thinks I plagiarized or had help. Which is quite the compliment, when you think about it. And the truth is I did have a little help. Delaney made some suggestions as to the order of things and such. But, the words. The words were all mine."

"Really?" Malvinia said. "You use words like 'plead'?"

George grinned at Jillian, still holding her eyes. "Yes, actually, I do. Although, I did use thesaurus.com when I working on it." He leaned a little closer and Jillian started to wonder if he was going to kiss her. "What'd you think of my list?"

Jillian smiled at that. "It was okay. Mine was better."

"Of course. You always top me." George laughed.

"But, um, your song choice was… interesting…"

He pulled out his phone. "I don't know if I want our song to be about a guy making a jealous fool of himself, but it does have a happy ending, and all." *Silhouettes* began to play from phone. "That's what your song list was, right? Looking for a song for us?"

Jillian was sure she was flushing again, knowing Malvinia was listening. She nodded. "Mm-hmm."

George was smiling at her again, when he suddenly sat up and shut off the music on his phone. "Geez. This really isn't the time to do this, is it? I'm sorry." He nodded toward Malvinia. "I didn't mean to make light when," he looked at Jillian again, "your friend is in such a condition. What was I thinking?"

"It's okay," Jillian said, and glanced at Malvinia, who was leaning with her chin on her hand and smiling.

"Jills," Malvinia said, "go home."

Jillian raised her eyebrows and sat back. "No. That's okay."

"Go home," Malvinia said. "Nothing's happening right now. Go on."

"No, I-" George sat back and put an arm around her shoulders and she leaned into him. "I want to be here for Lacey."

Rolling her eyes, Malvinia said, "Go home and make gooey eyes at each other. And then make-up the rest of the way. I'll hold down the fort with Kai and Christy. Come back tomorrow."

"I think I ought to at least wait until Lacey's parents get here."

"Suit yourself," Malvinia stood up. "I'm going to stretch my legs for about five minutes. I'll be right back." As she passed by them on the way out, she paused and leaned over toward George and faux whispered, "She's exhausted from an emotional day. Talk her into going home." She walked out of the waiting area.

Jillian glanced shyly at George and shook her head. "Oh, that Vi."

"Why don't we wait for Lacey's folks, share their concerns and burden for a few minutes, and then go."

She dropped her head on his shoulder. "You're wonderful, George."

"Am I?" He kissed her hair and she closed her eyes. *I'm glad you think so. I need you to think so.*

"Yes," she said, and then sighed. "I wish we'd started ages ago."

"Me too," George said, and reached his hand up to smooth her hair again. *None of this stupid stuff would have happened if only...* "Say, uh... how are you feeling? How's your back?"

Flushing beet red, Jillian turned her face into his shoulder. "That's all better. But... um... as for the, um, rest..."

"I was just checking on how you're feeling, Sweetheart. Nothing more." He laughed as she pulled back to look at him. "Come back here." He tugged her against him, again, and she laughed into his neck.

She sighed. "I want to be alone with you," Jillian said, after a moment and put her arm across him dropping her hand on his shoulder. "And Mal trying to help me do just that made it worse."

"Well, we'll be alone after Lacey's parents arrive. Right? I'll accompany you home. Maybe... you'll invite me to stay?"

"No explicit invitation needed, I should hope," Jillian said, sighing against his skin, warming in the familiar scent. She smiled at the thought that she'd have a pillow that smelled like him again and he'd have his space on the bed. *How it was meant to be.*

"No? Does that mean I've got a permanent invite?" His free hand reached up and rested on her arm.

"Yes. I like it when you're around. And Charlie doesn't seem to mind you, either, though he did sit in your spot on the bed."

George chuckled. "You know, he's a pretty cool cat. He doesn't seem too demanding, except at feeding time. And he's got good taste in movies." He kissed her hair again and left his chin against her head. "Say, Sweetheart?"

"Hmm?"

"Do you want your key back?" He could feel her mouth curl up against his skin, then her warm breath as she laughed just a little.

"*My* key?"

"Well, yeah. I've never given it to anybody else, so..."

She pulled back to see his face again. "Yes, please. I'd love to have my key back."

He leaned over, but she moved too and kissed him first. They twisted a bit in their chairs to face each other, while their hearts pounded. "I missed you so damn much," George said, against her lips when they paused.

"I missed you, too," Jillian said, thinking about lying in her bed with him. *Just having him there... Even if we don't touch...* "We have to stop on the way home to buy you a new toothbrush."

George smiled. "How are those thoughts connected?"

"They aren't. Except I want to be with you, all the time, so you'll need a toothbrush-" He kissed her again and when he stopped, she mumbled, "I'm dizzy, George. You've got to stop doing that to me."

"Never," he said, and kissed her again.

Thankfully, Malvinia had her voice raised as she headed into the waiting area with Lacey's parents and they weren't caught unawares. After a few minutes exchanging concern and get well wishes, Malvinia shooed Jillian and George out, this time truly whispering, "Go home. Get some sleep. But not *too* much."

As they started to walk down the hallway, arms around each other, George said, "You know, I really like her."

Jillian laughed.

"Now. You said, I need a toothbrush. Tossed the old one, eh?"

"Yes. I cleansed my apartment of you. Tossed everything. Washed the sheets." She hesitated a moment and then said, "Gave back your key."

"Viciously done, by the way. Subtle, but vicious," he said. "You were really angry."

"So were you, if I recall."

"Yep. Stupid angry."

She laughed. "Think you can stake a bit of a claim on my apartment again?"

George laughed too. "Should I mark the territory?"

"No!" Jillian laughed. "Let's not get carried away."

They weren't far down the hall, but they were far enough, George released her and dug his wallet out of his pocket while they kept walking. Jillian watched him open it and slip a key out of it. "Seriously?" She asked, as he handed it to her.

"I'm nothing, if not hopeful, when it comes to you."

"Covering all contingencies, purely precautionary," she said, with a nod and started fumbling with her purse. "You probably should have held onto this until we reached the car. I'll never get it on my key chain while we're walking."

"I could do it for you. Be happy to," George said, as he replaced his wallet.

"Oh, yeah? Go ahead." She handed the key back, as well as her key ring. George added the key with no trouble at all.

"For you," he said, and handed it back. "You know, your friend is right." He paused. "Is it Mal or Vi? You said both…"

"Either. She's answers to both. It's whatever…"

"Okay. Well, anyway, Mal was right. You've had quite a day. Why don't we worry about the toothbrush tomorrow-"

"No!" Jillian said, a lot louder than she intended, and she had to purposely lower her voice. "I want you to stay. Please."

"I was just thinking," George said, "if you'll let me finish the thought, that we should stop by your place to take care of Charlie, but head on over to mine and you can take a soak in the tub."

"Uh, no," Jillian tried to come up with an excuse that didn't involve say anything embarrassing. "I'd love a soak in your tub this weekend. But tonight, let's just crash. I'm exhausted."

"Whatever you say," George said, and put his arm around her again, where it belonged. "I love you, Sweetheart."

"I love you, too." Jillian said, and put her arm around him. "Oh, geez."

"What?"

"We'll need to get a cab. I took one here. I was too upset to drive."

"Let me worry about it," George said. He dropped a kiss on her hair; a gesture he realized was becoming a habit. *I like it. I need more habits like that.* "In fact, Sweetheart, let me worry about everything."

She squeezed him and leaned into him. It was too good of an offer to refuse; just like he was too good to refuse. *There is a reason I can't say no to this man. We're meant to be together.*

An hour later, George and Jillian fell asleep in her bed, with Charlie at the foot, in the corner, and a new toothbrush on the counter in the bathroom.

Thursday was an interesting mix of high and lows for George. Jillian had felt that she needed to be at the hospital, so he'd come into the office alone and found the women were all still shooting daggers out of their eyes at him. When Rachel had buzzed him for a call that had come through the main switchboard, and been overtly crisp, he'd decided to do something about it.

His visit to Rachel's desk had been short. He'd walked up, leaned over, and said, "Jillian and I made up last night. You can all stand down now."

"But…" Rachel said, and pointed toward Jillian's office, which was obviously empty.

"She has a friend in the hospital. I thought she'd call you, but she's probably got other things on her mind."

"Oh." Rachel's eyes slid down to her keyboard.

"Any questions?"

Rachel grimaced for a moment and then looked back at him. "Um, no. Sorry."

After that, the daggers stopped, although the peculiar looks had started. He didn't know what he'd done to warrant them, but he decided he didn't care. Jillian was back and frankly, nothing else mattered. Except that now that he wasn't insane with jealousy or torturing himself to get her back, he could almost think again and the interesting revelation he'd had while he was home reared its ugly head.

He looked around at his office. He didn't want to be there. Not just because he wanted to be with Jillian, but because he really didn't want his job. He'd been working very hard for a long time and it seemed so ridiculous. It was time for a change. But, what?

Ringo found his way to usefulness again, while George tried to decide what his next move should be. Internet job search? Seemed logical. Except...

He put Ringo back in his pocket and picked up and dialed his desk phone. "Vidar. Got time for lunch today?"

CHAPTER THIRTY

Lacey was moved from the ICU a little before lunch and everyone was breathing a sigh of relief. Seeing her, however, had taken some of the relief back. She was cut up, bruised, bandaged, casted, and looked very pale, but the doctor said that she was healing nicely. They kept her on a strong sedative that would keep her asleep for a while, a few more hours at least, saying that she was going to be in a lot of pain when she awoke.

That left the group propping each other up again. Jillian was the forceful one, making Malvinia go home for a shower and a nap, mentioning that her department hadn't yet exploded without her watchful eye. Reluctantly, Malvinia agreed.

Kai also ran out to her office for a few hours, promising to be back before dinner. That left Lacey's parents, who were also exhausted and decided to try to nap in the visitors' chairs in Lacey's room, with Christy and Jillian.

Christy motioned Jillian out of the room when Lacey's dad started breathing really heavily. "I didn't get to see you before you left last night, but Mal said you and George made up."

"Yes," Jillian said, and leaned against the wall. "We're back together."

"Good," Christy said, and then she crossed her arms. "I'm sorry. I was... really... bitchy when you told me. I was... I'm sorry."

"I'm sorry too, Christy," Jillian said. "I'd like to think I'm a better friend than that."

Christy looked at the floor. "You were fine. I wasn't. I was feeling sorry for myself." She looked up sheepishly. "The guy I told you about..."

"The married one?"

"He dumped me. I didn't take it with my usual flair. I took it out on you."

"Oh," Jillian said. "I didn't know. I also didn't think you were taking that seriously."

"I wasn't," Christy said. "But, it still hurt a little. You want a laugh?"

Jillian frowned. "I dunno. It isn't at your expense, is it?"

Christy shook her head. "I'm giving up on men for a while."

"That's not particularly funny," Jillian said, and reached out to rub Christy's upper arm. "Are you okay?"

"Oh, I'm fine," she sort of shrugged. "But, I'm a little... discouraged right now. I'm really happy for you. I just keep thinking that it's not fair. You weren't even looking and you found your guy. I've put in so many hours looking for mine that I can't even begin to tally it up and I've got zilch to show for it. So, I figure maybe the thing to do is take a break. Maybe even more than a break. Ban interacting with men."

"Won't that be tricky at work?"

"I mean socially."

"Right," Jillian said. "Well, it never hurts to give yourself a little time."

"It'll be hard," Christy said. "Kai and Malvinia are soooo busy with work. You've got George. Apart from Lacey needing some help with recovery, I think I'll be on my own quite a bit. I haven't been for a long time."

"Maybe it's a good thing then. You can get reacquainted with yourself. Maybe try some new things. Take a class or something."

Christy looked like she was fighting a smile. "Take a class? Like what, pottery? That's so you, Jillian. I'm not sure I'm really interested in getting in touch with my inner artist or anything."

"Who said art? It doesn't have to be art," Jillian said. "You could take some kind of... I don't know... theater? Join club for... wine tasting. Do rock climbing. I don't know."

Christy couldn't fight it anymore, she smiled. "Thanks, Jill. I'll remember that, if I get *that* bored."

"You know, you could always hang out with me and the band at The Blue Feather on Mondays."

Christy shook her head. "I'll remember that too."

Jillian gave her a hug around her crossed arms. "It'll be okay, Christy."

"Thanks, Jill," Christy dropped her arm and hugged her back. "Okay. Enough feeling sorry for myself. We've got a friend in there..."

"Yes," Jillian said. "I feel so helpless."

"Me too." Christy shrugged again. "Not much we can do."

Jillian nodded.

"All right," Christy said, standing up straight. "Let's go down to the cafeteria and get a coffee. You can tell me all about you and George."

"Is that a good idea?"

"Just because I'm off men, doesn't mean I've given up romantic fantasies. And you've got a real life one. I want to hear all about it."

Jillian patted Christy's upper arm. "Sure. Let's go." While Christy left a note for Lacey's parents as to where they were going, Jillian sent a text to George letting him know that Lacey had been moved from ICU and that she'd see how things were going and figure out whether or not she was going to be able to see him for dinner, or if it would be later.

Lunch with Vidar had been interesting and fruitful. When they returned to the office, George had taken out his copy of his employment agreement and assured himself that he wasn't stepping over any lines, he'd called Vidar and confirmed, setting another brief meeting for after work. Taking Vidar's advice, he then asked Irene if she'd take a short walk with him around the block. Irene was a bit hesitant, but agreed. When they returned, she'd agreed to meet with both him and Vidar after work for a few minutes.

By the end of the meeting, held just off of the Gardiner D property, George thought he'd either just begun on a road to brilliance or was exhibiting more signs of insanity. His idea was more than a little nuts. But, he had two others willing to be nuts with him.

He was starting his own software company, only he was going to make games. Vidar had told him a few years ago, when George had interviewed him, that he had wanted to work in the video game industry also. But, like George, he'd decided that paying his bills was more important. Just a lunch talking about their ideas had established that they could both see themselves working together to create something new. They'd even agreed on the basic structure for a game, what they wanted to see in a game that was a little new and different.

Apparently, his time as a manager at Gardiner D wasn't a total waste. He was able to lay out a plan, acknowledging it was a little aggressive, to getting a first release ready and out on an on-line platform in about six months. They'd keep the price down at first, and sell mods cheap as they were able to finish more of the intended final product. If it worked, if the game caught on, they'd be selling the entire thing for a little less than a comparable game from a big name company.

The risks were real, of course. Unless they wanted to goof around on it for years, they had to quit their day jobs and be serious for the six months. No income. No fallback plan.

Vidar had put away some savings since he'd started working at Gardiner D, so he decided he could take the risk. Irene was less sure. George told them both that he didn't want to quit Gardiner D and start officially until after the first of the year. *No health insurance.* Irene agreed to talk to her husband about it.

George headed to the train station feeling as high as he'd ever felt. He figured he was about to take a pretty big risk and it felt amazing! He had the space in his house for them to all work together. He also had a savings bond that he'd been sitting on since he graduated from college that would allow him to invest in the hardware and software they'd need to put the plan into action. He'd told Vidar and Irene that he'd handle the startup costs and the space, if they agreed that the company was his and he took fifty percent of the profits, as opposed to a third.

Vidar had agreed readily, saying that he figured he'd managed to put away about eight months' worth of savings and he'd rather keep the extra two for backup, in case. Irene had been neutral, uncertain if she could commit to the venture, and that made George nervous. Irene was a big piece of the idea, as she brought something to the team that neither he nor Vidar did. In addition to programming, Irene had a degree in visual arts.

Having a trained artist on the project left him only one hole. He didn't plan to fill it by adding anyone else to his company, he hoped to fill it with a consultant-type position, as it wasn't something he needed full-time over the six months. It was, however, crucial to have someone who could truly fill it. They desperately needed music, original music.

He'd not only started planning, but he'd started moving forward with all this, without even hinting at it to Jillian. He started tapping his foot on the floor. *No one has technically committed to anything yet. If she totally freaks out, I could back out.* If not, there were a lot of papers to sign and file. He didn't know much about starting a business, but he did know he wanted to incorporate for liability protection. *Shit, there is a lot to think about and line up before the end of the year.*

And he *wanted* to do it. If not then, he'd probably never have a chance again. Although he guessed it would be a while before the expectations started on her side, it was only too easy to see that he was going to be asking Jillian to marry him in the not so distant future.

He wanted that too. Not that it would change anything, as far as he could see. He wasn't going to be any more committed to the relationship with a ring than he was now without one. He knew what it felt like to be without her, and he wasn't going to allow that to happen *ever* again. On the other hand, if nothing else worked, a ring would probably get her into the house with him.

But, once he proposed, his responsibilities changed. He'd need to be looking at both their futures. And a risk like scrapping a perfectly good job was not going to win him a round of applause from her parents, or his for that matter.

What is she going to think about this? He tapped faster. The plan had a lot of nice side benefits. He wouldn't have to worry about going any rounds with H.R. when Jillian got the Director Job and he couldn't work under her. Of course, when it came out that he was taking Vidar and Irene with him... *Yikes. This could be ugly.*

But he *wanted* to do it. It was the first time he'd felt excited about something he could call work in years. And he had confidence in Vidar and Irene, assuming she joined them. And if Jillian didn't completely lose it when he told her, well, she might be just the music consultant he was looking for. She had connections too, if she decided she wasn't the perfect person or just plain wasn't willing to do it.

This could be perfect or a disaster.

He called Orville while he was still on the train, letting him know that he'd gotten back together with Jillian and then sharing his idea to start a new business.

"Well, if that don't beat all," Orville said, when George had finished. "You come by here tonight."

"I may have some difficulty with that. I've got a basketball game. And Jilllian-"

"You come by here. I don't care when. They can get me out of dinner, if necessary."

"I was heading ho-"

"Come by. Tonight. No excuses."

"Um, sure," George said. "I'll figure it out. Perhaps Jillian will come with me."

"Nope," Orville said. "Come alone. Thinking about it, come now."

"Well-"

"Now," Orville repeated.

"I'll tell you what. I'm nearly home. I'll change my clothes and then turn around and come over."

"Okay. But no other delays."

"All right. All right."

Jillian was torn. She wanted to go home to George and Charlie. She also wanted to be there until Lacey woke up. The doctor had said she ought to be awake soon, but 'soon' had stretched into more than hour. It was more than likely that she'd feel like she should stick around once Lacey was actually awake. She glanced at her watch and decided it was time to just accept she wasn't going to be home until late. She called George, his phone went straight to voice mail, so she left him a message that she would probably be at the hospital until late and that she'd call when she left.

Then she left a message for Rachel that she'd be back in the office in the morning. She figured she'd better at least put in an appearance. She could always leave a little early and head over to see Lacey before dinnertime.

Having made good time back to Orville's, George was able to check the voice mail that had appeared on his phone as he entered Whistling Elms. He must've been in a dead zone when Jillian called. He tried not to let it bother him that she wasn't going to make it to the game. Circumstances were as outside of her control as they were his.

He quickly texted that he'd check his phone again after his game and then knocked on Orville's door.

"Come in," Orville said, as soon as he opened the door. "You made good time. In fact, perfect time. I only just managed to dig the thing out."

"Thing?" George asked, as he followed Orville into the apartment.

"Yep. I was starting to worry I'd lost it. And after telling you to hurry over here. That would've been an unpleasant turn of events."

"Okay," George said. "What exactly did you want me here for?"

Orville motioned him to sit down, handed him a small flat jewelry box, the kind necklaces come in from department stores, and then seated himself. George looked at Orville's grinning face and raised his eyebrows. "Go on. Open it."

George opened the box and listened to Orville ramble as he pulled out a ring. The larger stone in the center was blue and cut in a sort of rectangular shape. It was surrounded by an outer ring of tiny clear stones.

"That was May's, of course. It's not worth much, I expect. It was the best I could afford back then, which wasn't much. Though I did go through some trouble a while ago to make sure that my kids knew it wasn't going to them in the will. My lawyer says it's all straight and they can't come and demand it back."

"Uh, Orville-"

"Now, since you've said, you're going to try this whole business thing, which, by the way, I'm *especially* proud of you for, I figure you're going to be pretty broke for a while. And since you and Jillian got back together, it won't be long until you're in the market for one of these.

"Jillian's a good woman. I know I haven't seen that much of her, but the way she was holding onto you the other evening when you stopped by here and were in need of, I'll call it comfort... well, she's clearly loving and kind. And there isn't a whole lot more you need than that. Except the fire, which I understand you already know you have.

"I don't know that this ring'll be to her taste, but I hope... If she doesn't like it, I'm okay with you selling it and using the proceeds to get something she does. I'm not going to get all sentimental or anything."

George searched for words. He finally came up with, "This was May's?"

"Yes. And if Jillian's superstitious, you can tell her that we never went to bed angry. We had a late night, here and there, but we always worked everything out. So the ring has a lot of years of good... what do you call it?"

"Karma? Energy?" George tried to supply a word.

"Yeah, I suppose. Whatever. Anyway, it's yours, kiddo. You can hold onto it until the right time. You can sell it tomorrow. It's up to you. But, I want you to have it. I hope it'll make a difference for you at some point."

"I'm speechless," George said.

"Fair enough, I suppose. Look, take it and figure it out later."

"No, really," George turned the ring over a few times. It was set in silver and the stone in the center sparkled like the light bouncing off a lake. *Blue. Not unlike her blue glassware, in a way. This is the most non-traditional, traditional ring I could have imagined. She'll...* "I think she'll love it," he said, quietly.

"If she's worth her salt, she won't care all that much about the ring; she'll be more interested in the man that gives it to her. But women... they can funny about these things."

"Is it a sapphire?" George figured he should know.

"Yep."

"I think she'll love it," he said, again. "I'm still a bit... speechless, Orville."

"Well, I didn't give it to you because I wanted to hear a speech. If you think it's good, say thanks and get on out to your game."

Closing the box with the ring securely back inside, George looked Orville in the eye and said, "Thank you." He tried to think of a way to ask the question that was coming to mind. After another minute, he stood and looked away. "Any reason you felt like you had to do this tonight?"

There were a few moments silence. Then Orville said, "Nah. Just figure there's no time like the present. And I didn't want you buying something you didn't need, when you're going to be in financial straits."

George tried not to frown at Orville. "Are you sure about that? You're feeling all right?"

"Of course, Kid."

"You'd better not be lying to me," George said. "I'll make you take this thing back and leave it to your kids, after all."

Orville snorted. "What a threat! You go on. When the time comes, I hope it serves." When George didn't move right away, Orville motioned him out. "Go on."

Hesitating, George took another look at Orville. He wasn't looking any different. His color was good. He was moving at about the same pace. He looked the same. But giving away May's ring...

Just in case Orville was lying, George gave him a very quick, very manly, backslapping hug and left before the scene was too emotional for either of them.

Giggling like school girls in the hospital cafeteria earned Jillian and Christy some entertaining looks. A few were smiles of envy, most were of annoyance. Christy put her hands on her hips and dropped her voice to a fake bass and said, "How can you girls be giggling in a serious place like this?" Bringing on another fit of giggles.

"Oh, Jill," Christy sighed after the laughter subsided. "It sounds like he's a man and half. Very dreamy."

Jillian nodded. "Apart from the irrational jealousy."

Christy waved her hand in the air. "I think you need to look at that from a different perspective. It's not that he's irrationally jealous, it's that he's hopelessly and desperately in love."

Jillian smiled. "Oh, I don't know. I think that's me."

"Hopeless and desperate?"

They both giggled.

"Hopeless," Jillian said, "maybe. I can't say 'no' to him, Christy."

"What would you want to say 'no' for?" Christy smirked. "I'd think after what you've told me, saying 'yes' is a real *pleasure*."

"Are you sure you're going to take a break from men?" Jillian asked, with a crooked smile.

"Definitely," Christy said. "I'm not going to date again until I think I've met one who's a keeper."

Toying with her coffee stirrer, Jillian thought about her 'keeper' and the one thing she hadn't told Christy, or Malvinia, or anybody. "Good idea."

"You've gone suddenly somber," Christy observed.

"It happens," she said, in as casual a tone as she could manage.

"Talk," Christy said. "You sigh and blush and everything else, and then go somber. Talk."

He gave me a key to his house. And I'm still trying to figure out what that means. After the fight, I couldn't take it back fast enough. And I've never even used the thing! Does he expect a key to my place? Do I want to give him one? If I don't, why not? I trust him there, don't I? What difference would it make?

Why do I worry about stuff like this?

"He's got a basketball game tonight. I'm going to miss it."

"I bet you can go," Christy said. "Lacey will wake up soon and you can get away." When Jillian didn't answer right away, she spoke again. "You should go. I bet Lacey isn't going to be feeling much like company. She'll be glad we're all here, but she'll be wanting to rest."

"Well," Jillian said. *He'd like it. I'd like it. And maybe I can maim Taro while I'm there.* "If Lacey doesn't need me. I don't feel like I've been here enough."

Christy stood up and Jillian followed her out of the cafeteria. "Hopefully she wakes up soon."

Just as Christy predicted, Lacey woke up just before dinner and after talking for a few minutes, wanted to go back to sleep. Jillian stayed a bit, helping ensure that Lacey's parents ate since they didn't want to leave her side. Malvinia was back and Christy told her about the basketball game. Malvinia pushed Jillian to go too.

She wasn't a tough sell at that point, wanting to be with George. So, like the first game she'd attended, she arrived after it had started, but before the half, and she sat with Melissa.

Melissa had welcomed her warmly and then said, "I'm really glad you two worked it out. George told Rachel you were back together, but since you weren't at work, everyone was a little curious..."

Jillian nodded. "I didn't think about that. I guess I should have said something to someone."

"No," Melissa said, "I understand you've got a friend in the hospital?"

"Yes," Jillian answered. "She's doing better now."

"Good," Melissa said. After a minute she repeated herself. "Good. Uh, Jillian?"

Jillian looked at Melissa.

"I know you weren't at work today, but... have you got any idea what's going on with the musketeers tonight? They're all acting really... mad or something? At Taro."

Jillian looked at the court. "Oh."

It was easy to tell then that George spotted her; he was taking the ball back up the court as they transitioned for offense, motioned a play call to Chris, and then looked around him into the bleachers. He smiled right at her, looking surprised and pleased. Jillian waved at him.

"Did he do something?" Melissa asked, beside her.

Debating her answer, Jillian cheered one basket and then looked at Melissa. "Look, I don't know much first hand. But, the second hand information I've been given plus the tiny bit of first hand I do have..." She cleared her throat, a little white lie for Melissa's sake was more difficult than she'd expected. "He said some things that contributed heavily to the fight George and I had. I'm not saying it's his fault. We're the ones that fought. But, that's probably what's it's all about."

"What did he say?"

Jillian definitely didn't want to say anymore. It was hard enough to think about the fight, but to bring it to Melissa... She kept up the pretense. "You should ask him what happened. Like I said, most of my information is second hand. It's hearsay."

Melissa crossed her arms. "Something's been up with him for a while. The timing... I thought it was Gardiner's news. But he's been acting so odd. Then I thought it was the wedding, that he changed his mind. If there's something going on with him and the guys... That makes more sense." She looked toward the court again. "Did he say something... on purpose?"

"On purpose?"

"To cause the fight."

"Well," Jillian said, as a delay, but then went on with the truth in the face of a direct question. "It seems like it. But, who knows?"

Melissa made a face. "I'm going to get to the bottom of it. Tonight."

"Melissa," Jillian started to say, but then she didn't know what else to add.

Melissa looked at her. "I'll get to the bottom of it."

Jillian didn't know what else to say at that moment, so she kept quiet. *Great. Now I'm responsible for a fight.* She hoped it wasn't going to lead to another break up. Perhaps, Melissa would do better than she and George did. Maybe she'd talk instead of yell. And listen instead of assume. "Give him a chance to explain," she said, before she realized she'd opened her mouth.

"Oh, I'll give him a chance. I think with the way things are going for him tonight, he'll be glad to have someone allow him a word." She nodded back toward the court.

Jillian followed her gaze. It was true. The team wasn't exactly playing very well, and if one took the time to pay attention, it was obvious who the odd man out was. Every pass to Taro seemed a little stiff and hesitant, as if they weren't sure they wanted to do it, like they couldn't trust him.

I think that's the first time I've seen men playing basketball while hindered by emotion.

She decided not to think about it anymore and watched George play. She loved the way he moved when he played, how his muscles flexed and his eyes flashed, all in a rhythm of his own making. It was like watching music, if such a thing were possible, the kind of thing poets attempt to put into words.

No wonder I'm so out of my mind. The man is the personification of absolutely everything I'm passionate about.

"Wow, look at that face!" Melissa said, from beside her.

"Hmm?" She returned her focus to Melissa.

"Does he," Melissa nodded toward the court, "know you feel like *that* about him?"

"I hope so." *I've told him. He'd have to know. Unless... have I shown him?*

At the half, George immediately jogged over to the bleachers, completely uninterested in anything to do with the game for the few minutes he didn't have to be. "Hi, Sweetheart!" He said, and Jillian leaned forward to kiss him on the lips.

"Hi!"

"I'm glad you're here. Does this mean Lacey's doing better?" He dropped to the bleacher at her feet.

"She's been awake, but not saying much more than to ask what happened and that she's tired. The doctors say she's doing really well." Jillian scooched down to the bleacher he was sitting on and he smiled and reached for her hand as he mumbled something about being a sweaty mess and she didn't have to get too close.

"You look fantastic out there," Jillian said.

"Thanks, you look fantastic too," George said, as his eyes focused on her face and Jillian felt herself inhale at his intensity. "Do you have to go back to the hospital soon? Are you hanging around for a little while?"

"I've been told to quit feeling guilty about not being there twenty-four hours a day and not to go back tonight. So, I'm giving myself a break. I'm also planning to go in for at least a half-day at work tomorrow."

"So, you're available for the rest of the evening?" George asked, with a little hope in his voice.

"Yes," Jillian said.

"Perfect. I've got some stuff I want to talk over with you. Maybe we can ditch these guys, go back to my place, crack open a bottle of wine, and relax."

"Stuff to talk over?"

George grinned. "Nothing bad, Sweetheart. No State of the Union speech or anything." He laughed. "We just did *that*. It's just some stuff to talk about."

"Um," Jillian said, "sure. Sure, that sounds fine. We'll need to stop for Charlie-"

"No problem. We'll stop for Charlie and get your things. We'll sleep at my place tonight. If that's okay."

"Do you want to get a drink with your team?"

"Tonight? No." George said, and wondered if Jillian felt like she was being bulldozed. He was being pretty pushy... again. But he needed to talk to her about so many things. Timing being what it was, he figured to start with the new venture. Keep it limited to that for the night.

It was still way too soon to be talking about anything that he wanted to talk about with regard to them, like moving in. She hadn't even used her key yet.

"Wow," Jillian said, without inflection. *What? What? What?*

"That's it?" George asked, expecting a reaction with at least some emotion from the woman leaning back against his sofa.

Jillian took another sip of her wine and smiled. "I'm just trying to form a solid coherent sentence out of the myriad of questions that are circling in my mind. It's incredibly difficult." *Why can I absolutely never, ever, anticipate anything that this man is going to say? Never!*

"Oh, come on."

"Okay. I think that you are probably the most... No, that's not it... You're the bravest man, I know." She shook her head. *My God, George.* "But, I guess I'm just confused. Have we, or have we not, been fighting over a job for the last year?"

"Yep," George said, as slipped his arm behind her. *She hates this.*

"And now, you're just going to walk away..." *Walk away with nothing.*

"Yep," George nodded. *And she's taking the long and sarcastic road to say it.*

"And risk everything you've got to start a company which may never pay back a penny of what you're going to put in." *You're... amazing, George.*

"Yep," George nodded again. *And here comes the boom.*

Jillian sat forward, away from his arm, and set her glass on the coffee table. She shifted on the couch to pull one of her knees up, so she could turn her body to look him in the eye. "Then... I guess... I have to ask the question... Are you going to take on any investors?"

"Huh?" He asked.

"I have some cash set aside. If you're going to do this, I would love to make an investment."

"You would?" *You would?*

"Oh, yeah." She stood up. "Where are you planning to set up? I assume here, in the house, right? A bedroom or the morning room?" *You are the bravest man I've ever known. Probably a little insane too. But that goes with the bravery. My Don Quixote doesn't tilt at windmills, he tilts at computer servers.*

She held out her hand and George grabbed it. They walked together to the morning room. "It's probably big enough to let everyone have some space. A bedroom would be too crowded with more than one of you. And if you each take one and have your own offices, it'll be hard to work together."

"You think?" George asked, putting his arm around her shoulders.

"Hmm. I'll do a little research into the current philosophy of color for work spaces." She looked up at him. "I'll buy in by purchasing the furniture. What do you think? Will you sell me a small piece of the pie while it's still on ground floor?"

"Was that a joke?"

"What?"

"The pun, the ground floor..."

"Nope," Jillian said, with a smile. "I wish I'd thought of that. But, I'm serious. Can I buy in?"

"Why would you want to?"

"Because if there's anyone in the whole world who can pour enough energy into this idea to make it work, it's you. I just hope you pick the right people to work with. And that they can keep up with you."

George nodded. "Yeah. About that. I've, uh, I've asked Vidar."

"Oh, yeah?"

"He wanted to be in video games when he gave up and came to Gardiner. Like me."

"Well, you'll have to make him smoke outside."

George chuckled. "I'll definitely do that. Maybe, he'll quit. He doesn't actually smoke that much. He doesn't go out every hour."

"Eh," Jillian shrugged.

George cleared his throat. "And, I've asked Irene."

"Irene! You're leaving Gardiner D and taking both Vidar and Irene with you? If I get the Director Job, I'll be down two managers and two programmers, one of which I was considering suggesting as a possible promotion to manager!" Jillian shook her head. "Geez, George. Could you do a little more damage on your way out?"

"Hey, now. Let's chill-"

"Sorry!" Jillian said, and ran a hand through her hair, pushing it back. "That was work Jillian having a total freak out." She leaned against him. "Girlfriend Jillian is back now."

"Oh, yeah?" George tilted his head.

"Yeah." She slid her arm around his waist. "And the girlfriend says, 'Excellent choices. You're assembling a great team. You're not only brave, but very smart.'"

"Well, girlfriend Jillian, thank you. Thank you for your support." George dropped a kiss on her hair.

"Just remember, girlfriend Jillian may bring the stress of her job home with her. Don't take anybody else or when work Jillian melts down, the overlap might be unpleasant."

George laughed. "I wasn't planning to take any more staff with me. Heck, I'm not even sure I've got Irene. Vidar, yes. But Irene, she wanted to talk it over with husband and so on. You may still have her."

"Oh, that's not fair." Jillian tilted her head up to see George's face again.

"What?"

"Now I get to be multiple personalities for real. Work Jillian hoping she stays and girlfriend Jillian hoping she joins you."

"At least you aren't referring to yourself as two separate people and in the third person." He said, with a chuckle.

"Oh!" Jillian playfully swatted him on the behind.

He reached back and grabbed her hand, turning her to face him, and pulling her up against him so his hands could slide around her. "Hey, does girlfriend Jillian want to celebrate?"

She wrapped her free arm around him. "With another sip of wine, definitely. But," she dropped her eyes, "some of the celebration needs to wait until tomorrow night."

"Ah," George said, quietly. "How about we just make out, tonight?"

Jillian laughed and shook her head. "Sure. A little more wine. Put on a little mood music."

George kissed her softly. "Can I take one minute to tell you how much it means to me that you're being so supportive of this?"

"Uh-huh." She said, and kissed him softly.

George smiled against her lips. "It means the world. Really. I don't know if I'd have the nerve otherwise."

Jillian answered him with her eyes still closed. "You've got enough nerve to do it all on your own. And enough drive for any five or six people. I'm just the lucky one who gets to watch you succeed."

"I love you so damn much," George said, and then kissed her dizzy again.

Around 2 am Jillian woke up from a nightmare where she couldn't breathe, and tried to keep still and not bother George. Shaking off the nightmare was hard enough, but listening to the chatter in her head once she'd calmed down, made it completely impossible to go back to sleep.

If anyone can do it, George can. Right? Of course. Assuming his idea is any good. It must be, since Vidar is on board. So it's good. Right?

But he's taking two people with him. And we still have to get the investment from a man I've sworn at and threw things at, to save the company, or there may not be work for any of us. Oh, my God. Can it get any worse?

I'll lose my job when Gardiner finds out what happened with Grec. For that matter, he may fire me if he finds out about me and George. And then I'll be unemployed. And George will be eating up whatever savings he has. And he might lose his house.

Oh, God. Can it get worse?

Even though, rationally, she knew it wouldn't affect the outcome of anything, she wasn't about to say any of her worries out loud. Not even to the Universe. It was better to just keep going, than to acknowledge the possibility of trouble and invite it to come faster.

She was going to have to ask George to handle all the presentation stuff, when it came time to deal with Grec, she would only be a liability if she was in the room, assuming George was still there. *Everything with George is 'right now.' He may just turn in his resignation tomorrow.*

How did he survive waiting for Gardiner to make a decision on the Director position? I can hardly believe that he didn't chew off his own arm. Then again, maybe the reason he was able to wait had something to do with this other dream. He didn't really want this job that badly.

If that's true, and his impatience is directly proportional to how badly he wants something… that's pretty flattering to me. He won't wait a minute for me.

She rolled onto her stomach and put her face in the pillow.

I have to admit to myself, at least, that I'm glad… when it came to getting back together, anyway. Now that we're on the other side, that is. I could have used more time before, but… I love being with him.

She turned her face toward him. He was breathing so heavily, it was just shy of a snore. He was so peaceful. *Hard to imagine this person being so driven when he's awake. He's on fire… all… the… time.*

Studying him a little closer, despite the dim light, Jillian propped herself up on her elbow. Unable to resist, she lightly touched his hair. *He's full of so much fire. That's what I saw, wasn't it? All that energy and drive… his fire. I don't have that much* fire *in me. But he does. So much fire.*

Sliding back down onto her pillow, she pulled her arm back. *Don't wake him just because you can't help yourself.* She rolled onto her back. *You've got impulse control issues too.* She exhaled until she'd emptied her lungs and thought she'd pass out from the lack of oxygen.

What are we going to do if we're both jobless and broke? Trying not to think about her parents' likely reaction to her losing her job, she took a few deep breaths. And then their reaction to her having put some of her savings into George's venture. A few more deep breaths. *I wish Charlie was here. He'd let me scratch his ears, right now, and he might even purr.*

It was easier to calm down when she remembered that George's morning room was about to become an office space instead of the lovely breakfast room she'd fantasized about. *Good thing I never mentioned that to him. What would he have thought?*

She rolled onto her side and then her back a few more times, until she finally fell back asleep.

At least it felt like a somewhat normal morning, as far as normal had begun to establish itself. George and Jillian walked into the office together, then ascended the stairs carrying their bags and coats, and moved across the floor side by side. Having arrived close to their usual time, only a few people were on the floor to notice them, but Ishi was one of those people, and she wandered over to Jillian's office after a few minutes.

"So, it's all good again?" She asked, from Jillian's doorway.

"What do you mean?" Jillian asked, as she booted her computer, trying to be funny.

Ishi crossed her arms. "Duh."

Jillian nodded. "It's all good."

"*He* said so yesterday, but you weren't around."

"Well, *he* was right."

"Good," Ishi said, and nodded. "You're good together." She immediately turned and left Jillian stunned at her keyboard to have received such a positive comment from Ishi.

The moment her computer had finished logging in, Jillian's IM popped up.

Ping.

Hi, beautiful.

Be professional, George. Enter key.

We have a meeting with Hardware in less than thirty minutes. Enter key.

Ping.

I know.

Ping.

I just wanted to say one thing.

Oh? Enter key.

Ping.

You're not just my love, you're my everything.

Jillian placed her hand to her heart. "Oh, my God, George. Do you sit around thinking up this stuff just to floor me?"

Ping.

I read that somewhere. Possibly a greeting card. But it's still true.

Jillian grinned. *My honest guy.*

That's sweet. Let's plan on lunch and we'll talk then. For now... work. Enter key.

Ping.

You're so right. Work.

The IM went silent then. For over five minutes the IM was silent. Jillian took out her notes from the last meeting with Hardware and looked through them. George had missed it.

Did you want to see my notes from the last meeting with Hardware? Enter key.

Ping.

Not right now. I'm working. Work. Work. Work.

Jillian raised her eyebrows.

Sounds to me like you're goofing off. What are you working on? Enter key.

Ping.

Trying to turn into an orange.

Jillian thought about it for a moment.

Why are you trying to turn into an orange? Enter key.

Ping.

So I can concentrate.

Jillian groaned and shook her head. *It's going to be a dilly of a day.*

CHAPTER THIRTY-ONE

Rachel interrupted the meeting with Hardware just a few minutes in, saying, "Jillian, George... Gardiner wants you both in his office immediately."

Jillian and George exchanged a look and then excused themselves from the meeting. Rachel waited for them, but she had no additional information to share. "He called up requesting you both, that's all I know."

George voiced the obvious concern that Jillian didn't want to acknowledge. "Did he ask for Sergei, Taro, and Neal too?"

"I don't know," Rachel said. "The request was 'immediately,' so I came straight down for you. I'm sorry, I don't know anything else."

Jillian nodded to George and held her notepad tight across her chest. Whatever Gardiner wanted to see them about, it didn't necessarily have to be bad. It was just *immediate*. But her nerves were on edge from the moment Rachel entered the room.

George was far less concerned, though still concerned. There was more than enough going on than to focus any worry on what Gardiner wanted to see them about so urgently. He was still waiting on an answer from Irene, which was far more concerning. Without her, he'd need to look for another artist. And he still hadn't mentioned to Jillian the idea of her helping as a music consultant, or perhaps referring him to someone else.

Rachel left them at Gardiner's reception area, though Jillian suspected she'd walked with them all that way in hopes of being admitted to find out what the fuss was about. But the issue at hand was clearly bigger than just George and Jillian as Sergei was close on their heels, whispering loudly, "Any idea what it's about?"

Jillian could only shake her head, George shrugged. The assistant told them to go in, so they didn't hesitate.

On the other side of the door, Gardiner was waiting at his conference table with Mr. Grec. Gardiner waved them to the table. Jillian paused momentarily in her stride, but took a seat opposite Grec. George and Sergei flanked her, taking their seats on either side of her in unison. Jillian wondered if Gardiner noticed the synchronization, or Grec, but regardless, she had and she was felt a wave of gratitude for the support.

Grec narrowed his eyes, almost imperceptibly, at Sergei, but Jillian caught it and then her stomach turned. *This will be... interesting.* She tried to think somewhat positively, rather than assuming the worst.

Under the table, George patted Jillian's leg in an attempt to be supportive and comforting. She placed her elbows on the arms of the chair and put her hands together in her lap. George wondered if it was a signal to him to back off, but she slid her shoe against his for a moment and he took it as a sign that she'd received his message and he quickly moved his hand before anyone else noticed it.

Once Neal and Taro arrived and occupied additional seats, Gardiner began the meeting telling them all that the unscheduled conference was about the competition and then turned it over to Grec.

Cisco Grec cleared his throat and no one in the room thought it was for any reason other than to command attention. He sat back in his chair and Jillian mused that he looked quite bored. Though, whether that look was a cover or not, she hadn't decided before he spoke.

"I have changed my immediate plans and will be leaving the country Monday evening. Therefore, your presentations will need to occur on Monday morning, so that Gardiner and I may conclude our business, one way or the other, prior to my departure."

Neal and Taro sat back in their chairs. Sergei didn't move a muscle as far as Jillian could tell, but she raised her joined hands just a little. *And he gets his revenge. Just like I was worrying about.* George crossed his arms. Gardiner leaned forward.

"I know that this is unexpected and that your teams are going to be... displeased with this news. We'll have the presentations..."

Gardiner continued to talk about how Monday morning would unfold, but Jillian only listened peripherally. Instead she looked at Grec and he met her gaze. She thought he looked smug, but with a touch of bitterness beneath it. The more she thought about it, the less she was convinced that his move was intended to punish her. *He's pleased to be exerting his power, but he's not enjoying it the way I'd have expected.*

Gardiner didn't take too long running through his information and he excused them without taking questions, the moment he'd finished. George, Taro, Neal, and Sergei all stood. Jillian continued her eye contact with Grec and rose slowly. She committed to the decision as she straightened. "Gardiner, might I have a word with Mr. Grec?"

The room had been silent, but George felt it get quieter. He turned his back to the table and leaned over sideways to speak in Jillian's ear. "You sure about that?"

Sergei mirrored George and whispered, "Is that a good idea?"

She stayed were she was, eyes locked with Grec, and made an 'mm-hmm' sound.

Gardiner looked at Grec who lifted a hand and shooed Gardiner away. Gardiner glanced at Jillian and then rose, walked to his desk to pick up a sheet of paper, and then lead Jillian's peers out of the room.

Jillian sat back down.

"Well, a few private moments, after all," Grec said.

After shutting the door behind him, Gardiner raced over to his assistant's desk and, while picking up her phone handset, asked her to leave reception. She gave a wide-eyed, quizzical look, but left and shut the double doors behind her.

Gardiner pushed a button on the phone and then placed the handset back in the cradle. The speaker crackled and George thought he could just make out Jillian's voice. *He must have turned on the intercom or something while he was at his desk.* Gardiner turned up the volume and, though the sound was a little hard to listen to with the intermittent crackling, all the men leaned over to listen to what was being said.

"So your protector works here. I didn't meet him on the office tour," Grec said.

Jillian replied, with a simple, "Yes."

"Still not your boyfriend?"

"No, the gentleman who was on my right side is my boyfriend."

Gardiner looked up from the phone to stare at George. *I guess word still hasn't gotten around. That's surprising.* He shrugged at Gardiner who shook his head and then looked back down at the phone.

"I see," Grec said, and began to rock his chair. "He's the one who interrupted our conversation when we were introduced, isn't he?"

"Yes," Jillian said. "He is."

Grec tilted his head. "I wonder if he knows you never mentioned him."

"I didn't ask to speak to you to discuss that."

"No?" Grec asked.

"No," Jillian placed her elbows on the arms of the chair again. "I want to ask you, directly, if I had anything to do with your change of plans and if there might be some way to change them back."

Grec smiled, a slow smile that made Jillian think that he believed he had her exactly where he wanted her. "Well, that's *the* question, isn't it?"

Jillian didn't answer, it seemed rhetorical. And she wasn't about to give the man any more openings. If he wanted to negotiate, it was up to him.

"I'm going to tell you a secret," Grec said, and leaned forward again. "Actually, show you, as well." He reached inside his suit jacket and produced a piece of paper that he opened and Jillian saw it was a check. He smiled without showing his teeth. "It could be done today." He laid the check on the table. "Cashier's check in the full amount."

"Really? So why isn't it done?" Jillian asked.

Grec refolded the check and put back in his pocket. "I could have my plane ready to depart in one hour."

"That doesn't answer my question."

"I believe it does. You needn't bring anything with you. My assistants will arrange for everything you need. And, at my direction, everything you desire." After a moment, he reached down to the floor next to him and produced a jewelry box. He placed it on the table and slid it to Jillian. "That belongs to you."

Gardiner mumbled, "Holy shit. I'm in a soap opera. I can't believe this."

"I can't believe you allowed this to happen," George said. "How is it possible that *this* is your only alternative?"

Gardiner didn't answer.

"No, thank you," Jillian said, and slid the box back across the table. "I thought I made myself clear this past weekend. Give it to someone else."

Grec picked up the box, stood up, and walked around the table. Knowing he was quite capable of using his body to make her feel small and intimidated, Jillian stood up before he came too close.

"I bought this for you and you alone."

"I disagree. I think you bought it for your ego."

Gardiner winced. "She's just going to make it worse, isn't she?"

"I hope she hits him," Sergei said, and then glanced at George.

George nodded at Sergei. "I hope so too." Sergei's shoulders dropped a little and George almost smiled.

"Perhaps, you are right. It's an interesting hypothesis. We should discuss it in further detail, on the plane."

Jillian held back a laugh and shook her head. "I don't understand. I mean, I really don't understand. There have to be hundreds, probably thousands, possibly hundreds of thousands of women in this city who'd be thrilled to be invited to fly on your private jet to Europe with you. Why me?"

Sighing, Grec turned the box over in his hands, but he didn't look away from Jillian. "You remind me of someone."

"Ah. Someone you knew a long time ago, right? Someone you loved very much."

"Yes," Grec said. "My mother."

"Eww!" "Ugh!" "Gross!" The chorus seemed loud enough that they all shushed each other.

"No, no." Grec turned the box again. "Not like that. It's not an oedipal complex. You look nothing like her." He started to move again, this time, he walked very slowly around the table and Jillian turned to watch him move. "She found money offensive too." He started tapping the table with the box as he walked. "I had every intention of walking away after your... remonstration of Saturday last. But, I've found that your refusal makes you that much more interesting."

"Just my luck," Jillian said. "What was your mother's problem with money?"

He sniffed and continued on his route around the table. "She grew up without any to spare and was putting herself through school working two and three jobs, when my father saw her. His attempts to court her proved a bit disastrous." He lifted up the box. "She objected to his ostentatious displays. He sent her dozens of flowers. She hated that. He asked her to dinner, she refused to go to the restaurants he chose.

"Their first actual date, he tried to cook for her because she refused everything else. She ended up cooking.

"She refused to accept presents from him. He found it very annoying."

"She sounds like a very smart woman," Jillian said, "with a good reputation."

"Mmm," Grec said. "She didn't want him coming around. He was after her for months before that first date. Eventually, she changed her mind. But even after they married, she wouldn't go shopping with his money without someone along to prod her, like my aunt or my grandmother."

He waved the box at her. "You're the first American I've met who's rejected something as beautiful as this. And like my father, it only makes me want you to take it more."

Trying to turn the conversation, Jillian took a step and then spoke. "I would hope that the others are sufficiently ashamed of themselves. But they probably aren't," Jillian said.

Grec smiled. "I doubt they've ever given it more than a moment's thought, if that."

"How incredibly sad."

"Tell me, do you really reject this due to the nature of the gift, or is it something less noble? A loyalty to your boyfriend, perhaps?"

"And loyalty is less noble?"

"I concede your point." Grec was nearly around the table and getting closer again. "Now, I shall make another one." He stopped short of her. "He works here. You probably have many friends here. I'm in a position to keep them employed."

Gripping the desk and gritting his teeth, George realized he was shaking. The fury was beginning to boil over. "Why are we all just standing around listening to this?!"

"Because," Sergei said, "she asked us to give her a minute. She asked you to trust her. I'm sure if he gets handsy, she'll make some noise."

"Yes, you are," Jillian said. "And it's shameful to think that you're making that decision based on something so childish."

"Childish? You think passion is childish?"

"I think you're having a temper tantrum. My two year-old nephew acts like this when he wants a toy and his mother says no." She crossed her arms. "And when he gets it, he's bored in less than hour. I think your interest in me would wane the minute I set foot on the plane."

"I, respectfully, disagree." He tapped the box against the table again. "I believe you'll outlast every woman I've ever met."

She snorted. "I'll lose my color the moment I become like all the others. I'm sorry to disappoint you, but I think you're chasing a fantasy. And I assure you that I'm not interested in an experiment to find out if I'm wrong. The fact is there is nothing you can offer me that I want."

"Even employment for those you care you about?"

Jillian shook her head. "You really don't understand, do you? Care and concern is a two way street. If they care about me too, they'd never ask me to do it."

Gardiner turned a shade of green and sat down.

George glared at him. *About time you felt some remorse, you miserable piece of shit.*

"Besides," Jillian continued, "you should really think about your leverage. Once they're unemployed, I'll have no reason to speak to you. The only thing you could possibly get out of letting this company fail is a sick satisfaction from punishing me.

"Truly, is that who you are? A man who has a temper tantrum when he can't get what he wants and who punishes people for being loyal? How sad for you. No wonder you feel comfortable making rude propositions. You've no manners at all and you might even be fundamentally damaged.

"Your mother would be mortified."

"My mother was also a very practical woman. I still question that you really understand what I'm offering," Grec said.

"I don't care about what you're offering, even if I am misunderstanding. I already have everything I need." Jillian waved her finger toward the box. "*That* may be very pretty, but I don't need that."

Grec exhaled. "That's sounds like a very definite 'no.'"

"It was a very definite 'no' on Saturday."

Gardiner rolled his assistant's chair backward and sat forward to put his head between his legs.

"Are you hyperventilating, Gardiner?" Neal asked. "Do you need us to get you anything?"

Gardiner shook his head. "This is the worst thing I've ever heard."

"Because you set up one of your employees," George said, "or because you foresee the money you need flying away on a jet?"

"That's very disappointing to hear."

"It's disappointing to say," Jillian said.

"Touché." Grec tapped the box on the table one last time and then lifted it up and extended it to her. "I understand that you won't be joining me, now or in the future. But please, keep this. I meant what I said, that this was purchased with you in mind."

Jillian closed her eyes for just a moment. "No."

"You could put it in a safety deposit box and pretend it isn't even there. Or you could sell it. Or give to your daughter, if you should ever have one."

"No."

"Why?"

"I told you, I don't want it. And, of course, and maybe even more importantly, he wouldn't like it."

Grec raised his eyebrows. "*He* wouldn't like it. I didn't realize the relationship was *that* serious. More than a boyfriend?"

Jillian sat on the edge of the conference table. "It's none of your business. But, what he thinks matters. It matters quite a lot."

"Love then, hmm?" Grec perched next to her, but not too close. "That's good for my ego."

"Yes," Jillian said.

"Engaged?"

"No," Jillian said.

"Fool," Grec said.

"Pardon?"

"A woman who gives up a fifty thousand dollar bracelet for a man is the woman to commit to."

"That's worth fifty thousand dollars?"

Taro grabbed George's arm and turned him to sit on the desk. "Remember to breathe."

Sergei lifted his hands. "I had no idea."

Fifty-fucking-thousand dollars. Holy crap.

"You have *got* to be kidding me," Jillian said, and took the box from him and snapped it open.

"I suppose you don't know much about jewelry, then."

"I didn't realize that anyone made a bracelet worth that much."

Grec laughed for a moment. "If you have the money, someone will make it." His lips turned up further. "If you aren't accepting it, why don't you at least try it on?"

"Still trying to tempt me? Even after all this?"

Grec stood again. "If you won't join me in Europe, it would give me immense pleasure to have you accept that."

Shutting the box again, Jillian actually smiled. "You know what would give me immense pleasure? If you handed that check to Gardiner and could fly off into the night as a hero. Then, I'd be able to think of you as a really good person. I might even feel a little sadness that I said 'no' to a good person. "

"Very good," Grec said. "That's a very emotionally charged argument. All right. I'll deal with you. You keep the bracelet and I'll present the check to Gardiner."

"I'm truly sorry, but I can't pretend for you. The answer is still no. Give him the check because it's the right thing to do."

"Perhaps, it isn't. I still haven't seen what you've all been doing for the last two weeks."

"You're right, but we both know you're decision isn't hinging on that, or you wouldn't have brought the check today." Jillian handed him the box.

"There's really no point in continuing this. You know it and I know it. Neither of us is budging."

Grec took the box and set it on the table and then crossed his arms. "I suppose you're right. I suppose I haven't provided you any good arguments on my side. You've given an interesting one, but it hasn't moved me either." He took a breath. "Stalemate. Very few of my chess games end in a stalemate."

Jillian snickered. "Nor mine."

"So what do we do? Both lose?"

Crossing her arms, Jillian nodded. "Starting to look like it. That's the problem with war in real life. No one willing to surrender until the casualties have piled up."

"And it turns out you're a philosopher."

"Actually, I'm more studied in game theory than philosophy, though game theory can be applied to philosophy. Do you know anything about game theory?"

Grec tilted his head. "I can't say I do."

"Probably for the best. I don't think I've been playing very well."

"No?"

"No. We are very much in a classic zero-sum game. When one wins, the other loses. The only attempt I've made to change that didn't give you much to win by, except a small ego boost, calling you a hero. Not very good.

"Unless one of us is willing to change the rules or the stakes, we're going to stay in this stalemate."

"Was I supposed to understand that?" Grec asked.

Jillian shrugged.

"The one thing I think I heard was one wins and one loses. I don't see it that way. I think we can both win."

"And I don't. Which is the root of the current stalemate," Jillian said. "Well, I give up. I'm not willing to budge. What you're asking, I won't do. So that's that."

"That's... that."

"Is the presentation on for Monday? Or will you being flying out tonight, after all?"

"I have yet to decide."

"All right. I suppose we ought to open the door and announce that our negotiations have failed and a state of war continues, unobstructed and without much hope for a cease fire."

"A bleak outlook, indeed."

"Indeed."

Jillian stood up from the table and dropped her arms. "You're a worthy opponent, Mr. Grec." She held out her hand.

He took her hand for a brief shake. "I wish very much that we were not opponents."

"As do I."

She turned and walked to the door, then waited. Grec followed her after a few moments and opened the door for her. "Thank you," she said, and walked out.

Gardiner had waited until the last second to disconnect the intercom, leaving them all standing around the assistant's desk, looking a particularly odd group when Jillian and Grec emerged from Gardiner's office. Jillian made a face. "Gentlemen," she said.

The only face she looked at, though, was George's. His face was indecipherable.

Mr. Grec walked over to the group and addressed Gardiner. "It's become painfully obvious that my presence here is not beneficial. I must apologize for the time that your employees have expended on a project that I can no longer wait around to see completed."

Looking mildly ill, Gardiner stood and slowly walked around the desk. "I see. I had certainly hoped for a different conclusion. Are you certain you couldn't even take a look now, before you leave? It wouldn't be organized, but I'm sure that in fifteen minutes-"

"I'm quite certain. Thank you. I'll pick up my things." He turned and re-entered Gardiner's office.

Jillian looked at the floor. "I'm sorry, Gardiner. I tried my best. But, I'm afraid that Mr. Grec and I were unable to reach any kind of compromise."

"Don't you dare," Neal said. "George, don't you let her act like she let anyone down."

With more than a passing glance at Neal, Jillian provided them all with a fake smile. "I did let you all down. I thought I could convince him. Instead, I've driven him off completely."

George wanted to put his arm around her, but had to settle for crossing his arms and looking at Gardiner, with raised eyebrows. "Gardiner?"

Gardiner shuffled his feet as he took a few steps. "*I'm* sorry, Jillian. You've been... I'm sorry."

The group turned as Grec emerged from Gardiner's office. "Gardiner," Grec said, and nodded his head toward the door. No longer shuffling his feet, Gardiner quickly joined Grec to escort him from the building.

Grec turned as the outer doors were opened and looked at Jillian. "I hope it will help you to know you were right."

Then he was gone and Jillian put her hand on her forehead and shook her head. "I think I need to have my head examined."

"Why?" George asked.

"I've never played poker and I'm not good at this game. Why I ever thought I could outwit or even just keep up with that man, I don't know. It's probably all my fault."

"I don't know anyone who could have won that setup," Sergei said. "I think you did quite well."

"No," Jillian said. "If you'd been there..." She noticed the look the four musketeers shared amongst themselves. "What?"

With Gardiner out of the room, George closed the gap and put his arm around her. "Let's go. You need a minute or two to regroup. We'll go get our things and go to lunch."

"What aren't you all telling me?"

The door banged just a little against the frame as Gardiner rushed back in. "I wouldn't have believed it if I didn't have it in my hand." He lifted his hand and held up papers. "He signed and gave me the check."

George tightened his grip on Jillian. "Well, we're heading out to lunch." He started to walk and tugged her along.

"Yeah, lunch," Neal said, and followed along, Sergei and even Taro joining him.

Gardiner's face dropped.

"Congratulations, Gardiner," Jillian said, stopping her stride. "We're all very happy that it turned out so well."

"I know," Gardiner started to say something and then stopped. "I'm in awe of you, Miss Braden."

George tightened his grip on Jillian. "We all are. You can thank her later, Sir."

"What's going on?" Jillian asked, as George tugged her on through the outer doors. "I appreciate the sentiment and solidarity, but, shouldn't this all be cause to celebrate?"

George lowered his arm as soon as they were out of the office, still leading the way around the floor toward the elevator, with Jillian next to him and Sergei with Neal flanking them, and Taro bringing up the rear. When they arrived at the elevator, George pressed the button and threw a glance over Jillian's head to Sergei. "We heard it all," he said, quietly.

"Pardon?" Jillian asked. *They couldn't have heard it all. There's no way.*

Next to her, she could see Sergei nod.

"What do you mean, you heard it all? How could you hear it all?"

"Gardiner turned on the intercom before he left. We listened from Liz's desk phone."

"Why? Why?" Jillian took a breath. "Why?" *No. No. No. NoNoNoNoNoNo.* Jillian pushed Sergei aside and headed for the stairs. *How humiliating. How mortifying.*

Feeling her move the moment it happened, George followed Jillian to the stairwell, glancing back to the guys and waving them on to the elevator. Even in heels, Jillian was taking the stairs as fast as he could. "Jillian," he called out, unable to catch her.

When she hit the mid-floor landing, she turned. "Why?" She asked, again.

George stepped onto the landing. "Curiosity and concern. There were a few moments I wanted to barge back in there and hit him. But you held your own."

Shaking her head, Jillian hit the stairs again. "The respect you all have for me is tremendous, isn't it?"

"What does it matter if we listened? It was all *you* in the room."

Stopping mid-flight, Jillian turned again and looked at George. "I don't know. I don't know anything. I'm so confused and irritated and exhausted and, and, and angry. I don't know…"

George took the remaining stair and stood on the one just below her. "I'm sorry, Sweetheart. I hate that guy." He tentatively reached out a hand toward her.

Oh, George. Jillian wrapped her arms around him to bury her face against his neck and he held her with one hand, while holding onto the railing with the other.

"Sweetheart, you were fantastic. Smart and tough. I can hardly imagine anyone handling him any better."

"I'm so embarrassed you heard all that."

George shook his head lightly so he wouldn't hit her with his chin. "You shouldn't be. You were marvelous."

"So are you and the musketeers. I'm not sure that walking out on Gardiner like that was the best idea, but it was really generous of you all."

"It wasn't generous, it was appropriate. Come on." He started to nudge her up the stairwell. "We're going to go announce to our team that the competition is over, they all have the afternoon off, and then you, me, and the musketeers are going to lunch and celebrate. Screw the rest of the details. The company is saved, so who gives a rip."

Not particularly feeling like facing anybody, Jillian suggested that a voice mail to everyone would be enough. But Sergei, Neal, and Taro had beaten them to the floor and by the time they opened the door to the stairwell, there was a small mob waiting for them on the other side. *Thank God, I didn't cry. I don't know if I could show my face, if I had tear streaks.*

There was a spontaneous round of applause. Jillian looked at George and he shrugged and then said, "Take a bow." She looked at him wide-eyed. "How about the cute, little curtsy you did the other week on stage?" He grabbed her hand and then stepped to the side, so she was front and center all by herself, but he still held on for support.

Feeling more than a little ridiculous, especially since she didn't know what everyone had been told, but also being on the spot, Jillian took George's suggestion to heart, and swept a foot behind her to execute a very small and modest curtsy. Then she said, "Thank you."

The people who had gathered didn't stop applauding at that. It took both George and Sergei waving them down to break it up. Then it started right back up again, when George told everyone that not only was the competition off and it was back to business as usual, but to take the afternoon off. *At least this time it has nothing to do with me.*

Finally, the impromptu celebration broke up and Jillian escaped to her office. She sincerely debated hiding in the ladies' room, but decided to get all her things together and just get out of the building. She'd have the whole weekend to try to get her mind together, assuming George didn't drop any other bombs on her.

Quickly shutting down her computer, she set her bags on her desk, and turned to grab her coat. Assuming the knock on her door was George, Jillian turned back with a somewhat plastered on smile on her face, wanting to give him the most positive moment she could, despite how she felt.

Instead of George, it was Gardiner.

"Oh," Jillian said, flatly, unable to come up with a more intellectual thought.

"Hello," Gardiner said. "I've…

Jillian crossed her arms. "You've?"

"I want you to know, Jillian, that I never expected things to go that far."

"Really?" Jillian asked, and began to load her computer into her bag. "Patty seemed to know exactly how far it was likely to go. Of course, she suggested that it be just dinner. So maybe I'm wrong and she really didn't see 'fly off with me on my private jet' coming."

"This wasn't how any of this was supposed to go. He was supposed to come in here, see everyone hard at work and just sign on. The competition was a surprise and his interest… in you, was equally unexpected. Really. I never meant-"

"You're lucky I don't sue," Jillian said. "I don't know that I had much of a case until today. But today, today was a setup."

Gardiner shook his head. "I didn't think it would be. Not really. You know that, right? I didn't send for just you. I sent for all of you."

"And you left it to me to fix everything for you."

Gardiner exhaled. "I'm really sorry that it came to that. Just remember, you asked to be alone in the room with him. I didn't force or even suggest it."

Jillian finished bagging her computer and grabbed her things. "I'll be taking the afternoon off."

"Oh," Gardiner said, and moved out of her office doorway as she stepped out and then locked up. "I don't suppose…"

"I won't be suing you, Gardiner," Jillian said, with a smile. "We'll all get back to work on Monday and dig ourselves out of this hole."

"Excellent. That's really great. Thank you, Jillian. I think things are going to be much better on Monday. We have our backing-"

"That's right. Don't forget to take care of that check. Get to the bank before it closes."

"That's my next stop. I just wanted to be sure that everything was okay here, first."

Jillian bit back a sarcastic laugh. "Everything's just fine," she said. "Just fine."

CHAPTER THIRTY-TWO

Everyone was looking at Jillian like she'd cracked or something. She wouldn't consider eating lunch with the musketeers just a few weeks ago and suddenly it seemed like such a great idea. She even agreed to eat at one of their favorite lunchtime haunts. When they'd arrived, they were all treating her like a fragile piece of china, except for Taro, who said absolutely nothing. Jillian couldn't stand for it. By the time the food arrived she'd told a joke and they were all in shock.

It was clear that Taro was still on the outs with the other musketeers and Jillian started to feel a little bad about that. He'd made his own bed, but that didn't mean he couldn't grovel a little and work his way out of it. "How are plans for the wedding?" She asked, during a slight lull in the conversation.

Taro laid down his fork. "Actually, they're going pretty well. But, I think my Best Man is backing out on me."

"What?" George asked.

"I thought we were trying for a party tonight. But, I guess that's off since... everything went down."

"Oh," George said. "I didn't mean that. I forgot about it. Completely."

"If you want to back out, just say so." Taro crossed his arms and locked his jaw.

Sergei sat back in his chair, as did Neal. *A showdown?* Jillian wondered.

"I wouldn't do that." He turned to Jillian. "Forgive me if I hang out with the guys tonight?"

It's been daaaaays since we were together and now you want to hang out with your buddies tonight instead of make love with me. "Sure," she said, trying to cover her thoughts and her hormones.

Focusing back on Taro, George said, "It'll have to be just us. Since I didn't get around to telling anybody else. What do you think?" He threw a glance to Sergei. "Poker?"

Sergei nodded and replied, "Sure." But then he glanced at Jillian.

George caught it but moved on and looked at Neal. "You in?"

Neal nodded and George looked back at Taro. "We can try again in another few weeks, if you want. Or, you got the three of us tonight for cards."

Taro also glanced at Jillian for a moment, then looked at George and dropped his arms. "Hey, you guys are the ones I want there the most, anyway."

George leaned over and kissed Jillian's cheek. "Thanks, Sweetheart. You're the best. Since we don't have to work tomorrow, we'll do something special."

Biting back her irritation and her thoughts, especially the sarcastic one that maybe she'd have plans without him for tomorrow, she smiled sweetly. "Call me later, then."

"Count on it," George said.

They split up after lunch. Jillian headed home to drop off her things and then go to the hospital telling herself that it was for the best she wasn't seeing George. She needed to visit with Lacey and see if her parents needed anything. Thinking of herself as being unselfish made her feel better.

As she headed out to the hospital, Mrs. Kerchner called to her from her doorway. Jillian joined her in her apartment and let her know that she and George were back together and that she'd be spending time at the hospital with her friend.

Mrs. Kerchner smiled at the reconciliation and then sent a jar of jam with Jillian for Lacey's parents. Not knowing what else to do, Jillian took it with her after a big thank you.

George and the guys got started early on the cards and the beer; it was still mid-afternoon. Neal was the one to call him on the idea he'd had that if he could clean everybody out, the game would break up early enough that he could still see Jillian. "It wouldn't ruin my night," George answered. "But I'm planning on buying pizza and keeping it going until everybody's really done."

The real challenge was keeping the conversation going. The stuff Taro had pulled still hung in George's mind and Sergei wasn't exactly acting like he and Taro were buddies again either. George knew he and Taro were going to stay friends, just like he knew he was going to stay friends with

Sergei, though it was going to help when Sergei started dating somebody, *anybody*. It seemed to be mostly Neal and Sergei talking, when conversation was actually called for.

When George took a large pot on a Straight, everyone called for a break in the action.

"You drew to a Straight?" Sergei asked, when Neal and Taro went into the kitchen.

"Sometimes you've got the cards. Sometimes you've got luck. Sometimes you've got both."

Sergei picked up another bottle of beer, opened it, and then said, "You've got luck. More than your share, I'd say. What are you *doing* playing poker tonight?"

George shrugged, wishing that anyone other than Sergei was asking him about Jillian.

"You know, I was just thinking-"

"Novel approach for you," George said.

Sergei hit George's shoulder. "I was just thinking that you're next."

"Next for what?"

Sergei gave George a knowing look. "A bachelor party."

George chuckled. "Oh, you think so, huh? For all you know, you'll meet a girl tomorrow and beat me there."

"Yeah, right. That'll happen."

"You never know. I don't even know how soon Jillian would be ready for something like that, let alone me." *I'm not going to screw this up. I've got to stop pushing her. No proposals until there's a chance she'll actually say yes.*

Sergei started laughing as Neal walked back into the family room with a bag of chips and more dip. "What's funny?"

Sergei ruffled George hair. "Dipshit here doesn't think Jillian's ready to commit."

"Really? Are you ready?" Neal asked, all innocence.

"I'd figured on maybe living together first," George said, while he smoothed his hair back, in an attempt to stave them off. "And, you know we've only been together a few weeks. I'm not walking up the aisle yet."

"You're not thinking about asking her to move in, are you?" Taro asked, returning to the table.

"Today? No." *We just got back together and she'd freak out.* With a glance around the room his mind wandered about the house, upstairs and down. Thinking of her there, talking, laughing, and even just sitting or standing. He thought of her soaking in the tub and sitting on the sofa. He thought of her cooking with him in the kitchen and next to him by the fireplace. *She loves it here.* He knew that. When she stayed over, she always settled in and moved about as though she belonged. *She belongs here. With me.*

Taro looked around. "You know, if you do, you're going to have to give up the bachelor look you've got going in here."

"What do you mean?" George asked, crossing his arms.

Taro rolled his eyes. "If she moves in, she's going to want to decorate this place. It's huge. I hope for your sake she isn't into lots of flowers. You could end up with a lot of floral wallpaper."

Neal made a face. "And the weird guest towels that no one is supposed to use with the lace. Guest soaps. I swear that one always made me wonder. Why do they call 'em guest soap or guest towels, if even the guests aren't supposed to use 'em?"

"And pink!" Taro said. "I've been in negotiations with Melissa. She honestly wants a pink bedroom. I talked her out of that, and now we're *discussing* a pink bathroom."

"What's Jillian into?" Neal asked.

"Lots of color," George said. "Mostly bright. Not pink. And her taste is just fine by me." He thought of her comments about his white walls. *Color would make this place more inviting. Hmm.*

"Oh, yeah?" Sergei asked, with a teasing lilt.

"Yeah," George said. "The first time she saw my dining room, she started this whole decorating plan for it. Very classic." *Maybe get a piano in here somewhere. That would be tempting for her. I wonder how much they cost.*

"Oh, yeah?" Sergei asked, again. "And just what does Jillian visualize for your dining room?"

George sighed. *It's going to be a long night.* He picked up the cards and handed them to Neal. "Your deal." *Gotta get everybody focused back on the game.*

Neal shook his head. "Not until we hear this. What does she want to do with your dining room?"

Malvinia had her arms crossed. "You're *not* seeing him tonight?"

"I don't know yet. It's complicated. Maybe it's for the best. I haven't had a moment of sanity in weeks."

"Sanity is overrated," Lacey murmured.

"Did we wake you?" Jillian asked, feeling instantly guilty.

"I've been doing almost nothing but sleeping," Lacey answered. "From time to time, I'm going to wake up." She tried to shift a little. "Now, I came in in the middle. What's going on?"

"It doesn't matter," Jillian said. Despite her brave words, she just wanted to find George and curl up together for the weekend, but since that wasn't going to happen… "Not really."

Malvinia opened her mouth, but before she could start to share her thoughts, Jillian's work phone started to ring. She tried not to groan. "And with my luck that will probably be a server going down and I'll be in the office tonight."

It wasn't a server. "Hi, Melissa."

"Hi, Jillian. I don't think I'm supposed to say anything, but I had to be the first... Congratulations! Gardiner started the paperwork last night. You'll probably see the official offer to be the Software Director on Monday."

"Last night? Are you sure?" Jillian asked. *That's interesting. I would have thought he would have waited until after he had the money in hand. I'd also have thought he'd wait until the end of the competition.*

"Completely sure. I just didn't see it because Becky's had it, but she finally decided she couldn't keep it a secret all weekend and called me and leaked it. I'm so happy for you."

So, he was going to give me the position all along. Wow! "Well, if you weren't supposed to tell, I'm glad you did. And thank you for the congratulations. I appreciate it."

"Of course, that's nothing compared to what's going on right now..." Melissa said.

"Oh, boy," Jillian muttered, putting her hand to her forehead. "What's going on now?"

"Well, Taro was supposed to be having some kind of bachelor party thing at George's now... and he just called. It's not a poker game, anymore. I think you might want to get over there."

"What are you talking about?"

Melissa giggled. "It's gotten interesting over there. You really should go. Bye, Jillian." Melissa hung up.

Kai, Malvinia, and Lacey were waiting for her to say something. "Well, it turns out the Director's job was mine already, regardless of everything else. Gardiner put through the paperwork." *What's going on at George's house? I can't imagine what I want to see.*

"Well," Malvinia said, "that's worthy of congratulations. You earned it. But what's with the face?"

"I don't know. Melissa said something's going on at George's and that I should get over there." Jillian sat back in her chair. "I don't think I want to know. If it's bad, I don't think I can take it right now."

"Did it sound bad?" Lacey asked, and tried to shift again. "I need to move a bit. Can someone...?"

Malvinia helped Lacey change her position just slightly, the others were too nervous to help because of all the stitches. Christy and Lacey's parents returned from grabbing a very quick bite and Jillian and Kai both vacated their chairs for Lacey's parents. The group stepped out of the room to allow Lacey's parents a few private moments to talk with Lacey.

"She's doing *really* well," Malvinia said.

A chorus of pleased comments sounded and then Kai asked Jillian if she was going to go see what was going on at George's house.

It was Christy's turn to be caught up. She then followed up with, "Oh, you *gotta* go."

"I'm leaving him alone. It's a *bachelor* party. I probably don't want to know…"

Malvinia nodded. "And yet, you've gotta go."

The doorbell rang and Neal shouted he'd get it. Then a few seconds later he shouted for George, who put down his roller and pushed up the sleeves on his sweatshirt passed his elbows. "How hard is it to pay for pizza, Neal?"

Opening the door in his ratty sweatshirt and shorts, to find Jillian on his doorstep with two of her friends behind her on the step below, all he managed to do was smile and say, "You don't look like pizza delivery."

"I wasn't going to bother you. Honestly." Jillian said, and he could see the color in her cheeks beneath the wind-chilled, reddened skin. "But Melissa said… And the girls…" She used her thumb to motion behind her. "Mal and Christy forced me. Is everything okay? You know what? Forget it. I should go."

George reached for her arm. "It's fine. *Really*. I'm glad to see you. I'm *always* glad to see you." He nodded his head toward the interior. "Why don't you come in? Mal and Christy are welcome too. It's cold out there."

Jillian smiled only faintly, but crossed the threshold. "Melissa said I really needed to see what was going on over here. I don't know why." He could tell when she caught a whiff as her face scrunched in confusion. "What's going on?"

He stepped to the side with her, so Christy and Malvinia could follow them in. "Don't let him smooth talk you if something's up." Christy said.

Neal shut the door behind everyone and said, "Nothing's up that she won't approve of, or at least be amused by." Christy turned to him. "Oh. Hey, twist. Still got the panties bunched, I see."

Christy turned to look at him and shot back, "Oh, it's the messenger. We shoot them, don't we?"

"Ha-ha."

Jillian and George walked into the family room and she got a look at the drop cloths all over the flooring and the furniture that had been pushed into the center of the room and the explanation of the smell became evident. "You're painting?"

"I was talked into it." He took her coat and carried it as he took her hand. "Come on. I want you to see this." He led her into the dining room and flipped on the light switch.

She felt like taking a deep breath, so she wandered over to the nearest cracked window, but couldn't take her eyes off the walls. "It's gorgeous," she finally said.

"The guys were giving me crap that sooner or later you'd be decorating this place and we came up with the idea to do some of it ourselves. You know, just to give me more control. But then I *had* to use your idea in the dining room... You have great taste. You were right about the color setting off the fireplace surround and mantel."

"I can't believe you're painting," Jillian said, turning around and taking in the completed room. "How long have you been working on this?"

"Much of the afternoon and evening. What do you think?"

"It's even better than I thought..."

Malvinia spoke from the doorway. "I have to admit that of all the things I thought we'd find this didn't even make the list. What's with the change in the party?"

George answered the question, but looking at Jillian instead of Malvinia. "The guys talked me into it, after a rather *colorful* discussion on the future of myself and this house. And Sergei and I told Taro that if he shut up and worked his butt off, we'd move on from his own *colorful* storytelling."

"Yes, but why...?"

George took Jillian's hand again and walked her the rest of the way through the dining room and into the kitchen, where Taro was currently painting along the edge of the backsplash in a yellow. "Hey, Taro."

"Hey, Jillian," Taro muttered.

Yeah, he's thrilled about this. "Yellow?" Jillian asked, taking in the deep yellow, veering toward a brown.

"Warm and cozy," George said, and then let go of her hand to open a cabinet. "Notice something else. Lots of room for dishes and glasses *of any color.*" He opened the one next to it that held his white plates. "If necessary, I know just where to donate these."

Realizing then what was actually going on, Jillian nearly sat down in a kitchen chair, but George shut the cabinets and snagged her hand again and she was moving back into the family room. *Just relax. Deep breaths. It's all right. You're putting the cart ahead of the horse again. He's just painting... and showing you where you can put your plates and glasses... eventually.*

Showing her the paint can lids, he said, "So, I know it's kind of... subtle compared to everything else, but I thought a dark beige in here. That way it's a neutral background and for the most part, anything can go on it... sculptures, prints, whatever. It'll be open to any color scheme for furniture. I also have some new cabinets waiting in the garage to hold the electronics on the sides of the fireplace and hang the television above, per suggestion." He smiled at her.

Then he showed her a few more cans. "This blue is for the first spare bedroom. This light yellow is for the second bedroom. And this green is for the last one. I just couldn't see red in a bedroom. So I figured a repetition of green, but in a different shade, would be okay.

"Oh, the library/parlor is getting a red coat right now, courtesy of Sergei and Neal. You should see that." He took her hand again and led her into the front room. "And, one other little thing, as well."

Thanks to the many bookcases, the red wasn't as overpowering as Jillian would have expected. It brought the whole room to life in the late autumn's fading sunlight.

"Wow, George," Jillian said.

"I remember you saying 'wow' about my house before. I'm just hoping you still mean it. We haven't started the bedrooms yet, so if you really hate it…"

"George," Jillian said to start, but then she turned and just ran out of words.

George's face tightened a bit. "Oh, no. You hate it. Which room? Or is it all of them? You know paint is cheap and it can be re-done."

"Is this…" She almost didn't want to ask as she walked to the object covered by a drop cloth against a bookcase. "Is this what I think it is?"

"What do you think it is?" George said, suddenly somber and when Jillian turned to him he looked like he was a puppy that had just been caught eating her favorite shoe. "Don't get mad."

"Oh, Lord," Jillian muttered, and then raised her voice. "What did you do? Where did you get it?"

"Well," he cleared his throat. "That's the part I don't want you to get mad about." He walked over to the drop cloth and uncovered the upright piano to pull out an envelope which he handed her but kept his hand over hers. "Okay. So, here's the thing. As you know, I'm about to be really, really broke. Obviously, I didn't buy it. I went to the people that I knew would care about you having a piano."

"Who are?" Jillian couldn't think of enough people at The Blue Feather that would care to pitch in enough to buy a piano.

George swallowed. "Your folks."

"What?!"

"Now, hear me out. I called your folks, and after a few tense moments, I convinced them that we were back together. By the way, you might want to let them know something like that, if there's ever a next time and you've been crying at their home about it. It took a lot of talking. Anyway, I told them I wanted to offer them an olive branch. We worked out a deal that they would buy you a piano and in return we're going to have dinner at their house once a month and you'll play for them after, music that *they* like."

Jillian shook her head. *I'm hallucinating. It wasn't Lacey who was in the car accident, it was me. I'm doped up on pain killers and having a crazy dream.*

George reached toward the piano again producing something wrapped in brown paper. "Now, I told them upfront that I hadn't talked to you about this and that you might reject the idea. And if that's the case, then the piano goes back and that's it. And I'll handle it. I'll make the phone calls.

"But, if you accept it, then it's a small bridge, right? And I picked this up."

Jillian almost didn't take the package from him, but finally did and unwrapped some sheet music. The top piece was Tchaikovsky. "Your parents like Tchaikovsky." Then she put that one behind the next. It was some kind of swing version of a melody by Tchaikovsky. "And that's for you. The same thing, but tailored to a different audience, you and me. I figured you can practice both and maybe it won't be so bad.

"While we were getting the paint, I kept thinking that when you do move in here, you need a room that's all yours, so you can feel like you really live here, you aren't just, you know, passing through. While having your furniture here will go a long way, it just isn't enough. The only thing that I could think of was a music room.

"But it's not like giving you drawer or closet space and saying 'there it is, fill it up.' You needed the piano to go with it. This is all I could come up with. But, like I said, I was really clear that you hadn't been consulted. If you want to reject this, reject it. I'll take care of it."

When I move in here? A piano... It was finally too much to bear. Jillian sat down on the piano bench, hard.

"Are you okay?" George asked, as he dropped to his haunches in front of her and put his hands on her legs.

"I don't know." Jillian said. *Does he ever take a breath? I can't even think and he's going a hundred miles an hour. I think. Is this what I think it is?* "I don't know. Is this, I mean all this..." She waved a hand in the air about indicating the whole house. "Is this really all for me? Is this... asking me to move in now? Or, am I misunderstanding? Or...?"

George sucked in his lips for a moment. "Yes. It is. But, you don't have to," George said. "I just really love having you here. I'd love it even more if you were here all the time. You and Charlie. So I could come home to you. And you could come home to me. But it doesn't have to be now. I did hear you the other night, when you said you think everything with me is 'right now' and I see what you mean. I've been pushing and pushing. And all I can say about that, about all of this, is I'm sure.

"Which isn't something I thought I'd be saying. Ever. But, I'm sure. I'm so sure. So, I hope that the house is inviting. And someday... Until then, I hope you feel really welcome and will want to be here."

"You really want me to move in?" Jillian asked, trying to be sure that she'd heard him right. Two days ago they weren't speaking and he had it in his head that she'd cheated on him with Sergei, of all people, and now...

"I do, if it turns out that you want to. But if the house doesn't work for you, we can always look for someplace else. I'll just paint all the walls white again to sell it. I'd be happy in your apartment, if that's non-negotiable. I think it'd be a little tight eventually. And I can't imagine where the piano would go. Whereas here we have much more room than we need..."

"We need to talk," Jillian said, and stood up. *Which isn't even the half of it.*

"I thought we were talking," George said, but followed when she took his hand and led him into the morning room to be able to talk truly privately for a moment. *This can't be good.*

Finding the center of the room to give the maximum amount of distance from everyone else in the house. "Are you really offering to move? I thought you needed it, the space, the house, for your venture," Jillian said, in a very quiet voice, wondering if he told any of his friends yet.

That's my Jillian. Worried about me and my plans. Concerned for me. "If necessary, another plan can be devised."

"I see." She glanced at her feet, tapped her toes once, and returned her gaze to George. "Gardiner filled out the paperwork last night. I'm the new director. It's supposed to be official on Monday." She took a deep breath. "Assuming I stay."

"Congratulations!" He smiled. "I knew it was going to be you," George said, quietly. "But after everything, I wouldn't blame you for walking."

"I already told Gardiner I didn't plan to sue. But, to be honest..."

When she didn't speak for a moment, George rubbed her arms. "What are you thinking?"

"Right now? I'm not. I was floored enough this morning with the meeting and then the promotion and now my boyfriend asked me to move in with him. I think my brain just shorted out."

"Hey," George said. "I just invited you to consider it. You don't have to. You can just say no and not even give a reason, if you want. Though, I'd certainly prefer something of an excuse, like 'we've only been seeing each for a few weeks and part of that time we were in a huge fight.'"

Jillian stepped up to George and put her arms around him. "I love you. You know that."

He hugged her. "I sense that's a no. That's okay. I promise. There's no crazy ultimatum here. Just me wishing we could be together all the time."

"And that's not pressure?" Jillian asked, against his neck and George chuckled. "I can't believe you decided to paint for me."

"Yeah, well, it's for me too," George said. "Hey, regardless of the answer to moving in, I'd like to know what you think of the colors."

"Excellent choices," Jillian said. "The rooms are looking fabulous. I think the bedrooms will be great too."

The doorbell rang. "I did one other thing," George said, and started for the door.

"Of course, you did," Jillian said, wondering what other shoe needed to drop.

She waited with him while he paid the pizza delivery man and shouted to the other musketeers that the pizza had arrived. Neal took the boxes from George and headed into the kitchen.

Noticing Malvinia and Christy were still milling around, George said, "I'm sorry. I forgot you were here. We ordered plenty. If you'd like."

The seven ended up in the kitchen, the ladies only having a small slice each, since they'd already eaten, but found the pizza hard to resist. George slipped out of the kitchen for a minute to close a paint can that he remembered was still open and Malvinia leaned over and quietly asked Jillian if she was going to stick around for a while.

Not knowing what else to do, Jillian nodded. She didn't want to be anywhere else, but she didn't know what to tell George either. The more she thought about it, the more torn she became. *I would love to live here, but I can't. How can I tell him that? How do I explain it? It sounds so... old fashioned.* She must have looked shocked or ill or something because Sergei jumped up and put her in his chair.

"What now?" Malvinia asked.

Jillian shrugged and then looked at Malvinia, dropped her voice, and said, "He asked me to move in."

She must not have been quiet enough, because behind her Neal said, "Ha! Told ya. Five bucks each."

"How did you call that?" Sergei asked. "She wasn't even supposed to be here tonight."

Neal was grinning when Jillian looked at him. "These two? Puh-lease. If she hadn't shown up on her own, do you really think he'd have waited until even tomorrow?" He looked at Jillian. "That guy *really* loves you." He shook his head and moved to be ready to take the bills from Sergei and Taro.

"So," Christy said. "He's really pushing you hard, isn't he?"

Jillian opened her mouth to say that she wasn't sure he was exactly pushing, but Neal snapped first. "You can just shut your mouth there, Twist. My buddy is just trying to show his woman how he feels, which is supposed to be romantic. If you don't like it, get out."

Christy blinked a few times. "Well, I never-"

"Probably, never will," Neal said, and Taro and Sergei laughed.

"Neal!" Jillian said, by way of a remonstration but she didn't think about it again until much later. George returned to the kitchen as Taro and Sergei were handing Neal their bills and handed her the envelope he'd given her before, saying, "You put this down unopened. So, you told everybody?" He leaned down and kissed the top of Jillian's head and even

Christy couldn't help but smile at that.

"Well, Mal asked."

"Mal asked about your promotion?"

The room went still.

"I'm now guessing the money changing hands isn't about the Director Job, like I thought," George said.

Neal seemed to recover first. "Well, how about that? Congratulations, Jillian."

"Thank you," Jillian said. "It's going to be announced on Monday, I think."

Taro walked out of the room. Sergei picked up another slice of pizza. "No wonder you look so shell-shocked. You've had quite the day. First the slime-ball, then the promotion, and now the paint fumes." He looked at George. "You should sleep at her place tonight. It's going to be strong in here for a while. It's too cold to open the windows all the way."

"Thank you for the advice," George said, and Jillian looked up at him. "Everything all right?"

She did her best to nod, looking up into the air to try to see him towering behind her. "I'm fine." *I think.* "What about Taro?"

Neal frowned. "He'll recover. He's just all bent out of shape that George is going to have to leave the group." His frowned lifted to George. "You okay?"

George felt like laughing, but he wasn't quite ready to tell the guys about his plans. "Me? I'm fine. It's all going to work out just fine." He looked down at Jillian again. "Is it okay that I'm proud of you?"

She smiled. "Yes. Yes, that's okay." *Time to change the subject.* "So, what's this?" She lifted the envelope.

"It's from your folks. I don't know what it says. Crossing my fingers about it."

"I'll read it later then." Jillian stood up and went searching for her purse. George followed. He didn't creep up on her, but he still managed to startle her when she turned and saw him.

"Oh. Sorry. I didn't mean to scare you." He got closer. "Did I go too far today? I got all ramped up about these ideas and didn't even think…"

Jillian couldn't help but smile. "I know. I would never have figured you for the impulsive type a few weeks ago, but now… I realized we both seem to have impulse control issues."

"I would have said that it was only when you were concerned, but I guess I kind of jumped on the *other* idea too."

Jillian knew he meant the new business. "I didn't see any paint for the morning room."

"You said," he stepped closer and slid his arms around her, "that you were going to do some research. I've yet to hear the results."

Placing her hands on his shoulders, Jillian sighed. "Not everyone operates at full tilt twenty-four hours a day, like you do."

"Huh. Who'd have thought it?" He pulled her closer. "You know something? You haven't kissed me since you got here."

"No?"

"Unh-uh." He shook his head. "We need to rectify that situation. Immediately."

Jumping into the mood, Jillian giggled and then got to her tiptoes and slid her arms around his neck. "Immediately?"

He wiggled his eyebrows and then tightened his grip on her, and she took a quick breath before he made her breathless.

It was Neal who accidentally interrupted them, talking as he walked up, "George, the pizza's almost gone, so if you want- Oops, never mind." He turned around quickly.

Both George and Jillian laughed softly. Jillian spoke first dropping back to her heels. "Best stop anyway. I'm starting to feel lightheaded. I'd prefer not to embarrass myself in front of everyone."

George dropped his forehead against hers and closed his eyes. "Anytime you feel dizzy, Sweetheart, just hold onto me."

"That's the problem. I'll hold onto you and the next thing I know, you'll be making me dizzier."

He bent over and kissed her one more time, quick and solid. "Okay. I should probably grab another bite and then get back to work. What are you going to do now?"

I'm going to do what you do, George, Darling. Throw myself in. "That depends." Taking his hand, Jillian started hurrying for the stairs.

"Uh," George said, but didn't fight the motion.

When they were halfway up, Sergei leaned around the staircase. "Should we all be leaving now?"

George glanced back and shrugged. Jillian shouted, "No! This won't take more than a minute."

Sergei laughed. "Good thing she's okay with that."

"Button it, Orlov!" George shouted and followed Jillian into his bedroom.

"Shut the door," she said, and pulled her sweater over her head. George pushed the door shut, his eyes traveling over the newly exposed skin and satin. "Uh," he said, again.

"Okay," Jillian said, and headed toward the closet, motioning him to join her. "What can I borrow to paint in?"

George would have laughed at himself, but he was still thinking about the satin and how great she looked in it and how great she'd look out of it. "Right," he said, and shook his head a little. "Uh, let me see."

He eventually found her a t-shirt from the dresser. She pulled it over her head and then gathered the excess fabric at her waist and twisted it into a knot, snugging the shirt in causing it to pull a little at her bust and a lot at her waist. "It'll do," she said, and then smiled at George. "Now, I guess I'll have to be careful of my jeans."

But George shook his head and then tilted it as he thought. It took a minute, but finally he found some of his sweatpants that had a drawstring waist. She pulled them on, rolled the cuffs, and tightened the drawstring until they hung about her waist, leaving just a patch of exposed skin. *I'm going to have to paint in a different room in order to keep my hands off of her.* "It's a surprisingly fetching outfit," George said.

"Fetching?" Jillian asked, as she sat on his bed and pulled off her socks. *And barefoot to boot.* "Yeah. Fetching."

Mal and Christy were discussing a cab when Jillian arrived in the kitchen and they both smiled at her. "So, not just staying, but helping," Mal said.

Neal handed her a paintbrush that was still attached to the packaging. "Good for you. Do *not* get any paint on the flooring. He's threatened to skin us alive, if we do." He grinned. "God only knows what he'd do to you. Of course, you might like it."

Jillian gave him a playful shove and then started to detach the paintbrush.

Neal gave Malvinia and Christy a tight smile. "Did I hear something about a cab?"

"Yes," Malvinia said. "We came in Jillian's car and since she's staying a while…"

"I'll call one for you. Any preference as to the cab company, Twist?"

Christy glared at Neal and put her hands on her hips. "You know, I think I'll stick around for a bit and help. If someone has some clothes I can borrow."

"Oh, *you're* going to *help*?" Neal asked.

"That's what I said," Christy said.

Jillian made a 'hmm' sound. "I think we can get another t-shirt, but I don't know about pants."

"I've got a shirt you can borrow," Neal said. "How about you stick to edging to keep you from getting any on your pants? Do you have a good attention for detail?"

"I can *paint*," Christy said.

Figuring that keeping Christy and Neal apart would make the remainder of the evening go more smoothly, Jillian helped her to work on the edging in the family room. That also served to keep Jillian away from Taro, who clearly wasn't taking her promotion well, though he did do a double take when he saw her dressed to paint and she was pulling her hair back in an elastic.

While Taro and George continued in the Kitchen, Neal and Sergei finished up the library/parlor/music room. Jillian plugged her mp3 player into George's stereo, turned the music down in an attempt not to bother the men, and started a playlist she used when she was working out and needed an energy boost.

Not long after, Melissa showed up, dressed to paint. "Did I tell you, or did I tell you? This you had to see. After you decided to stick around, Taro gave me another call. I figured I might join in too." She joined Christy and Jillian and after introductions, accepted a paint brush from Jillian, while Jillian picked up a roller and started covering the rest of the walls up to the edging.

The workers were enthusiastic for a few songs and started singing along to a few. When George walked through to take Neal and Sergei two beers, he asked them why they didn't sing a little louder and turned the stereo up a bit. "Because no one wants to hear this," Jillian said, and turned it back down.

On his way back to the kitchen, George turned the stereo up again. Jillian popped up and turned it back down. And he turned it back up. And she turned it back down. "You never told me what the other thing you did was," she said, trying to distract him.

"Oh, right," he said. "You want to see it now?"

"Uh, *yeah*, *now*," Jillian answered. "You're all about *now*."

"Ohhhkay." He walked around the furniture and dug out another flat package, this one was very large. "The guys disapprove of this..."

Christy turned around. "Now, I'm curious."

"Me too," Melissa said, and put down her paintbrush.

George unwrapped what turned out to be a large picture, bigger than her Starry Night, and when he turned it around it was the two of them, smiling at each other.

CHAPTER THIRTY-THREE

She knew the picture so well that she almost didn't need to look at it, except that it was so much larger than she'd ever seen it that she couldn't help but stare at the smiles and their eyes, the private look they were sharing. "It's… amazing. How did you…?"

"I took it to a real photographer. She printed it and then blew it up. Only took about two hours. And then, of course," he looked at the picture, "it's just fantastic. Look at you." He shook his head.

"So, why don't the guys approve?"

"I don't know. Nobody's naked or anything. But, they say it's too personal to hang in here."

Neal joined them and nodded. "Yep. It's nice, but too personal. It'll make other people uncomfortable."

"I don't think so," Melissa said, and Jillian looked at her. "I think it's amazing. Taro! I want us to take a picture like that."

Christy nodded her head. "Ohhh, Jills. Wow!"

Jillian took the picture from George and held it at arm's length. "Whatever made you think to do this?"

"What do you think of it?" He asked, rather than answering her.

"I don't know," she said, and turned to hold the picture up, eyeing what it might look like on the wall. George put his arms around her from behind and squeezed her tight against him. He dropped a kiss on her hair and said, "I love it. It's my lock screen on my phone. I thought it would be great to see it all the time, not just when I look at my phone."

Jillian tilted her head to try to see him. "It's my lock screen too."

"Yeah?"

"Yeah." She shifted to her right so she really could see him and he bent over and gave her a quick kiss.

"God," Melissa said. "You guys are so romantic. I had no idea."

Jillian looked at Melissa. "It's all George." She turned her head back to George. "The most romantic man I know."

He kissed her again. "It's you. *You* inspire me."

Melissa sighed. "You two are adorable." She stood up. "I'm going into the kitchen for a few minutes."

"Me too," Christy said, and jumped up.

"Was it something we said?" George asked.

Then Christy came scampering back through the room and headed toward the front of the house. "Sorry," she said. "There's romance in the kitchen now, too. I'm a third wheel in two rooms."

"Christy," Jillian said, "you're not a third wheel." But Christy was already through the room. "And she's heading into the front room with Sergei and Neal. That won't last either."

"Call it the music room," George said, and released her to take the picture back. "Now, what do we do with this? I like it. You like it. The guys say 'no.' I don't know. What makes it inappropriate?"

"You know, at this size, it is sort of obvious we're lying down. That may have something to do with it."

"Maybe the bedroom then?"

Jillian nodded. "And that would add the missing-" She stopped herself.

"Finally," George said. "Say it. I've been wondering what's wrong with my bedroom ever since the other Monday night. Come on. Tell me."

Jillian looked down and then brushed a strand of stray hair out of her face when she looked at him. "It isn't wrong. I just felt like it was... impersonal. There isn't much of you in it." She touched his arm. "It's just an opinion. And I'm not a professional decorator. I'm not even an amateur. Not really. So take it with a grain of salt, or a whole shaker."

"You think I didn't express myself," George said.

She shrugged.

"Well," he started for the stairs, "let's see if this helps."

After they ascended the stairs again, he took down the print from above the fireplace in the bedroom, hung their picture, and stepped back. "It's a little high. I'll fix it tomorrow." Jillian put her arm around him and he lifted his arm to put it around her shoulder. "I like it. You?"

"It's lovely, George. You are something... so very special."

"Thank you. Does that fix the room? A little?"

She smiled and shook her head. "There was never anything wrong, but it does make it much more personal."

George cleared his throat. "Think you'd like to wake up and see that every day?"

"Oh, George," Jillian said, shaking her head and stepping away from him. "I thought you were keeping the pressure off."

"That wasn't meant to pressure you to move in." He walked over to the door and shut it quietly and gently. "I just wondered what you're thinking. I mean, obviously, you didn't jump at the invitation. But you didn't exactly say 'no' either. So are you thinking about it? Are you putting off telling me what you think? Are you-?"

"Stop!" Jillian put her hands on the sides of her head and sat down on the bed. "You're doing it again. Everything has to be *right now*. We only got back together two days ago and now... It's a wonder you survived all this time at work waiting to know about the Director's job."

He sagged against the door. "It was far harder waiting for you and I didn't even realize I *was* waiting for you."

"Argh!" Jillian dropped backwards onto the bed. "You are so impossible."

"I thought I was something special."

"You are *and* you drive me nuts."

He walked over to the bed to stand next to her legs, towering over her and looking down at her with a tense smile. "I just want to know what you're thinking. If you won't tell me, I think I can safely assume it's because you think I don't want to hear it. But, I do. I want to hear it. Whatever it is."

Jillian sat up and sighed. George joined her on the bed and took her hand in his. "Just tell me. I'm a big boy. I can take it."

"I don't know where to begin," Jillian said, as she stared at her feet.

"It doesn't matter. Pick a spot. Backtrack. Hop around. I don't care."

She leaned against his shoulder. "Oh, George, I really don't know what to tell you. I mean, I'd love to live here with you. Who wouldn't want to? The house is great. And you... you're amazing. I love you. So much."

"But..."

Jillian tucked her head against his shoulder. "I just can't do it. I can't be you're live-in girlfriend."

"Okay. Why?" George asked.

"Because, I can't. If I were to move in, I'd be giving my apartment up. And if I have to do that and since you *own* this house, I'd need some kind of contract or something to ensure that if we break up, I'd be able to live in a bedroom for some period of time in order not to be homeless. And we'd have to hash out how the bills would be divided. And so on."

George took a breath. "That wouldn't be a problem. We can-"

"But, I don't want that. Who would want that? A lease is necessary to live in an apartment. But I don't want that kind of thing in my personal life. I don't want a lease from my lover. It's one of the least romantic things I can think of."

"Uh, okay," George said. "So, in order to live here, you'd need a contract. But you don't want a contract because it's unromantic."

"Exactly."

"I don't get it," George said. "Does that leave us any options?"

"Not really."

"Oh. So, you'll never move in. Never." *Well. There we are. Fucking never. What the hell are we doing if we're never going to be living together? What's the point? You have a relationship and it grows and you grow with it and eventually you're sharing a home. That's how it's supposed to work.*

"Well," Jillian said, "I wouldn't say never. Just not soon." *He's angry. I knew he'd be angry. And I can't say I blame him. And I can't figure out how to say this.*

"What breaks the circle of 'you'll only do this with a contract but you don't want a contract'?" *This had better be good.*

Jillian took her hand out of his. "Time, I suppose."

"No, you just said that you need a contract but don't want one. If it would change with time, you could say that. What changes with time? What do you need?" *There has to be something I can do. Something I can give you. Something I can say.*

"It's…" Jillian put her head in her hands and her elbows onto her legs. "I'm sorry. I didn't know. If I'd known… But I didn't. I've even fantasized about living here with you. Waking up late on the weekend, having breakfast in the morning room, coming back here to get dressed and start the day and then deciding to make love again instead. Spending the whole weekend here with more space then we know what to do with, and yet staying together the whole time."

George would have smiled. It sounded lovely. He wanted it. But she wasn't through yet, so he couldn't have it.

"I just didn't realize that I *couldn't* do it." She sat up again and looked toward him, but didn't look him in the eye. "I never came so close before. I never wanted to give up my own space. But I would love it, if it weren't for the fact that I wouldn't have any here."

"I'm giving you a music room," George said.

"That's not what I mean. As beautiful as the thought is, and it really is beautiful, Darling, it's still *yours*. All of this is *yours*. And as much as you want me to be here, I'd still be just a lessee."

George gritted his teeth. "You'd never be a lessee. You were more than that when we first went out. You've mattered for so long, I don't even know when it started. This doesn't make sense."

"Oh, George. It's not about logic, it's about how I feel. If it was solely about logic, I could talk myself into it with the contract and the thought of sharing the bills. It would have to cost less for us living together, than apart."

Jillian swallowed. "It's just about how I feel. And I don't blame you for being confused or surprised. I didn't know, so how could you? Even *I* thought I was this thoroughly modern woman. We slept together on the first date, for goodness sake. Why would you think I had a traditional bone in my body after that? I didn't think I did. But it turns out I do. I can't help it."

George shook his head. "I don't understand. What do you mean?"

Jillian swallowed again. "I don't know how to say this. Not exactly." *Maybe I could say this better if I used an example.* "So, um, let's take Cinderella."

"Cinderella?" George's eyes opened wide and crossed his arms. *What the hell is this woman talking about? Is this some kind of joke?*

"Yes. A perfect example. She's actually living a miserable life, right? So when the opportunity to get out comes, she's going to take it. But even she... she doesn't shack up with the Prince, does she? He doesn't say, come live a life of luxury in the palace as my girlfriend."

The light began to dawn. *She wants to get married first. Jesus. Why didn't she just say so? All the drama and rambling, just to avoid saying 'I don't want to live with you unless we're married.'* He sighed and then got up from the bed and headed for the closet.

"George?"

"Just keep talking. I want to get something."

"But," Jillian started.

"Just keep talking," George said, again.

Jillian stood up. "What are you doing?"

"Just keep talking," George called out from the closet.

Jillian exhaled. *He's not even listening to me now. Just keep talking. Just keep talking. Like I'm some kind of parrot who doesn't say anything worth listening to. He asked and now he doesn't want to hear my answer because it isn't what he wants the answer to be.* She rose and headed for the door. "Never mind. I'll be downstairs."

She returned to family room and picked up a roller. Christy looked up from the edging she was doing along the floor trim. "Okay. That is not a happy face." She sat down on the floor. "Why aren't I seeing a happy face?"

Jillian shook her head and loaded the roller. "It's fine. Just a little communication issue." She put more paint on the wall where the entertainment center had previously resided. It was almost too much. She knew that spot was where he'd meant she could put up some of her artwork. He'd been indirect, but his meanings had been obvious.

She put the roller back down, walked into the dining room, and flipped on the light. It was exactly how she'd imagined. And she could put a rug down and then her table on top of it and... Life was unfair. The perfect man in his perfect house and she couldn't figure out how to make it work. There were a lot more good moments than bad, but the bad ones, were they couldn't communicate, they were important. They were relevant. She moved around the room shutting the windows since the temperature was dropping outside and it was too cold to leave them open.

I want to live here. With him. Why does this have to be so hard? I want to come home to him.

"Why did you leave?" George's voice echoed a bit in the large empty room.

Jillian looked over her shoulder at him. "I didn't leave. I just came down here."

Yeah, right. "Okay. Why did you run away?" He asked, striding across the room carrying three smallish boxes in his hand.

"I didn't," she answered. "I was frustrated. So I came down to look at something I really wanted to see. Something I could enjoy." She took a quick breath. "And I love it just as much as I thought I did. So, it worked. I enjoyed it."

George shook his head. "You are a really terrible liar. You babble when you lie."

"Gee, thanks," Jillian said.

George shook his head again. "Are you going to tell me why you left?"

Jillian crossed her arms. "Sure. The way you started ignoring me and what I was saying, it was upsetting."

"I wasn't ignoring you. I was listening. I just wanted to get something."

Jillian shook her head. "That's not how I saw it."

"Well, that's how I saw it. Now, are you still upset, or do you want to see what I was getting?"

"Fine," Jillian said. "Why not?"

George took a step closer and leaned down a bit to meet her eyes. "I was getting your presents from Washington. I hadn't given them to you yet and I thought now was the right time."

"That would be sweet, except you kept saying, 'keep talking,' like it didn't matter what I said while you went to get the presents. And, by the way, I don't need a shot glass from SeaTac, so I hope-"

"Jillian." George cut her off. "Could we please take it down a notch? If it helps, then I'm sorry the way I did that was upsetting. I think you'll like your presents."

Jillian took a half-step back. "We were talking about something important, something you wanted to talk about, and you got up and turned your back on me."

"And, I'm sorry. I won't do it again. Okay?" He put his fists on his hips and tilted his head. "Don't tell me this offense is unforgivable. After everything..."

Jillian shook her head. "Of course not. But, that was hard for me and you just got up an-"

"I know. I'm sorry. Are we good?"

Jillian nodded slowly then a little faster and then dropped her arms like she was exhausted. "I'm sorry too. I feel like an idiot. That's part of why I came down here. I feel like such an idiot. I can't keep up with you. Everything is moving so fast." She put a hand to her head. "I'm starting to feel dizzy even when you aren't kissing me."

"Probably the paint fumes," George said, and held out his free hand. "Come on. Let's grab our coats and go outside for a few minutes. We'll get some fresh air *and* you can open these."

"I'm in my bare feet and my shoes are upstairs. Let's *not* go outside."

"Okay, then," George said, and took a step closer. "I thin-"

Bam! "Ow!" The scream came from a different room.

"Christy?" Jillian went running with George on her heels. She turned the corner in time to see Neal hauling Christy up.

"Ow. Ow. Ow." Christy kept repeating as she tried to put some weight on her right ankle.

"What happened?" George asked, from behind Jillian as visions of his homeowners' insurance activating jumped into his head.

"I tripped," Christy said. "Ow."

Neal got down on one knee and put her hand on his shoulder, then touched her ankle. She winced and sucked in her breath.

"Ow."

"I don't think it's broken. But it might be sprained." He stood back up. "Come on into the kitchen, Twist." He looped her arm around his neck and started to move.

"Ow. No. Give me a minute. And stop calling me Twist."

"If it's really sprained, you want to ice it right now," Neal said.

Sergei chimed up. "The guy's got some kind of basic EMT certification. I'd listen to him."

"Well, it hurts!" Christy said.

Neal rolled his eyes. "Fine." He scooped her up and headed toward the kitchen.

"What are you...?" Christy didn't bother to finish the question, she just held on.

Jillian followed them into the kitchen and watched Neal help Christy into a chair, lift up her leg, and examine her ankle one more time.

"I'm not sure it's a sprain either, but we should ice it in case it's going to swell." He hopped up and returned with a flexible ice pack out of the freezer, brought it back to the table, handed it to Christy and then turned around to leave the room. He came back with a throw that he folded and folded until it was pretty thick and put it on a chair and had Christy put her leg up on it. "Okay, about fifteen minutes with the ice." He looked at Jillian. "Does George have any ibuprofen? It's good for swelling."

"Uh. I don't know," Jillian said. "But I have some in my purse. I'll get it." She headed back into the family room. From there she could hear

Neal.

"I'll be back in a bit and we'll check it again. Keep it elevated and take the ibuprofen. Questions?"

Christy answered. "Just one. Did Sergei say you're an EMT?"

"Yeah, that's not true. I've had some first responder training. CPR. Use of a defibrillator. First aid stuff. Like for this kind of thing," he said, and motioned toward her ankle. "Sergei doesn't know how much more training and testing an EMT has than I do. But I've got some certifications, so, you know."

"Okay," Christy said. "Thank you for the help."

Jillian returned as Neal walked out, and she handed Christy two ibuprofen. "How bad does it hurt?"

Christy accepted the tablets and replied, as Jillian went to get a glass of water. "It's sort of pulsating. It really hurt when I put weight on it. But it's not too bad now that I'm off of it."

"So, not broken?" George asked.

Shaking her head, Christy said, "I doubt it." Then she tilted her head toward the front of the house where Neal had gone. "Your guy knows his stuff, I suspect."

George smiled. "Neal knows his stuff. No doubt. If he says it, he's sure." He glanced around. "What happened to Taro?"

Jillian handed Christy a glass of water and then looked out of a window. "He and Melissa are outside." She moved a little closer. "Why does that not look good?"

George joined her. Taro was waving his arms a bit and Melissa had hers crossed. "I'm definitely staying away from whatever that is. At least, while it's happening." He looked at Jillian. "I'll make sure he's okay later, if it doesn't resolve well." He lowered his voice. "I don't know what's going on with him, lately. The other night, he really acted like he'd done the right thing, breaking us up."

Reaching for George's hand, Jillian let out a long, slow breath. "He didn't do it by himself."

George took her hand and frowned in acknowledgement. "Yeah, I know. I'm sor-"

"*I'm* sorry," Jillian cut him off and squeezed his hand. "It took both of us." *It was definitely my fault too. I have to figure this out...*

George moved away from the sink, pulling her along with him into the family room. "Jillian," he started, but couldn't quite figure out what to say next, so he wrapped his arms around her for a hug. She molded against him, tucking her head against his neck. *I love you.* After a minute, he began to think about where he'd set down the boxes.

Stepping back before he could remember, Jillian sighed and said, "We've got to get back to work. With Christy out of commission, I better get it into gear in here. If Sergei and Neal finish the music room, I'll see if I can draft them. But if we wait too long we're going to have lines in the paint from where some dried.

"You best get back to work in the kitchen. If we keep it up, with this amount of help, we can finish this floor tonight."

Maybe it would be better to do it after everyone goes home anyway. George sighed in response and nodded. "Yep. Back to work."

Jillian knew when Taro was back to helping George, because Melissa returned to the family room. "Everything okay?"

Melissa shrugged and picked up a paint brush.

The late news was on when Jillian finally onto dropped to George's couch. "Oh, my word, I'm tired."

"Me too," George said, and dropped next to her.

"You have the best friends, and no, I never thought I'd say that."

George laughed and put his arm around her. "If we'd met anywhere else, you'd have had a chance to really get to know them before now. Of course, I'd like to think if we'd met anywhere else, we'd have been together ages ago."

"I wish we had been. But I'm going to stay grateful that we're together now," Jillian said. "Well…"

"Well, what?"

Jillian sat forward. "It's late. Charlie's overdue for a feeding by hours. I'm a terrible mom. So, we should get changed and if you'd like, you can pack a bag and stay over tonight. Tomorrow we can paint bedrooms. I'll work out something so I can stay here tomorrow."

George held onto her as she tried to get up off the couch. "Let me get your presents first."

Poking him gently in the ribs, Jillian wriggled out of his grip. "Please. I'm horribly late for Charlie. Please, let's hurry. The boxes you had were small enough to bring with us. I'll take care of Charlie and then give you *all* of my attention. Okay?"

It was impossible to disagree because she was off the couch and heading upstairs, leaving George to haul himself off the couch and drag himself up the stairs behind her. If she wasn't worried about Charlie, he would have suggested they both take a shower. Then again, he'd also have suggested they just drop into bed. "Fine," he said, gripping the railing to help pull himself along. *At least there's an elevator at Jillian's place.*

After changing his clothes and packing a bag, he went looking for the boxes. *I wonder if I'll be able to convince her to actually open these. Maybe I'd be better off not doing something cute and just pulling the ring out of my pocket.*

"Charlie?" Jillian called out as she opened the door, though she needn't have as Charlie was sitting just a few feet away and began to meow the instant the door cracked. "I'm so sorry, baby," Jillian said, and pushed into the apartment, scooping him up, and carrying him into the kitchen.

Although George thought it was obvious Charlie was indeed hungry as Jillian had thought, he grinned as Charlie was content to perch two paws over her shoulder and watch her get the plate. "I'll get the can," George said, and headed for the pantry.

"Thank you," Jillian replied, and after setting the plate on the island, she went searching for the can opener.

George watched the rest of the ritual and smiled broader at the simple scene of domesticity. He again reconsidered his idea of springing the ring on her via the gifts from Washington. It had seemed cute and fun when it was spontaneous. Suddenly, he couldn't help but wonder if he should be doing it up. A fancy restaurant, dress clothes, all the trimmings to make it special for her.

"Now," she said, and walked over to a cabinet to get some glasses. "I promised you that I'd give you all of my attention…" She looked at him. "Water? Wine? Something else?"

"You were right," George said. *If I delay, I can find something for the third box and plan a real proposal.* "It's late. Maybe we should just think about getting some sleep. The last few weeks really have been non-stop."

Jillian lifted her chin a little. "All right. Go ahead. I need a glass of water." *Well, that's a change for him.* She filled her glass and watched George take his bag into the bedroom. He tossed her a look as he reached the doorway and she smiled at him with tight lips. *Something's up.*

After putting her glass in the dishwasher and cleaning up Charlie's dinner, Jillian searched her purse for her phone and found the envelope from the piano. She glanced at the bedroom. George was in the bathroom, so she might as well.

The note from her parents was short and simple. *Enjoy. We look forward to seeing you.*

Jillian slipped it back in the envelope and nodded to herself, grateful it was so short and contained a kind sentiment and nothing that she could correctly or incorrectly interpret as a comment on her life. George must have been right about it being a peace offering. She was going to have to figure out how to talk to them at dinner, but at least now there were going to be dinners. So long as he was with her, it would be okay. If it was bad, he'd make it better. If it was good, he'd be there to share it.

While trying to imagine what the phone call he'd made must have been like, Jillian placed the note on her kitchen counter. She needed to make one herself in the morning and thank them. It would be safer to write a note back, but a piano was a sizeable gesture that needed to be acknowledged as closely to 'in person' as she could manage.

She found Charlie on the sofa and picked him up. He purred and rubbed against her cheek. "Hi, baby. I'm sorry I was a bad mama." She glanced toward the bedroom again. It looked like George was still in the bathroom. "I had another crazy day. You'd never guess in a million years. It's just change, change, change."

Her memory flashed to the conversation in the stairwell when George had talked her into going public and she'd been hesitant and he'd said something about how she was worried her life was going to change but that it already had. *That was an understatement. It didn't just change. Nothing is the same.*

Hugging Charlie, she walked over to the windows and whispered to him. "He's asked us to move in." Charlie rubbed her cheek again. "I told him no."

"Errrff," Charlie made a strange sound.

"Yeah," Jillian said. "I know. It surprised me too. I had to say no, though, because I want it all, Charlie."

"Fffft."

Jillian set him down on the window sill and then dropped to her knees next to him. "Think it was a mistake?"

"Errrff."

"Well," Jillian said, as she scratched his ears, "I don't know. It felt right at the time. It's one of those things you can't take back. I couldn't move in and then threaten to move out later if he doesn't want to commit. So, it just makes sense not to... until... Right?"

This time Charlie just purred and didn't give her any kind of sound to pretend was conversation. She sighed. "What am I doing, baby? I don't have any idea anymore. What is *he* doing? I'm so lost."

"Everything okay?" George called from the bedroom doorway.

Jillian looked over her shoulder at him, smiling. "Sure." Then she whispered to Charlie again. "If you decide you have any thoughts on this, let me know." She kissed the top of Charlie's head, rose, and started for the bedroom and *him*. "Just chatting with Charlie."

She slipped around George and shut the door to the bathroom while she brushed her teeth and washed her face, not wanting to face him because she felt like she'd just lied to him. By the time she'd finished her routine, she was chastising herself for being so silly. She'd made the decision that was right for her, so she shouldn't feel anything but good about herself. She'd definitely made the right decision.

Then she opened the bathroom door and George was sitting up in bed, clearly waiting for her, since he had nothing in his hands for entertainment. No book, no phone, nothing.

"Hi," she said, and slipped into the closet to change into a nightgown.

"Hello," he called out and took a deep breath, trying to be patient as he waited for her. It seemed to him that Jillian was acting a little different. She hadn't demanded much privacy since a few days into their relationship. Of course, that may have been because he'd hardly allowed her any. But he thought that, suddenly, she was hiding again.

Maybe she's nervous about being in bed together? They still hadn't made up completely. It was *possible* she was feeling nervous.

George ran his hands over his face. *Or I blew it by suggesting she move in and now things are strange between us. I was probably okay until I started pushing for an answer. God, George, where is your self-control? It's like you went to bed with this woman and woke up addicted to her and all sanity went out the window. All dignity with it. Reason too. But mainly, self-control.*

She walked out of the closet in a satin nightie that covered her to her knees and he could imagine the slip of the fabric between his fingers. "You okay?" He asked, again.

"Sure," Jillian said, and lifted the covers to slide into the bed. "You?"

"Yeah," he lied, and scooched down the bed to lie down. She joined him and turned out the light giving him the obvious cue that she didn't want to be intimate, made even more obvious when she rolled onto her side facing away from him.

He felt the urge to sigh, but fought it and instead scooted nearer her and put his arm over her, pulling her back against him. Thankfully, she didn't stop him. She just said, "Goodnight."

"'Night, Sweetheart," he replied, and put his chin against her shoulder, hoping she'd fall asleep quickly, so he could hold her for a few minutes and then toss and turn without her knowing, fully expecting to kick himself for pressuring her for an answer for a while before he could sleep.

He's so warm. The air from his breath along her back and side nearly tickled and the weight of his arm about her waist pushed her into the mattress and pulled her tightly to him. *I hope he falls asleep quickly, so I can relax.*

Jillian was able to see the clock and she watched the minutes slowly begin to pass. One. Then two. His breathing wasn't changing. Three. Four. *Definitely still awake.*

He was sure that it hadn't been more than five minutes, but Jillian was still awake. Whatever was wrong was keeping her up too. He lifted his head a bit to see the time. For once, he'd underestimated a little. It was seven minutes.

"Having trouble falling asleep?" Jillian asked, and he lowered his head again.

"A bit," he answered. "You too, huh?"

She shrugged and the motion bobbed his head. "I guess."

He cleared his throat. "What's wrong, Sweetheart?"

I'm having second thoughts. Second guessing myself. I don't know what I'm doing anymore. I haven't known for such a long time that it's amazing I even remember ever having had *any idea what I was doing.* "Nothing," Jillian answered and closed her eyes tight in the face of her lie.

"No goodnight kiss," he said, softly.

"Oh," Jillian said. *Right.* She tilted her face toward him and they managed to connect a slight peck on the lips, then she dropped her head back to the pillow. "I'm fine. Just tired and awake at the same time. That can happen when you're overloaded. Today was crazy from top to bottom. I still haven't thanked my parents for the piano. And I have a lot-"

"Jillian," he said, softly and she stopped talking. "You babble when you're lying."

She exhaled. "I'm not... I mean... Could we just sleep?"

"Except neither of us is," George said.

"Don't be logical," Jillian said, and looked back at the clock. "Not at this hour."

"Okay," George said. "Then I'll be emotional. *I'm* having trouble sleeping because I think I upset you. Did I?"

Jillian shifted to roll over and George moved to give her space to roll onto her back. "No. Of course not."

"Then what's wrong?" He reached over and smoothed her hair back and she turned her head to look at him in the dim light. "Come on. No need to keep it from me, is there?" He smiled at her.

"Well, no. I suppose not. It's just," she paused a moment. "I'm just second guessing myself. That's all. So much... so fast... I've told you before."

"Ah," George said. "Not regrets, I hope."

"No, George, not regrets. Just second guessing... second thoughts."

George tensed, but managed to rub her arm gently. "Second thoughts... about us?"

Her hand touched his arm. "Not us. I love us. Please don't think..." She rolled onto her side to be closer to him, but didn't elaborate.

"Just tell me," George said.

Jillian closed her eyes while she said, "Fine. I'm having second thoughts about living with you."

George rolled away to snap on the bedside light and then back to her, propping himself up on his elbow. "I'm confused. I thought you said no."

"I did say no."

"So, then... you're thinking you should have said yes?"

"Maybe," Jillian said, and then rolled onto her back again and crossed her arms over her eyes. "I don't know. I mean, I really don't know. It's just *so fast.*"

George was smiling at her when he peeled her arms down from her face, one at a time. "Is it really too fast? Or is it the other little thing you mentioned? Because if that's the dilemma, I think I can solve it."

"Oh, don't," Jillian said, and took in a stuttering breath. "Just let me think about it."

"But we can work this out. Easily-"

"Just until morning. Please. Let me have my own thoughts until then." She touched his cheek. "I know how this goes. You talk and I get turned around and before I know what's happened I'm saying 'yes' and I may not even know what I'm saying 'yes' to."

"Hey," George said, and pulled away from her hand. "Have I ever persuaded you to do something you regret? Honestly?"

"No," she said, and dropped her hand to his bicep. "No. But, maybe, just this once, I could let the idea marinate overnight. And in the morning, when I'm not exhausted and my head isn't spinning..."

George smiled a moment and then dropped onto the pillow. "Sorry. You deserve all the time you want. I guess I'm just excited about the future. I've been sitting in one place for a long time, long before you joined Gardiner, and now I've got new plans and I feel alive and like I'm finally going somewhere and I just want to get going. I don't have to be there this moment, but I want to get moving." He grabbed her hand and lifted it to his lips for a short kiss. "And to give credit where credit is due, you are a really big part of the why and the how. And having you alongside for the journey is just a lovely bonus."

"Stop," Jillian said. "You see, this is what you do. You don't even talk about the subject directly and yet..." She shook her head and groaned. "You say the most amazing things, George. You really do. And I wind up... dizzy."

I guess I better lay off on the future plans right now. "You say amazing things too." George squeezed her hand. "Have I ever mentioned how much I love it that you use my name so much?"

"What?"

"I have enough trouble with people using nicknames and stuff, but you use my actual name, *all* the time. Even in the most, ahem, passionate of moments. I can't tell you how great that feels."

"That's what you like to be called. Why would I use anything...? Now you're trying to distract me."

George chuckled. "If I was trying to distract you, I'd do this." He leaned over, placing a hand on her cheek, and kissed her slowly and thoroughly. *Mmm. Now that's fantastic...*

"Mmm," she breathed against his lips when he stopped. "Oh, yeah, that would do it."

He chuckled and then slid his lips across her cheek and to her ear, dropping kisses as he went. He whispered, "Do you know how long it's been since I touched you?"

She ran a hand up his arm and then down his back. "Four days and twenty-two-ish hours."

He chuckled against her neck. "I didn't know you were counting." His lips began to travel again.

Jillian exhaled sharply. "After we made up, I'd been counting the minutes until we could be together. I had such high expectations for tonight."

"I'll try to live up to them." His voice rumbled under her chin and she shivered. He pulled back a bit to see her eyes. "Tell me something."

"Hmm?"

"If you had high expectations, why'd you get into bed and roll away, without even a kiss goodnight? I know you said you're rethinking your decision, but that's no reason to hide. Not from me."

"It's not always that easy," Jillian said. "Not for me. I don't quite know how to live up to *your* expectations."

"Jillian, Sweetheart," George started and touched her lips with a finger. "I love you. I love you whatever you're thinking or feeling. How I feel about you doesn't change with your moods any more than it changes with mine. Even when I was angry and we were apart, I still loved you." His eyes roved over her face. "All I've ever wanted was you. All I want from you is you. Just be you." He leaned closer and Jillian took in a breath. "Just give me you."

CHAPTER THIRTY-FOUR

He moved to kiss her, but Jillian moved and kissed him first, running her hands over him when he kissed her in return, and they fell back into the pillows. *Just give me you.* Jillian couldn't help but hear the words looping in her head. He made it sound simple. It was never simple.

Still, she wanted to do as he asked, so while he touched her, caressed her, she tried to find whatever it was inside her that he wanted and she hadn't let him have. He made it a little easier, keeping his kisses light, instead of dizzying, his touches soft and gentle, making love so slowly that she had time to both enjoy it *and* think.

But thinking wasn't helping. By the time her nightgown was on the floor and his soft and gentle touches had begun to feel *too* slow, even torturous, she was no closer to knowing what he wanted than she'd been the first time he'd kissed her weeks before. So she tried harder with what she did know, touching him where he liked to be touched and enjoying the way he reacted to her, while slipping quietly into a happy haze as the dizzying fog finally swirled around her.

His pajama bottoms soon disappeared and they both relished the unobstructed contact, still moving slowly. The words came then, whispered repetitions of sweet and tender thoughts, and finally the most unpretentious and direct of all.

When they had to pause again for George to find what he'd left on the bedside table, Jillian thought of one thing she could give him. *Faith. In him. In us.* She took the packet from him and George thought at first that she wanted to help him with it, but she held onto it without opening it and asked him, "You weren't with anybody while we were apart, were you?"

"No, of course not," George said, his brows knitting together, "why would...?"

"Me neither," she said, and tossed the package to the floor.

George didn't react much for a few heartbeats, he looked from her to the where it lay on the floor, and back again. *Was that the wrong thing to do?*

Seriously? Does she know what she's doing? Please, God, let her know what she's doing. "You sure?" He asked, finally.

"I'm sure," Jillian answered and she reached for his face with a trembling hand. "Just you."

The slow and the gentle vanished with her answer. He pulled her to him and moved his lips down her body making her gasp and then his hands followed making her body shake and her breath stutter. He made his way back up and took her hands in his, interlacing their fingers, and pushing them into the bed, stretching their arms above their heads.

He stopped, poised just above her, and let out a breath. "Are you really sure? My feelings for you aren't contingent on this either." *Be sure. Be sure.*

"Just you," Jillian whispered. "I love you."

"I love you." *So freaking much, I love you.*

He didn't move, so she whispered again, "I love you, George."

George kissed her softly for a moment. "God, I love you, Jillian." He moved lower on her body, holding her eyes while he pressed against her. "No going back..."

Faith. "Why would I need to?"

His eyes held hers and then he was inside her in every sense. Her arms strained against his hands and her heart pounded and her legs shook. Every fiber of her being tried at once to both control and surrender. "Ah, oh, God, George!"

As she moved beneath him, George held himself still for as long as he could. It was the fight that was the winning for the losing, but he wanted more. He moved slowly, kissing her, looking into her eyes, loving her with all of himself. In return, she met him kiss for kiss and touch for touch, taking all of him and trying to give all of herself.

At first, as he moved with her, she stayed with him, but as the tension built, the memories flashed. The first time they were together and she was both safe and scared in his arms, overwhelmed by him as he made her feel so... as he made her feel. *Don't hold back. All of this means nothing if you're holding back.* Then she was telling Mrs. Kerchner and Malvinia that she didn't know what more he could want. But she did. She knew. He'd asked. He'd flat out asked. *Don't hold back.*

Jillian closed her eyes a moment and, though the sensations were stronger, she was still able to think. *That's it, isn't it? It's why he's jealous. He knows I still hold back. He's afraid I'm keeping part of myself to give to someone else. Oh, George.*

She pulled her hands free of his and reached for his face. He was with her, no doubt, all of him. He focused on her and in her and she wanted to be with him the same way. She held on to him, fighting the desire to close

511

her eyes, searching his face to see everything she knew was there, passion, trust, love…

Even as the peak was calling him, George held on with all his might, waiting for Jillian. As her hands touched his face he was certain even if the timing didn't work out, she was with him in other ways. But then he realized something was different. She hardly blinked. She stayed with him as he moved. For a fleeting moment he worried that he was wrong and she wasn't anywhere near where he was, until she opened her mouth to gasp, still looking into his eyes, and he knew she was with him in a way she hadn't been before.

Her eyes closed a moment, but she returned to him immediately and he saw her vulnerable and open, and it almost felt like she was calling to him. He moved to kiss her, but she held his face just short as she trembled under him. She mouthed his name, though no sound came out. Her lips parted again and she took a stuttering breath and he could tell she was nearly there.

His vision narrowed to her eyes as she gasped again and suddenly he fell into her, awash in the light and the warmth deep inside, until he could open himself and fill up all the dark places in him with her light.

As Jillian saw the fire, instead of retreating, she tried to open herself to it, knowing it was him, his power, his drive… his fire, and she soaked in the heat until she finally fell into it, swallowed it, and felt herself bursting from the energy.

They met each other at the fringe, their energies mingling and blending so that the climax was nearly a disappointment, ripping them both back into their own bodies as the release took them each, separate, yet together. He groaned into her shoulder as she cried out and they both shuddered.

He quickly struggled back to his elbows so he could see her face, and she looked at him with drowsy eyes that sparkled with the smile from her lips.

At first, it was too much to speak, but when she was able to raise a hand and run it through his hair, she whispered, "George."

He smiled at her and whispered, "Jillian." He smoothed her hair with one hand. Grateful he didn't have to leave her, he stayed and they gazed into each other's eyes for a while, until he felt guilty. "I'm not crushing you, am I?"

She chuckled. "Yes, you are." She wrapped one arm around him. "But, don't go."

"Don't have to," he answered and rolled onto his side, turning her with him, making a tangle of arms and legs that they laughed about as they sorted themselves, ending up next to each other smiling.

He touched her hair again. "I love you."

She laughed again. "I love you, too."

"What was…? That was amazing."

Jillian nodded. "Yes."

"Did you... do something? It was a lot like that first time, except more. I'd started to think it couldn't happen again and then it did..."

She kissed him and then said, "I guess, if it was me, I didn't fight it this time, because I wasn't afraid."

"You don't ever have to be afraid with me. I mean, I know I blew it once, but never again, honestly. I'll never let you go again. Never hurt you again. I swear I-"

She interrupted him with another kiss. "Darling, you babble when you're worried." She ran her hand down his cheek. "And you don't have to worry about me being afraid, because even when I'm afraid, you make me brave. I love you more... than I'm afraid." *Do you? Do you really? Are you sure?*

Her eyes dropped from his to his chest and he touched her face. "Sweetheart?"

... Yes. She looked at him again. "If the offer is still open, I want to move in with you."

"Jillian-" She looked nervous.

"If you want us, that is, Charlie and me. If you want us then we want you. I want everything you said, just like you said it. Come home to each other." She felt like her throat was closing up a little and her eyes were watering. "Let's make a home together."

He crushed her to him so quickly she didn't have time to breathe first. "Oh, Jillian. Oh, Sweetheart. Yes. I want you. Both." He released her enough to kiss her. "I called a vet's office nearby and asked about cat-proofing my house and how to settle a cat into a new home. She said we should pick a small room to be his for a while, so he can adjust. I was thinking the front bedroom. It's got a great view of the street and the trees. Lots of activity outside, when we're not there to amuse him. And he needs play time. We'll make a point to play with him a lot every day until he's ready to come out and own the whole place. I've got it all figured out. I want you both."

"Oh, George," she said, in a breathy voice and he pushed his forehead to hers. He closed his eyes and basked in the serenity. "When did you have time for all this?" She asked.

When he opened his eyes, hers were closed. "All what? Calling the vet? I did that yesterday. I've been thinking about having you move in for a while."

She chuckled. "I swear, I've never known anyone who could go this fast." She opened her eyes. "Don't let go, or I'll fall behind and I'll never catch up."

"I'll never let go."

"Me either."

He grinned. "Promise?"

"Promise," she said, with a smile.

"Good," he said. "Now, there's something I have to do." He started to roll away and she touched his shoulder.

"You'll ruin the afterglow," Jillian said, with a click of her tongue against the roof of her mouth, although the smile still played about her mouth.

"God, I hope not," he said, and heard the nervous tinge in his voice. Ignoring the nerves he went searching in his bag for the boxes, and finding them, returned to Jillian.

"Seriously?" She asked, but then she took the boxes, placed them on the bed, fluffed up a pillow and placed it against the headboard, and slid up the bed to sit against it. "Okay, then. Let's see what all the fuss is about." She winked at him.

He grinned and moved a pillow and himself so he could sit next to her, his pulse picking up as she lifted the first box. *At least they're in the right order. Please, God, let her like 'cute.'*

Jillian shook the box and it rattled. "Hmm," she said, and then lifted the lid to reveal the lion bracelet.

George had to bite his lip not to laugh at her expression of surprise and then how he could see her thinking.

"Well," Jillian said, and plucked the bracelet out of the box. "My nephew is really into animals right now. He's going to think this is amazing. I'll wear it at Thanksgiving."

George nodded and smiled, still trying not to laugh. *She really hates it.*

"Thank you," Jillian said, and put the bracelet back in the box and the box on her night stand.

She's wary now. George said, "You're welcome," as she slowly opened the second box.

What on Earth? Jillian pulled the bracelet out of the box. "And elephants, trunk to tail. Now that's-" She stopped and looked at George, seeing his widening grin. "My three ring circus!" She grabbed him for a hug. "Oh, you darling, you!" She sat back and laughed. "First the dancing penguin and now the circus. You really know how to sweep a girl off her feet."

He leaned over and kissed her. "Anything to see you smile."

She returned the second bracelet to its box and put it on the nightstand. When she picked up the final box, George's heart started to pound. *Oh, boy. Here goes... everything.*

"This ought to be the seal," she said, and glanced at him. "What's wrong? You looked flushed."

He shook his head. "Nothing. Just open it."

"Are you sure?" She touched his forehead. "You don't seem feverish."

"I'm not ill. Just open the box."

Jillian exhaled. "Well, we know you aren't having monthly cramps. What else could be-"

"Jillian, just open the box."

"It can wait." She put down the box and turned to him. "I'm not kidding, you look very flushed. Do you need a glass of water? I'll get it." She moved to leave the bed and he grabbed her arm.

When she looked at him, he said, "Sweetheart, thank you for the concern. I'm fine. Really."

"You weren't flushed a minute ago."

"I'm fine." He sighed. "I'm just a little nervous. Please, open it."

"There's no reason to be nervous, I love my circus."

"Please, open it."

"All right," she answered and picked up the box without taking her eyes off of him. "Just know I care."

"Oh, Sweetheart," he said, with a nervous laugh. "I know you care." He nodded toward the box.

Jillian nodded her head in reply and then returned her focus to the box. "It's different from the other two," she observed and he swallowed. She looked at him again. "They were coated with silver paper. This one's blue. Makes me wonder."

Oh, my God! Open the damn thing! He almost reached over and lifted the lid himself.

She took off the lid while she was still looking at him, and then turned her head to… Gasp! The sound she made was loud and long. The lid fell from her fingers and she plucked the ring from the box. "You bought me a ring?"

"Well, to be honest, no."

She dropped the box, but kept fingering the ring as she looked at him, confused.

"I didn't steal it or anything. Orville gave it to me. Yesterday. He said if you didn't like it, we could sell it. But it was May's, so unless you really hate it, I don't think I could. It, um, the stone, the main stone," he gestured toward the ring, "the uh, Sapphire, reminds me of your blue glass. Sort of. So I thought, you know, you'd like it. It's very traditional, and yet non-traditional, like you."

"He gave this to you?"

"Yeah, after he heard about my business plans and that we'd gotten back together. He said I'd need a ring eventually and was going to be broke, which is certainly true. Oh, and he said to tell you that, if you're superstitious, the ring should have positive energy because they were married for more than sixty years and they never went to bed angry. Full disclosure, there were apparently a few late nights, but they always worked things out. What do think? Like it?"

"I love it. I can't imagine a more perfect ring," Jillian said, glancing at it and then looking at him again. "But, um, I need a little more here."

"More?"

She held up the ring between them. "Is this what I think it is? Or am I just adding up one and one and getting three? I mean, you did go looking for it earlier when I said... And just... Is this what I think it is?" *Oh, please, let it be what I think it is.*

He couldn't read her. Not at all. Just like when he gave her the key. *Oh, shit. Oh, shit.* "Well," he said, and cleared his throat.

"If it is," she took a shaky breath and then swallowed. *Faith, right? Please, please, please, please.* "I'll say 'yes.'"

Will you? "Marry me, Jillian." The words were out before he even had a chance to think about them. "Uh, please?" He let out a nervous laugh.

She nodded. "Yes."

Their arms were around each other and they slid down on the mattress and both laughed. "Oh, God," George said, near her ear. "That was the scariest thirty seconds of my life."

"*You* were scared? I just asked you if you were proposing. What if you'd said, 'oops, no, slight misunderstanding'?"

They both laughed again, holding onto to each other tightly. "I *think* if I *hadn't* been attempting, so very badly, to propose, and you'd thought I was, I would have lied. I would have said I was and been all the luckier for it."

"Oh, my. That's a lovely thing to say."

"No. It's true." He ran his hand over her hair again. "You know, all I wanted from the moment I first saw you... before we even spoke... was to be next to you. And now, it, it sounds ludicrous, but forever won't be long enough."

She sighed. "Oh, keep talking. I'll be nothing but a melted puddle."

He chuckled again. "I have never before been accused of having a silver tongue. But you make it sound like..."

"Oh, you do. But, so long as you're being honest, what difference does it make?"

"It'll make a difference if you're nothing but a puddle."

They laughed again. Then he kissed her softly and whispered, "Best afterglow ever."

"*Mm-hmm.*" She agreed with him and handed him the ring. He slid it on her finger. She reached for his cheek, looked in his eyes, and breathed out, "Best afterglow ever."

They curled together for a few minutes. "You feel wonderful," George said.

She held up her hand and looked at the ring. "No, I feel like I'm floating."

"And that isn't wonderful?"

She giggled. "Since you mention it, yes, it is." She ran a hand over his chest. "You feel wonderful, too. Which is nothing new." Her eyes jumped up to his. "I just realized, I mean fully realized, we don't have to work tomorrow. We can sleep in. Or not. I guess I have a few phone calls to make." She looked at the ring. "I want to tell people."

"Good. I want to tell people too. Do you think you'd have time to see Orville? I'd like to do that one in person and it would make a difference if you were there."

"Of course," Jillian said. "I should swing by the hospital to see Lacey too, and I'll probably catch a few of the girls then. But, I'm not sure what to do about my parents. This news probably ought to be delivered in person."

"So, we'll go on Sunday. Drive out and share the news." When Jillian bit her lip, he asked, "Worried?"

"Yes and no. I don't know what they'll say. I expect it won't be all bad. They must like you. They agreed to the piano."

George chuckled again. "Don't worry, Sweetheart. Whatever they say, we're still getting married."

Jillian put a hand to her forehead and rolled onto her back. "Oh, I wonder. They might come up with something to make you change your mind."

George took her hand from her forehead and kissed it. "I don't think so. Your dad already knew I planned to marry you at some point. And he didn't send me packing."

"He knew? How did he know?"

"He asked when we all had dinner. You know, 'what are your intentions?' I told him I planned to marry you."

Jillian blinked. "You said that? To my dad? Oh, my."

"I think that helped my case when I was begging for the piano."

"Okay," Jillian said, and covered her face. "I can't think about that anymore. What do you plan to do about your parents?"

"Best I can do is a phone call. So, we'll call. How would you feel about me putting you on the phone? Just for a minute."

She lowered her hands. "Terrified. But I'll do it for you."

"Thank you, Sweetheart." He leaned over and kissed her. "You know, we did this in the wrong order."

"What?"

"I should have proposed first. Then we could have made love right after."

"Oh, no!" Jillian sat up. "Oh, I didn't even think."

"Yes?"

"What am I going to say when people ask how you proposed? Well, we made love and then while we were still naked, he-"

George pulled her down next to him. "Who's going to ask?"

"All the women," Jillian said. "That's how the conversation goes. 'Guess what, we're engaged!' 'Really? Congratulations! How did he propose?'"

"So I messed this up. Want me to take back the ring?"

"No!" Jillian lifted her hand away. "No. You're stuck now. You asked... sort of, and I accepted and that's that."

George smiled and took her in his arms. "You're stuck too. So how about you just leave out the sex. Tell them about my unbelievably clever mislead with the three ring circus. That should be enough. Don't you think?"

"Perhaps. If I can manage not to blush."

"Ah, blush. You'll look adorable. And happy. People can chalk it up to happy. You are happy, aren't you?"

Jillian touched his cheek, bit her lip, and nodded. "Deliriously." She smiled as broadly as he could ever remember.

Saturday passed in a flurry of activity. George spent most of his morning painting bedrooms while Jillian spent hers hauling clothes and some odds and ends to his house. A full move was planned for the next weekend, assuming that either a suitable moving company could be found and hired on such short notice or a truck was hired and friends helped with the carrying.

By lunch, George was questioning his ability to stay on his feet, until he saw Jillian hanging clothes in his closet, correction, *their* closet. She was bouncing with every step and singing softly to herself. When she turned and saw him, her whole face brightened further and she smiled. *And I get to see that every day.* He found himself next to her, unable to recall moving his feet, and then refreshed from a few short kisses.

Jillian continued her partial move after lunch, worrying about wearing down before she had everything she thought she needed for the week. She had debated and finally decided to move Charlie on the last trip. He'd hidden in the apartment after her third trip, so she figured she'd let him be until last. She also talked to George about his plan to keep Charlie in a bedroom for a short time while he adjusted, and they'd decided to hold off painting that bedroom to keep it fresh.

By two in the afternoon, Jillian found that she'd moved her clothes, books, music, and movies. She had practically everything but her kitchen supplies and her furniture. She also had boxes and suitcases stacked in a spare bedroom waiting for new homes. The bathroom hadn't been a problem; there was plenty of space. And the closet had taken most of her hanging clothes. But there were few spare dresser drawers, leaving quite a few items homeless.

She did smile happily at the thought of her books in the library. She also loaded her music and movies onto those shelves. Then, having checked on Charlie, settled herself into a bath and made a brief phone call to her parents, thanking them for the piano, confirming the terms of the deal, and then inviting herself and George to lunch the following day.

Having completed most of her chores for the day, she leaned back in the tub and sighed. It seemed both a pleasant and logical move, since they planned to stop by the hospital and then visit Orville, to get cleaned up first. *Spoiled.* The soak did wonders, as did the thought that she could enjoy it any and every day going forward.

George had a very charming smirk on his face when he found her there. "Look at you," he said, and knelt down next to her. "I don't know that I've seen you look that relaxed... ever."

She giggled. "Probably not."

"You've settled in already, then."

She sat up and leaned her arms on the edge of the tub. "Well, you did give me a key, and then asked me to move in, and then proposed. So..."

"I did, didn't I?" He lifted his right hand and ran his index finger along her arm.

She nodded. "Mm-hmm. And here I am." She sighed. "Taking advantage of every advantage that I possibly can."

"Ah. Good for you," George said. "Is this the real reason you said yes?"

"To your proposal? Just to soak in the tub?"

George grinned. "Yeah. Whenever you want."

"You caught me. I'm marrying you for your tub."

His brows knit together in a mock frown. "Of course. You've envied my bathroom from day one. This is all you want."

"Well..." She slid a finger along his hand. "Maybe not just your tub. Maybe there are other reasons." She looked at his hand while she drew a small circle on it, and then looked back up at him. "Like being made dizzy. I used to go on rides at the amusement park for that. Now, you make me dizzy without any help."

He grinned again. "So you marry me for my tub and as a cheaper alternative to amusement parks."

"Precisely," she said. "I started on this plan right after the first kiss. I tried to warn you, you know. I tried to tell you that kiss was a bad idea."

"Hey, now!"

She laughed. "*Terrible*, in fact. A *terrible* idea."

He dropped his fingers into the water and splashed her lightly. "Clearly. Look where you ended up, soaking happily in my- *our* tub." After she laughed again, he kissed her lightly and then stood up. "I need a shower before we go."

"No objections here," she said, leaning back against the tub and sliding down a little. "I need a few more minutes."

She couldn't convince herself to get out of the tub, even after he'd finished his shower and was combing his wet hair. "If you want to go to the hospital, you're going to have to get out of there. Orville doesn't take excuses."

Dragging his eyes back from Jillian's reflection in the mirror to his own, he tried to keep his face serious, so she'd agree and get out of the tub. *It took her about a minute to be comfortable here.* He was smiling again when he exited the bathroom and started looking for fresh clothes. *She's nearly moved in, too.* He looked up at the picture on the wall that he still needed to rehang. *This is good. This is really good.*

From the bathroom, he thought he heard Jillian getting out of the tub. *Progress.* He stepped into the closet and saw her things filling up more than half the space and shook his head. *I guess I asked for that.* He was going to have to do something about drawer space too. *There are far too many full suitcases in the other room.*

As he removed a hanger with a dress shirt on it, he glanced up at the shelves above the rod. She'd put a few boxes up there too. His were pushed to the end. That was okay. He didn't care. But he did notice one of the boxes on the shelf that it was probably time to be rid of.

Although he expected it to be dusty, George pulled the box down and carried it into the bedroom to set it down by the door. He could take it to the trash when they left.

He must've taken more than a minute in the closet. Jillian had already covered up with satin underwear and was lifting a sweater out of a drawer. "No lace today?"

She threw a look at him over her shoulder. "Maybe later." Then she tugged the sweater over her head. He held back a sigh. *Later.* But she was moving at a good pace then, so there really wouldn't have been time to admire the lace anyway.

"Dressing up?" He asked, as she retrieved a skirt from the closet.

"Shouldn't I? It gives us the option to get dinner somewhere nice after we visit Orville. Unless you want to hurry back here for more painting."

"Hurrying back would be all right, but painting isn't necessarily what I had in mind," George said, as suggestively as possible, hoping to get her thinking about later.

"I know. We need to spend time with Charlie to help him settle in." She zipped up her skirt and walked to one of the boxes, still open on the floor, and started rummaging for shoes. "And then after that, I still have so much unpacking to do."

Jillian looked at him as she sat on the bed to put on her knee-high boots. "So much to do. So little time." He must've frowned or something because she laughed, stood up, walked over to him, and threw her arms around his neck. "Don't worry. There will be time for *us*."

"I wasn't worried," he said, and kissed her for a few seconds before she pushed away and said something about her hair and makeup and disappeared into the bathroom.

He figured if she was dressing up, he'd better do the same and went fishing for a sport coat and tie. He wasn't about to go as far as a suit. When he was tying his tie, he walked into the bathroom to watch her. *This is better than television.* Not that she had much of a transformation then. She was mostly brushing out her hair and reapplying some cheek and eye color. But it was entertaining all the same. *I wonder if I'll ever get bored of just watching her.*

When she'd finished, she added her jewelry and he realized that she'd been wearing the engagement ring the whole time, even in the tub.

"What are you smiling about?"

"Nothing," he answered and took a step back. "Just marveling at you."

"Oh, no," Jillian said. "No smooth-talking, right now. We have places to go." She made one last inspection in the mirror and then headed passed him back to the bedroom and found her purse. "I'm all set," she said, and looked at him.

He picked up his sport coat and handed it to her. "Do you mind?" He picked up the box by the door. "I'm taking this out to the trash." He started out the door.

"Okay. Why the trash? What's in it?"

"Just stuff that can go. Probably should've gone ages ago."

"Liiiiike?"

He stopped mid-flight on the stairs. "Old girlfriend stuff." He looked over his shoulder at her. "Probably not appropriate to keep around."

She smirked. "Oh. Getting rid of the evidence, hmm?"

He started back down the stairs, shaking his head.

From behind him, she called out. "I see it's all taped up. And dusty. Haven't been in there in a while, I take it."

"No. I suppose not."

"Want to go through it first? Just to be certain you're not getting rid of something you want? I promise to behave and not look, if that helps."

He reached the main floor and headed toward the back of the house. "There's nothing in here you'd be curious about. It's all Sarah stuff. Mostly pictures. Should've dumped it ages ago. Not sure why I didn't. Anyway, if I haven't missed by now, I won't miss it."

Jillian didn't follow him. For some reason that seemed odd, so he stopped in the kitchen and looked back at her. She just shrugged when he met her eyes. "Whatever you say."

"I say, it's trash. I say, it's over. I say, it's done. I say, this house should only be about the future, not the past. What do you think?"

Jillian didn't smile, but she nodded. "If you change your mind, I promise not to intrude while you go through it." She shifted her weight. "I've got old stuff too. And, just so we're clear, I'm not sure I want to just dump it."

"Oh," he said, and set the box on the floor. "What do you have?"

"Letters, notes, cards, pictures. Stuff like that. Most actually have fond memories attached."

"Oh." Even as he said it, he was surprised by the flat tone of his voice.

"Don't get upset," Jillian said.

"Why do you want to keep old stuff?"

"Why did you?"

This is beginning to feel like a fight. He sighed and glanced at his watch. "Okay. Fair enough. If we're going to open up more wounds, we should probably do it later. I was trying for the easy way. Silly me. Let's go to the hospital, check on Lacey, and share our news. And save the blood-letting for later."

Jillian laughed loudly enough he knew it was forced, but at least she found her coat and slipped her arms into it. "Blood-letting. How dramatic." She took a breath. "Let's go."

George nodded to himself, kicked the box on his way passed it to the front door, took his sport coat from Jillian, and layered it and a heavier coat. He opened the door and motioned her through, realizing he needed to talk to her about parking in the garage instead of the street.

Jillian started forward and then paused in the doorway. "Are we fighting?" She asked, and then looked at him.

He shrugged. *Not much of an answer, I know. But not now…*

"Because I don't want to fight. Not now. Not *ever*. But, especially, not now."

He sighed. "Jillian." He sighed again. "I don't want to fight either."

"Okay. So…" She stepped back and shut the door. "Let's get your box and throw it out, so your mission will be complete. And later we can… deal with mine."

"You'll throw yours out?" He asked.

"We'll discuss it." She reached for him, placing a hand on his arm. "I think if we talk about my reasons, you may feel a bit different."

"Oh?" His arms itched to cross, but he battled the urge, not wanting to pull away from her.

"But… if you don't… well, that may be an option… throwing it out."

His arms quit itching.

Her hand squeezed his arm. "I love *you*, George. I'm with *you*, marrying *you*. If my box of memories hurts you, then it's not okay. I hope you'll understand. But if you don't... then... we'll move forward together... somehow. In a way that works for both of us. Right?"

He shrugged again.

"Can I at least make my case *before* you decide it has to go?"

He nodded and lifted his arms. She came into them quickly, wrapping her arms around him. He dropped a kiss on her hair. "Sure, Sweetheart."

"So," she said, into his neck. "Is the fight over? For now, at least?"

"Sure."

She exhaled and pulled back. "Okay. Fine. If that's what it takes. It's in the blue bedroom. Let's get it and take care of it."

Really? "Uh," he said, for lack of words.

She started toward the stairs. "I won't have our first full day of being engaged marred by this. We deserve to be happy. If this is what it takes, then so be it."

George clutched her hand and tugged her back. "All right. Gesture made and understood. Let's worry about both boxes later. We have places to be."

"No." Jillian tugged her arm free. "It's upset you now. *I* upset you. Let's deal with it."

He followed her up the stairs, taking one for every two she climbed. By the time he reached the landing, she was back out of the bedroom and handing him a pencil box. "That's it?"

She nodded. "Yep. That's it."

"Just this little thing?"

"Yes."

He flipped the lid and saw folded sheets of paper and photos. Pretty much what she'd described. *Not quite as daunting when you look at it and it's a tiny, little pile.* He closed the lid and handed it back to her. "Let's talk about it later."

"George, I-"

He kissed her lips. "It's okay. I'm fine now. We'll talk about it later."

"Okay." She said, quietly, her eyes still closed from the kiss. "But, really-"

He kissed her again. "Really. I mean it. Discuss later."

"All right, then." She returned the box to the bedroom and they headed for the hospital.

Taking less pain medication, Lacey seemed to be awake more of the time, so the visit had more conversation than previous ones had. Jillian could tell Lacey was putting on a good face. It was obvious to her that Lacey was still in a lot of pain. The nursing staff had her moving some during the day, leaving her tired in the afternoon, but not sleeping.

With Malvinia there also, the small talk didn't last long. She was focused on Lacey for a few minutes, but then had to go. Jillian stopped her, after sharing a look with George. He didn't like that she hesitated and waited for him to agree it was time to share. He wanted her bursting at the seams to tell. *I suppose that Lacey being in a hospital bed might account for some of it. I just hope that that's all it is.*

"Before you go, Mal," Jillian started and paused a moment to take a breath. "We have news." George saw her start to smile then, *really* smile, and he stepped close and slid his arm around her waist, trying to be a part of everything.

Malvinia shook her head and raised her eyebrows. "Well?"

Jillian looked up at George, and then back at Malvinia, and then Lacey. "Well, last night," she focused on George again, "George proposed." She put her left hand on his chest, nicely showing off the ring. "So, we're engaged."

"Oh!" Lacey said. "Wow! That's amazing." She lifted up a hand and motioned them closer. "Let's see the ring."

As Jillian and George moved toward Lacey, Malvinia took a step closer too. "Last night? After all the painting? What happened?" She focused on George. "How did you propose?"

Jillian started snickering and showed the ring to Lacey, who made appreciative noises and smiled broader than Jillian had seen since the accident.

George answered Malvinia. "It was somewhat spontaneous."

Malvinia held out her hand and Jillian showed her the ring. "Gorgeous."

"I love it. Not as much as I love George." She flashed him a dazzling smile. "But I love it."

"So," Lacey said. "Tell us about the proposal."

Jillian bit her lip over her grin and then told the girls the edited account that George had suggested the night before, while he felt himself flushing a little. *I can't remember the last time I felt this embarrassed.*

"Congratulations, George," Malvinia said. "You've got a real treasure."

"I know," he said.

"Oh, Vi," Lacey said, "don't be so formal." She looked at George. "Welcome to the family, George. We're so happy."

George smiled at Lacey. "Thank you. That's very kind."

"Not at all," Lacey said. "The look on Jillian's face is worth more than anything I can think of." She reached out her hand to George and when he took it and she squeezed. "Be happy."

"I think I can say 'yes' to that," George answered.

Jillian focused on Malvinia who walked around the bed and gave her a hug. "All my very best wishes."

"Thank you," Jillian said.

Malvinia whispered to her. "Call me when you have a minute and aren't too busy floating on cloud nine to tell me what really happened with the proposal."

Jillian giggled. "That was all true, Vi."

Malvinia stepped back and squeezed Jillian's arms once. "I agree with Lacey. That smile is priceless." She slipped her arm through Jillian's as she turned to head out. "I'm actually off tomorrow and Monday, if you can believe it. So call me if you need anything." She lowered her voice. "Have you told your parents yet?"

"No," Jillian answered. "We're going out tomorrow for lunch. And we'll share the news in person."

"Good idea." Malvinia started toward the door and towed Jillian with her. "How about Christy and Kai?"

"I'd hoped we'd bump into them in person, but if they don't drop by before we have to go, I guess I'll call them."

"Okay. If I see them in the halls I won't say anything, unless they do. Make sure you get to be the one to tell them."

Jillian cringed. "Christy just told me she was giving up men for a while. I hope this doesn't upset her."

Releasing Jillian's arm, Malvinia shook her head. "You can't make your life choices based on anybody but yourself. If she flips out, let me know. I'll talk to her. We'll commiserate about men and then dig up some happiness for you."

"Commiserate? Vi? Is everything okay with you?"

Malvinia shrugged and smiled sheepishly. "Just remembering our conversation from a few weeks ago and wishing I had one of those. But, I haven't exactly been making relationships a priority, so what can I say?"

Jillian gave her a quick hug. "Call me later, if you want to talk. I'd offer to do it now, but George and I have a date with a friend of his and..."

"It's okay, Jills. I've got to get back to work. I'm just glad I had the good fortune to hear your news in person."

They said their goodbyes and Jillian rushed back into Lacey's room. They spent another fifteen minutes chatting and then headed to Whistling Elms with Jillian feeling a little guilty to be leaving Lacey alone, but she consoled herself that Lacey's parents were returning by dinner time.

As George opened her car door at Whistling Elms, Jillian realized that she'd begun to expect George to drive whenever they went out together. He shut the car door and Jillian took his hand. "Remind me later to give you my spare set of car keys."

He released her hand to put his arm around her. "Thanks. I'll do that." He kissed her hair. She squeezed his waist.

Finding Orville ready to game gave George a twinge a guilt. *I should have called and at least mentioned I was bringing Jillian along.*

But the guilt couldn't have lasted even a minute, as Orville spied the ring by the time they'd said hello.

"Well, I'll be!" He stood up and held out his hands to Jillian and she walked forward and placed her hands in his. "Here I thought *eventually* the kid would make the leap, but I didn't guess it would be so soon." He lifted Jillian's left hand up a little. "He must be growing up. And you, dear, are probably the one to thank for that. May I kiss the bride?"

"Of course!" Jillian answered and Orville kissed her on the cheek. "And, I should tell you that he's been completely honest with me. So I know that I have you to thank for this treasure, as well as George."

"No, Dear. It's you who gives it value, by wearing it again."

Jillian took her hands from Orville's and hugged him. "What a wonderful man, you are. Thank you." When she released him, he was blushing from ear to ear. She gestured him to sit on the couch. "I only came along today to tell you the good news. I won't intrude on your fun." She looked to George.

He was standing quite tall, with his hands behind his back, looking a bit puffed out in the chest and showing his teeth in his smile. She blushed at his obvious pleasure. "I'll wait over there while you play," she said, and gestured toward another couch.

"Don't be ridiculous," Orville said to Jillian's back, and she turned toward him again. "We have to celebrate. Let me gather up a few friends and find something suitable to toast with. Stay here. I shall return."

"Orville, I can-"

George was interrupted by a grumbling sound from Orville. "Stay here with your lovely fiancée."

Once Orville had shuffled off, George gestured to Jillian to sit and he joined her. "You've made Orville very happy," he said, and put his arm around her. "Thank you for being so good to him. For thanking him. That was sweet."

Jillian leaned into him. "It was sweet of him to give you this ring. I hope he doesn't come to wish he'd kept it."

"I don't think that will be a problem. I'm more concerned about his health."

Jillian sat back. "Why? Is he ill?"

"He denied anything. He's had health issues for a long time. Nothing to worry about with proper medical care, diet, the usual. But, I don't like him giving away his stuff. Feels a little like he's preparing for... something."

"Oh," Jillian said. "Is there anything we should do?"

George tightened his arm around her. "Based on knowing him for as long as I have, no. I asked, he answered. That's the end of it. But, I'm glad we're getting to celebrate *us* with him."

"Me too."

When Orville returned, he had a few friends with him, including Delaney. George knew them all, but allowed Orville to make the introductions. Mariah joined them a few minutes later with a few cups and some sparkling grape juice that she'd liberated from the kitchen. After the lovely toast that Orville gave them, *May you find comfort in each embrace, joy in every smile, hope after every tear, and more love than you can imagine, always,* George found himself digging out the record boxes again.

The small celebration grew as a few more residents found their way into the common room. Jillian danced with most of Orville's friends and George finally met Marcia. He'd seen her, but hadn't been formally introduced.

The party lasted until dinner was called and Jillian told George she wished it didn't have to end. *We'll have to organize an engagement party then.* He put his arm around her and said, "We can come back. Orville would like it."

"Okay," Jillian said. "So would I. You know, he still didn't listen to *Cupid.* For someone who was so happy to see me wearing the ring, I'd have thought he'd enjoy their song too."

George thought about that as they walked to the car. Once he started the engine, he looked at Jillian. "It's probably mixed emotions."

"What is?"

"The ring and the song. The ring was special, but he's let go of possessions before. Her clothes, obviously. And he had to get rid of a lot of stuff when he moved in here. The song may be more memories than he can take, though."

Jillian nodded, but didn't say anything at first. After they'd exited the parking lot, she said, "I wouldn't want to cause him pain."

"You didn't," George said. "If anything, I think you made him happy." He released the steering wheel briefly to grab her hand and bring it to his lips for a kiss. "You've made me happy too."

She exhaled and dropped her hand to his leg. "I'm happy, too, Darling."

"So everybody's happy."

"Right," Jillian said, and took her hand back into her lap. "Which leaves only the boom to fall."

"What boom?"

She crossed her arms and dropped her chin to her chest. "My parents." She uncrossed her arms and ran her hands over her face and pushed back her hair and her head too. "Everybody is happy for us so far, but neither of us has told our parents yet. When were you thinking about the phone call to yours?"

"Tomorrow night, if you're okay with it. A couple of my brothers will be there for dinner, so I thought we'd catch most of the family at once."

"Three brothers," she said, and shook her head. "What am I marrying into?"

"A long line of lumberjacks, actually." George said, with a grin.

"But not you," Jillian said.

"Nope."

"You decided to be who you are instead."

"Yep."

"And who are you?" Jillian asked.

"Don't you know?"

Jillian nodded and put her hand back on his leg. "Yeah. Yeah. I know who you are."

George looked at her for a moment. "Good." He refocused on the road. "Dinner?"

"Please. Where?"

"Well, I know we dressed up, but how about we get takeout and eat *at home?*"

"*Home.*" Jillian twisted toward him and lifted her hand to touch his hair. "That sounds lovely."

CHAPTER THIRTY-FIVE

The dishes were in the dishwasher, but the glasses still had a little wine in them, and the bottle was still half-full. Jillian pushed the button on the dishwasher, snagged her glass from the counter, and looked out the window to watch George walking back from the trashcans. He was moving quickly, probably from the cold, but Jillian amused herself with the thought that his speed came from a desire to get back to her. She even wondered for a moment if she was right, when he came in and gave her a look that hit her in the stomach, as he reached for his glass.

Put down the glass and make me really dizzy.

He finished his glass and set it on the counter. "So…"

"Hmm?" She raised her eyebrows.

"Would it be to asking too much…?" He picked up the bottle and poured a little more wine into her glass, then a little more into his. "Would you play for me?"

"Play?" Jillian asked.

George nodded. "I won't exaggerate and say I crawled through broken glass to get the piano. It wasn't a pleasant conversation, at first, but it wasn't that bad. I'm not asking you as a payment for anything. But, I'd really love to hear you play."

"Um, sure," Jillian said. *Play the piano. For a one man audience.* By the time she'd set her glass on the counter, her heart was pounding and her stomach was flipping over. *Just me. Without anyone else to cover up my mistakes.* She tried to remember where she might have her books and sheet music. She must have brought them, but she hadn't seen them. Probably upstairs. "I need to look for my music."

"Really? The other week, you played from memory."

Yes, but I had others with me. If I stumbled, they were there to catch me. "I'll be more comfortable with some music in front of me."

"Okay. You could always try the new piece I bought."

Oh, dear Lord. Sight read? In front of you? "I don't think…"

"Oh," he said. "I thought you liked the music." He set down his glass. "I'm sorry. I didn't mean to say that. Not like that. I just thought…"

"I do like it. The idea was really sweet. It's just I haven't practiced it. So…"

George tilted his head. "So?"

Just tell him. Then he'll leave it alone. "So, I'd rather not embarrass myself."

He snorted a laugh. "Embarrass yourself? With me? Oh, please! Just give it a whirl. I know you've never tried it before. How could that be embarrassing?"

"Are you joking? It may well be mortifying."

"Death?" George snorted again. "And here I thought we were past this kind of thing." He lightly rubbed her upper arms. "Don't you know? I'll love hearing you, no matter what it sounds like. And since I've no ability and no skill of my own, I couldn't begin to judge it anyway." He grinned at her. "Take another swallow of your wine and play something. I don't care what. Twinkle, Twinkle, Little Star, if you like."

She couldn't help but smile at that thought. *Still…* "George, please. You're the last person I want to be in front of when I make a fool of myself."

"Oh, geez, Jillian. I should be the one person you'd be okay *with*. You know why? Because I'll never think you foolish." His eyes roved over her face, then dropped and followed his hands as they skimmed down her arms and clutched her hands. He grinned again and lifted her hands to his lips and kissed her fingers like he'd seen Freddy do. "Think you can 'tickle those ivories'? For me?"

"Oh, you don't play fair. Not at all." She shook her head. "All right. Fine. But you have to promise not to laugh. No matter how awful."

"I won't laugh." He spread his hands apart, taking hers with his, and he leaned forward and dropped his forehead against hers, not even noticing the sigh he let out. "Trust me, hmm? Let me admire you."

"It's hard to admire someone who isn't…"

"What? Perfect?"

"Yes," Jillian said.

"Trust me," George said, and lifted his head. "Please. Play for me."

"Okay," Jillian said. "Fine."

"Fine? Just fine."

"Yes," she said, and pulled a hand from his to reach for her wine glass. "I do this reluctantly. And only because I can't say 'no' to you."

"Let's change that phrase," George said. "How about you always say 'yes' to me?"

Jillian smiled, took a sip of her wine, and then nodded. "You're right. I always say 'yes.'"

"So?" George said, and raised his eyebrows.

Shaking her head and exhaling, she turned toward the front of the house and led the way, not letting go of George's hand. She stopped at the piano and then took a step to the side to place her glass on a bookshelf. "No drinks at the piano."

"Okay," George said. "I'll remember that." He watched Jillian slide out the bench and then adjust it after she sat down. After she'd fiddled with it to where she seemed to like it, she looked up at him for a moment. *She looks so tense.*

Then she slid the bench over a few inches and slid herself down, making room for him. "Please. Sit."

His smile could light the moon. She realized she was holding her breath until he sat down. She lifted the fall board and the light twinkled off her ring. Grinning, she put her fingers on the keys. "Remember, I'm not a professional."

"Jillian," George started but then she played a chord and he stopped.

After a few more chords, she began a melody and he started to laugh as he recognized Twinkle, Twinkle, Little Star. "Oh, very funny."

"You said…"

"I remember," George said, and kissed her neck sending a shiver, followed by a giggle, down her back. "Got anything else?"

"Um, Mary had a little lamb?" But she opened the music he'd bought and then tried the introduction very slowly. When she'd progressed as far as the familiar Tchaikovsky melody, she paused and said, "This is really nice."

"Yes, it is," George said, looking from her hands to her profile, enjoying the music and the warmth of her sitting next to him.

She played another line and stopped to turn the page. "I'll have to teach you to read music, so you can turn the pages for me."

"I'd like that."

She played the next page, still very slowly, feeling out the music through her fingers and approving most of what she heard.

"You're fantastic," George said, beside her.

"No," she said. "But thank you for saying it."

"I don't lie to you. You should know that." He leaned a little closer. "You're fantastic."

She blushed and dropped her hands into her lap. "Oh, George."

"Why is it so hard to take compliments from me?"

"I don't know," she said, looking down at her hands. "It's probably something to do with my actually believing you, that you're sincere. I don't know that I ever believed I could be appreciated by anyone else when I wasn't perfect. And I so want to be."

George covered her hands with his. "You *are* perfect. Oh, maybe not in every single thing you do. But you're perfect *for me.*"

She swallowed and looked up at him. Her eyes were moist. "Please don't cry. Do you remember what you said to me the night I was waiting for you when you came home from a night with your girlfriends? We hadn't even been together for a day, yet. But I was… upset. Do you remember?"

"I'm sure I do, but I'm not sure what you mean."

He reached up to her face and pushed back her hair. "You said, 'you're safe here.' Everything bad is outside the door. And you said that I could say anything and not to worry about how I said it."

"I remember."

"It goes both ways. And it goes for more than words, but actions too. Sweetheart, you're safe here. With me. I promise you. I'll always treat you with respect. And I'll always take care of your heart."

She laughed nervously. "You ought to write that down. That would make a lovely marriage vow."

"I promise it all to you now. Without the ceremony. Without the pomp. Of my own free will. Just you and me, right now. I love you so much."

She couldn't stop herself; the tears started. "Oh, George." She took her hands from his and put her arms around him, hugging him tightly. "I love you, too." She took a few moments to pull herself together, and then she turned back to the piano and wiped her face. "I'm sorry. I can't seem to control myself."

"It's all right. Happy tears don't bother me as much as sad ones. They are happy, aren't they?"

"Very."

"Then, okay." He draped his arm over her shoulder and gave a squeeze. "Enough of this for tonight? Want to watch a movie? Go to bed?"

She let out a breath. "Not yet." She looked at him again. "I'm not finished. My audience deserves to hear the whole piece." She looked back at the music, wiped her eyes one more time, and then put her fingers back on the keys.

She stumbled through the rest, wincing at the mistakes, but continuing on. When she finished, she closed the music while George applauded softly. When she looked at him again, he smiled at her. "Thank you. For everything. The music. The piano. The… understanding."

He leaned over and kissed her hair at her temple. "I'm just glad to be here," he said.

"If you're even half as glad to be here as I am to have you here, then I'm a very lucky woman."

He laughed lightly. "Now, that's a nice sentiment. Come to bed?"

"Um. How about this first?" She turned back to the piano and slowly played an introduction. "I haven't played this in ages. Not sure how good my memory is."

The melody began and George recognized it immediately. *Of course. Cupid.* "I'd say your memory is fine."

"I played this to accompany a friend in college when he was auditioning for a musical. I must have played it a hundred times in a row, over and over, practicing. But I'm not sure I remember the verses. The chorus is easy."

"I wouldn't know the difference, I bet. But it sounds great to me."

"Thank you." She kept playing. "I wish Orville was inclined to listen to the song. I noticed a piano in the common room."

"Yeah, we'll have to be careful there."

"Definitely."

She hadn't paused in her playing while they were talking, so George took that as a sign he could continue. "I keep thinking about a song for us."

"That's sweet of you," Jillian said. "I still haven't come up with anything I want to try to convince you is the right one."

"It's harder than I would have thought." He wet his lips. "I've never had a song before. Not even with Sarah. I seem to be putting a lot of weight on it."

"It would have been easier if we had had music playing at a special moment, like our first kiss. But we were lacking in musical score."

"That was ironic, after all the music earlier that evening."

She struck the final chords and then glanced at him. "We didn't need help setting the mood, like some people do." She closed the fall board.

George stood up slowly and stepped aside to watch Jillian rise and slide the bench under the keys. "Can we make this a regular thing?" He moved over to the shelves and picked up Jillian's wine glass.

"Make what a regular thing?"

He handed her the glass. "You playing for me?"

Jillian nodded very slowly. "I think that might be possible." She smiled at him, took a sip of wine, and headed toward the kitchen.

He followed her and when she put her glass in the sink he stood behind her and wrapped his arms around her. "Will you always be difficult?"

"I have to keep you on your toes. Besides, you know eventually I'm going to agree. I can't say n- I mean, I always say 'yes' to you."

"Come to bed." He said, softly next to her ear.

She grabbed his arms and leaned into him, tilting her head back to see his face. "Hmm, well, I suppose... *yes.*"

He chuckled and leaned down to kiss her.

George had to ring the doorbell and hold Jillian's hand to keep her from backing away. "Relax."

"I should never have let you talk me into wearing this," she said, as she tugged under her coat at the hem of the bright blue dress she'd regretted wearing ever since they'd left home.

Squeezing her hand, George said, "It's lovely. You should always wear color. That gray thing you were considering isn't you, at all."

"And my hair. My mom..."

"It looks better down," George said. "If she says anything, you can always say you're wearing it down for me."

"Oh, that'll score-" She cut herself off, as the door opened. "Mom!"

Jillian's mother opened the door wide. "Come in, Jillian. Welcome, George." Cheek kisses between the women and then George handed over the wine they'd brought as a hostess gift. "How lovely. Please let me take your coats and then head into the living room. Luncheon isn't quite ready yet, I planned a little extra time in case you ran into traffic."

"Thank you, Mom."

As they entered the living room, Jillian's dad put down a book and stood up to greet them, shaking George's hand, kissing Jillian, and then motioning them to sit. "We're very pleased that you could both join us today. And, Jillian, we're very much looking forward to hearing you after lunch."

Still standing, George found himself displaying a nervous smile and tried to soften his lips. Jillian took a grip on George's arm and it became painful enough that he turned to her.

She, too, had a nervous smile and was showing a lot of teeth. Through her teeth, she quietly said, "They think I'm playing for them today. Oh, my God. What am I going to do?"

He placed a hand atop hers. "Well, we could always tell them the news right away," he whispered. "I know you planned to wait until after the meal, but it would probably distract them."

"I don't know," she whispered as she turned to him. "Usually, they're more relaxed after they eat. I know I will be."

He took her free arm in his free hand and gently turned her, tugging her closer so he could whisper directly in her ear. "You'll be more relaxed the moment you've told them and so will I." He let out a soft sigh. "This is supposed to be *good* news. Remember?"

"I know, I know, but-"

"Why aren't you seated?" Jillian's mother asked, as she entered the living room. "I need to check in on the kitchen, but you all should sit. Jack, offer them a drink."

"I was about to," Jillian's father said, and her mother nodded with a smile and headed out of the room.

"Now?" George asked, in a whisper while squeezing her arm.

Oh, boy. "Uh, Mom," Jillian raised her voice a little so her mother could hear her. "Can you come back in here?"

"Is something the matter?" Her mother asked, and walked into the room to stand by her father.

"No," Jillian said, and turned and clasped George's hand. "Why don't we all sit?"

Her mother took a few steps closer, rather than sitting. "What is it, Jillian?"

Jillian smiled at George, took a breath, and focused back on her parents. "Mom, Dad, we came for lunch today to share some news with you." Another deep breath. "We... George and I... are engaged."

George hadn't thought much about exactly what he expected Jillian's parents' reactions to be, but after a moment he began to really understand the ice queen act that Jillian displayed at work. They were both inscrutable, still, completely unmoving except perhaps their breathing. There was absolutely no discernible emotion, neither positive nor negative, across from him. He released her hand and put his arm around her waist.

The silence lasted for a few ticks of the grandfather clock in the room and then Jillian's mother broke it, though her face didn't change. "This is a surprise."

"It shouldn't be," George said, and Jillian startled next to him.

"The timing," Jillian's father said. "That's what's surprising."

"The timing?" Jillian asked. "What of it?"

Jillian's mother took a few steps back and sat down, looking from Jillian to her father. "Jack," she said, in a flat tone, giving away as little as her face. She looked back at Jillian and George and motioned them to sit.

They settled and Jillian took hold of George's hand again, waiting for her father to sit. He didn't sit, however. Her father walked the room once, and then stopped next to her mother, put a hand on her mother's shoulder, and looked squarely at George. "I know you said that you were serious about Jillian. I'm sure you think that we should have expected this. And after our talk the other evening, I can't say we didn't expect it, but the timing... My concern, *our* concern, here, is that you two haven't known each other very long."

Jillian's mother cleared her throat.

Her father exhaled. "And, frankly, we have a few more concerns, including your financial situation."

George leaned back on the sofa. *You have* got *to be kidding me.* On his right, Jillian started doing her ice queen impression too, her face smoothed into an empty mirror. If she hadn't squeezed his hand, he would have thought that her mind had left her body. *Am I supposed to answer this? Or no?*

"I'm sorry?" Jillian asked. "What was that? You have concerns?"

"Yes, Dear," her mother said.

"You *have* concerns," Jillian said. "*You* have concerns." George turned his head completely to look at her. The ice queen was melting or morphing; he could see her jaw clench. "I can't even have congratulations. I just get *concerns.*"

Her father exhaled through his nose. "Well, Jillian, really. Did you really think we'd celebrate that our daughter wants to jump into a legal entanglement, with a man she barely knows, when her life is up in the air?"

"*My life?* What about my life?"

It was her mother's turn to answer. "You're still playing at this business thing-"

"Oh, Mom!" Jillian stood up and walked around the sofa to stand behind it with her arms crossed. "*Playing?* I'm not *playing!* I've got a career."

"You can't take this *career* seriously, Jillian."

George's mouth was open before he knew what was happening and he said, "She should. She got the promotion."

The momentary silence gave George the impression that no one was going to react to his announcement.

It was sweet of him to try. Jillian stepped behind him and dropped her hands to George's shoulders.

"Jack," Jillian's mother said, in a strained voice and she lifted a hand to her shoulder to touch her husband's hand. "*Jack.*"

"I heard, Karen." He looked at George and shook his head. "This is a disappointment."

"A disappointment?" George asked, since Jack was looking at him.

"We'd hoped that you'd receive the promotion." He looked up at Jillian. "And you'd come to your senses."

"George," Jillian said. "We're leaving."

George stood up. "Wait. Why doesn't everyone just take a moment?" He pivoted toward Jillian.

"George, it's better if we just go," Jillian said, and shook her head.

"Come on." He turned toward her parents. "Okay. You've had a few surprises. I'm sure if everyone takes a minute, we can find a little perspective."

"George, please," Jillian said, behind him.

Jack raised his eyebrows. "All right. Let's have some perspective. What is going to happen now? Will you be working for Jillian?"

"Actually, I'm starting my own company."

"Oh? Well, that *is* interesting. What's your business plan? How much capital have you raised?"

"Dad," Jillian said.

"Well," George said, fighting putting his hands in his pockets. "The business plan is still under construction. The actual work plan, however-"

"So, no capital yet, then," Jillian's father said.

"No, Sir. I'll be using my savings-"

"Savings?" Jillian's father took a step forward. "What will this company make?"

"A video game."

"A video game," Her father seemed to chuckle a little and looked at Jillian's mother. "A video game." He looked back at George and put his hands on his hips while his face clouded over. "Let me see if I understand. You're planning to leave your job and eat into your savings to start a company making a game."

"Yes," George said.

"Uh-huh. And you plan to marry my daughter and put her on the hook for your mortgage while you're spending your time playing at your computer."

"Dad!"

"No, sir. I most certainly do not."

Jillian's father looked at her. "You marry him, you'll be in the middle of any money trouble he has."

"Dad!"

"A pre-nup won't save you from creditors."

Jillian walked out of the room, shouting, "We're leaving!"

"Mr. Braden, that's not at all-"

"*Quite* the disappointment," Jillian's father said.

"George! I have our coats!" Jillian called from the hallway.

"Jillian!" Her mother stood up and headed for the hallway. George took another moment staring down her father and then turned and followed her mother into the hallway.

Jillian tossed George his coat and then slipped her arms into her sleeves. "Let's go."

Her mother walked over to the door and put her hand on the knob. "Don't leave," she said. "We can table this discussion and have lunch."

"No," Jillian said. "I'm leaving. *We're* leaving."

Her mother opened the door. "Very well." As Jillian picked up her purse, her mother seemed to focus on her again and took a step closer, reaching out to her and taking her hand. "What an... interesting engagement ring."

Jillian pulled back her hand with a snap. "George!" And she stepped around her mother to make her way to the door.

"Uh," George said, and then mumbled a good-bye.

Outside, Jillian was already halfway down the walk, so he caught up with her with a fast jog. "How do you feel about eloping?" Jillian asked. *I'll do anything to keep those people away from us.*

There's a certain appeal to not having a big wedding. "Uh, Sweetheart, you should think about this. For a few days." *There's no rush and I don't want an annulment due to emotional distress.*

"I didn't mean now. It can't be today, anyway. It's Sunday. We'd have to wait until tomorrow." She unlocked the car doors with her fob and headed to the driver's door. George followed and when Jillian opened the door, he stepped in close so she couldn't open it far enough to enter. She looked at him with a frown. "Trying to be subtle?"

"Let me drive." George said. "Please."

After a few seconds, Jillian released her grip on the door and stomped around the car to the passenger side. By the time George had buckled, Jillian was tapping her foot. "Let's go. Get me off this street."

He started the car and put his hand on the gear shift, but didn't move it.

"I'm not going back there, if that's what you're thinking."

He lowered his hands from the wheel and the gear shift, and then turned toward her. "That's not what I'm thinking. I'm thinking that they may have a point."

"What?!" Jillian looked at him and crossed her arms. "They do *not* have a point! They don't even know what a point looks like! They are so far from a point that... darn, I'm so mad I can't even come up with a good metaphor! This is *my* life. *Mine.* It's mine to enjoy or to regret. All my mistakes have been mine. They can't claim they've *saved* me from anything or *rescued* me after, either. No! They've no business in any decision I make."

George took a breath. "I mean about my video game company."

"What?" Jillian blinked. "No. No, no, no." She reached for his shoulder. "Do *not* let them in your head. Under no circumstances should you *listen* to them. They're doomsayers and they're unhappy with me. It's not about you. Not really. They can talk about the *timing* all they want. They're mad at me for not doing what they want. You, George, are an easy target because you're not used to it. That's all. Do *not* listen to them."

Nodding slightly, George turned back to the windshield and shifted into drive. "Okay. Let's go home."

"Mal, I don't know what to do. He's a wreck. I thought *I* was upset, but they really did a number on him," Jillian was pacing the kitchen and looking out of the window, holding her phone tightly against her head. "He was completely off at basketball practice, like he hadn't slept in a month, no coordination, no rhythm. I dissuaded him from telling the guys that we're engaged because he looks like death, not like he's happy. We came home again and he said he'd be outside a few minutes and headed straight to the backyard and climbed into the big tree. He'd been sitting there for close to half an hour so I went out and he said he's fine and just needed a few more minutes. That was over twenty minutes ago." She rubbed her face with her free hand. "What do I do? I have no idea what to do."

"I don't know, Jills. I don't know."

Jillian turned around and leaned on the counter, hoping he hadn't seen her looking at him and felt pressured, while at the same time hoping he had and would come in to talk or even just sit. *If he would just come in.*

Malvinia sighed. "You could try to entice him to come in. Go out and leave a trail of something for him to follow back into the house. Yell out the door that you have pie or something he likes." She coughed. "Take off some clothes and stand in the window."

"Nice try. I don't think he's in the mood for sex. Not when he's up a tree. What is he doing up a tree? Hiding? I don't get it."

"So, go back out and ask."

"He's already said he needs time."

"Okay. Give him time," Malvinia said.

"I'm trying, but it's *killing* me. It's all my fault. I should have told my parents over the phone. I should *never* have put him near the line of fire. I mean, I know they were aiming at me, but he isn't just some collateral damage. And clearly he wasn't ready for it."

"What did they say?" Malvinia asked.

Jillian repeated the brief conversation as accurately as she could remember it, realizing as she finished that she was gripping the counter so hard that her nails were bending. She crossed her arm over her stomach and walked into the family room. "I *hate* that they did this. Dad never gave him a chance." She stopped by the mantel and looked up to see her distorted reflection in the television. "I was so mad when we left and he was so calm, I didn't even realize how hard it had hit him. It's all my fault."

"Jills?"

"Yeah?"

"*You* still need to calm down."

Jillian sighed and leaned her head down on the mantel. "I failed him, Vi."

"Okay, deep breath," Malvinia said. "Very deep breath. The drama level here is much too high. Let's get some perspective. Yes, your parents were awful. Yes, they upset you *and* George. But the next steps are yours and his. You control where you're going from here."

"Not when he's up in a tree!"

"Jills, you know the old saying, 'if you can't beat 'em, join 'em.'"

Jillian began to pace the living room. "Are you suggesting I go climb into the tree?"

Malvinia let out a snort. "No. But I am suggesting that you support him in whatever it is he's doing, so he can do it faster. Take him a cup of coffee. Maybe that will help you too, give you something to do."

"Making coffee doesn't take long."

"But it's better than nothing. And it might open him up a little. Conversations can start with a simple gesture and a 'thank you.'"

Walking back into the kitchen, Jillian pushed her hair out of her face with her free hand. "You know Mal, you can be a fount of wisdom."

"I know. I'm so underrated." Malvinia said, and then clicked her tongue.

Jillian laughed. "All right. I'll try the coffee. Wish me luck."

"I wish you more than luck. But frankly, if he's everything you think he is, you don't need luck."

She started the coffee maker. *It's really not a bad idea. Something warm to drink.* "He is. I know he-"

"What am I?"

"Ahhh!" Jillian was so startled by George that she let out a soft scream, though she managed to hang onto her phone. "Oh! You scared me half to death."

"Sorry," George said.

"Tarzan came down from the tree? Or should I say George of the Jungle? Huh. I like that. George of the Jungle," Malivinia said. "George the jungle man. Mmm! Once you've set everything to rights, get a little of that jungle love."

"Yes, Vi. I gotta go now."

"Right. Bye. Call me later."

Jillian disconnected the call and set her phone on the counter. "I was just making coffee. To bring you some. Help keep you warm. While you were... whatever you were..."

George sighed a little and walked closer. "I'm sorry. I just needed to think. There's still more thinking to do, actually, but I did some good thinking out there. I guess I didn't think about what I was doing until you came out." He motioned toward the window. "It's my other... eccentricity... I guess you'd call it. My yo-yos are one and that's my other."

"What?"

"The tree." He looked at the coffeemaker. "We got a few minutes, grab your coat and come outside?"

"Ohhhkaaaay," Jillian said. "But, uh, I'm not climbing that tree."

"That's fine. I wasn't going to ask you to."

They walked outside and George walked up to the tree and patted the low branch. "I'm sorry I went... uncommunicative, but I've been coming here to think since I moved in. This tree is a great... silent... tower of perspective."

"Oh?" Jillian stepped closer. "Tell me."

"You see, based on her height and her trunk width and the location and well a few other things, it's easy to tell that she was here before the house. She was lucky to be sitting in the right spot when this area was developed, nobody cut her down.

"Anyway, she's a great deal older than us. And, well, assuming no disasters like a lightning strike or a deadly beetle or truly devastating wind or snow, she's got a really good chance of being here long after we're gone. That's perspective."

"Go on," Jillian said, reaching up to grab the same branch.

"Well, when I think about her lifespan, all the things she's seen come and go, the weather she's endured, and hopefully a few fun moments with children swinging on her branches or something like that, it reminds me to think about the important stuff and not to worry about the little stuff. She's likely had all kinds of things happen to her, good and bad, and she's still here."

"I follow. So, 'don't sweat the small stuff.'"

"It's more than that. It's also don't miss the big stuff. In comparison, you and I have unfairly short lives. Of course, there are insects with only a few days, so it's relative. But still, the point is that we have to make the most of the time we're allotted."

"And you've been out here thinking about what's small and what's big?"

George smiled at her in the light cast from the house, and then shook his head. "Yes, but there's more."

"More?"

George nodded. "Trees are, like all nature, amazing. I grew up with a deep appreciation for them."

"I can imagine." Jillian said. "So, what else?"

"Well, the else is balance. This little blue and green ball we live on is a precarious balancing act; everything on it plays a part. We have to live our lives in balance too." He paused for just a moment. "Even if I wasn't a programmer deep down, I was never going to be part of logging. I can't do it. It's not in me. But logging is about balance too.

"You cut down a tree, you plant another one. Balance."

Jillian tilted her head. "Still following, I think."

"So, that's what I was thinking about. The big. The small. Balancing everything. What I want versus what I have. What is right for me versus what's right for you, right for us. How to take a million pieces, put them together, and create something that lasts." He nodded toward the house. "At least for a while."

"Wow," Jillian said. "I was in there thinking he's been outside for nearly an hour. Now I'm thinking you were *only* outside for an hour."

George laughed. "I'm not finished thinking yet. I haven't solved the puzzle. I just believe I have a good grasp on what the pieces are, now."

"Oh," Jillian let go of the branch to rub her arms. "Care to share anything about that?"

George let go of the branch and placed his arm around her shoulders. "Let's go inside where it's warm first."

She nodded and walked with him. "Maybe I can help with the solution."

He dropped a kiss on her hair and then removed his arm to open the door for her. "Sweetheart, you are smack in the middle of the solution. I promise you that. I just want to mull over a few more things."

Walking into the kitchen, she rubbed her arms again and then took off her coat and poured the coffee. "I would really like to be a part of things. Decisions especially, if they'll affect both of us."

"I won't *do* anything without talking to you. But I'd like to think a bit more, so when we talk, I'm ready to present it."

Jillian turned and handed him a mug. "You make it sound like a business meeting."

He grinned. "You have the agendas. I have the meetings. But enough, don't you think, Sweetheart?" He took a quick sip from the mug and then set it back on the counter. "For the moment, let's focus on making dinner, hmm?"

He moved across the kitchen and opened the refrigerator, searching for a quick plan for dinner. Jillian moved behind him, taking the coffee mugs to the table. "How about fish?"

"Sounds good. Um, George?" Jillian called from the table.

"Yes?"

"Why do you call me 'Sweetheart'?"

He took a container out of the refrigerator and set it on the counter. "I haven't thought about it. It's always felt natural. Why?"

"I was just a bit curious." She turned the mugs around so their handles were facing opposite directions. "I knew someone in college... He called all the girls 'Sunshine'... saved him the trouble of learning any names." She snickered. "I'm not saying you don't know my name, of course. I just wondered if you'd *always* used 'Sweetheart' as a pet name or a term of endearment or..."

He took out a pan and turned on a burner on the stove. "No. I don't think so." He started going through the pantry. "If I remember correctly, usually I've used nicknames." Holding up a box of rice, he turned back. "You don't like nicknames, if I recall."

"Right. And neither do you." It was Jillian's turn to fetch some things from the refrigerator. "So... you and Sarah..."

"Me and Sarah, what?"

"Nicknames? Pet names?"

George laughed. *And now she's jealous...* "I never called her 'Sweetheart.'"

"No?" Jillian began to fetch plates and set the table.

"If you must know," George paused and cleared his throat, "and I promise you'll likely gag on the knowledge," he paused again, "Sarah's nickname or pet name or whatever was 'Sari' and sometimes 'Rah' like the cheer 'rah-rah.'"

"Oh." Jillian finished folding a napkin and dropped it on a plate. "'Sari' is pretty. But, 'Rah'? That is... awful."

The pan was heating up and George put in a small amount of oil. "Told you."

"What did she call you?"

"She picked up on 'G.'"

"Huh," she said, and started to the cabinet for the glassware. "Any objections to stopping at the apartment tomorrow for my glasses?"

"Nope. What about you and Sam?"

"He didn't like the blue glass."

George started seasoning the fish. "You know what I mean."

"Well, he called me 'Jill.'"

"And you hated it." George said.

Jillian murmured her agreement. "His full name was Samuel. But he went by Sam with everyone, so I wasn't special."

George turned and waited until she looked at him and he met her eyes for a moment. "Let's say *he* wasn't special."

Jillian smiled. "Whatever you say, George."

Playing with Charlie kept Jillian occupied for a while, easing some of her guilt about the move and then not being around enough. He responded to her presence with apparent pleasure and purred when she stroked his fur.

When she found George crouched in the morning room, taking measurements, she hated to distract him. "I think we'll need to let Charlie roam soon. He's already acting bored in there by himself, and I think you'd better be ready for him to sleep with us." She leaned against the wall. "Vidar and Irene aren't allergic to cats are they?"

George looked up from his measuring tape. "I never thought about that. I'll ask them." He looked back at the tape, picked up a pencil, and made a note. "I think I'm ready for a bit of a talk," he said, and then looked at her, "if you are."

Jillian crossed her arms. "That sounds serious. Is this about the 'great think' you had in the tree?"

He picked up his measuring tape and stood up. "Yes, it is." He took a step forward. "I know you don't want to hear this, but your father's right."

"No, he isn't," Jillian said.

George transferred his things to his right hand, so he could reach for hers, as he approached. "Sweetheart, I know they upset you, but that doesn't negate your father's logic. He's a smart man. Although he never said, I have a suspicion he practices corporate law, probably contracts."

"You're being right about his practice doesn't *negate* his being wrong about everything else," Jillian said, and she kept her arms crossed, even as his hand rested on her arm.

George exhaled. "Jillian, please take a breath and join me on the sofa. I'll bring wine, if that will help."

"I don't want to sit down. I certainly don't need alcohol to take the edge off. Generally speaking, it isn't wise to pour alcohol on a fire. Just say what you have to say. Do it quick."

"Alright." He put his hands behind his back. "He's right about creditors. That's why I never planned to borrow from anybody, just risk my own money. I'll incorporate as an LLC to limit my liability. The odds that someone will sue over a video game are quite low, I think, unless there's copyright infringement which brings me to the big issues.

"In order to protect you, I don't want you to put anything into this venture. That includes furniture."

"George!" Jillian dropped her arms.

"I don't want you exposed to any risk on my account. If you put something in, it might put you on the hook."

"Oh," Jillian said.

"Your support means everything, absolutely everything. I just want to be sure that you don't get hurt, if I screw up. I think we'll all be okay. Vidar and Irene and me. We'll be really careful. But, you. This isn't your project, so you have to be safe.

"And, uh, I was thinking. The ways to legally protect someone are… well, they're simple. It's like your father said, a pre-nup won't do it. So, we don't get married, not for a while. We haven't really talked about that. Setting a date."

"Now, I'm ready to sit down," Jillian said, and headed for the living room.

Following behind her, George didn't stop talking. "Are you upset? I have no idea where you stand on this."

Dropping to the couch, Jillian crossed her arms again. "How long are we talking?"

"How long?"

"How long do you think we have to wait?"

Letting out a long breath through his nose, George joined Jillian on the couch. "I don't know. It would probably be wise to wait until after the game is released and we see if anyone jumps at it. So, I guess, maybe a year and a few months, on the inside. That would be okay, wouldn't it? I mean, it takes that long to plan a wedding, doesn't it? I think that's right. When

J.P. got engaged it was just over a year, I think. I mean, it wasn't my wedding, so I didn't pay that much attention.

"My job was to make sure I'd marked my calendar and showed up when and where I supposed to, dressed as I was supposed to be dressed, and not get loaded at the reception and embarrass the family, not much to ask of me. This time, it'll be more important. I'll pay attention.

"But, a year and a bit isn't too long. Is it?"

Don't do this. Please. Don't let them dictate terms to us. Be stronger than that. Jillian kicked off her shoes and twisted toward him, pulling her legs up under her. *Calm. Be calm.* "A year and a bit... on the inside." She exhaled. *Calm.* "I'm not sure." She raised her thumbnail to her mouth, but pulled her hand away and dropped her arm on the back of the couch. "I was so excited when you asked me. And you're always so interested in 'right now.' I didn't think about it. I just assumed it would be soon." Looking away from his eyes, she lowered her head. *Say it.* "To be honest, I think I expected you to suggest we go to the court house tomorrow."

"Ah," George said, and sat back. After a moment he quietly said, "I see."

I see? That's all? Just, I see? "And now you're thrown. You weren't thinking about rushing this time. Everything up to marriage was 'right now,' but not that." She crossed her arms again. *I'm so stupid. So unbelievably stupid.* "I'm an idiot."

"Jillian, don't talk like that."

She turned away and jumped back up, grabbing her shoes as she went. *Okay. Find a way to be calm. Find some calm.* "I need a few minutes. I'm going to go get my glasses."

George followed her toward the front of the house. "Unh-uh," George said. "You're not walking out of here. This is important."

"I need a few minutes," Jillian repeated and grabbed her coat. *A few minutes to scream into a pillow.*

"Fine. Then, I'm going with you." George grabbed his coat.

"That defeats the purpose. I need a few minutes. I'm just going to get my glasses. And... think."

"You'll be gone over half an hour," George said. "I'll go with you and I won't talk. That way you can think. In fact, I could drive and you could just think."

"That's not..." She struggled with her coat. "Fine, I'll say it. I want to be alone." *Or more accurately, I want to be away from you.*

George shook his head, tossed his coat on a nearby chair. "No. No, you don't." He took her firmly by the arms. "I've figured you out. A little, at least. I'm sensing a bit of angry along with this running away thing. What you want is for me to take you in my arms and kiss you until you're dizzy and then suggest we get married tomorrow, just like you expected.

That's what you want, isn't it?"

"George, please. I don't want to fight. We can't fight again. I'm too tired."

"Who said anything about fighting? This is just an attempt to get you to tell me what you're thinking."

"Well," Jillian said, and pushed out of his grip, "I waited for you to think earlier. You can give me time to think in return."

CHAPTER THIRTY-SIX

"What do you need to think about? All I've asked is what you want. And you know what you want." Jillian threw up her hands and started walking toward the music room. George followed. "Or are you trying to talk yourself out of or into something?"

"What would I be talking myself out of?"

"Being angry? Being sad? Not getting married tomorrow? I don't know."

Jillian walked to the piano and lifted the fallboard almost absently. George closed the gap and pressed the lowest key and Jillian looked at him again. *At least that got her attention.* "Come on. On Wednesday we said we were going to be better at communicating. I'm trying awfully hard here. *Talk* to me."

Jillian tapped the highest key on the piano. "I *need* to *think.*" *I need to decompress.*

George tapped another key. *I hate it when she's like this. Why can't she just trust me? Just quit assuming everybody is judging her and trust me.* "About..." Then he pressed a key closer to the middle of the piano and held it down while the tone rang out and fell away into silence. "...what?"

Why can't he just give me a minute to resolve myself into something better than this? She moved to press another key, but stopped with her finger just barely grazing the key. "About... my feelings." She dropped her hand to her side and looked into his eyes, "I'm disappointed."

"That's what I thought. Were you just expecting me to suggest getting married right away? Or were you *planning* on it?" When she didn't answer right away, he nodded. "So, you want to get married tomorrow."

Yes. "Don't twist my words." *Yes, I do. Oh, God help me. It's crazy and totally reckless, but I do.* "That makes me sound reckless."

And you don't want to sound *reckless. You want to be swept away and blameless.*

547

"Which is my role in this relationship."

Pretty much. "Stop."

"It's funny. All this time I've been thinking that I was pushing you. 'Let's be together.' 'I love you.' 'Marry me.' But it turns out, the whole time, you were right there with me, weren't you? Maybe, even waiting for me?"

"I'm certainly waiting for you now." She shook her head and crossed her arms. "I knew it. I knew I shouldn't move in here until we were married. It's the free milk versus buying the cow thing all over again. You'd think one generation would actually listen to their mothers, but we never do."

"You're not a cow," George said, flatly.

"I'm not married either," Jillian said, just as flatly and started for the door again.

"So, what? You're going to move out?"

"No," Jillian said, as she stopped walking. "Who said anything about moving out? I'm not just going to leave. I'm committed." *Or I should be committed...* "So, I'm going to get my glasses and bring them back here. Maybe they'll make me feel better and more at home."

"I'm committed too. And this *is* your home. And I *do* want to get married. We started telling people. *Your* friends. *Your* family. It's not like I've tried to hide anything. But then you stopped me from telling mine."

Jillian's hands fisted and she placed them on her hips. "I asked you not to tell the rest of the musketeers because you looked like you were miserable. Did you really want to hear what they had to say when you were acting like that?"

"Fine. Whatever." He glanced at his watch. "Well, it's time to tell my family. Any minute now, we should call. So, will you quit running away and get on the phone with me?"

Still with her hands poised on her hips, Jillian tried to relax her face. "And what will you tell them?"

"What do you think?! Exactly what I said yesterday. I want to introduce you and tell them we're engaged." He grabbed the back of his neck and rolled his head to the right. "I'm starting to think you want to back out of the engagement."

"I don't want to back out," Jillian said, through her teeth. "I'm still here, aren't I?"

"Then, can we get on the phone?"

"Yes. Fine. Let's."

Soaking in the tub was Jillian's solution. Her whole body was aching and her mind felt thick like syrup. She'd been too embarrassed to write down names while she and George were on the speaker phone, so she'd struggled to remember his parents and the brothers' wives and the kids. Not that they'd talked to all of them, especially the kids who had just shouted to be heard. The call hadn't lasted long, about ten minutes, but by then she just wanted to hide and she was too tired to *run* as George had put it.

I should be happy about the phone call. She kept repeating the thought over and over to herself as she allowed her arms to float. *It means he's definitely serious. Men don't tell their families they're getting married, unless they mean it.*

But the disappointment hung over her like a cloud that she couldn't see her way out from under. Even in the tub, the gloom was there. *How is it possible I let my expectations get so high?*

Actually, that was an easy question to answer. She'd believed. She'd actually let herself believe. They'd fought and had a horrible break up and then he'd come back. He'd come back on knees. It may not have been literal, but it was certainly true figuratively. He'd argued them back together. He wouldn't take no for an answer.

It was wonderful. He loved me so much, he didn't want to be without me, which was perfect since I didn't want to be without him.

But the fighting was starting up again. She'd tried not to let it happen. She'd tried to get some space so she could calm down and not confront the issue.

It's ridiculous, wanting to marry someone I hardly know. Except that I do know him. And, I really want to marry him now. And he really doesn't want to marry me now, which means one of us has to give in. And, of course, he's got a legal reason, not just logical, but legal, which means, it has to be me.

She slid down in the tub to her nose. *I'm going to be stuck here waiting for who knows how long. It's a lovely place to be stuck.* The water swallowed her up for a moment. *But it's still stuck.*

Opening her eyes, she looked through the water upward to the ceiling. The ripples in the water obscured the view and the light overhead wavered and shimmered, as it came through.

Letting a few bubbles out of her mouth at a time, she stayed under for another minute until her air was nearly spent, enjoying the separation from the air above. The strange low hum yet near-silence of the water pushing against her eardrums made the disconnection from world above more substantial. Even as the air trickled away and she knew soon her lungs would be screaming to breathe, she felt safe and warm in the cocoon. *Maybe I can wait for him for a while. I'll just stay in here. Not show my face. Not see anyone else's either. I wonder how long I can hold my breath.*

She sat up and inhaled as she wiped the water from her face. *Yeah, living underwater isn't going to be practical.*

The knock on the door was more insistent than she'd have expected. "Jillian?!"

She wiped her face again. "Yes?"

"Oh, good," he said, twisted the doorknob, and cracked it. "I was worried when you didn't answer. Can I come in?"

"Sure," she said, and leaned on the edge of tub. "I'm sorry. I didn't hear you."

His eyebrows sunk and the edges of his mouth turned down. "You didn't hear me?"

"Uh, no." Jillian reached for a towel. "I, ha, went under for a bit."

George waited for Jillian to look at him again, but she climbed out of the tub and focused on drying herself. "So, this isn't the silent treatment," George said.

"No." Jillian laughed softly, still not looking at George. "I just couldn't hear you." She started rubbing her hair. "What did you want?"

He sighed and crossed his arms. *I guess I should have expected more drama.* "Well… I'd like Jillian back, for starters."

"What's that supposed to mean?" Jillian asked.

"I know you're upset, but can you please not act like this? At the very least, can we talk about it?"

Jillian sighed and wrapped the towel around herself. "And say what, George? You don't want to get married for over a year. You're not going to change your mind. What is there to talk about?"

"Good!" George said, and closed the gap between them. "There *is* a misunderstanding."

She looked at him warily. "Oh?"

"Sweetheart, you think I don't want to marry you, but that's not true. I only want to wait until it's safe. If it wasn't for that…"

"Yes, of course." She grasped her lotion bottle on the counter and muttered, "If it weren't for *that.*"

"So, it's worse than I thought," George said. "You don't believe me, do you?"

"Does it matter? The result is still the same."

He held out his hand, she glanced at it, and then handed him the lotion bottle. "It's not the same at all," George said, and opened the lotion. He squeezed a little onto his hand, began to rub it onto her back, and attempted to meet her eyes in the mirror. "Sweetheart, everything I've said to you is true. Believe me now. I wouldn't have asked, if I didn't want to marry you. You know that, don't you?"

She met his eyes for a moment and then looked away. "I believe you."

George sighed again and gently turned her. "I love you. We'll get married. I promise. Do you believe me?"

"I believe you," she said, quietly.

At least that time she looked at him. "But you want to get married now. Do you want me to give up the game idea?"

"No," Jillian said. "No. Not at all. I just…"

"I could… if it's that important to you."

"I wouldn't ask you to do that. It's something you've wanted…"

"For pretty much all my adult life, yes," George said. "But if it means losing you…"

Jillian closed her eyes. "I'm not leaving." She looked at him again. "I never threatened to leave. I just wanted some space to think."

"Well, if you're looking for a threat that will make me one-eighty, that's the one."

She shook her head. "Look, I love you too. I'm not asking you to do anything. I just…"

"Want to get married," George supplied. "And soon."

Jillian exhaled and lowered her head. "George, nothing new is being said. I don't see the poi-"

"The *point* is to come to some kind of understanding. Some kind of agreement. Something that will let us go back to where we were just this morning."

She looked at him again. "That's a nice thought, but we can't go back. It doesn't work that way. The only way is forward." She started applying more lotion. "The only way forward… is through. So we go through."

Yeah. "Yeah," he said, nodding. "Yeah, that's true. So… can we go forward… together?"

Another loud exhale erupted from Jillian. "I'm *not* leaving." She looked at him in the mirror. "Okay?"

"You're not here either." George said, with a swallow.

Jillian's mouth opened, just a little, but no sound came out.

"I can feel the distance between us. Hell, I can see it. You don't even want to look at me."

"Well," Jillian said, with a crispness in her voice, "what do you want me to do about it?"

George lifted his hands. "I'm sorry. I didn't mean it that way. There's no need to get defensive. You're upset. I get it. I just… I want to fix it."

"Well, you can't just fix it like that. You can't say 'this is how I want things' and have them be that way. Some things take time. I've been telling myself that same thing for the last hour." She put the lotion bottle back on the counter.

George dropped his own hands and followed hers with his eyes. Unlike the previous night, her ring was sitting on the counter. "Right," he said. "Right." He paused a moment. "So, am I sleeping on the couch tonight, then?"

Jillian shook her head. "That's a bit dramatic. No. I'm not kicking you out of bed."

Picking up the ring from the counter and holding it up between them,

George said, "That's good, because we're supposed to have good karma with this ring. No going to bed angry."

Her eyes darted to the ring and then back to his eyes. "Angry is different." She sighed again. "Look. I'm tired. Let's go to bed. Nothing is changing tonight."

"Are we going to be sleeping facing away from each other?"

Jillian's head tilted and she let out a strangled laugh. "Oh, George." He watched her eyebrows come together and the blinking start.

"Oh, no. Please don't cry," he said, before he could stop himself, and when he moved to take her in his arms, she didn't fight him like he expected. Instead she tucked into him and let out a small, shaky breath. "Jillian," he whispered against her hair.

She seemed to sob a few more times against his chest, but the sounds slowed and he kissed her damp hair. "Come to bed," he whispered and when she nodded her head under his chin, he reached between them, found her hand, and slipped the ring back on her finger.

"I love you," she whispered.

"And I love you," he replied, as he lifted her into his arms and headed toward their bed.

When Jillian woke, it was still early, which gave her time to think in peace. Nothing was quite normal, even their sleeping positions were different. All the other nights they'd fallen asleep with him on his back and she'd been curled up against him. But that morning, she'd woken on her back, with George turned into her, his arm possessively across her stomach. Of course, that was the probably the smallest detail rather than the big picture.

She couldn't stop the deep breath as her mind flashed back to the way they'd made love the previous night, slowly and tenderly, completely devoid of the usual passionate abandon that made at least some appearance every other time. *No wonder it feels like the first time every time, it's so different every time.* George had carried her to the bed and quickly joined her under the covers, kissing away the tears and holding her tightly. The gentle kisses and holding had gone on for a very long time, she couldn't even identify when it had turned into something more, but it had stayed tender. Afterward, he hadn't let go, even imprisoning her in his sleep. *He's really afraid I'm leaving. It would be sweet, if I hadn't already assured him I'm not leaving. He won't take my word for it. We've got problems.*

George felt the fog lift and was grateful that Jillian had stayed in the bed. Even before he opened his eyes, he heard her breathing and knew she was awake. The odd sleeping position gave him the opportunity to kiss her shoulder without moving. "Good morning," he said, after touching her skin with his lips.

"Good morning," she answered and began to stretch.

"Alarm didn't go did it?" George asked.

"Nope," Jillian said, and managed to roll onto her side.

George stretched for a moment and then draped his arm around her again. He scooted closer and pulled her back against him to spoon. "Good. Just give me two minutes of this."

That was *sweet*. She reached behind her to run her fingers through his hair. "I don't think two minutes is enough." As he kissed her shoulder again, she could feel the smile in his lips. *We are going to make this work.* "But, maybe we should get moving anyway. We *have* to go to work today." He made a groaning sound and Jillian rubbed his head again. "If we get moving, we could reward ourselves. That shower *is* meant for two."

"Tell me you actually are implying what you sound like you're implying and you've got yourself a deal."

Jillian laughed and pulled away from him. "You'll just have to find out. Won't you?"

"How do you want to tell people?" George asked, as he lifted her hand to his lips and kissed her fingers quickly, just below the ring, smiling the entire time.

"Good question," Jillian replied, flushing and grinning. "Did you already have an idea about that?"

He kept hold of her hand, gently twisted it up, and flashed the ring at her. "Well," he said, "there's the quiet move of flashing the ring around and waiting for someone to ask."

"Mm-hmm," Jillian murmured and leaned a little closer.

"Or we could send a group voice mail…"

"Nuh-uh," Jillian said, shaking her head just a little as her nose scrunched up, and she leaned a little closer.

George swallowed, licked his lips, started to lean over, and bumped his elbow on the steering wheel, causing him to snort a laugh and look away for a moment. "There's always the same method from before, tell a few people and let it go on its own."

"Hmm…" Jillian murmured as her eyes drifted up and she seemed to consider it. "I don't know," she said, and dropped her eyes back to his. "Maybe, we're overthinking this."

"Maybe," he whispered and leaned a little closer, "we are. Maybe we've been thinking, just a little too much." He heard Jillian inhale in preparation, and he quickly closed the gap to set about making her as dizzy as possible, before they left the car and headed into the office.

But she didn't let him go for too long. "Work," she breathed. "We have to work." He nodded and kissed her another minute, for good measure.

Wiping her lip gloss off of his lips with her thumb, she giggled. "I should wait to apply my lip gloss until we're actually in the office. Save you the trouble of wiping it off and me the money for the wasted lip gloss."

Grinning behind her thumb, George replied, "I thought the point of lip gloss was to make your lips more desirable to kiss."

The edges of her mouth curled up. "So it is." She sighed. "Let's go."

"We still don't have a plan on how we want to handle this," George said, as he opened the car door.

Jillian stood up, looked at him over the roof of the car, and shrugged. "Do you care? I don't mean, 'do you care?' I just mean, does it matter to you how this goes?"

"Not really. So long as people know. Well... I guess, I'd prefer some kind of announcement from us," he closed the car door and began walking toward the building, "rather than a slow leak."

"Trust me, it won't be slow, no matter what we do. Once it starts, it'll be wildfire."

George nodded. "Yeah. I bet you're right."

"Will you trust me to get the word out?"

His eyebrows raised, George looked at Jillian as they approached the front doors. "Got a plan, after all?"

"Of sorts. If you're okay with my way."

He opened the door for her and they began the walk to the stairwell. "Any reason I shouldn't be?"

"If you aren't, say so now," Jillian said.

"I trust you," George said, with a quizzical look.

"Great!" Jillian said, with a smile and detoured into the HR cubes. "Melissa!" She called and started walking up the aisle flashing her left hand. "You'll never guess..."

George laughed and slowly began to follow Jillian. When the squealing started, he shook his head. *Yep. Wildfire.*

The floor was mostly silent when Jillian and George left the stairwell. "It's quite the feat to have escaped from downstairs," George observed. "I thought they'd keep us there all day."

Jillian giggled and then flushed at herself. "Yes. It's kind of them to all want a moment of celebration with us."

It wasn't until George was alone in his office that the thought crept back up about having an engagement party. Jillian loved the attention, which frankly seemed out of character for her. But twice it had happened; she'd enjoyed the party at Whistling Elms and now the attention downstairs. And even more, he'd enjoyed her enjoyment.

There was the little side thought, too, that a party might help hold her off for a bit on the actual ceremony. She'd put on a brave face for him that morning, and though he had little doubt that she'd come to accept that they had to wait, it didn't mean she'd come to like it. In fact, her enthusiasm earlier that morning had made him wonder if she wasn't acting.

Thankfully, she'd been as enthusiastic announcing the engagement as she'd been when they'd had their private moments, so he was able to believe that in regards to them, she was still committed, still all in, ... still loved him more than she loved the idea of being married. *He* was her *choice*.

But, she still wanted the ceremony and the paperwork. *So much for not wanting a contract with her lover.* And he couldn't give it to her for a while.

It wasn't going to be easy, the next year. Between the time he was going to be putting in on his game and what he guessed would be a constant downward trend in Jillian's attitude about not being married, the future looked... bleak.

A party is definitely in order.

While he pondered the logistics of the next few days, his commitments, her commitments, and, of course, their commit to move her furniture on Saturday, he also tried to imagine slating in a party. His mouth turned down a little as it became more obvious that he'd need to schedule it for at least a few weeks out. And that put it during the holidays. Which meant it would be harder to get people there.

His IM popped up with a *Ping.*

Hi there. HR just called.

His desk phone rang.

Ping.

They want us downstairs again in about thirty minutes.

George answered the phone and agreed to be downstairs in thirty minutes. No doubt it was about their relationship and her promotion. At least, he couldn't imagine what else it could be about. It was the proverbial other shoe Jillian had mentioned. Well, he'd known it was coming. *They'd* known it was coming.

He looked at his computer screen and typed. *I just got a call too. See you then.* Enter key.

Ping.

Nervous?

He shook his head and smiled.

No. We already have a plan. Enter key.

Ping.

It's not too late. You could change your mind and I'll turn down the promotion and everything can stay the same.

He snorted.

Not on your life. Enter key.

Ping.

Ok. Just making sure. After this there'll be no going back.

He jumped up and walked swiftly to her office. "Do you want me to…?" He stopped short and turned to close her door. "Do you want me to stay here?"

"No," Jillian said, rising from her desk. "Not if you want to go. I just wanted to be sure because this is a real door we're going through. A one-way door. If for any reason you aren't sure, now is the time. But I'm only asking because of that."

He ran a hand over his mouth. "You're sure. This isn't cold feet on your part?"

"No. No, I'm behind you. This is just the last point where we can quietly turn around. That's all."

He dropped his hand and nodded slowly. "Okay. So long as you're in for this. I know that you want some things to be different." He moved to her desk and sat on the edge. "I know you don't want to put off other things." He reached for her hand and she slid hers into his and squeezed.

Meeting her eyes again, he swallowed. "You cried last night. I don't want to make you cry."

"George…"

"I don't just love you, I like you. I like who you are. I like the sensitive, caring woman you are. But when you cry, it just kills me. I don't want you to be the ice queen. I want to know what you're feeling. But it just *kills* me."

Her lower lip seemed to tremble a moment and she blinked.

"I don't want to be the reason you cry. And… it looks like I'm causing it again." He whispered, "Damn."

"George, I'm with you, okay? I won't lie for you and say I'm *glad* about the other thing, but I'm with you. I want you to be happy. I want you to do what makes you happy. I won't have you unhappy just to give me what I want. Because then neither of us will be happy."

"You really are too good for me," he said, quietly.

She squeezed his hand again and then lifted her other hand to his shoulder. "It'll be okay. *We'll* be okay. I just wanted to double check that this is how we're going forward. That's all. Are we good?"

He nodded and then lifted her hand to kiss it. "We're *so* good." He sighed and then laughed quietly. "I'd kiss you properly, but we don't want to mess up your lip gloss right before the HR meeting to discuss our relationship."

She squeezed his shoulder. "Love you."

"Love you, too," he said, jumping off the desk to hug her and then head back to his office.

She fucking deserves better.

Irene knocked softly on George's door a few minutes later. The conversation was brief as she turned down George's offer in as subtle a manner as she could, remaining cryptic enough that if anyone did overhear, they'd be hard-pressed to guess the topic. He'd smiled and thanked her, trying not to give away that he was anything more than a little disappointed.

Now, what? He needed a third programmer and worse, he really needed Irene's artistic training and eye. *Shit. Catastrophe.*

He glanced at the clock. He was going to have to either find someone else in the next twenty-two minutes or make the leap without all the players in place.

Twenty-one minutes.

"I'm sure you're both aware of the pertinent information in the employee code of conduct," Marlene said, as she spun a copy of the book around to face them.

Jillian and George both nodded, but neither said anything. In the elevator, George had suggested that they let HR show their hand first.

"So," Marlene continued after a moment, "as you know, then, there is nothing at all against a personal involvement between two individuals who are peers. However, I've been asked to speak to the both of you because there is about to be a change.

"I expect you're also aware that Gardiner has been looking at both of you for a promotion. He's planning on making the offer today; the paperwork was started last week. Normally, Human Resources has a very specific, rather simple, involvement in this kind of scenario. But, your relationship was officially noted last week also, and that relationship will be an issue once the offer is made, if it's accepted."

"Yes," Jillian said, and George lifted his hand to cup his chin, letting his little finger touch his mouth as he leaned onto his arm.

Marlene exhaled and shifted forward. "I'll make this short, we're in a quandary." She placed her hands on the table. "If this had happened after the promotion, we'd begin disciplinary action. But, since you've done nothing wrong," she paused and looked away for a moment, "well, I've been asked to present some possible solutions to the situation."

"Uh-huh," George said.

"Before I say anything more, I suppose I ought to ask, has word leaked out?"

"Uh-huh," George said, again.

"I figured," Marlene said, and turned her gaze to Jillian. "Congratulations."

"Thank you," Jillian said, and she looked at George. *He's awfully quiet.* Then she looked back at Marlene. *I guess he's still waiting on those cards.*

Marlene cleared her throat. "So, that leaves... you." She focused on George. "We're hoping this can all be done very amicably."

"I'm out, then," George said.

"Er," Marlene said, "not exactly. But you can't work under the reporting structure you're currently in, once Jillian's over it. Now, there is an opening for a technician in Hardware. It's a substantial downgrade, though, and you're not really qualified for it."

George nodded slightly, moving his head against his hand.

"But, um, no management positions are open," Marlene continued. "Unless you're interested in the technician job, and we'd certainly work with you on that, it's up to us to come to a mutually beneficial agreement." She transferred her gaze back to Jillian. "I suppose I may have put the cart before the horse. You are accepting the position, correct?"

"Well-" Jillian started.

"She is," George said, firmly. "There isn't a reason in the world not to."

"Yes, um," Marlene said, quietly, "Some might say there is a reason. That's why I decided to call you both down, even though this really is a single person issue."

"That reason isn't a consideration," George said, and lowered his hand, sat up straighter, and looked at Jillian. "No matter what."

She nodded back at him. "Is-"

"I can't help but wonder," Marlene said, over Jillian, "if you're sure. It would be easier for everyone if you just turned it down. Then nothing would need to be done, at all."

"I'm sorry, that's not an option," George said, quickly, still focused on Jillian. "You earned it, you deserve it, and you're taking it."

"Maybe, I don-"

"And you want it," George said, softly with a slight smile on his face and shifted toward her in his seat. "We've been through this. Multiple times. It's yours. I'll never stand in your way."

Oh, George. I love you. So very much.

"Oh, my," Marlene said, and then sighed. "That's a terrific sentiment." She looked at Jillian. "That's a rare one, you've got."

"That's true," Jillian managed to get out before anyone spoke over her.

"Well, then," Marlene continued, "it's time to hammer out details." She returned her focus to George. "Should this be private?"

George shook his head. "Not in my view."

"Okay. The offer I've come up with is that you'd resign; we'll provide you with a letter of recommendation, as well as a reference. This won't be the usual, generic, acknowledgement that you worked here, but an actual reference. And there will be some kind of severance pay. I can't say anything about that until Gardiner looks at it.

"He's not happy about this, by the way."

"I'm sure, he's not," George said, and Jillian mentally finished the thought with, *he's had enough potential legal trouble in the last week to give him an ulcer.*

Marlene went on. "So, how does that sound? As a beginning? Would you be willing to resign, if the considerations are adequate? Um," she looked at her notepad. "Naturally, your 401K is yours. We'll help you roll it over to your next position or an IRA. Any outstanding awards, we'll vest. And we will definitely pay you for your outstanding vacation. I have approval for that."

"My vacation?" George sat up. "I was hoping to work here through the end of the year."

"Oh," Marlene said, flatly and took a moment before she answered. "I'm sorry, that's just not possible. Your last day will be Friday."

Ouch.

CHAPTER THIRTY-SEVEN

The remainder of the meeting was almost pointless in Jillian's mind. Until Marlene had a number, there was really very little to talk about. And George's other expectations had been bashed against the rocks.

"You were right about that one-way door," George muttered as they took the stairs. "Geez. Friday! That wasn't exactly what I had in mind."

"I know," Jillian said. "How big a setback is it?"

"I'm not sure. But I was counting on the paycheck through the end of the year."

Jillian sighed. "I could-"

"Don't say it again. Please!" George said. "I just hope the offer covers more than a few weeks."

"They are asking you to voluntarily resign. I'm sure it'll be something more than that. If it isn't, you could always ask for arbitration. That's in our employment agreement."

"Yeah," George said, with a sigh, thinking again that he needed another programmer for his new project. *This is rapidly deteriorating. If I'm going to steal someone else from here, I have to do it before they throw me out. Shit. Shit. Shit.* "Do we have any meetings with Hardware today?"

"In about thirty minutes, I think," Jillian said, in a higher pitch.

"Based on all this, do you think anyone would care if I missed it?" George missed her quizzical tone, opened the door at the top of the stairwell, and let Jillian pass through.

"They'd rather neither of us were there."

"Then, I'll skip. I've got to figure some things out. And quick."

"I could always-"

"No," George said.

"*Help*," Jillian said, and both she and George laughed quietly, cutting the tension just a little.

"You *are* helping. Just stay you. Do your job. I'll figure this out."

Jillian nodded. "Okay, tough guy. But, I'm here for you." She patted his arm as she left him at his office door.

George smiled at her back. *She's a rock.*

This is not going to work. I've got to do *something. I know he doesn't want me involved, but...* After checking her calendar and assuring herself that none of her meetings couldn't be rescheduled or missed, Jillian called Gardiner's office and asked his assistant for ten minutes, any ten minutes, he had on his calendar. When she was told he could see her in fifteen minutes, she opened the Hardware shared drive, looking for an agenda to see who was officially chairing the meeting she'd either miss or be late to. She still hadn't convinced anyone to add her or George to the email invites. As she looked through some folders, her eye caught on a file that had appeared to have been saved in the wrong directory.

Budget revisions. Curiosity won without even a bit of debate. The file wasn't even password protected. She glanced through the columns and then the numbers. *Cripes! Now I know where all the money's been going.* She shook her head and looked a second time. *Where has Gardiner's head been?*

She printed a copy to take with her. *I'm going to need more than ten minutes.*

After staring at the walls of his office for at least twenty minutes, George began wondering again if Jillian's father was right about him. Was he about to commit financial suicide? Hoping that it would distract him from his latest problem, he had begun putting together some hand-off material. But trying to put together the materials only emphasized his new deadline. *Friday. Geez. Friday.*

How am I gonna find somebody that quick? And if I do, I really need to move up my timetable since I don't have the cash to wait until the New Year. What if Vidar bails?

Thinking wasn't helping; perhaps talking would. George crossed the floor and surprised himself by choosing Neal's office. "Got a few minutes?"

Neal nodded and gestured to a chair. "Hey. I would have figured it was time to say congratulations, but looking at you I've got to ask, who let the air out of your balloon?"

George blinked at the odd expression, "Uh, I guess you could say HR did." He closed the door and perched at the edge of a chair. "I guess I misjudged. They want me out faster than I'd expected. My last day is Friday."

"Damn," Neal muttered under his breath. "Sorry, man."

"It's not like I didn't know it was coming. I just thought they'd let me work through the end of the year. I can't imagine Jillian will be handling your appraisals after only being director for a month and a half. I figured Gardiner would take care of that and they'd give me a little time."

Neal's eyebrows jumped to his hairline. "That was very optimistic of you."

"Yeah," George said, with a little bit of a laugh in his words. "Guess I should have been a little more realistic."

"Got any prospects?" Neal asked.

"I was working on something, but I don't know if it's going to come together now." He rubbed his palms against each other. "Perhaps, I didn't think things through."

Neal stood up, walked around his desk, and sat on the edge near enough to George that he could place a hand on his shoulder. "Look, you may be in a tough spot career-wise, but you got the girl. And while it's easy enough to make fun of the romantic garbage in the movies and on TV, the truth is that having the right people in your life makes everything else work. Unless you think you made a mistake and that Jillian isn't really the right one for you, I'd say any consequences are worth it. Another job will come along. But she's one-of-a-kind."

George sat back and Neal's hand fell off his shoulder. "You really think that?"

Neal quirked a smile and his shoulders bobbed. "I know *you* do. And I wasn't kidding when I said I've seen how happy she makes you. I'm just getting to know her, so I can't say a whole lot more. But from what I have seen... I don't think she's the person we all thought she was."

"She's definitely not the ice queen," George said.

"No," Neal agreed. "Look. It'll take a little while. And, frankly, with her being the boss, it might be a little challenging, but we'll acclimate and eventually it'll be like she was always part of the group."

"Really?"

Neal nodded. "I know Taro's been worried that she's going to drive a wedge between you and us, but I don't think she's planning anything like that. I was impressed on Friday when she jumped in to paint. And she's been great at our games. Just be patient and give us more than three weeks to start thinking of her as an honorary sister."

"Yeah," George said. *Had it* really *only been three weeks?* "Thanks, Neal. And I suppose Taro will be telling me 'I told you so' about the job, so thanks for not..."

Neal snorted. "I don't know why he's so sure Jillian is the devil, but if after all of this, he says 'I told you so,' I volunteer to hold him while you hit him."

George blinked and then started laughing. "Yeah. That'll fix everything."

Neal shrugged. "He's lucky you don't want to kill him. I had to talk Sergei down for over two hours after his little stunt. Sergei was beyond pissed." He shook his head. "Starting to wonder if Taro has a death wish."

George nodded. "He's not himself. You, uh, tried to talk to him?"

"Taro? Well, no. Think I should?"

"He's not going to talk to me or Sergei, at this point. And I was wondering if something's up with him and Melissa. Jillian said something a while ago…"

Neal stood up and circled his desk. "Yeah. I've picked up on it too. Maybe I'll see if he wants to go to lunch."

"Good," George said, and stood up to go.

Neal absently tapped his desk with his knuckles a few times. "George," he started. "How are things with Sergei?"

Shrugging, George looked at the floor for a moment. "It's fine. Awkward as Hell. Haven't had a private conversation with him yet. But it's fine. Once he's with somebody else, it'll be easier."

"I suppose that's as good as could be expected. And things *are* good with Jillian, right? Despite the job situation."

George tried to smile and knew it looked really fake. "Of course."

"Yeah?" Neal nodded and crossed his arms.

"Yeah."

"Okay, just checking." Neal shrugged. "I know it would be hard on me if I was getting forced out like that. Might take a toll on the relationship."

George sighed and sat back down. "No. That's all fine. To take your words, 'it's worth it.' And if I can get some things to fall in place, who knows, it might turn out to be a good thing for me."

"And yet," Neal's eyebrows knit together and his lips turned down, "I'm sensing not all is well."

"Has life ever been perfect?"

Neal grinned. "Well, three weeks ago, you seemed to think so."

George grinned back. "Yeah, well… extenuating circumstances. Eventually, real life intrudes."

"So long as you get to live in the 'extenuating circumstances' part of the time."

He let out a breath followed by a genuine smile. "There's a lot of fantastic in my life right now. You can go ahead and laugh if you want; I am so frigging in love with her."

"I know," Neal said. "Glad she feels the same way about you." He cleared his throat. "I was surprised I had to hear through the grapevine that you were engaged."

If yesterday hadn't been so insane… "Well, HR wanted to see me pretty much first thing."

Neal nodded. "Do you already have plans?"

"We haven't set a date yet," George replied, trying not to think about the tears. "But I was thinking about trying to have a party."

Neal seemed to perk a bit at that. "Parties are good."

"But it's so close to Taro's wedding next week and then the holidays. I don't know if we can squeeze it in."

"This week," Neal said.

"Could." He started thinking about everything on the calendar. Their lives were only going to be crazier and crazier in the short term. "Do you think people would come to something tonight?"

"Tonight? Well, I would. I guess you could ask around a little and see if people are available. Your place isn't too far. Sure you want to do that on a weekday? Between cleanup and hangovers…"

"Actually, not having it at home would be better. Maybe do it as a sort of surprise for Jillian. Every Monday night she's at the Blue Feather, so we could do it there."

"That's the place you ran into each other three weeks ago."

"Right."

Neal tilted his head. "Nice symmetry."

George snorted a laugh. "Yeah. It would be perfect symmetry if we got married there."

"Think she'd like that?"

"Maybe. She wants to do it as soon as possible. Like tomorrow."

"Is she pregnant?"

George shook his head. "No. She's not pregnant. I swear that's all anyone ever asks."

"Come on, it's gotta be the first thought anyone has when there's a rush on a marriage…"

"Taro and Melissa announced they were getting married in only four weeks. You been asking him if she's knocked up?"

"They've been dating for a while. Like six months."

"Doesn't that make it more likely he's put a bun in her oven?"

Neal shrugged. "Okay. Got it. I won't ask again." He tapped the desk. "So, tonight. Who's invited?"

George leaned back. "Why not everybody? I'll ask Rachel to get the word out."

"And keep it a secret from Jillian? Or was that just a thought?"

"I think it'll be fun. She'll love it." *I'm pretty sure she isn't playing tonight. Better double check that.*

When Gardiner looked up from his desk, Jillian shut his office door behind her. "Good morning."

Gardiner stood up. "Good morning. I was planning to drop in to see you later today, but Caroline said you needed to see me urgently. Did something happen?"

"Yes." Jillian walked to the desk, sat down, dropping her printouts on the desk. After Gardiner sat, she sighed. "Originally, I wanted to see you about George. I was hoping to convince you to give him a better parting package. But I think that will have to wait for a few minutes." She turned the pages around. "This was sitting on the Hardware shared drive."

Gardiner picked up the pages, flipped through them, and then frowned and leaned back in his chair.

"Has Hardware really spent twice their budget the last two years?" Jillian asked.

Gardiner tapped his fingers. "Three, actually. R&D. It's a tough business."

Jillian took one of the sheets back. "I see half a dozen projects that were cancelled about two months in, after equipment and supplies had been purchased, and then the projects are replaced by something else. Did you approve this?"

"I'm not a hardware man. I'm a software man. I started this company with two friends, in our spare time, making financial software. I have to depend on my Hardware folks to know what they're doing."

Jillian closed her eyes a moment. "Okay. I don't mean to sound... just tell me if someone's verified that the equipment arrived."

"Of course. Why?"

"You're sure? This wasn't some kind of embezzlement scheme?"

"It wasn't and isn't. We've been depreciating it."

"So, why aren't we returning any of it when the company's going under?"

Gardiner leaned forward. "I told you, I depend on my Hardware people to make decisions about Hardware. My understanding is this was all non-returnable."

Jillian shook her head. "It might be now. But some of these projects were cancelled before the boxes were opened, I bet. Are you listening to Brian about this?"

"He's the Vice President of Hardware."

And, apparently, he's either a complete idiot or a thief. "Gardiner, are you really sure that the equipment is here?"

He tapped his fingers again. "Shall we go look?" Jillian nodded and Gardiner gathered the papers and slipped them in his desk drawer. "Just a visit. A quiet visit. We'll just look around and see what we see and what we don't."

"Sounds like a plan." As they stood up, Jillian had a thought. "Did Grec know about all these expenditures?"

"We gave him copies of the books."

"Oh, boy," Jillian muttered. "If the equipment isn't there and Grec put his money down... then..."

"He wasn't given *real* copies of the books." Gardiner stopped at the doors to his office. "That's what you're thinking, isn't it?"

"It's a logical assumption." Jillian answered. "Even if he really did give you the money just to impress me, I can't imagine he would have considered it if he saw this."

"What do we do if we don't find the equipment?"

"I'm thinking we get a lawyer and then bring in law enforcement."

"Shit!" Gardiner said, and then muttered, "You don't know any good lawyers do you?"

"As a matter of fact..."

Not finding Jillian in her office, George wandered over to Rachel's desk. "Have you seen Jillian?"

"Earlier," Rachel said. "But only in passing."

"Okay, thanks," George said, leaned on the cubicle wall, and dug out his personal phone, hoping Jillian was carrying hers, and sent her a text. *Hi. Are you playing at BF tonight?*

"Urgent?" Rachel asked, from her chair.

"Yes and no. I gotta figure something out." He glanced around. *Lots of people.* "Come into my office for a minute, okay?"

"Sure," Rachel said, and followed him with her notepad and pencil. "What can I do?"

"Well," George answered as he pushed his door against, but not closed. "I could use your help arranging a surprise party... for tonight."

Rachel lowered her notepad and pencil. "A surprise party?"

Snooping while trying to hide that you're snooping is very time consuming. Jillian and Gardiner were touring the line facilities looking for additional storage locations. If they failed there, it was back to the labs and offices and, unfortunately, needing to become less subtle. Next to her, Gardiner nudged her arm and gestured toward the far wall. *There is some warehouse space just off the loading dock. Nice thought.*

Her phone had buzzed a few times and she'd hated ignoring it, but she didn't want to give Gardiner the impression that she could be distracted from something so important; particularly when she was still planning to ask Gardiner for a better package for George, assuming the whole company didn't end up under a receiver with the whole fiasco. Then her phone rang and she knew whatever was going on with George, he wasn't going to just give up. "This is Jillian."

"Hi? Why are you answering like that?" George asked.

"I'm sorry, I'm in the middle of something right now. Can I help quickly? Or may I call you back?"

"Alright. I won't ask where you are or what you're doing. Just answer a few quick yes or no questions, huh?"

"Sure."

"Are you playing at the Blue Feather tonight?"

"No."

"Are you planning to go?"

"Yes."

"Good. May I join you?"

"Of course."

"Great. Thank you. Talk to you later."

"Okay," Jillian said to the silence, he'd hung up so fast. *Well, that was interesting.*

Gardiner opened the door to the warehouse space, and then quietly asked, "Was that George?"

"Yes," Jillian answered, feeling the blush start in her cheeks. "It was obvious?"

"The stilted conversation made it obvious."

"Ah," Jillian mumbled, and finally found the light switch panel.

The overhead fluorescents brightened and began to hum. Gardiner stepped away from the door, and then two of them looked around the area piled high with boxes.

Jillian began reading the labels. "I think we've found the stash."

"This is good," Gardiner said. "The purchases were legitimate."

"Yes," Jillian concurred then stepped back to look around the room again. "There's just so much of it. All this stranded investment. We've got to use it or liquidate it." Sidestepping to some shelving, she tipped a box toward her. "This doesn't even look like it's been opened to check the contents. I hope the packing slips were correct."

Picking a box off the top of a stack, Gardiner set it down, produced a small pocket knife, and sliced the tape. He slowly opened the top and looked inside. "I have no idea what this even is," he said, and Jillian returned the box she'd tilted to its place, and joined Gardiner.

"Me either," she said, as she peered in. "Maybe that's the next round. We found it. I'm guessing it's all here. Maybe the next step is to get Brian down here to explain. And while that's happening, have someone else come down here and do an audit." She sighed. "And we need to get a copy of the information that was sent to Grec and make sure it wasn't fraudulent. If it wasn't, then no attorneys."

"I have confidence in our CFO."

Jillian tilted her head and raised her eyebrows. "I think we all had confidence in Brian, too. After this, I don't think it would offend anyone if we performed some audits."

"And you wouldn't mind an audit of Software?" Gardiner asked.

Jillian shook her head. "I can justify any and all expenditures for Software. And they've all gone by you anyway. But if you're worried about appearances, we could keep it quiet by starting with the email server. See what was sent to Grec and his people. Did you give them a hard copy of anything?"

"I didn't. You know, the more I think about it, I'm pretty sure he didn't pour over the books. I think all we really shared with him were the annual reports. He asked a few specific questions, here and there. Was vitally concerned about Software. I can't say I disagree with him. It's our real strength.

"He said it would be wise to put more emphasis there. That's what he was interested in. Seeing what you folks were capable of. Supporting it. I really think that's what he wanted his money to do here."

"Once this is over, ask me about my ideas for Software. In the meantime, let's make sure we've got all the past straightened out and then we'll look at the future," Jillian said. "I'll get Ruby on the emails to Grec. And we can have a conversation with Brian." She pulled out her phone and started searching for Ruby's contact.

"You've got ideas for Software? What kind?"

"I'd prefer to present something more formal to you, but generally speaking, I've had some thoughts about expansions of our more popular products and a few new directions that might be worth pursuing." She found Ruby in her list.

"That's good," Gardiner said, and then cleared his throat. "Do you want to be part of the conversation with Brian?"

"Oh," Jillian said, and froze her hand over her phone. "Right. Probably not appropriate. I'll just-"

"What do mean? Not appropriate? It's completely appropriate. You found this," he gestured all about them. "You should be part of the rest. The thing is I don't know how seriously he'll take you."

"Oh?" Jillian resisted crossing her arms as she thought of all the reasons Brian might not take her seriously. *Better not be about George or I'll-*

"No. I had planned to start a conversation today with words of congratulations. I chose you for the Director position."

"I, um, heard," Jillian said. *It'll just be easier if he knows.* "It leaked."

"Not surprising. We'll need to see what you have in mind for your team, of course. But, if you've got a vision… and you can handle this, well, I think I made a mistake. "

This time, Jillian put her hands on her hips in order to resist the urge to cross her arms.

"If we're going to have you turning the entire company on its head, we'd best pay a visit to HR and make that promotion to VP instead."

Jillian's phone dangled precariously from her hand when her arms dropped to her sides.

Pacing his office and working his yo-yo wasn't helping. *I need an artist. I'm jobless on Friday. Jillian wants to get married.* Essentially, nothing had changed since he'd met with HR. And it wasn't going to change if he kept pacing his office. *There has to be something I can do. Something...*

It was a little early for lunch, but not so much so that people would look at him funny if he left. *Come to think of it, people will probably be wondering what's going on with me if they see me all tense.* A quick text to Jillian saying he was slipping out to see Orville and he was free. It felt great to get out of the building and into the air and even better to be moving around. The season had definitely taken a turn, the wind had a harsher bite against his face than it had previous days, and he'd have been in real trouble without a coat.

But it wasn't the chill in the air that made him catch the bus; it was the desire to shorten the time it was going to take to get to Whistling Elms. He wasn't certain what he expected from the visit, except maybe he'd feel a little better about the jump he'd made. Not so much a jump, more like he'd flung himself off a bridge. "Would I feel this way if Irene had accepted?" He asked himself, under his breath, realizing as he started speaking that he wasn't alone on the bus. He still answered out loud with, "who knows?" and a shrug.

Not one to care for pleasantries when the unexpected happened, Orville started off their conversation at his door saying, "What are you doing here?"

When George didn't answer immediately, Orville followed up, "Shouldn't you be at work?"

"Yeah," George mumbled. "That kind of caved in on my head."

Orville didn't say anything at first; he just opened the door wider and shuffled backwards, leaving space for George to enter.

A few minutes later and George had told Orville everything. *My entire life can be encapsulated between a few sips of coffee.*

Orville just shook his head. "One step forward, two steps back, eh?"

"Unfortunately."

Orville let out a heavy breath. "Did you come here to get it off your chest, or are you looking for advice?"

"Advice," George answered.

"Okay, Kid," Orville said. "I think you've let the number of things that are happening distract you from your focus. This happened. That happened. So what? Focus on what's important and it'll all come together."

"That's just vague enough to sound wise and be completely unhelpful at the same time. Thanks."

"Well," Orville said, while shifting in his chair, "you're in quite a mood. Relax! It'll work out. Now, answer yourself this question. Of all the goings on right now, what is the most important one?" He shifted again. "And don't play stupid. We both know the answer."

"What do mean? Being jobless? Being partnerless? Being a disappointment to my woman? And her parents? Hell, being a disappointment to myself?"

"Yep, that's what I mean, though you're only a disappointment to yourself at the moment because you haven't done anything. Once you've started moving again, that'll pass."

George frowned at Orville. "If this is the kind of help you're going to be, maybe I'll just go."

"Coward," Orville said, as George stood.

"What?"

"I said, 'you're a coward.'" Orville didn't bother to move. "You've got all the answers right in front of you, but you're scared to do what you need to do. You finally decided to take a leap with work, but the tiniest setback and you're cooling your heels again. It's a good thing you're getting kicked out; it *might* just keep you motivated. And Jillian," Orville sighed. "You run as fast as you can toward her, get all the way to the finish line and then stomp on the brakes." He shook his head. "To provide you with a sports analogy... false start on the offense. Twice!"

"It's not that simple!"

"Sure it is."

Rather than going back and forth, George decided to try to pry Orville out of his Yoda-like advice mode and get something more concrete. "Fine. Then dumb it down for me. What am I supposed to do?"

"Marry the girl," Orville said. "If it's what you both want then just do it. There is nothing in the world that will make everything else work or at least seem less important than having the *right one* there with you."

"But I can't do that to her. The risk-"

"If she's willing to take it, then don't make that decision for her. *That's* who you want to look at every night and again at breakfast the next morning, the person who believes in you. The person who sees you the way you wish you were. It'll make you feel like you can conquer the world. And when you feel it... you can do it. Everything will fall in place.

"That was the difference between May and June," Orville said, in a hushed tone. "June wanted me along for the ride; her ride. May wanted me to be the best I could be and wanted to come along to wherever it took me, and I wanted the same for her. When she came with me for school, I made a point to look for lodgings that would give her a very short walk to work. I didn't let her settle with her job either, she was considering a typing position, decent pay, but no challenge for her at all. I convinced her to wait for the bank job she'd interviewed for. She got it, she loved it. We looked out for each other. Took care of each other. The rest followed along.

"You're better off broke with a good wife by your side, than rich alone or with a shrew making you regret waking up in the morning." He paused. "If she's really the right one and you're both ready, don't hesitate."

"But I *am* looking out for her. Protecting-"

"Tch. Coward." Orville shook his head and struggled to his feet. "Okay, big business man, let's go get you some business advice."

The growl from her stomach snapped Jillian out of the spreadsheets she was reviewing. *It must be really late.* She glanced at her watch and realized she'd missed lunch by over two hours. *Ugh. Where has the day gone?* It was rhetorical, of course. She could account for every minute. But without the incentive of spending time with George, she'd ignored the coming and going of the lunch hour.

Thankfully, what she'd gleaned from the emails Ruby had tracked down, there hadn't been any fraud. There was no likelihood of legal trouble. Gardiner D was a privately held company, so no stockholders were going to complain and the SEC didn't have any interest. The only issue left was the IRS, and there... so far it looked like they were all right. *Thank God.*

Gardiner hadn't been kidding about the VP title. Marlene had seemed a little irritated with the sudden change and had made comments about having to redo the paperwork. Gardiner told Marlene to take care of it, that Jillian's official start date was still the following Monday, news to Jillian, but then nothing had been done quite the proper way, and there wasn't any excuse for delayed paperwork.

Jillian cringed again just thinking about it. She didn't need to be part of any irritation in HR. Her name was already on the list for misbehavior, though technically she'd done nothing wrong. There was no doubt in her mind, they'd be watching her.

She sank back in her chair and wondered *and worried* about the new responsibilities she was taking on. The worst, of course, was still going to be managing the guys and being *involved* with their friend. How was she going to balance that? How was she going to be social on *that* level and a boss in the office? That was the answer, she supposed. She was going to have to become a multiple personality for real, not a weird joke she'd made.

Wait. If I'm a VP, I wonder if I can get a director in-between us. The thought had enough merit, whether it was possible or not, that she was able to take a deep breath, get up from her desk, and begin a search for food.

It was late enough that the cafeteria had closed so her only option was to leave the building. She glanced in George's office as she passed by and saw he wasn't in. *Is he not back yet? Huh.*

It isn't like I've never accepted a favor before… George looked around the waiting area. Glass tables, uncomfortable white couches, expensive art, a receptionist bringing the clients coffee or cappuccino or lattes or whatever. *I can't afford this guy.*

As if he could read George's mind, Delaney tapped him on the arm and quietly said, "Don't worry. I've got it covered." He started for the desk and the receptionist scurried back to her post and welcomed them with a smile that faded a little when Delaney said, "Tell Roy that his uncle's here."

"Oh, um, Mr. Greene, I believe I told you on the phone that Mr. Rais is booked all afternoon and evening. He really ca-"

"He can. Tell him I'm here and that I can call his mother, if that will help speed things up."

The receptionist's expression went from pleasant to alarmed and she picked up the phone. "I'm so sorry, Mr. Rais…"

Delaney pulled George back a few steps. "He'll see us. Five minutes or less."

George was less sure, though the Mom card probably had some pull. "He's one of the best corporate lawyers in town. I doubt the threat of his mother will make much difference."

"We'll see."

"Oh, Mr. Greene?" The receptionist wasn't quite back to her fully pleasant self when George and Delaney turned back toward her, but it was close. "If you'll take a seat, we'll squeeze you in before his next appointment."

"That's lovely, thank you."

"Can I offer either of you gentlemen a beverage?"

"No, thank you," Delaney answered, and then said, in an aside to George, "He keeps the good stuff in his office. We'll drink there." Delaney took his arm and steered him to one of the fashionable and uncomfortable couches. "And don't let his reputation make you nervous. I watched him grow up. He's a guy like the rest of us, puts his pants on one leg at a time, and all that. He just happens to have gone to law school and risen to the top of his profession. That's all."

"Uh-huh," George said, and thought of Cisco Grec and Jillian. *She wouldn't even blink at this.* He squared his shoulders. *Nothing whatsoever to be nervous about.* He managed not to sigh. *Except the bill.*

Gardiner pulled together the Software staff, just before the early birds would be quitting, in order to make the *big* announcement. He kept it casual, just asking everyone to gather at the area near the elevator, rather than traipsing down to the cafeteria or packing like sardines into the large conference room. People took several minutes to make their way to the meeting, which was fine with Jillian, who used the time to look for George. When she couldn't find him, she texted his work phone, telling him the announcement was imminent.

Still having no answer, she tried texting his personal cell phone. Gardiner started looking around, taking mental attendance. Jillian lowered her voice and asked Sergei if he knew where George had gone. Sergei just shrugged.

When it looked as though everyone else had made it to the gathering, Gardiner made the announcement, calling Jillian up to stand beside him after he announced her name. The floor went silent for a moment, as he followed up with the decision that rather than have her as a director, he'd decided to promote her to vice president. Then the applause started, some fervent, some less enthused. Jillian registered Taro's reluctant applause with pleasure; she'd been sure he'd turn and walk away. Perhaps, things were better with him. Perhaps, he'd had time to think about it since Friday, decided that he had no choice, and had best learn to accept it.

Following the applause, Gardiner asked Jillian if she would like to say a few words. Her world had been so crazy with the engagement that she hadn't thought about the likelihood of speaking. *Ulp!* Off the cuff, after thanking Gardiner, she decided to acknowledge the contributions of all the staff in the most recent challenges and to announce that she had no plans to make any changes with regard to the staff, she thanked the managers for their hard work also, and then wrapped up with a positive comment about looking forward to continuing to work with such fantastic people.

As her words were met with more applause, she felt as though she'd been a bit trite. It seemed the best thing she could do, though, to attempt to reassure the staff that their jobs were secure and that she had no intentions of cleaning house. If pressed, her only real concerns were her managers, not their employees. Thankfully, she wasn't pressed and the next fifteen or so minutes were filled with congratulations and handshakes from those who felt they needed or wanted to do so. She managed to keep her smile in place and focus on the present, until the gathering began to break up and Gardiner asked someone behind her 'what had become of George' and someone answered 'maybe he couldn't bear to watch' and another said something about him 'having something more important to do' in a sarcastic tone.

She thought of her phone and then steeled her back and shoulders;

she'd have to ask him later. He wasn't there and that was that. *Certainly, what he's doing is important.*

Finding herself alone again, Jillian remembered Malvinia was off from the hospital and called her to meet up for a quick drink after work. She didn't tell her that they were having a quick mini celebration over her promotion or that George hadn't been there.

Jillian hadn't mentioned the surprise promotion to VP in an effort to ensure the plan of a quick drink would remain the plan, but for some reason Malvinia had latched onto her and wouldn't let go. She followed her home and they had another drink, a cup of coffee instead of an alcoholic beverage, and the talk around the table had turned to Malvinia's lack of male companionship.

"The problem is, I don't do well putting in the time for an actual relationship," Malvinia said. "I've attempted a couple of things in the last year. Both with doctors. I thought they'd be easier to talk to about work and be more understanding about my hours and my schedule."

"But they weren't," Jillian said.

"No," Malvinia said, with a snort. "I think they're looking for wives, proper doctors' wives, who stay home and make certain life is perfect for them when they do come home. I don't mean cook and clean, necessarily, probably tell staff what to do and when to do it. They always expected me to revolve around their schedule."

Jillian found herself chuckle. "Maybe *you* need a doctors' wife."

Malvinia laughed lightly. "Yeah. But where do I meet one of those?"

"No idea," Jillian said, and then sighed. "You know, I understand why you thought to look in the hospital for someone who would understand, but I wonder if you might not be better off looking outside. Someone you can dazzle with your medical knowledge. Someone who…. complements you, rather than mirrors you."

"Oh? Is that what you have? I seem to recall you met yours working identical jobs at the same company."

A brief glance at her *perfect* ring and Jilllian smiled. "We have a lot in common. Yes. But he has other interests. I told you about his video game company. Well, that's happening." *I think.* "What we have in common helps us talk and what we don't, keeps it interesting."

"Hmm," Malvinia murmured with a tilt of her head. "So, what kind of person am I looking for?"

"Oh, Mal," Jillian said, and sat back in her chair. "I am so *not* the person to ask about this. I'm just barely holding my relationship with George together."

"What?!"

Suddenly, it was time to come clean. She didn't mention his absence at the promotion announcement, not wanting to convict him on that issue until she knew where he'd been. But she did share her concerns about his not really wanting to get married and his jealousy. Naturally, she was fair and explained *why* he said they shouldn't be married soon and that it was hard to tell about the jealousy, as they hadn't been in a situation since they got back together to see how he'd react. As she spoke faster about her concerns and disappointment and fears, her pitch increased and when she'd finished with that, she found she still had steam and her other fear, that the reason for their problems lay with her, came pouring out again.

"I thought we talked about that," Malvinia said. "His jealousy issues are his and his alo-"

"But there has to be something," Jillian said. "Something that I can do to really show him that I'm... oh, I can't think of anything but a poker analogy... I'm all in and I don't *want* anybody else." She stood up and Malvinia joined her as she walked the main floor.

"Honey, he'll get over it," Malvinia said, as they entered the music room. "And as for his commitment issues..." She lifted an arm toward the piano.

"I know," Jillian said, and her shoulders drooped. "I know. He's nuts about me. And he's got a good, solid reason not to get married. But I..." She looked at Malvinia and bit her lip. "I can't believe I'm saying this to you. I *want* to get married. I feel more complete with him. And I want the ring and the papers and the... the... happily ever after." She sat down on the piano bench. "I don't know *why* I need it all right now." She hung her head and laughed bitterly, then looked up at Malvinia. "I don't know why I need it at all. He's told me he's committed and I believe him. But I just want it."

"Oh, Jills. I'm sorry," Malvinia said, and dropped a comforting hand on Jillian's shoulder. "It'll come. Why don't you just sit down with him and set a date? Then you can focus on planning and not worry so much about not getting it at the moment." She paused a moment. "The man isn't going anywhere. He all but dragged you into this house and he crawled on his knees to your parents to get a piano to make you stay. I don't think he asked you to marry him on a whim."

"No. I don't either." Jillian sat up straight and ran her hand over the piano. "It's about feelings, not logic." The memory struck her. Sitting at the piano just two nights before, playing for him. How pleased he'd been. How much he'd loved it. Even when she wasn't perfect...

Jillian stood up as she looked around for a clock. "Mal, I've got an idea and... oh, boy, no time to put it into action. I need a favor."

Malvinia's mouth quirked. "In the name of true love, sure."

Jillian almost made a derogatory comment about true love, but then stopped herself. *I believe.* "True love," she said, with a sigh. "Most definitely." Taking the stairs two at a time, she called back to Malvinia, "Please find my music player and bring it up. I need a song… the right song. And I need to buy and download the sheet music. And I need to call Freddy and see if he'll let me up on stage for one song. And I still need to change and fix my hair and makeup and…"

Her eyes wide and her mouth open, Malvinia just tried to keep up.

"I don't even want to think about the bill for all this," George groaned as he and Delaney left the law office. "Your nephew will be enough, but that video conference with the music copyright guy – I'm going to be paying for this after I'm retired."

"I'd expect some gratitude," Delaney said. "You just picked the brains of the top guys in the business. And it sounded to me like they were giving you good news. I'd say it's time to celebrate, not sulk."

"You're right, of course," George said. "Thank you, Delaney. Thank you for getting me in to see Roy Rais. That was incredible."

"You're welcome," Delaney said, and adjusted his jacket. "It's always a nice feeling to do a favor for a friend."

George gripped the file folder full of papers that he'd newly acquired. "I owe you really big for this one. This is so much bigger than the date at your restaurant."

Delaney smiled. "Invite me to the wedding."

"Naturally," George answered and he found his phone to turn the ringer back on and noticed the time. "Oh, shiiiit."

Delaney glanced at him and pressed the elevator button. "Hmm?"

"Did you know it was this late?!"

Delaney shrugged. "I suppose, why?"

"Well, it's after work, I have to run back to the office to pick up my stuff, and then run home and change to take Jillian to this jazz club… and I'm going to be late… by a lot." He stepped onto the elevator and started checking his text messages. He'd missed the promotion announcement. *Fuck! I forgot. Okay, well, at least I have a way to apologize for that one.*

His eyes lit on the message from Rachel and he slowly lowered his hand. "*And,* I invited the office to the club tonight for a surprise engagement party." *I'm going to be late and Jillian doesn't know about it. Oh, just Hell!*

Thumbing a quick message while he listened to chimes of the elevator bell tic off the floors, he debated telling her about the party.

I'm so sorry I missed the announcement
Have news that should make up for it

She didn't reply right away. After thinking for another moment, when the elevator doors opened, he decided against telling her about the party. It was supposed to be a *surprise,* after all.

And, I'm probably going to be a little late tonight
Can you wait for me at the house?

That could work. If she'd just wait for him, so they'd walk in together. He'd be able to tell her all the good news first, and then the whole night would be just one huge celebration, moment after moment.

But no reply text came, as he and Delaney got to the car. Delaney still drove, so that let George hold his phone and stare at the screen, willing her to answer. Perhaps, he should actually call?

CHAPTER THIRTY-EIGHT

"Okay. Here's the next one," Malvinia said, and skipped to the next song while Jillian twirled another lock of hair around her curling iron.

"You don't have to keep saying that. Just play the song until I say 'yes' or 'no' and then either skip to the next or stop."

"Wow, are you feeling sassy!" Malvinia said, and the music cranked back to life.

"I'm sorry," Jillian said. "I'm completely freaking out. I don't think I can do it... even if they let me." She looked at Malvinia. "Next, please."

Malvinia nodded. "You can do it." The next song began. "If it's that nerve-wracking, you could always just play something you know and dedicate it to him."

"Nope," Jillian said, and looped another curl. "This is my big move. *This* is how I show him that it's the real thing for me. I'm going to sight read for him in front of my friends. Then, he'll know."

"Should I call Kai and Christy?"

"Uh," Jillian muttered to give herself time to think. "Next song, please." She prepped another curl. "I don't know if this is really the time to have everyone finally check out the Blue Feather. I mean, this isn't really somewhere you all are comfortable."

"So, that's a 'no' then?"

"Well, I don't know. It'll be harder to play the more people I know."

Malvinia skipped to the next song without being asked. "I thought that was your point. Besides, *we'll* all cheer for you."

Jillian released the curl and prepped her last one. "I guess you can invite them."

Malvinia skipped to the next song. "Can you tell me what you're listening for? Maybe I can help more."

"I'm looking for a song that I know the tune by heart in my head, so I'll

578

know what it should sound like when I play it from the sheet music... for the first time. Oh, my," she said, as released the final curl and leaned against the counter. "Just thinking about this is making my stomach hurt." She took a deep breath and then unplugged the curling iron. "He'd better realize this is my version of a three ring circus for him."

Malvinia skipped to the next song. "Don't worry. He'll get it. I think it's a little odd, but I get it."

"That's it!" Jillian said, and pointed to the player. "That's *soooo* it. Can you get my laptop and turn it on? I have to buy the sheet music on-line and print it in the next," she glanced at the wall, "oh, *minus* five minutes would be good."

"I'm on it," Malvinia said, and rushed out of the bathroom.

Jillian looked in the mirror and started to setup her makeup while her curls set. *If I'm going all in, I'm going* all *in.* She started on her forties movie starlet look as she thought about which of her dresses to wear.

Orville tried to hold onto George at Whistling Elms, asking for a play-by-play of the meeting with the lawyer. George only succumbed for a few minutes, knowing he was late and figuring that Jillian would only be getting madder and madder by the minute. He was finally able to take a breath when he unlocked Orville's car and his phone chirped Jillian's ring tone.

His jaw released the tension that he hadn't quite realized it was holding and he took out his phone.

Hope you don't mind
Met Vi for a quick drink after work and she wants to join us tonight
Running to her place for a change of clothes
Can we just meet there?

Well, at least she wasn't angry. Or was she? He dialed her.

"Hi," Jillian answered in a somewhat strained tone after the third ring.

"Hi," George said. "I just wanted to be sure you wanted to meet at the club." He looked at the car that she couldn't know he was borrowing. It would help, but he was still running late. "It might take me a while to get there."

Jillian must have thought that he meant to take the train. "No worries about that. Mal and I are taking her car to her place. Mine's still at home and the spare keys are on your dresser."

George smiled. "Thanks, Sweetheart. That's really good of you. But, uh, I thought we'd go together."

"Well, you might still beat me there. But don't worry about it. We'll go home together. That's more important. So what's the news?"

"I'd like to share it in person."

"Okay, I have news too. Unless somebody else already told you."

"I don't *think* so. All I've had today were 'where are you' messages. I had my phone silent, not even vibrate, so I missed them." He started Orville's car and put on his seatbelt. "I am really sorry about that."

"I'll see you at the Blue Feather," Jillian said.

Wishing she'd said that she forgave him, but not surprised that she hadn't, he nodded. "Alright, Sweetheart." He hesitated a moment as he wondered if he should tell her about the party. "I'll see you there."

Jillian called Freddy while Malvinia dressed, knowing that she'd be too late to converse before the club opened. He agreed to assist her with her plans, even promising to speak to the club owner about it, so she'd have permission to play her piece as the first set concluded. "Well, I think I am committed now. Freddy agreed and is taking care of additional arrangements."

"You shouldn't make this sound like such a big deal," Malvinia called out from her bedroom. "You'll make yourself more nervous."

"I'm not certain that's possible." But it did prove possible to become even more nervous and Jillian was grateful that Malvinia had driven and would drive to the club.

"You look fabulous," Malvinia yelled.

Jillian scoffed and realized she was about to chew on her thumb nail. "Thanks. I just realized that you and the rest of the Fab 5 have never seen me dressed like this." She put her hands behind her back while she paced.

"Well, I like it! You remind me of the glamour girls of early Hollywood."

"Thank goodness for that. It was the idea."

"Jillian," Malvinia said, and stepped out of her bedroom for a moment. "Calm. Down."

Jillian took a deep breath and let it out like a steam whistle, in a series of blasts. *Not quite what I was trying for.*

Malvinia shook her head and turned around. "Based on that... when you have kids, don't try natural childbirth. Go for the epidural."

"Hey!"

The bedroom had been left in a mild state of disarray. Jillian's day purse was on the bed, opened and rummaged, and even tipped over. Her laptop was on the bed next to her purse while her work clothes were on a chair with the shoes dropped on the floor in front of it. *She even left some of her jewelry sitting on the bathroom counter. At least her engagement ring isn't here.*

George looked about and wondered why she was in such a hurry. He still wished she'd waited for him. But since she hadn't and time wasn't on his side, he also changed his clothes as quickly as he could manage and raced to beat Jillian to the Blue Feather; only pausing long enough to upright Jillian's purse and put everything back in it.

The business card that flitted out of the pile shouldn't have caught his attention any more than anything else from her bag, but he noticed the handwritten phone number on the back and flipped it over in curiosity. *Sarah's doctor? What in the Hell is Jillian doing with this?*

The first note of the first song of the first set rang out when Jillian and Malvinia entered the Blue Feather. *Too late!* Jillian hoped that Freddy had managed to get permission for her to take the stage and play. *A serenade. That's what I'll be playing... a serenade. Oh. My. God. How ridiculous am I going to look?*

Malvinia took her elbow and led her to the bar instead of letting her think and panic. Jillian opted for a glass of wine and looked around the room. It was nearly full, as usual. *Plenty of regulars to embarrass myself in front of. Perfect.* Of course, she wasn't entirely certain when George would arrive. The set had only just started, but would he even be there in time?

George found Sergei outside the Blue Feather, as he walked up to join the line. *I'd forgotten this was supposed to be a party.* He glanced up the line before stepping in. He didn't see anyone else from work. *Perhaps, that was never a concern.*

Sergei stepped out of line, walked back, and joined him. "Well, where'd you get off to? I was wondering if you'd been in an accident."

I'm in a train wreck. Taro may have been right. "It's been a long day; bad, then good, then bad again. Anyone else coming to this thing?" *I really don't want to have a scene in front of everybody.*

"I think so," Sergei said, with a small hesitation. "Rachel told everyone to show up at least twenty minutes after opening. Probably to make sure you were here. I'm early. You know, as moral support."

The line was moving pretty fast, so George just nodded in response while he reached into his pocket and fingered the card he'd picked up from his bed. *At least this time I've got proof. It isn't my imagination. It's real.* He flipped the card over in his pocket. *Why?*

He shook his head and then felt Sergei poke him. He followed Sergei's gaze and saw Huey was motioning him to come forward. He debated a moment. *It's past 'too late' to cancel the get-together. I need to get inside and figure out where this relationship stands, before anyone else arrives.* Waving at Huey, he stepped out of line and tilted his head at Sergei to join him.

Huey let them cut the line with a word of congratulations as George entered the club. He said thank you in passing and peeled off his overcoat, focused on finding Jillian. She was at the far end of the bar with her friend and he started toward her, his coat over one arm and the other hand jammed in his pocket, fingering the card.

Jillian was taking a sip of her wine when Malvinia nodded her head over Jillian's shoulder. She turned and spied George who didn't smile when their eyes met. Her teeth clenched and she gripped her glass a little tighter. "Well, hello." *What's the matter with you?*

"Hello," George said. *We need to talk.*

Out of the corner of her eye, Jillian caught Mal throwing her a quizzical look. That's when she noticed Sergei. *What's he doing here?* Sergei was looking at them strangely too. She quickly threaded her arm through George's and lead him a few steps away. "What's going on?" She asked, through tightly held lips, trying to ensure no one could lip read the conversation.

"I could ask you the same question." George pinched the card between his fingers.

"Me?" Jillian asked, but then closed her mouth completely as Sergei followed them and tapped George on the shoulder.

"Whatever is going on over here, you might want to knock it off, if you don't want it public," Sergei said, and lifted a fist with his thumb pointing toward the door.

Blinking a few times to ensure that she was seeing correctly, Jillian took a half-step back. "What is Ishi doing here?"

"Great. There isn't a single person on this planet that isn't against me tonight."

"Against *you?*" Jillian muttered, thinking about her sabotaged piano plans. "How is this against you and what is Sergei doing here?"

"You brought Malvinia," George said, in low and slow tone.

Oh, yeah? "I can't bring a friend? At least I told you I was. *You*, on the other hand, disappear without a word and miss my promotion announcement and-"

Sergei held up a hand. "From the tones you guys are using, this has the makings of a really nice fight, but I have to stop it. Ishi's coming over. Do you two want to cancel this party and have the fight, or do you want to go ahead with it?"

"Party?" Jillian asked.

"Yeah," George said. "You had such fun the other night, and since I've felt like I've been letting you down, I thought another engagement party might make you smile. But, I come home and find-"

"Seriously!" Sergei said, putting a hand in-between them like a wall.

"Shut up."

George leaned toward Jillian, bumping Sergei's hand. "I thought you deserved this."

"Who all is coming?" Jillian asked.

"I don't know. But everybody in the office was invited."

"Oh, *great!*" Jillian looked at the stage. She had to get a note to Freddy. *This isn't happening.* She tried to move toward the bar. One of the waitresses could probably help her with transporting a note. She lowered her glass and realized what she was wearing. *Oh. My. God.*

Ishi had already made her way to them and attached herself to the group; she snapped her bubblegum. "I guess Rachel wasn't kidding about coming later. *Nobody* is here yet. Bonus for me." She snapped her gum again and Jillian looked at her. "What? The whole *surprise* thing didn't work for you, did it?" She rolled her eyes toward George. "I don't know why *people* insist on this stuff." She glanced at Jillian again. "Like the outfit. Different. For you."

Jillian glanced around the group then forced a smile onto her face. "It's so nice of you to come. Ladies, let's see if we can get a few tables." This time she snagged both Malvinia's arm and Ishi's and led them toward the stage. They managed to take possession of four tables near the wall, so people standing wouldn't block other patrons who were seated from being able to see the stage.

As more people began to arrive, Jillian continued to do her best to greet them and act like she wasn't completely thrown, all the while trying to catch Malvinia's eye for help cancelling her intended foolishness. She found herself quickly trapped with George next to her, which would normally have been a comfort while people gave her strange looks as they took in her clothes, hair, and makeup, but not just then. When Rachel asked them for a picture, it was an awkward moment, but she put an arm around his waist, when he put his arm around her shoulders, and leaned into him.

It was Ishi who leaned in, after the picture was taken, from behind her shoulder to whisper, "The phony smile is starting to droop." Jillian clenched her fist and took a breath. But before she could respond, Ishi moved and whispered to George, "This totally backfired." Jillian started to laugh.

"Yeah," George said, through his tight lips. "I noticed." He had a moment of pause as Jillian laughed next to him. *Why would she do it? I don't get it.* He leaned over and whispered against her ear. "We *really* need to talk."

She snorted in response and smiled more broadly as Vidar walked up to them. He was trying to say something and mumbled, finally coming up with "Congratulations," and Jillian thanked him very graciously for coming. Vidar gave a lopsided grin and wandered away.

Jillian leaned over and whispered, "You bet we do. But that's not going to happen for a while thanks to this party."

George ground his teeth. "I don't think it can wait."

"Fine. You go first. Where were you today? You missed my promotion to vice president."

George's arm fell to his side as Jillian took a step back from him, a haughty look across her features, and then turned from him to side-hug Rachel who was saying something George couldn't hear. *Vice president?*

Smiling for real at the look of shock on George's face, Jillian introduced Malvinia to a few more coworkers, *er*, employees and kept looking for an opening to cancel her performance. *If this keeps up, I'll have to excuse myself and flag down Freddy, personally.*

Sergei gave George a bit of a shove to encourage him to sit. "What is going on?" He asked, in hushed tone. "You went to an awful lot of trouble to get back with her. If this... unpleasantness is the new normal with you two, I don't think I can stand to be around it."

"How did the promotion to director turn into a vice president?" George asked no one in particular. "That's unreal." He noticed Taro and Melissa arrive and jumped back to his feet and pushed his way to Jillian, not even registering Sergei's look of surprise. "Look. It's time we talked. Taro's here and I don't think I want to fight in front of him."

"How do you propose we get even a minute to talk?" Jillian asked, and then turned to smile and shake hands with Irene, who made a comment about how great it was to have two celebrations in one day. *Everyone but Ishi is pretending I don't look like a freak. She's the only totally honest person in this room. Ugh. How am I going to walk into work tomorrow?* George touched her arm. *This is all his fault. A surprise party! I could kill him.*

"Jillian," George said, and when she didn't turn to him immediately, he reached into his pocket and crumpled the card as the shock of her announcement wore off and the reality of her turning her back to him became his focus. He opened his mouth again, intending to demand her attention, but he stopped as he glanced up to see Taro coming his way. *Not here.* He took a breath. *We're not going to have this out in front of everyone.*

George placed his arm around Jillian's shoulders and squeezed, saying in a low voice. "All right. Later. Just keep smiling." He felt Jillian tense up her shoulders under his arm. "And, maybe, act like you can tolerate me."

It was like fingernails on a chalkboard. Jillian's hands balled into fists, but she relaxed them enough to grab his free arm as she turned and tossed an "excuse us a moment" over her shoulder to Irene. At least, he didn't resist following her.

They weren't alone, but the edge of the hallway leading to the office and bathrooms was as close as they were going to get. Jillian didn't even take a breath. "Look, I don't know what your problem is tonight. I've got my grievances too. But you *planned* this. So get over it quickly, or talk even faster, because I'm about as embarrassed right now as I've ever been and I don't need to be even more embarrassed by our fighting in front of all the people *you* invited to see me looking like a complete freak-"

"Hey! This was *for you.*"

"I don't recall asking for it."

"No, but, I thought-" His peripheral vision picked up something that made his eyes dart toward the door. "Ohhhh, shiiiiiiiiiiit."

"Oh, what!?" Jillian said, her hands rising with her shoulders and then she turned to follow his eyes. Her mouth opened as she saw her mother and father and she whispered, "Noooooooooo."

Her mother was holding onto her father like they were in a very dirty foreign country and she expected to be mugged, or at the very least offered crack, at any moment.

Jillian's hand gripped George's arm like a vise. "You didn't."

"No," he answered shaking his head vigorously. "I didn't."

"Then what... how... God, why..."

George watched as Jillian's father had his bearings with one gaze around the room and then began to move through, escorting his wife with ease. *I will never have that kind of confidence in a place I've never been.* The man's eyes narrowed a little as he scanned the room, presumably looking for his daughter in the sea of faces. *I wonder how much of that is learned... studied. Like Jillian's ice queen impression. She wasn't born doing that. Maybe I can look that confident too.*

Next to him, Jillian certainly didn't look confident. She looked a bit pale. He held in a sigh of exhaustion. *I'm going to have to get confident pretty damn quick, if I'm going to salvage any of this night.*

When George took hold of Jillian and started toward her parents, she tried to wriggle out of his grip, though only for a moment, and failed. *This is a no-win situation.* She looked longingly at a table that she might be able to hide under and then tried to wish her hair and make-up to magically transform, and while she was hoping for miracles, perhaps her clothes would change too and she'd resemble someone her parents would actually socialize with rather than their embarrassment of a child. And, maybe they'd all suddenly transport to a better location, too.

Jillian quit fighting the confrontation; there was no way out of it anyway. She glanced up at George and suddenly felt a wave of gratitude. Her parents might say any number of things, but he wasn't going anywhere. *He isn't going anywhere.* It felt like a new idea, even though she knew it wasn't and shouldn't be. There was something so real and final about it at that moment. *My parents unexpectedly appear and he takes my hand to go deal with it.*

She took his arm with her free hand, touching him lightly at the elbow in an affectionate grip, and he glanced at her and loosened his grip.

The ice queen has left the building. The soft eyes gazing at him with adoration made George's stomach flutter and he told himself, *she doesn't look at anyone else like this.* He smiled at her, trying to telegraph that everything was going to be okay.

The card in his pocket forgotten, George held out his hand to her father. "Jack. This is a surprise." In his periphery, he saw Jillian's eyebrows shoot up for a moment. *Now* that *seemed confident.*

"George," her father said, and took George's hand to exchange a handshake. The brief handshake over, Jack focused on Jillian. "Jillian."

"Hi, Dad," she answered in a voice just barely audible in the loud room. "Mom."

"There seems to be quite a crowd," Jillian's mother observed. "This is a very popular place."

"Yes," Jillian said.

"And," George said, "It's even more packed than usual. We're having an engagement party with our friends from work."

"Oh?" Karen asked, and looked around and then turned her gaze on Jillian. "These are work people?"

"Yes," Jillian said. "It's been a big day. Please don't feel you're unwelcome, but I'm surprised to see you here. May I ask what brought you?" *I must be crazy to ask that. Here it comes.*

"Several things, actually," Jack said. "First, we didn't leave things well. And that isn't something I can abide."

Jillian crossed her arms. "I can't abide it either, but that's how it went."

George put his arm around her and spoke to Jack. "I know I would like to see us all getting along better." He looked at Jillian. "You do too, right?"

"Yes, right. Of course," Jillian said. *And pigs will fly.* Malvinia waved at her from nearby and then pointed toward the stage. Looking over her shoulder, Jillian realized that Freddy was looking at her. She waved her hand to signal that she wasn't going on.

Freddy held out his arms for a moment with a look on his face that Jillian read as *you're kidding.* But all the same, he spoke into the mike. "I guess we'll do one more before our special guest comes up." And they started up another song.

Great. Another communication problem. Jillian pushed the thought of Freddy and the stage out of her mind. "What else?" She asked.

"Well," her father said, but didn't smile. "I received a call from Roy Rais today."

"You have *got* to be kidding me!" George said, and his arm left Jillian's shoulders. "What happened to lawyer/client confidentiality?"

Jillian's head turned toward him. "Roy Rais?! You have Roy as your attorney?"

"You know Rais?" George asked Jillian. *I can imagine your dad knowing him, but you?*

"He's been coming to our annual Christmas party since I can remember," Jillian said.

"I mentored him when he was first out of school," Jack said. "He struck out on his own after a few years and has really made himself."

The walls are closing in. "Well, I'm certainly surrounded by a swiftly shrinking circle," George muttered. "Here I thought it was expanding…"

"I don't understand," Jillian said, and looked back her father. "Why did Roy call you?"

"Can I sue him?" George asked no one in particular.

"He was calling…" Jack said, and then paused for a breath, "to congratulate me regarding my daughter's upcoming nuptials."

"Oh," George mumbled.

"He also said that he was very impressed by you," Jack looked him in the eye. "He said you were in his office today for a consultation. Apparently, you blew him away. He said if you don't make a splash with this venture, he may consider putting in a little money toward your next. Says you're going to be one hell of entrepreneur."

"Me?" George almost shook his head. "I'm not trying-"

"He thinks you've got the right combination of intellect, courage, and a natural sort of charm to pull together new enterprises."

"He's also got the drive," Jillian said, and when he turned his head to her again she was beaming at him. "If anyone can…" She said, softly and let him fill in the *'you can'* on his own.

Jack spoke again. "He said a few other good things too. That you listened to the advice you were given, asked excellent questions, and let him connect you with an expert you needed. Basically, he thinks you're sure of yourself *and* smart enough to listen to those who can help you. He said you are a rarity in his office. Apparently, he has a great number of clients who want his help without having to take any advice or change how they do business, and plenty who seem to think he can pull everything together for them without any thought on their part." Jack exhaled through his nose and shook his head slightly. "He said he wasn't going to make much money off of you because you needed very little from him, but you're the kind of client that makes him look good."

"Well, I…" George stalled, trying to form a useful thought. "That's very… flattering."

"I assure you, he didn't really give me any details. When he first called, it was about Jillian." Jack looked at his daughter. "I guess you came up in the conversation today."

"Well, yes," George said.

"And he was awed by your fiancé."

"Oh," Jillian said to George. "You won't really sue Roy, will you? He's a bit like family. And *we're* family. I'm sure he didn't mean to-"

"No," George said. "But I may have to say something to him the next time I'm in his office."

"Oh, George, ple-"

"Like, thank you," George said, and tore his eyes from Jillian to look at Jack. "I'm hoping you're a little less against us."

Jack inhaled deeply. "I still think you're rushing things a bit. But, I would be interested to hear more about your business." He patted Karen's hand that was still gripping his arm. "And we'd both like to try another lunch or dinner, and get to know you."

His mouth still tasted a little bitter from the previous day. "Because now I come with a good reference?" George asked.

Jack's chin lifted slightly. "Because you're my daughter's choice. Unless you intend to back out of that, it's as Jillian said, we'll be family. I never objected to you personally, just to a plan to take advantage of her. It appears I may have been wrong." Jack held out his hand again and lowered his chin.

Beside him, George felt Jillian stiffen. He didn't hesitate, though. He quickly shook Jack's hand. *Literally seize the opportunity. No telling when it will happen again.* Her hand touched the small of his back and then slid to the side to curl her arm around him.

"I guess, you'll see," he said, with as much authority as he could muster. "There's a reason I'm doing this now. This is my perfect chance, but it's also my last chance. One day the magic word 'kids' is going to come up in conversation. And I'm not going to be a father who works his day job, and then hides in the den or the garage, trying to make his dreams come true, while he misses everything that happens with his kids. If this flies, it's a new beginning. If it flops, then I'm done, I can cross it off the list, and it'll be back to the regular grind. I'm not taking advantage of Jillian, at all. This is for us as much as for me."

As he released his grip, he looked at Jillian again and leaned down to whisper. "That's done it. No choice now. We've got to work out our problems or prove your parents right."

She couldn't stop the nervous laughter. But she managed to respond with, "What problems?" and planted a kiss on his cheek. *When he's like this, I can't even remember any problems. I can't believe he's thinking about kids.*

He nodded at her, wishing they didn't have problems, as he recalled the card stuffed in his pocket and he lied, "yeah."

Noting that George had tensed rather than relaxed after coming to a truce of sorts with her folks, Jillian paused. *What's been eating him?*

Malvinia poked her in ribs. "It's time."

Glancing at the stage and seeing Freddy motioning to her, Jillian shivered and started to sweat. *Not now. Not like this. Not with everyone here. I can't even begin-*

Malvinia poked her harder.

Jillian shook her head and turned toward Freddy to give him a solid signal that she was backing out. Beside her, George had followed the interaction and caught her hand before she could raise it. "What's going on?"

"Nothing," she said, and considered wiping her forehead, despite her mother's presence and the comment that would inevitably follow about her unladylike actions.

She pulled her hand free from George and as she lifted it, intending to signal Freddy, he said, "That's not true. Why can't you tell me?"

She froze for a moment and then looked at him. "Beg pardon?" *He still wants to fight?*

"Another problem," he muttered.

When Malvinia poked her again, she realized she'd been staring at George and he'd been staring back and it hadn't been good. *I love you and you love me. I'm not sure I know what's wrong with us. I thought I did. But clearly I don't. I'm not sure what this is about, but I think I know how to end it. One way or another.* To no one in particular she said, "I'll need a strong drink when I get back."

Behind her, George exclaimed, "You're leaving?!"

But she wasn't leaving. She grabbed a hold of Freddy's hand to hop onto the stage, and then turned back to Malvinia, who had read her mind and held out the pages. She mouthed a 'thank you' to Malvinia and took a very deep breath. She hadn't heard what Freddy had said by way of an introduction, so she approached the microphone and tried not to swallow her tongue.

"Some of you know me," she stopped and mumbled, "sort of." Another breath and she tried again. "I'm being humored tonight with a favor. You see, I've recently become engaged…"

Someone in the house whistled and a scattering of applause echoed.

She felt her cheeks redden. "And I wanted to share something special with him." She looked at George, who was looking back at her perplexed, his eyebrows together and his fists on his hips. "It's not likely to be particularly great, because I haven't had time to practice this, not even once." George's eyebrows shot up. "Which actually quite fits with the evening, since nothing has gone as I planned."

Malvinia frowned at her.

Jillian shook her head and then let her eyes drift around the room. "And it's off genre. So anyway, please don't feel you need to listen to this." She looked back a George. "Except you. Please."

She took a single step toward the piano and then stepped back to the microphone. "George, I hope you-" She pushed ahead. "This is for you."

Fumbling with the pages, she set them up on the piano, watching her own hands shake. *Not now. Don't let the nerves get you now.*

In her head, she could not only see the people from work watching, she could feel them too. And her parents. *Oh, God. Not Mom and Dad.* But they couldn't matter.

Freddy brought the microphone to the piano and Jillian noted her stomach dropping. She sighed and turned to the microphone. "And I can't sing either."

OhmyGodOhmyGodOhmyGodOhmyGodOhmyGod. There is no graceful way out of this.

Another deep breath and she started the introduction, so grateful she'd picked a song she knew so well. From the corner of her eye, she could make out Malvinia nodding her head.

Even though the fingering wasn't familiar, the notes and the keys were, so for the most part, she found them. It wasn't a difficult piece, but it was made more challenging as she concentrated to speak the lyrics as rhythmically as she could.

A few feet from the stage, George stood as still as he'd ever been, hardly breathing and swallowing hard in empathy, all irritation vanished. When she'd first walked away, he'd felt his pulse quicken and the blood pound in his temples. Eventually, as her intentions had become clearer, he'd calmed some.

And then, Jillian was up on the stage, in front of *practically everyone* they knew. He could hear her voice trembling when she spoke and the pages in her hand fluttered. Once she sat at the piano, her hands seemed to steady, but her eyes were darting around the pages, her fingers, and then into the audience and back again.

He began to recognize the tune and tried to place the song, choosing to focus on the music for a few moments. The first lyric certainly gave it away. "Have I told you lately that I love you?" Involuntarily, he smiled. It was an old, sappy love song that made its mark in most of the wedding receptions he'd been to over the years, and she'd dedicated it to him, in front of *everyone.*

After the warmth began in his chest, George stepped closer to the stage and smiled broader at her, hoping that the next time she glanced his way, she'd see him there, hoping she'd know that he knew what it meant for her to do it. And, of course, what it meant to him.

As she continued to play and made a stumble in the music, he stepped closer again. Her face had faded from the nervous red to a pale, terrified off-white. *Don't pay attention to anyone else. Ignore them.*

He tried to send soothing thoughts to her via telepathy. *You're marvelous. Relax, there's nothing to fear. I love this. I love that you're doing this.* All the while, he tried to pay enough attention to the music and the moment, so he'd never forget it. *Never forget.*

I hate this. Jillian's fingers were heavy and didn't respond as fast as she expected. In a way, that was all right. The song was slow and she was feeling a great desire to get it over with. If her fingers had been in the mood to fly, she'd be through in half the time. *Ugh. Nerves!*

She could hear her voice trembling and nearly closed her eyes in embarrassment, which would only have caused her to lose her place in the music. *Yikes. What a disaster.*

After another stumble in the notes, she almost stopped. There wasn't much dignity in jumping from the stage and running, but it was as appealing as hiding under a table had seemed when her parents turned up.

Her stomach moved. *My parents are watching this. Oh. Dear. God.*

I am never *going to forget this. Every time I hear this song…* When her hands started to tremble again, his jaw tensed. *Come on. Enjoy it.* He took a step closer, ending up at edge of the stage. *This is so perfect. Enjoy it with me.*

Do not cry. Do not cry. You can do this. Slowing her pace just slightly in hopes of eliminating a few more mistakes, Jillian found a spot in the lyrics to take a slightly deeper breath. *Oxygen. Oxygen is good.*

She tried to play, speak, and think despite the litany of names running through her head of all the people that were witnessing her performance. *Too many people from work. I'm their boss. Oh. Lord.*

This was stupid. This was so stupid. I'm making a fool of myself.

It was the movement near the edge of the stage that caught her attention and drew her eyes, despite her attempts to keep them on the page.

He was there, so close she could reach him with only one long step and some stretching and leaning. *So close.* She paused in her rendition; it was enough to be noticeable.

Wanting to climb up onto the stage and sit with Jillian at the piano, to whisper that it was okay, George had to hold himself in check until she looked at him. He couldn't join her. It would disrupt her flow. But he could send her a signal.

CHAPTER THIRTY-NINE

George winked at her and she felt herself flush from the tips of her ears to the soles of her feet and recalled the moment when he'd winked at her a few weeks prior, when he'd been watching her play, and she'd glanced toward him. *I've known for so long. This isn't about me. It's not even entirely about him. It most certainly isn't about anyone else in the room. It's about Us. It's so he'll know too.*

An upturn of her lips and she winked back, then returned to the music and finished out the song with more confidence, even singing the last line softly and mostly in tune. George realized he'd held his breath as she did. As she released the keys and began to lower her hands, he waited to see what she would do. Duck her head? Grab the music and run?

Before her fingers had dropped to her lap, she turned toward him and flashed him a dazzling smile and his heart skipped along to a different beat. *Is it fair that I'm the one being rewarded for her hard work?* He lifted a hand out toward her and she left the music on the piano to move toward him.

And then, she was off the stage, whisked into his arms with her feet off of the floor, and being held so tightly it was hard to breathe.

"That was wonderful," he whispered. "*You're* wonderful. I..." *You are so wonderful.* "Thank you."

She hugged him back, smiling against his hair. "I'm glad you liked it." *I love you.*

He let her slide down a little so he could see her face, and then muttered, "Oh, Hell." *You can't do something like that and not expect to be kissed. I don't care who's watching.*

Her eyes widened a little at his declaration. *What is he swearing abou-?*

His lips were on hers and they weren't bringing a sweet little peck, but rather a knee-weakening, pulse-accelerating, passionate caress that caused Jillian to move one of her feet just to try to keep her balance.

When he'd made her head swim and the world spin around her, he stopped, pulled back just enough to look into her blurry eyes, and whispered, "I love you, Jillian."

The proper response is 'I love you, too.' But instead, Jillian slid her hand behind his head and pulled him back to her to kiss him as thoroughly as she could.

He hadn't expected her to kiss him then, in front of everyone. He'd expected a rebuke for his own lack of propriety. Instead, he found himself locked in a fire-filled, consuming kiss that took away not only his breath, but his internal gyroscope as well, and while one arm tightened around her again, the other reached out, just catching the stage and allowing him to throw some of his weight against it and taking her with him, so that they were at an angle.

When he heard the whistling and clapping, he waited for Jillian to end the kiss, but she didn't, and after a few more moments, he found that even the stage was not enough to keep him from feeling like he was falling.

George tilted his head back a bit, releasing them both, and tried to look her in the eyes, but the world spun around him and his eyes seemed unable to focus. "God. That was something."

"Are you all right?" Jillian asked, softly, as her hand slid from his head to his shoulder.

"I think so. That was really something. Is that how you usually feel? Dizzy seems like such a small word."

Jillian laughed and dropped her head under his chin. "Did I actually get to you?"

"Every minute of every day," he answered, and found himself able to see her clearly when she lifted her head and eyes to him once more. "And the littlest bit more so, just then."

Jillian laughed again.

He managed to get a second arm around her and not lose his balance. "You've such a great laugh."

"Did you really like it? The song, I mean."

"Yes, Sweetheart. I liked it. I even loved it. And I've got the perfect thing to reciprocate."

"Oh? What's that?" Jillian asked, and pushed back enough to meet his eyes.

"Where I was today. The lawyer. He's helping put together the legal papers to start my company. He hooked me up with an expert in music copyright. He had some ideas about using music from the jazz era, where the rights had reverted back the songwriters' estates or that had never actually been sold.

"It's brilliant. We'll record the music, use it in the game, the old song gets exposure and maybe some fresh sales."

"Jazz?"

"Yeah, and the setting is moving to New Orleans. It'll be a bit more noir now." He paused for breath. "Know any combos that might be willing to record some jazz in exchange for some possible exposure?"

"You know, I just might," Jillian said.

"What's more," George continued, "He's absolutely certain he can protect you, both of us actually, from litigation. We can get married anytime."

Her lips parted and she let out a tiny gasp of surprise. "Are you sure?" *We can get married.*

"Jillian," her mother's voice cut through the low din of the crowd. She and George looked simultaneously to see her parents disapproving scowls. Her mother took several steps toward them and dropped her voice. "You might want to stop sprawling atop that man in public."

"Oh, really?" Jillian said, as she pushed herself upright and out of George's arms.

"Yes," Jack said. "You work with these people. And this…" He waved his hand at the piano on the stage. "And then, this…" He motioned up and down toward Jillian and George. "This isn't very professional."

"Well, Dad," Jillian said, "we're in love. And *that man* is my fiancé. And it's still new. And this is the one chance in our adult lives we get to act like idiots, so I'm going to take advantage of it." *We're getting married.*

George draped an arm around her shoulders. "And she'll still be a kickass vice president tomorrow, regardless."

It was Jack's and Karen's turn to not react to the news. Karen blinked a few times and George knew without a doubt where Jillian had learned that particular expression. Jack stared them down for a few heartbeats, and then said, "We thought this was a director position. Congratulations, Jillian. That's really something."

"Thank you, Dad. It *was* a director position. But it changed to VP." *And I'd be happy to scrub floors, so long as I'm with George the rest of the time, so look as gloomy as you as you want. I'm so happy.*

Jack and Karen exchanged a look. George could almost feel the disappointment between them. *What is wrong with these people? How can they not be celebrating?* "I'm so proud, I could burst," he said, and squeezed Jillian.

She tilted her head to see his face with her eyebrows raised.

George grinned at her. "I knew what you were worth *before*, you know. Now everybody knows. And I'm the guy who won you."

She giggled. "Won me? Was there was a contest?" *I'd have seen to it you won, if there had been.*

He nodded. "Just because there weren't other competitors, doesn't mean I couldn't have lost."

Oh, George. She kissed him again, this time lightly and quickly. "I won, too." *Boy, did I win. My champion. My Hero. Bursting with pride.* "I'm proud of you too-"

"Your father and I are leaving now."

Jillian refocused on her mother and let the words come automatically. "Well, I'm so glad you came tonight. Please consider coming back some other time. I usually play with the band. Something I know, something I've practiced. I think you'd enjoy that much more."

Her mother smiled faintly. "I'm sure, dear."

"You'll let us know when we can try lunch or dinner again?" Jack asked.

"Yes," George said. *We are going to have to thaw these people out.*

With her smile growing just slightly, her mother said, "And we can start talking about the wedding."

Jillian lost her breath. *But we're eloping.*

Before she could even think of how to respond, George tugged her back against him, and said, "Thank you for being here. Have a safe drive."

Jack nodded and Jillian's parents turned to go.

George lowered his mouth to her ear. "We can talk about it later."

She nodded. *Right. Not now. It can wait. We'll figure it out...*

"Let's get back to the party," he said.

She nodded again and turned her head, so she could see him. "Yes. Let's celebrate."

When they'd turned their attention back to the group, there was applause from the nearest table of party-goers. Some even stood in an ovation.

"You two should be more careful. Try not to burn the place down," Ishi said, from off to the side.

Jillian blushed and George squeezed her. She let out a short laugh.

He looked around at the people who'd accepted the invitation. *I think I'm going to miss them. Truly.* When his gaze fell on Sergei, he saw the tight smile and decided he needed to begin the process of repairing things. "Will you excuse me a minute?" He asked Jillian, and tilted his head in Sergei's direction.

Jillian followed his motion with her eyes, her mouth twitching slightly as she saw his destination, and then she nodded. "Going to patch things up?"

"Going to try to start, anyway."

"Good luck." She moved away from him and sat down at the nearest table.

He still hadn't told her why everything was so tense between him and Sergei, not wanting to add that mess into the mix. Silently, he praised her for not prying. But then, George hesitated a moment, wondering if he should leave her side. When Malvinia joined the table, he knew Jillian would have support, if she needed it, and he was out of excuses. He was free to deal with… things.

Sergei seemed surprised when George sat down next to him. "I thought you two'd be glued together all evening." Sergei said, and gestured toward Jillian.

"Sometimes we have things to say that don't need an audience."

"Uh, oh."

"No," George said, and shook his head. "Not… Look, I'm not going to pretend that I'm totally okay with… things. But, we've been friends for too long to let something like this come between us, right?"

"Yeah. I should hope so." Sergei shook his head. "I mean, you *know* I wouldn't. Not now. Not if… Just never."

"Yeah. I know." George said, and signaled the waitress. "So, I'm buying this round and we'll do our best to ignore it."

"It'll pass, man. It's just a stupid…" He stopped and looked around. "It'll pass."

George leaned a little toward Sergei, lowered his voice, and said, "I know. Anything you can do to speed it up would be appreciated."

Sergei snorted. "This wouldn't even be an issue if you hadn't ditched me three weeks ago. None of this would have happened."

"*You* were late."

Sergei nodded toward Jillian. "You were right on time."

George grinned. "No. I was late too. But better late than never."

Picking up his mostly empty glass, Sergei said, "Here's to your good fortune."

George slapped him on the shoulder. "Thank you." *It's still going to be awkward for a while, but at least it's improved.* "When the next round comes, we'll toast the infinite possibilities that are still open to you."

"That *almost* sounds good." Sergei grinned. "Between you and Taro, I'm feeling the boom lowering. Time slipping away. The possibilities decreasing."

"You *definitely* need another drink," George said.

"Nah. But I'll take it."

"I have to go," Ishi said, leaning in and interrupting the conversation. "I wanted to give you this before I left."

She handed Jillian a napkin. "Okay," Jillian said.

"I know it was supposed to be no gifts, but… anyway… Have a good night and thanks for the invite." Ishi pushed away before Jillian could respond again.

Malvinia was the one who took the napkin and flipped it over, revealing an inked drawing of Jillian and George. "Okay, that isn't half bad. That's actually quite good."

"I think it's more than quite good," Jillian said. "It really looks like us."

"You could frame it."

"I might," Jillian answered and tried to figure out how to put it in her purse without creasing it.

"Huh," Neal said, from behind them. "Ishi has some talent."

"Mm-hmm." *There's another artist in the office.*

"May I join you?" Neal asked, and pulled up a chair when Malvinia agreed. "Best wishes," he said to Jillian.

"Thank you, Neal."

"That was *some* performance."

Trying not to react much, Jillian nodded.

"George said something about you being a pianist, but I didn't realize you were so talented," Neal said.

Oh, you mean the piano… not the kiss. Well, I'm not talented.

"Was that your song? Yours and George's?"

Jillian shook her head. "No. But the choice was intentional."

After a few moments of silence, Neal spoke again. "So, did I understand you play here regularly?"

"Sometimes," Jillian said. "I usually play with the combo that's playing tonight, but only when they need someone to fill in on the piano."

"Ah," Neal said, and the silence fell again.

Malivinia and Jillian shared a look while Jillian tried to think of something to say.

"How's your friend?"

Malvinia answered. "Lacey is doing much better. Thank you for asking. There's more hope for a full recovery."

"Good. And your other friend. The ankle. She's not here tonight. Is she okay? I wasn't wrong about her ankle, was I?"

"No," Jillian answered. "Christy is doing just fine."

"You're on a basketball team with George, right?" Malvinia asked.

"Yes," Neal answered, and spoke for a minute or two about the league and how the team was doing in the rankings, and then he looked at Jillian. "George has been really happy to have you come to the games."

Jillian could feel the unsaid and opened her mouth without thinking. "What about the rest of you?"

Smiling suddenly, Neal nodded. "*I've* always liked having support in the stands. Works for me."

"Okay," Jillian said, smiling back. "Works for me too."

"All right," Neal said, and stood up. "I guess I'll see you tomorrow at the office."

As soon as Neal had moved out of ear shot, Jillian touched Malvinia's forearm and said, "Thank you! I don't know how I'm going to work out the social aspects with the guys. Or the work ones for that matter."

"It's just a matter of time. And the more you put in each day, the faster it'll go."

Jillian sat back. "When did you start spouting this kind of wisdom?"

"Oh, I've read my share of philosophy. I just prefer to use the Art of War as my guide in my life." Malvinia said, in an off-hand tone, waving her hand in the air until she and Jillian looked at each other and laughed.

"Perhaps, you should consider a different one for your love life," Sergei said, and sat down in the chair Neal had vacated, as George pulled one up next to Jillian.

"No," Malvinia said. "I believe in 'take no prisoners.'"

"Yikes," Sergei said, and looked at George. "Dangerous women."

"Show me *one* who isn't," George said, and sat, grinning, waiting for Jillian to look at him. She didn't disappoint.

"The only difference between Mal and I... I *do* take prisoners," she said, and ran a hand across his cheek. "Get us a drink, will you, Darling?"

He laughed. "Yours to command."

When he began to rise, she grabbed his arm. "I'm only kidding."

"All right," he said, and sat down putting his arm around the back of her chair. "We saw you talking to Neal."

She nodded. "Mal was just saying that it's a start."

George inched closer. "Thank you. It *is* a start."

He watched her bite her lip, and then smile tightly.

"Taro," she said.

He shrugged, and then gestured toward a table where Melissa and Taro had taken a seat. "He came here tonight. That's a step in the right direction."

Jillian almost whined, *Do I have to talk to him tonight?*, but refrained. She was going to deal with what came her way, but she wasn't going out to meet that one.

As if he'd read her mind, George said, "I've got to talk to him. I'm not going to push you to come with me, but if you're feeling up to it... Melissa is here with him."

"You were so close with the 'not pushing me to come,' and then you fell apart." Jillian said. "You going now?"

"No time like the present."

Jillian reached over to Malvinia who grasped her hand. "I'll pray for you."

"Thank you. If I don't return, please remember to feed my cat."

Sergei rolled his eyes. "Even in jest, this is nauseating."

Jillian shot him a glance. "Says the man who gets to remain out of the war zone."

Malvinia laughed. "Take no prisoners."

George took Jillian's hand as they left Malvinia and Sergei. "I love you for so many reasons, I can't even count them. Now add this to the list."

Even at a distance, and with the music filling the room again, Jillian had no trouble figuring out what Melissa said to Taro when she saw Jillian and George approaching and she smacked him in the arm. She said, "Behave."

"Hi!" Jillian said, with too much enthusiasm when they reached table.

George squeezed her hand.

"Congratulations, again," Melissa said, and stood up to give Jillian a hug. Taro stood up too.

"Yeah, congratulations to you both," Taro said.

"Thank you," George said, and shook his hand.

They all sat down and the conversation came to a halt.

Desperate for something to say, Jillian blurted out, "I hope this party isn't stepping on your toes much. The wedding is so close."

"Oh, no. Not at all. This is fun." Melissa said. "We can't stay much later though, a million things to do."

"Of course," Jillian said.

The conversation died off again.

Jillian glanced at George and then Taro. Both of them were looking at the table. *Why on Earth did you drag me over here if you aren't even going to talk?*

"Hello, everybody!" Neal said, in a louder than necessary voice, as he stepped to the table. "This group isn't having enough fun. Something must be done. What shall it be? Ah!" He rubbed his hands together. "I've got it." He sat down in a vacant chair. "Let's play clear the air."

"Uh, Neal-" George started.

"We all know that Taro here," he shook Taro's shoulder, "wasn't being particularly nice the last few weeks. Don't we?"

Jillian tried to stop Neal. "Neal, I think you've-"

"Perhaps we could *all* apologize?" Neal suggested.

Taro snorted and everyone focused on him.

Melissa jumped in. "Alright, what's been going on?" She looked at Taro. "I've given you plenty of opportunities to tell me, openings of every kind. I've asked. I've hoped. Now it's not an opportunity, now it's a necessity. What's been going on?"

Taro glanced at George and then to Neal, and then gazed at the table.

"Enough," Melissa said, and jumped to her feet. "I'm finished here. And if you don't want to tell me what's going on, I may just be finished with you too."

Taro closed his eyes and exhaled loudly through his nose. "Hon..."

"No. No, 'Hon.' *This* is it. Tell me."

Jillian felt around the table without moving her eyes. Everyone held stock-still. In fact, apart from Taro, no one seemed to be breathing.

Melissa leaned over Taro. "Alright, I'm going." She smacked the table next to his hand and everyone jumped, but then she paused a moment and Jillian thought she was probably giving Taro a chance to say something. After a few more seconds, Melissa removed her engagement ring, dropped it on the table, spun around, and headed for the door.

Jillian counted to four before Taro grabbed the ring, jumped to his feet, and ran after Melissa without a word.

The table remained silent while everyone took a breath and finally looked at each other.

"That was… intense," Neal said.

Jillian and George both nodded.

"Not good," George said.

Jillian couldn't say anything. *I really hope that's fixed. Soon.* She swallowed and looked at George. *That can't be us. We can't ever let that be us.*

"Ok," Neal said. "Let's regroup. Let them… whatever. You two," he pointed one finger to Jillian and his other hand pointed to George, "are having a party. And we… we are celebrating." He stood up. "Come on." He motioned them to join him, as he headed toward Sergei.

George tilted his head toward Jillian. "That's true. We're having a party."

Jillian shook her head. "Oh, sure. And it's been… interesting."

"Sorry," George said, and slumped a little in his chair. "I don't know what's going on with him… I guess we shouldn't have…"

Jillian put her hand to the side of her face. "I don't think I want to worry about him anymore tonight, at least, not with respect to us."

George sighed and leaned over to kiss Jillian on the cheek. "Yeah." Glancing around, he realized the conversations at other tables were dying out, little by little. "Is it just me or is everyone winding down?"

Leaning against his shoulder, Jillian said, "Monday nights are tough."

"Should we go?" George said. *… before something else happens to make this night unforgettable?*

"I don't know. Should we?"

Malvinia chimed in from the next table. "You don't have to stay. Anybody who wants to stay will stay. But there may be a few people who want to say goodbye."

"Make the rounds?" George asked.

"Sure," Jillian said, and let George lead the way around the tables so they could thank people for coming to celebrate and wish them a goodnight.

Jillian made a show of using her key to open the door, making George laugh. "About time, eh?"

"I used this the other day when I was bringing my stuff, but *you* weren't here to see it." She answered, and leaned against the door jamb to partially block the entry way.

"As I recall, I was painting. But, you're right. I didn't see it." He said, and pushed the door wide, motioning for Jillian to go inside ahead of him.

"That was very good," Jillian said, over her shoulder, as she began to take off her coat. "There was a little bait and you didn't take it."

George helped her with her coat. "I wouldn't want to risk a fight starting."

"I was just joking."

He put away both her coat and his.

Jillian wrapped her arms around his chest from behind and buried her face in his back. He could just barely make out her voice. "I love you."

He smiled and patted one of her hands that sat across his stomach. "I love you, too." He tried to look over his shoulder. "Did you hate the party?"

"No," she said, into his back. "And the thought behind it was lovely."

"I'll never forget you taking the stage." He started to turn around. "You were... magnificent."

"I was terrified." She loosened her grip so he could turn in her arms.

"For the rest of my life," he said, and lifted her chin with his finger, "I'll remember that. No one has ever done anything like that for me. It's the best gift I've ever received."

She blushed and wondered how many times she could be embarrassed in one night. "I'm glad you liked it."

"*Loved* it." Instead of a mushy sentimentality in return, Jillian's eyes narrowed and her head turned.

"Do you hear that?" She asked.

"What?"

"That... chirp."

He listened and then heard the faint chirp too. "I think that's my work cell." *Shows the state I was in earlier. Didn't even manage to turn it off.* He stepped away from her to open his work bag, which he'd left resting on the couch. The chirp repeated louder. "Yep, must be." The phone was louder still when he raised it out of the bag. "Voice mail." He thumbed the caller id. "Oh, boy. It's Marlene."

Jillian didn't last more than a few seconds. "Well, check it!"

He nodded and started dialing.

"I'm heading upstairs," Jillian said.

He nodded again and shoved his free hand in his pocket. *HR leaving me a message after hours... Hell. Am I out on my ear tomorrow?* George followed Jillian up the stairs while Marlene's voice began to chime in his ear.

Jillian pulled off her shoes and let out a sigh of relief. She'd intended to put the shoes directly in the closet, but instead she dropped the shoes, sat down on the bed, and rubbed her feet. They hurt even more than usual; she'd been up on them quite a bit. *Perhaps flats tomorrow.*

George lowered himself to the bed next to her. "I've news."

"Good or bad?" Jillian asked, and then bit her lip.

"The offer from Gardiner D to leave quietly... changed this afternoon."

"For better or worse? What did Marlene say?" *Did I get through to Gardiner?*

George shook his head and then looked at her and the smile broke through. "I don't know what happened, but they're giving me everything that was mentioned before and six months' salary on top of that."

"You're worth more, but that's more than you'd hoped, isn't it?"

"I wanted to *work* through the end of the year. This is a gift." George sighed and dropped backwards onto the bed. "I can start working on the game right away and I've got more money than I expected."

She turned at her waist, so she could see him. "You're letting them off easy. But then again, if you're leaving anyway..." *Of course, I told Gardiner what a great guy you are, making things easy for everyone but walking away quietly, that you deserved more than a reference, vacation pay, and a handshake.*

"I am. And you, Sweetheart." He picked up her hand and squeezed. "You, get the promotion you deserve without anything to get in the way. It's perfect." He sat back up. "Another thing to celebrate. But I've had enough booze for today. Either we have to think of a different way to celebrate or celebrate later."

"Hmm," Jillian tilted her head and quickly raised and lowered her eyebrows. "I can think of a few possibilities for celebrating."

"Me too," George said, and sat up and leaned over toward her, but then stopped. He ran a hand over his jaw. "I should shave, shouldn't I? Give me a minute or two?"

"Sure. I should... get more comfortable, myself." Jillian watched him step into the bathroom and forced herself back onto her aching feet, planning to use the spare bathroom. As she turned, she noticed a small crumpled piece of paper on the bed. She picked it up and then exhaled sharply.

George lifted his electric razor to his face and started to move it. He paused in mid-motion when he saw Jillian in the mirror, standing near him, holding up the scrunched card.

"Did you go through my things?"

Ah, crap.

Before he could form any words, she raised her voice. "Did you *actually* go through my things?"

"No," He said. "Your purse was on its side on the bed and things had spilled all over. I put them back-"

"And went through them while you did."

"I noticed the writing on the card when I picked it up and flipped it over. It caught my *attention*."

Jillian took a step back, grinding her teeth. "If you need to see my stuff, let's do it." She turned and headed out of the bathroom, through the bedroom, and toward the spare bedroom.

"Jillian." George called after her. "I *don't care* about your stuff." He looked in the mirror for a moment, slapped the counter, and walked to the bedroom. *We are so messed up.*

She was back, coming through the doorway from the hall, as he came through the doorway from the bathroom, carrying her pencil box with her.

She upended it onto the bed. "You've been through my day purse. This box is everything else," she said, and looked at him with a tight face. "Except, of course…" Her phone came out next.

"Don't," George said, but Jillian punched in her passcode and held the phone out to him. His hands balled into fists.

"Anything else you want? My work bag is downstairs. My clothes are mostly in here. You know which drawers have my underwear. That's a classic place to hide things. My coat pockets might-"

"Stop!" George rushed out of the room, Jillian on his heels with her phone saying something, but he could hardly hear over the pounding in his ears and head.

He left her at the top of the stairs, or more likely, she stopped following him.

"Are you leaving?!" Jillian shouted from the top of the stairs and then stomped back into the bedroom. "Fine! Then go!"

The phone next to the bed rang and she scowled at it, and then she thought she heard the back door slam. "Well, I guess George won't be answering this." She grabbed the receiver and did her best to sound calm. "Hello?"

After a few moments, a feminine voice spoke. "Hello? Is this Jillian?"

"Yes."

"This is George's mother. Sorry to disturb you."

"It's no bother. None at all. He's just stepped out." *Probably in his tree. That is, assuming he didn't leave the property. Hmm. It's a bit late here for a phone call. I hope it isn't bad news… for real.* "Can he call you back? Or is it urgent? I can go get him."

"It's not urgent. I tried to call him at the office today but he didn't answer, and then earlier this evening at the house. I just wanted to be sure he's all right. We can talk tomorrow." She took a breath. "How are you?"

A masculine voice in the background came over the line. "Sweetheart, if he's all right, then leave him alone. It's late there."

Sweetheart? Jillian swallowed and her pulse sped up a little.

"He's okay, but I'm talking to Jillian," George's mother said, away from the phone.

"Um, Mrs. Crewes," Jillian said.

"Call me, Mary, dear," she answered. "Or 'mom' if it's not too uncomfortable."

"Thank you. Um. Can I ask an odd question?"

"Sure, Dear. What is it?"

"Does your husband usually call you 'Sweetheart'?" She sat down on the bed, waiting to hear the answer, and her day purse, which had been up against the pillows, fell over. Jillian glanced behind her to see the contents spread halfway down the bed. *Oh.*

"Yes, he does. Why?"

"No reason, ma'am, er, Mary." *Your son calls me his sweetheart. I think I just figured out where it came from.* Her eyes lifted to the picture on the wall. *From the very beginning.* "It's really very beautiful."

The box was right where he left it, sitting in the garage. He meant to put it in the trash, but every time he thought about it, Jillian's voice was in his head, and he hadn't.

Excellent. He picked up the box and carried it back into the house, through the kitchen and living room, and up the stairs.

He pushed open the bedroom door, which was against the door jamb but not shut, and only noted it long enough to wonder why she'd moved it. Once on the other side, the placement of the door was forgotten.

The box landed at his feet with a thud. "Here," George said, and kicked the box. "My phone is downstairs, but the passcode is…" His voice trailed off as he spied Jillian sitting in the middle of the bed, her dress pulled up a little, so she could sit cross-legged. Her bigger purse was tilted and spilled on one side of her and the stuff from her box on the other.

Her face wasn't twisted in anger anymore. It was downcast, perhaps… sad?

"Oh, George."

"Sweetheart?" George stepped around the box. She pressed her hand to her heart and smiled tightly. "Are you okay?"

Sweetheart. Jillian shook her head. "I'm so stupid." She motioned at the mess from her purse and then the mess from the box and flicked her phone, so it bounced a few inches on the bed. "I don't want to fight with you."

"I don't want to fight with you either." He squatted down in front of her, she reached out her hands to him, and he took them in his.

"And I don't know why I insisted on picking that one." She shook her head again. "I let myself *really* think you were combing through my things looking for... whatever. It took the purse spilling to make me see how ridiculous I was acting." She closed her eyes a moment, took a breath, opened her eyes again, and said, "I'm sorry. I'm so sorry. In the end, I ruined the evening."

Jillian pulled her hands out of his and continued, "I could have let it go when you said you didn't go through my things, but instead..." She waved a hand at the box he'd brought in. "I drove you to this. And you wanted to be rid of it."

She gave him a pitiful look and then motioned to the crumpled card. "And I never even addressed this. Is this card what was bothering you all night?"

George reached for her hands again. "Well, it *was*. But I just wanted to talk to you about it."

"Why didn't you say something?" She dropped her hands back into his.

"Well," he said, "I tried, but the atmosphere wasn't conducive, was it?"

"Not early on, but we could have stepped aside for five minutes, after my parents left."

"I didn't care about it then." He swallowed. "I wondered what and why and all that, when I found it. But, after that song..." He shrugged his shoulders. "It just wasn't important anymore. It didn't matter."

Then it worked. He knows. He really knows. She lowered her voice. "Tell me. When you found the card, did you think that I-"

"No. No to everything and anything you might think that I could have thought about you. I just wanted to know why. Why you had it."

"For you," she said. "I had it for you. He gave me that card in case you ever felt a need to say something to Sarah or ask her something. You didn't respond when she was here." She squeezed his hands. "I'm not saying you should have... just that you didn't. And if the time ever came when you wanted to... I held onto the card to help you.

"He gave it to me because he figured you'd toss it. Maybe I should have done the same thing. But if you need... anything... I want to help. I just... want to be there for you."

He smiled. "You're here right now, aren't you?"

"Yes," she said, and bit her lip.

"And you'll be tomorrow."

"Mm-hmm."

He looked at their hands. "And for the rest of our lives?"

"Yes. Absolutely."

His eyes lifted and looked into hers. "Me too. So then... we forgive each other and move on. Right?" He sort of chuckled. "Chalk this up to another fun bump in the road for us."

"Fun? I wouldn't call this fun."

"Well... I don't want to fight with you, but making up might be okay."

Jillian blushed faintly. "Yeah. It might be."

"Come on," he stood up, keeping hold of her hands, so that their arms stretched toward each other. "Let's clean this up. And all this," he said, releasing one of her hands so he could indicate his box and the pile she'd made from hers, "is going in a spare room. If you want to keep yours, that's fine. Tomorrow, mine's out to the trash." She started to open her mouth, but he quickly overrode her. "Really, I don't care about yours. Keep it if you want. I just don't want it in the same room we sleep in."

She nodded and climbed off the bed. "You're right. It definitely doesn't belong in here." She glanced over his shoulder at the picture on the wall. "You know, I might just be ready to get rid of mine too. I've got something so much better."

Jillian turned and scooped all the paper and pictures back into the box. She smiled at George as he paused from putting all her things back in her purse to look at her. He smiled back.

After she'd collected her things, she picked up both boxes and took them to the spare room. She placed them in the corner. *It's time to let them go. When I felt sorry for myself, I could take them out and remember feeling loved. I don't need them anymore. That picture on the wall takes the place of the whole box, of a hundred boxes.*

She stopped in the hallway bathroom, just in case George had decided to finish shaving, and then returned to their bedroom. George had set her purse on the nightstand and had zipped it up. The note she'd scribbled about his mother having called had moved to the nightstand on his side of the bed. She could just hear the razor going, so she wandered back into the bathroom.

He shut off the razor as she entered and rubbed his face. "I can't believe I forgot to shave before meeting you at the club. But I think... yes... I think I won't scratch you now." He put down the razor, turned around, and gave her an evil grin. "I went through your stuff."

"What?" Jillian asked. *Uh, what?*

He took her hand and led her to the stereo in the bedroom. "I needed this. Hope you don't mind." He had her mp3 player connected to the stereo.

"Oh. You mean you were looking for that in my purse. Just now."

"Yeah."

"Why?"

He turned on the stereo and then the player. "Because, by the most amazing coincidence, I need this…" The music started where she'd turned it off; playing the same piece she'd played for him.

After starting the song from the beginning, George set the player down and held out his arms. "Would you care to dance? To our song?"

Jillian's eyebrows lifted subtly and her lips parted and she let out the softest sound he almost never heard. *Our song? Of course. It's now our song. How perfect.* "Our song," she whispered.

As she nodded, he took her into his arms and started to sway, and then step with her slowly around the room, focusing entirely on her eyes at first, and then pulling her in tight against him. "I'll never forget what you did tonight. Playing like that. It was… so… words fail me. I'll never forget it. I can't believe how lucky I am."

Jillian relaxed into his arms and allowed herself to breathe deeply.

He dropped his cheek to her hair.

Jillian leaned her head against his cheek in return. "Me too. Let's not fight again. Let's just love each other."

"I like the sound of that." George grinned against her hair, feeling light as a feather. "But, uh, the last time we called a truce, we still ended up fighting and our lives turned inside out and upside down. It might happen again. What do you think comes next?"

"I don't know." *Until recently, I'd have only been willing to face the unknown with the one person I could count on, me. But, now…* "But I'm not afraid of whatever may come, so long as I'm with you."

Nor am I, as long as I'm with you. "Then let's try," he said. "Let's get married tomorrow."

She tilted her head back to look at him with a smile brighter than any diamond. "Are you sure?"

"I'm sure. No matter how it goes, we can take the consequences." George dropped his forehead against hers and reveled in the feeling of belonging. "Together."

Jillian closed her eyes and ran her palm against his smooth cheek and strong, dependable jawline that had become not just familiar, but irreplaceable, in such a short time. *I was always meant to be here. With you.* "Together."

The End

ABOUT THE AUTHOR

Kelly Lopushansky lives in Colorado with her very patient husband, two amazing children, and one darling, shelter-rescue cat named Roo. In addition to writing, she works full-time in the telecommunications industry, enjoys reading, knitting, crocheting, and computer programming. She's a graduate of Colorado State University with a degree in Electrical Engineering. Her favorite work experiences include her other passion: teaching, whether it was in a formal classroom setting or just answering questions one-on-one, Kelly loves to share with others.

ALSO BY KELLY LOPUSHANSKY

Heavenly Matchmaking: Meant To Be
(e-book format only, available at most major on-line booksellers)

CONNECT WITH KELLY LOPUSHANSKY

Blog: http://kellylopushansky.blogspot.com/
Twitter: https://twitter.com/klopusnow (@klopusnow)